Heirs to the Kingdom
Book Six

Last Arrow of the Woodland Realm

Robin John Morgan

www.heirstothekingdom.com

First published (Paperback) in the UK in 2015 by Violet Circle Publishing.

Manchester, England, UK.

Print ISBN: 978-1-910299-07-4
Digital ISBN 978-1-910299-15-9

British Library Cataloguing in Publication Data.
A catalogue record for this book is available from the British Library.

All papers used in the production of this book are sourced only from wood grown in sustainable forests.

www.violetcirclepublishing.co.uk

In Memory of
Henry Hancock - Walter Renwick

The inspiration behind Fagan and Albanlin

*The fight for what is right on the side of good is the hardest fight
of all. It is the most difficult path to walk, filled with challenges
nd obstacles, that will test you to the depths of your fibre. It can
be a lonely road filled with self doubt and little reward, your only
consolation being that no matter how hard things appear, you know in
your heart it is the right thing to do.*

*The road of goodness will indeed test you, but as you near the
end, you will understand that in taking this road, you choose to face
yourself, and pass into the realm of understanding.*

(Sapphire of Callanish)

Introduction

Destiny

Look to the coming of the Bowman, for he shall herald the start of new days.

We all have a path to follow, it is the sum total of all who have walked before us that guides us through the difficulties of life. The love we hold, the wonders we have seen, all add to our ability to feel instinctively, which is the right and only way to go.

The pain and hurt we feel and hold inside, and the horrors we see can also shape the way we view the world, and they can be lessons to guide us, or corrupt us from what is right onto a path less travelled, your only companion being loneliness or the few other misguided and damaged souls you will cross paths with. It is a recipe that will lead to a distorted view of the world, and a lust to be heard and seen as one of the more powerful and less damaged than any other. The mortal soul we hold can mislead us into thinking we have a right to what we do not deserve, and when you encounter these people along the road, it would be prudent to avoid them, and try not to be drawn into their ways of deception, for they will make them appear far more appealing than the reality on which they are based.

Greed will always manipulate and use the defenceless to attack those of value, for greed will always carry the weapons of power, and show no mercy in their use. The path of truth and decency is by far the hardest path, but it is also the most rewarding, so when you are forced to choose, think carefully and choose wisely.

A young Saxon princess was born to the line of a man of great power, who had everything the world could offer at that time. She was doted upon and spoiled, and lived life in the lap of pure luxury, gaining attention from all who surrounded her. She was never unloved, if anything it was quite the opposite, no young girl could feel more loved or cared for as little Morgan was.

Her father was all the people expected from a knight of his own realm, he was strong and brave and fought with the strength of ten men, he was admired and many who were weak flocked to him for protection, where they fawned over him and his family. The Duke of Cornwall took what he wanted and gave little in return, for there was no man who could consider himself an equal. Born of the land of iron stone in Saxony, he sailed to the shores of the Britain's and took a castle and lands to do with as he wished, and his daughter admired and worshiped him, for he appeared more than any man, even more than a king in her eyes.

Morgan's mother was a Celtic queen; she was beautiful and fair, and gifted with many of the Celtic traits of her people. Her beauty was unrivalled and Morgan saw the admiration given to her and to all who viewed her, the life of the duke and his family was idyllic.

Morgan learned quickly, and grew to like the power she could wield as a four year old girl, she was not aware of the changing world, and the new lords of power rising within the realm. One such lord was proclaimed king of a Celtic line, and the others saw him as the one king to rule all, and through the age he ruled most of the land except that of her father who resisted, as he had the power to hold back the king.

But he did not have a wizard to aid him, and for the first time Morgan saw the power of magic when used against her father. Cornwall was slain and her mother taken as the queen to a new king, and in her grief a strong and powerful hate began to grow. It was a hate that twisted and warped her, and yet from the outside none would know, and it festered within her as she brooded on the death of her father and the changes within her life.

It is fair to say her life was not much different, the new king tried hard to please her and show his affection to her, but she resisted, filling herself with hate, and when her brother was born the new heir to the throne, she swore she would do everything in her power to take back what she saw as rightfully hers. What began then, all those years ago, festered and grew within her as it poisoned her soul and corrupted her mind. She learned to be sly and weave her deviousness around everyone, using others to act keeping her quietly plotting in the dark. It became a way of being and was hidden well from sight, so much so that she wove her way into the trust of the old wizard that aided the king in her father's downfall, and as his apprentice, she began to see the real power of magic and how easily it could be corrupted to bring down the rule of all men. She began in secret her devious ways that started with the hidden imprisonment of her teacher Merlin, and the downfall of the one true king, her half-brother Arthur.

Morgan loved the magic and the power it gave her, and she studied in seclusion moving from land to land hiding always where those who sought her could never quite reach her. With the power of her rapidly advancing magic, she gained more information on how the world was formed and who created everything, and she hated and despised them. Once she discovered their secrets on how they helped shape the world of men, they became her targets for revenge when she discovered that her half-brother, and one true king, had a son born in secret whom they had hidden until such time as a new heir could rise up and rule the land with a fair hand, she planned in secret to take back everything they had stolen from her father.

But she had secrets too; the lines of the Saxon were just as good at hiding what had befallen far from the prying eyes of the world. There was no coincidence in her father's ability to take and rule the land, and build an empire to face off a king of Celtic decent. Her family was also from the old world, and had many dark secrets hidden under rocks and behind closed doors. The Ruling Council had always been far too preoccupied with the affairs of the line of Pendragon, to notice the quiet workings of a family equally as powerful lost in the mountains of Saxony. Like her family, she sowed the seeds of hate and revenge, and lusted after darker powers with which she one day intended to rule the world.

Morgan never expected that the lines of the council and those they created in the early days, would gain greater powers as they passed them from one generation to the next. In her lust she had not always paid enough attention, and as she focused on extending her life, which she tied to a raven, she had not prepared for the rising of power that would march out to meet her son from a town constructed of timber in the north. Morgan made an error, but felt it was one she could correct; after all she had the knowledge of a thousand years to match against the woodcutter's son and his flower girl wife. So began a battle of wits as they met and sparred, with both sides convinced they were the most just in a fight to unite a world destroyed by disaster.

Morgan had meddled with the lives of men for centuries, and had been very successful in corrupting them into her ideal of lust for greed and power. Without realising, she brought about their downfall as the Ruling Council fought back and destroyed much of what she built. Then came the one they called Red Stone, marked with the sign of a rune, and more capable than Morgan realised. Her husband the woodcutters son, faced and defeated her son in battle, and in a desperate bid to gain the ground she lost, she used the darkest power she knew to bring her son back from the dead and then plotted a trap so elaborate, she knew an innocent girl would never see what she had in mind. So began the fight to rule, and it excited her to find she had a worthy opponent, for Runestone Sapphire was indeed far more powerful than her previous adversaries, and it relieved the boredom of time, as she hid herself and planned her fight to gain control of everything, in a battle that would ultimately shape the fate of the whole kingdom.

CHAPTER ONE

AWAKENING NATURE

It was just before dawn, in the long warm summer of 2034, when a tall dark figure crept silently through the fields of Loxley, guiding the small excited figure of a young girl toward the outer edge of the hidden farm village contained within the high walls.

Without a sound they passed like shadows, and left Loxley by the side gate that few of the inhabitants knew about. Under the stars that shone brightly above them, they passed through the gate, and for the small figure holding tightly to her guide's hand, there was a gasp like stifled giggles of happiness, below the deep violet hood that hid her face.

The long walk from the stockade wall, round into the woodland of Sacred Rowan trees, and up past the Loxley burial grounds, to the stone circle high above the western wall of the stockade, had been a morning of pure adventure for the young Runestone. Accompanied by her grandfather, her first ever secret walk out of the walls was indeed a very special treat for her.

It had been dark as they made their way along the path at the side of the high rough wooden wall, but sat on the grass, as the sun rose over the edge of the old stone circle, she could see the wide five miles of the town of Loxley, hidden within the immense skirt of thick dense trees that gave it the protection of keeping many passers by unaware of its presence.

Leenard sat in thought as his granddaughter ate her thick sandwich of cheese, and drank her freshly made lemon cooler from her metal flask. The sun was high in the sky and the morning was becoming very warm indeed. Runestone was enjoying every moment as if it was the best moment in her twelve summers of life, for her world had suddenly expanded, and she now had a bigger picture of her surroundings, one that was far greater than the small stone street that had played such a large part of her life in Loxley.

Deep inside she felt her emotions stir; somehow looking out on the world she sensed some deeper longing to connect with everything that was there before her bright blue eyes. Leenard gave a small smile to himself as he felt her longing for the land and woodlands growing inside her, it had been precisely his objective, in bringing her here to such a powerful and sacred spot. In his mind, he wanted to see her reaction, and find out if she had begun to understand the strong feelings that were starting to grow inside her, as she approached the start of her womanhood.

Runestone spoke quietly, almost as if she felt she should show respect to all that surrounded them. "Tell me the story again Grandfather. Tell me of the creation."

Leenard gave a chuckle. "Have I not told you a thousand times?" Runestone gave a giggle and leaned against her grandfather, happy and content.

"It's my favourite story, and this place is so beautiful, I think it will become my most favourite place on earth. You tell it so well, and I love to hear the way you say it. Oh, please Grandfather; it will make this the best day of my life."

He gave a mighty laugh as he lifted his arm up her back, and gave her shoulder a soft squeeze. "Well my dearest Granddaughter, there is little I can say to such a well placed request, and so my child, if you really want to hear your old bookworm recite the tale, I would be delighted to do so." Runestone gave a huge smile as she settled on the soft fine grass, her gaze fixed with love on the long white hair, and bright green sparkling eyes of her beloved grandfather. He gave a deep cough, and smiled.

"Let me see now. Oh yes darkness." Excited she gave a soft giggle as she felt the wonder of her grandfather, and prepared for the tale she loved the most.

"Darkness... You see my child, in the beginning that was all there was. In the old tongue it was known as Merle, for deep within it there were things that existed, although it would be hard to call it life. One could however say with relative accuracy, that whatever it was, it was not for the good of anything... I would say without doubt it was considerably more evil than we could ever imagine."

Runestone gave a gasp at the sudden deepening of her grandfather's tone, and she smiled as he gave a nod of agreement. She crossed her legs and moved slightly forward to get a better view, and the old man, happy in his heart, continued to tell the tale.

"The Earth as we know it today was all those years ago, a cold empty ball of mud and stone enriched with many particles, but it was not a place of life sat alone in the darkness. The day the light came into this universe was the start of everything, and what a splendid beginning it was." He gave a huge smile, and the young Runestone's eyes danced with adoration. "The light as you know was the entrance of what you know today as the founders of the Ruling Council. Much has been said in the text of old of their adventures, but we know little of where they came from, some have said they came from a race of distant people in another world entirely, and that they were stripped of their form for using the power between them to talk with their minds. I suppose we shall never know, but that is simply a matter for other tales. The Ruling Council began at the moment of their arrival, and such was the power of it that the sun exploded into flame, and light entered the world throwing the Merle into the furthest corners of our known universe."

"Oh Grandfather, how wonderful." Runestone's eyes burned with the thrill she felt at the thought of the five spirit like beings exploding the sun into flames.

Leenard gave a smile.

"It was indeed a most wondrous event for us, for the light twinkled off the smooth surface of the earth and caught the attention of one of them."

"Erathome." Runestone almost bounced on the spot with delight. Leenard gave a slight cough to clear his dry throat.

"He was known as the curious one, and yes indeed, he saw the place we call Earth, and it was he who travelled here first, and using the vast powers of his mind, he sculpted the rough ball, and created the Earth, for it was named such by him, and I might add it became the first word of a new language that would be established here."

"And home Grandfather, for was it not Tideguyde, his cousin who also named the place home?" Leenard gave a soft chuckle and lifted his hand to her face.

"Indeed it was, and such was her admiration and feeling for the work of her cousin, she took all of the debris from around the space of the earth, and she created a small replica, and it was to become the moon. If I do not mistake myself, I feel your favourite part of my tale is almost upon us, is it not?"

Runestone gave a burst of joy as her eyes widened with her excitement. "I love Rundalba and Hearlearn, they made everything." Her chuckles of happiness escaped as the old man watched feeling the joy of his most precious granddaughter overflow her.

"Indeed so my child, for Hearlearn fell in love with the Earth Home, and he came down to it, and found that he had the power to separate the minerals within the mud and rock, to mould and mix in strange fashions that created much that we see in the world today. Great was his skill, and such was the force of creativity inside him that he worked endlessly in the making of many new things, and one in particular, was so beautiful in its construction that it touched deeply within the consciousness of Rundalba, and she too descended to the earth, and took it as a garment to wear for all time, and so the form we know today as human was created, and her entrance into it brought it to life."

Runestone sat with a huge smile, not moving, as deep within her mind she saw the pictures of that first being, Leenard continued, feeling he would be wrong to disturb her precious thoughts.

"There was much that Hearlearn created, but he was spoiled for choice, as he liked the form of the human, but his heart was also captured by the finer workings of his creativity, and Rundalba took up the man form, and worked it carefully into that of a tree, and she created the garment for Hearlearn, who slipped inside and knew she was right in her choice. In that moment a power existed between them, and it was named by the oldest and wisest of the Council, and it was Albanlin who named it love."

"Oh how wonderful, Oh Grandfather, it must have been the most incredible thing, to wear the clothes of creation, made by the source of all life."

"It was indeed my child, and I think it is safe to say, that such was the power of the moment, that many things of greater wonder were created in this world, and all that was made by Hearlearn, had the life of Rundalba added to it. So began mankind with the trees and the flowers, and all of the beasts and birds of the land, and earth lit by the brightness of the sun thrived as a paradise. All of those mysterious powers played their part in adding gifts to the earth in aid of Rundalba and Hearlearn. Albanlin noticed how Tideguyde, who as we know was quite emotional at times, would sit on her own small ball in the space around the earth, and she scattered her feelings across the new world as it slowly revolved around it, and Albanlin in his wisdom noted the duration it took to pass round the whole of the earth, and he named the segments and called them the passing of time, and soon he found other things he could measure with his time, and through his skills we began the passage of time and called them days, weeks, months and years."

"Erathome grew bored didn't he Grandfather?"

"He did indeed, he was very adventurous, and it has been said it had been that adventurous nature that had got the group in trouble in their own world.

However there came a time, where he had sculpted many of the planets that we know surround us today, and yes Runestone, he did indeed become quite bored with everything. He announced he wanted to move onwards in search of more, and thus began the lessoning of the Ruling Council, for Rundalba and Hearlearn wanted to stay, and Albanlin did not wish to leave his youngest sister, so he decided to remain here with Rundalba to watch over her. Tideguyde was torn, as she loved her cousin Erathome, but wanted to remain together as a group, finally Erathome left alone, to travel the cosmos in search of wonder, and poor Tideguyde became very mournful. Hearlean called it mooning around, and Rundalba felt sorry for her."

"That is when Rundalba made the three suits for her, isn't it?" Leenard had begun to say the very same line, but Runestone in her excitement had beaten him to it, and he gave a deep chuckle.

"Again, my dear sweet child you are quite correct. Rundalba made three garments, which she presented to Tideguyde. They were fairer than anything made by Hearlearn, although it is said that they did not have the purity of beauty that Hearlearn had contained within the garment of Rundalba. Never the less, Tideguyde chose her garment, and when she slipped inside and she felt the emotions of wearing it, her power passed through it, and it shone with the reflections of the sunlight, and from that moment onwards, the whole of her little moon gleamed out in the sky. Rundalba took the two other garments she had made for her friend and placed them in safety unsure of what she would do with them."

"They would be Fae." He gave a nod.

"Indeed they would, but it would be many years before they were to be used."

"I have drawings of clothes I want to make one day; I have saved them like Rundalba did."

"It is wise to look forward and plan for the future, preparation can be everything in this world."

The two of them sat together, high on the hill that contained the old stone circle overlooking the hidden town of Loxley, and the woodlands and fields that now formed the border of Yorkshire and Derbyshire. Leenard took a long drink and loosened his coat, the sun was high in the sky as the morning marched towards noon, and the temperature was rising. The young Runestone with her long bright red hair, which reached the centre of her back, sat quietly as she watched the birds flying above the woodland below. The story had been told her a hundred times, and yet she never grew tired of hearing it, and her thoughts drifted around inside her head as she tried to put it all into pictures.

"Grandfather?"

"Yes My Child."

"This is the start of the Earth Faith, you know how Hearne created everything and Eve breathed life into it?"

"It is My Child, why do you ask?"

"It's nothing really... I just wondered, because you have told me so much about the others... You know Christians and Muslims and Jews and stuff, if this story is true, then how can there be others?"

Leenard was pleased to see his granddaughter questioning all she had been taught, as she applied her knowledge of what he had taught her. For him it was a sign that she was at the beginning of discovering her own real destiny, and the truth of who she really was.

"Well yes... I don't understand how if Hearne was the creator of everything, then how can any of the other stories be true?" She turned to look at him. "I mean we believe in Earth Faith, but the others equally believe in their faiths...which one is right?"

Leenard gave a nod of understanding at the confused look on his granddaughter's face. "Runestone child, this story is far more complicated than you realise, but to give you some answer to your question, I shall continue the story, as we have reached the most important part of the tale, and that is the part of knowledge." He put down his cup and loosened the button on his collar. "The Ruling Council had invented so many new words, yet at that time they all spoke with their mind, none of these words had sounds, and it was Rundalba who first began the process of working out the sounds and the meaning of the words. You see Runestone, she had trouble remembering all of the new words, Albanlin and especially Hearlearn would chat away freely using the new language, and she had trouble at times keeping up with them. Rundalba took her deepest feeling and gave it a symbol, which she carved into a tiny piece of stone. All of the ruling council as spirit forms emitted a colour that in a way showed their real skills, Rundalba was red, Hearlearn was green, Albanlin white, Tideguyde was blue, and the strong minded Erathome was Yellow." He took a brief pause as he hoped this new part of the tale would make some sense to her.

"Rundalba took the small stone with her symbol on it and it absorbed the essence of who she was, and the stone burned bright red with the power, it grew very hot and she placed it down to cool. That cooled stone became the very first letter in the alphabet of the new language that would evolve with wisdom and knowledge into the words we speak today. Do you understand what I am telling you my child?" She looked a little confused and uncertain, he gave her a gentle smile.

"The letter on the stone was the symbol of Rundalba, and it became the first runic letter. My Dearest Child you carry its name." She looked up surprised.

"Grandfather... It was the first Runestone, wasn't it?" He gave a slight chuckle.

"It was indeed, it's why you carry the name, it was I who named you at birth, because you are as special to me as that very first stone." Her mind reeled with excitement, this was new to her, and it thrilled her to know she was named in honour of something as significant as the first letter ever written.

"Runestone my child, Rundalba created words and language, and she decided at that moment she would sound out each of the names of the symbols she created. All the small red stones were lined out on the floor as she showed the others, and this became the foundation for the education of mankind. From that day forward man was given something that allowed him to have an identity, he could choose and write down his own name, and so began the thirst for knowledge. The council were so taken by it all that they too thought of taking other names, Hearlearn got Rundalba to write out his name, and it looked much too long, so he chose his favourite symbols and Rundalba rearranged the symbols and called him Hearne, I might also add that it was because of looking for a shorter name that she came up with two new words of her own. He was a patient man who would listen, and although at times he made many mistakes, he would never repeat them, and from those attributes the words of hear and learn were born." Runestone giggled.

"Why have you never told me this part of the story before, it's simply wonderful?"

"Like all things my dearest child, the process of learning must be structured."

"Oh Grandfather tell me more."

"Rundalba decided to use none of the symbols from her own name; she used two new ones that looked as simple as life itself."

"Eve... I know that, but it's wonderful knowing that she called herself that because it looked so beautiful."

"She was the lady of life who gave so much to the world, and I might add, it is a name you will see in many ancient texts, much of this story is similar to that of other faiths. You see my child, like naming themselves, mankind found a way to communicate and record all that had gone in the past, and so with time and a great deal of reflection, there were many who entered this world in the early days of time, who did great things that reflected those of the founding ruling council, and around them great tales rose up, and the seeds of many religions were mixed into the tales of old. You see my dear child, why so many have similar themes of respect and tolerance and love, they are there for a reason." Runestone gave a happy smiling nod; she had never heard her grandfather talk with such passion.

"Tell me about Albanlin... In Earth Faith they call him Lord White Line."

Leenard pulled on his white goatee, as he thought for a moment. He raised a finger and shook it as he began to speak.

"Alba as you know from your studies, means white in Latin. There are many words from the old language that have not changed much, and have appeared in similar forms all over the world. Lin in the old language means line."

"Whiteline." Runestone giggled.

"The Whitelines were the term applied to the power contained within Albanlin, for out of all of the group, he was indeed very strong. His power was based in his vast knowledge, which in turn gave him great wisdom. When he summoned the forces inside himself, they say it came out of him in a blinding flash of the purest white, and there are many who today believe his power is that of pure force. Albanlin never took on a new name, but yes my child, there were many who called him Lord Whitelines. I suppose in many ways, to the group he was like a father, never forget that they fled here from a terror in their own realm; I suppose him being the oldest, he naturally assumed a parental role. It is said that he felt great awe at the work of his companions, and even though he was the one responsible for time, he made a request of his sister Eve, to create for him a single man. When it was made, she breathed extra life into the man, and Albanlin lifted him up and took him deep into the Merle, there away from all eyes, he filled the man with all his knowledge of what surrounded the earth, he gave him the Whitelines of power, and named him Guard, although later on he became the guardian of the Whitelines. It is written in the oldest text, that this guardian was taught everything about the Merle, and when Albanlin returned and set him on the earth to live amongst the others, they feared him and named him Blackline, which was their translation of the word Merleline."

Runestone gasped. "Not Merlin... but he was good... how can that be, grandfather? Merlin was the protector of Arthur." The sheer look of horror on his granddaughter's face made him chuckle, as he lifted his hand to calm her and smiled.

"Dear child calm yourself, never forget that he was taught by Albanlin, he knew very well the secrets behind his own name. It is true his name carried the element of the Merle, but it was not darkness within him, it was the mark to show he above all others had been instructed in what really lived within the darkness. He carried the Whitelines of power, a power of purity remember; never forget Runestone, to know your enemy is the first step towards defeating them. Even at that time, there were elements of the Merle drawn towards the earth, and mankind became an easy target for them, the Ruling Council could easily resist them because of their strong minds, but not all men were strong, and soon after their education began, it became apparent that there were many in this world who actually courted the powers of the Merle."

"Witches and demons." Leenard gave a chuckle.

"They are just words created by the Christian church to name things they had no understanding of, witches were merely herbalists and midwives who chose to shun Christianity, and demons were terms applied to many people who did not behave as the church would wish them to, they never really existed, but there has been many over the years who have found ways of drawing power to themselves, and not always for the better. Never forget child that we all came from the same makers, and humans have traces of those who created them buried deep within them. Mankind has many of the gifts given them at the start of time, the most powerful I might add being love."

"Love Grandfather... how can that be powerful?"

"Runestone Sapphire, you stand on the edge of womanhood, and yet I see there is much still for you to learn. Never underestimate the power that two people can form in a union, for deep within them lies a force so powerful it could destroy the earth."

"But how Grandfather? I do not understand." Leenard rose to his feet and gave a wide stretch of his arms. He arched his back to stretch out the aches and then gestured to his granddaughter to stand. "Let us walk a while, the day grows hot, and I would rather move with the breeze than bake here in the full glare of the sunlight."

Leenard took her small hand in his, and lifting his bag on to his shoulder they turned their back to the sun, and walked towards the tall grey stones set in a large circle. He pointed at the stones stood proud with straggly grass at their base, set deep into the peaty earth of the moorland.

"These stones were erected in a time when there was little means of lifting and building, they were a labour of love to mark the moment a faith revealed itself to the world in its celebration. They were built with love, and remain here after all the time that has passed them, tell me my precious child, is that not a tribute to the love that built them?"

Runestone looked at the tall stone, which had weathered countless years here alone. "But it was not magic that built them, it was men with a lot of hard work."

"And child, there was some power at work to aid the efforts of such men. Something motivated and drove them to erect a monument that would last a thousand lifetimes. Was that not the love of their belief?"

He slowed his pace, and glanced down at Runestone, who he could see was pondering on his words. The breeze blew gently off the top of the moor, sweeping her hair backwards to the sun, and her face looked pale, he knew that she was coming to some understanding. "You have to understand Runestone that magic is just an ordinary simple word, for something that goes beyond our understanding. There is a force contained within all of us called life, yet we cannot see, touch or taste it. That force can be strengthened or weakened, it fills our hearts with love and drives the thoughts to help us understand it and come closer to it. It is all around you, and all you have to do is open yourself up to it, and you can draw on its power and achieve things of great wonder. There will come a time when you understand more, and maybe then you will recall these words today. Time will always get you to where you to want be."

This was the first time in a long time, that Leenard had been able to spend a great deal of time alone with his granddaughter, he felt a little of the pressure lift as he knew now the time had finally arrived, to begin in earnest his preparation of Runestone for what was still an uncertain destiny. The young twelve year old was simply having a wonderful day, her love for her grandfather mixed with the freedom of being outside of the walls of Loxley, filled her with delight, but she also felt that these moments alone, somehow were very important. Maybe it was the way her grandfather studied her reactions, or his tone edged with concern, deep down inside she knew that this was very important to him, and she felt he was trying very hard to ensure she remembered everything with clarity. It felt like the time was right to have some of her own questions answered.

"What is the White Circle Grandfather? I have heard you and mum talk about it at times." Leenard stopped and eyed his granddaughter, she had picked up on more than he had realised, and yet knowing who she was, in a way he could not understand why it had surprised him at all.

"Well now let me see... We know the powers given to Merlin were very much that of Albanlin, and we call them the Whitelines. Well Hearne had an immense power, which he used in his creation of all things, his ability to command the qualities of the earth where over time named the Green Circle, I think you know a little of this from your mother." Runestone gave a knowing nod. "Well then, Eve, who carried the real name of Rundalba, as you know was the sister to Albanlin, and she became the wife of Hearne, Rundalba means "round white," and it was at that time she decided to bring out the two spare figures she had made for

Tideguyde, and at that moment White Circle was created. Let me see now... yes... You see Tideguyde as you know missed her cousin, and over time she began to regret her decision to stay on her moon and watch the others. One day out of the blue she decided that it was time to go after him. None of them knew where Erathome had gone, and they tried to talk her out of it. The legend says she cried for two years, and such was her floods of tears falling from the sky, she created vast oceans on the surface of the earth. There is a rumour that is where salt water came from, although I cannot say with any accuracy. She returned to the moon to think and then just disappeared, it was obvious she had taken off when they were distracted, but by the time they all realised; it was too late for them to do anything. Eve missed her friend, and travelled up to the moon, where she found Tideguyde's smashed garment, she returned it to the Earth, and took out the two matching remaining garments. Eve crushed the old garment to powder and mixed it with salt water, and painted each of the new ones with it, the effect was that it enhanced the figures and gave them a very strong essence of Tideguyde. Just before she breathed life into them, Albanlin added the power of fellowship to bind them together, and Hearne added some of the power of the earth, so that never again would they be missed by the remaining members."

Runestone stopped walking and looked up at her grandfather. "Fellowship and Earth.... FAE." He gave her a big smile; he was very happy to see she was working things out a lot quicker.

"Very well done, and yes indeed it was the creation of the Fae. The first figure was given the seat on the moon, and was called at first simply Ofmoon, although Hearne named the second and called her Bridge, as he thought their union would bridge the gap between the two planets. Eve gave them a longer life span than any other, and she added a few small tricks of her own. Eve decided to use the Whitelines, which all of them contained, and she bound it in a circle of succession."

"Sorry Grandfather... How do you mean succession?"

"Actually, it's quite simple really. You see the way it worked was that like the force of life that created them; the power that was given would intensify as it passed to the next generation. The Fae were a fair and noble people, who believed in peace and friendship. Eve was no fool; she also had the mind to mix the Fae into the population of man as the natural peacekeepers, and used them to solve disputes. They were indeed very skilled in what they did, and when Bridge, who was later named Bridget, by her people finally reached the end of her long life, her powers passed onto her granddaughter Gwendolyn, and such was the power she contained that those who studied these things made the link between the Whitelines and the Green Circle, and linked it with the power of life, Rundalba, or round white, and so they named Gwendolyn White Circle."

"So the White Circle, is only the power of the Fae, it's not something a mortal can have?"

"As always My Child you are quite correct. The Fae suffered a great deal after the rule of Arthur and dispersed from their home on the Violet Isle, although they are still to be seen around many places, they have an elegance that almost shines out of them, it's really most captivating and touches the soul." He stood for a few seconds staring into space across the moor. Runestone noticed the almost sad look in his eye.

"Have you ever met one Grandfather?" His voice seemed almost as lost as his thoughts.

"Just the one, it was a very long time ago." Runestone smiled.

"Was she very nice?"

"What?" He gave a loud cough as he came out of his thoughts, and appeared to be suddenly quite flustered. "Well yes, as I say just the one, but yes my dear child she was indeed quite a remarkable person." He coughed more as he lifted the bag up his shoulder and then fumbled in his pockets, Runestone gave a cheeky giggle.

"She was really beautiful then?" Leenard somehow thought for a moment, he saw an almost Jade like quality to the cheeky twinkle in Runestone's eyes. He straightened his jacket and turned on the path, his voice was almost brisk.

"Yes I suppose she was, nice girl, very calm and clever." He walked forward and Runestone chuckled as she hurriedly followed him.

"Tell me more tales Grandfather." He strode on a few paces as he thought, and then with a smile he turned to her bright attentive face and took hold of her hand as he walked.

"Have I ever told you the tales of this place, and the rumours of Robin Hood coming from these parts?"

"Oh no... does he come from here?"

"He most certainly does.... Let me see now, where do I begin? Oh yes, Loxley..."

It was long after dark when they both returned to the high gates of Loxley. Runestone was feeling very tired after such a long hot day walking and talking with her grandfather. They made their way up the long dusty road toward the two rows of stone built cottages, and soon stood beside the gate with a flower shape cut out of it. Leenard stopped and took Runestone's hand to hold her back from opening the gate, and she turned and looked up at him. "Wait a moment Runestone."
She could feel he had something important on his mind, but she knew him well enough to know that he was looking for the right words.

"Is everything alright Grandfather?" He gave a reassuring smile.

"You know I love you Runestone? You are so very precious and special to me." She lifted her hands to hug him.

"Grandfather I love you too, I love the times we have together."

"Runestone there will be many moments in your life when things will not make a lot of sense, you must none the less try your hardest to understand that things have happened in the past that you have no knowledge of, but it will all become clear. I want you to try very hard to remember everything I tell you, but you must not say anything to anyone of the things we discuss, not even to your sister. Can you understand that?"

There was an almost urgent tone to his voice and it scared her a little, yet she saw the love and concern he held in his bright green eyes for her. "I understand Grandfather." He gave the softest of smiles.

"Good girl, believe me, I do think you are a very smart girl who has a lot of magic all around her. Trust your old bookworm, I will never let you down." She pulled him closer and hugged him hard.

"I know Grandfather, I love you very much, and I do trust you." He patted her gently on the back.

"Excellent, I think from now on we should have regular special lessons. I think the time is right to upgrade your education." He released her and gave her a soft kiss on the nose, she giggled. "Go on get yourself inside, I bet your mum has your tea ready."

"Alright Grandfather, I will see you tomorrow.... Good night."

She turned through the gate, and skipped up the path towards the door, the old white haired figure stood for a moment as he listened to the sounds of Rune's arrival in the house. "Watch over her Opal, she means so much more than life to me." The breeze lifted around him, and he smiled. "Thank you my angel."

Leenard turned, and walked the few paces to his own gate. The darkness deepened as he lifted the key from inside his coat pocket and fitted it to the lock, it turned with a resounding click and the old door creaked open. He took a step forward, and then looked back towards the direction of the high gates. "Dam you Mason, I should have killed you when I had the chance." The old door banged shut, and the street fell into silence.

From the moment that Runestone came into the world, her destiny had been pre-written on the stone, and as she stood on the edge of becoming a woman, Leenard could see a lot of similarities to his second wife Opal. It was obvious who she would become, and what her fate had in store for her, but it was still very difficult for Leenard. Mason was on the move having taken total control of the south, and Leenard knew that at some point his hideous mother would appear from her hiding place. It was something that made him shudder, for she had proven herself in the past to be as devious, and she was very talented with her powers.

Runestone was a quiet and studious girl, and although he could see the massive intelligence behind her eyes, at just the age of twelve, she showed no signs of the strength she would have to muster to control the force, which would soon push its way to the surface to shape her destiny. All the old scholar could do now was hope, it was his duty from that day forth, to educate her in a way that would show when the moment finally came. In the mean time he would observe, and wait to see just how soon the force of the red stone given to her by Eve would surface. The game was in play and the waiting had begun, soon like a flower she would burst into the bloom of her womanhood, and she would have to rise to the challenge in victory, or she would be slain, and the world would crash into the chaos of the Dark One and her vile children.

Alone in a dark world, a solitary figure dressed in a tattered black hooded robe gazed into a wide pan of silver containing the waters of Avalon, as he watched the rippled pictures unfold. The long red hair flew through the air as the young figure of Runestone fought against Morgan le Fey, deep below the Citadel Mount, she twisted as the black clad figure of Jett shot into the air between them, and the watching robed figure gave a loud gasp.

"NO YOU FOOL!" The rippled waters flashed, and the figure in black for the first time in his long life felt a sudden twinge of fear in his heart. "This is not good." He turned, and with a click of his fingers he was gone.

The water in the bowl rippled as the pictures showed Rune hit the floor hard, and gasp as her body hung limp on the end of the broken white bridge. Her eyes flickered for a moment, and the violet light flowed across her cheeks, and then went out. The touch of the black Star of the Merle had defeated her.

CHAPTER TWO

TIPPED SCALES

Look to the Bowman, for he will herald the start of new days.

New days could mean many things. In 2012 when the red death struck, it had been Mason Knox with his army of Cutters that had closed the roads, and prevented the death of many of his people in Cornwall. They had heralded the start of new days, as the rest of the country fell, with the earthquakes that followed into decay.

When Mason had walked out into the fields of Devon, and laid out his plans for the building of a new wall, again it had been heralded as the start of new times of fortune. The people of the south rose up in cheer, and celebrated the coming of a new king to lead the land.

In Loxley, as the young son of Robert Lox sat nervously in his seat, having blown a perfect pitch on the old bone horn, the gathered woodsmen of the north spoke of the coming of better times. When Robbie set forth and prevented Mason Knox from taking the crown at Canterbury, everyone looked up and proclaimed that the prophecy of old was true, and now was the time when the Bowman would deliver new days.

When Mason Knox fell at Liverpool and was washed into the sea as Runestone cast the land down, hope grew in the hearts of many, and yet as the days progressed the bright light of hope began to fade. Mason returned, as his mother brought him back from death, using the ancient ways of a devious Saxon past. When Robbie discovered the identity of the new king, hope began to rise, but York fell to the power of Mason's black clad army, and news from the realm of Avalon ceased.

The hooded man had disappeared, and as the country fell to the might of the army of the red dragon, despair now crept into the hearts of everyone, for now the new days as foretold, became the reign of darkness. Merlin was gone, and the

Houlen had proved to be a mighty enemy, Robbie and the group had achieved their goal, and placed Amethyst on the throne of the castle in the centre of the Mirrored Waters, but Morgan le Fey had proven to be as smart, and taken the realm for her own using the deadly black Star of the Merle. Hope on both sides of the fight waxed and waned on a daily basis.

Jett had been lost to the deadly Mirrored Waters, Treen and Jaz were on the edge of death, Rowan lay with a broken leg beside Robbie, who had split his skull and lay motionless below the blood streaked white rock wall on the edge of the Mirrored lake. Many of his group lay around him, knocked to the floor by the blast of the Dark One, and Rune lay motionless hanging off the edge of the white bridge, having been hit in the face by the Star of the Merle. Jade stood white faced, beside the slightly trembling William, as they gathered their thoughts for a moment to try and understand what had happened. The Dark One lay many miles away, on the far shores of the vast underground lake, as her assistant ran blindly towards her in the darkness.

They had all achieved their tasks, and recovered the sceptre of the lost king of old, but Avalon was about to seal itself as the Dark One's magic took hold, and the power of the people of the Fae of the moon failed. All was now lost, as the only hope for the green realm became trapped in the new domain of Morgan le Fey, and York prepared and planned to move forward and destroy Loxley. The balance had shifted away from the woodland people, Mason Knox had the upper hand, and in those bleak moments, to those around the Hooded Man, it felt like there was no hope left, as no one was left who could help them, or was there...?

Deep inside the thick ancient woodland, on the southern borders of Avalon, the fat swollen trunks of the oldest Oak trees alive groaned and moaned in rhythm, around the open glade that contained a long two storey wooden house with a large rough timber barn, set by an old forge made of crude handmade bricks of mud. The moon was high, although slightly obscured as the dark clouds flooded into the sky above, and the last of the silvery light glinted off the small glass window, that stood open in the warm night air.

The flicker of candles inside splashed the frame yellow, as an old owl swooped from a nearby tree, and swept a small squealing brown mouse into its talons. It landed silently on the windows edge, and gave a soft hoot, its wide saucer like eyes cast in on the silent old figure, sat under the candlelight in a heavy wooden and crudely built rocking chair. He was lost in thought as he puffed on the black stalk of a Meerschaum, with a wide round white bowl. The end of the pipe glowed bright orange, and was followed with a thick fog of white smoke, the old man's head turned to the window and stared at the bird, from under a pair of thick bushy white eyebrows.

"I heard em chatting hours ago Brooke my old friend, that's the trouble with them old buggers, they gets an idea of what's a foot, and blow me, they just wail and moan all night." He nodded to the old owl as it tore at the mouse held tightly in its grasp. "Too bloody talkative at times is Oak, not like the beech, they thinks things out before they speak." He gave a push with his woollen stocking foot on the dark smooth floorboard, and the heavy chair began to move, as he slowly drew in another long breath from the old pipe. "It's gone ill tonight, and I dare say it may look darker by the morning, I can feel her in the trees, and she is restless, it's been a long time since she walked these paths." The chair stopped rocking as the old figure grabbed at one of the arms. "Oh well, I'll stoke the fire and set a pot to boil, it will be nice to have company after all these years."

Two miles to the south, where the water fell from the high cliff, down into the wide bright pool, surrounded with thousands of flowers of every colour, a faint glow of red rose from the water, as every bloom in the clearing of colour bowed towards her. The colour intensified as it hovered over the water towards the northern most bank, and as it hit the dry sand on the water's edge, it solidified into a solid shape of a woman, who wore a long hooded robe of red edged with silver runes. The figure bowed to the flowers, and a soft caring voice spoke quietly. "Thank you, my children, I love you too." The figure turned to the path of dark flattened earth, where another dark figure stood dressed in long robes of tattered heavy black cloth, she smiled. "It has been long since you walked here my brother." She took a quick step forward and embraced him, his voice was calm, yet she knew him well enough to know he was deeply troubled.

"I cannot give you much time, but things have gone ill, and we must do what we can to protect her. Know now she has the star, and we may lose everything we have built here." The red clad figured gasped.

"How? It was hidden and protected with many cloaks." A pale almost transparent hand slipped out of the tattered black sleeve, and rose to her soft white face.

"It matters not, the fact is that she has grown more powerful than any of us saw, and she has it." His voice softened, as he touched her cool skin. "I have missed you My Sister, and now all I can do is give you a brief moment to put into plan whatever you can to aid the redstone, for I must leave here and seek the council of the moon, for this land was given to their care, and the door to the depths are closed to me." She slowly lifted her arms and embraced him.

"I will do what I can here, you must make haste, for I feel the powers around us are being drained, and time will run short if we do not hurry." She released her grip, and her brother stepped back.

"Come back with me when this is done?" Her face softened and she gave a slight smile.

"You ask always, and yet you know my reply? I made my choice for my own reasons, and even though I know you do not understand, my spirit will remain always here where I brought the first of my gifts to a world built by all of us. He is here in this place as well as my heart, you know this." The black hood gave a silent nod.

"Go with speed for the fate of all of us will hang on the coming days." She turned and walked into the trees, and out of sight, and the tall robed and hooded figure stood silently watching her.

There was no one to notice the hooded and cloaked figure as it walked slowly along the path towards the cabin. Inside the old man was sat waiting by the brick fireplace, as the flames licked the insides of the chimney. All around the room was the evidence of a life alone in the woodlands, as the woven baskets, and handmade pots lined the shelves, containing a life unseen by any. The silent figure sat rocking in his chair, a man of great age, with wrinkled tanned skin, and hair as white as snow that stood out from his head in every direction. He scratched with a hand as brown and worn as his face from his labours, at the thick wide sideburns that almost hid his enlarged ears.

He gave a gentle smile, as he rocked in his chair, and then came the shadow in the glass of the door behind the curtain, and he leaned forward, and looked back at the shadow that gently tapped on the wooden frame. "Come on in My Sweet." His voice had a ring of happiness, in the old high pitched tone that squeaked out of him.

There was a resounding click, and the door swung open as he gave a broad smile. He slowly stood up from the chair, and bowed with great reverence. "Ye took yer time My Sweet, it's been an age, and I now have the look of the bark I tend. It is good to see ye, come sit, and tell me of the world and ye new troubles."

The figure dressed in all red stepped into the room, and lifting her arms, her hood fell down, and her long almost floor length red hair glinted as it fell down her back. "Hello old friend, as I said I would, when the time of need comes, I have returned to you. I feel joy in my heart to see you again."

The bushy eyebrows of the old man twitched, as he peered out from underneath them like the old owl still sat on the window bottom; he slid back a highly polished wooden chair, and gestured to it.

"I think My Sweet that a root juice is in order to mark this occasion of meeting between old friends. Oh my, I must say it has been long since company graced the happy cabin of the Keeper." He turned almost as if he was young again, and scurried across to the wall of cupboards and swung back the doors. Eve took her seat at the long table of snow white ash; he turned with a cheeky grin, as she smiled feeling her own happiness. "I take it, it's sesame bread and goats' cheese as usual?"

Eve gave a giggle. "You remembered?" He gave a familiar wink, and hummed a soft Celtic tune as he gathered the bread, freshly churned butter, and the soft white cheese. Eve, who appeared very young and very Rune like, sat and watched with glee, as one would at a dear old grandfather.

Fagan Sylvester Hammond was indeed a great age. When Rhiannon had made the decision to leave Avalon and return her people back to the realm of the moon, Fagan had asked to stay; he had been a very popular figure in Avalonia as the Maker. His role had been to make whatever was required by the town's folk, and his skills in the lines of the Fae arts and crafts was well known. In his youth he had spent a great deal of his time in the old forest, a place not visited often by the other members of the community, and his love of the Forest of Time, was at that moment in time, unrivalled.

Many in the town had seen him as eccentric, and never really understood his love of the forest; to them it was a source of timber and precious foods. Fagan thought it was a realm of magic, filled with hidden pathways, with streams and waterfalls of wonder. To him, every plant and tree was a single life, and as precious as any other human. The Forest of Time held many secrets of the first years of creation, and deep within the centre Fagan found trees of extreme beauty, with fruits that had never been given an earthly name. When Rhiannon decided to leave, he had sought a meeting, where he had begged and pleaded to remain behind, and manage the forest for the next queen of the realm when she came. Rhiannon had listened to his words filled with his love and passion for the life held deep within the forest, and she had granted him the role of Keeper to the Forest of Time.

As the Fae of the Moon left the realm forever, he stayed alone and built his cabin, where he was happy and contented, at peace in his magical world. His life as a Maker blended with his role as Keeper, and he used the world around him to decorate his home and provide his food and warmth. Fagan had a knack of using everything, so that nothing he took from the forest was ever wasted, in his eyes to waste the smallest of twigs, would be an insult to the world he served.

There had been many rumours about the new Keeper as he packed his cart, and trundled down the white road away from Avalonia. Many said he had meetings with a strange woman deep in the woodland, and he talked to the trees, which could speak back to him. The strangest rumour was that when he made his arrows, he asked the trees to give him the straightest and longest twigs they had, and as he bowed to the trees, they would snap off their own twigs, and donate them with love to him.

His eyes sparkled as he sat down at the table, and cut a slice off the bread with his razor sharp knife. Eve took the plate as he offered it, feeling at home, she smiled as he stood, poured the drinks and then sat back down. "It has been too long My Sweet, did ye notice the barn and the new fence?" Eve gave a smile as she took the wooden goblet from her lips.

"It is dark, but yes I noticed. The place is looking better than ever, you have been busy in my time away." He chewed on his bread and cheese, and then swallowed.

"I like to keep busy, now the barn is done I intend to repair the forge, and I think a new kiln, the pots don't last as they did." He gave a smile, and then looked straight at her. "The trees are talking again."

Eve smiled; she had always loved his way of talking on one thing whilst thinking of another. His conversations would ramble, and then suddenly the subject would change, and have far more meaning than the words he had spoken. Eve knew he had heard of the events, he had ways of learning that had no need of people.

"And what do the trees tell you my old friend?" He gave a chuckle as he lifted his goblet and his eyes danced.

"Oh My Sweet, stones of such value cannot be hidden, especially moonstones, opals and the red stone." He put his drink back on the table. "They say she carries more than others, and the green one is much like a little wood nymph that once walked in these trees." Eve gave a big smile.

"The Green One is much like Opal was in the days after the creation, and the Redstone is far beyond any of us thought she would be." Fagan cut another slice off the loaf and offered it to her.

"The trees say that something eats at the life here, and she is in need of help. Her battle is greater than everyone expected and the trees whisper in fear, for they say that she is the one to fight the sky. The new queen is here but is cloaked in darkness; the waters have seen this and talked to the trees. I feel the change in the earth as I walk, even the poppies are nervous, there are strange folk and stranger deeds in this land of the beginning, and it does not bode well."

"Then you know why I have come this night old friend?" He sat back and gave her a long stare as he chewed.

"They have wounded, the trees have heard the river whispers. I will aid them where I can, but long has it been My Sweet, since I made weapons, I swore I would never make them for any other than my queen." Eve slid her arm across the table and took his large hand in hers. Her eyes burned a radiant violet, and Fagan could see the concern behind them.

"I understand that you turned away from violence to a life of love and nurturing, but they are in great danger. Their supplies are low and they will need use of a smelt, with a time of rest under a careful watch, they will find the strength they need to fight for all of us. I have come this evening to ask you my oldest and greatest of friends, to please watch over my line, and help Runestone protect all we built here." He wiped his mouth on a soft green cloth, and rubbed his long stubbly white chin.

"If I had meant to refuse ye, I would not have welcomed ye. It has been a long age since I made the weapons of man, I will ask the trees to show favour to these who defend our lord of the woodland and set us a new queen." She gave a smile and squeezed his hand tightly. He considered the moment and looked back up. "What has happened to little blue eyes, the trees say she has returned to the land of her prison, and talks to the dream people?"

Eve thought for a moment of her daughter, she gave a sad smile. "As told of old, and like myself, her powers have passed on, but she is happy and contented watched by her father. The Sandling's of that realm need her, and she protects them for the benefit of all others." Fagan watched as the wave of sadness clouded her eyes, he gave her hands a gentle squeeze, and he spoke in a low soft voice.

"She is the daughter of ye, will the white lord not let ye go to her?" Eve shook her head with sadness.

"He has only given me little time here; I shall return to the watch soon. I must do what I can here before my time is finished, I am lucky he relented and allowed me to return." She gave a soft smile to her oldest friend. "I miss her more than I ever imagined." Fagan gave a smile and lifted the jug; he refilled her goblet and then began to pour his.

"I cannot help them with powers while they are underground, below the rocks I can only walk as a man of the realm, ye know that My Sweet?"

Eve gave a nod. "They will still face many challenges before we can bring them aid, we must wait to meet them when they surface. I must admit I am concerned old friend, Little Morgan has more than her usual bag of tricks this time, she has prepared well, it is not like before when the soldiers of the town hunted her down with you." She gave a long sigh. "She has a power in her grasp that has even concerned my brother."

This was news to Fagan, the thought of Albanlin the high white lord being even the slightest bit worried, was very sobering news indeed. "The White Lord is worried? That is not something I ever expected to hear My Sweet. How could Little Dark Eyes become such a threat?"

Eve sat back as she sipped her drink. "Morgan has had many years to study in secret. Her powers have grown stronger than even the council thought possible for a mortal. She has defied all logic, and entered the realm unspoken of to take the Star of the Merle for her own." Fagan gave out a loud surprised gasp.

"She has the black stone?" His large ears almost flapped, as he shook his head in disbelief. "Well if she has brought that into this realm, it's no wonder the oaks are shouting like they have coral spot." The sudden seriousness of the moment hung between them for a minute, before Fagan almost breathed out his thoughts. "Is little Redstone ready for this? Does she understand what will be asked of her?" Eve was sat in thought and stared into space for a second before coming back to her senses.

"She is the daughter of my line, and from the union of the guardian of the Whitelines, she has long been the hope we have all carried. Whether she is ready or not, this will be her destiny, and it is now our task to help her achieve it. She has the White Star and what it holds, I just hope that it is enough to save her." Fagan gave a solemn nod as he listened. "Once she understands all that was written, then she alone will wield the power to shape the destiny of everyone, none have seen further than these days, all we can do is hope."

Fagan gave a happy chuckle. "She has a sister who I feel has gifts that maybe it was not the wisest of decisions to give to her." Eve joined in with a small laugh.

"Jade can be a little wild like her grandmother, but she is no fool, Little Morgan has had a small taste of the trickster in Jade tonight, I think it will balance her own methods a little. It gives me great hope seeing the love she holds for her sister, Runestone will be well aided with our little green eyed nymph in the shadows."

The owl on the window hooted loudly across the forest of mighty trees, and the clouds above slipped quietly past as the night moved onward. Inside the cabin two old friends moved from the table and sat by the fire, they sipped hot goats' milk, as they talked of times long past and young family. The Keeper of the forest, and the Lady of Life talked of prophecies, and bringing aid to the realm of the hooded man, and ways in which Avalon could be freed from the cold firm grip of the Star of the Merle, as the rest of the world moved steadily forward.

It is wise not to forget that life is uncertain. None of us really know what is just around the corner. Like a flip of a coin; events can turn and twist in ways that no one expects. At best all we can do is face what it is in front of us, and do our best to get through. It is a philosophy that young Robbie had used since the moment he had been pronounced the new lord of Loxley. In the times that came as he fought against Mason Knox, he would take a deep breath, and do his best to fight for an outcome that would benefit the people of the woodland realm.

It is true that Robbie came to the game late; Mason had after all spent the last twenty years in preparation for the taking of the land as his own. On countless occasions Robbie was told how this was his destiny and his task alone. It felt like a huge burden, but he faced the challenge, and after a year of endless fighting, he had left his children in the care of the two servants of the Fae, and made his way into the lost realm of Avalon.

The high sorceress Opal had warned him in his early days that his group would lessen. He had not expected to lose Melanie, who had remained at Loxley, and when Rafe left with Sapphire to visit his dying mother, Robbie noticed the change to his team. The loss of Alley to the Houlen had greatly affected the spirits of the Specialists, and as he fought his way up the tunnels, deep below the Citadel of Rhiannon, he had begun to wonder if his destiny was to lose the fight, and allow others to follow in his stead.

In the space of just one day, the fate of the woodland realm had slipped in favour of a man who had oppressed, and murdered so many innocents in his rise to power. Suddenly it looked like the magic, which had woven its web around Robbie and Rune had failed. He had achieved his task, and fulfilled his destiny, but it had come to nothing.

The new queen had taken her rightful place on the throne of the Mirrored Lake in the large caves of crystal, deep below the Citadel Mount in the realm of Avalon. As her powers began to grow, and Avalon lifted itself and repaired after the long sleep since the departure of Rhiannon, the Dark One made her move to take the sceptre of the one true king from Rune and the Specialists. Casting the power of the Merle into the air, she had begun the charm of binding, and begun to seal the realm against all who would oppose her, and the new queen found her powers were blocked, unable to be drawn down to aid her.

The Specialists had fought their hardest, as they met the greatest enemy they had ever faced. The Houlen had been a tough opponent, and some of the group had wondered if the secret hidden realm hadn't proven to be the unluckiest they had ever entered. After the final confrontation of the Dark One and her evil guard, the Specialists were now in the worst condition they had ever been.

Woody was distant, sat alone in the long grass, as he grieved for the loss of his companion Bess, Treen and Jasper who were injured in the fight with the Houlen, now lay close to death in a small clearing below the high series of thin rocks, on the south western edge of the Citadel Mount. Deep below them on the shores of the Mirrored Lake, the rest of the group were in disarray.

Bear and Big John lay on the path concussed, twenty yards away from the main group, having been thrown with great force by the spell of the evil sorceress.

Hornet sat stunned her head bleeding, slumped against the wall, and Crystal sat having just recovered from the fall. Steph and Smokes sat together as they came around from their crash on the floor, and now as Jade ran to her sister on the broken white bridge set above the Mirrored Waters, William the future king turned back toward the rest of the group. Steph was starting to understand the danger all of them were in. Todd, Blades, and Jay, were far ahead of the group, scouting out the tunnels, and not even aware of what had happened to Robbie and the rest of the Specialists behind them.

Jett Amber had gone; she had been thrown into the Mirrored Lake, of which everyone knew was a certainty of death. The Houlen were still loose in the labyrinth of passages, and the black vested soldiers of the Raven and Dragon were all over the place, with orders to hunt down the Specialists. In two separated groups, and unable to communicate, as the crystal rock of the cave prevented the passage of power, it was looking very bleak. The world of the woodsmen had suffered a mighty blow, and the balance had now been tipped in favour of Mason

Knox, as he finally took control of the battered walls of York. For the first time since the red death, the realm of the Green Lord looked like it was in mortal danger of collapse.

Rayne and Gwinne had moved their forces into the heavy woodland south of the city of York, as the Howling Fools helped organise in the trees, and they prepared for Mason to celebrate his victory, then begin his campaign to move south and march to try and destroy Loxley.

Jessica Lox had no idea of whether her son was alive or not. With her brother in law, John Lox, she prepared for the coming of the black army to the lands of her home. David Williams took greater control of the internal forces, as he prepared for a long siege on the stockade walls. John Lox commanded the forces encamped all around the large stockade, to ready the first lines of defence in the trees. The feeling deep within everyone, was one of great concern, all hope had been placed in the Hooded Man securing the throne of the king, to bring the country into balance and unite the whole land. It was not looking good as the fates had appeared to move into Mason's hand. Lost to them all in the realm of Avalon, Robbie and his group had no way of knowing what was happening, and no way of letting anyone outside the realm know of their dangers. Things looked very hopeless, and morale was ebbing away, and slipping into fear.

Destiny had written many years ago that a new queen would come to the Violet Isle, and the realm of Avalon; the question in everyone's mind now, was would the White Queen at Avalon remain seated, or would she be overthrown within a day of coming to power? She was still weak as she waited for the moon to pass into its final phase; it was a time of nervousness, with no idea of where the following days would lead.

On the south western side of Avalon, the lands where thick with heavy rough grasses, which in the past had been used to graze the large beasts that were slaughtered for the daily meat supply of the people, and also supplied the vital reed that thatched the roofs, and wove the baskets. It was wide open prairies that led from the town of Avalonia, to the base of the high green mound of the Tor, which housed many large scattered areas of woodland at its base. Here in the deep thick undergrowth Harry sat with Hawk, and watched the soldiers in the distance as they sealed the ruined town, and guarded the long road.

With the passing of power, most of Rhiannon's sealing spells had lifted, and the Dark One had bided her time until this very moment, where she seized her opportunity to allow her soldiers to venture down the long white road, to restart their supply runs from the curtain of light, sent to them by Mason. Torches flickered in the darkness all along the road, and it was obvious that with the hundreds of carts and soldiers now arriving, Mason had been planning this for a very long time.

Hawk was worried as he sat on watch. He did not want to move back into the tunnels again, but he needed to make contact with Robbie. As he watched, he knew the soldiers were now doing everything in their power to find Robbie, and with injured members of his group, he was stuck hiding in the trees. He felt torn, as he needed to find the others, but could not leave his team unprotected. He looked back into the clearing where Una sat with Maggs comforting a distraught Maddy. Woody and Rags sat in the trees opposite watching their flanks, and Gaynor worked beside Milly.

Gaynor looked up at Milly; it was not hard to see the fear in her eyes, and hear the scared tone to her voice. "There is nothing more I can do Milly."

The tears welling in her eyes formed, and ran down her cheeks. "I don't know a great deal about herbal cures, I have done everything Saff showed me, but it's not enough."

Milly smiled and pulled her close.

"Hey come on now, we cannot give up. It can take time with these medicines; all we can do is sit and wait. You are very tired, have something to eat and rest, I will watch them for a time." Gaynor looked at Treen's red face as she burned with her fever; she gave a gentle nod, and turned to move over to the fire where Maggs sat with the steaming pot tending the can that gave her a smokeless flame. Milly wrung out the cloth and folded it neatly, placing it on Treen's head to cool her, she lifted the other cloth, and with a tear in her own eye, she turned to Jasper and wiped his red hot face. "Don't leave me Jaz, I need you."

Ursula held her hands to the wall as she ran down the wide white path at the side of the Mirrored Lake. Three Houlen led the way sniffing as they went, they were still a little blurred as Ursula watched them through her burned eyes, but they had the scent, and she knew she must get to her mistress as quickly as possible.

Morgan le Fey lay on a beach of small white stones, where she had slammed with huge impact. A wide groove had been scored out of the stones, as she had landed with the force of Jade Opal's ripple of air. She lay still, her eyes closed, her feathered cloak torn with the impact of the sharp pointed stones on the beach. Her eyes blinked open, and she screamed with all her might, the stones on the beach vibrated as her shrill cold scream echoed across the surface of the calm water, and bounced across the high ceiling and walls of the cave.

She sat bolt upright, her eyes burning a fiery red in the dim light. Her hand clenched tightly on the black star shaped stone that she had snatched from the floor as she had struggled onto the white rail at the bridge. The moments of her confrontation with Rune now came back to her mind as she felt the pain throughout her body; Rune had proven to be an immense power, not unlike that of Eve. It was hard for her to accept the defeat, and she quietly sobbed to herself, as she felt the pain of her insides, that still held the contorted feeling where Rune had gripped tightly at her life force, and pulled at it in hope of tearing it from her. Twice now in the space of a few months, Rune had come very close to destroying her, she knew there was something she had done wrong, but as to what it was, she was not sure.

Morgan sat on the beach, and worked her mind backwards, as she tried to puzzle out where her mistake was. There had been a moment where she had brought Rune to her knees with the black stone, where it had gone wrong, she was not sure, she just knew that somehow Rune had found a way of drawing back her power, and had overcome the effects of the stone. She stared across the water into the distance of the huge cave where the white castle of crystal stood glowing white, and small in the centre of the vast underground lake, radiating light on to the high walls of white stone streaked with the violet seams of amethyst. "That has got to go." Her words spat the malice that now burned inside her.

The Houlen gave a screech, and through the blurriness of shapes, Ursula could just make out the dark shape of her mistress on the white beach in front of her. She knelt down beside her, and threw her arms around the very startled looking Morgan le Fey. "Oh Mistress I was so scared, I am so glad you are safe, I thought you would leave me forever."

For someone who had spent a thousand years alone, to have someone actually show concern, let alone hug you, was a very strange experience for her. The Dark One stiffened, an odd look on her face, and raised an arm up Ursula's back; she patted her twice very stiffly, and gave a small wince like looking smile. "We are safe my little apprentice, have no fear. Tell me did you follow all of the ritual?" Ursula pulled back, and looked into her mistress's red eyes.

"It is all done, including the containment charm. They will not leave this land, we have them trapped." The Dark One moved back, and then stiffly she stood up, and looked around the edges of the Mirrored Lake.

"Good. Come we have much to do, we must return to the cave and prepare. We have a lot of rats to round up, this time we shall be more prepared for them; the Flower Girl shall not evade me twice."

Ursula gave a smile as she felt on the floor for her bag, she stood up and the Dark One took her face in her hand and peered into her eyes. "They are healing fast; it will not be long before they are recovered. Come, we have a long walk and much to consider."

With the help of the Houlen guard, Ursula and her mistress made their way into the long tunnels, which took them to the edge of the northern border marshes above the Scree. Together they walked out into the night, and hurried through the woodland to the Hollow Rock, where the cave of potions and instruments waited.

In the realm of Avalon where the large Lake of Passing always shone in the moonlight, things had changed. The temperature was rising again, and there was little relief in the darkness from the heat of the day. The sky that had always shown the moon at its brightest and best was now dark as thick clouds rolled in, blotting out the open sky. For those soldiers dressed in black bearing the crest of a red raven or dragon, as they walked the ramparts, and manned the lookouts waiting for dawn, there was to be one more surprise. The following day, the sun would rise as always, but in Avalon, there would be no coolness of night to raise cheer to all. Morgan le Fey was now in control using the black star that contained the deadliest of all the dark powers, and while she reigned supreme, there would only be one more dawn. From the moment the sun rose, there would be no night time to follow and cool the earth, the power of the Fae for now was failing, as the Star of the Merle absorbed it and gained more strength. While the moon was high there was a chance that Rhiannon could interfere with the plans of the Dark One, and she was not going to allow that to happen.

Darkness still hung over Avalon, as it fought the powers of the Merle. While the moon still rose there was hope for Amethyst, as she entered into the new phase of the Queen of the Realm. Dawn was close, and so time was running out for Rhiannon as she watched from her garden in the Castle of Crystal at the centre of the Realm of Moon. Her mind was focused as she fought to restrain the coming dawn and give her granddaughter more time; the arrival of the black clothed figure of Albanlin was a distraction she did not need.

"My Lord it is long since you walked here, and as glad as I am to see you, this is not a good time for us." Rhiannon kept her eyes fixed on the water that bubbled and rippled. Albanlin knew she would not remove her gaze, as it could break the connection and give the full control of the land to the Dark One. He watched her closely knowing she was using all of her strength.

"I come to ask a great favour of the Queen of the Moon, at a time of great need." She had an idea of what he wanted, yet her gaze remained fixed on the water.

"I knew you would come, I felt Eve walk back into the realm in solid form."

"Then you know the true owner of the realm has returned, and your guardianship is over, yet you still fight to keep your kin in power?" Rhiannon's fingers tightened on the delicately carved rail of the viewing pool.

"Eve cannot assume power, most of her gifts are now Rune's, she will have to return back to her resting place, and remain the spirit of a realm she chose, and her time for now is limited."

Albanlin gave a small chuckle as he walked up to the side of Rhiannon, and placed a hand on her shoulder. "You must let me in, I want to take Little Redstone out to protect her until she is ready." Rhiannon shook her head.

"I cannot... Do not ask this of me, for you know what you ask means I must abandon my kin and risk everything that was prepared."

"You must let her go my dear child of the night, her fate is tied like all of ours to Little Redstone, we must work quickly to ensure she is safe until the moment of their meeting, everything hangs on the gifts of our lines finally facing the destiny set by all of us."

"If I abandon Amethyst now, she will be trapped at the mercy of that witch. She has not received her gifts; you are asking me to condemn her to death."

"I will not let that happen, but you must understand that we must act now or lose everything, for if we fall now, all that was written will be erased forever, you know this?" Rhiannon shook her head slowly, her voice crackled with emotion as she spoke, still holding all of her power, and focusing it on the castle deep below the Citadel Mount.

"How can you be so sure we were right? None of us saw this."

"Trust me, and allow me passage into the realm below the rocks, and I promise I will protect your line from the powers of the Merle. Open the gate and give me entrance, and I shall do all I can for her." His fingers gave her a reassuring squeeze on her shoulder, but she shrugged it away.

"What if you are wrong? Mistakes have been made throughout all that we have done, I cannot risk it."

"I am not wrong; you know this and I know you know why. Was it not you who counselled the Green Lord to have faith? Trust to that faith now, and guide me to Little Redstone. Rhiannon use the wisdom you have gained over time and open the gate, we have little time to waste here."

His words were soft, and yet carried the weight of their truth. Rhiannon knew he was right, and yet somehow as she watched Amethyst in the gazing pool, turn from the slumped figure of Rune far below her and swim back toward the castle, she knew she must place her faith in the most powerful and wisest of the Ruling Council.

"I know you know more than the rest of us, yes I do know of the aid you gave to my seer of old, there was no guarantee she was right, and to trust to the inexperienced is far more dangerous than my ability to hold on to Amethyst. Promise me, you will not fail her, for that stone is draining all of the powers of the realm and if I let go she will lose my protection. I cannot allow that witch to take another member of my line, I will not bury Amethyst beside Eleanor and suffer the grief I have endured again, promise me you will not fail her." She lifted her gaze slowly from the water, and Albanlin saw the fear and the grief contained within her soft grey coloured eyes, his voice was soft and filled with care, yet Rhiannon still held on driven by her deepest fear.

"Open the door, and I will show you."

For a moment Rhiannon closed her eyes, as her concentration shifted, her voice was a soft whisper. "Go... Forgive me Amethyst."

CHAPTER THREE

WITHIN WHITE WALLS

It had all seemed like it was going to plan, there were soldiers and Houlen within the tunnels, but they had been expected. All of them had known it would be a tough fight, and they were prepared to hold off as many as possible in the tunnels, which in turn would give Rune the time to get Amethyst safely seated, at which point it was just assumed that when the new queen took her rightful place, the power of the Fae as commanded by Amethyst, would come to their aid. Robbie had fought with all of his strength, knowing that fifty yards down the tunnel behind him; Rune was in full control, and about to place the new queen. Amethyst had been very nervous, but with Crystal to reassure her she had taken her first steps, and was ready to begin her new life in the seat of the Crystal Castle.

On the signal from Rune, Amethyst had travelled across the Mirrored Lake carried by the misty figures of the past queen's handmaidens, known as the boat of the Mirrored Waters. She had been placed upright on the steps of a large white ornate castle of crystal. She was nervous and slightly afraid, and yet as she saw the castle she had been filled with an unexpected joy. Her fingers and toes tingled as she took a step forward, and began to walk up the steps, through the lavishly carved archway of moons and trees; she peered into the side rooms of the vast entrance hall, and saw the large white stone table with a violet coloured sword inlaid within it. Amethyst knew this was the resting place of the one true sword, and walked quickly toward the table.

Almost holding her breath, she stood before it, and then raised her palms above it, as she had seen Rune do many times on her own table. The shimmering mist rose out of the centre and swirled into the air, as the voice of Rhiannon spoke.

"Greetings Granddaughter, now is the time of the passing of one queen to another, as I watch the realm of the moon pass into another phase on the mortal earth. Be at peace and know you are cradled in the centre of protection of my realm on your earth. Ascend the steps and take the seat of the watcher of the moon, and you shall be known as Vivian, guardian of Avalon."

Amethyst looked round to the high walls of the oval shaped room, with its white marble floor, and saw the ornate stair of platinum that spiralled up through the ceiling, to the highest tower of the castle. She turned with excitement, and hurried across the white shiny floor, and took the delicate rails as she quickly made her way up the spiral staircase.

At the top of the stair, she found herself in a room of brilliant white. Four smooth pillars held aloft a dome of clear crystal, on which somehow the moon seemed to shine. She looked up in awe, as she saw every contour and crater on the white shimmering surface. In the centre of the room stood a silver chair with a deep blue padded seat, in front of it was a small round table of clear crystal with silver legs, on which stood a large and very old looking basin of pure silver. She knew it was the water of the mirrored lake that was contained within it. At its side lay the sceptre of the one true king, she marvelled at the long golden handle that was inscribed in a very ancient tongue. The end was a large fist size ball of pure amethyst; it was a kingly jewel indeed. The voice of Rhiannon spoke softly.

"Take the seat and speak the words held deep within you, and be the queen and new ruler of this realm." Amethyst moved across the room, and turned to sit. For a moment she hesitated.

"Oh this is lot to be responsible for, am I really up to this? My only real talent is swimming."

"This time was long set for you my darling, never fear, for I will always be with you."

"Daddy, is that you?"

"Amethyst honey, relax. You are of the line of the moon, and I am connected to you always. Trust me and take the seat, you will understand everything."

Taking a deep breath, Amethyst sat back and felt the soft seat of the chair push into her. "I am Amethyst Diamond, daughter of Rayne of the Moon, and I have come to this place as was seen many years ago to claim my seat, and become ruler of the land of Avalon and the Fae Ofmoon here on Earth."

Her eyes blazed with deep blue light that swirled around the room. She swallowed hard as figures of light and smoke passed before her eyes, and bowed to her. The light faded and her eyes of violet emitted a soft blue light, her whole body seemed to fill with a tingling sensation, and she gripped the sides of the chair, and closed her eyes feeling slight nausea.

For several minutes she felt like she would swoon with the light headedness that pulsated through her, voices seemed to whisper to her telling her of things in the realm that had to be done, but she was sure she would not remember such a long list. The secrets of the moon were passed into the new queen, and Amethyst became the human embodiment of Vivian on earth. Her mind cleared as a wave of peacefulness passed over her; she relaxed in the chair and opened her eyes. The waters in the bowl like goblet began to swirl, and she swallowed hard as she leaned forward, and saw a picture forming. Rhiannon's face smiled at her.

"Greetings Granddaughter, and Vivian returned. Take the ring and listen carefully." A ring of silver rose out of the swirling water, and nervously she took it and slid it on to her finger. The moment it touched the bottom of her finger, the crystal within the castle began to glow, and as she looked out through the open wall between the pillars of white stone, and across the huge underground cave of the Mirrored Waters, she saw the light moving forward in a wide band, illuminating the whole inside of the cave. Rhiannon spoke again.

"You have accepted the seat, and now as the moon rises in your world and passes the phase of this night, so shall your powers be passed to you. These gifts have laid dormant within you for your whole life, relax and accept them as the day draws on. You now have the powers of the waters, you can enter the lake and choose one other to reign beside you, choose them quickly as it will aid the moment, for there is still much to do. When all of your powers are completed, the ring will glow in the silvery blue of the moonstone, use your powers well and be fair in your rule. All of this realm will be yours, and all in this realm will respond to you. Avalon will live again and rebuild itself anew, treasure your time with your chosen partner, and know that the Mirrored Waters will extend the lives of those who swim in them. Live in peace and be happy, we will talk often from this seat. Good luck my dearest Granddaughter. Now take the sceptre to the new future king of his realm."

Rhiannon's face faded away, and Amethyst sat back feeling relieved, as the world around her grew with the light. She descended the spiral stair and walked back out on to the steps, the misty figures that had carried her across the water were now solid and in human form, they bowed to her gracefully, which felt a little odd to her.

Amethyst wasted no time, and dived straight into the water. It parted as she moved into it, and when it surrounded her, it felt warm and made her tingle with pleasure. Her strokes in the water seemed to propel her ten times further than normal, and the great distance back to the white bridge, seemed to pass in a few moments. As she rose to the surface of the water, she felt a pressure under her feet, like many hands were lifting her upward; it was an odd sensation, and one she felt she would have to get used to.

Her time with the future king felt strange, he was so young and she felt she understood his feelings of not being prepared at all for the role of king. Rune and Jade had been as normal as ever, except to now be referred to as Vivian felt a little odd. She had taken James by the hand and they had lowered together into the water, and suddenly Amethyst had felt a joy like no other. They swam back to the castle and both happily laughing came out of the water; it was when James commented on her clothes that she looked down to see she no longer wore the garments of a woodsman. When exactly her clothing had changed, she had no idea, she just knew that it had something to do with the power of the place.

The next few minutes had been fun, as together they walked around the castle exploring the rooms that were now theirs. James had taken her into his arms and kissed her, she had felt happier than ever before in her life.

The scream of the Dark One echoed loudly all around the castle as it bounced across the water from the white bridge, and both jumped with fright.

"The crystal! Rune has not got it yet." Her eyes blazed with violet, as she looked about. "We must find it, Rune will need it." Amethyst ran back down the corridor into the room at the side of the great entrance hall and the white table, and without thinking she placed her hands on the table and asked the question. "Where is the White Star of the Mirrored Waters?" The table beamed brightly, and a voice she did not know spoke.

"There are many secrets in your realm My Queen. Know that the sacred crystal of my line is kept in the keep of the Mirrored Waters. Only you may take this thing that lies with the one true sword, take it to my daughter, as her need now is great. Look deep My Queen."

It took a second to understand, and she turned, and ran through the arched doorway and down the steps. Running at full pace, she lifted her arms, bounced into the air and bent over. Amethyst dived into the water without even leaving a ripple. She kicked her feet hard, and plummeted down into the hidden depths of the Mirrored Lake. The lake was as deep as an ocean, and somehow, without understanding why, she could breathe, it was a strange experience as she sank deeper into the lake, and the light behind her began to grow dim. Her violet eyes flared, and the light from them lit up the water all around her, her head moved from left to right as she searched the depths of the lake. It had been several minutes, when she noticed a faint glow below in front of her.

The star of white crystal seemed to glow brighter as she approached; she stretched out her hand, and her fingers closed around it, and was surprised at how small it was. Amethyst lifted it up and felt the electric pulse contained within it, it looked so small in the palm of her hand, somehow, she had expected something that belonged to Eve, to have somehow been a lot bigger and grander. It was just a star cut from white crystal that seemed to glow and pulsate with life.

Amethyst twisted in the water to swim to Rune, but stopped and looked back as a glint of something caught her eye. Slowly her body moved in the soft water, and she felt her heart beat faster as she began to descend. She could not believe her eyes, for there stood like a crucifix on a shelf in the rock, was Excalibur, the one sword as carried and wielded by Arthur. It was very similar to Robbie's, and yet she felt the great power within it, her eyes marvelled as she softly stroked her arms in the water to keep her level with it. It was the symbol of everything that Hearne and Eve had created in the world, all that Robbie and Rune fought for, all of their dreams and hopes for everyone, seemed to be rolled up into the one glance at the blade. She was mesmerised by it, and could not seem to draw her eyes away. The temptation to touch it was huge, but the tingling in her fingers brought her back to her thoughts, as the white star gave off a large pulse. Rune was in danger from the Dark One, and with one last look, she turned, kicked off hard, and swam back toward the white bridge.

It was odd swimming below the water and being able to breathe. Her hearing was also intensified, and although she was under water, she could hear everything perfectly, it was the strangest sensation ever. Amethyst heard the fight begin, and knew that Rune was gaining in strength, somehow, she felt that as she approached the bridge where Rune stood face to face with Morgan le Fey, the star in her hand pulsated more, was it sending power to Rune? She was not sure; she just knew she had to get it to her as quickly as possible.

The sudden intervention of Jett, brought a large pulse from the crystal, and Amethyst realised that Jett had lunged, and been deflected. Her response was almost instinct as in her mind she saw Jett head towards the water. It took a second to think the words. "Not the Water!" The flash of blue light flowed from her through the water, the lack of a loud splash calmed a little of the panic inside her, and she kicked harder towards Rune. The crystal star gave a mighty shudder, throwing Amethyst slightly off her stroke; she twisted under the water as she saw the edge of the bridge rippling above the surface.

As Rune's arm came over the edge of the bridge, Amethyst felt another shudder; it was like something had taken her heart in their hand and squeezed it hard. From deep within her warning bells seemed to ring. She kicked hard, and came up through the surface of the water, her arm stretched upwards, and she felt the star as it made contact with Rune's hand. A voice echoed inside her head.

"Leave here now, go or you will lose the gifts you have been given, protect this realm from the Merle. Leave now."

It felt like her legs were grabbed, and she was dragged back under the water. Amethyst felt the pressure on her chest, as if something was pushing at her, fear rose within her as her heart began to beat faster, and she twisted in the water, and kicked out hard to push herself away. Amethyst swam as she heard the voice of the king in her mind. The Dark One screamed, and she felt the water ripple above, as something passed over her. Her thoughts now turned to the castle and James alone waiting for her, and she feared that he was in danger. She pushed her arms back hard in the water, and instantly her speed increased. The new Queen of Avalon had to await her powers, and now as she swam, they began to build slowly. Her place for the time being was within the walls of the Crystal Castle, protected in her vulnerability by the powers of the Fae. The fate of Rune and all the others would rest on her shoulders, for the powers of the Fae would soon be hers to wield, and then and only then, would she be able to protect all of those she loved so dearly.

The four riders cloaked in black, streaked down the road towards the walls of York, where mounds of the dead still burned, casting the foul reeking smoke across the sky. The dust formed a thick cloud behind them, as at high speed they clattered through the smashed gates, and onto the smooth tar, road that ran from the green mounds of earth behind the walls. They turned into the central avenue that would take them down toward the new headquarters of Mason Knox. The horses skidded to the halt on the smooth floor, and the figures dismounted and the two guards turned, and blocked the door with their long silver spears. "HALT! Announce yourself or suffer."

The leader of the group dropped his hood, as he walked up the steps with an air of annoyance. His grim face scowled at the guards.

"I am General Mark Richard Dale of Canterbury, get out of my way and don't waste my time." The soldiers snapped into a salute, as he roughly brushed past them, and entered into the halls that also now formed the living quarters of Mason.

Dana Knox was walking slowly down the stairs as he entered, and looked up toward her, she smiled at the sight of her good friend. "Mark, you made it? How wonderful to see you. Mason will be overjoyed." Her pace quickened as she came down with a large happy beaming face, and she opened her arms and hugged him warmly. He seemed equally pleased to see her, as General Dale put his arm round her and walked along the long hall.

"You are looking good my dear, I do believe being up North you have blossomed. I am so pleased he has done it Dana; this was the best news as I stepped off the boat. Mason must be delighted, now we have just one more task, and he will have everything he has worked so hard for." Dana smiled more at his charm and obvious compliments.

"I must admit, I have not seen him so happy in a long while, it now looks like his plan is beginning to come together. I feel soon we shall walk in Loxley and then with luck, be back on route to London. He will be so happy to see you Mark, it's been too long."

He gave a chuckle. "His work at Glastonbury has kept me very busy; I just wish he had chosen me instead of that drunken oaf Walters. Did I not warn you he was past his best? You should have called me sooner, then I could have personally handed him York."

The large doors opened, and Mason stood at the new operations table, he looked up and his face broke into a huge smile to see his best friend at the side of his wife. "Mark you old rogue." He walked round the table as everyone in the room looked up, and watched Mason walk down and give him a huge hug, and slap him hard on the back. "It has been too long my friend; I am delighted you could get here on time to help celebrate." He slipped back holding him by the shoulders as he smiled and then turned to the staff.

"Food! Bring food, and wine for my guest, and your new commander in chief."

Mason guided his old friend to a long highly polished table at the end of the room. "We are very fortunate my dearest of friends, come we have a wonderful kitchen care of the ex-duke, he was indeed a man of a discerning palette, we have found a very well stocked larder and some excellent wine. Only the best for you as you tell me of Glastonbury and the wall."

The staff scurried as the table was laid with great speed; Mark Dale sat with Mason and Dana as they spoke of his last command, before taking on the new role of leading the attack on Loxley.

"It has gone very well Mason. They walked right into the trap as you predicted. The whole region is now sealed behind the wall, if they do make it out of Avalon, they will have no place to run, the circle is sealed, and we have twenty times the soldiers in place now." Mason gave a broad smile as he broke a leg off the duck, and placed it on his plate.

"I take it Lance has settled in and is ready?" Mark gave a nod as he chewed on his food.

"He is a chip off the old block that one, when I left, he was more than exerting his new authority. He reminds me a great deal of you old friend, I think the circle is in more than capable hands." He paused for a moment. "I must admit Mason I was surprised to see the church had a mission there." Mason barked a hearty laugh.

"I am a man of God haven't you heard?" Mark gave a laugh as Mason rapped on the table. "That mad old monk will give us no trouble, he hates the woodland pagans more than I do." Mason began to chuckle, as Dana gave a sly smile. She lifted the bottle and gestured to him for more wine. "Believe me my friend, the church can be a very persuasive force for our cause and with them in my control, we will find many stay right where we need them and will oppose the woodland dwellers in the fight to come."

Mark Richard Dale had been a member of Mason's inner circle for a very long time. He had helped with the early planning of the wall in Devon, and had played a vital role in the organising of the men to construct it. Not only was he a very accomplished leader of men, he had in the days of modern man been a structural engineer. He was very unlike the rough Cutters, he was a businessman, who was very confident and had no understanding of the word impossible, and he was used to getting his own way and had no qualms about how he achieved it.

He wore the uniform of a general, which had been altered to make his clothing more comfortable and highly presentable. Unlike the heavy vested troops he commanded, Dale wore a black heavy canvass shirt, with a black tie bearing the red dragon crest of the soldiers. He wore a sleek fitting suede black waistcoat and carried a long heavy velvet black hooded cloak with no crest, but four small red dragons to denote his rank. Dana had sought his advice many times during the period where Mason had laid in state at Tintagel. Lance saw him as an uncle, and he was one of the very few people that Lance actually showed his few emotions to.

Mark sat back in his chair, as he sipped his wine. His dark eyes observed the room in front; Mason smiled knowing that he was already assessing the place. "I take it you will find this place to your liking? It's a shame Franklin isn't here, he proved to be a very talented tactician in the end." Mark leaned forward placing his glass on the table.

"I have heard many things about him, he was highly respected at all levels, I always thought we would have worked well together." He looked up at Mason's bright blue eyes. "Did he have anything in mind for Loxley?" Mason gave a broad smile.

Mark Richard Dale had been very fortunate; he had boarded his boat at the base of the Thames, and enjoyed a leisurely journey. The boats that followed were not having quite such a peaceful time as they journeyed along the ancient river. The Sage worked his men in shifts; there was no point along the river, where woodsmen were not set ready to attack, and maintaining a constant watch. Twelve boats sat along the edges, burned out with large explosive holes in their sides. Louisa and her group of rough looking Outlaws had been moved from the riverside, and now took on the new role of aiding the Sage as he targeted the large buildings of Mason's industry.

Mason's commanders within the London circle were now on the defensive as they began to barricade and strengthen buildings that for years had known a peaceful routine. The attacks were so scattered that no one had any idea of who would be next, as the Outlaws struck with heavy force in the south, only to appear several nights later much further north. They sat below ground with the Sage in the tunnels looking at a series of warehouses that once were the facilities of Customs and Excise. Louisa looked at the table and the drawing of the cluster of warehouses.

"You are surprisingly well informed Master Sage. This place is a fortress; have you any idea of where we get in and out?" The blue eyes of the Sage twinkled behind his white mask.

"I would think Miss Louisa, to a company such as yours this would be a simple task." He gave a slight chuckle as he rubbed the white bristles on his chin. "I know this is a tough place, but this is the golden goose of Mason Knox. This is the place where most of the new weapons are stored ready to be shipped around the country." Louisa looked at Ox sat next to Rigger.

"What you think guy's?" Rigger leaned over Ox, and pulled the drawing towards him.

"It's big, but there is always a door if you look for it. Dove and me will find it; you and Doc look at the spread, let us worry about making it in and out." Louisa nodded and looked back at the Sage.

"When do we go?" He sat back in the chair, and marvelled at the casualness that they projected, although he knew already deep inside the whole team, they were already taking the place apart and looking for weak spots.

"This one is your own special project, take your time and plan well. I want this one more than all the others, have a look at all the info, and then let me know." The Sage stood up and gave a smile. Turning, he made his way across the tunnel, where he left the group surveying their next target. The door ahead opened as Nathan returned from his observation of the docks along the east of the river.

"Commander, all well I take it?" Nathan looked across at the group behind the Sage huddled together as they planned their attack, his face changed to one of contempt as he passed by.

"It was fine.... For a Sergeant." The Sage looked back at him.

"You are not happy with your placement Commander?" Nathan turned back to the Sage.

"In Caerleon I command a whole battalion, here I just sit and watch boats, while others with less experience do far more important work... I guess... I just feel I would be better placed back at the castle where I am needed." The Sage took a few paces back toward him.

"I am sorry you feel you are not used as you feel you should. I have to say Commander; I feel that stopping boats attacking Loxley to be a priority, and it is not a task I would trust to an untrained man. If you desire a more active role, I can arrange that you lead a strike mission, we have several in play at the moment." Nathan stared at the Sage as he spoke.

"I am not complaining, I just feel I can do more than is being asked of me. I would welcome a chance to prove myself; I believe you are planning a big job on the eastern docks?" The Sage gave a nod.

"You seem well informed yourself. Yes, we have something going on over there, but I have allotted a crew to that task. I shall find you something though, take the next few hours to rest as I talk with Brian, I will advise you of your command presently." The Sage watched as Nathan walked to his room, his eyes never left the quietly planning group of Outlaws. Martin Jarrod wandered in through the doors, and looked at the Sage as he watched Nathan.

"Problem?"

"What?" Martin smiled.

"You seemed preoccupied; I just wondered if there was a problem?" He watched the group and then the door as it swung behind Nathan.

"Our commander is restless and seems unsatisfied with his position." He turned back to look at Martin. "Keep an eye on him Martin, call it intuition, he bothers me at times." Martin gave him a nod and patted his shoulder.

"Come on, there is rabbit stew on the menu." Together the two of them went back through the door, and headed into the maze of tunnels in the direction of the new kitchens.

Louisa felt tired, she had been up all night and now as the day stretched into the afternoon, she was feeling exhausted. On the lower platforms, a series of new rooms had been built. They were small with enough room for a small bed and a wardrobe, with a little cupboard and a shelf next to the bed. It wasn't the easiest place to be, Louisa found that at times she felt very penned in. She had taken to sitting on her bed with the door that opened outwards wide, as she felt the little breeze that moved slowly through the old tunnels. Doc had managed to acquire a stack of books from somewhere, she was finding the Outlaws were very self sufficient, and asked for nothing, whilst obtaining everything they wanted. Sitting quietly with her boots off, she read the book and relaxed as her eyelids fluttered.

"Some people seem to be getting on better than the rest of us." Nathan's voice with its usual hints of sarcasm broke the peace; Louisa didn't even lift her eyes from the page.

"What's biting you now Nathan?" He leaned in through the door.

"Oh, I don't know, I just find it strange that one or two down here seem to be high in the favours of others, whilst the rest of us seem to be treated as lesser officers." She looked over the book.

"Oh, please get over yourself. If my lads have anything more than you it's because they get off their backsides and go out looking. They work really hard Nathan, when are you going to get that chip off your shoulder, and realise they do the most dangerous jobs?" She turned the page of her book, and began to read.

"That is sort of the point though isn't it? I mean one has to ask what exactly goes on behind closed doors to get such preferential treatment."

"WHAT?" The book hit the floor, as Louisa stood up and scowled at Nathan with anger. "Just what are you implying?" He gave a smile.

"Well to be honest, you didn't exactly resist slipping under my sheets, I just have a scar, and maybe there is more than meets the eye under that white mask."

"OUT! GO ON, GET THE HELL OUT OF HERE BEFORE I DO SOMETHING I WILL REGRET."

Louisa was ready to explode, as she pointed to the door. Her eyes burned with her rising temper. "I have had it with you Nathan; don't ever remind me of my stupidity in the field again. No one regrets that more than me now." Her nostrils flared, as she stared at him in disbelief. "Is that what all your bullshit is about? Has this come down to your childish level of the boys in the schoolyard? I work just as hard as anyone here, and you can bloody well believe me Nathan, it has not been easy. If I get the most dangerous jobs and that pisses you off then hey... You bloody well be my guest, because I have no idea if I will return every time I leave here. It's got bugger all to do with bed play; the Sage unlike you, has more manners, and would never expect that. NOW SOD OFF!"

Louisa pushed him hard in the chest, and he took several steps back with the force. "I mean it Nathan; leave me the hell alone, do you hear me? I am under the command of Jett Amber, never forget she has regular reports from me." Louisa grabbed the door and pulled slamming it back into the frame, which shook violently, as she slipped the bolts in place. Nathan turned, and walked straight into the tall muscular frame of Tiny.

"You not upsetting Miss Louisa again, is you?" Nathan pushed past him roughly.

"Get out of my way dung hill." He walked briskly down the passage muttering. "Bloody Jett this, and Bloody Jett that. That woman is becoming the bane of my life." Tiny tapped softly on Louisa's door.

"You alright Miss Louisa? He has gone now; you want me to stand here and watch?" Louisa's voice sounded calmer as it came back through the door.

"No, it's alright Tiny, thanks. I will be fine; I just need some sleep. You go get your head down." He nodded as she spoke through the woodwork.

"Alright Miss Louisa, but if he comes back causing a ruckus, you give me a call, I can always bend him a little so he understands." Louisa gave a faint giggle through the door.

"No, it's fine honestly, but thank you that is a very sweet offer." Tiny smiled.

"Sleep well Miss." He turned, and walked back to the door at the end of the white tiled passage. Louisa sat on her bunk and smiled, Tiny was huge, and she imagined that not many would survive him bending them a little. She picked up her book, and took a long deep breath, and began to read again.

The day had moved on, and the night was over. Amethyst had felt nervous all night, and now her nerves were increasing. For a while as she wandered around with James, she had felt fine, their new home was better than either of them could have dreamed of. She felt happy and laughed as he joked and they explored, the bedroom had been a real surprise, and he had pulled her softly on to the huge luxurious four poster bed and held her tight. The night had passed in each other's arms, and she had risen feeling more alive than ever before. The servants whose names she was trying to learn, had been very nice and welcoming and treated both of them with such courtesy, although it made James feel a little uncomfortable. He was used to being called Fish, not My Lord, and he usually hunted for his own food, which he then cooked. He also called Amethyst, Amy, where as they all now called her Lady Vivian, this for him would require a lot of getting used to.

He had noticed how Amethyst kept looking at her ring, she began to look very worried, and as they sat on the steps of the castle and watched across the calm waters, he lifted his hand and pulled her close. "You are alright, aren't you?" She smiled and gave a nod.

"Yeah, I am fine, it's just..." She lifted her hand with the large ring on it up. "My grandmother said as the moon rose this ring would turn bright silvery blue, and I would know then that the phase of the powers would be complete. Look it is still clear; I guess I thought by now it would be blue. Does that mean something is wrong?"

Fish gave a shrug. "All this is beyond me Amy. A nun in poverty brought me up, the only powers I was taught was that of Sister Mary's god. To be honest most of the time I was so busy daydreaming, I hardly heard a word of that. Since meeting Rune and all of her family, I have been lost in it all. It does take a little getting used to you know?" Amethyst gave a small laugh.

"Yeah, I suppose it does. The thing is, I am a little worried, mum has told me so many tales over the years to train me, and yet now actually being here and being treated like a queen, I guess I feel a little out of my depths. I am really worried something has gone wrong and I don't even know it."

"Can't you talk to Rune?" She gave a long sigh.

"That is what is bothering me. I cannot get in touch with anyone. I have been trying for an hour, but it feels like they are all blocked to me, even Crystal and dad." His understanding of the magic was minimal, but even Fish knew that was not right. He had never known a time with Rune when she could not contact everyone. He stood up and looked round nervously, suddenly he felt a chill in his spine and he felt very isolated.

"I don't know much Amy, but Rune would never leave you out of touch. I think you are right, all is not well, and it's not too hard to work out who is behind it." He grabbed her arm. "Come on let's get to higher ground, if we are going to have visitors, I want to see them in advance whilst holding a bow." He walked backward up the steps as he spoke. At the arched doors, he turned and headed for the spiral staircase. "We will have a better view from up there." Amethyst followed him, as he grabbed a silver bow and a quiver from the side of the stairs. "It aint rowan wood, but it will do."

Up in the high tower, Fish walked round checking every direction. Amethyst sat down in the chair and looked at the goblet of water. She gave a slight squeak as a small hand came up out of it. Fish turned quickly, and blinked as the small woman in red, rose up above the clear water. She gave a long bow to Amethyst. "Greetings My Queen of the realm." Both of them just stared in wonder.

"Rune?" The figure smiled.

"I am not she, although I wear the garment of her likeness. You are troubled My Queen and you are wise to listen to your feelings, for they are bound to this realm and show you the right paths to walk on." Fish crouched at Amethyst's side as she leaned forward.

"It's the Dark One isn't it?" The figure in red gave a smile, and turned to face him.

"The mortal Le Fey carries a gift of darkness, from the moment of her entrance into this realm; the balance of the magic has been tipped in her favour."

"The Star of the Merle?" Amethyst almost breathed the words out. Eve gave a nod of recognition.

"It does not belong in this realm, and from the moment it arrived, it has been drawing power to itself. I saw your attempts to save the child of the red queen; they went adrift did they not?" Amethyst suddenly looked embarrassed.

"I tried to help Rune. My mother told me the queen of this realm had to simply think, and it would be done. I wanted to send Jett away from the water, and on to the bank, I think Rune did something at the same time as I thought, and we exploded her." Amethyst hung her head. "I am so sorry; I thought the powers were with me, I think I killed her." Eve gave a small chuckle.

"Relax my child, the daughter of the red queen is safe, although she is further from home than expected, she is well have no fear." Amethyst gave a long sigh of relief and smiled; Fish just looked at her with wonder. Eve's tone became more serious.

"This thing of evil coming to this land was never seen, the daughter of life now is starting to grow in strength, although it will be some time before she has her full powers back. The white star will aid her and resists the black one; the powers of the moon will not be fulfilled until Life has dealt with the black star. You must be patient, as you sit here and wait; the whole of your realm has been sealed. The soldiers of the Raven now command your towns and islands. If any enter the lake they will die, and no boat can float on the Mirrored Lake without your command, even the mortal one cannot overrule the commands of old."

They both felt a little relieved, Fish looked at the figure in red. "So we are safe for now, and just have to sit and be patient?" Eve thought for a moment before looking at both of them.

"This is unseen, and the black one has in the past done many unexpected things. This castle has many protections, but there was never any protection from something as powerful as the black star, by all of the rules of this land, you should be protected, but I have to honestly say I cannot be sure. You are right to watch the lake and prepare, it is good council, and I would advise it. Soon I will go to Life and speak with her, she will know of your plight, time here is short, but know we will help the lord of the woodland realm, and bring aid as swiftly as we can. You will know the moment when the seal breaks, for then the powers will flow true and the ring will turn blue. Until that time, be on your guard." The figure turned, and Amethyst gave a small murmur.

"Please do not leave yet... Tell me, who are you, and how do you know of these things?"

The figured turned back and gave a smile that was very Rune like; it was then that Amethyst noticed the violet eyes. The figure nodded. "Yes, My Child, I am still here in the garden I created with your high lord of the woods. As with all of my lines, when we pass from the mortal realms and leave behind the garments we wore, we then are bound to one realm to keep and protect it for eternity. I chose the realm of my happiest times, and I am now a servant of this realm and its queen. Have no fear for I will not desert you, my granddaughter of my line will come to the aid of my queen and her kin." She gave a warm smile, and Amethyst smiled back.

"Thank you, mother of all lines. I am comforted greatly knowing you are with me."

The figure bowed and Amethyst bowed back. Fish watched not really understanding. "Yeah, thanks granny what's it, it's a big relief." Eve gave a loud laugh as she disappeared back into the calm waters within the goblet. Amethyst gave a giggle, and sat back in her chair with a long gasp.

"James what were you thinking, do you know who that was?" He shrugged.

"No, who?" She began to giggle.

"That was Eve, the power of life herself, it was because of her gifts that all of us are here." He gave a nod.

"Yeah, I get it now. That's why she looked like Rune isn't it?" Amethyst shook her head.

"You're hopeless, you know that?" He gave a broad smile.

"Yeah, that's why you love me isn't it?" She slid her arm round him, and pulled him close. She did love him there was no doubt. What she doubted was the fact that Eve could give no promise they were safe. In her mind the words 'Hurry Rune' echoed.

Across the huge underground cave, the ceiling reflected the twinkle of the water below, and the crystal castle set at its heart was silent. On the round dome above the tallest tower, the moon was still visible as it crested the top of the sky above, and then began to fall as the dawn approached; outside across the realm of Avalon all was still in total darkness.

CHAPTER FOUR.

HARSH REALITY

Rowan moaned in pain at the side of the motionless Robbie, Crystal, a small cut to her cheek crawled over towards him, as the others stirred on the ground regaining their senses. Steph was on her feet, as Smokes leaned against the wall, his legs still feeling a little shaky; he glanced around at the sight of the others, who had all felt the power of the Dark One, as she blasted them down with huge force. "God, I hate that woman, what the hell happened anyhow?"

Steph caught the glint of his bright blue eyes, in his hot dirty face, as she looked toward him, then back towards Jade who was running along the long wide path, back towards the ornate bridge that stretched out into the start of the Mirrored Waters.

"I am not really that certain, I think William did something to protect Rune, then all hell broke loose, and I ended up here on my back." She surveyed the damage and noticed the slumped figure of Robbie and the thick trail of red down the wall behind him. It took a few seconds to survey, but she quickly assessed the situation and realised it was not a good one. "We got big trouble honey, help everyone; we are not out of this yet."

Crystal looked down at Rowan's leg. "Urgh!!" She glanced back at his face. "Don't look." It was too late and she saw the look of horror pass over his face, as he saw the section of bone sticking through his pants just below the knee.

"SHIT!!" He flopped back on the floor and clenched his teeth. Crystal gave it a closer look, as Steph knelt down next to Robbie. Crystal gave a sigh as her eyes met Steph's.

"We are going nowhere until we fix this, he cannot be moved whilst his leg is like that." Steph gave a nod of agreement, and screwed up her nose as she viewed the leg.

"Can you do it, while I check Robbie?" Crystal nodded and looked towards John who was sat watching, not able yet to stand on his feet.

"I need you to hold him while I do this." He gave a nod as she looked down at the frightened look on Rowan's face. "I will freeze your leg to dull the pain, just keep as still as you can and it will be fine." He did not speak, but it was clear from his look he understood. The sweat rolled down the side of his face, as Smokes knelt down beside him to lift Robbie for Steph to inspect.

John crawled over and took hold of Rowan, and a bleeding Bear staggered up with a stunned looking Hornet. Crystal took off her long white gloves, and Rowan tensed, he swallowed hard. "I thought you were deadly with those things off?" She gave him a cheeky wink.

"I can control it; just be grateful you won't feel a thing." He gave a slight attempt at a smile and lay back, turning his head to look away, and Crystal went to work. Robbie had been knocked out, and had a very large cut on the back of his head. He groaned as he slowly came back round. The blood had soaked his collar and the right side of his face and hair. Smokes held him sat up, as Steph made a pad from a scarf, and bound it on to the back of his head. She took out her knife and cut a wide strip from her cloak and tore it into bandages.

"It will need a proper looking at, but that should hold until we get you up top." Robbie gave a nod and wished he hadn't, as his head pounded. With the help of Bear, Crystal pulled on Rowan's leg and the bone disappeared through the skin, Rowan gave a loud moan, even with his leg frozen, the pain was still intense. Robbie looked round at everyone, with their dirty sweaty faces from the fight, and the slightly dazed look in their eyes. There was a loud crack, as Bear snapped a bow to make splints for Rowan's leg, and Hornet tore up his cloak to make more bandages.

Shakily Robbie got to his feet with the help of Smokes, William was watching out half way between the bridge and the group. His back was to the bridge where Jade had just ran up the steps, and was looking at the floor at the end of the bridge, the final moments were beginning to come back into Robbie's pounding head, as he remembered the fight with the Dark One. He looked at Jade who turned and shouted across to him. "ROBBIE SHE IS NOT HERE, WHERE IS SHE?"

Her voice echoed inside the large cave, and bounced across the water towards him. Jade was quite far away, but he could see the look of panic on her face, the questions stumbled into his brain. Had she fallen into the water? Did the Dark One take her? Had she opened a window and slid through, so that she could return any moment to help them? Holding the wall, he was already moving swiftly towards Jade, although his legs felt hollow and he shook.

William grabbed his arm to steady him, and Robbie gratefully accepted the extra support to help him move faster. He could see Jade looking over the rails along the bridge, as she checked the crystal clear waters for any sign of her sister. Robbie felt a cold tingle run down his spine, and panic rose in his chest as his pace quickened towards the steps leading up to the bridge, where she had last been seen. Steph and Smokes now aware of Jade were right behind him, as they ran to catch up. Still shaking and leaning slightly on William, he made it on to the empty bridge in front of the long tunnel that ran up into the heart of the Citadel, where he had fought off the soldiers. The dim lifeless shapes of the dead littered the floor at the far end of the tunnel.

He scanned the bridge and looked in hope to Jade. "Where was she when you last saw her?" Jade pointed to the very end of the bridge as a tear ran down her cheek.

"She was there... Robbie she fell on the bridge, but she never fell off, I was watching, she fell right here but she has gone into thin air, I have tried to talk to her but she is nowhere to be found." Robbie lifted his arm to her as her tears streaked down her dirty face.

"Come on Pebbles, don't cry, she must be somewhere, we just need to find her." Jade gave a huge sniffle, and wiped her face with her sleeve.

"Why would she leave us Robbie?" He pulled her close as they walked down the bridge to the edge of the tunnel, where Steph now stood with Smokes and William.

"I don't know Pebbles, I just know that she would only go if it was important, maybe she has gone to Amethyst." He looked up at Steph as he drew closer; he could tell her mind was already connecting with his.

"Something is wrong here Robbie, I am not sure what, but I can tell you, I don't like it." His instincts were telling him the same.

"Rune did get Amethyst to the castle didn't she?" Steph gave a nod.

"Yeah, everything was fine, until the Dark One turned up." Robbie turned and looked out across the water, where in the distance the castle shone brightly.

"So, if Amethyst is now the new queen, why do I feel that something has gone horribly wrong?"

"Let's face it.... Man it's been a shit day." Smokes gave a long sigh as he sat on the steps on the opposite side of the bridge with William, his long red hair hung lank across his dirty cloak. "Since the moment we came here, they have been lining up to nail us. I'm telling you Robbie, Mason knew we would come, and this whole place has become one big nightmare of a trap." Robbie patted his back as he slipped onto the step beside them and took the weight off his shaking legs. Jade walked down to the bottom of the steps.

"What we going to do Robbie?" It was a very good question, and not one he had the right answer for at the moment. He lowered his aching head to his hands and rubbed his eyes. Steph answered before he could speak.

"We are separated, so we need to find the others, and fast. Blades and Todd were scouting ahead with Jay. I cannot believe Keith would stay put with all the soldiers around, I would have thought he would have made it to the surface."

Robbie looked up.

"Getting everyone together is our only objective, after we are together again, we will look at the situation, and when I say everyone, I mean Rune as well, I want her found and fast."

"GET DOWN!" Robbie lurched forward as Smokes twisted on the step and pulled at him, his unstable legs gave way. He slithered onto the lower steps as Smokes pushed him harder, and he crouched above Robbie. William was facing the top of the steps and peering across the bridge to the other side, where the rest of the group now sat, surrounded by black vested soldiers, who were pouring out of the tunnels ahead of them. Smokes pushed on William shoulder.

"There are too many, we are no match for that lot, get the others back." He gave another soft push and William slid down to Robbie's side. Smokes looked back at them. "We got more trouble Rob, it looks like they got the others, they are binding their hands, and I think they are taking them prisoner. No offence Rob, but we need to get the hell out of here, and then find out where they are taking them, we are no good to them caught in a bag." Robbie was not sure; his head was pounding and making it hard to think clearly, he looked at Steph, who gave him a slight nod.

"Pete is right, if we get caught, they have no hope of being freed, although at this moment in time, I am not that sure there is anywhere safe for us. I think we can pretty much agree that there is no queen in control here... well not one we would want to serve. We need to find Rune; without her we have had it."

He knew she was right, but the thought of his friends in the hands of the enemy was a chilling proposal. There had to be a reason for Rune to disappear, and he knew that Steph made sense, without Rune they could not help Amethyst or contact the others. Reluctantly he gave a nod of agreement, he looked at Jade who gave a slight nod and put her head down, William agreed and he looked back to Smokes.

"What you got in mind?" Smokes looked back across the bridge for a moment, and then back down to Robbie.

"They have them tied and are leading them off, so they must have some sort of cells or something. Dad has a house up there, I reckon we should get back on top and head there, you can pretty much guarantee it will have some sort of protection from her on it. I think we need to hole up, do a little scouting, and then find a way to get all the others together again, and then break Rowan and the others out."

In the tunnel just above their heads, came the sounds of pounding feet, Smokes slipped down the steps quickly. "We better move out of sight, come on get under the bridge." Moving as quickly as was possible, they slipped round the side of the steps onto the thin ledge, and carefully moved into the protection of the dark space right below the bridge, doing their very best not to touch the water, which they knew would be instant death. Above them the sounds of trudging feet grew louder. With their back to the wall, and hidden out of sight, all they could do now was wait for the moment when it was clear enough to move out.

At his side Steph sat still holding Jade in her arms as the reality of the last hour began to sink in. Robbie heard Jade sniffle as her mother pulled her close, and her weak words leaked out from under her mass of long shaggy hair. "They have Rowan, and I have lost Jett forever." Steph squeezed her tightly and Robbie felt the wave of emotion pass over him. A feeling of utter helplessness seeped into him as he sat in the dark with his back to the wall, while his head thumped repeatedly. He looked down at his wrist and the white bangle, and closed his eyes as he thought of Rune.

"Where are you Runestone?"

Morgan le Fey and her assistant had made their way back to the secret cave in the Hollow Rock, as the sun had risen over the mountain and begun the new day. Morgan had felt weakened by the fight with Rune, and although she had escaped with her life, the memory of a young Pendragon facing her and demanding she knelt before him stayed close in her thoughts.

Ursula ran around the room as her sight improved, and collected up cooking ingredients to feed her mistress, as the Houlen, who were looking more human now, paced around outside the cave. The Dark One sloped off to her corner where an old padded chair was wedged between two large tables stacked high with old dusty leather bound books. She lifted a worn old book down and sat in the chair as she flipped the parchment pages over muttering to herself.

Ursula watched from behind the stacks of bottles and jars, her mistress was very quiet and still. The book lay open in her lap, and yet Ursula was sure that her mistress was silently reliving her moments alone with Runestone. Ursula had been blinded and her only connection to her mistress had been that of the power of the black star shaped stone. The feelings that had passed through her in the moments when she knew that she was fighting with Rune had been those of extreme pain and also fear.

Ursula looked down at the rough wooden table, as the cold shiver ran down her back. Rune had beaten her mistress in a fight, and in the final moments Ursula had felt her mistress lose the will to continue, her incantations had been the difference between life and death. She thought as she chopped the vegetables, how she would have felt knowing her assistant had played a vital role in her survival; again, she looked up at the figure sat quietly staring into space. Ursula shuddered, was the violet witch really that powerful to put such a great fear into the heart of her mistress?

It was a sobering thought as she stirred the pan and watched the stew boil. Morgan sat lost in thought, and for the second time in weeks Ursula knelt before her with the bowl of steaming food. "Please Mistress you must eat to gather your strength."

The Dark One blinked and looked down, her arm slid slowly forward as she took the bowl on the plate with a large chunk of bread set at the side. Ursula smiled. "Eat it, you will feel better." She rose slowly to her feet, to go and get her own food, but as she turned, she felt the hand of the Dark One close on her wrist. Ursula looked back at the harsh white face and red eyes that looked up at her.

"He told me to bow to him, and then from nowhere he hit me... How?"

"Mistress?" Ursula was confused. "Who did Mistress?" There appeared to be a flicker in the eyes of the Dark One as her thoughts seemed to end and she began to slip back to reality. Ursula watched thinking that her mistress had aged almost over the evening. Morgan le Fey looked up at her as her face began to show her returning to reality.

"He said he was the king, that boy ordered me to bow." She let go of Ursula and lifted the chunk of bread from the side of the plate and pushed it into the stew. Ursula watched as the Dark One bit deep into the bread and began to talk as she chewed. "That brat actually told me to bow; if I had not been as tired as I was I would have ripped out his heart and eaten it in front of him."

The change in her over the meal was almost miraculous, as she rambled on cursing and swearing, as her anger at the indignity of the request burned inside her. Ursula returned to the stool by the table, where she sat in front of her mistress as she consumed her food as if it was part of the boy king. Relief washed over the young assistant as she saw her mistress return to normal, and the morning passed with her looking into her books and preparing new spells for the oncoming battle to finish the job.

In many ways she thought it was strange. Ursula had always known of Runestone and her line of power, she had felt the pain and fear of her mistress and now to look at her; it was like it had never happened. The Dark One screamed her new orders from the entrance to the cave at the Houlen outside. "Go to that useless officer and tell him I want all of them found, I have given him everything he wanted so tell him now it is time he earned his pay. Find them and kill them, bring the witch and woodsman to me and I want that BOY!"

Ursula heard the squeals of the Houlen as they disappeared into the distance outside, her mistress returned and looked across the cave at her. "Put those jars in your bag, we have much to do before midnight." Ursula turned and saw the lines of coloured powders in small thin vials. "Hurry girl, we have a queen to dethrone and a witch to catch." Morgan le Fey slipped her hand in her pocket, she looked relieved, and Ursula noticed as she gripped the black star shaped stone, she also noticed how the rash had moved another inch up her arm.

She snatched up the vials and put them in her bag with her other bottles and jars, she turned to see the entrance to the cave was empty. Quickly she crossed the large stone cave and blew out each candle as she passed. Outside the sun was blinding after the dim light of the cave, and she blinked and lifted her hand to shield her eyes.

Morgan le Fey was already some distance ahead walking briskly down the trail that led back to the mountain above the Mirrored Lake. Ursula hitched the large bag on to her shoulder and ran down the path to catch up, she noticed as she got closer, the bag in her mistress's hand twitched and moved as she walked. Ursula gave it a wary glance and moved across behind her mistress to walk on the other side of her.

As they came out of the trees along the wide dirt path, toward the base of the mount and the Scree, over the lake on the edge of the crumbled old town of Avalonia, the Houlen had delivered their message from the Dark One. Samuel Knots had wasted no time, and his archers trooped out on to the long white road and dipped their arrows into the hot coals of the metal baskets that six young boys carried between them.

The burning arrows lifted into the air, and as they sunk into the soft ground of the wide grassland meadows, the flames fanned into the air and thick black smoke drifted across the old town. The woodland had been searched, and now Knots looked to the tall grass as cover for a woodland force. As the smell of the burning grass lifted into the air, the long line of bowmen followed by the Houlen began to walk slowly onto the smouldering black soil, as they combed the realm for the trapped Specialists.

Hawk watched through the trees as the others hurriedly gathered their things together. Skip watched beside him as the flames leapt into the air. "The team have not had anywhere near enough rest." Hawk looked back through the trees as Harry prepared everyone with Woody.

"We have no choice, we will have to dig deep and summon enough strength until we find a safe place...Come on it's time we moved." Hawk and Skip came back through the trees and slung their packs over their shoulders, as they both took one end of the stretcher that contained Jaz. Woody had the front and Harry the back of Treen's stretcher, as Woody took them out of the trees towards the tall blades of high rock, at the edge of the mountain range, on a path that wove round the large tor and down to the lower southern marshes of the realm.

Una and Rags kept look out up front as Maddy and Milly covered the rear, Maggs with Gaynor, watched the stretchers and the two patients as they moved quickly out of the trees and into the tall finely spiked grasses that grew well above their heads. Una and Rags moved quickly, trampling down the tall grass as Woody trudged along with the stretcher and Harry panted.

Maddy looked back and raised her bow. "If those vile things want to find us, it won't be our scents they find. All they will sniff is soot and ashes; I will burn every trace of us away." She closed one eye and aimed into the centre of the camp and fired, the trees ignited into a roaring inferno as she turned back with Milly and ran to catch up with the others.

Round the Tor, the grasslands expanded into a maze of thick clumps of the fine deep green bladed grass. Small mounds grew up in a scattered pattern, on which there were old gnarled and twisted trees. Rags had the job of running up them, and climbing into the trees to get above the grass to navigate as the group trudged on. The day was growing hot as the sun began to burn down on them, and the flies in the grass buzzed around their faces. It was hard going and their stops became more frequent as their feet dragged, and got caught in the mass of tangled dead grass that knotted their boots from years of growing wild.

Hawk signalled yet another stop, the sweat was dripping off his nose. Gaynor and Maggs were glad of the break as they collapsed beside the stretchers red in the face and soaked with sweat. Una sat down, as Rags once again wove through the grass to another mound, where she gripped the old woody trunk and climbed up to her look out. Una drank the last of her flask and screwed on the top as Hawk sat down beside her. "This is murder, we are being cooked alive. At this rate we won't need to worry about the Houlen, we will fry to death first." Hawk lay back and wiped his face.

"We cannot stop; if we do we are as good as dead. We need a place we can rest and then find the others. We must make it to the swamps, and then try and find our way to the river." Una gave a nod.

"At least in this heat, being near the water will help, those two are not getting any worse, but to be honest they are not improving either." Hawk took another long swig from his bottle and offered it to Una.

"Still no word from Rune?"

Una shook her head. "Nothing... Although if she is in the caves, I will not be able to contact her until she comes above the ground." Hawk rose slowly to his feet.

"Then until we hear something, we keep moving, and hope to hell Rune can find us all a safe way out of this trap."

As the hunt continued through the smoke filled grassland of Avalon, Hawk burdened with the two stretches pushed on through the tall grass, toward the marsh area that surrounded the whole of the south of Avalon. It was a hard torturous journey, burdened with the two heavy stretchers, soaring heat, and in a marshland that was getting harder to navigate safely by the second. The Houlen finally picked up on the scent, and screamed into the air as they changed their direction, and began their pursuit through the tall grass that led away from the cinders of the trees, and round the base of the high Tor.

The heat increased as the sun climbed through the morning and into the afternoon. From the ground wisps of vapour began to rise into the air, and a mist began to grow across all of the swampland. As the heat increased the water was starting to evaporate, and Hawk and his team found it harder going as the humidity increased to an unbearable level, which brought with it a host of black biting annoying flies. Their pace slowed as the sweat ran off their brows and clothes, and all of them felt exhaustion creeping into their legs. Skip gave a gasp as he tripped on a clump of matted grass, and staggered forward gripping Hawk by the shoulder. "This is madness, I am sorry Hawk, but I really must take a break, at this rate, I feel I may even be glad to meet a Houlen." Hawk gave the signal and the group groaned with delight as they slipped down on the damp floor, doing their best to find some shade below the high tall blades above them.

In the cool darkness below the white bridge on the edge of the Mirrored Lake, Robbie opened his eyes as Smokes gave him a soft pat on the shoulder. "Come on Robbie it is all clear, we better be making a move." He felt weak and very weary, and dragged his feet up to stand.

William and Steph were getting up and lifting their bags. Robbie looked round. "Where is Pebbles?" Steph gave a shrug.

"We think Rowan, she just disappeared and slipped off, I am sorry Robbie, it's just been so much to deal with, I lost track for a moment, and by the time I realised, she had gone." He understood, he too had drifted off into an uneasy exhausted dream filled sleep.

"Pebbles will be OK, she will fade from view and find Rowan and the others, when we find them, you can pretty much guarantee she will be beside him. OK let's get the hell away from here."

They came out from under the bridge, and under William's guidance as he had been studying the map made by Leenard, they hurried along the wide path at the side of the mirrored waters, heading away from the bridge and where Rowan and the others had been taken captive. Robbie's mind felt a little clearer, he thought about his situation, and all that made sense was to find the others and Rune, and then come back better prepared to help Rowan and the others. He had no idea how he could do it, he just knew that he had to find a way.

The Dark One with Ursula moved deep into the long white tunnels below Citadel Mount for a second time. Morgan le Fey marched briskly into the tunnels with no fear; she knew that all the tunnels were under her command and that the new queen was trapped in her tower. Amethyst Queen of the realm had nowhere she could go, caught in the crystal castle with Fish, all she could do was watch from the tower, now understanding she was a captive of the power from the Star of the Merle. The whole of Avalon was being influenced by the black stone that was held tight in the grasp of Morgan le Fey's hand, and any chances she had of calling for aid from Rhiannon was gone.

Several hours after leaving the cave, Ursula with her mistress arrived at the long white bridge, that led out into the pure waters of the Mirrored Lake, the Dark One gave a shudder. The memory of her previous night's visit still held captive her fears; she needed time to find some way of combating the violet witch, but for now her task was the final seal of Avalon. Ursula viewed the wide cave of white crystal with broad violet seams with awe, as she looked round and gasped. The silence of such a large space seemed eerie, back in the tunnels behind her the sound of a slow drip echoed. Her mistress was already hard at work untying the squirming bag, as she knelt on the edge of the bridge where Rune had landed with such force previously.

A soft cackle left her lips as the cord came away and she pulled at the bottom of the sack, tipping it over the edge, there was a soft splash and the waters rippled. "Come Ursula and see how the powers of the moon have drained and given me the seat of this house."

As Ursula walked to the edge of the bridge, the Dark One pulled the Star of the Merle from her pocket; it looked dull and lifeless in her hand.

The black skin of her fingers now ran to her elbow, as she held aloft the star. Ursula could not help but look at the black arm and the cold star of stone in her hand. The Dark One gave a smile. "It is a small price to pay to have the honour of a gift so powerful, see how the mirror fractures with my host?"

Ursula turned to what had been on their arrival a calm mirrored lake, now as she watched the waters shuddered and broke with ripples, as what looked like the flapping tails of rapidly growing creatures thrashed in the water.

"Go my children of the deep, swim to the queen and hold her for me. Find me my gifts and guard this water from any who try to pass." The water thrashed and splashed as long slimy tails broke the surface wriggling like huge eels, and the ripple extended across the water towards the centre, where in the distance, Ursula could see the towers of gleaming white.

Fish loaded his bow beside Amethyst, and watched as the creatures moved across the lake towards them. On the table behind them in the centre of the room the goblet of water showed the pictures of the lake filled with slimy foul creatures of destruction. Fish leaned on the ledge of the window and took aim. Amethyst rested a hand on his.

"Do not waste the arrows there are too many, she has put her guard around us, they cannot enter here, even without Rhiannon there are spells on this place that exclude all but the race of the moon." He looked over at the large shapes under the water as they circled the small island in the centre of the Mirrored Waters.

"We are trapped." She gave a nod.

"For now, Rune will come to our aid have no fear. We must wait and at the right moment your arrow will have its targets, be patient my love." Her voice was soft and he turned and looked at her stood radiant beside him, it was as if now she understood all that was happening and had accepted it, to fight for the moment would be pointless, and as he looked into her intense violet eyes she smiled. "Let her think for now she rules here. We have nothing but time and the tables will turn in our favour, the powers are rising as we speak."

Far away across the water on the white bridge, Morgan le Fey, with the small figure of Ursula stood at her side, lifted the Star of the Merle high. Her eyes flickered with a dull deep red as she focused her mind, and drew in the power from above her through the star. Feeling the power flowing into her she began to quietly speak her curse as her wrist began to vibrate, the water of the lake began to swirl and bubble and Ursula stepped back in fright, moving slowly to the side of her mistress and using her as cover.

The large grey creatures rose up in the water and raised their long slimy necks into the air. Ursula slipped back further as she saw the long oval head with deep orange eyes, her heart missed several beats, as she realised the bag of small wriggling creatures had grown within minutes to these monstrous beasts. Rising out of the water looking almost like dragons with huge fins they were terrifying, the Dark One continued to murmur as she commanded the beasts using the star, and with a gigantic roar of a scream, the huge creatures sunk down into the water with a crashing splash. Ursula ducked as the huge wave rose up and smashed over the edge of the white bridge, and she drew a long breath as the cold water hit her and she clutched at her mistress's cloak as her feet slid slightly on the wet floor.

Soaked to the skin and shivering, she looked up at the white face of her mistress. Le Fey gave a smile as she lifted Ursula to steady her on her feet. "Never show them fear, you must learn to control your feelings in the face of these creatures. The Bronteal are savage if they smell your fear." Her face twisted with her smile. "Fear not you are safe with me; they know who they serve and will not harm you."

Ursula swallowed as she looked back at the wake of the huge beast as it swam into the centre of the lake. "They will keep watch for us and prevent anyone interfering with my plans. Go back to the tunnel and wait for me."

Wet and afraid she did not argue, and scurried back into the tunnel, where she stood watching her mistress and dripping onto the floor. The Dark One stood on the end of the bridge and began to chant. In the castle Fish stepped back from the window in fright as the massive Bronteal leapt up out of the water all around the base of the castle. The large oval heads opened their mouths revealing the long rows of white sharp teeth, as they roared into the air, suddenly his bow felt like little protection against a beast of such size. They rose out of the water reaching halfway up the tower wall. Amethyst gripped at his sleeve with terror, as they both watched the massive beasts fall back into the waters and the wave of water crashed up onto the wall spaying all the insides of the lower floors and soaking everything. Fish peered down over wall and watched the swirling water.

"What the hell were they?" He looked back at her. "Did you know those buggers were in there when you went swimming?"

Frightened as she felt, Amethyst had to give a small smile. "They are not of this realm; it is her work. Those foul things come from somewhere very dark; she is just making sure we do not use the water to escape her." He looked back over the wall.

"She has done a bloody good job, there aint no way I am leaving this balcony. Hell did you see those bloody teeth?" Amethyst gave a nervous glance at the water.

"Come away from here, we will be safer inside the centre of the room." Fish turned toward her as the cave at the far end lit up with a bright blue flash of light. Ursula shrank into the wall as the streaks of lightening shot out of her mistress and up into the air. It danced across the water as the surface of the lake bubbled. Back in the castle of crystal, Fish jumped back as the lightening leapt up from the water onto the walls. The light expanded out into wide beams and formed a large wall of light. Slowly as it widened, he realised that the light now encased the whole castle, it spun and pulsated in the air, and although he was not happy about it, he thought it might keep the water creatures at bay, which in his mind was the worst of two evils. Fish stepped back to Amethyst as she sat in the chair. "Looks like we are here to stay." She nodded as she watched the water in the goblet.

"Rune will come, I know it. She must be busy; the dark powers are stronger than any of us thought."

In the distance behind them as they found the tunnel they needed, a bright flash filled the end of the cave near the white bridge, Robbie and Steph turned quickly at the rear of the party. Steph looked at Robbie. "She is back." Robbie gave a nod as his pace quickened, and he followed William and Smokes into the long arched tunnel. Just for a moment he saw the clear glass surface of the water ripple, something inside him stirred with caution. He turned back to the tunnel feeling his head pound with the massive headache and his pace became faster.

"Come on let's hurry, whatever she is up to, for once I don't want to be a part of it."

Will and Smokes were a few paces ahead and their pace quickened as they ran blindly up the tunnel, which felt like it was rising. Robbie's head was filled with questions, for which there were no real answers. He had seen Rune fall as he turned back to the bridge, her violet cloak had been pressed up against the stone rail, and yet when they had reached the spot she had gone. Had she gone after the Dark One alone? Was she in another realm? Endless questions and concerns pounded through his mind, but the only question he really wanted answered was.

"Oh Rune, where the hell are you?"

"Robbie is that you?"

CHAPTER FIVE

DARKNESS

Colours flashed behind her eyes, as her mind began to wake from the long dream state she had been in since her moment of falling on the bridge. A familiar sense flashed in her thoughts. "ROBBIE IS THAT YOU?"

Rune opened her eyes in the darkness and blinked. She felt light, as if floating and tried to sit up, her body tilted and her arms flung out sideways to look for support, but there was nothing to hold on to, and nothing but darkness. Her head swam, and she blinked again trying to gain her bearings, before her was nothing but the darkness, vast empty cold darkness. Her breathing increased as she drew in a breath, and tried to compose herself, but deep down inside she felt a strong sense of panic and unease growing, something around her was moving.

The scream of fear was in her throat, yet her instincts warned her to stay silent, her eyes tried to focus, but the darkness was total as she floated around not knowing where. There was nothing familiar at all, no sense of Robbie, or Iona, nothing. Rune took a long deep breath and tried to concentrate, her mind felt empty and lost, all of the feelings she had felt in her realm with her sisters of the table were gone, the only sound was the dull thump of her heart as it pumped inside her. Her mind opened within itself. "Focus Rune, come on pull yourself together. Something hit you in the face and you fell, this is just you dreaming, it will not last long and then you will wake."

The sounds of a million voices rushed into her mind, they screamed and raged with a hideous language, she was not expecting it, and her senses felt the fear and the evil mixed together with the rage and hatred. She pulled her hands to her face almost as instinct and screamed for all her might. Her head felt like it exploded, and her body swung violently backwards, and Rune snapped her arms out sideways, but there was nothing but empty air between her fingers.

"Shut up! What are you trying to do? If you let them in, they will devour you."

The voice was loud and deep, and almost familiar, she snapped her mouth shut as her mind swirled and tried to focus on the voice. Her heart beat five times faster and clouded her thoughts, her breathing was rapid and she could feel the fine metal chains of her jewellery round her neck, as they lifted and fell with her gasps.

She fought with all her power to clear her mind and think straight.

"Who are you, where am I, where are Robbie and the others?"

"Relax, a friend is coming, you will not be alone for long, summon your power and protect yourself child of violet and the red stone."

Rune turned in the darkness as her breathing regulated, and the sudden fright inside her began to lessen. It was pointless to look, the darkness was total, and there was no sense of anything within close proximity to her.

"Are you still there, please don't leave me?"

"I never have. I am always with you child of the stone; be at peace all will be revealed when the time is right." Rune felt a wave a calmness flow into her, and a familiar feeling washed over her.

"Will you not tell me where I am, or who you are? The sense of you feels familiar, but I cannot recount who you may be."

"Now is not the time, and this most certainly is not the place... Just know that in a moment of great peril, you were lifted and brought to safety." A mild panic beat into her heart.

"I am no longer in Avalon, Oh please tell me this is not true, Robbie is alone and needs me."

Her eyes searched through the darkness, but it was pointless, and she knew in her heart that the voice did not lie to her. Nothing around her felt familiar and what she could sense frightened her, for the feelings from whatever surrounded her were vile and hideous. The voice in her head softened.

"He is watched over, and the most trusted guardian we have has been sent to his aid, relax Little Red Stone, and know that for this moment you must be safe from the dark power that is destroying the realm you know as Avalon."

"But if Avalon is at risk, I should be there, why have you brought me here when everyone is now in even more danger?"

Lost in this dark place and knowing that Robbie was alone in a realm now being controlled by the Star of the Merle terrified her. *"You have to take me back."* The tears welled in her eyes. *"He will need me."*

"Hush child, you have been weakened, and you need to rest before you can summon the power to protect them. Believe me, he is safe and watched over."

"Eve?"

"I am here child, be at peace Life, for you have encountered the touch of things unknown in your world. Come and be beside me, for you have many things to learn before you return."

Rune felt her body relax as she suddenly began to move forward through the darkness, the sense of Eve all around her. *"Where am I?"* There was a faint chuckle inside her head from Eve.

"You would be more relaxed if you did not know, but you are the red stone with the violet power, so you should know where you are. Be prepared for when you

*know, you will be open to all your senses and feel what is around you, it will not
be pleasant for you hold a powerful combination of gifts that will appeal to what
surrounds us."* Eve's voice carried a note of caution, and it frightened Rune, she
drew a large breath, and tried hard to focus her mind. Her concentration flowed,
as she felt the strong presence of Eve move closer. "Are you ready child?" Rune
nodded in the darkness, and then realised what she had done and smiled.

"I am ready."

*"You appeal to all here as you are life. The appeal is far greater for you are the
source of life and the food of what surrounds you."* Rune drew a breath and stared
into the all-consuming darkness. *"You are cast into the Merle my child of life, but
fear not, for you are not alone."*

It was hard to concentrate knowing she was cast deep into the darkness that was
the outer edge of her world. It was even harder to fight the sudden surges of panic
that exploded inside her, knowing the Merle was the pure evil that fed from the life
and the love of others. She felt Eve within her and tried to relax, in front of her she
saw a shimmer of white, voices began to murmur in her head, thousands of them
broke into a hideous evil tongue she did not recognise, and the murmur began to
increase as the shimmer of white grew brighter into the shape of a ball.

*"Behold the doorway, for you are the stone on which all shall be written,
learn from this."* The voice of Eve seemed to echo as the thousands of voices
began to talk rapidly, their tone increased from the silence to almost a deafening
scream. The white ball of light flared, and Rune snatched her hands to her ears
as the deafening roar of fear exploded in her mind, and billions of terrified wails
screamed and scattered into the vast open darkness around her. She bit down hard
on her lip as the voices yelled and wailed, the light turned orange, and she closed
her eyes it was so bright.

The voices now seemed to be talking and screaming faster, although they were
also growing quieter, as they travelled further away from the bright light, and soon
they were a distant terrified echo, and Rune felt the sun warm her face. She was
travelling backward and not even aware of it, the bright yellow ball she had known
all her life burned into the outer reaches of space before her.

Eve spoke and Rune turned, it was not the face and body she had met on the
Isle of Tears, but almost a picture, made of millions of tiny sparkling spheres that
glowed with the faint tinge of red. Eve had appeared in her true form, but she
had brought herself together in the picture she knew Rune would understand.
She looked like she was made from a mist of tiny water droplets, and Rune gave a
smile and felt her insides settle. Eve gave a smile back. "You are lucky, no one has
witnessed what you are about to see, stay close to me, but fear not for this is the
past and has been and gone."

Rune witnessed the start of all things, from the moment the sun exploded into
life, as it became the doorway from one realm into this one. She watched and

gave a smile as she saw five glowing shimmers of energy streak through the space towards an odd shaped smouldering lump of rock; the excitement began to grow in her. "I know this, my grandfather has told me this story a thousand times."

"Behold my true family Child of Life. Erathome, Tideguyde, Hearlearn, and my brother Albanlin, and of course, there I am with my true name, Rundalba. You know of this story and how those from my realm sculpted your world?" Rune nodded with joy.

"It was my bedtime story when I was little; my mother told me and then my grandfather. I know how you went to the world sculpted by Erathome, and you sat beside Hearlearn who moulded the rock and the clay to make all things." Rune gave a giggle of excitement as she spoke and saw it happen before her eyes. "We all know of how you changed your name to Eve, and Hearlearn shortened his to Hearne. This is my most favourite story, I loved how you made two garments when Tideguyde decided to leave, and followed Erathome into the vastness of space, and you all poured into one of them the gifts you had, and created Ofmoon, the vessel that would be touched by Albanlin who gave magical fellowship as his gift, and Hearne who gave powers of earth, and it became Fellowship and Earth, F,A,E. Then you gave it life and Rhiannon was born to take the watch over all things as the first line of Fae Ofmoon."

Her giggles flowed up as she saw the golden hair and the familiar face of the Queen of the Moon travel up to her seat. Excitement bubbled like a brook over stones, and Rune watched her story that she had written in her violet book come to life before her eyes. Eve watched her happiness, and felt her joy.

"This is not just a story of the past Runestone Life, this is your family history, now watch my brother for here is a matter of importance to you." Rune watched as Hearne made the shape of a man, he passed it to Eve who blew life into it, and the man stretched and opened his eyes. They were as green as the moss that grew all around Hearne, and Rune recognised them instantly. "Grandfather?"

"His name was Merleline; he was taken as you can see by my brother into the deep darkness for a long age. There alone deep within the Merle, Albanlin taught him everything about the darkness and the power that was contained within it. The power inside him was the power of the Merle blended with the huge forces of my brother. Alba means white, and Lin as you know is line." Rune whispered quietly to herself.

"Whitelines." Eve nodded.

"The power inside your grandfather was part Merle." Rune's head turned sharply to Eve.

"No, that cannot be true, my grandfather was good and fought to help everyone, it is Le Fey who harnessed the dark lines." Eve lifted a hand to Rune's.

"Be at peace Runestone Life, there is still much to tell. He chose to shorten his own name and became Merle and lin. Merlin was balance in every single way, an equal amount of dark Merle, and an equal amount of white power. That is what you are seeing before you now. My brother is as I am, not from your world, we wear the garments of your form, but as you see here, I am a force, an entity, I have no shape or form you would recognise. Your grandfather was the first and only one to hold the forces of the Whitelines, there is no Merle within my brother."

Rune struggled a little as she tried to understand all that Eve was telling her, Eve smiled. "You have time to work it all out. Now watch again for we have little time left here." Rune turned back to see her grandfather return, he went down to the Earth and talked to Hearne and Eve. Eve took the second garment she had fashioned similar to Rhiannon and Hearne made a few changes. Merlin added a white light, and Eve drew a single hair that turned violet, out of her long hair and wove it into the figure, she then breathed life into the woman, and Rune realised this was Bridge. The one created to bridge the gap between the earth and the moon, who later became Bridget Violet's mother. Suddenly Rune understood completely.

"Gwendolyn's great grandmother and first Queen of the Fae on Earth." Eve smiled knowing that Rune would put all the pieces together in her mind, and then begin to understand.

"Come, for we have more to see." For a moment Rune's eyes blurred, and when they cleared, she was stood against the wall in a room of towering white stone encrusted with jewels. All around the floor there were piles of gems and golden objects; Eve leaned in closer to her. "This is the meeting room of the Ruling Council; it is buried deep below the Forest of Time." Many figures stood around the huge white stone table cloaked, as a voice that she now knew was Albanlin spoke. His back was toward her, and all she could see was a long cloak cast over the white stone seat.

"It is settled then?" His arm dropped into the inside of his cloak and lifted something out and placed it on the table, with a jerk, it slid across the smooth surface to the figure in a powder blue silk hooded cloak. The soft hand of Gwendolyn slipped out of the long sleeve, and stopped the sliding object. Rune gasped as she saw the Star of the Merle, and Albanlin spoke. "You must keep it safe White Circle. That has every bit of the worst and most devious power contained within it. It must never be found or it will undo everything we have worked so hard to build, that small star could destroy this world and others we have built. Now what do you have as protection?"

The powder blue cloak separated and Gwendolyn lifted a bundle wrapped in dark blue velvet up onto the table, she unrolled it and revealed the shining sword. "How did you get that? I just gave it Arthur." The dark robed figure at the other end of the table was clearly Merlin, Gwendolyn smiled.

"This is not Excalibur, this is its sister Destiny, and is not a sword for this age. Destiny shall only rise if the world is in peril. I am sorry my husband, for I know how you complain I keep too many secrets, but this will be needed in times I have seen, I have arranged for it to come forth when the time is right and certain conditions are met. This is my gift to the future as you give your staff." Merlin muttered under his hood as Rune had seen him do a thousand times, a smaller figure in white placed something small on the table and Albanlin nodded.

"Those will serve greatly your line little Green Circle; I see you have much of your father's wisdom." The deep voice of Hearne boomed from under a wider than normal cloak of what looked like green leaves.

"They are small and look insignificant, but one day they will rebuild the line of the green circle as was foretold." Hearne placed a small object onto the table beside the two small coloured marbles. "This is the most important gift of all, place this in your keep for it is vital to the future, it is the only one of its kind and shall carry the name of its owner in time." Rune stretched to see, but Albanlin had already lifted it and slipped it into his pocket.

"Then it is done, we shall see what befalls this land and others when the darkness falls, all we can do is watch and hope." Eve lifted her hand and touched Rune on the shoulder.

"Come, there is one more thing you must witness to understand what has befallen you."

The scene before Rune seemed to blur, and she blinked as her vision stretched, and spun before her making her stomach churn. For a brief moment she felt her body shake and felt the floor press harder into her feet, and as she opened her eyes, she found herself stood on the white path at the side of the Mirrored Waters. Over on the opposite side of the bridge to Robbie and the rest of the group, Rune saw herself fall as the black star hit her in the face. Her stomach gave a mighty wrench as she watched herself drop out of the air and on to the floor with a heavy thud. Eve leaned in to her side. "Watch carefully, and see the power of the star in its true form."

As Eve spoke, Rune saw the long wisps of dark smoke leave the star in the hand of the Dark One as she snatched it back off the floor, it swirled like campfire smoke into the air and wafted across toward the collapsed figure of Rune on the floor, a cold shiver ran down her spine as she watched the smoke surround her, she looked to Eve who watched her carefully. "Why have I never seen it do that before?" Eve gave a small smile.

"Because a small part of you inherited from your grandfather, has now been awoken as a result of what happens next." She pointed back to the bridge, and Rune turned to see the still water below the bridge ripple. A long white clad arm rose out of the water, and pushed the white star of crystal into the hanging hand of Rune. It was a startling moment for her as she watched from across the water. From the moment the white star touched her hand the dark smoke that surrounded her gave a violent jolt. From her hand white light shone in a bright speck that travelled down her arm and covered her entire body.

As the Dark One confronted William with the hidden figure of Jade, Rune saw the light rise from her motionless body and form the shape of a tall white hooded figure. It lifted her into its arms, and with a bright white pulse, the two figures disappeared as the dark smoke streamed away from them, and swirled around the dark figure of Morgan le Fey as she screamed at William. Eve took Rune's hand in hers.

"It is time." Rune's eyes closed and she felt the numbness of her limbs as she relaxed in white light. Her mind wandered and darkness drew round her, and she felt a slight pressure on her back, she gave a long deep sigh and slipped into sleep as her mind went blank. The soft voice of Eve echoed for a second. "Rest and grow strong for we shall talk more in good time." The pictures of all she had seen danced through her head, but somewhere distant there were voices.

"Go easy on her, she is still very weak."

"I know what I am doing, believe me My Sister she is ready, have you felt the power she holds, now is the time, I am not wrong in this."

"I have always trusted you, but I fear for her mind if you release so much upon her, I understand My Brother, honestly I do, but we must not risk the outcome by passing it to her too early, please I beg you, give her a little more time and ..." The voices began to fade, and Rune slipped deeply into a calm and restful slumber.

As the sun passed noon, high on the top of Citadel Mount, Ursula fanned herself in the scorching heat as she looked down on the clouds of mist floating over the realm of Avalon. The Dark One seemed pleased with her days work, and gave a weak smile. Ursula had carried out the spell on her mistress's behalf, but was still unsure of what she had done. "Mistress can I ask what is happening? I do not understand all that I have helped you achieve." The Dark One lifted a hand to her shoulder.

"You have impressed me greatly, for you have unique gifts for a half mortal." Ursula did not understand her, and turned to look up at the deep red eyes of her mistress. The Dark One gave her another pat on her shoulder. "The containment spell you carried out sealed everything within this realm, including the daytime. No moon will rise over Avalon to aid the new queen; she is now powerless as the sun rules this sky." It was quite a surprise to her.

"Is that possible? I thought the Merle would have more influence in the night." The Dark One gave a slight strained chuckle.

"You still have much to learn, the power contained within the star cares not what time, day or year it is. As we speak it is seeking those of power to strip, and all in Avalon is now losing the hidden power stored within, and it is strengthening the star. Here it will remain forever daylight, and prevent the return of the power of the moon and its heirs. You see my Apprentice, I told you, beside me you would witness great things."

"But what of the Whitelines, will they not destroy the stone or weaken it?"

Morgan le Fey looked out over the clouds above Avalon with a satisfied look on her face. "Old Lord Whiteline underestimated the power held captive in the darkness, the force he used to contain the heart of the Star became its food, and for a long time now it has craved more. Have no fear Ursula of the boat people, the time of the Whitelines is finished, and here in this place together, we shall begin the unravelling of those meddlers the Ruling Council in every realm." Morgan turned on the top of the high edge of the mount with a happy look on her face. "Come we have more to do, but first we shall rest and give the charms time to work, we have much to prepare for the coming days."

With that she strode off across the top of the high plateaux, leaving Ursula to scramble and gather her bag. For one brief moment she gazed across the white clouds of the heavy mists far below her, and thought for a second, she saw the thick green of the large forest in the far distance appear through the haze and then disappear again. She turned and ran to catch up with the long flowing black cloak of her mistress, as she strode with confidence towards the tumbled ruin of the old Citadel.

Alone in the labyrinth of white tunnels, Jade had lost all track of time. She had moved with caution up the long tunnel to follow the path taken by the soldiers who held captive Rowan and the others. The biggest problem was there were so many tunnels leading off her path, which hampered her progress of slowly investigating each side tunnel and it had taken up hours. Her heart was heavy, and she was feeling dispirited as she reached another tunnel on her left, and slid up to the side of it to peer round the corner.

Once again, the tunnel was empty and silent; she gave a long depressed sigh, and slowly moved round, leaning on the wall as her legs ached. She slid down the wall and rubbed the back of her calves. "Ooooh that feels good."

"Ye should take ye boots off, and walk bare footed, it will cool ye legs and ease the pain." Jade gave a nod, and then realised she was no longer alone.

Her arm came up with great speed as she straightened and rose back up, with the glinting of a silver dagger; it swept through the air in a flash. The clash of metal on steel rang in her ears and white light flashed in her eyes, as she felt herself lift into the air, and then with a bump, she hit the wall opposite and slid onto the floor. Her eyes sparkled with silver flashes for a second, as she saw the blurred figure lean over her.

"Ye have great skill Little Green Eyes, but will have to do much more if ye want a slice of old Fagan." Jade blinked, her eyes clearing as they focused on the huge hand, and thick bushy eyebrows that had appeared behind it. "Come now Little

Green Eyes, ye have wasted too much time bouncing about like a rabbit with fleas, we must work fast before all has been robbed." Jade took the hand feeling confused.

"Do you know me? Who are you, and what are you doing sneaking about down here?" The happy old face came into view, as Fagan pulled her back to her feet. Jade was unsure of what to do, yet his eyes sparkled so brightly, and in her mind, she thought they looked quite kind.

"Well, I must say, it's been a while since ye line and mine crossed paths, but ye have his eyes and her mischief, and so therefore in a way we have met, although in the skin I must say we have not met before. But not to worry, there is much to do and many things before us, I am sure a nice cup of Jasmine and some sesame seed cakes will be nice to chat over later." He lifted her dagger off the floor, and passed it to her as she watched lost in confusion.

"What?" It was then she suddenly realised, and looked at him in wonder. "You can see me?" The figure that towered above her with thick white bushy hair and rather large ears, gave a big smile, and his old lined face creased up.

"Well of course I can, ye think I would miss the tricks of Little Blue Eyes a second time?" Jade stared unable to understand. She was invisible, and yet this very peculiar stranger could see her clearly.

"You can see me, right?" He stepped back and gave her a long look.

"I just told ye, as clear as day, did I not mention Little Blue Eyes?" Jade frowned.

"You mean Rune, right?" He gave a hearty laugh, and stretched out his hand to hers. Jade took it still feeling very lost.

"My name is Fagan Sylvester Hammond, and I am the son of Sequana, previous Maker and the new Keeper. The Lady of Life asked me to look in on ye all and provide some assistance, she is the mother of Little Blue Eyes, who I believe is ye grandmother." He gave a smile and looked back at the tunnel Jade had recently come up. "Well I am glad we got that all straight, come on then, those vile dark wood vermin have been sniffing about, so we should hurry, it won't be long before it's all gone and we are left to fend with just our hands." He gave her a sharp nod, and stepped into the tunnel, and disappeared as he walked briskly away.

Jade felt her mind swirl not understanding a word of the conversation at all. She hurriedly slipped her dagger back into her boot, and then ran round the corner back into the tunnel, where she saw the long green cloak waft, as the tall stranger walked at a great pace away from her. She felt a little uncertain, but he had not killed her and seemed friendly in an odd Harry sort of way, so she hurried behind him assuming he knew for certain where Rowan might be.

Fagan strolled up the tunnel, turning into side passages without any hesitation, it was obvious to Jade he knew the place very well indeed, although she followed him silently still unsure of whether or not she could trust him. The fact he could see her when she was invisible worried her, she had only ever known Rune to be able to spot her after she had faded, and her thoughts spilled out before she could stop them sounding out loud. "Are you a wizard like my grandfather?"

Fagan gave a soft chuckle and stopped; he turned to his side and looked down at her with a broad smile. "Well then that is quite a question... As I said, I am the Keeper and I have been sent to aid the party ye are with. To be a wizard would not serve my purpose, although I must admit, I would be happy as a daffodil if I could be one for a day."

"But you can see me... I mean, no one else can, so you must have some power in you, because only Rune can see me." Fagan thought for a moment, and he lifted a finger and rubbed it inside his large left ear.

"Well, ye clearly see my little green eyed friend, I have been here for a long time, and it's my job ye know? I tend everything in the forest, and keep it in balance; I know many things and have many tasks before me. I suppose that we are two of a kind in these days of the things connected to the earth. I walk unseen and yet see all, as ye do, for I can be hidden to all when I choose, and at that time I suppose only ye will see me, after all ye do come from the line of little blue eyes."

"Who is Little Blue Eyes, are you talking about Rune?" Fagan gave another smile.

"Ye know, I thought we had done this?" He scratched his wild tufted white hair and gave a sniffle. "Bad air down here ye know? It plays havoc with the nose. Well now, let me see, ye have the gifts of little blue eyes, who after all is ye grandmother, and she too would sneak about and try very hard to trip me up in the woods." He gave a fond smile of remembrance. "I always fell ye know? Never told her I could see her; oh she was so lovely. Talks to the dream people now, the trees missed her when she left." He looked down at Jade and patted her face. "Ye have much of her inside ye, she was quite a little rebel when she was ye age as well." Jade was starting to understand that he was talking about Opal as a small girl.

"I miss her too, she was cool." Fagan frowned for a moment, and turned, then strode on, Jade hurried to his side. "Do you know where Rowan and the others are?"

"There is only one place left in here they can use, so I would think that ye friends will be there, that's why I am going this way." Jade gave a happy nod.

"Cool... we can get em fast and then go looking for Robbie."

Fagan gave a nod as he walked quickly watching the path up front. "We must work fast, time is running out, ye must take them into the woods and ye grandfathers house, ye will be safe there for a while."

"Cool, I have never seen granddads place before." Fagan stopped and looked back down at Jade with a strange look on his face. Jade shrugged. "What?" A curious look came over his face, and his white bushy eyebrows twitched.

"Why is the temperature so relevant?" Jade looked confused for a second and then gave a wide smile.

"Oh, I get it... Cool." She gave him a big smile. "Where I come from, cool sort of means good." He gave a slight nod.

"I see, but why not just say good?" Jade shrugged.

"Not sure, I suppose it just doesn't sound as cool." He was not sure he fully understood, but he gave a slight nod of understanding.

"Does that make hot bad?" Jade gave a giggle.

"No way, hot is smoking like Rowan is."

"Really? I would like to say I understand that, but I am afraid I don't. Still happy trees sing on a warm summer wind, let's see now... Oh yes, three more right and one left, and we will be almost there. Well time is pressing and we have much to do before the sun boils the rivers, come on then." He strode off down the first tunnel on his right, as Jade gave a happy sigh and quietly spoke.

"You don't understand me, man I aint understood a thing you have said since I met you."

"It's nice to have good understanding, and a common bond isn't it?" Fagan's voice echoed slightly off the walls as he walked down the long tunnel. Jade loosened her bow on her shoulder, and followed him.

Crystal stood up from the side of the rough bed in which Rowan lay sleeping; she stretched as she crossed the small room cut out of the stone, sealed with a heavy metal door, where Bear and Big John stood listening through it to the guards outside. Jay sat on the other bed with the frightened looking Hornet; Blades stared out of the window cut out of the stone wall that overlooked Avalon. Todd stood quietly beside her looking at the steel bars that were cemented deeply into the white stone.

Rowan's swollen leg was raised on the end of the bed, tightly bound and splinted with a snapped bow. Crystal leaned back on the wall and gave a long sigh; she looked at John and Bear with their ears pressed firmly to the door, close to the small window in the centre. She whispered quietly. "Any news?" Bear leaned back, his face dirty and marked with dried blood, his eyes looked tired.

"Nothing... They have something in mind for us, but I am not sure what." He glanced back at the bed on the far side of the room. "How is he?" Crystal looked back to the sleeping figure.

"I have numbed his leg the best I can, I am finding it harder to do, I think I am so tired I need to recharge a bit before I try it again. Hopefully he will sleep for a while." Big John gave a nod.

"It's not going to be easy, even if we can find a way out, with that leg he won't be able to run for it, I guess we have to wait and see what Robbie and Rune have in mind." Bear tensed, and leaned back off the door.

"We have company." He took two long steps back, as the sound of many feet clattered on the stone floor outside. They all moved back from the door, as Todd turned and leaned back on the wall. Keys rattled as the footsteps drew to a halt, and then the sound of the large key being pushed into the lock clunked, and with the sliding of old rattling bolts, the door swung open.

Outside the door a tall and muscular man, dressed in tight black leather pants and a heavy canvas tunic, with thick heavy crossed sword belts stared at them with dark shining eyes. His long ragged dark blonde hair hung over his shoulders in thick matted curls, this was one of Mason's Cutter's, and he seemed to swell with pride as he viewed his captured prize. His voice was rough and coarse. "I want no trouble while you stay here. Behave and you will be treated well, soon you will be moved from here and sent to our Governor in London."

Bear gave a surprised look. "What does Mason want with us Cutter?"

The officer gave a smile, as the soldiers and two well dressed men in black seemed to rise with delight. The Officer showed little fear faced with the large imposing figure of Bear, as John stepped up to his side. "You will be executed in public to set an example to those who break the laws of the Governor of England and its surrounding lands." Bear gave a smile.

"His rules mean nothing; I answer only to the Hooded Man and the new king." The comment made an impact on the Cutter, who seemed to disregard the remark with a slight laugh; yet Bear could see in his eyes, the mention of a new king did draw a little doubt in the mind of the Cutter. Bear continued to smile with his bright white teeth. "You are no match for the Hooded Man and the new king, I shall rest here a while and enjoy it when I face you and kill you in combat, sharpen my sword for me, I will be needing it soon." John gave a big smile and agreed.

"Aye, some water and towels would be nice; I want to look good when I slice up your army for my king."

The soldiers behind the large Cutter shuffled their feet and looked a little edgy, the group had been sentenced to death, and yet here they stood confined to a small cell, talking of a new king and attacking them all. It felt strange and made them very nervous, all of them had expected to see fear in their eyes. Bear stood proud, he was dirty from his fights, and yet his stance commanded great authority, the soldiers felt the intimidation that emitted from him, the others in the room all stood resolute around him. None of it made sense, they were prisoners and yet they appeared like this was just a temporary disruption, and that they would soon be back in the thick of the fight.

The large Cutter officer gave a smile. "I admire faith... but yours is unfounded." He stepped back and the door swung shut with a deep boom, which echoed down the tunnels, Crystal turned to speak and Bear lifted a large dirty hand.

"Shush, wait a moment." He looked back at the door, and they all knew the Cutters were listening.

CHAPTER SIX

OUT OF TOUCH

The sky above was the deepest blue, and the sun shone down across the top of the trees. High in the branches of the tallest trees ever grown, the birds sang, and looked down to the wide pool that was filled from the waters that fell down the high falls of the tree covered rocks, and brought life to the glade of Eve.

The large open area was smothered with the brightest flowers, mixed in a rainbow of lush colour, as it spread its carpet across the floor, and surrounded the simple path of short grass, that came in from the trees and skirted the cool clear pool. Across the wide expanse of the rock strewn glade, the flowers swayed in the gentle warm breeze, as they hummed to the sound of the working bees.

Butterflies of every colour danced in the air with the long tailed Dragonflies of blue, orange and sparkling green, as the hover flies wove between them, darting around in a frenzy of labour. Set back in the cooler shade of the heavy oak, was a small paved area, on which stood a roughly woven canopy of willow, thatched with the dull mustard brown of reed, and woven together with the seeking strands of heavy lilac laden flowers of wisteria. Below on a long bed crafted by the most skilled hands from beech and ash, lay the sleeping figure of Runestone.

She was washed, and her hair was braided back, and flowers of many colours had been woven into her braids. She was dressed in a long gown of the palest green, and her long fiery red hair was pulled round in a long ponytail, and laid neatly across her front. Her eyes were closed, and her long eyelashes rested gently on the top of her pale white cheeks, deep inside herself, she was calm and relaxed with a strong sense of feeling safe, unaware of the figure dressed in all red, and looking so like herself, who stood by the side of the wide pool of clear water holding a large jug made of stone.

Eve knelt by the side of the pool, and lowered the jug into the water to fill it, the sun caught in her hair and it glistened with red and a bright golden yellow. She lifted the full jug up on to the stone slab at the side of the pool, and then looked down into the rippled water. Slowly she drew her hand across the surface and the ripples ceased, and the surface of the water cleared and settled to a smooth glass like mirror. Eve looked deeply into the water, and the picture of Opal dressed in her long white robes came into view. The small wide-eyed figures of the Sandling's, gathered happily around her, and Eve smiled at the happy scene of her daughter.

The picture faded and changed, and she saw the tall old figure of Hearne as he stood on the edge of the wide plinth of rock, above the woodland in Loxley. She felt the tug at her heart, knowing they would remain forever apart, and she leaned closer to the water. "I am watching my love, as I do every day."

A single tear ran from her eye, and dripped into the clear surface of the water, and the ripples ran outward changing the picture. Sapphire lay asleep in her bed at the old farm in New Avon, she was restless and moved erratically, as deep inside her, pictures and visions flowed into her mind of the past and the future. Eve waved a hand across the water. "Rest easy my child of the White Circle, now is your time as the power of the sapphire opens your heart and mind, and brings you the gifts of your grandmother, for you will inherit all of her gifts of vision. Now is the time for you to take your place, as the centre of sight, you soon will have the task of aiding the new queen of your people."

She gave a small flick of her wrist, and Sapphire stirred in her sleep. "See the star of your new circle, for it is like your centre, sapphire blue on white, and set within a violet circle." Eve's long white hand bearing the platinum ring of woven oak leaves slid out from under her long red sleeve and touched the water, and the picture faded.

Eve lifted the jug and rose slowly on the water's edge, the flowers all around her seemed to rise, as if standing at their best for her. She walked amongst the rows of bright flowers, following the path of green grass, and on to the dusty brown paving that formed the small area of stone beneath the arbour that Rune slept below. She carefully lifted a small silver cup that stood on a small shelf attached to the arbour support, and poured out the cool clear water. Gently she sat down on the side of the bed beside Rune.

Sweeping her hand across the length of Rune's sleeping figure, Rune gave a small murmur and stirred. Opening her eyes, she saw the smiling face of Eve.

"Welcome back My Lady of Life, your slumber has been deep and I feel of great need. Come, lift yourself and drink, it will refresh you and give you the strength to begin your destiny in the world against darkness."

Rune felt like she had been dreaming, and this was yet another, she felt a little disorientated and confused, she lifted her arm that felt heavy, and rubbed her eyes as she slowly sat up in the bed and received the silver cup from Eve. "What is this, do you not have any coffee?" She took a long drink and felt the coldness of the water as it quenched her hot throat; Eve gave a smile and patted her leg.

"That is the source of all life, for it is water drawn from the beginning of the mirrored waters. You drink the greatest source of all we created here, for it is the contents of that cup that intensifies your powers." Rune swallowed another mouthful and blinked in the brightness of the daylight.

"But it's just water, how can water intensify my powers?"

"Water my child is the centre of everything, is there not water in the heart of every Opal? Is she not the symbol of life to you in your woodland realm? You have much to learn my child and there is little time." Rune looked around in deep thought at the colourful garden all around her, and the high waterfall that fell into the clear pool.

"I understand that most things require and are composed of water, my grandfather taught me that, but I still do not see how it can intensify powers." Eve sat straight and her bright violet eyes shone at Rune.

"I reside here in my home of Avalon, your grandmother lived by the castle on the coast of the seas, and even your home is set beside a wide expanse of water. Has it never occurred to you, that you have used your greatest powers beside areas abundant with water?" Rune had just woken from some strange dreams, and now she had to think about all the moments when water was close by. It was confusing and she still did not feel fully awake.

"I am not exactly sure I understand you." Eve looked to the large pool across the wide glade filled with flowers.

"My Child, water has carried the message of life since I first arrived here in this the first realm. Think of all you have done, the woodland beside the river on your way to Caerleon, Tintagel, even Windsor has a lake. Robbie's Mere is your home and centre, and even here at the side of the Mirrored Waters you faced and fought the mortal Le Fey, it is no coincidence that you were beside water, for you are life, and water is its central ingredient, your powers will always be enhanced when you are close to the source of physical life." Rune knew that Eve was right.

"I have never really thought of it that way, I mean it never really occurred to me, now that you have mentioned it, I can see the link." Eve gave a satisfied nod.

"Good, now drink and feel your strength return, you have much to prepare before you return to face the darkness. Come walk with me in my garden."

Rune slid her legs off the bed and dropped them down to the cool stone floor. Her legs felt weak and shaky as she stood; slowly she walked onto the warm grass at the side of Eve, and marvelled at the garden of immense floral beauty. For a moment she was lost in the wonder of everything that surrounded her, and she felt like she could see every colour, shape and wonder of the natural world compacted into this space of lush living beauty. Eve felt her happiness and linked her arm as she guided her to the water's edge. "You have done much Runestone Life for your limited years, as I have said before, you have gone further than any of us expected, but your road is long, and you have only just taken your first steps along it, so you have been brought back to me in the last of my time to learn the final steps that will aid you in the toughest fight you have faced to date."

Rune stopped and turned to Eve. "How do you mean the last of your time?" Eve gave a smile.

"I gave most of my powers to my daughter, who in return has passed them on to you. There will come a time when I shall cease to walk here and return to my natural state, and remain forever held within the Isle created by my husband for my time of rest." Rune looked surprised, and Eve lifted a hand to her soft white face. "This is a choice I have made for the sake of my line and their future, I chose it freely, fear not my child, and do not feel sorrow, I have lived a time of such great happiness here, I have no regrets as I pass beyond all in this and the other worlds I have helped create." It made no sense to Rune; she could not imagine having to leave Robbie or her children.

"What about Opal and Our Green Lord? Do you not feel pain being here lost to them?"

There was a long moment of silence between them, as Eve stared out across the water, and into the trees on the far bank. Her voice was soft and filled with love.

"I love my daughter, for she is the greatest source of happiness to me, knowing that she carries my line and that of my husband, who I love more than anything I have ever known. You must understand the responsibility we all have faced and borne in our role as rulers on the council. It was decided long ago that we must give all we have built to the lines of men, for they are still our greatest creation. Do not be saddened, for I have no regrets in the part I have played, and will play my part to help keep what we have built alive and safe. When the time comes, you too will understand everything and it will help you in your final tasks." Eve turned to an arched tunnel of hawthorn trees. "Come we shall move to the shade and eat, and I will tell you the answers to many questions, and begin the process that will lead you to your true destiny."

Rune was unsure of exactly what Eve meant, but she did have many questions and wanted to know the answers, she also felt hungry at the mention of food. With Eve linking her arm she stepped under the trees and walked into the long corridor. "Is Robbie safe, can you tell me if he is alright?" Eve squeezed her arm tightly.

"Have no fear, he feels at the moment he has failed, but it is a minor setback he must overcome, he has friends' unseen to aid him, and soon you will be reunited." Rune gave a slight smile.

"I cannot feel him, and it scares me. I cannot feel any of them and I was scared I was lost to them."

"You are hidden here from everything, it is important that you above all others are protected for a short time, fear not you will go back to Avalon in time. For now be happy, for you reside in the heart of the Forest of Time, and this is a place like no other you will ever enter, for this place was the start of all things in all worlds. Now rest awhile and let things move forward in other realms before your part to play."

In the cell carved into the mount, high above the city of Avalonia, Blades continued to stare out of the window, as the others huddled tight, close to the sleeping Rowan and discussed their options. John was positive that Robbie and Rune would come to their aid. "It makes more sense to prepare, and then when he gets here bust out and take out the weakest to get their weapons." Bear considered the prospect, but Fox had been paying more attention to their surroundings than the Cutters when the door was open.

"All our kit is piled on the table at the far end of the room, all we have to do is get across there, and we will be back to full strength. I reckon they have about ten guards out there, the rest of them were with the leader, and from the sounds of it, they left with him." Bear gave a nod.

"OK, so we seize our moment, and pile out towards our stuff, I assume Robbie will know the way out, so we just follow his lead." Blades turned at the window.

"What about Rowan? We cannot leave him, but he won't make it alone with that leg." John looked back at her.

"Keep me covered and I will carry him." Bear agreed.

"Ok you get him out in front, and we will protect him from the sides and rear."

"No offence guys, but aren't you forgetting the Houlen?" Jay's bright green eyes watched from under her matted long black hair. "Those vile things are everywhere, and we are only half the number we were in our last encounter. If we get caught in a tunnel with them it will not be easy, we are almost out of arrows, and let's face it, we all need more rest." Crystal gave a long sigh.

"She is right, I for one am exhausted, my powers are drained, I will not be much help if we meet them."

"It's her; I can feel her gaining in strength." Everyone turned to Hornet, her voice had been quiet, yet somehow it carried round all of them. Blades gave her a funny look.

"What do you mean, you feel her?" Hornet looked worried.

"Rune told me it might happen, there will be times when I feel her more than others, I hate it, but she is family and some bonds cannot be broken. She is right above us as we speak, and her power is growing very strong. I felt it down by the bridge when she fought with Rune, I also felt her fear, and then when the star grew stronger, I felt her power increase. I think that thing she has is trying to steal all the powers from us, I have tried to talk to Rune, but she is out of reach." Crystal shook her head.

"Yeah, me too, but I cannot seem to reach her."

"I feel the Houlen too, they contain her power, and so I connect with them." Judith swallowed hard, and looked even more nervous. Bear gave a smile at her.

"Then little Hornet, we have an edge, and that is a big help to us." He gave a big smile, and she relaxed a little and smiled back. Bear turned back to the others. "OK we have the makings of a plan. Once in the tunnel, Hornet can monitor the

Houlen, so at least we will have advanced warning, it won't be much time, but at least we can prepare. I reckon it will take Robbie and the others a little time, so I suggest half of us sleep while the others stay vigilant, at least that way we will be better rested if this comes to a tough fight, agreed?" They all gave a nod. "Good, OK John, you Crystal, Fox and Jay get first sleep, and we will keep a close eye out." Bear stood up and took his place at the door as the others moved around the cell. Crystal and Jay shared the other bed, and John sat in the corner with the sun on his dirty face and closed his eyes. Blades walked over to Bear and leaned on the door.

"I will feel happier with my mother's swords back in my hands." He patted her shoulder.

"All in good time Blades, don't worry, I know Robbie, he will be planning now to help get us back." She smiled.

"Yeah, I know he will."

Under the heavy mist that now blanketed the whole of the vale of Avalon, deep inside the thick marsh, the heat was becoming unbearable. Flies buzzed unhappily in thick clouds through the tall reed like grass, and Hawk with his party were finding it harder and harder as they pushed forward. Woody led the way carefully watching the floor to ensure they travelled by a safe path, all around them deep water filled pools marked the areas of great danger, and it was crucial that Woody kept them on solid ground.

Their pace was slow hindered by the two stretchers containing Treen and Jasper, who burned red in a delirious fever, Milly and Gaynor kept close doing their best to keep them cool, wiping their faces with damp cloths. Behind them the mist swirled and clouded their trail, somewhere in the distance the eerie calls of frustrated Houlen, seemed dulled by the heavy mists. With each wail the group felt the cold tingle of fear and concern creep down their spines.

Woody sliced through a tall stack of reed, and opened another path through into a wide space. In front of him was a wide pool of water that surrounded a raised mound in its centre, on which stood an old and twisted solitary oak. Its jagged limbs spread out across the top of the mound, which had a single track of heavily tufted grass across the water towards it. Woody tested the ground with his heel to ensure it was firm enough; Hawk cut through another high wall of reed at his side, and looked out on the pool surrounding the mound. "What is it?"

Woody wiped his face and neck as he studied the terrain. "I have seen places like this at home; I have used them in the past to protect my sheep from the wild animals in the night." Hawk understood him.

"We can rest up here protected by the water?" Woody crouched down and inspected the floor at his feet.

"We can use this as a way in, and hope there is another on the other side, but it looks like it is very well protected, it might be a good place to rest safely." Hawk gave a smile.

"Well done Woody, we need somewhere desperately to rest up, this pace is killing all of us, some rest and a good meal will give us a much needed break. Ok let's get everyone across to the island and set up a guard, we have some protection from this mist, but it also hides them, take Rags and scout it out while I get the others organised."

Hawk moved back into the reed and informed the others of what was happening, it was greeted with a great deal of relief, all of them were soaked with sweat and very red faced, and on the edge of exhaustion. Rags and Woody slipped off across the path marking a safe route as everyone stayed sat on the ground with relief. Una looked spent having helped carry one of the stretchers, and Hawk gave her a pat on the shoulder as he stood at her side while she stretched her aching legs.

"Ooh this is the worst thing I have ever done; I could sleep for a week."

"You might get the chance if this mist does not lift soon." Hawk took a long swig from his flask. Una looked up as she wiped her face for the thousandth time that day.

"Are we going to hole up here for a while?"

"We are blind, the compass is just spinning, and the sun does not seem to be moving, I have lost track of time, and I am not sure which is the right direction. Something here is wrong, and to be honest until we know more, I would rather keep us together in a safe place. We need to contact Rune."

"I am trying, but I feel so drained, it's like I can barely throw a thought to my feet." Hawk wiped his smeared dirty face and neck, as he waited for the signal from Woody.

"Something is very wrong Una, call it a gut feeling, I have never known Rune be out of contact for so long, and the day here is not as it should be. I want to play things a little safer and rest everyone up, until I know more, I think staying put is our only option."

"What about the Houlen? They have our scent, they must be somewhere behind us." Hawk crouched down to her side and looked at her red face.

"I have been thinking about that, we have been slowed down greatly by the stretchers and these tall reeds, to be honest I expected them to catch up with us hours ago. I know it sounds odd, but I am starting to wonder if they fear water, you know in the woods on the path to Avalonia they were not spread out wide, but gathered in small groups close to the road. I am beginning to think that they do not like it and do everything they can to avoid it. We have been trampling down everything as we ploughed on through all this, our path is as clear as day, yet they have not followed us." Una thought about it.

"I suppose you are right; they are beasts with a keen sense of smell, they must have picked up our trail back there. Oh god I hope you are right; I will rest easier knowing surrounded by water we are all a little safer." He gave a smile, as a shrill whistle sounded through the reeds announcing the return of Woody, and he patted her leg.

"Come on let's go and make camp, I think a good meal and a long sleep will aid all of us."

He grabbed her hand as he rose, and pulled her up to her feet; looking back at the others as they wearily got up off the ground and lifted the stretchers, he gave them all a big smile. "We have found a camp up ahead, Maggs get a smoke free fire going using the can stoves as soon as we have everyone in place, I think a good meal and some rest will benefit all of us."

Weary, yet happy moans lifted from the tall reeds as they made one final exhausted effort to take them to a sheltered place of safety. Una and Hawk took a stretcher and led the way on the narrow path and took the party across the wide clear pool, and onto the small island sheltered under the arms of the ancient twisted oak.

Maddy lifted her bow at the rear, as the others moved slowly forward onto the narrow path. Behind her she heard the reeds crack as if trodden down, she stopped and spun round raising her bow with a loaded arrow, waiting to see what was lurking behind her.

The thick mist swirled before her, as she stared at it trying to make out if anything was there, the rest of the group carried on without her across the path, leaving her alone surrounded by the tall reeds. Deep down inside she felt something stir; it gave her prickles up her spine as she tried to see if they had been followed. For the briefest of seconds, a dark hooded figure appeared and then disappeared as the mists swirled back and concealed them, her heart skipped several beats as her sweaty hand clamped harder on the warm wood. "Who's there? Name yourself or I will fire."

The damp water glinted on the tip of her arrow, as she held it fast ready to fire the moment, she had a target. The voice was soft, yet carried authority. "I am no enemy of those who fight to free this world of darkness White Circle."

Maddy swallowed hard at the sound of a voice, her senses were picking up no one, yet there before her was a voice announcing the presence of another. The tension deep down inside her rose as she croaked out her words. "A friend would show themselves openly, yet you hide in the mists, come forth and give me a face to talk to."

The sweat dripped off her nose, as the mist swirled forward toward her; she pushed her feet firmly into the ground and pulled back more on the string. The dense white mist rolled backwards and she saw the hooded figure in a tatty black cloak, stood on the path cut through the reeds; his face was hidden in the shade of his hood as he watched her. Maddy felt nervous, she was all alone and confronted by a stranger who proclaimed to be a friend, but deep in her mind, she knew there had been no one in the realm when they entered who had not been an enemy. He did not move, and it unnerved her that he had used her name of old.

"Name yourself stranger, and state your business here, for we trust few who walk in these lands."

"You are wise to exercise caution at this time, but you have no fear from me. I have come only to offer you advice."

"Yet you sneak up and do not announce yourself, which does not instil me with confidence stranger." His hood moved slightly, and Maddy felt that he had smiled at her lack of trust in him.

"Times are dangerous, it is safer to proceed with caution, and after all, you are the one holding a weapon, as you can plainly see I am unarmed."

It was something that she only realised in that moment, as she looked at the frayed hooded robe with no belt for a sword.

"You say you are here to advise us; tell me what advice you could give us that would win you favour with us?" Her arrow remained fixed on the figure who still remained stood on the path ten feet in front of her.

"You have two wounded by the dark beasts; I believe one of them is kin to you? They will die soon if you do not find an antidote to the poison within them. I can show you a way to reverse the effects of the poison; your numbers are small for the tasks you face, so the addition of two more will aid you greatly." It worried Maddy that he knew so much about the group, but she felt a little hope rise inside her, as she had suffered the pains of losing one daughter, and in her heart, she knew she could not lose another, her voice softened as it showed her rising emotion.

"How can I save them?"

"Lower your bow White Circle and I will tell you." She was alone and frightened, and as much as she desperately wanted to save Treen, she was afraid if she lowered her bow, he would kill her and maybe the others, it was a trap of faith, and in this place of hell, much of hers had disappeared.

"How do I know I can trust you not to attack?"

"You don't, but you have the choice to put your faith in the right place, and know it will bring back your daughter, the choice is yours." Her hand shook slightly on the bowstring, it was at full tension, and she knew she had to fire, or lower the bow. Her arm was very tired and she knew she could not hold it for longer. "My time here is short White Circle, what is your choice?"

Slowly and cautiously Maddy lowered the bow, she had no choice and she knew it, the life of her daughter meant everything, and if there was just one small way to save her, she had to take it. The figure took a step forward, and she felt her hand grip tighter on the bow that now faced the floor. "Look to your feet and the white flowers that grow there. Gather the flower heads and infuse them in the water from the pool behind you. Let them drink it slowly, and the poison will retreat. This is not a cure, but it will inhibit it long enough to get them to the Lady of the Woods, for she has the only real cure." Maddy looked down quickly, not wanting to take her eyes off the stranger. All around her feet white flowers grew in abundance, she looked up and the figure had gone.

"Wait don't leave us." The mist swirled back around her, and suddenly she felt very much alone, and gave a slight shiver. Maddy stood watching the empty place for several long moments, before she quickly crouched down and gathered the heads of the white flowers, she was not sure how many to use, so unwrapping her handkerchief, she filled it with as many as it would hold, and slipped it into her shirt pocket. Feeling hope surge inside her, she grabbed her bow, lifted her bag, and then ran onto the thin path, following the markers towards the island mound that rose out of the wide pool of water.

Robbie trudged along with his head down, at the side of Steph. Up ahead; Smokes and William ran on, as the sight of daylight flooded the end of the tunnel. Steph felt a sense of relief as she looked at Robbie almost dragging his feet. "How's the head?"

"Pounding." He had lost a lot of blood and felt weak, and the crashing pains going through his head did not help, as it jumbled the thousands of thoughts of recent events bouncing through his mind.

"Let's get out in the fresh air and I will look at your head properly, it will need stitching, your bandage is soaked with blood, I think the sooner we attend to it the better for your headache." He gave a slight nod and wished he hadn't as his head almost exploded with the movement. William stood in the opening that was the entrance to a large cave that led back into the tunnel, the light was blinding after the dimly lit cave, and as he looked down at the parchment map, the light reflected back off it and he screwed his eyes up to reduce the glare.

"If this map is right, this should be Eagle Heights." Smokes leaned over his shoulder to look at the map.

"Where is that then?" William looked out into the thick swirling mist in front of him.

"Well, that must be right, because according to this we should be just on the edge of the lake near a place called Misty Bank." Smokes stepped out and peered through the heavy white mist, at what looked like woodland just across the grassy area in front of the cave. He looked up at the high wall of rock that disappeared into the heavy cloud above them.

"I would say you are right, man, I can only see about twenty feet, how close are we to Merlin's place?" Will looked up from the map and pointed north.

"It's that way, this map is a little out of scale, so it could be a few hours or a day away, I am not really that certain." Smokes gave a nod and turned to look in the direction of the faint trees.

"Well I must admit if it's trees we have to go through, that will suit me better."

Robbie and Steph came through the cave and into the daylight; Steph shielded her eyes, as even with the mist, the sun felt blinding.

"Somehow I expected it cooler than the tunnels." Her Mind exploded.

"Steph is that you? Steph it's Una where are you? Steph it's Hornet, Oh Steph we are stuck in a cell and need help, Steph! This is Crystal is Robbie with you? We have been trying to get hold of Rune, but cannot contact her. Steph Maddy and me are trapped in the marshes with Hawk and some of the others, Treen and Jasper have been badly wounded and we fear they will die if we don't find Rune."

Steph swayed as her hands went up to her head, and Smokes snatched her into his arms to support her.

"Hey Baby are you OK?" Her face looked drained of colour, and she swooned a little holding her face.

"BE QUIET, STOP YELLING AT ME THE LOT OF YOU, YOU ARE STRAINING MY MIND!" Smokes held her firmly by the elbows.

"Hey sorry Baby, I didn't know I was shouting." Steph dropped her hands and opened her eyes to look at him.

"Not you, them." He turned and glanced behind him.

"Who?" Steph smiled.

"I got Crystal, Maddy, Una and Judy all asking me about a hundred questions at once." Smokes understood, unlike Robbie after years of marriage to Steph, he had learned to understand the powers and communication that his wife had constantly going on in her head.

"Yeah, OK Baby, have a chat and then let us all know what is happening, I think I will get a fire going and cook something." He looked across at Robbie who had slid down the wall inside the cave and was sat with his eyes closed; he gave a wink at William. "Not sure about you lot, but I am starving, it feels like days since I last ate." Will gave a happy nod; he too had spent the last few hours listening to his stomach as it groaned from lack of food.

As the two of them got busy, searching the bags to see what food they had between them, Steph sat on the grass, and one at a time she went round the circle of her sisters and found out where they were and what was happening. Crystal seemed very worried about her powers.

"I am not sure what is happening Steph, I am sat right beside Judy, and yet up until the moment you appeared, I could not talk to her using my mind. Is there something wrong with me?"

"It's not you Chris, Maddy and me are the same, we have been talking about it, I think that somehow the Dark One has found a way of diverting our powers away from us."

"It's the star, I have already told the others, I am not sure how, but Rune did say that some family links could never be broken. I think because she is my grandmother, I can feel the star as she wields it, and it has been growing in power

since we got here."

"Well that would explain a lot."

Smokes smiled as he watched Steph with her eyes closed talking with her mind, but nodding in agreement with the others, as she would if they were sat in front of her.

"OK girls, I think Judith has a point, I cannot get hold of Rune, so she must be somewhere that prevents her talking to us. I need a rest and Robbie needs his head seeing to, I am going to do what I can and have something to eat. I want all of you to stay in touch and keep me posted, we will look at the situation and try and work something out. All of you rest and conserve the powers you have, as soon as I have news, I will talk to all of you."

Steph opened her eyes and looked at the group sat by the fire, she gave a long sigh as she stood up and walked toward them, and Robbie opened his eyes and looked up at her.

"How bad is it?" She gave a slight smile.

"It's been better, but at least we are all back in touch, well most of us."

"None of them have heard from Rune then?" Steph shook her head.

"Sorry Rob, there has been nothing since the bridge."

Steph watched and felt the huge surge of disappointment run through him, as he lowered his head and stared at the white bangle on his wrist. "She said she would always find me with this, I just wish it worked the other way, and I could find her." Steph crouched down and took his hand.

"Don't give up on her Robbie, she is somewhere, and she is missing you just as much, you know that. One thing I know about my daughter is if it is keeping her from you, well, there must be a very good reason. Don't give up on her."

His eyes lifted and met hers; she had the same strong searching eyes of her father. "I will never give up on her." Steph gave him a big smile.

"And she knows that Robbie, have faith in her, she will appear before long." She patted his shoulder as Smokes passed a steaming cup with the rich smell of coffee, and he gratefully took it. Steph opened her bag and searched for her sewing kit. "Ok let's sort that head of yours out, and then hopefully your thoughts will clear a little, and I will tell all of you what is going on around Avalon."

CHAPTER SEVEN

QUESTIONS

In a clearing surrounded by the tallest oak trees, where all the branches stretched out and met high above the centre of the circle to form a roof, casting dappled shade through the leaves, was a simple table of stone. It was cool and clear as Rune sat on a raised smooth stone, cushioned with soft dark green moss. Eve sat opposite as the two of them helped themselves to fruits and nuts of the woodland, laid out on the table in roughly carved wooden bowls. Two silver goblets held a clear liquid poured from a tall stone jug, and Rune recognised the scent of rose petals, and the familiar taste of elderflower.

Rune had noticed many small changes in Eve since she had met her for the first time high up on the Isle of Tears. The look of youth seemed to have lessened, and when she moved, Rune could see, as the sunlight passed across Eve's hair there was a faint trace of silver. Rune felt nervous, Eve had told her that this would be the time of answers to many questions, but deep down inside, she was uncertain as to whether or not she would like what she heard. Eve smiled and passed her a bowl made from walnut, which contained many berries, some of which she had never seen before. "I feel your apprehension Runestone Life, never fear the truth, for even if we have no care for what is said, it still brings clarity and wisdom for future use."

Rune looked at the table avoiding Eve's gaze, there were so many things that made no sense to her, and she wanted to know the answers to them, but it was finding a place to start, which was her greatest trouble. Eve leaned forward and took her hand in hers. "The order is irrelevant, ask what is in your heart and mind, the answers have their place. Like a patchwork quilt the squares are made first, but the final design is in the order that they are stitched together to create the whole." Rune smiled a sheepish smile.

"There are so many things that I find hard to understand, but the one that I ask myself more than any is why me, when I am the second born of my house? Jade is the true heir to Opal, why did she not inherit the powers and the placement of centre?" Eve sat back and gave a nod of understanding.

"It is a good place to start. Jade was the first born of the line of Opal's, but you misunderstand your destiny and power, for Jade is the heir to the line of Opal, and in her is the future of the Green Circle, that was never your destiny." Rune felt the huge wave of surprise run through her.

"But I am the centre, I am the one marked to carry forward the violet lines, it is my destiny as the one all shall be written on." Eve gave a small smile.

"You are indeed the future of all things, but you misunderstand what has passed to you. Runestone Life, your sister is Green Circle as was always preordained in her line, but you have to understand that the gifts that have passed to you were never given to Opal, she has never possessed the power of the red stone, that alone was yours."

"But if Jade is the heir of Opal, then how can I be an heir?"

"You forget that Opal was born of two lines." Rune shook her head trying to understand.

"That's another thing, everyone talks of two lines, which is why I replaced Sapphire, but she has the power of Gwendolyn and my grandfather, as I have Opal and my grandfather, it makes no sense." Eve took a drink from her cup and thought for a moment.

"It makes more sense than you realise, you complicate your thoughts when you should be simplifying them." Eve leaned forward again, and her eyes shone brightly as they met with Rune's. "Think of the tales of the Ruling Council and you will understand better. Gwendolyn was a descendant of Bridge, and your grandfather was the guardian of the Whitelines."

"But that is two lines, Sapphire should have been made centre of her circle."

"That is one line created from two very strong sources of power; never forget Runestone Life, that Bridge and Merlin were both created by the Ruling Council. We all gave a gift to add to their powers, but they were not the original source of the powers. I must confess that my brother Albanlin did place a mighty force inside Merlin, and it was a strong force from Tideguyde that was placed in Bridge and Rhiannon, yet it was still diluted considering your line. Together their powers at their best, would equal that of one of the council founder members at their worst, yet it was far stronger than any given to the lines of men. They equal one line Runestone Life, not two."

"I have your power, and that of my woodland lord?"

"You and your family have the power of two lines in their purest form. My daughter Opal was very powerful in her time, but you have exceeded the expectations of all of us." It made some sense to Rune, but it still held other questions.

"But it does not change the fact that Jade was born first, Jade should still be the centre of all things." Rune gave a sigh trying to understand the process of power, and then she had another sudden thought. "But actually, if you think about it, then my mum should have had the power before either of us, yet it passed over her and came to me... Oh none of this seems to make any sense." Eve laughed.

"Take a drink and do not put so much pressure on yourself, look for the simple solution, you are in exactly the right place, but you are clouding your own thoughts by thinking too deeply. Keep it simple and use plain logic."

"But it does not matter how simple it is, the fact is that my mother missed out on the powers, she just got a sleeping gift and the ability to weave, and she is also more intelligent than most people I know, I think she gets that from my grandfather."

Eve raised her hands in the air. "Ah ha! See, I knew you would get there?"

"What? How do you mean... do you mean that my mother is the heir of my grandfather and not her mother?" Eve gave a happy smile.

"My dear child it means exactly that."

"So, my mum is really a wizard?" Eve chuckled.

"We never created wizards, that was a name invented by man to label those with abilities they did not understand. But your mother is the heir of your grandfather's power, and therefore she could not continue the line of the green circle... The ability to weave power is a gift that is only possessed by my brother, which is why he is so powerful and the head of the council. He has great wisdom, and he saw long ago many tasks that would be destined for Merlin, and so it was written that in the time of greatest need to mankind, Merlin would move on and allow his heir to work beside those who came of greater power. I must admit none of us realised it would be the union of the White Circle and Merlin, which would one day be blended through his heir with the union of the Green Circle and the red stone, to create the new line of power. You are the result of many chance moments through time to get to this place in time."

"How?"

"I think My Child you should look to the work of Gwendolyn, for she was very powerful and had greater wisdom than most in her age. Gwendolyn had a mighty power of sight, a gift that is part of the gifts of fellowship as given to the Fae by Albanlin. She saw many things and prepared much in secret, even now we are unsure if she saw the moments of your life, we do know she knew that the mortal le Fey would rise up and strike at man. Gwendolyn took the core of her power and hid it deep within Opal; I can only guess that she did it because she knew one of my line would have the power to carry it. On the night Opal gave you the gifts of your line at the Mere in Loxley, something passed from her that recognised a signature implanted in you at birth."

"The mark of the Fae, Gwynfor told me of that in Scotland, he said it was my grandfather who recognised it and changed my name from Rutile to Runestone." Rune gave her first big smile as she began to understand the mysterious way her powers had been bound together; Eve gave a happy smile, noting the change in Rune.

"That mark is also the symbol of the first rune made, and it has dual meaning, for it signifies Fae, but also Rundalba. It is the mark of my most precious gift to the world, for it binds the knowledge of all of us, and it marks our passage from the lives of men to lead them finally into their own destiny. Your birth was the beginning of a new way of life for everything, and it matters not if you were first or last born in your household, the mark was set long ago to mark the one who could wield it. You are my true heir Runestone Life."

As the pieces fell into place, it was a very sobering moment for Rune, her mind wandered as she put together all the facts in her mind, and Eve watched as she understood the process, and was glad to see that Rune was finally beginning to understand, and coming to terms with who she really was. Rune looked at her for a moment and then paused again. A few seconds passed, and then she asked her next question.

"If I am your heir, your colour is red, so why is my power called the violet lines and not red?" It was a simple question, and yet Eve found it funny and profound.

"The answer is simple, yet in many ways very complex. Firstly, each member of the council is marked by the colour they omit in their true form, as you know mine is red. Hearne is green, but more importantly, Erathome was yellow, and Tideguyde was blue." She paused for a second as Rune waited silently.

"Yellow and green were never meant to be your destiny, for to some extent they passed to your mother and sister, although you do have traces of both those lines mixed within you, for you are of Erathome's earth, and of the line of the Green Lord." Rune understood that, but it did not explain the colour purple, Eve smiled.

"In the beginning everything was built in balance from myself and from my husband, in everything that we did, there was a balance of the feminine and the masculine. When the mortal Le Fey came along and created her troubles the balance was thrown out, as she understood the true nature of power, and she placed men to rule alone, and it was said there could never be balance in the world until the two elements of masculine and feminine came back together."

"Robbie!" Rune almost jumped off her seat with excitement. "Grandfather said there was something strong between us; he said he wanted to study it because it was more powerful than he had ever seen before." Eve gave a chuckle as she saw the bright smile on Rune's face, and she nodded gently as Rune put the pieces of the puzzle finally together in her mind.

"Robbie was tainted by Gwendolyn's power, which was influenced by Tideguyde and that was blue, and if you mix that with red it's purple." Rune seemed happy at spotting the simplicity of it. Eve agreed.

"You are quite correct, and it pleases me to see you use simple deduction, but as I said, it is a little more complex in its nature. Powers mingle and react with each other, your gift from my line is very pure, and so therefore a very strong red, but to fully understand how it all came about you must look to the lines of the Fae."

Rune frowned.

"The Fae, I was just starting to get the hang of it, and now I am lost again."

"It is simple enough, have no fear. When Bridge was created as a copy of Rhiannon to link the Fae Ofmoon to the Earth, Hearne mixed the powers of the earth with those given by Albanlin of fellowship. Never forget who made the earth to begin with, for Erathome moulded it with his own hands spreading his own power all over it. I added the final touch, which created a force that would increase and intensify with each passing to another queen. Bridge passed her power to Gwendolyn who increased its potency, which made it the darkest of blues and as you now see that was then combined with you through your union with Robbie, but even so, such was the purity of those powers contained within you that they could not mix easily." Rune gave a sigh.

"You don't make this easy at all." Eve laughed out loud.

"My poor sweet child you already know the answer we have spoken about it."

"We have?" Eve wiped her eye as she laughed.

"Power can only be woven together." Rune jumped with the sudden realisation.

"My grandfather... Of course why did I not see that? He was the one, who first noticed the mark and he was the one who changed my name. He understood the meaning because he has studied everything that has been written in the old text, why did I not see that? I have part of his line in me to weave together all the powers, dark blue and red make deep purple, or violet, I cannot believe I never saw it. All this time it has been there in front of me, and I missed it. By making my mother his heir, she helped weave together all the hidden magic to create me." Rune lifted her goblet with joy and took a huge gulp of the ice cold drink and felt happiness grow deep inside her. Eve rested on her hands on the table with a happy look on her face.

"Let's not forget that when Sapphire was born, he noticed the gifts had not been passed to her. Meeting a direct descendant of Gwynfor helped, after all he was the brother of Gwendolyn, we all knew then that it was the right time for the coming of a new line of power. Gwendolyn was very shrewd, and she passed the power to a line of the masculine. From the moment you and Robbie met as young children, I think that you recognised the elements hidden deep within him, but we all knew for sure the moment that you became involved with him, for within a very short time you saw the first traces of the mixing of power." Rune looked up at her.

"I did?" Eve shook her head.

"Oh Rune... Think about it, was it not within a few weeks that your eyes began to glow with lilac? Opal knew straight away, she told her father who I must admit was not that sure, but to everyone else it was a sign that the power was mixing and weaving around you."

"So that was what caused it, all this time I have been trying to understand everything, now I see how simple it all is. The power was still weak, but as I grew stronger in my ability, and my relationship with Robbie deepened, the colour became more intense." Eve lifted her glass and took a long drink as she saw everything making full sense to Runestone. She placed her goblet back on the old table.

"I am glad to see the wisdom growing stronger inside you, with every moment that passes, you will understand more, and it will strengthen you, and guide you and Robbie in all you do."

The sudden mention of Robbie brought Rune back to earth with a bump; she put her goblet down on the table and felt the pangs of separation. "I miss him, and I fear for him without me." Eve took her hands in hers and gave them a soft squeeze.

"I understand how hard it is to be parted from those we love, but it will not be for long. Your young woodland lord needs this time to understand where his strength is, for he needs to look into his heart and find a way of seeing that he has not failed. The outcome is not as he would have wished, but he has achieved all that was asked of him, the heirs have been found, and he has brought them together, his task is complete. Give him this time to learn as you have, and let him find out who he really is, for in that path lies greater power for both of you."

Rune gave a nod, she was not sure she fully understood, but she knew him well enough to know that he would use his strong instincts, to steer himself back onto the road that was right for him and everyone.

"Why was I taken away from Avalon?" Eve was happy to find that Rune had asked the one question she had expected.

"The Star of the Merle will kill you." She saw the impact it had on Rune. "It is a thing created by Albanlin in his attempt to rid all the worlds of the most terrible forms of evil. I must admit none of us thought that the mortal Le Fey would be able to find it, let alone use it. She has gained a lot of power in secret, and in order to protect you, Albanlin entered the realm and brought you out to safety." Rune had already guessed that, hearing it confirmed her fears.

"What must I do to go back and face it?" Eve admired her bravery, but her face changed and she showed her concern. Her voice was soft and quiet.

"I wish with all my heart it was me in your place, but the gifts have passed on, and so you will in time face her with that evil and vile thing. For my part I am helping you understand yourself and the powers you hold, but there will be one more task from another before you can truly fight her and the star." Rune gave a soft nod.

"I understand now, this task is mine, and mine alone. Will the white star help me?" As she lifted her head, Eve felt a pain in her heart as Rune's eyes connected with hers, and she saw that Rune was starting to truly understand her task.

"I cannot tell you, for I do not know the full power of the white star, I just know that my brother fears what is contained within the Star of the Merle, and in the coming days two others have been chosen to guide you."

"Will I live, do you know if my children will know their mother?" Eve's eyes clouded with tears, she rose from her seat and moved round the table. The fear in Rune's eyes was too much for her to bear, and she dragged her up in her arms and held her as tight as she could.

"Oh, Runestone my child, I have tried to see in the mirrored waters a thousand times, but they cannot show me, all I can say is that no matter what you face I will be with you in spirit to aid you." Rune lifted her arms and pulled Eve close burying her head deeply into her.

"I am so frightened I will not live and Robbie and my children will be left without me." Eve felt the fear inside her and gripped her tighter; it seemed so unfair that someone so young had so much responsibility to burden her. She understood the fear and the deep pangs of separation from her children, she too had paid a high price, and suffered at times being alone with only a reflection in the water to show her how the life of her only child lived. Eve pulled Rune gently back from her and looked down into her white frightened face. Her voice contained a small amount of desperation.

"Listen carefully to me My Child." Eve unclasped the long red cloak from her shoulders and swung it around the shoulders of Rune. "Take this, for it has many protections, close your eyes for a brief moment and listen very carefully for we have little time. Go to them and take them away from the castle, take them home where they will have the protection of your table, for it has powers even you have not discovered. They will be safe with the guards of Fae, for they are two of the most powerful maidens of their line. Move quickly, and when they are done return to me by closing your eyes and thinking of me." Rune gave a nod, understanding that what Eve was doing was against all the rules set by the council. Rune closed her eyes and she felt Eve kiss her softly on the forehead. "Go with speed my precious child."

"Rune! Rune when did you get back?" Rune opened her eyes to see Alice running down the garden at the rear of the castle in Caerleon to meet her; she looked round not understanding what had happened, half expecting to see Eve stood there. Alice came running up and threw her arms around her, and Rune snatched her with huge joy into a full embrace.

"Oh Alice, how are you? I missed you, where are the children?" Alice beamed with delight and pointed behind her.

"They have just been taken inside; I was about to collect up the toys when I saw you." Rune pulled her back into another big hug.

"I have very little time Alice, we must hurry, the children must go back to the house in Loxley, come on and gather all your things, and I will tell you everything."

Rune hurried across the long lawn, and up the steps to the back doors of the castle; her eyes burned a bright violet as she walked and sent a message to Sapphire. *"Sapphire hear me."* Sapphire sat bolt upright in bed.

"Rune, I have been trying to get hold of you."

"Sapphire listen carefully, I have very little time so I am going to pass you all of the information about Robbie and the group. I need you to head to Loxley and brief John and Jess, then go to York and talk to Rayne, all is not well, so close your thoughts to everything else."

Sapphire lay back on her pillow and closed her eyes. Her body gave a jolt as Rune pushed everything she could remember through her mind to Sapphire. Sapphire's cheeks flicked with a vivid purple light as her eyes twitched.

Rune moved quickly up the long corridor, to where she could see Filomena and Isolde with the children, the large tiger lay at the base of the pram, and sat up with a deep rumble as it saw Rune. Her eyes filled with tears as she saw the two servants lift the children from their pram, and she rushed forward and swept Hal into her arms and pulled him tightly to her. Isolde smiled as she held Iona. "My Lady we did not expect you." Rune looked down at the small face and bright blue eyes of her son as her tears rolled down her cheeks.

"Oh my darling, I have missed you so much." She squeezed him hard as Iona gave a happy little squeak, and lifted her small hand to her mother. Filomena helped her take Iona into her arms, as she crouched on the floor and held both of them tightly. Iona's eyes were bright, and watched her as she quietly spoke the words of a mother who had missed her children desperately. For a few precious moments, the two servants of the Fae stood beside a beaming Alice and watched her.

Rune looked up from her children to the two staff. "I am taking the children back to the house; I think they will be safer there for the time being. The Dark One is in Avalon and has sealed the way out, we are doing everything we can to restore the new queen to her seat, but things have gone ill. Gather all the children's things, for my time here is short."

The servants gave a brisk nod and disappeared. Rune sat with her children on her lap as Alice knelt down beside her.

"Is everything alright, has it really been awful?" Rune felt the apprehension rising inside Alice, as Furry Face walked over and rubbed his huge head on her shoulder. Rune rubbed the back of his ears hard, and he gave a whimper of happiness, she turned and looked at Alice.

"We confronted the Dark One and we fought, I really am not that sure what happened, but I ended up with Eve and the others as far as I know have scattered." Alice looked pale and swallowed as she gave a small nod. Rune felt her fear and slid Iona into her lap and then squeezed Alice's hand tightly. "Bear was fine when I last saw him with Robbie." Alice gave a weak smile.

"Is it really dangerous? I wish you had taken me I would have helped." Rune gave a soft smile.

"I am glad I didn't, it's felt like a trap since we first arrived, the Dark One is in control at the moment and she has sealed the realm, I was lucky to be able to get out with the help of Eve." Alice looked frightened, and Rune understood, she too had not heard from Robbie and was afraid for him. Rune squeezed Alice's hand; her voice softened. "Alice, we lost Alley."

"What?" Alice looked startled. Rune took a breath.

"I know you were good friends; I truly am sorry. She died saving Gaynor from a vile creature created by the Dark One called a Houlen, we were outnumbered and surrounded, it was total chaos. She was taken very quickly Alice, and would have not felt anything." Alice lowered her head and the tears dripped from her cheeks. "I have so little time Alice, you must go and get your things, but I promise you, I will get back as fast as I can to help them, I will bring Bear home to you." Alice lifted her arms and pulled Rune into a hug, the two children made little chirping noises, and Alice withdrew and stood up and wiped her eyes.

"I will get little Jessie ready... Thanks Rune." Rune gave a smile as Alice turned and ran off to the stairs to gather everything together and have a small weep for the loss of her friend. Rune settled with her children on the floor in between the doors of the main hall, and treasured each second, she had been given alone with them.

The dark hooded figure stood by the waterfall on the edge of Eve's garden in the Forest of Time, as Eve looked at him defiantly. "It was not your place, we agreed." Eve flicked her hair back over her shoulder; her bright violet eyes smouldered with anger.

"Neither was it yours to go to Rhiannon and obtain passage into this realm, this place is under my domain, yet you chose to ignore the rules, and take her from the bridge."

"That was different, at that moment her inexperience showed, I had to act to save all of us, if I had left her to the mercy of the stone, she would be dead now, and none of us would have hope." Eve turned with a snort.

"How very convenient Brother. You act against the rules set by you because of her youth and vulnerability, and that is fine." Eve turned back and her eyes flashed deeper violet. "I did it because she is a new mother who was being torn apart from the inside, because of the loss she felt being separated from her children. She should never have been asked to leave, have you no feelings or understanding for kin?" Albanlin felt the pain and anger in her words.

"You chose your place freely Little Sister."

"THIS IS NOT ABOUT ME, IT'S ABOUT RUNESTONE!" Eve felt the rage at her brother coursing through her. "Do you not understand a thing? Has living up there in the clouds taken every scrap of feeling from your heart? Runestone will never focus her powers while she feels the strong emotions of separation from her children, have you learned nothing from my death?" Albanlin stood for a second hurt by the remark; he took a step toward her.

"That is not what I meant; you know my regrets? I was slow and never realised; I never wanted you lost to this world. I didn't see the pain you felt when Opal was taken to the woodland realm. Eve, my sister, you must believe if I could undo that moment of terror I would."

He moved closer, and she looked up at him with tears in her eyes. They dripped to the floor and small red poppies burst into bloom. Albanlin snatched her into his arms and held her close; Eve pushed herself on to his shoulder.

"I missed her so much; she was so perfect and beautiful. When she left, it hurt so deeply I could not think of anything else. No one, not even you saw the force building in the mortal Le Fey. I care not I broke your precious rules; I cannot allow that to happen again, she has but a small moment with them, but it will give her the strength she needs in the coming days. Believe me Brother, those few moments will increase her strength and power tenfold, give her these few moments alone with them." Albanlin held her tightly, and he finally understood everything.

"I am sorry Sister. Until this moment I think I have never truly understood that day, even now after an age I see I still have much to learn. I will watch over her as always, but this you know. The Red Stone will have her time, although allowing her the use of your cloak will cost you, and in that there is little I can do." Eve moved back and looked into the hood that hid his face.

"I have had my time, if this small time alone with her children costs me a few moments of my age, it is a price I will freely pay." Her face was as pale as Rune's, but her face now bore the look of age as small lines appeared under her eyes. Her long red hair that hung almost to her feet now bore a wide band of white, without her cloak her power was lessened, and she had lost some of the look of her youth. Albanlin gave a deep sigh.

"So many ages and yet still we seem locked in the same fight with man, I had such high hopes and yet at times I feel despair. Even as we speak your beloved Hearne is set on the destruction of everything rather than allow Le Fey to lead the destruction of it all." Eve gave a soft smile.

"He has always had that wide stubborn streak within him. You will convince him; he has always accepted your council. He grows lonely like all of us, and his hope is in the child that lives close to him, I have felt his love for her deep within her, she gives him back his memories of times long since passed that we shared. When next you speak, tell him I love him." Albanlin raised his hand to her face.

"I will... Go and rest now, save your strength for her return." Eve turned, and her brother watched as she walked slowly to the arbour, and lay down in the soft bed. He stood for a few moments and watched her as she closed her eyes, and then turned toward the waterfall, and the entrance to the cave behind it. As he walked behind the fast flowing water, it lit up with a mighty blast of white light, and all in the garden of Eve settled into slumber until the moment when Rune would return.

Jess was busy at the farm, in the greenhouses, as they were busily cropping tomatoes, and she stood by the large double door directing the young boys who had recently come to work for her. They struggled as they lifted the heavy packed boxes of soft red fruits stacked in piles of eight, and with wobbly legs walked to the front of the greenhouse and the steps down to the cart.

The glass of the greenhouses illuminated in a bright violet light, and Jess turned to see the window open, and a huge tiger walk out of it. There was a high pitched scream behind her followed by a crash, and she turned back to see one of the young boys running with all his might down the centre of the house, as the large tiger bounded happily up the steps towards her. From behind a large stack of filled crates several small terrified faces peeped over. Jess gave a chuckle, and turned back to the yard as a bright blue flash of blue exploded. Jess hurried down the steps and dragged Rune into her arms as she stepped through the window. Sapphire gave a big smile as she walked out into the yard, and the window closed behind her. She winked as she saw Rune in a tight hug almost being suffocated by Jess.

"OH, Rune you are fine, how is everybody, is Robbie alright? When is he coming home?" Rune slipped back with a smile, happy to be back on familiar turf, and she enjoyed the warmth radiating out of Jess.

"I have only a short time Jess. Robbie was fine when I left him, but I must get back as quickly as possible." Behind her, the two servants of the Fae came through with the children and Alice. There was a scream from the other house across the yard, and Beth rumbled towards them waving her hankie, her eyes filling with tears as she saw Alice. Sapphire gave a giggle at the look on Alice's face. Rune took Jess by the hand and walked over to Sapphire.

"Jess there is a lot you must know, I want you to go with Saff, and she will update you and John. I have so little time and there is much to be done." Jess gave her hand a tug as Rune went to let go.

"He is alive isn't he?" Rune gave a smile.

"He is fine, things have been harder than expected that's all. I want to get back to him as quickly as possible." Jess sensed her concern, but agreed, and let go of Rune's hand. Rune turned to the two Fae holding the children. "Take them to the house; the table will protect all of you. If all goes well, we will return as soon as possible... If it does not, you know what to do. Take the buggy, it is in the stable and keep them safe." Filomena gave a small curtsy and Rune smiled. "Don't let Robbie see you doing that." Filomena gave a soft giggle.

"Sorry My Lady, it's just being in the castle with the other servants, I have sort of got back into doing it." Rune took Hal and gave him one more big hug, she kissed him on the head and handed him back.

"Goodbye my little woodsman, watch over your sister for me." She took Iona who gave a happy squeak, and Rune smiled. Iona's eyes were large and bright with violet. Rune kissed her softly and pulled her close. "Goodbye my little princess, watch over my realm while I am gone." Iona chattered happily in her mother's arms, and Rune gave a soft giggle and handed her back. "Protect them, goodbye my sweet children, Daddy loves you and will be back soon." The two servants gathered their things, and Rune watched as they made their way towards the stables. Sapphire stood at Rune's side, and Rune turned to her. "Walk with me a moment."

Rune walked onto the long drive that ran between the two houses. "Sapphire as you know all is not well, we will have no contact as soon as I set foot in the realm again. Brief John and Jess with Fuse, and then get to York as quickly as possible, tell Rayne he must hold out as long as he can, so I can get Robbie back." Rune noticed the look change on Sapphire face. "What is it?"

Sapphire shook her head. "Yeah sorry, you don't know, you have been in another realm, York has fallen, it's now under the command of Mason." It caught Rune's breath.

"So soon? Scarlet thought they would hold out much longer. OK well if that is the case Rayne will know what to do, Scarlet planned for everything." Sapphire gave a nod of understanding and Rune smiled. "I have missed you cousin, tell me how is Rafe?" Sapphire gave a shrug.

"He is not good, he is pretending he is fine, but it's been very hard on him. Do I really have to keep all this secret? I don't feel right hiding it from him, especially the news of Jett, is she really lost to us?" Rune touched her hand.

"I know it is not easy, give him space to deal with what he has been through. Rafe is tough, but I feel not ready for duty yet. Let him grieve, and tell no one there you have seen me. I know how hard this is, but you must not mention anything at all about Jett. Help out there and then in a few days contact Louisa in London, and check on their progress. Mason will be feeling particularly pleased at the moment, and if so, he will make a strike from the south. If Rafe is restless find him something to do in London until I return." Sapphire still looked concerned. "What is it you hide from me Sapphire?"

"It's OK you have little time, it's nothing really, I have just been having some really weird dreams and strange feelings." Rune gave her a warm smile.

"I feel the changes within you. Embrace them Sapphire, for your circle is finally forming around you."

"What? But you are the centre; you are the centre of both circles." Rune grabbed her and pulled her close.

"I am the centre of all circles, including yours. Never forget Dear Cousin, your name carries the mark of the sapphire and that is the mark of sight. You are Fae although I think at times you forget, speak with Rayne, he will help you understand what is happening... Right, I really must go, I will see all of you soon, stay alert and I will call to you soon."

Rune stepped back and waved to Jess. She gave a shrill whistle and the tiger raised his head, and then bounded down the path towards her. She gripped the tiger hard and closed her eyes and thought of Eve, there was a blinding flash of red, and Sapphire stepped back, Rune and Furry Face had disappeared, and Jess walked up to her side.

"John is down at the hall with Fuse; fill me in as we walk down."

In less than a blink Rune opened her eyes, and was back in the garden of Eve. She opened her fingers and Furry Face gave a small growl, and sniffed the grass. "It's alright Baby Boy, you are safe here, this is a very special place." The tiger gave a long whine and looked round at the rest of the large garden; he sniffed the floor and walked through the masses of brightly coloured flowers towards the arbour where Eve was asleep. It was as if he instinctively knew who she was, and he whimpered as his large head rose over the side of the bed, and looked down on her. Eve raised her arm, and her eyes opened as she reached over and scratched the back of his ear.

"Well good day my fine young friend, I see you have chosen to companion your mistress and ensure her safety." Rune slipped off the long red cloak decorated around the edges with silver runic symbols, and she folded it neatly in her hands as she walked through the flowers towards Eve. When Eve sat up and smiled, Rune caught her breath at the sight of her looking more like the middle age of her mother, than the young woman she had been only a short time ago. She looked at the cloak and realised.

"You should not have loaned me this knowing it would reduce your life force." She handed the cloak over, and Eve slipped it back on to her shoulders.

"I see a great weight has lifted, there is great joy in your heart having visited your kin." Rune beamed a very happy smile.

"It has made a big difference, I knew they were safe, but seeing for myself has helped me."

"Good then take my hand and we shall walk together, for I shall take you to a place that is very special, and there we shall wait for your guide." Rune gathered her things which were neatly set at the base of the bed; she noticed how all her clothes were clean and smelled of the flowers from the garden. Eve seemed in happy spirits as she led Rune into the trees, and onto a long path lined with poppies under the high arching branches of many trees that Rune did not recognise. Furry Face scampered in front, and would disappear from view as he slipped into the large blue, brown, and golden yellow ferns to investigate. Rune felt a deep sense of calmness growing inside her.

"Who is this guide that will help me?" Eve gave a happy chuckle.

"Fagan is very special to me; he is a very old and dear friend, who has served our line for many generations. He is in Avalon at the moment with your sister." Rune turned quickly.

"He is with Jade?" Eve gave a nod.

"I asked him to take aid to your party, and from what I have seen in my mirrored waters he is with your sister guiding her to some of the others."

"Only some, can you not tell me what has happened?" Eve watched as Furry Face gave a yelp and pounced out of the ferns, and then ran happily along the path towards them.

"Your party has been separated. Your sister is currently making her way towards the group that contains her husband, for they have been captured and are imprisoned in a cell at the top of the high wall of the Citadel Mount." Rune's stomach twisted violently.

"Imprisoned, how? When? Are they alright?" Eve lifted a hand.

"Calm yourself child, they have not been harmed, although I believe that the one named Rowan who is husband to your sister has suffered a broken leg. I believe they are to be taken out of Avalon and sent to the snake in London, but fear not for them, Fagan has ways of helping that many will not see coming." Rune was still panicked.

"Is Robbie with them?"

"No, he is safe with your mother and father and the heir of the line of men. The young king is showing some of the line of Arthur, he has been leading them out of the tunnels, and as I speak, they are resting and preparing to seek out your grandfather's house. The rest of your party is deep in the marshes to the south, where two of them have suffered at the hands of her vile creations, and have been close to the edge of death." Rune gave a large draw of breath, but Eve waved her hand. "Fear not they have aid, and although they cannot be cured where they are, the poison will be halted and reversed to give them an aid towards recovery." Rune felt her tension ease, and thought deeply of their situation.

"We have been trapped, Mason knew we would have to come here, and he has sat in wait for us." Eve gave a nod.

"I feel you are right; you must always remember that the will of mankind is very strong, and there are many amongst them who can pose threats when not expected. The Merle weaves in just the same way as the force for good, like all things Runestone Life, there must be balance in everything."

"But there isn't is there? I mean the Star of the Merle is not meant to be here; it must be tipping the balance away from the centre?" Eve stopped as they met a crossroads in the path, she turned and walked to the right, and the trees changed to varieties Rune recognised.

"Runestone Life, you have to see the full picture. Avalon was closed to all except those of the lines of Fae. Others have been frequent visitors, but that did not throw out the balance. Avalon was a force for good that contained all of the powers for good things, at this moment in time the mortal Le Fey has sealed the realm to only those she allows to pass, and the star in her hand is slowly absorbing and feeding off the power for good.”

“But that is terrible, if she succeeds the balance will tip forever and chaos will come to all the worlds, we must stop her.” Eve gave a smile, which confused her.

“I agree we must stop her, but the truth is Runestone Life, if she soaks up every drop of the power of good within Avalon, nothing will change and balance will be achieved, for here the balance is very different from any other place.” Rune could not understand why and she looked confused.

“How can that be possible, if you absorb all the power here, it has to affect all other places, because this is the centre of everything.” Eve smiled at her and took her arm and began to walk down the path again.

“That is exactly what the mortal Le Fey thinks, and as you have, she has missed the point, although you are much closer to understanding than she is. You are right to say that this is the centre of everything, but I would like to add that here isn’t Avalon.”

“What? But it is isn’t it? We are walking in the Forest of Time; it is the heart of Avalon.” Eve gave a cheeky giggle that reminded Rune a little of Jade.

“The Forest of Time is known as the heart of Avalon, for it sits within the realm. Here where we walk is the first realm and it sits within the realm of Avalon, but the two are very different places, it is why here I can walk in my mortal form for a while longer, but when I walk in Avalon, I appear somewhat fainter. Do you understand? You are right to say this is the centre, for it is the centre of everything, but it is not part of Avalon, that is separate from here, that is the reason you are safe from her, the two overlap.”

“But that does not change the fact that if Avalon is turned to evil, the balance will change.”

“In Avalon yes. Think Runestone Life, what does this realm contain that increases with every passing moment?” Rune thought deeply but was very unsure.

“All I can see is trees and plants; I have no idea what else this realm holds.”

“Exactly correct.”

“What? You mean the plant life?”

“I mean Life, of which I might add you are a big part of it.”

“Do you mean that as the trees and plants grow, so does the power of this realm to allow it to balance other realms?” Eve pulled her close and gave her a big hug.

“You amaze me how quickly you apply your mind; I can see the time spent with your grandfather has served you well. Do you now understand? This realm is expanding all the time, and as it does, new life springs up and the power grows stronger. The Forest of Time is the centre on which everything is balanced and it is directly connected to you Runestone Life.”

"To me, are you sure?" Eve smiled at the funny look on her face.

"The power flows from here into you, and as you undo the wrongs of the world, the force within you repairs it and new life grows. As you are the centre of all circles, the Forest of Time is the centre of you." It made sense to her at last.

"Mason has killed the life and covered it over, but we fight and replace the damage as we succeed, undoing his evil and creating new life as we go. Now I understand you, yes, I can see how it works. I helped my lord replace the ancient forests in Scotland, and threw down her castle, we all helped undo her evil and put life in its place. I built a garden for Rose, but I never thought why, it just seemed a natural thing to do."

"That is Nature, Runestone Life, a natural urge or thought is exactly that...!"

A cold shiver ran down her spine and for a brief moment a picture entered her mind. "My grandfather warned me... He was so angry when I devastated the forest in my pain; he saw it as weakness because he thought I had helped Mason increase his hold. He asked me to find my control and focus, or he would have to kill me." Eve gave a serious nod.

"He was always a little over dramatic, but yes, when you first received your gifts, there was a danger you would lose control of them. He was right to show you the right path, although he did labour the point a little. I am pleased to see you grow with the knowledge you hold."

The trees broke, and they walked out into a small meadow filled with brightly coloured wild flowers, which wove up through the lush green grass. A neatly cut path led through the centre to where a long wooden two storey cabin, sat beside a large rough wooden barn with an old brick forge chimney at the side of it. Rune looked round at the place and it felt so much like home in its idyllic setting surrounded by trees. "Oh this place is beautiful." Eve walked with her up to the wooden steps and stopped.

"I must return, so for now here we must part." She pointed to a small window on the bottom floor beneath the large balcony above them. "I have arranged with Fagan for you to rest here that will be your room. This place is very quiet and well protected so rest and gather your strength, for when the Keeper returns with your young lord, you will have much to do." She pulled Rune into her arms and gave a warm tight hug. "Fear not for you will gather soon, and then begin to make your plans to right the wrongs of the mortal Le Fey."

Eve pulled an arrow that was woven between the laces of Rune's empty quiver out and looked at its split shaft, and tattered white feather. "This place has a forge, it does appear you need more arrows, and some repairs to your equipment." Rune gave a smile and gently took the arrow from Eve's hand.

"This arrow will never be fired; I carry it with me always as a memory of my first time hunting with Robbie. It was damaged and unusable, but I kept it as a keepsake." Eve smiled.

"The last arrow of your woodland realm, and one it appears that carries much of the love that binds you both together. Keep it safe, for if the love it holds is as deep as the love I see in your heart, then it carries the hopes and dreams of all the realms." Rune looked down at the arrow in her hand, and for the slightest moment she felt her heart flutter as it had the day she ran down the steep bank at Joe's cabin, and into Robbie's open arms. Eve gave a happy nod and gently placed the arrow back into Rune's hand and then turned to leave. Rune looked up and asked one more thing.

"If I may? I have one more question." Eve stopped and waited patiently. "I saw the black mist... you know from the star, when I visited the bridge and watched myself fight the Dark One. Why did I not see it when I was fighting her? If I had, I would have known it was coming towards me." Eve turned back and lifted a hand to Rune's face, and softly stroked her cheek.

"Your eyes have been fully opened by the White Lord. At the time you faced the mortal Le Fey, you had not been in the heart of the Merle." Rune felt her heart give a little skip.

"Was that where I was when you came for me, in the heart of the Merle, so I did not dream that, it was real?" Eve gave a gentle nod.

"Your lord took you there to awaken the part of you that is your grandfather, for he contained traces that gave him the wisdom to see the evil within it. When next you face her, you will see the way the evil weaves around its prey, and it should help you in your fight."

It gave Rune a little hope, knowing that she would at least be able to see the dark force approaching her. The thought of having to face it still frightened her, but she felt a little more prepared. Eve gave a soft smile as she saw the ease building inside her great granddaughter. "I must leave here now. Prepare yourself and think deeply about all we have spoken of, for we will meet again my dearest of children, for you have one more task to face before the final moments of confrontation. Be all that was written and bring love and life in all your footsteps."

"Goodbye... Thank you for all you have done for me, how will I ever repay you?" A tear welled in Eve's eyes.

"You have many times over already by honouring me and my line, I love you so deeply my daughter of the woods, I am proud of what you have done for my lord and husband, for he holds you above all others, as he once did me. Remember Runestone, crystal can hold out power, but some crystals hold all powers. Goodbye." Eve turned and walked back down the path; she stopped and gave Furry Face a big scratch on his ear. "Protect her lord of cats." He gave a deep rumble of a growl, and she turned and waved goodbye, then headed back into the trees.

Rune stood quietly, and watched her go from view, as Furry Face came up the steps and sat by her side. She felt a strong pull at her heart knowing that their time together would lessen, and it saddened her. Rune stood alone dressed in all green wearing a green cloak that Eve had handed her, and all the trees around the meadow tipped their high branches in salute. Deep below the earth strange rumbles and squeaks emitted and Furry Face tilted his head right and left as he listened. The trees were talking excitedly to each other, and spreading the word that the Lady of Life was amongst them.

Rune looked down at the arrow in her hand, its feather shone with the bright white of the goose feathered end, she smiled again as she thought of Robbie and the love she felt for him. She turned to walk inside as she thought again of Eve, and she stopped at the doorway. "Crystals hold all powers... whatever does that mean?"

CHAPTER EIGHT

UNEXPECTED HELP

Maddy sat beside Una, a few feet up from the water's edge, both of them had washed, and together they watched the path across the water to the far bank, and the cut down reeds, where they had been guided onto the rough tufts of grass and weed by Woody. Maddy's eyes stared at the gap in the wall of what looked like brown thatch; Una lifted the cup of her tea and cradled it in her hands. "If those flowers work, why worry? I mean they must be a friend of ours." Maddy blinked as she stared at the far bank, behind her up the mound Maggs boiled up the water as Milly prepared the two burning figures of Treen and Jasper.

Harry sat pulling the heads off the white flowers and dropping them into Maggs spare handkerchief, he would absentmindedly pop the odd flower in his mouth as he stared at the filling piece of cloth in his lap. Skip sat in front of him, having had a wash in the water at the base of the mound, and felt much better to be free of the sweat and dirt. Hawk watched the far side of the mound, where Woody had made a spear by binding an arrow to a long stick, and was now stood up to his waist in the water, stabbing at the large orange fish as they swam by.

Skip leant back on a rock and gave a long sigh, the sun was still high in the sky, and the mist across the marshes was as thick as ever. "I am exhausted; I really don't think I could have walked another foot. It feels like we have walked for a day." Harry flicked a flower into his mouth and chewed as he looked at Skip.

"We have." He slid his hand into his jacket, and pulled out his pocket watch. The lid popped open and Harry glanced down at it. "Yep, it's just gone twelve." Skip looked up at the haze above them, where the sun shone as a bright dull ball through the mist.

"Well, no wonder I am famished, it's lunch time." Maggs leaned across to Harry and took the handkerchief containing the white flowers off his lap.

"I think Skip, you will find it is time for supper, my poor Harry pops is looking almost a waif it's been so long since he has eaten." Harry gave a large smile as Maggs blew him a big kiss. "Poor Baby, I shall feed you as soon as these are ready, you keep your vibes mellow my big hungry baby, and I will get you something to fill up those unhappenin places." She rolled the flowers up in the handkerchief and dropped them into the boiling pot of water.

Skip gave her an odd look. Harry looked at the large bunch of flowers still piled at his side, and picked them up and began chewing on the heads.

"Wow, you know, these are kinda of addictive, they really do hit the spot."

Skip looked back up at the sun, and then back to Harry. "That cannot be right, it's Mid-Day look at the sun." Harry shrugged as he chewed.

"The watch don't lie Skip, check it out." He passed the silver watch over to Skip who looked down at the face of the clock showing just past twelve. Under the small number twelve was a window, which had a moving dial in it; the picture in the front of the window was of a small brass moon.

"How the hell can it be midnight, when the sun is still up?" Harry shrugged.

"It's something to do with the power of the star I reckon, I mean, what else could it be? After all she is trying to stop us putting a new queen in power here, and this place has always been linked to the moon. It stands to reason if you stop the moon rising, and keep the sun high, you can defeat the influence of the moons power and gain control." Skip stared at Harry with a very strange look on his face. Rags dropped out of the tree and came down to the fire to sit with them.

"I can't see bugger all now the mist has got thicker, it makes me bum ache sittin on that branch, don't reckon no one will try walkin in that lot, it's bloody impossible." She gave a happy smile as she looked round them all, and then grabbed a cup. Rags looked at Skip who was staring at Harry with a confused look on his face, as he sat chewing the flowers, she watched as Skip sat up and leaned forward and stared at Harry's face. Harry stopped chewing as he noticed the scrutiny from Skip.

"What's with the fixed stare?" Skip's voice seemed to carry a cautionary note of bewilderment.

"My God Harry... Are you... Are you actually sober?" Harry seemed a little surprised, and a little offended.

"Just what is that supposed to mean?" He looked a little nervous, as Skip stared even harder at him, Una and Maddy turned to look, even Rags seemed engrossed in what was very quickly becoming an almost shy and obviously embarrassed Harry. Skip turned to Una and Maddy as they looked up the slope of the mound at him.

"Look at him; I do believe he is; he hasn't got so much as a twitter." Harry gave a very deep gulp and lifted his hand, in hope of proving Skip wrong. As he stared at the raised hand, which was motionless and as steady as a rock, the colour ran from his face and a look of abject terror crossed his eyes.

"Oh shit... It's those flowers man.... Oh Christ they have gone and done it to me. Oh bugger, they have done me in they have, they crept up on me and cured me." A look of instant panic crossed his frightened face, as he looked at the others one by one. Maggs looked back at all of them as she stirred the pot on the fire.

"I don't know what you are all talking about, Harry is never drunk, he just gets a little unstable with his nerves, the poor baby, that's why he uses so much tonic."

She gave a small hiccup, and smiled a big loving smile at Harry; it was hard for him to smile back as he faced a fear deep inside himself that he had never expected. It was a great source of amusement to the entire group, his eyes looked very clear, and he spoke in a very ordinary way. He put his head into his hands and tried to concentrate on what he thought reality should be like, the slightly glazed edges of his world had gone, and in an instant, everything had become very clear and it was too much for him to deal with.

While Milly and Gaynor watched the brew and prepared to cool the liquid to administer to Treen and Jasper, Harry stood up and walked in a very sure footed fashion to the edge of the water. He took a long deep breath as he faced reality for the first time in as long as he could remember, he had no choice but to deal with it, but it was the most frightening thing he could comprehend, in fact, it was ten times more scary than heights or the dead.

Skip lifted a small white flower from the grass, where they had fallen as Harry had stood up; he held it up in front of his face to look at it with a questioning eye. "Nature provides us with such wonder, it's so small, and yet miraculous and I feel dangerous at the same time." Rags gave a cheeky giggle as Una and Maddy smiled watching the frightened figure of Harry.

Treen was bright red, and her clothes stuck to her with the dampness from her sweats. She mumbled as her eyelids twitched, as if she was in some sort of bad dream, her French words were understood by very few of them, although Gaynor who was wiping her brow, muttered quietly back to her in French, and held her hand tight. Skip joined them and helped to sit her up, and held her straight, as Milly put the cup to her lips. It took quite some time for her to coax Treen into drinking half a cup. Everyone watched holding their breath, as Milly turned to Jaz.

Harry took the watch, and walked steadily along the water's edge. He felt his cheeks and rubbed his chin, his mind felt fragile, was this being sober? He could not remember. Nervously he slipped his hand into his inside pocket and slipped out his nerve medicine, there was laughter a little way off and he turned to see Rags sat in the grass. "Welcome to Earth Harry." She gave another laugh. "You know what? If you really are sober, it will break Joe's heart. Just think of the money he will lose." She giggled as he lifted the flask to his lips.

"Hey don't joke Rags, this is serious, I might have to see the world all normal, and that is a fate worse than death." He took a long swig of his nerve medicine and retched violently. Rags could do nothing but giggle, as she saw him fall to his knees and vomit. Harry moaned on his hands and knees like a whimpering child. "Oh God it's true, the spirits have cured me, oh shit I am done for." He retched again and was sick. "Oh god this is hell, I can feel everything." Rags tittered as she sat watching him, and keeping a wary eye on the mist covered water.

It had taken over fifteen minutes, but there had been a significant drop in Treen's temperature, and Jaz seemed to be following. Milly smiled at Maddy. "I think she will be fine." Maddy knelt down at her daughter's side and turned to Milly.

"Thank you." Milly gave a smile.

"You have no need... I didn't do that much; it was you who told us about the flowers." Maddy gave a rare smile.

"You tried everything, whether it worked or not is irrelevant. You tried and did all you could, to me that means a great deal." Milly blushed a little, as the others all gave a nod of recognition for her efforts. In many ways she had always felt a little on the edges of the group, it gave her a lift to see they all recognised her efforts. Jasper had always told her how a show of ability was important within the group, and maybe now after patching up their cuts and bandaging their limbs, she felt that they had understood her role and actually appreciated it.

While Harry sat alone with his head in his hands moaning to himself, something that did seem to get everyone smiling, Woody helped Maggs with the dozen fish he had speared, and he filleted them as Maggs set them to cook. Una moved back to her watch, and Maddy stayed with Skip close at the side of Treen, as her mumbling stopped and her temperature seemed to fall. Hawk breathed a sigh of relief as he carried a plate down to Una, and offered it to her as he sat down at her side. Una noticed the chopped white flowers on the fish, and smiled as she looked across, and saw Harry flicking them off his food with a look of deep suspicion. "We have hope again." Hawk gave a long sigh.

"We bloody need it." Una patted his leg.

"You worry too much, you have got us this far, have more faith."

"I will when we are all back together, and can look out for each other, I think in this place, we need all the numbers we can muster to survive." Una gave a nod as she ate.

"Although we do have a guardian watching over us, I have no idea who, but I am mightily glad they told us about those flowers. I think any longer and we may have lost two more, we should count ourselves lucky."

"Maybe... I will be glad to get out of this hellhole of a place; it's been one long stitch up since we arrived. As soon as this mist lifts, I want to get the hell out of here and find Robbie; I just wish the sun would move so I could tell which way north was."

"It's that way." Hawk turned to see the steady white hand of Harry pointing across the water.

"How do you know that, the compass has gone haywire?" Harry pointed a sober thumb behind him.

"Look at the tree, it's green only on this side." Una gave a smile as Hawk looked back; with everything going on he had forgotten the most basic woodsman skill known. He gave a small chuckle and winked at Una.

"The moss grows on the northern side; I should have known better." He gave his head a shake. "Harry sober and leading the way, this has been a very surreal time." Una sat quietly giggling as she ate her fish.

At the end of the tunnel, Jade carefully peered around the corner. "There is a door at the far end."

"I know."

"Oh yeah right, I keep forgetting you used to live here." Fagan smiled.

"Well my little green eyed friend, it is time to get as mad as a willow in a drought, are ye ready?" Jade gave a nod and slipped out her short sword.

"Do willows get mad in a drought then?" Fagan rolled his old eyes, and his ears gave a slight wiggle.

"Oh, I should say so, ye should hear em carry on, they scream like smacked babies they do, it's a hell of a racket, ye can hear em right across the wood ye can. Spoilt buggers ye know? But that is what ye get when ye let em hang their toes in the water all day."

Jade giggled as she followed the old man round the corner, and up towards the wooden door.

Jade stood on her toes, and peered in through the small barred window, and saw the three guards sat playing cards at the table. She slid her hand across the rough wood and felt for the cold metal loop that lifted the latch, Fagan's hand touched hers and gently lifted it away, he whispered quietly into her ear. "I think a few friends would be quicker and quieter."

Jade moved back from the door, and watched as he slipped his hands in his pockets and felt around for something. Fagan gave her a wink as his hand stopped on something, and then he drew out a small leather pouch.

Unsure what he was up to, she watched as he slipped his fingers inside it and pinched them together. Fagan lifted out his fingers and held them up in front of the small window. "Be swift my little friends, we have great haste here." He took a long deep breath, and then with a big puff, he opened his fingers and blew hard. Jade blinked.

Inside the room, the three guards were oblivious as they tossed coins onto the ever growing pile of silver bits, and took fresh cards. They didn't notice the fast silent movement across the floor, and under the table. One of the guards was a fat man dressed in heavy chain mail beneath his black vest with the roughly printed symbol of the red dragon on it. He gave a smile as he looked at his cards, and then tossed four silver bits onto the pile. The other two guards looked at each other and gasped, it was the biggest bet of the day.

It was hard to describe the moment, as Jade on her tip toes watched. The three guards were sat happily playing, and then for a second there was a loud sort of rustle of leaves. She gasped with shock, and almost slipped off the door, as the three guards seemed to jump slightly in their seats, and then simply exploded with leaves. It was almost scary, but it happened so fast, she had barely the time to think. In the blink of an eye the guards disappeared without a sound under the dense thick growth. She looked at Fagan who was grabbing the door ring. "Are they dead?"

Fagan pulled open the door and looked into the room. "Oh yes, it's a bugger of plant is bindweed, it gets its tendrils into everything and hangs on for dear life, ye have no worry about them three, they will be compost by now."

Jade looked round the door at the large pile of leaves that covered the table, chairs, and the guards. She gave a slight shudder as a cold feeling ran down her back.

"Good job Harry aint here, that is a lot worse than his uncosmic monsters." She saw the door to the cell, as Fagan approached the throbbing pile of leaves, and quickly ran across to it. A large bunch of keys hung on a rusty nail on the wall; she snatched them quickly and began inserting them into the lock to find the one that fitted. With the lock undone she slid back the two heavy bolts and the door swung open.

Two brown boots stood in the doorway as Big John and Bear stared at the open door. They clumped across the room quickly, and both of them jumped back in fear. "Rowan, Rowan talk to me." Big John leaned slightly forward and looked at the bed where Rowan seemed to shake.

"Pebbles, is that you girl?" Another voice spoke from the doorway and all of them turned to see nothing.

"It's draining her powers, she will be visible soon as it soaks everything up, we have not got much time, so come on before the bindweed notices ye, I doubt three will be enough to satisfy it." Bear felt a little confused, but he was swift enough to act, and soon he herded everyone out the door, as Big John gently lifted Rowan on to his shoulder.

"He is alright Pebbles, just worn out from the pain, let's get him out of here and then we can sort him out proper." Jade came back into view with tears in her eyes, she gave a nod at John, who turned to the open door, where the strange voice seemed to speak.

"It's not good, but I know a few plants who can help, and I think a little friend who can put that to rights, we will soon have him up and romping around like the cornflower on a wild meadow."

John gave a confused nod, he had got use to Pebbles fading in and out, but her friend had still not appeared and it made him nervous. With Rowan on his shoulder, he headed out of the door to where Bear was fastening his bright golden sword back on his belt, as the others grabbed their weapons and bags. Fox handed

Jade Rowan's sword and quiver, which she slung over her back, and then as quick as a flash she saw Fagan hold open another door at the far end of the room.

"This way my green eyed friend. Follow this passage for ten on the left, then go fourth on the right and eleventh on the left, follow that tunnel to its very end, and ye will come up level with the white pool. Ye will find your grandfathers house due west, now hurry, she is gaining in power and I have to rush." Jade felt the disappointment rise inside her.

"Are you not coming with us?" Fagan gave her a big smile, and leaned forward.

"We shall meet soon, as sure as the rushes cover the rocks below the Crystal Falls. There is much to be done, and I have to aid the others. When ye all meet the lord ye follow, head along the edges of the marsh going southeast, and then follow the paths into the Forest of Time, I will be waiting. Tell the lord ye sister is safe." He gave her the softest kiss on the forehead as the others rushed past her. "Go and spare no time, it will not be long before ye friends are missed." Jade flung her arms round his neck.

"Thanks Fagan you are a cool guy."

"What not hot and smoking like a Rowan?" Jade gave a giggle.

"Sorry Fagan, that is just for Rowan." He smiled as he pushed her back from the door.

"Go; be as swift as the breeze in the morning leaves." His bushy eyebrows rose as he smiled, and Jade turned and ran down the tunnel after the others.

It had been an exhausting time, and before they moved away from the shelter of the cave, they had rested and slept. Steph had stitched up the back of Robbie's head, and some more sleep had helped to clear his mind. He sat outside the cave in the humid air as he waited for William and Smokes to wake up. Steph sat at the fire with a small orange pot and poured out two cups of coffee, she came back out of the cave and handed one to Robbie. "Lucky you don't have sugar, it's in Blades bag." He took the cup as she squatted beside him. "How's the head?"

"Better thanks." He sat on the grass with his back to the rock wall, and his bow across his lap, his quiver lay at its side, and Steph noticed.

"We are very low on arrows; we could use a place to hole up and make a few more. I am not sure my dad's place will have anything hot enough to make arrowheads." Robbie seemed unconcerned.

"The wood has sticks and birds for feathers, I can make a fire hot enough for our needs, I carry a tool kit, so it's not really a problem. We will need a little time though, that was a hard fight, and equipping everyone will take a few days." He looked really low and Steph couldn't help but feel for him, she patted his leg softly.

"Things always look their worse before they take a turn for the better, don't let everything get to you, Rune will appear, and we will find a way of getting the others out, you will see." He gave a smile, but deep down inside he couldn't help but feel like everything had fallen apart, his thoughts were spoken softly as he closed his eyes and rested back on the wall.

"We have done everything that was asked of us, yet Mason still has the advantage. I walked right into his trap, and just did not see it coming."

"Don't be so hard on yourself, none of us realised. You know, I think at times you forget, Mason has been planning this for over twenty years, hell we have been fighting none stop for just over a year, we are all tired and battle weary, but what choice do we have? No matter what Robbie, we have to keep going because there really isn't that many who can do this. Give yourself a break, hell you have just had kids and all that worry, let alone leading the woodland world."

The thought of his children seemed to warm him inside, he sat quietly picturing them in his mind and felt a little happiness rise inside him. Maybe Steph was right, looking at it all, maybe he had not thought it through as thoroughly as Mason. But Mason had been given the time to plan all his strategy's, it was actually obvious that if he wanted to seat a king, he would need to get the sceptre. He opened his eyes and noticed Steph watching him; she sensed the question coming and waited.

"Just why exactly do we need this sceptre thing anyhow? Does it really make that much of a difference? I mean after all, as long as it's Wills bum on the seat and his head, we put the crown on, what does it matter?" Steph gave a shrug.

"To be honest I am not that sure, my dad seemed to think it was of the utmost importance, but like all the plans he made, he never actually said why it was so important."

"Well, I suppose if he felt it was that important, it must be, we will just have to make sure we keep it safe." Robbie watched the mist swirl in front of him. "You know, I am starting to really hate this place, will this bloody mist ever lift? I can barely see the tops of the trees. I thought Avalon was supposed to be a place of wonder to feast the eyes on, not much feasting happening in this." Steph stood up, and walked onto the grass just in front of him.

"To be honest Robbie, I am not sure this is normal for here, Una seems to think it's the Dark One. Have you noticed how the sun has not gone down?" He looked up at the sky, and could just make out the bright orb hidden by the thick cloud.

"No, I thought it was early morning when we came up, I just figured it was somewhere around mid afternoon." Steph looked down at him with sparkling water drops from the vapour building up in her hair.

"Check your watch, it's only just mid morning." He fumbled in his pocket for his dad's old pocket watch.

"No, that cannot be right." He opened the case and looked at it. "It's 10:46 and July twelfth, how bloody long were we down in those tunnels?"

"It was just before midnight when we sent Amethyst across to the castle, so that was what, just over thirty four hours ago, and the sun has been shining none stop since. I tell you Robbie, this has to be her work, I think she is using it to keep Rhiannon from gaining any influence here and helping out, it does sort of explain why we have heard nothing from Amethyst and Fish." Robbie got up off the floor.

"We have wasted too much time; I have been sloppy."

"Robbie, you took a huge blow to the head, not to mention the fact that just about all of us were exhausted after a very hard fight." Robbie looked back at the cave entrance and the two sleeping figures.

"That is not the point; we need to get a move on. Rowan is going to need our help, I want those guys back in the fold, and then I have to find Rune. Come on wake the others, we are lucky we have not been attacked while we were here. We need to get to your dad's house and work out how the hell we can get back under that mountain and free the others." Robbie lifted his quiver and slung it over his back, he lifted his bag, and threw his torn cloak over his shoulder and stood watch, as Steph went and woke the others.

As Jade ran through the tunnels with the others, and Robbie prepared at the cave entrance at the edge of Misty Bank in Avalon, Sapphire finished her briefing in Loxley, and after walking to the gates to see her mum, she opened a window and left for York.

Two miles out from the large stone city, Rayne had set up a new headquarters high in the trees. Sapphire was impressed when she saw the high platforms covered with wooden huts; high in the branches of trees bigger than any she had seen. A young corporal guided her up the steps, and onto the long runway, that ran from tree to tree connecting all the buildings, and into the largest set in the centre of a huge Oak, which was the operations room. Rayne and Gwinne took her into a small office attached to the room filled with personnel, and she sat with a drink and a meal, and gave her report on the progress of Avalon.

Rayne was very worried, after all it was his daughter trapped in the castle at the centre of the Mirrored Lake. He paced up the room as he tried to think of a way to bring her aid. Sapphire could only relay what Rune had told her. "There is nothing you can do at the moment it's sealed tight, and Rune has not found out how the Dark One opens the entrances for Mason's men. Rune only got out because of the cloak Eve lent her, and she only had a very limited time then."

Rayne gave a nod; he had a very concerned look on his face. Gwinne could see his worry and tried to comfort him as best she could.

"Rayne darling, she has Eve and Rune watching over her, let them help her from the inside, we are shut out, there really is nothing we can do until she is freed." He stopped pacing and thought for a second, his deep violet eyes glinted in the daylight.

"Eve is no longer mortal, and she has given up most of her powers to Opal and Rune. Rune is still in the forest, which must mean the star will drain her if she tries to approach it, unless?" He stood frozen voicing his thoughts quietly, more than actually having a conversation with them. "I wonder if he has passed it on, he must be there?" Sapphire looked at Gwinne who seemed equally confused.

"Passed what on?" Rayne came out of his thoughts and looked at Sapphire.

"Oh nothing, it's just things of the past, it's a little frustrating as I know that place like the back of my hand, having spent my entire youth there. If Rune contacts you, I want to know the moment she does, I can help her a lot." Sapphire sat back in her chair.

"Yeah, no prob's, to be honest I would imagine she will contact you first." He nodded.

"Hmm I would think she would." Rayne seemed to snap out of his moment of concentration and gave Sapphire a large smile. "So what are you up to next? We have a lot on here at the moment; you are welcome to muck in." Sapphire waved a hand.

"No, I have to get back, but thanks. Rafe is still adjusting to the death of his mother, and I want to be there for him, it's been pretty tough on him." Gwinne gave a sad look.

"Poor lad, it must be very difficult for him, I would imagine his loyalties will be very much split now." Gwinne's comment surprised Sapphire a little.

"Why would Rafe's loyalties be split? He is a Specialist attached to Loxley." Gwinne seemed quite sincere.

"Well yes he is, but his mother and father ran New Avon, it's the closest woodsman settlement to the large wall south of Birmingham, they have had skirmishes all over that area from months now. We have sent them another ten units to help maintain the defences. I am not sure he will want to leave his home, and he also is allied to Jett, she is now the next queen at Caerleon, I would think things are a somewhat confusing for him at the moment, sooner or later he will have to choose a direction. Soon there will be a few who will have difficult decisions to make; this war is spreading right across the whole country."

Sapphire had never really thought about it before, she had assumed that Jett would live in Loxley with Rafe. Gwinne gave her a knowing look, and Sapphire did wonder if Gwinne knew far more than she was letting on, after all, she had spent the morning thinking of what Rune had said about her own circle forming. Gwinne noticed the change in her face and smiled.

"We all have a destiny, maybe you should take a walk with me, it's quite beautiful up in the trees close to the canopy."

There was something in her tone of voice that gave Sapphire the distinct impression she should take Gwinne up on her offer. She rose out of her chair, and Gwinne led her back through the operations room, and out on to the long wooden walkways.

Gwinne was right, this high up in the trees with the sun beating down through a soft breeze, the whole of the woodland felt more alive than ever. Bright shapes with soft green edges to the light danced across the wooden floors, as the sun found its way between the leaves, and lit up the decking. The trees softly stirred above her moving in an almost hypnotic rhythm. Gwinne linked Sapphire's arm as they walked slowly along, while some distance below, woodsman ran about preparing the defences of York. Gwinne wasted no time in approaching the subject that had occupied Sapphire all morning.

"I sense the changes within you, I would imagine so has Rune. For a long time you have been unsettled inside, I think soon many answers will flow to you."

Sapphire was a little nervous; she had no idea that others could see so deeply inside her.

"You know something of what is destined for me?" Gwinne chuckled.

"In many ways we all share the same destiny, but it is true, I have often thought of you, and I would hazard a guess and believe I would be correct in saying, so has Rune."

"So you know what is planned for me?" Gwinne stopped and looked Sapphire square in the eyes. Her bright blue eyes shone with the life that coursed inside her, and Sapphire felt that Gwinne was reading deeply into her.

"You are descended from a queen of Fae, none other than the White Circle herself, and you are named Sapphire. It takes very little to deduce that one day you will be the head of your own circle, for Sapphire is the mark of sight, and as your powers intensify, you will find you will have a gift that will enlighten many."

It was the second time that day she had been told a circle would form around her, and she felt a strange twisting inside herself.

"Why me? I have nothing but doubts, I really do feel so isolated at times, and I wonder if I am honestly doing the right thing most of the time." Gwinne began to walk slowly along the deck again, and Sapphire walked at her side.

"You have a gift that is not the most certain of gifts, to doubt at times may be prudent, for there is no guarantee that if you begin to see things that they may come to pass. Isolation has always been a mark of the seer, Gwendolyn moved to Carnac just so she could be apart from the rest of the Fae world, you remind me of her at times."

"It all feels so confusing, I really am not sure I can do this." Gwinne smiled.

"I remember my sister saying much the same when she was told her circle would be a table of swords, she too felt like it was something that carried too much responsibility, yet as you know, Scarlet became the ultimate source of knowledge on the swords she guarded, and she found their rightful owners against all of the odds. I think it is early days yet, forming a circle is a very natural thing, and never forget that the centre of all circles, including yours is Rune, she will guide you as she has to date." Sapphire gave a long sigh.

"I just wish I could sort myself out before all of this happens. I have so many doubts inside me at the moment, and no idea in which direction I should go." Gwinne gave a nod.

"I think that fate has been decided, although I would like to say that to feel love for any is a wonderful thing, even when unrequited it is still a worthy feeling."

Sapphire felt a little embarrassed, her feelings for Robbie had been a source of inner personal conflict during her times alone, but to know others could see it worried her greatly.

"I have struggled with my feelings, which again makes me worry, because if I do not understand my own feelings, how will I ever understand what I see?" Gwinne took her hand and gave it a squeeze.

"No one would blame you for loving the Lord of Loxley, you are young and have been isolated for most of your life, it is very natural to feel a romantic notion towards a man whom so many hold in such high esteem, but I would say this

Sapphire more out of concern for you. Do you love Keith, because he has the same love for his lord and leader as you do? Or do you love him for the man he is? That is a question I think you need to understand and answer before you expand your horizons into other things. Resolve that conflict, and I think everything else will fall into place."

Gwinne was more insightful than Sapphire had realised, and to hear her talk about something she had spent a great deal of time thinking about alone felt frightening. Gwinne simply smiled and carried on walking.

"Have the dreams started yet?" Sapphire gave a nod.

"Yes... I have been having one in particular, and I just don't seem to be able to make sense of it. I just keep seeing this young gypsy like boat girl, but even though I know there is a connection, I am unable to find it."

"It's early days yet, these things will not rush, when the time is right you will understand, and things will fall into place. Just remember that what you see could be the past, present, or a possible outcome for the future. Nothing is set in stone; never forget that all things change as the magic weaves its way." Sapphire gave a nod of understanding, and although she felt a little embarrassed, she also felt grateful.

"How will I know who is in my circle? I mean we all sense each other, how will I know who has the sight and belongs in the circle?"

"You will know, as your powers increase so will the feelings of who is suitable, it is a very natural process, although as the heir to the white circle of the Fae, I would imagine as the new queen grows, you will be responsible for some of her education." Sapphire stopped and looked at Gwinne with surprise.

"Iona... are you sure? What could I teach the daughter of the creator of theViolet Lines?" Gwinne laughed.

"Oh, Sapphire relax, by the time she is old enough to begin to understand her gifts, you will be at full power, and will have no worries when it comes to helping the young queen. Rune is your centre, but she is not Fae, I am quite sure there will be things you understand on a much deeper level, and will have the benefit of the experience to teach her. Have a little faith in yourself... The day wears on and I feel that if you are to return to our grieving commander, you will need to depart shortly. Never forget we are kin, if you feel you need to talk, you know where I am." She leaned over and kissed her softly on the side of her cheek. "Relax, and let it flow into you, and you will be fine." Sapphire slid her arms around Gwinne and gave her a big hug. "Thanks, you have really helped." Gwinne smiled as they turned on the walkway, and began the slow walk back.

The preparations were ready, and in the small town of New Avon everyone was in a sombre mood, as they got ready to say their final farewells to Connie.

Outside the white fence in front of the old farmhouse, there was a bright flash of blue light. As Sapphire stepped through the window from York, she heard the voice of Rafe, as he came quickly down the path towards her. "Where the bloody hell have you been? What's the big idea of just buggering off without a word, and not checking with me first?" His face was red with anger, as he loomed up in front of her; Sapphire reeled slightly with the force of his aggressive manner.

"HEY!" She lifted her hands and pushed him back a little to give her space. "I was called off in a hurry by Rune, you were asleep and I didn't want to wake you, considering you have hardly slept in the last few days." He backed off, and his manner softened.

"Oh... I thought... you know?" Sapphire felt her anger grow inside herself, she felt he had no right to shout at her, after all she had been there helping him get through a difficult time.

"Really... I would say you didn't think, don't you dare shout at me like that!" She pushed past him roughly, and entered through the gate, Rafe turned and called back.

"That's still not the point, I asked you where you had been, and I want an answer. You know round here it's simply courteous to let others know when you are leaving."

The front door slammed behind Sapphire and Rafe gave a long sigh, for a while he had thought she had left to return to the group without him. It had crossed his mind that maybe she had been sent to ensure he was fit for duty, now he felt rotten for losing his temper with her, after all she had been really good over the last few days, and had been a huge help around the place. He kicked the gate back open hard, and it banged on the large rock at the side of the flowerbed and shuddered.

CHAPTER NINE

HAVING FAITH

The coming of the Red Death had done much to change the landscape of the country as it had been at that time. Hearne's decision to release a virus that would destroy the lives of men was one of many beginnings for the destruction within the country.

For centuries the power of the Dark One had controlled the minds of men, her whispered words of the Darkmares had convinced Hearne that more than just a virus would be needed. The earthquakes and freak weather that had followed in specific parts of the country had been very successful in removing the tall buildings, and concrete jungles of the age of modern man. Vast holes opened in the earth and swallowed the burnt out remains of the cities and sprawling towns, hurricanes and typhoons raged tearing away the fabric of man.

By the year of 2015 the country looked very different, as the weather turned back to normal. The growth of plants became fast and invasive; as they began the decay to remove all that was left. For the survivors there were many questions and very few answers. Communities such as New Avon and Loxley chose not to concern themselves over the last remnants of an old way of life, they worked hard to start a new life and rebuild a better way of being. Yet a few thought deeply about the destruction of the country, Mason Knox had been one who had for a very long time occupied his mind with the destruction. Even Leenard had also asked many questions of Opal and her father.

London had large parts that had been flattened to the floor, and yet in other areas of the large city there were parts almost untouched. The motorway from Bristol to London was almost unaffected, yet many of the large built up areas around it disappeared forever. Birmingham had been swallowed, as was Manchester, as the city burned to the floor, yet Bristol and most of Gloucester survived. The other strange phenomenon of the whole affair had been how the large Cathedrals had not suffered so much as a crack.

Fuse had spoken for a long time with Skip and Leenard on the subject. Canterbury cathedral had been surrounded by devastation and yet up until the coming of the golden arrow, it had been completely unaffected. The whole area along the coast and inland, had been wiped from the land and replaced with green life. Robbie had not at the time given it any thought at all. It was the one question unanswered, with a world turning to the Earth Faith, why had the Lord of Creation decided to spare a church that for centuries, had done all in its power to demonise the true beliefs of what had been the strongest faith of the land under the rule of the Celts?

Father Peter Mathew Warren had taken the early writings of Column Cille, and translated them. He understood much of his thinking and the ways in which he blended the beliefs of the early Christians with that of the Earth Faith. Time after time he read the preaching's of tolerance and brotherhood between all, and the facts did stand that the aged old Celt had in fact managed to bring together Celts, Vikings and Picts on the small remote island of Iona in peace, it was a mighty achievement for one man, and Warren admired him for it.

Father Warren had re-established his church in Hathersage on the same preaching's of Cille, and now as the news of the king came to him, he decided it was time he made the journey to Lincoln to talk with the bishop, who would if all went well, unite the land by placing the crown on the new king's head. As Robbie headed south to Caerleon, he had packed his bag and several books, and travelled off to meet with Bishop John Stevens.

John Lox had insisted on him having a guide, and so had assigned one of his guards to ride with him. Bowman Jersey became quite a conversationalist on the long road to the gothic cathedral. For Father Warren, who had for much of his life been contained within his churches, especially that of the one at the Black City in Scarborough, he enjoyed the open spaces, lush green pastures, and woodlands on the journey, and the normally quiet man found inside he had a very social side. The two men became quite good friends as they rode along slowly debating the fall of the Age of Modern Man.

As the afternoon of July 12th 2039 slipped towards the evening and various groups within Avalon moved closer to reuniting, Father Warren and his companion stopped on the edge of the vast woodland and looked out over the green plains of Lincoln, and the Cathedral stood above the crumbled remains of the ancient city.

Lincoln like so many other places, in parts had been spared, and Father Warren spurred his horse forward with Jersey beside him. He enjoyed the bright hot sunlight on his face and shoulders, and it was now very evident by the colour of his face that he took the pleasures of being outdoors more often these days. The dark eyes and pale skin was no longer a feature of the Father, who spent a great deal of his time outside the church visiting his parishioners. With the cathedral coming closer, they pushed hard to make it in time for the evening meal.

Bishop John Stevens welcomed Father Warren with a large smile, and as a host of high standing, he provided a lavish meal for his guests. There did appear to be a slightly nervous characteristic to the bishop, and Warren held his tongue unsure of whether he should even mention Loxley. Many of the other guests seemed to talk of minor issues and parish life, yet they watched Father Warren with great interest. After the meal John Stevens suggested a walk in the garden and he seemed to relax a little.

"I am sorry my friend that things seem to be cooler than you expected, things in the country are taking some very different directions. There are great divides in the church at the moment." They stepped out past the large stone pillars, and onto the wide lawn under the moonlight. Father Warren lived in Loxley and although he knew much of its day to day happenings, when it came to the country, he really had little idea of what was going on.

"What is happening, I was led to believe that the church was reforming in a much better light than of the last council?"

Bishop Stevens stopped in the centre of the lawn; he looked around and could see that both of them were out of ear shot, even so he lowered his voice. "You must understand Peter that Mason Knox is a very powerful man. For many years he has funded large projects within the church, and there are many who still see him as the future. Robert of Loxley has achieved a great deal, but you must realise that he is of another faith, and the church finds it hard to support someone who will not support them." Father Warren understood the problem, but he had spent his life studying both sides of the faiths, and he knew that there could be a happy medium.

"Mason only supports the church for what it is worth to him, I know Robert of Loxley and his wife, they may believe in a different faith, but their intentions to make this a better land for all of us is of the highest priority." He turned to Bishop Stevens; "They will defend everyone no matter what their faith if Mason puts them at risk."

The bishop smiled; he lifted his hand to the shoulder of Father Warren. "I have seen what they have done, but I am not the one who needs to be convinced my friend. Believe me when I say, that Lady Runestone made more sense to me in one night than many lectures delivered in my youth at college, but that is beside the point. Peter the church is a slow beast to change; we have many who support the coronation of a king who can be traced to a true line of this country." He gave a long sigh. "There are many who feel that Knox will rule the day, and they are unwilling to make a stand against him, especially in the south."

Father Warren looked around at the long lines of stone pillars and the elaborately carved windows of the Cathedral. "Is that why we must talk in a place where we cannot be heard? Has it really got so bad that even you, the leader of the church is afraid to speak openly?"

The bishop, who had always had such energy, did seem to be very sedate; his voice was low and rung with caution. "Peter we must now be more careful than ever before. We must be able to stay in the positions we are so that we can be of use to the future king of this realm. Loxley has a great deal of supporters, but there are men of high position in this land who are influenced by Knox. I am asking you to aid me here, so that we may be able to support this heir brought to us by Robert of Loxley."

For Father Warren in many ways, it was an honour to be thought of so highly, but he knew the bond he had with the community of the woodland was far greater, they had in many ways saved him as much as he had helped to save them, he could not leave them behind. "My friend, I will help you in any way that I can, but it must be from Loxley. I cannot leave those who are in need of me; it would be a betrayal I could not live with." John Stevens gave a nod as he looked at his friend.

"I thought you would say that, in many ways I envy you Peter. You do have something of great value in this world, I would not swap it either." The two clergymen walked slowly to the wooden bench set back from the flowerbed, and quietly, in the warm evening air they talked of Loxley and of the state of the country. It was quite late when Father Warren asked the old Bishop, why he thought all the Cathedrals had been spared by Hearne.

The Old Bishop sat back in the seat and looked up to the skies of black, dotted with a million stars. "I have given such a lot of thought to this. You know Runestone and how she claims the red death was a symptom of her grandfather?" Warren gave a nod. "I have seen and read a great deal, there is a force within this world that none of us can escape, some call it nature and some God. I like to think that maybe the churches were spared because there is still a greater good for all within them."

The bishop sat quietly for a moment to reflect. "Hearne has been proven not to be the myth we all believed him to be. Indeed, for many long years there have been signs in the world of the devotion shown him by the people. Much of what we have known as Pagan has been dismissed, and yet I have met with someone who claims to be a relative of this mythical Pagan wizard or god or whatever he may be, for I really am not sure which."

The bishop sat forward and looked back at Father Warren. "My meeting with Lady Runestone proved to me that there is much in our faiths that walk hand in hand, and my answer to you must be exactly that. It is why I feel that Robert of Loxley should be supported, even if half of the church I serve is against him. I think my friend, that if they really are telling the truth, then their green lord recognised much of the similarities, and as a sign of respect for our faith, he chose to preserve what he could have wiped away." He gave a small smile. "I suppose if you do believe what they say, I would like to believe that my lord would have done the same in his place. There is a reason my friend, but as to what I am unsure, what I can say is that regardless of how it happened we are here, and therefore we have a duty to the people who survived."

It was not what Warren expected, but he gave a nod and smiled at the bishop. "I have pondered the point for many years with no conclusion either, tonight you have enlightened my thoughts." The bishop stood up and offered his hand.

"It is late and I must rest, but I will leave you with this thought. The longer I live, and the more I learn, the more I see that there is a road that all can walk on. I feel my dear friend that you more than most have walked further." He gave a smile as he shook his hand. "I will see you for breakfast, goodnight."

Bishop John Steven returned to his room and wrote in his journal, outside in the darkness Father Warren sat lost in thought; the world in which he lived was now beginning to change fast. For a long time, it had been so quiet and simple, and then one night out of the darkness a hooded figure of a youth had entered his church and looked up at the statue of Mary and the child. From that moment he had felt the change begin, and he could see how his destiny had changed from that of a humble vicar doing his research. His work in many ways had come to life, and he now faced the same task of his mentor and writer Column Cille. He now had to find a way using tolerance to help unite the church and the land around him.

It had been a long hot day for Father Warren, but he had at least had the benefit of the cover and trees, followed by the cooler outbuildings of the Cathedral in Lincoln. Deep within the realm of Avalon the temperature was reaching unbearable levels; these were not made any easier by the flies in the damp marshland, to the south of the realm and across the lake.

Hawk and his group, had spent most of the day sleeping, the heat added to their exhaustion. Woody and Harry had taken everyone's cloaks and tied them together to hang from the large tree branches, and create a place of shade to sleep below. The group rested as they waited for Hawk to decide what their next course would be. All of them were simply glad to sit, rest, and recover a little from the oppressive exhaustion they all felt. Far across on the other side of Avalon, once William and Smokes had been awoken and had eaten, with Robbie and Steph, they set off into the mist and the dense woodland of trees, which stretched along the western edge of the long Lake of Passing.

Progress was slow, mainly due to the fact that as the day wore on, it got hotter, and the mist thickened. Visibility was just eight feet in the dense woodland, and Robbie had to slow down to prevent the others from walking into the wide trunks that loomed suddenly out of the white swirling vapour before them. Steph had wondered how Robbie could navigate so well with the limited visibility, and a sun above them that did not appear to move in the sky. Robbie had taken note of the fact in Avalon his compass did not work, for most of his time there; he had been using the trees and the sun to navigate. With the thick mist and no aid from the sun, he had returned to his teachings from Joe in Loxley, and used the surroundings to navigate.

The trees parted and Robbie stepped out into a wide clearing where the mist appeared to be a lot thinner. From the moment he stepped clear of the green leafy edge, he felt a change in the air that was almost electric, his eyes fixed on the old, gnarled, twisted trunk and the heavy branches above him, of what was a tree of great age. Long threads of every colour hung from the branches by the thousand, all of them attached to items of jewellery or small cloth pouches. They moved gently in the breeze bumping into each other, giving off a faint tinkling sound that was almost hypnotic. Robbie stared at the huge tree as Steph came out of the trees and up to his side. "The Tree of Lost Souls, I wondered what it would look like." Robbie looked at her.

"This place is very sacred; I can feel it in the air." Smokes stopped, and gave a shudder.

"It feels sort of spooky in this mist, not sure I want to linger round here for long." He slipped a brightly coloured rag out of his pocket, which Robbie recognised as being the one Steph had tied on his head as a headband on Honey Hill, and he wiped his face and neck free of the sweat, as he watched Steph take a step under the wide branches below all the chiming items on the long strings.

"This tree marks a special ritual, for it is a monument to the memory of every member of the Fae lost in battle. Each of these strings contains an item returned from the battlefield that belonged to each person lost. The Fae believed that to bring something so personal back to their home would permit their lost soul to return to their homeland and be at peace. I think it is a very beautiful gesture, and in a strange way it reminds me of the tree of chimes at Jade's house, they seem to strike the same tones." She walked slowly, looking up at each of the tokens hung above her as she spoke, comparing it to the tree of chimes gave Robbie a little comfort as he listened, and he could see how she felt the tone was the same, Smokes was not as convinced.

"There is a lot of string hung there Baby, not sure you should be walking about disturbing them, you know it's better we leave well alone." Steph gave a smile.

"You have spent too much time listening to Harry, if there is any karma here; I will bet my last bit it's peaceful. The Fae are a deeply spiritual people, there will be nothing here to harm those who respect their culture."

A blood curdling scream echoed in the woodland behind them, and Smokes gave a shudder as he jumped. Robbie turned and faced the trees as William came through on to the grass below the tree.

"We have company." Robbie looked round the wide glade below the huge tree; he glanced back towards the thick heavy trunk.

"Get to the trunk, the visibility here is better than under the trees, we can use the tree to guard our rear, and face anything that comes at us head on." He looked back to Steph. "Let's hope the spirits of all these Fae understand we are on their side, this land may be sacred to them, but for us it's our best chance of survival."

They all moved quickly into the centre, and placed their backs to the tree trunk, which was so wide, it would have accommodated a few more of them across its girth. Robbie loaded his bow, and the rest followed as they prepared to face an attack. Smokes stabbed his long silver spear into the ground just in front of him, as he prepared with just twelve arrows to face the Houlen.

"We are low on arrows, don't miss and make every one count." Robbie had the same thought going through his mind; he was down to just ten. Nervously they waited, as the screams in the trees got louder, and the Houlen smelt fresher scent. William wiped his face on his sleeve, and Robbie winked at him.

"You OK?" William gave a smile back and nodded.

"I'm fine, just hot; this heat is not for me." Robbie's hair hung lank around his shoulders as the sweat ran onto his face.

"Yeah, a good blizzard about now would be very welcome, just stay close and aim for the head, they will not find it easy to attack us here, our back is safe and they can only come at us head on, when your arrows run out, use your sword, but stay close to me at all times, they will only succeed if they separate us OK?" William gave a long breath and prepared.

"Got you."

"Good man."

The screams were louder, and the sound of breaking branches echoed around the open glade below the tree, it was obvious that the Houlen were coming fast. Robbie lifted his bow, and pulled back on the string, his arrow resting on the first finger of his left hand. Gripping the bow tightly, he looked down the arrow waiting for that moment when the dense foliage parted. The moment came, and he moved like lightening, as he turned slightly and released his arrow.

The grey contorted face with red burning eyes came screaming through the parting leaves, as the Houlen bounded into the open. Within less than a second Robbie's arrow hit it right in the centre of the forehead, its head whipped backwards as the rest of its body moved forward with the momentum of its pace. It disappeared back into the leaves as the legs shot into the air, and it hit the floor with a deep grunt and lay motionless. A second came out a few feet down and Smokes fired, Steph hit another almost at its side and Robbie and William both fired together as two others came leaping out in the air in front of them. Howls and screams filled the air as those behind saw their dead comrades and the lust for blood increased.

Robbie moved with pinpoint accuracy, hitting each of the vile beasts dead in the centre of their forehead as they appeared. The following two minutes seemed to last an age, as the arrows in the quivers of the small woodland group lessened. Robbie pulled his last arrow and fitted it with high speed to the string, William hit the next one as he lifted his bow and waited. A tall slender woman with the face of a demon screeched into the air through the thick wall of new green leaves, and Robbie let his arrow go. She was moving towards him fast, and she tried to dodge the arrow, it hit her in the neck and the power of the arrow dragged her sideways to the floor.

A murderous rage lifted into the air as she hit the floor thrashing and kicking, her eyes burned with a deep intense red of hatred, as she thrashed wildly screaming with hate. The arrows had run out, and it was as if the Houlen sensed it, they came out of the trees in a wide row as the injured one rose into a frenzy of rage. Robbie lifted his sleeve as he wiped the sweat out of his eyes; at his side William held his long golden sword with both hands as he waited for the first Houlen to lunge at him. Smokes held his long spear in front of him, and Steph had her sword out ready. Robbie dropped his hand to the cool metal hilt of Destiny as he prepared for the first to attack.

The Houlen stood in front forming a wide circle around them; they stared with red evil eyes, their mouths vibrated with their lust, making them murmur in unison. The hum of their yearning for the death of the party began to rise in tone and quickened with rhythm, it was obvious they were building up to a slaughter. Robbie swallowed hard as he grasped Destiny, and pulled out the long shining sword, the eyes of the Houlen widened and the murmur stopped.

The sudden silence unnerved Robbie as he waved the sword in front of him softly; it was something he had not expected. The Houlen stared at him with hate, but something had changed, and he was not sure what. Steph whispered from the other side of Smokes.

"The tree... Robbie look up at the tree."

Robbie took his eyes away from the Houlen for a split second and looked upwards. Above him hanging on a thousand threads bright deep blue light shone from every pendant and pouch, the light seemed to dance down and illuminate Destiny, which shone brightly in a deep blue haze of light. The Houlen dropped to the ground with fear, and looked away from the light hiding their faces in the grass. Robbie took a step forward, and the Houlen seemed to sense it, they gave off frightened little yelps like scalded puppies, and crawled backwards towards the shelter of the trees. "What's happening Steph?"

Steph shook the wet hair out of her face. "To be honest Robbie, I haven't got a clue. I am just bloody happy you pulled out that sword. The only thing I can think of is that maybe this lot have met your swords brother."

Robbie looked at the sword beneath what was now a deep blue pulsating light. The blade of Destiny seemed to pulsate in rhythm with the lights above, and it was very obvious the Houlen were afraid of it.

"What do you mean? Do they think this is Excalibur?" Smokes gave a rapid nod.

"Who the hell cares, if it freaks these bastards out, use the bugger, go on lunge at em." Robbie lifted the blade high above his head and the Houlen began to whimper louder. He gripped the hilt tight, and then with all of his effort, he screamed as loud as he could, and jumped forward three paces as he swept the pulsating blade across his path.

"ARRRRRRRRRRGH!"

It was chaos. The Houlen leapt backwards, emitting deafening screams of terror and flew into the air. In their panic they smashed into each other and the trees. They scrambled wildly as they tried in their desperation to get away from the sword, smashing and bumping into everything. Robbie swung the blade across his path as he took another step towards them, and they wailed into the trees in blind panic. Steph and Smokes gave a long breath of relief as William began to giggle. The sight of Houlen yelling and wailing in terror and bouncing off the trees or falling over each other did look very comical. Robbie kept yelling and sweeping the blade across his path until the glade was free of any living Houlen, and the rest had fled into the woodland, and only their wails could be heard as they smashed their way as far as they could get from the sword. Robbie turned and lifted the sword ready to drop it into its scabbard, and Smokes lifted his hands.

"Keep it out!" Robbie looked behind him where the scene was clear.

"Why?" Smokes gave a shrug.

"I don't know, maybe just in case, it seems to me that they are pretty bloody scared of it, I just think as long as they can see it, they will stay the hell away, after all there was loads of the buggers, I am happy to be here and whole, I kinda want to stay that way." Robbie looked at Steph.

"What do you think?" Steph slumped to the ground and leaned back against the stump of the old tree.

"I suppose it might be better for a little while longer, although it does seem that the tree has responded to the sword. Maybe the power of the Fae in the sword, and the lost spirits that linger here are a source of great fear to the Houlen; after all they were once Fae themselves." Smokes looked back at her with a surprised look on his face.

"How can those vile buggers be Fae? The Fae are supposed to be elegant gentle people." Steph took a long drink from her water bottle, and poured some water onto her hankie. She wiped her face and neck and she looked at the three men, who all now had her undivided attention.

"If you think about it, before they transform with their blood lust, the Houlen are very elegant well dressed creatures, they look very similar to the Fae of old. My dad told me that the Dark One would capture the wandering isolated Fae, and then take them to her place and corrupt them with the dark power, which is how she created the first Houlen that Rhiannon destroyed. I figure she is still doing it, but has improved her methods."

William walked over to the tree and collapsed at it base, his face red and dripping with sweat. "It does explain the sword, if they think it is the one sword, it will be a memory from the earlier times, when Excalibur was seen as the ultimate destroyer of all things evil. It is the one thing they know will defeat them, that must be why they fled when they saw it." Robbie looked back at the trees and the scattered bodies of the dead on the grass.

"My only question is will it keep them away permanently, or will they be back?" Steph screwed the top on her water bottle.

"They will be back. At some point they will regroup, and no doubt their mistress will fill them with wild hate and send them back at us." Robbie agreed.

"I think we have a good opportunity to get the hell away from here. Just through those trees is a road, we will be faster in the mist on the road, it should lead us to the main track to your dad's house. I think we would be better to get a move on, I don't fancy meeting the Houlen in the trees." Steph gave a nod of agreement.

"Yeah, it makes more sense; we will be better protected at my dad's place." She dropped her water bottle into her bag, and lifted her bow and empty quiver. "Come on then, let's get out of here." Robbie dropped Destiny into the scabbard, and the lights in the tree went out, he smiled to himself as he lifted his empty quiver off the floor. Grabbing his bow, he looked to the trees and the direction of the road.

"Come on then, let's get the hell out of here." He turned and headed for the trees. William sheathed his sword and followed him, as Smokes kept a wary eye behind them with Steph.

As the evening wore away with the solitary watch bell to mark the funeral of one of New Avon's founders, the sun slipped slowly into the west, and painted the sky with a tinge of pink, before the bright red of sunset. The funeral had been a large and solemn affair, and Sapphire had stood alone set back from the others and respectfully watched Rafe and his father hug in their grief. She had only just been able to get back in time, and the glance of Rafe's dark eyes had told her that he was still unhappy with her. As the funeral ended Rafe remained at the grave with his head bowed, Sapphire stood waiting patiently for him. As she quietly waited beside the grey stone wall that surrounded the community plot, her mind had raced, as Rune's words and those of Gwinne's had played over and over in her mind. She felt tired and confused, and deep down inside she had a strange feeling, and was not sure what it was.

Lost in her thoughts she could only feel that there was a deep yearning growing inside her. It felt as if some part of her was blindly searching for something it knew was close, but was unable to find. The feeling had been growing inside her for several days now, and she could not figure it out and felt very frustrated. Lost in her thoughts she did not even notice Rafe as he walked up and yelled at her. Her eyes blinked for a few moments and then she came back to reality and the blast of Rafe's temper. "Sorry Rafe, What?"

"I SAID, I STILL WANT AN ANSWER TO WHERE THE BLOODY HELL HAVE YOU BEEN? I HAVE SPENT HALF THE DAY SEARCHING ALL OVER FOR YOU!" It hit her like a shock wave and she recoiled backwards away from him. "WELL?"

She blinked again, and looked back at his red angry face, as he stood with his hands on his hips as if waiting for her to justify herself. She could not help but feel somewhat annoyed, after all she had spent her day running about trying to fill everyone in and make sure she was back in time to be with him at what she thought was a tough time for him. Her anger showed.

"I have told you I was called away on urgent business, not that I have to justify myself to you, I answer only to my family." Her tone was sharp, yet it seemed like it had no effect on Rafe at all.

"Well the next time you decide to bugger off without a word, bloody well ask if it is convenient, have you any idea how much trouble it's caused?"

"WHAT?" Rafe did not even wait for her to get the rest of her words out, he turned and stormed off down the road, Sapphire felt the anger rise inside her, and she very quickly ran to catch up with him. "Hey hold up and just you bloody well wait, who the hell do you think you are talking to? I do not need your permission, I can come and go as I please, you have no bloody authority with me." Rafe spun round quickly on the spot.

"When you are here in New Avon you follow the rule here, and as the commander of forces here you will inform me if you leave here. Do you understand?" She was completely lost for words.

"Here...Here? It's funny that Rafe, because that crest on your shoulder says you left here and became a resident of Loxley, so which is it? You either command here or in the north, you cannot have it both ways, and by the way, even if we were at Loxley, you would still have no authority over me, I answer to my centre, and no bugger else, especially an ego driven idiot in a cloak. I bet you don't talk to Jett like that, she would slice that ego of yours right off." She brushed past him and walked across the road to the driveway of the old farm, Rafe stared at her and then seemed to calm down, he took a few hurried paces after her and called out.

"Look hang on Saff, I am sorry, I was worried you know, I got up and you were gone, and I thought you had left without me. Come on Saff it was all a big mistake, let's not fight." She stopped at the garden gate and looked back at him.

"I have had a really busy day running about all over for Rune, and believe it or not, I have my own problems, yet I have been here for five days doing everything I can to help out." Rafe gave a smile.

"Oh yeah, what problems have you got then?" Just the look of him stood halfway up the driveway with that boyish smirk on his face was enough, and Sapphire felt the anger inside her grow.

"You know what Rafe forget it.... Just grow the hell up and leave me alone." The gate banged loudly as she headed up the path towards the steps.

"Oh come on Saff, I said I was sorry."

"Bugger off." The front door swung shut behind her, and Rafe gave a long sigh, as again he stood in the driveway alone. Just above the trees the sun grew into a fiery red ball and prepared to slip down into the trees, and send the woodland realm into darkness. Upstairs in her small room Sapphire flopped down onto the bed feeling exhausted, it had been a very long day, and she had barely slept since she had arrived at the farm. She buried her face into her pillow, feeling the exhaustion take her and her eyes closed, as she slipped into a restless sleep.

The pictures came quickly. The young girl walked along the street almost in a daze. There was noise all around her from the heaving stalls laden with bread and fish. People were shouting, and she could hear the clatter of feet running all around her, she caught a glimpse of herself in a large glass window, and for a moment she stared at the young slender figure of a girl dressed in a white flared skirt embroidered with intricate coloured flowers along its hem, and a small cotton torn blouse. Her hair was long, sleek and very dark, as it hung past her shoulders, and she felt the strong sense of anxiety that came from the eyes that stared with fear back at her.

As with all her dreams, she saw the pale hand laden with golden rings take a hold of hers, the voice was abrasive, yet soft. "Come with me child, you will be safe." Sapphire turned and looked up at the white face surrounded by jet black hair, it was young and very pale, and the dark cold eyes twinkled as she smiled an almost twisted smile.

Sapphire sat bolt upright in bed with a huge gasp, her heart was pounding and the sweat ran down her face, she took a long deep breath to gather herself as she realised it was just a dream. She breathed out and whispered quietly to herself. "Le Fey."

CHAPTER TEN

MOMENTS OF CLARITY

The tall figure of Jonathan Rafe stood out at the top of the bluff, as he looked down on the place that had been his every dream of his early life. It rolled across the plain nestled in the surrounding woodland, a small oasis of neatly ploughed fields, and narrow lanes that contained the wooden houses of the town he loved so dearly.

Rafe carried the loss of his mother on his face. It had been a very difficult time, and suddenly he felt confused and mixed up inside. Life until now had been simple, all he had ever wanted to do was to be like his uncle and become the best woodsman he could be. Now as he looked out on the small community that his parents had helped to build, he felt a tug at his loyalties, his time with the Specialists had given him a greater sense of who he was as a man. The village looked so quiet and peaceful, and yet now he felt like walking away would be a betrayal of his mother's life work.

In the past five days he had hardly slept, and his soft brown eyes seemed dull above the dark lines on his face. Rafe looked tired and exhausted as he walked slowly from the bluff and back into the deep woodland. He had spent the night sat in the dark trying to find his direction, Jett was high in his thoughts and being so far from her side, he missed the chance to talk to her. She was wild and in many ways very unconventional, but she had been the one to sit for endless hours into the night quietly talking. Now the thoughts of those times came to mind and he knew he needed to see her, she had a way of putting things into place and he felt even more isolated not being able to talk to her.

Rafe slowly walked between the trees as the hundreds of thoughts passed through his mind, the sadness of his soul surrounded him as he stopped and sat on a fallen trunk. He slid down onto the leaf covered earth as he drew up his knees and leaned back on the rough bark of the trunk and closed his eyes. The weariness of the last few days had caught up with him, and as the sun rose slowly in the sky, lost and confused, sleep finally took him, and he slumped back and drifted with the pictures of his life swarming into his mind and slept.

Rafe was unaware that the group were in trouble, his argument with Sapphire had left him alone and isolated, he knew nothing of Robbie and his party, who had been separated and scattered to the three corners of the realm of Avalon. In many ways he was lucky to be free of the knowledge that Jett had been lost. Blades had been very quiet as she held in the grief of losing a close friend. Jade had cried sat under the bridge held tightly by her mother, and as Rune slept alone in a soft bed, under the roof of Fagan the Keeper of the Forest of Time, her mind wandered trying to understand what had befallen Jett.

The flash of bright blue light had bounced across the Mirrored Waters, as Jett was flipped over the rail and headed towards her death. She had closed her eyes accepting her fate, and had felt a strong and sudden lurch in the pit of her stomach. Jett spiralled out of control and lost consciousness, her mind raced into strange dreams, where she heard the voice of Rune scream, "Jett...No!" over and over, and yet behind it somewhere lost in the background she heard the strange voice of another.

"No, you fool!" It echoed as she felt herself spinning in darkness, with speckles of the blue flash dancing around inside her tightly closed eyes. The voices trailed away as if they were lost in the distance behind her, and other sounds that began as faint whispers grew louder. A tiny voice grew stronger as she heard the sound of a skipping rope hitting the floor, and somewhere in the back of her mind, she could hear the same small voice singing nursery rhymes. Her mind spun in the haze, as the little voice grew louder, and for a second everything seemed to suddenly clear, as she felt a warm soft hand touch hers. The voice was shrill and very loud in her ears.

"I knew you wouldn't leave me; I knew you would come for me. This place is so lonely, can we play now?"

The earth slammed into her back, and she gave a loud scream, as the pain coursed through her, and she gasped out the air trapped inside her lungs. The light flared through her eyes almost blinding her, and she snatched her arms instinctively to her face, she was still holding the long golden sword, and felt the cold hilt on her cheek.

The long grass felt soft and warm underneath her, as she sat up with a jerk. She opened her eyes, and blinked in the brightness of the light. "Ruby.... Ruby is that you?"

Her eyes slowly came back into focus as the ground that was spinning around her slowed down. Jett stretched out a hand to the grass to steady herself as the dizziness slowly wore off. The blade of her sword glinted in the sun as she looked down at it. One part of the edge was blackened where it had taken the force of the Star of the Merle. She pressed her hand to the ground still feeling a little sick, and looked around at the forest of enormous trees. "What the hell happened, where the hell is Rune and Jade?" She shook her head to clear her blurred thoughts.

"Ruby are you here, or am I dreaming again?"

Slowly she got to her feet, her legs were still shaky, and she wobbled slightly as she got a full view of her surroundings. "Oh this is not good, this place aint Avalon, where the hell am I?" A branch snapped to her left and she lifted her sword almost by instinct, and held it out in front of her, as a figure stepped out from the cover; she looked at the strangely clad man with dark searching eyes as she took in his full appearance. "You aint no Cutter, who the hell are you, and where the hell is this place?"

Sapphire walked slowly through the woods; she knew that Rafe would be somewhere around, she was just not sure where. The feeling inside her was strong and she just instinctively knew that he was in danger. Her dreams had kept her awake half the night, and she also felt guilty at having shouted at Rafe, after all she had seen the level of grief he had gone through, and in a way, she understood his anger. Although, it did not excuse his two outbursts, she also understood that at the moment, he was the only connection she had to her life with the Specialists. Her pace quickened as she scanned the trees and watched the high bluff, the strong feelings inside her were growing, and she knew she had to get to him soon.

Rafe was still asleep with the sun warming him, it was deep and he was not aware of anything going on around him. Two Cutters who were on a scouting trip, laughed quietly as they approached him, they signalled each other with large smiles on their faces as they tip toed towards Rafe with their swords out. "Shush Jed, this will be a right laugh, see what I mean about em being easy pickings?"

Jed was a tall well built man covered in hair, and wearing a bloodstained vest, the two of them had already dispatched two other woodsmen that morning and now with their swords in hand they planned to dispatch another. Jed leaned into Rafe who snored in his sleep. "Hey sleeping beauty wake up." He pushed his sword on to Rafe's chest. Rafe gave a grunt as he disturbed, he flicked his hand across his chest and knocked the sword away.

"Sod off Jett, I am knackered." Jed flicked the sword and it hit Rafe on the side of the head.

"Watch it mate or you will find this stuck somewhere very unpleasant."

Without warning Rafe's eyes snapped open, he leapt up from the floor, and with a flying fist, Jed rocketed backwards. The other Cutter lunged at him with a yell, and raised the sword back to swipe at Rafe.

Rafe twisted, and lunged at the Cutter smashing into his arm and plunging his teeth deep into the Cutters shoulder. The Cutter screamed out in shock and pain, as he fell back with Rafe growling like an animal on top of him. The dagger glinted, and Rafe pushed it hard into the soldier's chest. Jed bounced up off the floor, and snatched up his sword; he swiped the blade towards Rafe, but suddenly went upright and coughed. Rafe pulled away from the dead Cutter, and watched as

Jed dropped to his knees. The Cutter gave a moan and a wheezy cough and blood sprayed out of his mouth; he stared at Rafe with a look of complete surprise, and then fell face down on the woodland floor.

Up at the top of the banking in the tree line, Sapphire stood still holding her bow with her second arrow fitted. Rafe spat at the floor, and the blood splattered onto the brown leaf litter. He kicked at Jed who rolled over, the arrow giving a loud crack as it snapped, and he stared at the wide lifeless eyes. "I do not like being woken up without a coffee, you get me?" Sapphire came down the hill holding her loaded bow up and looked around making sure they were alone.

"Well, I see you had breakfast." She tossed a blue cotton handkerchief at him. "You, Ok?" Rafe wiped his mouth and gave her a cheeky smile.

"Yeah, I am fine, cheers Saff I owe you." She looked down at the two dead Cutters' and then back at Rafe before lowering her bow.

"Yeah, you do, so don't forget it." He could tell she was still annoyed with him; he gave a slight nod and looked at her.

"I won't... Look Saff... About last night." She turned looking around the woodland.

"Forget it, we got bigger problems, these are scouts, which must mean there is a raiding party around." She bent down, and lifted his bow and threw it at him; he caught it with one hand. "I think we should get back fast and report this; your uncle will want to know as soon as possible." He gave a nod of agreement and glancing round the woodland he slipped his dagger back into his belt, and then followed Saff as she headed back up the track in the direction of the bluff.

The mist was becoming so thick, that what had looked on the map like a short walk had turned out to be hours. Steph slowed down as she panted. "Sorry Rob, I need a break my legs are killing me." Robbie was feeling frustrated, it was impossible to see more than a few feet in front of him, something that was also impeded by the sweat running down his face and into his eyes.

"It cannot be much further; we have been walking for most of the night." William was stood up front staring into the thick white swirling mist.

"I don't think it is, is that a fence?" Smokes gave a long sigh of relief as he walked slowly past Robbie up to the young boy.

"Oh thank god for that." He took a few steps forward as the mist swirled showing the track ahead and the start of a neatly made wooden fence, before swirling forward and hiding it again. "It looks like we made it." Steph gave a moan as she straightened up, and hoisted her bag onto her shoulder. She gave Robbie a pat on the shoulder as she staggered forward to the others.

"Time to put a kettle on... oh and by the way, if there is a bath, I get first dibs."

Robbie gave a smile as he trudged on the dry earth floor of clay and small stones, toward the others, who were walking along the edge of the white painted fence looking for an entrance. The small party felt their spirits lift as they reached the gate with the small carven sign 'The Homestead', and without thinking Steph swept her hand across it and the gate gave a small click. She led the way in lifting her bag towards the old white stone built cottage. Robbie watched as Steph rooted around inside her bag. "I have my dad's spare keys in here somewhere, I am sure that old metal one will fit."

Smokes examined the old lock plate and leaned against the door slightly. "I can always force it, if not Honey." Robbie gave a smile.

"Considering who's house this is I am not sure you should try that." Smokes gave a smile and nodded.

"Oh yeah.... Hmm see what you mean, it's a wizards house, yeah you're right we don't want anything unnatural jumping out on us." Steph gave a giggle.

"Here it is." She pulled out a large bunch of keys, of which one stood out from the others, it was much bigger and looked very old indeed, Steph held it up in front of her to examine it, and the door swung open. Smokes who was still leaning on it, gave a slight yelp and fell straight through landing in a heap on the floor. Steph gave a chuckle as she grabbed his arm and pulled him back to his feet. Robbie smirked with William, as they both stepped in behind a slightly surprised looking Smokes, who was following Steph down the hallway.

"Pretty cool key that, especially if you were drunk, I can't tell you how many times I have struggled trying to fit the bugger to the lock in the darkness. I could really use one of them, just show it the door and you're in, that's what I call cool magic."

Robbie was not really sure what to expect. Leenard's house in Loxley was to say the least very interesting, it was filled with much of the things he needed in Loxley for his medicines, and as expected there were shelves of books. The Homestead was very different from anything he had imagined, and as he watched Steph walk around the main room, he could see that she too was learning and understanding a great deal about a hidden part of her father's life.

There was an element of slight surprise for Robbie, for which on the surface appeared very much to be a plain and quite ordinary house. It felt very cosy with its low ceilings and exposed beams, and the walls felt very much like he had seen in other homes, decorated with small cross stitched pictures, and some very nicely painted portraits of Leenard and a very beautiful woman who he naturally assumed was Gwendolyn, she looked younger than the woman he had seen come out of the wheel of Carnac, but the likeness was there.

Steph lifted a small frame containing an unfinished needlework off the cushion of the old rocking chair by the large open fireplace and sat down in it. Her gaze went slowly round the room as she absorbed the story of her father and Gwendolyn from the paintings and the stitched pictures. Smokes had disappeared and from somewhere behind Robbie, he could hear him rattling round in the kitchen. Robbie looked back at Steph. "Are you Ok?"

"Hmm... Fine."

"Not quite what you expected?" She looked back round the room.

"It's not that Rob, it's just... I am not sure really... It's just that here I am sat in the middle of his early life, and I guess that this is it." He was not sure what she meant.

"How do you mean?" She gave a small sigh.

"These pictures, this house, all of them memories of a very important time, and as much as I have worked with him for all these years, I know there is so much more to whom he was and what he has done, but this house is just a reflection of it all. I will never be able to sit with him and talk to him about it all, he has left me forever Robbie and as much as that has hurt in the last few days, sitting here I think I can see how much more I needed to learn from him."

A cold shiver ran down his spine; as he listened to her quiet voice reflect the loss she felt. He understood her perfectly; he too had felt the same way earlier that year walking around his hometown of Loxley. He knew there was so much more to learn and understand about his own father, but he also knew that he at least had his mother and the rest of his family to help fill in the gaps, for Steph there was no one left from the time when Leenard had lived here with Gwendolyn, for her there would be no answers. Robbie knew that there really wasn't anything he could say that would help.

Robbie turned to look through the long timber framed windows, where blue roses pushed up against the glass, and he saw the swirling mist block out the view of everything beyond the small neat white fence. Avalon was as good as a million miles away from everything, and hidden under a blanket of deep white, he felt the cold fingers of isolation stroke his spine, and he knew that here for now he was a prisoner, and that he had no one to aid his plight, Avalon had been sealed, and although he had achieved his goals, he knew that he had failed the world of the woodland by walking into Morgan le Fey's elaborate trap. His thoughts sounded out of him without him realising. "How the hell does a rabbit break free of the snare to escape its fate?"

"It fights to the death and chews its way out." Robbie noticed Will looking up at him from the chair next to him, and he gave a smile as he nodded in agreement.

"We have a lot of fighting and chewing to do then." Will agreed.

"We will do it." It was a simple remark, but Robbie could see how the young boy had changed so much in his brief time with them, he admired his faith in the group to overcome their current difficulties, when he felt so much doubt.

"The stove is lit and the kettle is on the boil, we are quite lucky I found a big tin full of coffee beans and there is plenty of sugar as well as a cupboard full of herbs. We have bread and cheese left in our packs and a few carrots, sadly John and Maggs have most the other food, so it's either cheese on toast or just a sandwich?"

Smokes gave a big smile pleased with his efforts. Robbie and Will both gave him a smile, the sudden thought of food was more than appealing, it had been almost 12 hours since any of them had eaten.

Jade hit the foot of the steps that led up to a cave, where the light of day flooded in illuminating the white walls. She spun on the spot, dropping to one knee as she loaded her arrow. John puffed and panted up the tunnel giving Rowan a piggyback ride, Rowan's splinted leg stood out in front like a battering ram. Judy was not far behind laden with John's bag as well as her own, Jade smiled as she trudged up red in the face gasping for breath. "Nearly there now." Judy gasped for air as she passed her and began a weary climb onto the steps.

From down the tunnel the sound of the dog was getting louder. Bear and Crystal came next, both of them looked exhausted, and Bear who was sweating profusely looked the most unkempt that Jade had ever seen him. Bear gave a nod as he breathed heavily. "Fox and Blades are keeping cover; Jay is on her way stay sharp, if they let that dog off the lead it will come at us fast."

Jade gave a nod, and watched the long tunnel in front of her, where she could see Jay sprinting like mad from the corner. Bear thundered onto the steps to follow the others, and set up the next line of defence. Jay came panting and skidding to a halt, as she crouched down on the opposite side of the path and lifted her bow. The walls echoed with her rapid panting and gasping for breath, she swallowed hard trying to regulate her breathing.

"Seemed to have spent my whole life running along stone walls, I tell you Pebbles, if we get out of here, I am living in the woods away from stone forever." Jade gave a smile and winked.

" Joe has a spare room, you will love his place, and there is not a brick for miles."

The escape from the cell had gone relatively well; they had been fast to move and with Fagan watching their rear they had made up good time. The biggest problem had been that it had indeed been many years since Fagan had walked in the maze of tunnels below the Citadel Mount. The new occupation of the Mount had brought many soldiers underground, and there was also the hunt for Robbie and William, so the tunnels were not as empty as Fagan had expected. There had been a few tense moments where they had run into a search party, and Bear with John had seen some very brutal fighting. Blades had found it difficult using both swords in the confined tunnels, and so had resorted to using just the one; even so with one sword spinning in her hands she was just as efficient at despatching the enemy.

The biggest problem had been that the soldiers up at the cellblock having discovered the breakout had brought out their dogs. There had been a couple of occasions where a huge dog had been let lose off the leash, and one had almost got Hornet as they all ran down the tunnel. It had been a swift action on Blades part that had killed the dog and seen them all to safety. The journey through the tunnels had been long and exhausting, the heat below the surface was now increasing as under the bright glare of a twenty-four hour sun, even the rocks were starting to heat up, and hold in much of the burning temperatures of the surface.

All of them looked like they had been swimming in a mixture of dirty water and blood. Their clothes hung with the wetness of them, and their hair hung matted with sweat and blood splatters. It had been a very long hot and uncomfortable night, as they dug deeply into their reserves to fight off those they met on route. Their only saving grace had been that to date they had not met any of the Houlen. The sound of Fox and Blades pounding feet came down the tunnel, as Jay and Jade tensed and pulled back on their bowstrings. Arrows were now in short supply, and both of them knew that they would not have much longer before their supplies were exhausted.

Hand in hand, Fox and Blades ran as hard as they could up the tunnel. Fox gasped as his feet pounded on the stone, they slowed as they saw Jade and Jay keeping cover, and Blades gasped for air as they got closer, Fox pointed behind him. "Watch the dog, I got the other one, but it will not be too long before they let it go. As soon as we hit the top of the steps, get the hell out of here, I reckon there is about ten of em following with crossbows." He patted Jade on the shoulder, and then ran up the steps with Blades. Jade scanned down her arrow and watched the tunnel, as the bark of the dog grew louder. Behind her she heard Bear scream out.

"Pebbles... Jay, get the hell out of there now!"

Both of them rose off the ground together and turned with speed. They ran onto the steps to see Bear at the top with his bow raised, behind them the sound of the dog was growing louder. Jade felt the aches in her legs as she ran with all her speed up the steps; they were steep and rose swiftly towards the bright light of the sunny day. After being for so long in the gloom it felt dazzling and she screwed up her eyes, as she ran with her head down. The twenty steps to the top felt like hundreds, as her tired body rebelled against the strain on her with twinges of sharp pain. As she neared the top, she felt Fox's gloved hand snatch at her sleeve as he helped haul her over the final step, and she opened her eyes wide to get a lay of the land.

The entrance to the tunnel formed a wide round cave, it was not as big as Jade had first expected. John had placed Rowan down on the floor just outside, where Crystal was doing what she could to help ease his pain, Hornet watched from the other side of the cave entrance. Outside in what should have been the open view of the grassland leading down towards the White Pool, everything was hidden under the thick veil of the heavy mists. Jade walked out into the bright hazy sun and felt the temperature increase instantly. "This place is worse than the tunnels."

"Well at least there is more room to run, it's not that bad." Jade gave a smile,

Hornet was right; at least it was a wide open space, although Jade doubted that in a thick mist like this, they would have little chance of getting very far ahead of the dog. She lifted her bow as she watched back inside the cave covering with Hornet. Bear was stood at the top of the steps with his bow raised as Fox and Blades carefully walked backwards to the opening to take cover. John was watching Jade from across the other side, somehow, she felt he was thinking the same way as her, he voiced his thoughts to the rest of the group.

"Not sure about you lot, but I am knackered, I am not sure I can go much further. How about we take a stand here while we have them caught in the tunnel?"

It was already on Jade's mind, and it seemed to make the best sense, after all if they held the doorway, they would have a much better chance in the short term of holding the Cutters back, which would buy them a little time to get their second wind up.

Bear turned and ran towards the cave entrance as the others lifted their bows with the last of their arrows, the sound of loud barks and snarling came up the steps, they had released the dog and it came growling up the steps, and rushed across the cave towards Bear.

As bowstrings went taught, Bear turned as the huge dog leapt up at him. With a vicious snarl it opened its mouth, and Bear hammered his fist with all of his last strength into its head. The dog lurched sideways as Bear took hold with both hands and twisted with a violent rage. The snap echoed around the cave, as Bear gave a murderous roar of rage, the dog left his hands and flew to the wall, where it smashed to the floor dead. Bear watched the steps his eyes blazing with rage, his face streaked with sweat and blood. Jay swallowed hard as he turned to face the others, he looked very angry, and it was a terrifying sight to behold. Across the floor at the top of the steps there was no sign of movement, but the sounds of Cutters preparing rose up in the air. Bear planted his feet hard and pulled out his long golden sword, his rage was building and everyone could see, he would run no longer.

Metal clashed on the steps as Bear gave a roaring scream that bounced off the walls, and echoed in a sinister deafening tone. "COME ON YOU COWARDS AND FACE ME!"

Steel helmets appeared on the steps as the soldiers raised their swords and ran up them. Arrows launched, as Bear gripped the hilt of his sword and prepared to wade in. The first six fell with arrows in their chests, Blades somersaulted into the air and landed at the side of Bear as four more guards came up the steps, and ran towards the centre of the room and the two waiting Specialists. Blades, was like lightening as she gave every ounce of her last strength to two flying surgical slices of her swords. The first man fell as she passed the second, and with a wail like a banshee, she brought her sword slicing round behind her with speed and it connected with the back of the Cutters head, it flipped into the air and hovered for a moment, before it dropped behind the body that had continued to take a few more steps.

Bear lunged at the other two hitting the first hard with his fist, as his sword came round like a guillotine on the other. The Cutter took the heavy blow to the face, and he crumpled, as he hit the floor. Bear's huge sword came crashing down into his chest, and drove right through to the marble floor below him. The three others who had appeared were hit instantly as Jade, Jay and John took them out with the last of their arrows, they staggered at the top of the steps as their legs gave way, and then crashed backwards, the sounds of the their weapons echoing as they rattled down the steps and back into the long tunnel.

Bear grabbed at the cloak of the dead Cutter and pulled hard, the pin gave away and the cloak slid out from underneath him, rolling the body over. He gripped it firmly and pulled tearing it into two halves; wiping his face with one of them, he threw the other to Blades who stood staring at the steps covered in blood. "Here you go girl, wipe that scum off your face." She lifted the cloth coming out of her daze and lifted it to her face, her chest heaving slightly as she gathered her breath.

Jade lowered her bow and leaned on the wall, for a few brief moments there was total silence, as the outside was insulated by the heavy mist and inside the exhausted Specialists stood motionless, and stared into space as they felt the weariness of the last five days finally take hold of them. Jay broke the silence as she lifted a small stick from her bag. "I need a sleep, what say you we blow this end of the cave and seal the rest of them in? I am not sure about you guys, but I seriously cannot take another step." Bear turned and gave a nod he looked thoroughly spent.

"Let's clear this scum and bury the lot of em, Fox get a fire going."

He bent down and took hold of the dead Cutter by the scruff of the neck, then dragged him to the top of the steps, and thrust him down. John lifted another and carried him to the top of the steps and heaved him down them. Just outside the cave Fox worked at pulling together bits of dead trees to make a fire, he struck his flint stick into a small piece of wadding and blew at it, it glowed brightly as it caught flame, and he gently placed it on the floor, and surrounded it with the shavings Hornet had cut from an old dead branch, the flames crackled as he began to build up the fire.

Jay worked on the fuse and measured it out. She cut it away, and pushed it into the top of the explosive. Bear came out of the cave as the others cleared away from the entrance, John was last and he walked out with the huge dog on his shoulder, he dumped it onto the ground in front of Fox, Jade was not sure why.

Jade looked at the large dirty matted haired animal, from a few feet away she could smell it, and she screwed up her face, she looked back at John. "God that stinks, why bring it out of there? What could you possibly do with it John?" John stretched his arms to pull out the aches.

"Dinner." He gave a huge smile. "That bugger wanted to eat us, well, I am gonna return the favour and eat his ass instead." Jade screwed up her face in utter revulsion.

"You want us to eat a dog?" Hornet and Crystal both looked equally as put off, Bear gave a broad smile as he saw the humour return to the group.

"You won't find it easy to hunt in this Jade." The thought of eating a dog just corrupted her stomach, as her face clearly showed.

"I think I'd rather starve." Blades gave a giggle stood guard at the entrance to the cave, keeping an eye on Jay as she worked.

"I have eaten it before, honest Jade it's really quite succulent." John started to laugh as he slipped out his knife and went to work. Jade gave an unconvinced look at Blades, after all she had tasted her cooking before, and she knew that once Blades cooked something it was pretty hard to distinguish what it had started off as. Somehow it was not the glowing endorsement Jade had wanted.

Bear gave a hearty laugh and patted her on the shoulder. "I too have never partaken of the beast, but I am assured by my brother Brett, it is quite palatable, so what say you that we both give it a try, and judge for ourselves? After all we need to gain back our strength, and that my dear Pebbles, could be just what we need." She was not sure at all.

"Yeah, but guys it's a dog... and not a very clean one...you know? It licks its own things and stuff; I mean I cannot see how that could be healthy." John gave a loud giggle as he cut with skill, dividing the carcass for the fire.

"Way I see it Pebbles, I have quite a hunger, and considering our circumstances, it's better than stale bread and a few boiled spuds. I wasn't planning on touching its tongue; they say that bit is very salty."

Jade gave a mighty shudder, and John burst into laughter, even Crystal who was not that keen started to giggle.

Jay with a broad smile lifted a glowing stick out of the fire. "Ok everyone heads up." She lit the short fuse and walked into the entrance of the cave, as Fox and Blades gave cover as she approached the steps. Crouching down at the top she gauged her line of vision and then tossed the fizzing explosive as far down as she could. The three of them left the cave as quickly as possible and took cover outside.

The cave amplified the ear splitting blast of the explosive. Deep inside there was a huge rumble as the walls collapsed, and a massive cloud of dust came billowing out of the front of the cave to mix in with the heavy mist. All of them lay still on the ground as the cloud floated past them. A few coughs echoed in the mist as the group sat up and spat the dust from their mouths. Jay walked slowly back to inspect the damage. The steps were no longer visible as the roof had collapsed in on them. Very little of the cave was left as it was filled with huge smashed boulders of white streaked with the violet seems of amethyst. "Well, that will help; no one is getting through that lot."

Jade lifted her head from the grass and gave it a good shake, her hair was so wet that hardly anything moved, and the dust stuck to her scalp. She sat up and ran her fingers through the lank knotted mass; her hand came away covered in grime. "I need a wash." Blades nodded in agreement; her face was still streaked with red from the fight.

"Yeah, me too, isn't that pool close by?" Jade looked into the heavy mist.

"Fagan said it was just in front of here, I don't suppose it can be that far away." Bear looked into the mist; he was not very keen on having the group divide, although the thought of being able to clean some of the stench and dirt off was very alluring. He looked at Jade who he could see had already made up her mind.

"Go in threes and stick close to each other, leave a trail so you don't get lost, and if you walk for more than five minutes without finding it, I want you to come back, we can all search as a group later when we have eaten." Jade gave a suspicious look at the meat hung over the fire that was now dripping fat into the flames.

"OK, we will stay close and I will mark the trail." Bear gave a nod.

"Take Fox." Blades face lit up with happiness and she jumped to her feet, and grabbed his arm. Jade felt the happiness inside her bubble up as the thought of washing the stale sweat and dirt off her felt like the best thing that had happened for days. Excitedly the party set off into the thick mist across what was a very rough uneven land, filled with big tufted grasses; it was obvious that at some point in time it had been a marshy area. There were few trees, and the ones that were growing looked very old and twisted, they loomed out of the mist in front of them in an almost sinister fashion.

The White Pool as Fagan had referred to it, was less than two minutes' walk away, in a perfect straight line from the camp. Jade discovered it when she had not noticed that the ground suddenly fell away. Her mind was so focused on staring into the mist ahead; she walked right off the edge, and fell three feet on to wet dirt and sand. She heard the water rippling ahead as Blades and Fox both looked down surprised and giggling at her.

Getting to her feet she walked slowly watching the ground, and her heart leapt for joy as she saw the edge of the water lapping up the sand, it took less than a few seconds to slip off her jacket and sword belt, and strip down to her undershirt. Blades giggled excitedly as she undressed at the side of Jade, within a minute Jade in just knickers and her lose shirt was in the water, Blades in her usual vest and tight shorts waded out in the warm water and sunk below the surface. Fox in his shorts carried out his shirt, which he washed and then used as a cloth to wash himself with, it was not long before Jade scampered out laughing at the sounds of delight coming from behind her, where Blades made the most of a good bath.

Jade grabbed her clothes and ran back into the water, just the thought of having clean clothes felt like the ultimate treat, and she revelled in the moment. It was a good hour before the three of them came scampering back into camp, dripping and giggling and feeling fresh and revived. "Oh that was wonderful, Crystal you want to get down there, you have no idea how good I feel being clean again." Bear looked at the fire and John watching the meat cook with a very hungry look on his face.

"Ok you guys keep watch, Hornet and Crystal you come with me. How far is it to the water?" Jade pulled a brush with broken teeth out of her bag.

"It's just a couple of minute's dead ahead, you can't miss it." She lifted the brush and began dragging it through her hair, Blades sat across from her with a towel rubbing her hair, which had lost some of its spiky shortness. Jade smiled. "Your hair is starting to grow, are you not going to cut it?" She shrugged.

"Not really sure, I use to have it quite long, but it gets in the way of the swords, I do like Treen's hair, I like how wavy it is, mine grows a bit like that, it's just that short makes the fighting easier." Jade screwed up her eyes in pain.

"Yeah, I bet it's good being knot free as well."

John gave a happy moan as he cut the first slice of meat off the dog, and dropped it on to his tongue. "Oh wow that is really good." Jade stopped brushing and stared at him.

"Oh man, I cannot believe you are eating a dog." He gave her a big smile and rubbed his large tummy.

"I am telling you Pebbles, it's delicious." He cut another long slice off the meat and dropped it on a wooden plate with his knife. "I am telling you; not eating this is depriving yourself of an experience in life." He offered her the plate.

Jade felt torn, her stomach had groaned several times in the last hour, and even though it repulsed her, she felt the saliva building in her mouth and licked her lips. John smiled as he held the plate in front of her, knowing how hungry she must be. "Well... what's it gonna be, because I can eat all of this if you don't want it?"

Hunger can be very persuasive, she took the plate and stared down at the long thick slice of meat, John cut another thick slice and handed it to Fox who showed no hesitation at all in getting stuck in. Blades soon followed, and Jade felt the pressure building as she lifted her knife and cut a small piece of the meat away. The others all smiled as they chewed quite obviously enjoying it. Jade stabbed the meat with the end of her knife and lifted it to her mouth. She took a deep breath and closed her eyes, then slipped it in to her mouth.

It had been so long since she had eaten and her body desperately wanted food, her mouth flooded with moisture as the meat hit her tongue, and she hesitantly gave it a chew. Her eyes snapped open and everyone was sat watching and smiling at her. She chewed more as the flavour soaked into her cheeks. "Wow this is actually really good, I just thought it would be horrible, but this is fantastic." She chewed harder as John gave a bright smile and began to cut more off the cooking animal.

By the time Bear arrived back looking much cleaner with the others, Jade had eaten her full and was lay back in the grass with a look of pure contentment on her face. Rowan sat at her side resting on the bags as he ate, and with the addition of food, he did look like a little colour had returned to his face, Crystal was glad to see him sat up, his leg was still numb, which pleased her; because she knew that her powers were almost spent. Back in the water she had tried to freeze some to use as an ice pack, and had failed, she now knew that she had no means of easing the pain in Rowan's leg. They had to find a safe haven and fast, where he could rest up free of moving about while his leg healed.

Crystal lifted her plate without even considering what she was eating; she took a bite and chewed as she looked at the group. "What now? We cannot stay here for much longer, our powers are fading fast and we are too exposed out in the open." Bear swallowed his food and looked round.

"Jay and John need to have a wash down, and you too Rowan if you need to, although I have brought some water up in a skin if it's easier?" Rowan gave a nod of appreciation.

"We need a safe place, I pretty much think Robbie will make it to Merlin's place, so I think we need to get there as soon as we can, I need somewhere to hole up, with this leg I am no use to anyone. Not sure how long this mist will last, but for now it will give us some cover, I say we finish our meal and when everyone is washed and ready we strike camp and get to Robbie as fast as possible."

The agreement was total, and as John and Jay slipped off to the White Pool, the others got busy repacking their bags and striking the camp. Jade cut the rest of the meat away from the dog and wrapped it in brown paper and stored it carefully in her bag. Crystal gave a smirk as she watched.

"I think anyone who owns a dog in Loxley better keep it on a short leash from now on, I think Pebbles may be up for a spot of inner wall hunting." Giggles ran round the camp as Jade stood up with a smile on her face.

"Oh, come on guys, it was a big brutal ugly thing, how was I to know it would taste so good?" She gave a giggle and lifted her bag on to her shoulder.

Within the hour they were all back on the trail, negotiating their way through the mist and skirting the edges of the White Pool. Bear carried Rowan piggyback style, with his bound leg jutting out in front of him, as Jade led the way. Fox and Blades watched the rear. Bear had been deep in thought for some time, and Rowan felt curious as to why.

"You got something on your mind Bear?" They trudged along as he thought for a moment.

"It's this mist that has me thinking.... You know when we first got here, it was hot and sunny, and yet the whole place was clear as day, so why all of a sudden has this mist come down?" Rowan had not given it much thought.

"Well, it's only appeared since we went underground; maybe it's the season here." Bear shook his head.

"No, I think it has something to do with her, I looked at the pool, don't forget I come from York."

"How is that relevant?"

"We have had a few droughts over my lifetime. I know what a pool that is slowly draining looks like and I am sure as hell that looking at the amount of water that has dropped in that pool, it's been fast, because where I come from, when a bank is that exposed from drought, the sides become baked hard."

"And they are not?" Bear gave another shake of his.

"No they are not, I am telling you Rowan, that pool has dropped three feet, and its dropped pretty bloody fast, if you ask me this mist will lift only when Avalon becomes a baked desert free of all water." It hardly seemed possible to Rowan, but Bear made a lot of sense.

"So you think that she does not want to rule here, she has actually come here to destroy it forever?"

"To be honest Rowan, yes I do, it's bothered me since we first got here and found her here. I can understand Mason wanting this place, he wants every square inch he can build on and dominate. It's her; it makes no sense when we know she has a place tucked away where no one can get at her. Avalon is the centre of all worlds, which we know is a fact, look at it from her point of view, if she can bring this place down, she will have an impact on every world. From here the cracks will spread out across everything."

A sudden cold feeling ran into Rowan, and it was a very sobering thought. The Dark One wasn't attacking the woodland realm, she knew Robbie would come here and she had prepared, but they had all thought she was here to trap them, when in fact it had just been convenient timing. Her goal was far bigger than Loxley, she was hell bent on destroying everything starting from its very beginning and working outwards. Morgan le Fey was attempting to undo everything the Ruling Council had built since day one.

"Bloody hell Bear, I think we need to move faster. We have got to get to Robbie and let him know. Him and Rune have got a bigger fight than they ever realised, and if we fail it's not just us, it's everyone else who is doomed."

CHAPTER ELEVEN

THE CONTROLLING POWERS

From the moment that Morgan le Fey had taken power in Avalon, she had opened the curtain of light to those who had been invited by Mason to come. A steady stream of carts rolled into the realm, and onto the long Queens Road up to the small town of Avalonia. Cartloads of building materials and supplies wove in a long convoy up to the base of the Citadel Mount, and mixed amongst them were carts filled with monks and priests from every monastery and abbey in Britain.

With the Citadel destroyed, Mason had given the mount to his most faithful member of the church to build an abbey dedicated to the teachings of Brother Argus. For two long days, the convoy had moved like a slow snake up the high pass and onto the top of Citadel Mount, hundreds of monks unloaded the timber and stone, and began the long process of clearing the site to build their symbol of devotion to their own lord. Behind the scenes Mason had found the whole thing highly amusing, and could think of no better way to insult Hearne and Eve, than by defiling the very realm they loved the most.

Brother Argus had promoted himself to Abbot in preparation for his new seat of power, and he began to lay down his plans to slowly infiltrate and seize control of the church in Britain. His power and greed knew no bounds as he sent out his spies and aids to Lincoln, where the newly appointed Arch Bishop, John Stevens had his base. The fight to control the church and prevent the heir found by the hooded man from being seated had begun in earnest.

Bishop John Stevens had been right to inform Farther Warren of his need for secrecy. The truth of the matter was that the church was split right down the middle. There had been many within the church that had not agreed to the crowning of Mason Knox, they had been more than a little relieved by the sudden appearance of Lord Loxley, and his halting of the ceremony. Within the hierarchy of the church Mason had great influence, and there had been a great backlash on those who had fought in the cathedral to prevent the crowning. For a moment it had looked like nothing had changed, and then suddenly the Church Council had been found dead, allegedly killed by rogue Cutters.

Brother Argus had been quick to act, and his voice had risen, as he proclaimed the deaths as murder by the witches gathered within the walls of Loxley. Many in the church had listened to his argument, and his demands to storm Loxley and kill all the family related to the wife of Robert of Loxley. He won many supporters, especially when he named the new Arch Bishop as a pagan sympathizer and demanded he resign or split the church forever.

Brother Argus had left the abbey and made his way south to Wells Cathedral, where he sat in the library of manuscripts and books saved from all over the land, and wrote to all of the churches and religious establishments that had survived the great plague of the Red Death.

In his letters he told of a church based in the gospels of old, and a church that would rise to be the tower of faith in the communities of Mason Knox as it was in days of old. It would shape the lives of everyone, and guide the new nation of the Knox Empire into an age of salvation. Many had burned his letters and laughed at him, yet a very large majority had seen his vision of a church that would partner up with the Knox Empire as a way of moving the church and themselves into a prominent position of power in the future. The effect was like the breaking of a dam, and soon priests and monks from all over the country were packing their things and making their way to Glastonbury, where Brother Argus had promised them a new beginning from an entire city devoted to worship, Avalon was about to become a Vatican like state, and the new Abbot would have the same power as a Pope.

For Bishop John Stevens, as the head of the church, he was being undermined by the ruthless monk. In private he had many supporters, but as the church watched the efforts of Lord Loxley, they felt their hopes falling as Mason swept to victory and took York. Father Warren's visit to Lincoln was at a time of deep apprehension, as the church watched to see who would be placed on the new ruling church council. For the Farther from Loxley, all he could do was wait and listen to the few who would talk to him, and their news and only hope, were the rumours they were hearing from London.

Across the river in the city of London, the thick clouds of black smoke drifted on a windless day. For as far as the eye could see, the black clouds spread out and hung in the air hiding the bright sun. The Sage sat on the edge of a crumbled wall high above the river bank and passed an apple to young Ben Winters, as they sat and watched most of the east of the city burn from the largest attack that the forces of Mason Knox had witnessed to date. From dawn, in one continuous sweep the Sage and Brian had drawn Loxley supporters from throughout the grey stone cities, and had masterminded over seventy attacks on as many ammunition factories as possible. Even now over twenty groups belonging to the resistance movement were still fighting, and setting off explosives all over the city. The Sage bit into his apple as his dirty faced young companion chewed on his. "It has been a good day for Loxley my young friend, we have done well." Ben gave a nod as he chewed.

"Is that it, can we go home now?" The Sage gave a soft chuckle.

"We still have much to do; this is just the start as we fight to stop anyone who supports the army of the dragon. One day the king will sit not far from here, and then we can all begin a new life."

Ben had grown a little, and now had a new set of woodsman's clothes, which had been made for him by Louisa. Tiny had made him a woven leather belt, and Dove had given him a small stainless steel dagger in a leather pouch. In his breast pocket was his most precious possession, a small brass compass that had been given him by the Sage just after the raid on Tintagel. He sat beside the Sage and swung his legs off the wall, as he thought about what would one day happen. "Where will you go when this is all done? Have you got a mum or dad to go home to?"

The Sage gave a smile as he looked out across the river. "I am not sure to be honest Ben. I have not thought of what will happen when all of this ends. All I have is a sister, and I do not know where she is, I guess I have nowhere else to be than here, so I will probably travel as I did before." His voice carried a heavy note of sadness; Ben was not to know of the heaviness of his heart, knowing the one place he would want to go was now beyond his grasp. Ben watched the eyes through the white familiar mask.

"I haven't got a mum or dad either, the Cutters killed em. What happened to yours?" Ben saw the flicker in the eyes of the Sage.

"I had a mum Ben, she was kind, gentle, and elegant, I watched her all the time as she went about her day caring for everyone. I have never met anyone who had a bad word to say about her, there has never been anyone who gave out as much love as she did." He sat up and took a long thoughtful breath, Ben was not sure if he was talking to him or just voicing his thoughts out loud as he watched with keen interest. "I never told her how much I loved her, it's my biggest regret, I should have said something before I left. It's too late now, she has gone forever." Ben put his head down.

"I am sorry, I should not have asked, forgive me I didn't want to make you sad." The Sage gave a smile and ruffled Ben's hair.

"Don't be sorry my little friend, I am glad you asked, because although it does make me sad at times, it is also good to remember someone so precious, I hope in my life I can do a little of the good she has done. There was a time where just for a while I had forgotten the lessons, she gave me in life. It's a good thing to remember what she taught me; I will never lapse as I did again." Ben smiled a big smile and his eyes danced.

"She must have been really special?" The Sage gave a happy nod.

"She was Ben, she was very special, there will be few like her in the future I am sure." The pair sat for a moment longer watching the smoke blot out most of London. Ben felt the urge to talk again.

"What will you do though? Will you stay here or move away?" The Sage bit into his apple, and chewed for a moment before swallowing.

"There will be much to do in a new world ruled by a king, I suppose I will move around and help out where I can. Maybe one day I will settle somewhere and live out my days working the land, I am not really that sure."

"Will you leave me behind?" It was not a question the Sage had expected to hear, it surprised him, as he had not given any thought to the future at all. He looked at the frightened eyes of his small companion and felt a tug at his heart.

"I will never leave you, if you truly wish to be my companion, you know I would not leave you behind, I just thought that maybe you would move on with some of the others or stay and help out with the king. You know Ben you have done much to help his cause, your reward for this should be equal to all of the others." Ben kicked at the wall below his ankles.

"I know it sounds silly, but you are the first real friend I ever had, you were good to me and looked out for me. I just hoped you would want to take me with you, but I thought if you settled down with someone, you know and had kids... I thought you might not want me anymore." The Sage lifted his hand up to the shoulder of the young boy.

"You think too much kid. As for settling down and kids, I don't think that is a path I will walk again. I think you and me are best off moving around together and selling wood and seeking our fortune don't you?" Ben gave a big smile. "Finish your apple, we will have men returning soon and a lot to do, get a fire going and get some food organised."

Ben swung his legs round over the wall, and onto the heavy stone section of floor with a happy chuckle. "Yeah, I am hungry too." He dropped off the wall as the Sage dropped down beside him.

"Now why doesn't that surprise me?" He gave a laugh as Ben scurried off to light the wood, and get the water on to boil. The Sage stood for a moment and looked to the north; his voice was quiet and reflective. "Nice dream, Alice would never buy into it though. You should have told her too Billy boy, who is the fool now?" He slowly turned and walked towards the old broken steps down to the ground floor, Ben was already far ahead of him stacking the wood ready to light it. Slowly he walked off to join him and help.

F ar across the river on the eastern side of London, Louisa dropped from the ten foot wall into the low bushes beside Rigger. She was tired and dirty and splattered with blood. "Hell that was rough." She sat back against the wall as Rigger quickly connected the wires to his portable charger. Both of them had been in some fierce fighting with the rest of the Outlaws, and the group of forty fighters had taken some heavy resistance costing them some of their team. Rigger wound the handle and waited for the signal; he gave a long sigh as he considered the moment.

"I hope this is enough, it's only half what I planned, let's hope it will start a reaction and take out the rest." Louisa gave a nod as she looked up hoping to see Ox and Dove.

"What's taking them so long?" Rigger patted her shoulder.

"Give her time; she has never let us down yet."

Louisa leaned out from the wall and stared at the high grey wall above her, the two ropes hung in place, but there was no sign of either of them. From high up the alarm bells rang in constant alarm, and the sound of gunfire echoed. Louisa could hear her heart pounding in her ears, as her eyes searched every window up the huge wall in hope of seeing the last two of her group drop to safety.

"They should be out now, what the hell is keeping them?" She felt a wave of relief run through her as Dove leapt out of the window, and grabbed one of the ropes. Her thin legs coiled into the rope and she began to slide down with speed. Just above her the large heavy frame of OX jumped out on to the rope. Louisa's heart skipped a beat as a black clad soldier jumped out behind him.

He clamped on to Ox hard, and both the men struggled, Dove stopped moving and she looked up to see Ox hanging by one arm, and hitting the man with his free arm, she began to climb back up her rope towards him. Ox hit the man several times, and it was clear to Louisa who had stood up to watch holding her breath, he was having an impact. The soldiers face was red and glistening with blood, but he hung on to Ox preventing him from slipping down.

Dove was climbing fast, as Ox took hold of the soldier by the back of the head, he thrust his face forward with power and the man recoiled as the thunderous blow from Ox's forehead collided with his nose. Louisa cringed as she saw the man's nose explode and the blood rained down on to her. The soldier seemed to go limp as Ox grabbed him roughly by the front of his shirt and dragged him off his overstretched arm and shoulder, with a wide swing of his free arm, he launched the soldier into the air, and Louisa watched as the soldier came rushing towards the floor ten feet to her left. He landed with a heavy thud, smashing through the brambles and small shrub like trees with a crunch.

Ox gave a smile as he took the pressure off his right arm, and began to slide down the rope quickly. Dove waited until they met and then followed him down, Louisa gave a gasp of relief, and began breathing again. Ox landed beside her with a smile, he winked at Rigger. "Blow the bugger."

Louisa slipped her arm around him and gave him a smile. "Don't scare me like that."

High above them out of the windows faces appeared followed by rifles, in the heat of a moments worry they had dropped their guard, Rigger's large hand gripped Louisa by the shoulder, and before she realised what was happening, she found herself flat on the floor as the bullets whistled down into the earth around her. With his large wide left hand, Rigger slammed it down on the plunger as he pushed Louisa into the wall, and the plunger whined as the voltage built, and was shot down the wires to the explosives.

High above, behind the soldiers, the air was lit with the flashes of a hundred sticks of explosives, the explosion roared in their ears, and they were lifted into the air and were tossed screaming out of the building. Louisa buried her face into the floor against the wall, as the ground below her shook violently, the noise that bounced into her covered ears was deafening, and she closed her eyes and tried to blot out the moment of fear she felt.

The wall above them bowed a little, and then tore away from the rest of the building. It exploded out into the sky and then rained back down to earth, battering everything four feet away from the wall, and crushing it into the ground.

Louisa lifted her head to see what was happening and rolled over to see the dense smoke and dust above her. Stones and dirt rained out of the sky and she brought her arms up to protect her face. Just above her Ox leaned into the wall, his large bucket like hand grabbed her shoulder and lifted her slightly, rolling her over to face the wall. "Stay close until it's over Miss Louisa; there is a lot of shit coming down."

"Ow! Tell me about it." Lumps of concrete were falling out of the sky the size of tennis balls, and bouncing all around them smashing the plants down as they hit at high speed, Louisa was as close as she could get to the slight protection of the wall, but her hips and sides had already received a few big hits that were starting to bruise as she lay there.

The few minutes it took, felt like forever, and when Rigger patted her leg to give her the all clear, she felt sore all over.

Louisa sat up and coughed as the dry dust clogged the inside of her throat, she blinked several times as the dust filled with tiny particles swirled into her eyes,

Rigger was sat back a few feet surveying the damage, he was dusted from head to foot in a fine layer of cement, and looked grey. Louisa looked up and the high wall had gone, what remained was a huge hole filled with splintered timbers and crumbled masonry. Fire raged all over the torn floors, and smoke bellowed high into the sky, it was utter chaos.

At her side Ox was packing up their equipment, he too was covered in the grey dust. Dove was looking up holding her bow, but there was nothing to shoot at, the few soldiers that could be seen were limp and dead, either blackened and burning, or crushed in the rubble. Louisa got up and lifted her bow. "Come on we have a rendezvous to make, the others will be blowing their charges soon, let's get the hell away from this place."

As the group ran through the undergrowth, littered with large pieces of smashed concrete and splintered wooden beams, behind them more explosions rumbled into the sky. From four different points the Outlaws had attacked and blown up large parts of Mason's number one armoury, and he had lost over two thirds of his supplies. It was a huge victory for the Sage and his forces, but it had taken a heavy cost from the group of forty outlaws. As the main store burned, twelve of their men lay dead from the brutal resistance of the Knox forces, there had been triple the soldiers they had expected, and Louisa was convinced that they had known they were coming.

Louisa panted as she slowed her pace next to Ox, as they approached the river wall, where the boat would pick them up. She drew in deep breaths to regulate her lungs. "We were expected." Ox stopped, and bent forward resting his tired arms on his knees; he took a long deep breath and turned to look at her as he crouched down beside her.

"I know, someone is talking to them, we aint safe anymore." Louisa gave him a nod.

"I know, we need to warn Master Sage as soon as we get back."

Ox stood back up and looked behind him as the other explosions shook the ground and took out the rest of the large storehouses. "When we get back you go down and tell him, I am done with hiding under the floor. If we have a spy in the camp, then I am staying out in the open where I can see em coming. I don't like living like a rabbit waiting to be trapped, from now on we stay in the trees as we should have done all along, it aint right woodsmen living in burrows."

Rune had eaten and rested, she was alone in the large wooden house of the Keeper with just Furry Face for company. Her mind had circled as she thought of all that Eve had told her, and Rune was starting to realise that she too shared a destiny that would bring her face to face with the Dark One again. The heat in the old wooden house was rising as outside the temperature soared, and Rune felt like getting out in the open to feel the breeze. From the side of the barn a thin worn track led into the trees, and as the large tiger walked casually beside her, she followed it under the shade of the dense large beech and hawthorn.

Her mind was occupied, and her right hand softly fingered the deep fur of the tiger beside her, she was unaware of the high canopy of the trees that seemed to shift and close together taking the brightest light off her, and keeping her in dappled shade. The Forest of Time was like no other place that Rune had ever seen, and even though she had much to think about, occasionally her mind would stop as she saw a flower or a coloured rock that she had no knowledge of. The woodland around her had many colours, and the floor was strewn with mixed colours of grasses, and brightly coloured flowers. Here in the world of wonder, the poppy had many forms, and she soon began to realise that like Opal and her daisy, Eve too had a favourite flower, for there were many drifts of deep red small poppies growing everywhere.

Crossing a small stream, the woodland to her left thinned, and a large wall of rock rose high into the air, Rune knew from the map that this place was known as the Lookout. From its flat top a person could see out across the forest and view the high cliff wall of the Citadel Mount on the far side of Avalon. From where she stood it was impossible to see the top, as the trees closed in high above her obscuring the view. She walked along the path that now ran parallel to the rough blue surface of the rock wall, and the path became wider and more defined. Rune had studied the map given her by her grandfather a great deal, and she knew at the end of the path was her goal, for even under the trees the heat of the day mixed with the damp ferns and grasses, and the humidity was high, causing her clothes to stick to her.

Her walk had lasted for over half an hour when she finally found what she was looking for. Walking out of the trees onto a smooth ledge of rock, she saw the deep cool pools of crystal clear water, and gave a happy smile as Furry Face padded up to the edge of the first one and bent low to drink. "Oh, you poor boy, all that fur on a day like today, I am wearing the thinnest cotton, and it feels like too much."

The tiger sat up and gave her a rough rattling purr, she smiled as she stroked his neck, and then she turned to the water and undid the tie on the front of her dress. Dropping her belt the dress hit the floor, and she moaned with pleasure as she walked down into the deep cool pool.

The walk from the White Pool, across the old marshland had taken far longer than Bear had expected. The heavy mist hampered their journey, and also having to carry Rowan slowed them down. Fox was as ever, keen eyed and had found an old dead tree with long white branches, and with the help of Bear and John, they had managed to cut away two long poles with his wire saw, and constructed a crude stretcher with the addition of Jade and Rowan's cloak. It had made a big difference as now Rowan's weight was distributed a little more evenly between John and Bear, and the pace quickened a little.

Rowan was unhappy at having to be carried like an invalid on the stretcher, he sulked for some time, but deep down inside he knew it was the best sense and at least it was more comfortable than being carried on the shoulder of John or Bear. Jade and Blades had given off quiet giggles as they saw Rowan, a proud Loxley general bouncing up and down with a long unhappy face.

As the long day stretched towards the late afternoon, the party finally came through the woodland and onto the road just above the Homestead. Had it been a clear day they would have seen the little cottage decorated with bright blue roses, and surrounded by a white picket fence, unfortunately the mist was thicker than ever, and so they looked at the soft dirt and gravel road unsure of which direction to take.

The group looked left and right. They knew they could not be far away from the cottage as they were on the road, but the mist made things impossible. Visibility was barely six feet, and the sounds all around them were dulled by the thick insulating blanket of the mist. To make things even harder, the heat of the day was at its highest, and it was becoming unbearable, as breathing alone caused the sweat to flow down their face. Jade was feeling very impatient. "We have to choose one direction; I say we go left."

Fox looked to the right. "I suppose we could send someone either way to check, then we know for definite." Bear was not keen.

"I think we should stick together, it's bad enough as it is like this, I mean I can hardly see all of you as it is." The irritation in Jade's voice showed.

"Well, we can't stay here; I say try this way, after all it's most likely considering Fagan's directions."

"Shush!" Crystal stood just in front of Jade, her hair was flat, yet her clothes seemed to still dazzle with whiteness from between the gap in her green cloak. She leaned forward as if listening hard; Jade stepped up beside her and whispered as she stared into the swirling mass of white cloud in front of her.

"What is it?"

"I am not sure... Listen." Everyone in the group had gone very quiet. Crystal twitched. "There... did you hear that?" Jade frowned.

"Nope... Why what was it?"

"Shush. There it is again... Is that chopping?" Jade stuck her finger in her ear and gave it a good wiggle, there was so much sweat and grime stuck to her from the long walk, she wasn't sure if it had clogged her ears.

"I can't hear a bloody thing." Fox walked slowly up to the side of the girls as he stared into the mist.

"I heard it... There is something down there, just not sure what." A dull thud came through the heavy air followed by a tiny cracking noise, it was so faint Jade was amazed any of them heard it.

"That's an axe." Crystal nodded with Fox.

"It most certainly is Pebbles, and it's an axe swung with a familiar arm, whoever that is knows how to cut wood." Jade gave a beaming smile.

"A woodsman.... Robbie?" Fox gave a happy nod.

"Certainly a woodsman, there is good rhythm to the cut of the wood... I think you were right; this way seems far more promising."

Round the back of the house Robbie swung the axe high, as he prepared the wood for the kitchen stove. There was quite a large pile of dried out logs, and he felt a need to do something. With his shirt off and glistening in sweat he swung the axe high, and it came crashing down on to the log with a resounding thud, followed by a loud crack as he twisted the axe and the log sprung apart.

Smokes was on watch by the front door, and the sound of footsteps brought him to the gate to try and get an advanced view of who was approaching. The small figure of a very wet and grimy Jade came out of the mist, and he felt the joy jump in his heart as the rest of the group followed. The gate swung open and he pulled her into his arms in a huge hug, the others all wearing smiles, passed him and he took their hands and patted their shoulders, as they walked into the garden and up the path to the old wooden door.

The sight of the group inside the cottage brought a huge sense of relief to Robbie and the first smile for some time. They all looked exhausted from the heat, and the long walk through the tunnels and across the marshland. Steph was delighted to see Jade, and her first question was of Rune, Robbie felt his heart drop as he saw the look of disappointment on Steph's face, when Jade explained she had not been able to contact her at all.

Like Steph he had thought that the unique bond Rune and Jade shared might have kept them in touch. As the party laughed and joked at being back together again, Robbie slipped out of the room into the kitchen where the back door was still open.

Stood in the frame he felt utterly lost as he stared at the piled up wood beside the door. He did not at first feel the hand that gently touched his shoulder and gave it a squeeze. "We will find her Robbie, there is a reason she is not here, don't lose hope she will be back for you."

Robbie turned to face the dirt smeared face of Rowan. He leaned against the wall supporting himself with a deep look of concern in his eyes. Robbie tried to smile, but he felt a deep emptiness inside himself and was not quite able to bring it to his lips. "Where is she Rowan?" Rowan patted his shoulder softly.

"I wish I knew, but believe in her Robbie, you know whatever it is that is keeping her from you, must be very important." Rowan's faith in Rune increased his respect for him, but Robbie could not understand why she had left them at such a dangerous time, the conclusion that had been floating round his mind came onto his lips.

"What if she is...?"

"She isn't... how can you even think that?" Rowan's answer snapped out of him before Robbie could finish the question, he looked at Rowan who lowered his voice and softened his tone.

"She is the centre of the circle Robbie; don't you think they would all know if anything like that had happened? Come on use your wits, something has happened and we have no idea what, but I can tell you one thing for certain, if she was dead or that vile woman had her prisoner, they would have delighted in telling us back in that cell, and they didn't. Rune is very much alive and out there doing something that will help, mark my words. Robbie you have got to pull things together, the group are two thirds back together, so chop more wood if you have too, but when you go back into that room, you must hide what you feel, because they are exhausted and weary after the hardest fight of their lives, and they need to see you as their hope and their leader, because if I am right you have got a bigger fight coming, and you need them secure in the thought they fight for the hooded man, do you understand me?" Robbie gave a gentle nod.

"Yeah... I know what you are saying." Rowan patted him harder on the shoulder.

"Good... because my leg is buggered, and at the moment I am no use to you, unless you can find me a seat above the whole lot of em, and then I can at least shoot at the buggers." Robbie gave a small smile.

"Thanks." Rowan gave a long sigh.

"Good.... Now help me to a chair, my leg is bloody killing me stood here."

It was not long before the small cottage became a hive of activity, Steph was first to fill the bath, and in the kitchen two large pans were put on to boil to keep the flow of hot water running as the women all sat together as they washed and cleaned. Smokes took over the kitchen using more provisions now that John and Blades who had two of their food bags had arrived, and a large pan of stew was set to boil out in the garden next to the back door, as the small wood burning stove was being used for the heating of the water. John decided not to mention the source of the meat as Smokes stirred the stew with pride.

Most of the men gathered in the garden, and Robbie listened to each of them as they gave their own views on their situation. Steph had been keeping Robbie up to date on how Hawk and his party were doing, and with the views of each of them, he could form a bigger picture of his position, and begin to gain some understanding of what he faced.

As the day wore on he sat alone on a small bench just outside the front door, and took the watch as the others sat inside and ate their meal. Alone in the heat and the silence, he suddenly felt his exhaustion creep into his limbs. The laughter inside seemed to die down as the group settled in the safety of the old wizards house, and one by one they drifted into sleep, the stillness seemed to creep around the tiny cottage and wrap them all in slumber, and alone with his thoughts Robbie without realising it, slipped into a deep and exhausted sleep.

Somewhere deep in the back of his mind, voices echoed. "All men have their own destiny young Robbie, don't ever forget that. You have a path to follow like all men, and if it forks from what you know into the unknown, do not be afraid to let your instincts guide you. Time will lead you to where you need to be." Robbie mumbled in his disturbed sleep. "Len?" A familiar feeling washed into his dream and he settled again, he felt a warmth around him that seemed to radiate through him and in his mind a dark pair of eyes watched him with care and love.

"Robbie Lad, you listen to me now and understand what I tell you. We are woodsmen born and bred: our life is the way of nature, because we live on the land, and with the land, and that is a special sort of life. It is a hard life but we do not always notice, and that's because we are accustomed to it. I am proud of you Boy; you are a true man of Loxley never forget that, because when things are bleak, that is when we are at our most dangerous. No matter what happens be a man of Loxley and show the buggers no fear, I love you son." Robbie jumped in his seat and his eyes snapped open. "Dad?"

An old face with a long nose and big white bushy eyebrows was a few inches away from his face. Robbie was startled at having the strangers face so close to him, and his hand rapidly went for the hilt of his sword, the old man gripped his hand tight as it touched the hilt, and Robbie blurted out in panic. "Who the hell are you?"

The man was strong, and Robbie felt his hand pinned to the hilt of his sword, the old face broke into a thousand lines and smiled.

"My word, aren't ye more jumpy than a buttercup? Here's me watching ye sleep all restful like the lilies, and then up ye jumps fidgeting and jumping like a daisy with root rot." He released Robbie's hand and stepped back to give a sweeping bow.

Robbie was unsure of what to do, and stared at the old man as his green hood fell back and his hair jumped out, snow white and sticking out in every direction, Robbie wondered for a moment if he was some sort of long lost relative of Crystal.

The old man swept a very well practiced and regal bow. "If I may good Lord of the wooden town north, and he of the hood. I am the Keeper, and sent here by both my ladies of my woods to bring aid and fair passage into the realm of safety and fair living. Like the moss on the trees, I am ye guide across a land blighted with many troubles worse than canker, and if it pleases ye, I shall show the way."

Robbie had been in a very deep sleep, and for a moment his mind felt mixed up as he tried to make sense of what the strange old man had said. All he could focus on was he had mentioned both ladies of the woods, and he struggled to make sense of it. Uncertain he asked.

"Has Rune sent you?" The old man stood up and gave a broad smile.

"No... although I must admit I am as excited as a Starburst Poppy at midsummer to know she is going to meet us. I have been sent to aid the Green Hood by the fair lady of the realm who cares for ye safety." He stopped for a second and thought. "I am sure little Green Eyes was told this, after all she was as happy as a daffodil when I left her." His bushy eyebrows moved up and down with his thoughts as he considered the parting moment. Robbie was unsure of what to do, and felt common courtesy should be applied.

"Well then good Keeper, will you not enter and inform us all of your plans, I am sure we have coffee or tea to offer you." It appeared to strike the right chord as the old man gave a beaming smile.

"Oh well, yes...my word. Does ye have sesame bread? I find it gives the legs the strength of the beech and the twist of a willow."

Robbie was not certain as he pushed the door, and it swung open, the tall old man dressed in a long green hooded cloak stepped through with a smile. "Oh it's been some time since Father Whitelines and I sat with the pansies and discussed the affairs of all, over lemon tea and barley crackers."

Robbie watched as the old man walked down the passage towards the living room, and then realised he should be following. He quickly stepped inside and felt a calmness wash over him, regardless of his strange manner, this man was going to meet Rune, which meant she was safe and was waiting. He hurried down the hallway to catch up with the strange figure and introduce him to the others.

CHAPTER TWELVE

TURNING THE PAGE

Deep in the marshlands to the south of Avalonia, Hawk and his group had used the small island surrounded by water to rest up in safety. Skip and Woody had used all of the cloaks to create a canopy using the branches of the old tree, and although the temperature had reached unbearable levels, the shade it created had given them some respite. Treen and Jaz were much cooler to the relief of Milly and Maddy, and although they had not regained consciousness, they both seemed to be sleeping more peacefully.

Taking it in shifts they had all been able to sleep, and it was clear to Hawk that they had begun to recover some of their strength, although there was still an air of melancholy about them, being around them with no jokes or wisecracks was a strange sensation. Harry had been the quietest of them all; he had taken very little sleep and sat on the edge of the bank staring at the water. His face looked very pale under his familiar wide brimmed black hat, and his eyes had lost their usual sparkle, Maggs watched him with concern in her eyes, even she had never seen him like this before.

Una felt the confusion and the fear deep inside him, and felt sorry for him; she lifted a cup and walked slowly down the bank towards him.

Harry continued to watch the water as she sat beside him and offered him the coffee. "This is the last of the coffee; you should drink in this heat." Harry took it with a slight nod, his eyes never leaving the water, Una sat quietly down and looked out at the tall grass and reeds on the far bank, Harry took a sip of the coffee.

"It's dropped two feet in a day." Una turned to him.

"What has?" Harry gave a nod across the water to the far side of the bank, where Una noticed the water level had sunken leaving a wide tidemark of damp mud below the grass.

"The water is evaporating, that's her goal. I tell you Una; she will bake this place and kill everything in it. There is nothing we can do now; she has complete control." Harry's voice was as clear as his head, and that was quite disturbing for Una, she had never seen him like this, and it felt very wrong.

"Come on Harry things just look bleak; you know Robbie and Rune would never allow her to do that. What's happened to the fighter and master of the samurai I know? You need to be more positive." Harry turned to her and looked her right in the eyes.

"It's gone, whatever I had it's not in me no more, them bloody flowers killed it dead. I know what I see Una, and we have not been able to stop her in a whole year of fighting her, if Rune had the power she would have used it in the castle, and killed her, but she didn't. I am telling you straight, everything here will fry, and when it does, so shall we." Una stared hard at Harry in complete disbelief, she shook her head slowly.

"You are wrong Harry, you might be sober for the first time in a long time, but you are anything but straight. Rune will find a way, and so will Robbie. You know I never thought I would see a day when you of all people would give up on those two, Robert Lox trusted you to look out for them and protect them, and you gave him your solemn word, and look at you now feeling sorry for yourself, and turning your back on the two people who love you the most. Let me tell you this Harry Lox, you aint too cosmic at the moment, so I suggest that before we pull out of here you get your act back together and find some of that cosmic ability, and fast, Robbie and Rune need us all."

She could not help but feel anger, even though she knew it was just the fear in him causing him to act that way, but she also knew they would need him, and she hoped it would at least have an effect. Harry did look a little shocked, but he just turned back to the water and began watching it again, Una got up and walked back up the slope to the camp, where Hawk had decided it was time to move on again.

Rune sat at the top of the flat rock high above the Forest of Time. She had bathed for a long time, and felt cool and refreshed for the first time in days. Having walked slowly up the steep path, she now sat under the canopy of an old twisted Hawthorn tree, and relaxed in the shade, as she looked across the white mist, and saw the top of the Citadel Mount. The whole of the valley of Avalon was buried under the mist, and on top of the mount she could see the bright sunlight glint off many moving things, it was more than obvious that there was a great deal of activity going on.

Without Robbie's telescope she knew it would be impossible to see anything in detail, so she closed her eyes and relaxed as she tried to sense the life of those at the top of the Mount. Her powers felt stronger with rest, and she felt the sensation of floating as her mind wandered out across the trees towards the working monks, who laboured in the hot sun building the scaffold to allow them to begin working on their new monastery above the clouds. Rune gave a broad smile as she sensed their thoughts, and understood what task had been appointed to them, her mind wandered as she learned more of what was going on in Avalon.

She had been sat there for some minutes when she realised what she was doing. In the past it had been natural to scan the area ahead to warn Robbie of danger that she did it without thinking, the moment impacted on her suddenly. "I am safe... I am in the Forest of Time and protected, my powers here are stronger, and they can only be weakened if I leave this area." It hit her like a bolt of lightning. "I can walk unseen in Avalon."

It was a defining moment of clarity, as Rune realised that her essence could travel anywhere, as it had in the past, it was her physical being that would be drained by the Star of the Merle. Her focus dropped to the mists and the valley of Avalon as she swept across it looking for her party, it had been a few moments before a very weak, but clear message connected with her. *"Rune is that you.... Rune can you hear me... Rune we are in the marshland, can you hear me?"*

Her excitement bubbled up inside her as she searched back towards the source of the signal. She concentrated as she looked for Una; it took a few moments before she got a fix and focused all her powers onto her. *"Una hear me."*

"Rune, Oh Rune it is you, we have been so worried, where are you, we are stuck in the marshland, and Treen and Jaz are very ill, can you help us?"

Una stood still at the water's edge, as she tried to focus all her might onto Rune. Her heart pounded with the joy of finally being able to contact her, Maddy was already on her feet trying to focus on Una to help her, but her powers felt very weak, and she was not sure if it was helping. The water, which had dropped another six inches and had now left a wide circle of mud in front of the bank suddenly glowed a deep violet. The pale violet figure of Rune rose out of the water and walked towards the smiling Una.

"I am here my sister, although I cannot be here for long, as this realm is under siege." Una opened her arms and embraced her warmly.

"Oh Rune, I was so afraid we had lost you, you have no idea how happy I am to see you." Rune gave a smile as she pulled out from Una's hug.

"We have little time, let me see Treen and Jaz." Una walked with Rune up the slope to where Hawk and Skip had taken down the shelter, and were busy preparing to leave, everyone smiled with great relief to see the violet figure of Rune come towards them. They all tried to speak, but Rune went straight to Treen and knelt down beside her, Milly gave a smile.

"The white flowers have brought down their temperature, but as you can see the poison within them still holds on to them." Rune raised a hand to Milly's shoulder.

"You have done well for them, thank you; it may have saved their lives."

It was an important moment for Milly, as the rest of the group all gave a nod of recognition for her care of their sick comrades. Rune placed her hand onto Treen's forehead and closed her eyes, everyone watched as for a few moments little flashes of deep violet lit up Rune's cheeks. She opened her eyes and took her hand away from Treen. Maddy sank to her knees at the side of her.

"Can you help her?" Rune gave a soft warm smile.

"Be at peace Madeleine my sweet sister, your daughter will return to you." Two tears ran from Maddy's cheeks as a wave of relief passed through her. Rune opened her palm and a small flower grew out of it, the violet flower opened its petals and bloomed. Rune picked off each of the petals, and then placed the small green plant on the floor. Within seconds the small violets spread through the grass bursting into fresh bloom, colouring the whole of the mound. Rune blew gently on the petals in her hand, and squeezed them hard. Holding her fist above Treen's lips she watched as a small drop of violet liquid dripped into Treen's mouth. She held her hand tight as more drips followed and Treen twitched.

Maddy gave a soft sob as her daughter moaned and moved her head; Rune looked at Milly who was watching fascinated. "Watch her, it will be some time before she is restored to full health, I leave you with more violets, boil them with the white flowers, and let her drink it every hour." Milly nodded understanding, as Rune turned to Jaz and began to repeat the process. As Jaz moved, Milly felt the lurch deep inside her stomach, and her tears rolled out onto her cheeks. It was a few moments before Treen and Jaz opened their eyes to the relief of all the party. Rune stood up and turned to Skip and Hawk as they watched with great relief.

"You must leave here as soon as they can walk. I cannot open a window here, it is too deep inside the realm of Avalon and will bring the attention of the Dark One straight to you, you must head northeast to the forest, and there I can bring aid to you. Travel until you meet the river, the curtain of light opens in front of a large rock face, you must not risk the road, travel round behind the rock and it will see you safely to the other side, I will get help to you. My time here is almost over, so travel with as much speed as possible and I will greet you all soon." Rune turned and walked to the side of the slope where Harry stood watching with a worried look on his face, he lowered his head as Rune approached him.

"The name of Loxley carries with it great responsibility Harry, remember the skills of a sword were never borne from a bottle, they were grown from a heart that had great love, and the desire to protect its kin. These people Harry have been more than family to you, lead them with courage for me." She lifted a hand and touched his chest. "Your family needs you, do not fail them." Two large tears dripped on his black boots, and Rune lifted a finger to raise his face to hers. "Harry we are all afraid, but we must conquer the fear inside us, Robbie needs you, and I need you." Harry lifted his hands and took her hand in his as tears ran down his face.

"I don't want to let you down honest, it's just like all I can feel is the fear, but I promise, I will try my best to come through for you." Rune gave a smile and stood up on her toes and kissed his cheek.

"I have never doubted you Harry, and I love you dearly, as does Robbie." Harry gave a sniffle and gave her a weak smile.

"I love you guys too."

"Then guide your party well, and soon we shall all be reunited in a safer place, trust me, and I will not fail you." Harry gave a nod, and Rune began to fade away, he held her hand until she had vanished, and then pulled out his bright spotted handkerchief and gave his nose a long hard blow. Rags gave a little giggle, and he wiped his face and looked at the others.

"Time to move on, so let's get packed up." The group sprang into action packing up the rest of their things as Maddy wept on Treen's shoulder happy to see her sat up. Milly gave Jaz a huge hug and held him as tight as she could, as Woody and Maggs quickly boiled the flowers to make a healing potion before they moved on.

Rune opened her eyes, and Furry Face nuzzled up against her, she gave him a big smile and scratched the top of his head. "I am safe my big baby boy, thanks for watching while I was gone. Come on we have work to do."

The large tiger gave a gentle rumble of happiness, and stood up at the side of Rune ready to leave. She walked out from the small patch of grass that grew beneath the old tree onto the hot dusty surface of the rock. For a moment her gaze lingered across the mist that blanketed Avalon, somewhere down there she knew Robbie was waiting for her, and yet she could not feel his presence, was he still below the ground in the maze of tunnels? She really had no way of knowing, and until he surfaced there was little she could do. Her bright blue eyes shone with life, and yet somewhere near the corners, there lay a hint of disappointment, Rune had wanted desperately to know how he was and where he was, not knowing felt hard and she felt the pangs inside her that needed to feel his warmth around her.

If the mist would clear, high to the west of Avalon she would have seen the wide band of green that marked the Forest of the Line, and there in its centre a thin wisp of smoke would have marked out the position of Robbie. In the heart of the little cottage, and under the protections placed on it by Merlin, Jade bounced around with glee, having given Fagan a huge hug. It was a great relief to all the others to see that her invisible friend now looked a little more solid, and had plenty of colour on his red rosy cheeks. John for one was very pleased to actually see the solid form of her friend, for a brief moment back in the cell he had wondered if his mind had been playing tricks on him.

The arrival of a visitor had felt like an occasion, and although most of them had eaten a great deal of the stew cooked by Jade and Smokes, it seemed polite to offer Fagan a meal, and it would be very rude not to join him. After much talk and happy banter, the group sat down to yet another meal with their guest taking a place of honour in the old rocking chair by the fireplace.

Fagan was positively delighted as they discussed their theories on the Star of the

Merle, Steph was now convinced that all of the powers of her circle were being slowly drawn into the star, and Fagan gave a very positive nod of agreement.

"Ye are of course good Mother correct, it was exactly for that reason Little Redstone was taken out of here so fast, she was much too precious to lose to Little Dark Eyes." Robbie felt his heart skip a beat as he held his spoon in mid air between his chest and his mouth.

"Rune is not here in Avalon? You do know where she is though, don't you?" His dark eyes stared at Fagan filled with hope, and the old man gave a smile as his thick bushy eyebrows twitched.

"At this current moment, I must confess I have not that knowledge." Robbie's face seemed to drop with disappointment, and Fagan spoke with a softer tone and kinder smile. "I do know that she is safe and protected by the White Lord himself, no harm will come to her." Steph stopped eating and looked at the man unsure of what he meant.

"Excuse me please Master Keeper, but which white lord do you speak of?" He gave a happy chuckle and leaned forward to pat her knee softly.

"Father Whiteline has left as I see ye know, so now there can be only one white lord, although I see we have a lady to continue the line of Father Whitelines, maybe I should call ye Mother Whitelines." Steph looked positively shocked.

"I am his daughter, but my dear Master Keeper, I have not the force of him within me, I can assure you." Fagan winked at her.

"I too like secrets, this is turning out to be most rewarding, I fear I have not enjoyed company as much since the sneezeweed ran amuck in the barn field."

He lifted his large spoon and took a large mouthful of the stew; he gave a contented sigh as he swallowed. "I must confess, the marsh hound is quite a beast, yet it has such wonderful flavour, ye must be very skilled indeed to hunt and trap one of these rare beauties."

Steph gave a cough as her face turned to a look of complete horror. She gave a very enquiring look at Smokes, who put his spoon down and looked at her innocently.

"What?" She gave another large choking cough, and her face seemed to hold fewer colours. Smokes shrugged unaware of why his wife seemed to be suddenly scowling at him.

"Pete, for god's sake, please tell me you have not cooked a dog?"

He looked at his spoon and the pale coloured meat. Robbie looked up from his bowl; his chewing had slowed as he looked to Smokes for his answer. He gave a broad smile as he looked at Fagan sat calm and relaxed chewing with pleasure.

"Your joking right?" Robbie and Steph both looked at Fagan.

"What about?" Smokes looked to his side where Jade seemed to have slid back a little, and was peering sheepishly out from under her fringe.

"Jade Opal.... You gave me this, just where exactly did you get it from?" Rowan gave a titter beside Bear who had looked away, and was staring at John who suddenly became very interested in his boot. Steph looked round the room at the others.

"OH MY GOD!" The spoon fell in the bowl with a clatter. "I CANNOT BELIVE WE HAVE COME DOWN TO THIS, WELL THAT IS BLOODY WELL IT, MIST OR NO MIST I AM NOT EATING THIS, I WILL GO AND BLOODY WELL FIND SOMETHING MYSELF."

The bowl thumped on the ground as Steph rose out of her seat, Smokes jumped up trying to stop her, but for Steph, she had reached the final straw. She stomped across the room towards the door. "I will take the heat, I can handle the worry and the fighting, I will face the Houlen and any other shit that bitch throws at me, but I will be buggered if I will stoop to the level of a bloody Cutter and eat dog."

She snatched her bow and quiver as she headed into the passage, Smokes quickly followed trying to calm her down. "Steph... Baby... Come on we already ate a bowl an hour ago, come on honey it's not that bad, you cannot go out there in the mists trying to find food, it's impossible."

Steph heaved on the door, as Smokes tried his hardest to convince her, but her temper was at its highest and the door flew open banging on the wall, she stopped in her tracks and Smokes bumped right into her. "Come on honey...oomph!"

Jade and Robbie both slid to a halt just behind them. Outside in the mists the dark shapes of the Houlen had stopped and were sniffing the air, it was an eerie sight as their heads twitched and jerked. Steph stood frozen as she watched them move slowly along the fence as if following a scent, and yet she stood in front of them just a few yards away in clear view, but unseen by them. Smokes felt her shudder as he watched them, and he lifted his arms around her and gently pulled her back whispering in her ear quietly.

"Come on Baby, get back in here where it's safe." She gave a gentle nod and took a slow step back.

Robbie pushed past and stood in the doorway with his bow; Jade came up at his side and whispered nervously. "Robbie, why haven't they attacked us?" He shook his head slowly.

"I am not sure Pebbles, it's like they can smell us, but they cannot see us, which is weird as hell because they are a few feet away on the other side of the fence." Fagan's large nose came past the side of Robbie's face.

"Ye can shout as loud as ye like, they won't hear ye... go on yell and scream, they will only jump and twitch like they have grass up their skirts." Jade did not understand at all, she could see and hear them, and she knew how keen their senses were from the fights they had with them.

"That's silly; they are there right in front of us look." She pointed with the arrow in her hand. The Houlen continued to move slowly along the fence sniffing the air and twitching with a hideous curiosity. Their red eyes scanned the area, and actually looked Robbie right in the eyes; it gave him a cold chill as he saw there was no recognition there. Fagan stepped out on to the garden path, and Robbie felt his heart jump, Jade stretched out her hand to grasp his cloak, but Fagan walked out on to the path without a care in the world.

"This is the house of Father Whiteline, did ye really think a man of his talents would leave ye all unprotected?" He gave a large happy smile as he walked right up to the gate, and stood within a foot of a large drooling Houlen as it sniffed the air and licked the side of one of its fangs. "My word, vile as they are, I do believe this one is prettier than his mistress."

Jade gave a giggle and stepped out into the garden, Robbie was cautious, he liked the strange old keeper, but he was not that sure he wanted to get too close and personal with a Houlen.

Jade stared at the beast with a contorted face that looked like stretched sinew. Its red eyes burned with hate, and yet she could see the confusion, she knew it had her scent, but she also knew that it could not see or hear her, which presented her with a moment to study what was in Avalon her greatest enemy. She blew across the gate, and the Houlen twitched, its eyes darted across the scene and its bottom jaw gave a sinister shudder, she stepped back as a cold chill ran down her spine. Fagan put his hand on Jade's shoulder and pushed her back. "Be careful little Green Eyes, they may not see ye yet, but we still have no idea of the power here, and the black star could be working as we speak."

"So let's use our best opportunity to deal with these vile beasts now while we have the chance." Jade looked back as William stood watching the Houlen with a look of abject distaste. Bear and Big John flanked him with Robbie. William took another step forward; his sword was already in his hand. "The way I see it, if they cannot see us, we should strike and even up the numbers a little." John was up for it, and he pulled on the hilt of his sword.

"Yeah, we owe them one for Alley, I say let's have em now while we can, it will save time later." Jade looked to Robbie who gave a nod, it made sense not to use this golden opportunity, she gave an evil smile and pulled out her sword and stared at the vile Houlen stood a few feet in front of her.

"Cool, let's give them the fright of their lives." Jade lifted her sword and thrust it hard into the chest of the Houlen. The scream was deafening, as the rest of the group moved with speed across the grass to the fence. The Houlen leapt into the air with shock, its thin claw like hands gripping its stomach, the others jumped with surprise and began looking from side to side to see their enemy. What they saw gave them a taste of fear like they had never known.

The first Houlen hit the floor screaming and thrashing around, two others stood close to it felt the burning pain as it slashed out in agony and tore into their legs. The others screamed in hate as they saw weapons appear in mid air and slice into them. Destiny came out of nowhere, and two Houlen screamed as the blade whistled past them and took off the head of another. John and Bear struck hard and fast with mighty blows, Smokes came out with Crystal and Blades, Todd was already out and at the very end of the fence where he loaded his bow, and hit those stood routed with fear out of arm's length in the face.

The scene was one of utter panic, as Houlen thrashed on the ground screaming and wailing, slashing anything within reach, others wailed and ran round in circles trying to find the source of their attack. As they lifted into the air, arrows appeared from nowhere and struck them deep in the head. Robbie felt the hate he held for the beasts roar up from deep inside him, and with both hands gripping tightly to the hilt of Destiny he hacked and chopped indiscriminately at them.

On the other side of the barrier created by Merlin, the Houlen wailed in pain and screamed for blood, but they could not see or hear their enemy. The air was filled with the scent of men, yet for the first time in their existence the scent of fear from the men they hunted was not there, the scent of fear that they could smell, was their own. The attack of the invisible enemy was just too much for them, and for the few who had managed to get into the cover of the thick mist; their fear followed them into the sky. In utter panic they shot into the air and collided with the trees as they fought their way in terror away from the scene of chaotic slaughter of their own kind.

As they screamed into the air and shot out of the mist into clear skies, they looked back with a frozen fear in their vile black hearts, but there was nothing to see as the mist covered everything with a protected blanket of white. Far below the ground echoed with the screams of those left dying in rage, and all they wanted to do was get as far away from them as possible. Fagan looked at the rusty old scythe he had found by the door. "Hmmm I remember making this; Father Whiteline was never a gardener, good thing I made tools to last." He wiped the blade with respect. Big John wore a satisfied smile as he watched the last of the wounded Houlen die.

"That felt bloody marvellous, those buggers will think twice before they mess with me again." Robbie stood panting next to Jade; Destiny held firm in his hand. He felt a warm glow of satisfaction and it felt good to even the score a little. The atmosphere of the group was very different, and a little like it had been in the past, having a chance to match the Houlen had lifted their spirits, after a week of hard exhausting fighting, winning one back made a great deal of difference. Robbie looked round at all the others.

"Is everyone OK?" They all gave a satisfied nod, with smiles on their faces, it felt good to see it and Robbie took a deep breath. "OK, some of them got away, so it's not hard to know who they will go too. This place might protect us from them, but I bet my last bit she will have other ways of getting in. Let's get prepared, grab as much stuff as you can, we will need to move out of here as quickly as possible."

Fagan noticed the change in all of them, as they jumped into action and he gave a soft smile as Robbie walked up to him. "Well Master Fagan if you would, I could use a good guide. I need to find Rune, and I think with you in our company, I shall find her much faster." Fagan lifted a hand and patted him on the shoulder.

"We have a long walk with many things to talk to; there are trees out there that will bring us news faster than anything else. Get ye things and I will take ye to a place of safety." He paused for a second and thought. "Hmm do ye think he will mind me taking this? It's a little dull on the blade and could use a sharpening." Robbie gave a shrug and smiled.

"I think Father Whiteline won't really be needing it, and if he does, you could always return it to him." Fagan gave a happy smile.

"I could polish the handle as well, ye know there are many grasses that like to be cut and kept trim. They wail and make a hell of a din if ye use a dull blade; I think it's best for everyone if I give this a little working back up."

"That is a grand idea Master Keeper, you do that." Robbie chuckled as he walked back into the house to gather his things, and Fagan eyed the blade of the scythe with the eye of a keen craftsman.

The following ten minutes were hectic. Smokes, Blades and Jade raided the kitchen; Robbie was more than pleased to find ample amounts of coffee beans. Most of the quivers were empty, so they packed them with extra supplies. Jade stuffed herbs and spices into her bag, and John shared out a large sack of flour with Bear and Smokes. Todd and Blades improved on the stretcher for Rowan, and Steph found some powdered pain killer in a cupboard, which although she knew it was very old, she thought if it was dried, it might still be safe to use. She gave a quarter of the measure written in a neat hand on the side of the bottle to Rowan, and he relaxed as they put him back on the stretcher.

Fagan suggested they leave by the back door; William had watched for a while and found a pear tree in fruit, so he filled his bag as he kept an eye on the fence line. The mist was so thick it was hard to see much further, but there had been no more signs of the Houlen, and when all were assembled outside the back door, Fagan gave the word, and they quickly slipped over the fence and into the trees.

Like Robbie, Fagan walked quietly and quickly. Bear and Todd walked right behind him holding the stretcher, which contained Rowan, as the rest followed closely behind. With a victory under their belt, and having a guide who had great knowledge of the area, had a very positive effect on the group, and Robbie found himself feeling light hearted and almost excited as they trooped at a great speed through the woodland.

It felt like he had turned a page, and was now heading in a new direction, the last week had been the toughest he had ever known, and for a short time he had buckled under the pressure. As he left the old cottage, he had begun to realise that he had no choice but to press forward and continue the fight. It was true the odds were against him, but they had been since he had begun to fight Mason. Making that important decision to fight on had changed everything, and he felt a little hope grow inside him. The thought of finding Rune was also playing a big role in his new found optimism, he knew she was somewhere and safe, that alone lifted a huge weight, and knowing his new guide had some idea of where she would be, lifted his spirits tenfold. His mind drifted as he thought of holding her again in his arms, it had felt like so long, and now he could not wait to pull her close again.

Deep in the Forest of Time, Rune sensed something change, she gave a smile as for the briefest of moments she felt a very familiar feeling. In the blink of an eye it was gone, but it was enough, and she gave a big smile as she looked at the huge tiger stood beside her. "He is coming I know it." The tiger gave a deep rumble, and rubbed his large furry face against her. Rune turned feeling joy rise up inside her and looked to the path she knew would take her back to the cabin. She gave a happy giggle and set off towards it with the large tiger bounding along beside her.

Steph looked up as she walked, just for a second she had felt Rune, she gave a smile and Smokes blew her a kiss. Steph gave him a scowl, and his smile faded. "I have not forgotten Peter Lane."

Smokes gave her a pleading look. "Awe, Come on Baby, I didn't know honest, they just gave it me and said they had caught it that morning, I didn't know what it was, it looked like venison."

Jade gave a giggle a few feet behind, and Steph turned and glanced back at her. "Don't think you are off the hook either Missy, you should have told your dad what you caught, I cannot believe a daughter of mine would eat something so foul as a dog, I have no idea what we are all coming to these days." Smokes gave a smile.

"See Baby, as I said, I had no idea."

"You're not off the hook yet." Smokes stopped, and held out his arms in disbelief.

"But I didn't know... How can it be my fault? I am innocent." Steph gave a smile as she looked straight ahead and carried on walking.

"Peter Lane you were never innocent, that's why I married you." Jade giggled as she caught up with her dad, he winked at her.

"She loves me see, I will be forgiven by tea time." Jade gave a big smile.

"I can hear you... Oh and by the way, it's gone tea time."

The rest of the group all smiled as they walked through the thick swirling mist following the tall dark figure of Fagan, as his long green cloak flapped behind him, and his thick white hair shone with the droplets of water from the mist. All of them felt a little happier and felt their hopes rising again. They had rested a little and had some good food, even if Steph did not agree, and with fuller stomachs they followed their guide, and wondered what another day in Avalon would bring.

Rune came to the turn in the path, and looked ahead to the clearing where she knew the cabin would lie. Furry Face came to an abrupt halt and gave a deep growl as he viewed the mist in front of him. The mist swirled and faded, and for a second a tall figure in a black tattered cloak appeared, and then disappeared back into the mist. Rune stood silent and watched, she could sense no presence and it worried her. The figure appeared again, but it was hard to make out any of their features. Her finger slipped into the deep fur of the tiger's head and she gripped it. "Who are you, and what is your purpose here?"

The figure remained motionless and spoke with a soft calm voice. "It is time. Prepare child of the Redstone, for soon you will see all that was written, make haste for the fate of all things will rest on your shoulders. Your destiny stands above all others; soon you will be called upon, and shall begin the fight that will decide the fates of many." The mist swirled and he disappeared from view again, Rune felt uneasy as the mist began to swirl backwards away from her, she shouted down the long path.

"Who are you? Tell me who you are and what do you mean prepare?" The mist evaporated into the air and the road was clear, Rune felt a tinge of fear run down her back and held on to the tiger firmly. There was no reply, and she suddenly felt very much alone. Her fingers trembled in the soft fur, and she felt her stomach twist. "Oh, hurry Robbie, I don't like this, I want you close to me again." Her voice felt empty in the vast quiet woodland, and for the first time since arriving in the Forest of Time, Rune felt very uneasy.

CHAPTER THIRTEEN

SAFE HAVEN

Fagan took Robbie and his party from the back of the Homestead, across the thin woodland and into the White Marsh. Fagan had quickly begun to understand the objectives of Morgan le Fey, and as the mist became even thicker, he knew that the marshland would be much drier and safer than it had been in days of old. Although he had said little to Robbie, he now felt a strong sense of urgency, having seen the large numbers of Houlen that had been sent to find the small party. Fagan remembered the final days of Avalon, when he had been living in the town, when the Houlen had struck. In all those years of the past, Morgan had only ever needed half a dozen to complete her work.

The fact that there had been several dozen at the cottage, and according to the group there was a much larger number somewhere else in the realm, he felt concerned about what she had planned. In the thick mist they would be very exposed to a dark beast that hunted by smell, so rather than take the most direct route across the woodlands and plains, he quickened his pace and headed for the higher ground of the pass that ran along the high rocks of the Giants Shoulder.

As expected, the marshes had dried out a great deal, it was hot work surrounded by the flies that were breeding at ten times the rate they would normally do, but the soft short spongy grass was easy to walk on, unlike the taller reed of the southern marshland. The group made fast progress to the start of the pass; they were in high spirits and felt stronger thanks to the large meal they had eaten. Fagan knew it would give them the burst of energy they needed to tackle the start of the steep climb upwards that was the beginning of the seldom used pass. Robbie puffed at the side of Fagan as he climbed up the steep gradient cut out of the rock, as it weaved slowly upward towards the top of the thick blanket of heavy mist. His hair shone with the fine droplets that had settled on his long main of dark hair, as he looked ahead into the gloom hoping to see an end. "I have no idea where you are taking us Master Keeper, but surely there must be a route that is easier than this?" Fagan breathed heavily as they trudged forward.

"I fear My Lord of the Wooden Town, that down below ye would make too easy a target for her beasts, on this high pass above the cloud, ye all have a better chance of spotting her beasts as they approach." Robbie gave a shrug, and stopped to catch his breath.

"I see your wisdom; it makes good sense.... Please call me Robbie, out in the wilds I prefer not to use a title, it makes for quicker conversation, and keeps everything simple." Fagan gave a nod back to him.

"Less words in thin air, I can see how that would work... Robbie."

He gave a warm smile as the group came panting up to a halt behind them, he pointed up the path to where the pass turned. "One more turn, ye will be at the top and in the daylight again above the mist, I do believe ye will feel as tickled as Day Lilies on a May morning." He turned with a smile and walked off again at great speed. Smokes took the end of the stretcher off John who was bright red and sweating profusely, behind him, Bear groaned with relief as Todd took the other end, and once again they all began to move forward slowly, with Steph and Jade watching the rear.

The climb was slow going, and although it felt like midday when they finally walked out of the mist and into brilliant sunshine, it was actually ten o'clock at night. For the first time in days, Robbie actually felt as if he was outside, he stood on the edge of the high shoulder and looked out over the mist towards the Citadel Mount. Everything below from the high rock wall he stood on, right across the vast valley to the mount in the distance, was hidden under the white blanket, and it was like standing on a cloud watching the rest of the world under the blazing hot summer sun. "Wow I cannot believe how far we have travelled."

"I can, that run down the tunnels from the prison cell, felt like it would never end, I can see why now, we covered most of Avalon underground." Jade's hair flowed backwards in the gentle breeze as she stood beside Robbie; he lifted his arm and pulled her closer.

"What is important Pebbles, is you made it, you went in there alone, and brought everyone out safe, I am really proud of you, that took guts." She gave a soft smile.

"Not really, Fagan showed me the way, without his guidance I think I would have just gone round in circles; he was pretty cool down there." Robbie gave a small smile.

"I still think it was brave." He turned to face the group who had all collapsed on the grey stone floor, and were laid back resting. "Ok ten minutes to get our breath back, and then we press on...Jay, Blades, keep a good watch."

Both of them sat wearily back up and gave a nod, they faced the edge of the high rock wall overlooking the mist and rested as they took the watch, Robbie wandered along the path to where Fagan stared out into the distance, he had a curious look on his face. "What is it Master Fagan?"

The old man scanned the surface of the Citadel Mount, but it was miles away, and he was not sure exactly what he was looking at. "Tis long since I stood up here, yet even to my old eyes, it seems this realm has more guests than I first thought."

Robbie slipped his hand inside his lower pocket and took out his brass telescope; he pulled it apart and put it to his eye, then scanned the pass up from Avalonia right up to the old Citadel.

Robbie had expected a lot of troop activity, but what he saw surprised him. Cart after cart wove in a long procession up the steep road toward the top of the mount. Each cart was loaded with heavy supplies, and monks walked in an endless line at their side. At the top of the mount, he could just make out the shape of the scaffold that was being erected around the site of the old Citadel. "It looks like Mason and his mother have got a bad dose of religion, in fact looking at the numbers I would say a very large part of the church has arrived, there must be hundreds of them up there swarming around like ants."

He scanned along the top plain of the mount, where he could see the smoke rise from the many fires, which provided the endless supply of food to the working monks. Long rows of tents had been erected, almost like a military camp; Robbie could see the organisation of such a large amount was being executed with precision. It was the final conformation he needed to understand that this had been planned for a very long time. Fagan squinted to lessen the glare of the high sunlight in his eyes.

"Twinkle by daylight is metal on the move." He pointed a long finger to the northern side of the Citadel; Robbie glanced back at him, and then trained his scope across the rock shelf towards the source of the glint from the sunlight. There were many large boulders obscuring his view, but he could just make out the slow movement of a small party. "Now that is interesting... What are you up to Le Fey?"

High on the wall of rock that was the Citadel Mount, the wind picked up its pace and blew the dust of the hot cracking rocks across the paths, and into the large fragments that remained of the old building. The cooking fires burned bright, flickering violently in the wind. The Mount that had remained empty for such a long time was now a hive of activity. Cartloads of monks had arrived from all over the country on the promise of the new monastery that would be built on the highest rock in Avalon. As the sun increased the heat of the day, already the wooden scaffold had been half built in preparation for the long process of rebuilding. The news that the strict Brother Argus, would head the monastery when completed had attracted far more members of the faith than any had expected.

Morgan le Fey viewed the start of the work with little interest, she had no use for their lifestyle or religion, but even so she was not foolish and recognised that Argus had done a great deal in the aid of her son, especially when it came to helping swing the opinions of many of the people in favour of his coronation. Argus was very influential in the church, his devout attitude had gained him great favour with the previous administration, although on a personal level, Morgan had nothing but contempt for a man she saw as a two faced greedy, sadistic hypocrite. In her mind you are both greedy and despicable or else you joined the hooded man; you could not be both saint and sinner. But at least turning Avalon into a community dedicated to the God of man, did give her a twinge of happiness knowing that one more nail in the coffin of Hearne would bring him closer to his demise.

Four Houlen led the way with burning torches, as the Dark One and her assistant followed along the long road that made its way down from the Citadel, across the wide rock plain to the second smaller peak of The Rest.

In the bright light of the day the dark shape loomed rough and stark, devoid of all plant life. Ursula was enjoying the walk in the cooler air of the breeze so high up, even though the Star of the Merle had caused the freak weather conditions; its owners were equally as uncomfortable with it.

The cool air across her face and through her long black hair lifted her spirits, and she smiled in the breeze as she walked slowly down the steep incline, which would bring them on to the plain of the resting place of the first true king of the realm. Ursula was interested in the carved out tomb that contained the last remains of Uther, Igraine, and the mighty legend Arthur Pendragon. "Mistress why do we need to visit this place?" Le Fey walked with long strides as if in a hurry, her long black dress snapped in rhythm as it blew in the wind.

"I have been here often over the years; this is the only place I can come when I feel the need to be close to my mother. Although tonight we have other business, we are vulnerable to the Flower Girl, she has found a means of touching our central life force, and I cannot allow that to happen again. It is my hope that certain elements of the past lines of the king, can help me make a potion to keep her out of our hearts, and therefore give us a chance of destroying her forever." Ursula seemed a little confused.

"How has she touched us mistress? I have not met with her or faced her in combat." The Dark One gave a shrewd look, the flickering shadows from her blowing hair, lit her face in a sinister way, and it worried Ursula.

"I cannot be sure as to how she overcame the force of the star, but during the fight I felt her take hold of the life force within me and try to extract it. If she has the ability to reach inside of my defences, then I think it is obvious she will attempt at some point to attack you, after today I shall ensure she remains well away from meddling with both of us."

The Rest was a large towering mound of solid stone. In an age when man put great efforts into his craft, it had been carved out into a tomb fit for any king.

To the people of Avalonia, it had been a symbol to the king they loved, that they made it on the second highest peak, so that the king who had passed could still be seen from every part of the realm. At the western side where the sun set, was a great carved doorway, which depicted the life of Arthur from the sword in the stone, to the final moments where he had been carried back to the realm of Avalon. The Dark One sneered at the sight of the carvings, depicting their hero and symbol of a true king. "He was as arrogant as his father; he certainly had no concept of family he barely recognised me."

She pushed on the large solid door plated in gold, and it swung soundlessly open to reveal a small chapel. Long shafts had been bored into the walls, so that the light shone down them with the sunrise to light the isolated altar of stone that bore a large golden Celtic cross. "Even he turned away from those who gave him his right and turned to the god of men, how that old wind bag of sticks Hearne must have felt I have no idea, but I would imagine it came as a real betrayal, yet they supported him no matter what. Do you see what fools they all are my little assistant? He betrayed them, and yet still to this day they honour him, they are pathetic."

Ursula looked around the round room, she had not really thought about the fact that Arthur had become a Christian. Here in the anti chamber to the tomb it felt strange, after all it was the granddaughter of the Green Lord that they faced in the battle to seat his relative. The walls were decked out in elaborate tapestries that once again depicted every aspect of the king's life. The altar was quite plain except for the golden cross, which was three foot high and elaborately engraved with runic symbols of a language Ursula could not read.

The Dark One paid it little attention as she made her way across the room toward the flight of steps that led down below the chamber, Ursula looked round at her. "Isn't this place guarded?" Her mistress sniggered.

"They were so proud of their king they thought no one would enter here to do harm. Foolish thinking, but no one has ever tried, they just wandered up here at all hours to weep and lay flowers. Not one of them ever placed so much as a weed at my mother's tomb, and she bore him for nine months, and suffered the pains of bringing him into the world for them. No one ever said as much as a kind word of thanks, all they care about was how wise Merlin was to ensure his survival after the death of Uther. They have treated her like a whore; she was the one who was wronged."

The Dark One rattled on down the stone steps, and Ursula hurriedly followed, she was intrigued more than ever by the talk of her mistress. In all the years she had been there as a crone or herself, she had never heard her speak so openly, she pressed her hand to the wall as the Houlen guard lifted the torch to light the way down. She ran down to catch up with her mistress, and skidded to a halt as she reached the lower chamber and stared at the three large tombs.

At the far end of the large room stood two huge works of stone, the first was white polished marble inlaid with golden runes; it bore the wide letters that spelt the name of Uther. At the northward end of it, was a tall white statue of the massive king holding aloft a mighty sword. Ursula felt her breath as she slowly drew it back in. The tomb of Uther was decked with hundreds of bunches of bright white lily like flowers, she walked slowly towards it, but it was not his tomb that held her breath.

The tomb of Arthur was as big as his fathers but was solid gold. On the top lay a golden life size statue of him lay with his sword of power along his chest. Even in the partial darkness, it shone like a beacon, she walked almost in a trance towards it, and marvelled at the craftsmanship and the skill put into the work. All around the base of the tomb, a band six feet thick of flowers covered the floor; Ursula walked round looking at them in a strange way. "If Avalon has been empty for hundreds of years, then who has been placing all these flowers here?"

From somewhere far behind her, the scornful voice of the Dark One echoed in the chamber. "Who cares, the tomb is empty, Rhiannon trusted no one with the body of her precious Arthur, only she truly knows his resting place. These fools have laid flowers for hundreds of years believing he was here, but he isn't I looked about two hundred years ago and the box is empty." Ursula gave a gasp.

"You looked?" The Dark One gave a sly smile.

"Hell yes, one of his bones and the right spell, and I would have had his entire line walking right towards me. I might have known that bitch would spoil everything and hide him where I could not find him, Uther's bones were useless." Ursula noticed the sly smile on the lips of her mistress, and then she saw the plain stone small tomb, and felt a twinge inside her stomach.

The tomb that held the remains of Igraine was a very simple oblong of stone with a thick slab on the top. The Celtic runes carved into it simply spelt her name; there was nothing to state that she was queen to Uther, and mother to the legend that was King Arthur. She ran her hand along the top of the smooth granite slab and felt saddened. Igraine was a true Celtic Queen of standing, and yet to see the tomb it felt like a slap in the face, she could not imagine how her mistress really felt considering it was her mother; in many ways she now understood her anger at those who surrounded Arthur. Her mistress watched her with a curious look.

"Is this the tomb you expected for a Queen of high Celtic standing? For generations they have slandered my name and fought to suppress me, and yet here I stand beside the tomb of the woman who gave the life to my half-brother. Tell me my young assistant; am I wrong to oppose them?"

There was a tone to her voice that hid the bitterness and the pain that she felt deep down, it was the most human that Ursula had ever thought her mistress to be. Here at the side of a plain stone tomb in full view of other tombs of high splendour, she could not disagree with her.

"You are not wrong, your mother deserved to be treated better than this, she should be honoured and praised, for without her they would not have had their hero and legend. I wish I had not come here this night." The Dark One gave a small nod of recognition.

"In a world that has seen so many women of power, my mother had no place, a day will come when everyone will see her as the true Queen of the Celtic lines, I will ensure it... Now come we have work to do."

The four Houlen guards placed their torches in the brackets on the walls decked out in shields and weapons all bearing the Pendragon crest. Taking a corner each they lifted the huge white slab of marble off the top of the tomb of Uther. Ursula was more than a little surprised at their strength. Morgan le Fey was quick to set to work, she peered over the side of the tomb where below laid the dressed corpse of Uther Pendragon. "No sword, his sword was never buried with him, I came here with Mason some time ago to try and get it. No one knows what became of it." She lifted the arm and slid off the metal glove revealing the dusty bones of a large skeletal hand.

"All we need is a finger." Ursula blinked as she pulled it clear of the hand with a snap, and slipped it into her pocket. "That's enough."

She gave a nod to the Houlen who slid back the top of the slab. "Make sure all the flowers are neat, we need to leave no signs that we were ever here."

Ursula gave a nod and bent down and picked up the flowers that had slipped off the top. She placed them back neatly and then walked around the large white tomb ensuring all was left neat and tidy. When everything was right the Dark One headed back to the steps and returned outside, the Houlen lifted their torches off the brackets and lit the way as they moved out of the chamber. Outside the Dark One walked briskly back along the path towards the Citadel.

"When we get back to the caves below, we shall use the heart of this realm to perform the charm in, we have time as the ritual will need to be made just before dawn, even if there is not going to be one, the timing must be perfect. Draw out the symbols and place the candles, then we shall rest, and at the given moment we shall take the protection we need."

Ursula nodded as she trotted along trying to keep up with the brisk strides of her mistress; she clung to her woven black bag, where the bottles of powders for the marking of the symbols rattled. The path wove through the large rough boulders, and dangerously close to the edge of the high cliff, Ursula looked over and saw the vast drop into the white mist below, she moved closer to her mistress as the breeze blew into her, and kept her head down concentrating on keeping her feet well and truly in the centre of the path.

Robbie lowered the scope. "I think Master Keeper; we should move and move quickly. I have little trust of this woman, especially when she visits the tomb of a king she despises. I am not sure what she could possibly be up to, but I will bet my last bit it's trouble for all of us. We need to get to Rune and let her know of this." Fagan gave an agreeable nod.

"We will cross the shoulder quickly, and then it's down into the forest, have no fear, ye will be in a place of great safety by midnight."

Robbie gave the signal, and the group began to stand and get ready for the last leg of their journey, over to the south Harry was taking the lead with Hawk, as they approached a large wall of stone, edged by what had once been a fast flowing river. They crouched down in the tall reed, and watched as cartloads of monks and soldiers came out of a large decorative archway in the rock that shimmered with white light, and trundled down the road toward the ford that crossed onto the long Queens Road to Avalonia. Some distance behind them, Una sat with a very happy Maddy, as Treen and Jaz sat in the grass and sipped the tonic that Maggs had made for them. Both of them looked a thousand times better and they both had gained in strength over the last few hours. It had given the group a strong sense of relief, and a new sense of purpose. Woody and Rags both sat at the rear, ever vigilant for the slightest sounds of any hunting Houlen. Harry looked down at the riverbed, which was now just a small trickle of water about a foot across, the rest of the river was sand, mud, and stones. "Well at least we don't have to swim." Hawk gave a chuckle.

"To be honest Harry, I wouldn't mind a dip in the water, it's so bloody hot, I think wading in deep water would be delightful about now. Ok I have seen what I needed to, that wall of stone is not that wide, and there looks like there are enough trees on the other side to give us cover. What do you think, move a little further downstream and then come out behind the rock?" Harry gave a nod.

"Yeah, I wanna stay well out of sight of those soldiers." Hawk turned and relayed back the signals, and the group rose up from the grass and made their way further down the river. Harry found a rough stony place to cross, and like lightening, in small groups they crossed the dried up stream, and made their way onto the opposite bank.

It took less than twenty minutes to cross the water, and weave round the back of what looked like a massive one hundred foot boulder, which housed the opening to the Curtain of Light. In the midst of the tall reeds and grasses on the other side there was a long island of solid earth littered with trees, Hawk guided the group up on to it and looked back as they scurried past him. The mist here was a lot thinner and his vision was clearer, back on the road quite far away the carts continued to move slowly out of the stone arch at the curtain, and move in a long line toward the town at the end of the long white road. Having taken a mental note, Hawk turned, and followed the group along the long island towards the bank of the next river, which marked the boundary of the marshlands and the start of the forest; he felt a strong sense of relief growing inside him as he hurried to catch the others.

Fagan stopped at the top of the long pass that wound round and down the steep side of rock into thick green trees. "Make ye way down and onto the path, ye will have no trouble if ye head in a straight line towards those rocks, for that is the Look Out, and marks the border of my home." Robbie felt a little confused.

"I thought you were going to guide us?" Fagan patted his shoulder.

"Ye have all arrived, and I am needed elsewhere." Jade looked at him with sad eyes.

"But I thought you would be staying with us?" Fagan gave her a soft smile.

"Does Little Green Eyes trust old Fagan or not?"

"Of course I do... It's just that I thought we would be going to your house with you. I don't want you to leave us." Fagan pointed down at the green canopy of the trees below.

"Ye see all of them down there?"

"Yes."

"Well, my little green eyed friend, they is chatting like ye never heard, they are in a positive dizzy with excitement as they feel ye coming, and they is chatting like that because that is my forest and those are my trees. My home starts there, and if ye follow that path to the large pools and turn right at the base of the Look Out. Well, that path goes right to my door, so if ye pop along like bramble does, I will be back there as soon as I have helped ye friends in the marshes." Jade gave a huge smile.

"Are they really talking, and you can hear them?" Fagan gave a chuckle.

"Blow me, ye has no idea of how much strength they have used, chatting like old women in the market they are, such is their excitement, I tell ye, I can barely hear meself think." Robbie smiled as Jade looked down the path and giggled.

"You can really talk to them, and they can talk back, and you understand them?"

"I can indeed, I am more blessed than the spores of a whistle fern at midnight, I will tell ye that much." He patted her shoulder gently and smiled. "Ye hurry on to safety and I promise ye over the next few days I will introduce ye and see if this old keeper can't get em talking to ye to." Jade's excitement seemed to rise rapidly at the thought of talking and learning how to talk to trees.

"Really you promise?"

"I does, now hurry and get into safety." Jade turned and scurried down the path as Fagan gave a nod to Robbie. "Ye will be fine from here, hurry to safety, I will not be long." The others were already heading down, as Robbie turned and began to follow. Fagan watched for a moment from under his thick bushy white eyebrows, and then pulling his cloak tight around him, he turned and took a different path; and with the blink of an eye he was gone.

The group hurried down the steep road and underneath the heavy canopy, the first thing they noticed was the lack of mist. A long path headed in a very straight line away from the rock road towards the high stone outcrop that Fagan had pointed out, for as far as the eye could see it was clear, a long lush path lined with trees, flowers, and ferns of many colours, everyone stood for a moment and enjoyed the vision of the Forest of Time, there was no doubt at all, this was the woodland to beat all others.

Rune sat bolt upright in her chair on the porch of the old wooden house, making Furry Face jump.

"Robbie?"

"Rune... Rune is that you, where are you?"

Tears flowed into her eyes and rolled onto her cheeks, and violets sprung up and raced across the floor of the open glade in front of Fagan's cabin.

"I am coming."

Steph jumped with fright as a massive explosion of bright violet light burst out in front of her on the path. Rune came hurtling through it, and launched herself into Robbie's arms weeping, he snatched her tightly, and pulled her close ending the yearning to hold her again as he squeezed her shaking body with all of his might. She buried her head in his shoulder, and he held her for a few moments soaking her up into his body again with happiness. Releasing her slightly, she slid back in front of him with bright blue happy eyes filled with tears and he kissed her.

"Oh Rune I have been so worried, I thought I had lost you." She shook in his arms and just snuggled as close as she could get, everyone stood smiling, and feeling a huge sense of relief at seeing her again.

Smokes nodded at the others and they understood, slowly they walked onwards and left the two of them alone together holding each other. The violet archway stood open, and Jade took the lead with a huge smile next to Rowan on his stretcher, and guided them into the archway, and out on the other side where they all came to a halt as they looked upon the cabin of the Keeper of the Forest of Time.

Robbie stroked back her red hair and smiled as he looked upon the familiar pale white face, dusted with the faintest of freckles. Rune's bright sapphire blue eyes sparkled with happiness. "You have no idea how much I have missed you, it's been hell out there trudging through tunnels and fighting in the woods, when all I wanted was this." She smiled and moved closer.

"Don't think about it, we are back where we belong again, I missed you too, so much has happened Robbie I hardly know where to begin." He lifted a finger to her pale lips.

"Then don't, we can discuss all that later. I don't care if she blows up the whole bloody woodland, this small time here and now is ours, and I want to savour every moment of it." She snuggled into him and he held her close.

"Ok Robbie." Furry Face sat down in front of the window and watched Robbie holding Rune in his arms, above them in the trees, birds fluttered and sang their songs of happiness as the bees buzzed in rhythm, and for a brief time there was peace throughout the Forest of Time.

Back at the long wooden house Steph took control, as rooms had to be allotted and provisions sorted and stored. The house was very long, and downstairs the door opened into a large kitchen come living room. Two thirds of the way down the house was a large fireplace built of heavy stone in the centre of the room, and both open sides led through to the stairs and two bedrooms. Steph found that Rune had placed her things in one, and so allotted Rowan and Jade the other room to make it easier for Rowan.

The upstairs was similar; in so much as it had two rooms, the stairs, and then a long corridor with adjoining rooms on either side. Trying to establish who was coupled up took a little time, but with a little extra help from Jay, both of them worked out who would require what, and the two large rooms which contained bunk beds served for the single men in one, and the women in the other. Steph and Jay came down and sat at the long kitchen table as they set each of the team to their allotted places to rest.

Rune gave a happy sigh in the arms of the man she loved more than life itself. "This is nice." She snuggled into his chest, as he rested his head on the top of hers.

"It's been a hard few days, but it seems irrelevant now. You had me really worried Rune, I came round after the fall and you were gone, for a moment I thought she had killed you." Rune gave a shudder in his arms.

"Don't talk about it, I woke up alone with no sense of you, it was horrible, I don't ever want to be like that again." He gave her a tight squeeze.

"Let's not talk about it then, come on we should make a move, the others will be waiting." Rune stepped back as he released his hold, and she took his hand as she smiled at him. They began to walk toward the tiger that sat watching them. "Rune didn't we leave him at the castle?" She gave a giggle.

"I have been with Eve, she helped me return to the castle and take the children home, he came back with me, I think he was worried about us." Robbie stopped and looked at her.

"Avalon is sealed, how can Eve get you out and back in." Rune's eyes sparkled with devilishness.

"It is, but we are not in Avalon." She let go of his hand and giggled as she moved toward the shimmering violet window. "You really need a bath you know? No offence Rob but you do stink a bit."

"Hang on... What do you mean we are not in Avalon, that's not possible?"

"You will see, I will tell you all about it when you have had a good long bath." Rune turned and stepped through the window; Robbie hurried feeling a little confused, but also very hopeful.

Inside the long wooden home of Fagan, Crystal and Blades found a large pan and began a meal with a little extra help from Smokes, Steph kept a wary eye from the table to ensure the contents of the stew were within her parameters of taste. Jade helped Rowan to bed, and with a little extra powdered painkiller, it was not long before he was asleep. Feeling wide awake she went outside for a little peace and quiet.

The house was set in a wide open glade of long grass filled with flowers. At the right hand side of the house was a very large barn filled with livestock. The long grass was neatly cut back into paths to allow Jade to walk without harming the wild flowers, and she peeped in through the doors to see all the animals content in their bays either sleeping or chewing on the bountiful supplies of hay.

Next to the barn was a tall and old crumbling brick chimney; she felt a small tingle of delight as she investigated the old forge. It was obvious it had not been used for some time, but she could see it would not take long to get it back into operation, although the bellows looked a little worn out, and she knew they would need a lot of repairs if they were going to use them to make weapons. Lost in her thoughts she did not notice as Rune came walking through her window closely followed by Robbie. Rune saw her and smiled, as she walked toward the doors and came over towards her. Jade did not notice she stood just a few feet away, Rune could sense the feelings trapped deep down inside Jade and spoke quietly.

"Jade... is everything alright?" Jade sat on the edge of a pile of new stones and looked up to her younger sister as the sadness buried deep inside her came bursting back to the surface. Tears welled in her bright green eyes and then streamed down her face as Rune moved forward.

"She left me Rune, I have lost her forever, and I feel so awful without her, I have been trying so hard to be brave, but I miss her so much, and I just don't know what to do about it."

"Oh, Jade sweetheart." Rune knelt down and snatched her sister into her arms as Jade wept bitter tears of loss. She held her as tightly as she could, as Jade shook with her sobs. "Jade you are wrong, I know she fell, but please believe me, Jett is alive, she was caught in the middle of several spells to save her, she got shot off away from here that's all. Please don't cry, I promise you we will get her back." Jade gave a huge sniffle as she swallowed hard. Her voice was higher than usual as she tried to overcome the huge feelings of pain that seemed to have got stuck in her throat.

"She is alive... but where? Rune I will go and get her." Rune released her sister and brushed the lank hair from her face, she gave her sister a smile.

"Jett was sent by accident into another realm, I am not sure which one yet. The power of the black star is preventing me from finding her. Jade, Avalon is sealed, none of us can look further than its borders, but do not give up hope I will find her and bring her back to you." She smiled and wiped the tears from her cheeks. "No more crying now, we have a big job ahead and Robbie and Rowan need their girls tough and together OK?"

Jade beamed a big smile and gave a nod. "Got you Rune." She pulled her back into a hug. "I love you sis, and I really missed you."

"I love you too... come on let's go help out; we have a lot to do." She took Jade by the hand, and they talked and giggled as they made their way past the barn and back to the old wooden long house.

Harry trudged in the thick mist through the thick slimy mud that had up until recently been a wide river filled with small boats, his visibility was less than five feet and dark shapes loomed up in front of him, he twisted back and called out to the line behind him. "Watch it, there is another boat here, and it's a big bugger." The dark shape of a large boat lay on its side, loomed up in front of him as he skirted round it, pulling his feet hard as they squelched out of the thick black foul smelling mud. Behind him the others groaned as they fought their way through.

"This eez orrible, why did you wake me Skippy, I would ave been happier being carried on the stretchy thing." Skip looked down at her brown boots that had a wide band of black slime attached to them; they gave a squelch as they sunk back in.

"I am really sorry darling; I mean if you want, I would be more than happy to carry you." He pulled with all his might to free up his right foot; it gave a huge burping sucking noise as it came up out of the mud.

"None... I am fine, it will take more than this boggy dirt slime to put me back on the stretchy thing, I ave not forgotten the who is responsible, and ave every intention of taking her to the bakers when I am through this."

"I do believe that is cleaners darling, but that's the spirit, we are almost there now."

Harry staggered up the steep bank, and dragged himself onto the rough grass, he gasped as his feet slipped, and he pulled hard on the grass to drag him over the edge puffing and panting. From nowhere a large tanned hand gripped him tightly and lifted him on to his feet. A face with rather large bushy white eyebrows and massive tufts of wild white hair smiled at him. "There ye go... Oh my and blow me, if ye is not the wheeled son of the old master of the wooden town, well I must say I am as tickled as a hare bell to meet ye at last." Harry stared with complete disbelief.

"WHO THE BLOODY HELL ARE YOU?"

CHAPTER FOURTEEN

MEN OF POWER

The tall cloaked figure in green, gave a broad smile as his bushy white eyebrows twitched. "I have been sent by the good lady of this realm to aid ye Harold of the wooden town, tis but a short journey now to safety, where ye will find all ye friends and comrades." He gave a sweeping bow as the others scrambled up the bank. "I am the Keeper, and am known as Fagan, in the service of all who bring aid to My Lady of Life. She requested that I wait here a little after dawn to greet ye, and in honour of her wish, here I stands to serve ye." Una gave a broad smile and returned the bow to Fagan.

"Master Keeper is it now? You were once Maker here as I recall, I was but a small girl when I last saw you. I visited you with my mother, when you made a belt for the sword of Arthur. You have aged well Master Fagan." The old man's face narrowed as his eyebrows met in thought.

"Well blow me... I do recall a certain small girl of the whitest hair stood quietly beside the White Circle. Could it be that you are Little Una violet eyes?" Una gave a hearty laugh.

"I am impressed Master Fagan that you would remember so long ago." With a large smile he took her hand, lifted it, and gently kissed the back of it, Una gave a broad smile.

"Ye always called me Master, when most would call me just Maker, how could I forget such manners, no matter how long a man may live my dear lady, he never forgets those who do him great service."

Woody and Skip helped pull Maggs and Gaynor up onto the bank as Fagan looked around them and greeted them.

"Ye is not safe yet, but if ye permits, I will take ye through paths seldom trod where ye can rest with your lord and his companions in safety, there is food and soft beds."

After what had felt like the worst two days of their lives, the spirits of the group lifted with great relief, and smiles crossed their faces, as Fagan turned and pointed into the thick white mists.

"Tis but a short walk to the borders of the forest, and then with a good pace under trees that chatter like happy children, we shall be home in time for a good hearty feast."

With a flick of his heavy green cloak, he spun on the spot and began to stride into the thick mist. The group hurried on very tired legs, and found themselves trotting to keep up with the long strides of their strange guide. Harry walked along with relative ease, as he was tall enough to match the pace, Rags who was quite small in comparison was almost running beside Harry.

She slipped out a flask, and with a gasp she took a huge gulp. "Man this heat aint right for me, I tell you Harry, I would be happier sat on old Bags at the moment with the wind flappin under me hat."

She took another long gulp and offered the flask to him; he took it gratefully as he wiped the sweat from his red face with his sleeve. Harry took a long swig and his face screwed up.

"Urgh! It tastes sort of musty and uncosmic." He licked his lips as Rags gave a broad beaming smile.

"It's tonic." Harry's eyes narrowed at her bright happy face.

"What do you mean tonic? You aint giving me them flowers again are you, they aint that cosmic and do weird thing to your vibes." He scowled as Rags gave him a slap on the back.

"Chill out Dude, I figured if them flowers did your vibes in, Rune's tonic would put em back. Looking at your weird face Harry, I reckon they have." Harry's pace slowed as he stared in disbelief at Rags.

"You aint messin with me Rags, I mean it aint funky playin with people's heads you know? Man you could cause some seriously bad karma with tricks like that." Rags giggled.

"I reckon you are safe enough; I mean hey Harry your vibes were seriously jangled, if Rune's tonic has only unjangled them a little, I reckon it will help."

Harry thought for a moment as he felt the strange warm sensation that had grown inside him. A little hope mixed in with his inner panic and he felt himself relax, he patted his waistcoat where his metal flask of Joe's tonic had waited patiently. Carefully he lifted it out, and unscrewed the top. Rags watched with a twinkle in her eye, as he lifted it to his nose and took a good long sniff.

The memories mixed with his longing, as the potent odour ran up the inside of his nose, and down into the back of his heavily watering mouth filled with tingling taste buds. Rags giggled as he licked his lips and closed his eyes; he lifted the flask to his lips and poured a small amount of the hot burning liquid in.

Skip had noticed Harry and slowed his pace as he came up level with Rag's. Both of them watched as a look of pure delight crossed Harry's face and he seemed to slump slightly as he relaxed with utter relief. Harry then seemed to shudder slightly and lifted his head and stretched out his arms. "Oh man, whoa it's a miracle; I am cured from the flowers." Skip was just about to speak, when Harry gripped his stomach and crumpled to his knees, Rags jumped with a shriek as Harry vomited violently.

"Urgh... HARRY!" Both of them took a step further back as he lifted a very sad looking face.

"It's no good I tell you, them flowers cured me, I am done for." His voice was one of utter misery as he retched again.

The group stayed close together as they walked behind Fagan in the thick mist. It had been a long hot day trudging through the marshes, and they were very tired. Their clothes stuck to them with the wetness of their sweat, and they were dirty and uncomfortable. Like walking through a doorway, the mist suddenly stopped, and they were below the sunlight under the canopy of tall ancient trees. Madeline looked behind her to see the wall of white mist; it seemed odd to see it just hanging like a huge white sheet obscuring the view of the woodland they had travelled through. In front of her she could see the path that ran into the deep wood for as far as the eye could see, Fagan gave a smile.

"Ye is in my world now, she has little influence here for now, ye can all be at peace to know her arm does not stretch long enough to touch these trees, here we all walk with the Lady of Life." It came as relief to know that the Houlen would not swoop out of the skies to attack them. The whole atmosphere felt like it had completely changed, and felt a lot lighter. It may just have been that all of them could now see clearly where they were heading, or what was behind them, whatever it was the spirits began to lift and their hearts felt happier.

The age of the trees was very noticeable, for most of them the Sacred Oak at Loxley was the oldest tree they had seen, and yet compared to the ones that surrounded them it seemed very young. The branches of the Oaks were so large and heavy, that they bent towards the ground with the weight, and in some cases, they had rested on the moist soil and taken root, sending new young trees upwards towards the dappled sunlight. The ferns were bigger than any they had seen before, and in some parts, they were so high Maggs could have stood easily behind them and been completely hidden from sight. The most noticeable thing though was poppies; they had sprung up everywhere creating scattered mats of bright red that ran through the grass like the spots of a ladybird. Every plant looked lush and filled with life, their colours were vibrant and seemed to glow in the sunlight, this was a woodland like nothing any of them had ever encountered.

As a new day started outside the realm of Avalon, the sun rose to another hot day of activity. Deep in the woodland on the outskirts of York the preparations for war continued. In Loxley the Kirk sisters set up their tables for the sale of daily bread, and across the empire of Mason Knox, the work bells sounded calling those enslaved to work. Far to the south along a woodland road two young boys stepped back as a group of riders hurtled past them, their horses straining as they drove onward. They stood in the trees at the edge of the track, and watched as they disappeared into the distance.

Fifteen minutes later, the group of six riders hurried out of the trees, and onto the main road at high speed. The dust in the hot day lifted like a cloud behind them, hanging in the still air and slowly settling to the ground as it dusted the white daisies that had pushed up through the short grass beside the road.

Moving swiftly, the horsemen swerved from the road and onto the wide driveway that headed in a wide straight line to the high wooden doors, set in the old heavy carved stone walls of the Cathedral at Wells.

The gravel rattled across the bottom steps as the horses slid to a halt, and the horsemen dismounted quickly. The first man down was a broad stocky soldier of six feet; his long black cloak flapped behind him as he paced on the steps and lifted a large hand to pound on the doors. Behind him the tall slender frame of a well dressed man in a black hooded cloak waited patiently for entry into the ancient building.

It was several minutes wait when finally, the door creaked open slightly, and brief words exchanged before the large heavy wooden door swung open, and the party of six dressed in all black entered. In the large entrance hall shaded from the hot sun of the day, the monk who had answered the door gave a regal bow to the guest of high honour. set in the midst of the cloaked party. The figure gave a nod and lifted his hands to the front of the hood, and slid it back and let it fall behind him, as the long almost white sleek blonde hair fell down his back. The eyes of piercing blue stared at the monk. "Tell him I am here and wish to see him immediately."

The monk gave another bow, and scurried away as Lance Knox looked round the heavy stonewalls of the Cathedral. "It appears our brother has a taste for grandeur, this is somewhat more upmarket than the houses of the church at Hull."

The group around him gave a laugh, as Lance looked round with an air of disapproval. It was several minutes before another monk appeared; he was older with short almost grey hair, his face was stern and yet his eyes seemed to smile with a dark malice, his arms remained momentarily within the folds of his long grey sleeves; he gave a polite nod to Lance and slipped out his hand to shake.

"My Lord Knox, this is a very pleasant surprise."

Lance looked at the man, and he too felt how unpleasant it all was having to visit. Lance gave a smirk of a smile, as the monk waved a hand to gesture inside. "We were not expecting you to arrive so soon, please My Lord will you follow me, and I will take you to see the young lady."

Lance stepped forward and followed the monk through the Cathedral, and on to the steps below the arched lintel that wound down below the ground, Lance seemed eager for more detailed news as he followed behind the monk.

"You are certain this is the girl, I find it strange she would end up here in your care hundreds of miles from her home, tell me Brother what information do you have?" The Monk walked briskly along the dim passageway just ahead of Lance.

"My Lord she was badly battered and bruised when she was brought into our care, she had taken a very brutal and severe beating. It was many weeks before she would tell any of us how she came by her injuries, it was actually the grounds man's wife who got her to talk, before that all she would do is sit huddled in the corner and stare with a blank expression. We were preparing to leave the headquarters of the church at the new priory and make our way here to prepare for our mission. It was Brother Argus who heard about her and decided to bring her with us, he has I believe been in contact with your father My Lord?"

They stopped at the plain wooden door, and the old monk tapped gently. "If you would not mind waiting My Lord, I shall inform the lady you are here to see her."

Lance gave a nod, and the monk opened the door and slipped inside, it was several minutes later when the door opened. and Lance was beckoned to enter, his guard waited outside.

Inside the room was larger than Lance had first thought. The ceiling rose high above them painted in a bright white, which was illuminated by the large ornate candle stands filled with long white candles. Slanted shafts rose upward to the surface where leaded windows provided more illumination, the heavy stone slab floors were covered with brightly floral patterned rugs, and a small polished table and chairs sat with a vase of freshly cut flowers opposite. To the right was a wide high four poster bed, and two polished oak wood cabinets beside a dresser and wardrobe. Lance viewed the room with approval, and turned to see the fragile pale figure dressed in white that gave a small curtsy as he turned. "My Lord."

Lance was surprised at first; she was not at all how he had perceived her. The girl looked at him with dark eyes from a small and delicate face, which was surrounded with short tufted, almost boyish hair. Her forehead carried the small red scar that was evidence of her beating, yet she was by all accounts very attractive. "You know who I am?" His voice seemed to carry less of the stern and bitter tone it usually had, as his blue eyes fixed on her and watched her every move. It was obvious she felt uncomfortable and embarrassed, yet her gaze remained fixed on him.

"Yes My Lord, you are the Lord Knox and son of the Governor to England."

He gave a faint smile, her polite manner and use of titles was very much to his liking. "You know why I have come here then?" Nadia lowered her head.

"I am well taken care of, my wounds are healing, I will be fine My Lord, although I thank you for the visit. It is nice to know at least one member of your family has recognised the brutality of your brother."

Lance stared at her, he was unsure of what to say, the documented evidence had conclusively proved that Mordred raped her; all the servants had testified to the bishop that they had carried her out to safety, and brought her to the church.

Lance gave a heavy sigh.

"You are with child and that child whether or not you like it is of my family line, from here on in you will be under my protection and that of the child's family." He turned toward the door as she looked up at him, somehow the quiet girl inside her broke, and she screamed down the room at Lance, as finally the tears flowed into her eyes.

"IS THAT ALL YOU CAN SAY, IT'S A KNOX? I DON'T WANT YOUR PROTECTION, I WANT SOME JUSTICE. THAT BASTARD YOU CALL A BROTHER BEAT ME AND BIT ME, HE RIPPED OFF MY CLOTHES AND HE KICKED ME UNTIL I WAS ALMOST DEAD, AND THEN MY DEAR LORD KNOX, HE VIOLENTLY TOOK ME."

She fell to her knees as the monk stared on unable to move with shock. Nadia wailed into her hands as Lance turned back almost cold and unmoved, he stared down at her as she lifted her head with tear filled eyes, her voice dropped to a sorrowful grief filled sob. "He took me in a brutal way, and it hurt so bad I thought my soul was being torn away, and when he had finished, he laughed and poured a drink as if it was nothing, then he turned and urinated on me." Nadia broke down on the floor and wept as the old monk crouched down to comfort her.

"My Lord I am sorry, but I cannot permit anymore of this, see how distressed she is? I cannot allow this here in a house of God. No one should relive such things, you have no fear the child within her will be well cared for, she has the very best to care for her here." Lance looked down at the sobbing figure, for a moment there was a flicker in his eye that almost gave a hint of feeling.

"My Brother is dead; he met his justice at the hand of the man who trained him. If you wish to lay blame, blame the heathens that he grew up around, because it was they who took the Knox out of him, blame the hooded man and his rabble in Loxley. I shall return and we shall discuss your future and the future of your child."

The old monk gave a nod to Lance as he held the weeping girl tight in his arms, and Lance turned. He walked to the door and stopped, just for moment he hesitated as he looked at the scene of the girl on the floor clinging to the monk who rocked her gently.

"What is your full name, and how old are you?" She turned her head from the monk, and looked across the long room with defiant eyes, her lip trembled but she swallowed hard and spoke with some pride.

"I am Nadia Lord Knox...Nadia Worthington, my father was your general's closest aid until he was killed on the moors, I am twenty four summers of age." Lance gave a nod and turned; he opened the door and walked out. The old monk lifted her from the floor as she dried her eyes on the baggy sleeve of her dress, he watched with great concern, and she gave a small smile.

"Thank you, Brother Francis, I will be fine now, I will sleep a little I think, but do not concern yourself I promise I will be fine."

He gave her a comforting smile. Brother Francis had been called several times when Nadia first arrived, finding out she had the child of a man she considered to be a monster inside her, she had on several occasions tried to kill herself. For weeks she had to endure three people with her at all times, Francis now feared the visit of Lance, which seemed to have distressed her so much may just incite her to try another attempt. Nadia had promised, and to date she had kept her word, but he still felt very concerned and uncertain. He sat in the chair as she rested, and when he was convinced that she was asleep he headed off in search of the gardener's wife.

Lance had been escorted to the library, where a hot meal and the company of Brother Argus awaited him. Argus was a fat overindulged bald headed monk, who had a far greater opinion of himself than those around him did. Lance had changed much, he was now looking very much like a young son to a powerful man, and he had much of his father's air of conceit, and was indeed cool in all his responses. Like his father, he dressed in all black, and wore only the very best hand tailored garments, he now wore a great deal of golden jewellery handmade and chosen by his stepmother Dana.

The influence of Dana Knox had changed Lance forever, gone was the small frightened boy, and now he was a stronger and more business like man of confidence, his father had also taught him well, and now Lance exerted his authority with ease, something the fat old monk found annoying. In the case of Nadia, it appeared Argus saw himself as some sort of hero, and his pious lecturing was beginning to bore Lance. Lance looked up as he screwed up the linen napkin and dropped it on the table.

"Spare me the rhetoric Argus, my father has rewarded you well for the care of the girl, just don't give me the caring man of the cloth speech, it wasn't that long ago you were equally as vile in your treatment towards women, have you forgot the violet witch's cousin?" Argus stared back with anger in his eyes at the young Knox's lack of respect for a man of his position in the church.

"That was work in the name of My Lord God, how dare you compare me to the likes of your brother's behaviour." Lance gave a smirk.

"You violated twenty women with your toys, frankly neither I or my father see the difference, use the name of your god if you must, but do not sit and lecture me on the morality or your actions, we have all done what it takes to seize power, and you Brother are no different, your lifestyle is far better than that of most."

Argus turned red with his anger, although he knew better than to pick a fight with his benefactor. He sat and contemplated his wine as he fumed inside at the insults given him by Lance.

"You have been paid well enough Argus, you have your new monastery, just don't forget the deal we made. My father has paid up front, so make sure your people keep that wild card bishop from crowning the so called new heir."

Argus looked up at the cold eyes of Lance, he knew well the power of Mason Knox and he had no doubt that the backlash would be severe if he failed. Lance knew his point was made. "Remember Brother, your new place of worship is guarded by our soldiers, we know Loxley is there, it would not take much to bring it all tumbling down, and he does have a reputation for blowing things up."

Argus gasped. "I am a man of the church; my word is my bond... You have no worries about Steven's; I have my people all over Lincoln. He would not dare appoint any supporters of Loxley to the council." Lance gave a nod

"My father will be pleased to hear that, as we speak, riders have been despatched from York to inform that wood loving rabble that he is firmly in control again. We are committed to rebuilding this land, but it does cost money and their little piles of green come at a price." Argus looked up with the new news.

"You are introducing taxation?" Lance smirked at the look of concern on the old monk's face.

"The church for now is exempt, so as long as you continue your effective support you have no worries Brother. Your own little hoard is safe for now, but never forget who protects it, failing my father will come at a high price."

Lance stood up and looked around the vast library of old books. "I shall return in one week with a proper medic and some staff to assist the girl, after that she will be back under the care of myself. I am sure you can keep her happy for just a few more days. I will expect an update on how things are going at Lincoln, my father is very busy, but he is growing impatient as he waits for results. I am travelling now to meet with him in London, and make arrangements for the girl." Lance lifted his heavy black cloak off the seat at the side of his chair. "Until then Brother." Argus rose and offered his hand, but Lance swept the large cloak over his shoulders, and headed out of the room.

Brother Argus watched Lance leave with a scowl; his large round face was still very red with his feelings of anger. "Impudent little bastard, thinks he is as powerful as his old man does he? We will see." He turned to look at the old monk Brother Francis. "It was only last year he was hiding behind the skirts of that whore Knox married, I have the measure of Lord Lance Knox, you mark my words, he will not be so disrespectful to me again."

Although Brother Argus was in many ways right, he had failed to see the changes going on inside Lance; Argus was indeed a powerful man within the confines of the church. His order of monks now wielded greater power than ever, with the death of most of the church's ruling council at the hand of Sapphire and her sisters of the table, Argus had become very vocal.

He too had suffered a greater indignation at the hands of Rune, and so his attack had been swift and bitter as he took on and publicly denounced all of those who sympathised with the worshipers of Earth Faith. His announcement to move from the large new Abbey and build a massive monastery and monument to the Christian Church brought him greater support, and now from his temporary base at Wells, buried deep within the ancient reference library, he used his new gained power and influence, to wrestle for control of the church. It had not taken him very long to court the support of the most powerful man in the country.

Mason knew people, and the moment he met with Argus he knew that Argus was a greedy man who craved the power of ruling. Mason was wise enough to pander to him knowing his greed would blind him, to which Mason would be able to exploit him. The deal was made to hand over the Citadel above Avalon, and Argus began informing those who supported him to make their way to Glastonbury, and wait for Mason to open the new realm to them, and the new sect of Brother Argus. Mason as ever demanded payment, and as he had done in the past, he used Argus to gain support and use his influence to hinder the new Arch Bishop John Stevens. To date he had proven effective in the task, and as a result when the Dark One took over the realm of Avalon, Mason opened the door and let in the long lines of the new monastery order of Argus.

Argus had a great deal to lose and he knew it, but he knew that Bishop Stevens was his greatest weakness in his plan to dominate the church; he had at all costs, to gain full influence over the new church council. He turned to Brother Francis, a deep feeling of unrest inside him. "We must gain control in Lincoln, we cannot allow those heathens to blind the bishop to their way of thinking, everything hangs on his choice of members, I think we should play a more influential role to convince the bishop of where his loyalty lies." Brother Francis looked a little distressed.

"You cannot mean The Brethren?" Argus gave a slow nod.

The Brethren were a group of monks who also bore the duties of knights, all of them were ordained monks, but also served as a full combat force to uphold and enforce the will of the church. Argus had known many occasions when they had been called upon to remove obstacles.

"The stakes are very high, this bishop has to understand that the church must rise up and rule in the new world as it has in the past, there can be no room for deals with heathens. He will listen to my words or he will have to be removed for the sake of the church." Francis looked shocked at the suggestion, and wrung his hands as he shook his head.

"Brother there must be some other way... We are talking about the cold blooded murder of our Arch Bishop." Argus sat back down in his chair, a stern look on his face.

"I cannot be held accountable for a bishop who would destroy all we have rebuilt, there can be no Pagan king as the head of this church, Bishop Stevens must conform to the will of the church, or suffer the consequences of his actions, there is too much at stake for us to fail in our sworn duties now."

For Brother Francis it was a grim thought indeed, and as he left Argus and attended to his duties, he felt a great unease within him. Argus knew his reputation and head were now at stake, and with the building of his new monastery he felt the pressure more than ever, failure was not an option for him.

With plans and plots looking as if the new Arch Bishop had stalled in his attempts to raise support for Loxley, Mason felt reassured that with York under his control it would not be long before the woodland realm began to fail. Word was already moving round the country at speed and with no visible sign of the hooded man within the country, the talk around most towns for the moment was of doom and gloom. Mason was delighted by the sense of foreboding coming back to him from the many plants and spies he had working all of the country, although, he was disheartened to hear time after time, of the mysterious masked stranger who was creating trouble all over his land of industry, London.

The Sage sat quietly with Martin Jarrod and Markus, as Louisa explained the previous day's events, she was convinced that Mason had known that the factory was going to be hit. "I am sorry Master Sage, but my boys and myself can see no other explanation, we walked into a prepared compound and its cost us men." Her eyes fixed on the bright blue eyes behind the mask, she could see that the Sage was giving it great thought; it was Martin who spoke first.

"I know Mason and his tactics, and yes, he has planted spies everywhere, but I find it hard to believe he could get one in this camp. We more than any, all have a valid reason to fight him; there is not a man down there that has not suffered in some brutal way under the hands of the Knox Empire." He shook his head slowly. "I am sorry Louisa; I cannot believe we have a spy." He turned to the Sage with a questioning look; the Sage gave him a pat on the shoulder.

"Your faith does you great justice Martin, but we must consider what we have heard. I agree that alarm bells were sounding all over London, and maybe they have faster communication than we realised, and brought extra men in. I really do not know, I think we would be wise to consider the points of view of Louisa's men, after all they are Loxley trained, and I find they have good instincts. I think for now we should close the circle of those in the know, from now on we shall keep the plans for future strikes quiet until the very last moment, a little prudence may save many lives, agreed?" They all nodded their heads. "Good, I will talk quietly with Brian today and see what he thinks, but for now just to be safe, I will take the advice of men of Loxley, I want all of you to get your things and stay on the surface. Being underground with Mason above suddenly, sounds a little unsafe."

They all rose, and made their way to the station entrance, to head down under the river and collect their things, as the Sage stood and looked out across the river and the smoke filled sky of London. On the other side of the river there was a lot of activity, as men in black unloaded carts, and ran about the streets as if preparing for something. The Sage watched with curiosity. "What are you up to father?"

It was just past midday when the group arrived at the long wooden house, deep in the Forest of Time. They had been on their feet for over twenty hours, and they were filthy, tired, and very hungry. It was a time of celebration and joy as the group reunited, and for Robbie it came as a huge relief as he hugged Skip and Hawk and his Uncle Harry. Rune was delighted and laughed and giggled as she hugged everyone, in the kitchen Jade and Smokes worked side by side with Steph and Blades, as they prepared a meal, which Rune suggested would be better if it was eaten out on the grass in front of the cabin.

Within one hour, everyone had been shown their bed and stowed their bags, and had taken a few moments to wash, before sitting down in a happy gathering of close friends and comrades. Robbie had noticed that Harry was subdued and not at all the happy cosmic guy he was normally. Rags filled in Rune and Robbie as Gaynor sat and giggled, Rune could not help but laugh, even though she thought it was very sad for Harry. She leaned into Robbie and spoke quietly.

"Poor Harry, the tonic was never going to work as it contained some of the white flowers; the cure for his impediment is really quite simple, when all he needed to do was just eat the violets. As long as the tonic had those flowers in it, even mixed with violets it would only half work, he looks like seeing reality as it really is, is far more frightening than the dead." Robbie had to smile as Rags gave a huge giggle.

"It was funny Rune, for a moment he thought he was cured and then he retched." She started to laugh. "I know it's cruel, but his face was so funny, I almost peed me self."

Rune giggled as Robbie lifted his cup to drink; he gave a smile as he put the cup down. "I need him fighting better than he ever has, the coming days will be tough. I think I will let my poor old uncle have something to eat and a good sleep, and then I will let him in on the secret to his cure. I think for once his tonic may be what we need to revive his bravery." Rune leaned against him as she sat on the grass and watched the happy party eating and laughing.

"You will need Rowan up on his feet." Robbie gave a nod as he turned to see him sat on a chair on the long wooden porch with his leg bound up and on a box for support.

"It's a big setback for us, I know he is frustrated, Rowan is not the type to sit back and watch others risk themselves, can you help him Rune?"

"I can heal minor stuff, but not that, although Jade has skills which I can combine with mine, it's just..." Robbie turned to see her watching the pair.

"Just what?" Her bright blue eyes flashed across her cheeks, as her eyes moved to look at him.

"It's finding the right way to convince Jade to use them, the power she needs to heal him, is still very new for her, and up to date she has only used them to destroy things. My sister will need much greater control if she is to help Rowan; she will need far more confidence in her abilities than she has now."

Robbie was not exactly sure he understood everything Rune meant, but he did know Jade and her ability for mishap was strong in her. All he could do was hope that with Rune she could master her control, Rowan's leg depended on it, he also felt the chilling thought of going into his hardest battle without his strongest friend and general. That alone was not something he wanted to think about.

He sat back in thought and watched them all eating together. They were all dirty and looked exhausted, he felt humbled to realise that they had gone through hell to follow him. His mind slipped back to April the previous year, where he had left Loxley with just a handful of men, and slowly over time they had grown in number, but also in the hearts and minds of everyone in the woodland world. He knew there was no question that he would fight to his own bitter end in order to save them, for to him they were as close as family, yet here they were pushed to their limit and still ready to stand beside him. A cold shiver ran down his spine and he shuddered. "Are you OK?" He came out of his thoughts as he noticed Rune watching him, and he gave a nod.

"Yeah... Just thinking... you know?" Rune smiled.

"I know... They need rest that's all, it's been hard on everyone Robbie, give them time. You look equally as tired you should get some sleep; I am going to take the girls up to the bathing pools later, you and the rest of the guys should visit them when we are done." He gave a long sigh, he was tired but he had a lot to think about, he gave a nod.

"Yeah, I think a long soak in cool water will help all of us, is there nothing you can do about this heat? Honestly Rune, I feel like I am being slowly roasted."

It was mid afternoon and the sun was set high in the sky, burning bright as Avalon sat below, shrouded in a white mist. Along the Queens Road, carts continued to trundle along with long rows of black clad soldiers. In the town of Avalonia, Samuel Knots monitored his Cutters, and felt the frustration of the heat, and the lack of any news about Robbie or the heir to the Pendragon line.

At the tall wooden gates of Loxley, Henry the Sergeant at Arms, watched from the high gantry as David Williams paced along the line of carts with his men, checking all who entered were not there to attack. It was a warm day with a faint breeze, and David was looking forward to the end of the shift and his first evening off in ten days with Melanie. The pounding of hooves came up the road from the valley and he turned to see the fast rider approaching up the side of the carts.

David waved the rider down to get them to slow their pace, and the horse slid on the dry floor, as the rider pulled up hard.

It took less than a second for David to notice the small red crest of a dragon, set on a shield neatly sewn onto the man's black tunic, his sword came out in a flash, and his men turned swiftly raising their bows. "Halt and announce yourself, and be swift for that crest on your chest marks the sight of our arrows."

The rider held up his hands, one containing a rolled piece of mustard coloured paper sealed with a red ribbon, and a black wax sealed stamped with the crest of Knox. "Hold your fire, I am here to deliver a proclamation from the Lord Knox, I carry no arms, I am only a despatch rider." He looked afraid, as he eyed the line of bowmen who all aimed at him with loaded arrows. David walked slowly toward him his sword still raised as he checked to see if the man told the truth and bore no arms.

The rider lowered his arm to pass the parchment to David. "I am only here to give you this; I have no need to wait for a reply."

David took the rolled up parchment and examined it, it was clearly addressed to the Lord of Loxley, he gave a nod to the rider, who pulled the horse and turned around, with a sharp kick of his heels, he bolted off down the road leaving a cloud of dust blowing in the breeze. David stood and watched as he disappeared into the distance.

Henry signalled his bowmen to lower their arms and turned to look over the wall where David was walking back towards the gates. "What is it Davie?"

"We have a proclamation from Knox, no doubt it's another ridiculous demand, hold the fort for me while I take it up to John, I would imagine he will want to see this straight away."

David slipped round the back of the barracks, and walked up the footpath toward the Village Hall, John Lox was sat with Fuse at his desk in the centre of the large operations room, he eyed the letter with great suspicion as he lifted a silver letter opener and broke the wax seal.

"What the hell does he want now?" He unrolled the long document and began to read, David and Fuse both waited in anticipation. John sat back in his chair and gave a long sigh. "The man is as mad as a hatter, bloody idiot thinks he runs the place, here have a read for yourself." John handed the document across the table to Fuse who began to read as David read from over the shoulder of Fuse. David could not quite believe what he was reading.

"Is he mad? He wants a tax payable for every soldier we have, or else we have to disband the army, who the hell does he think he is?" Fuse gave a smile as he took his glasses off and began polishing them on his shirt.

"He is the Governor of England and its surrounding nations, I must admit this is quite an inspired document, his madness really does not know any bounds."

The long list of the new taxes to be imposed by the new offices for Tax Administrations seemed endless. There was a tax for every house, every horse, every cart and so on, all of this was to be collected on the first day of every month and payable in advance. The details were clearly laid out stating a tax collector would be accompanied by two units of armed guards to help enforce the payment, across the bottom was clearly stamped. 'It is the duty of every Englishman to uphold the law and make suitable contribution to the revival and redevelopment of the country, to the care of every community.' Fuse dropped the document on the desk.

"It is actually very clever, I mean if you think about it, this tax collector will visit every town. I am quite sure that Knox knows that no woodland town will pay, which can only mean we will tie up our forces to protect each town, and thus reduce our frontline forces, he is not as big a fool as we thought he was." John Lox sat forward in his seat; he rubbed his hands together as he thought.

"We need to send out word to every town and prepare them, the way I see it, this so called collector will have to come out of York. I think it's time we begun to close the net a little, let all our scouts know I want this Tax Man found and disposed of. Get the word out he is to be stopped within the boundary of York, the way I see it if anyone is fool enough to apply for this job working for Knox, then bugger his stupidity and end it with an arrow."

Fuse listened carefully as he thought out the possibilities; he lifted the document off the table and scanned down the long list of taxes imposed by Mason. "I think we can see the final game plan of our enemy; he is not aware we have had contact with Rune. I do believe he feels that Robbie will be trapped forever, and he will just sweep the land and take the crown by force." He looked over the top of the sheet with his small horn rimmed glasses. "When he is king this document will give him the authority to crush Loxley for tax evasion. It is quite a subtle plan." David gave a nod.

"He is preparing for every eventuality, which is quite a good thing." John gave a frown.

"Just how exactly is that a good thing?" David gave a big smile.

"Well let's be honest, if he has to set a plan for the future in motion now, it means he is still unsure of the outcome, he still thinks he is going to get the fight of his life." David flicked the paper in the hand of Fuse. "And that tells us he is not convinced he can win." Fuse gave a small smile as John suddenly understood the whole picture and smiled.

"Well then, with that in mind, let's up the stakes and begin to strangle his hold on York."

The women had all gone up to the bathing area, and most of the men had cleared up the grassy area outside of the cabin, Harry stood just on the edge of the clearing staring into the trees, his mind filled with doubt and confusion, being sober was a very different experience, and not one he could clearly remember.

Robbie walked up by his side and lifted an arm to his shoulder. "Harry."

Harry blinked and looked at Robbie. "Hey Rob." Robbie smiled.

"What's on your mind Harry? You have hardly said a word since you got here, even Maggs is worried about you, and she says you have not spoken to her in two days. She seems to think you have lost your faith in your abilities." Harry put his head down.

"Got a lot on my mind Rob, it's been a tough few days." Robbie pulled a small slip of paper out of his pocket; he pressed it into Harry's hand.

"Follow these instructions to the letter, and Hearne will help you overcome the white flowers." Harry's head jerked up and he stared at Robbie with wild eyes. Robbie patted his shoulder. "I need you back and fighting like the uncle I know and love." Harry snatched Robbie into his arms and squeezed him tight as tears welled into his eyes.

"Oh, thanks Rob, you have no idea of the pain. I love you Rob." Robbie walked back as Harry took out his hankie and wiped his eyes to study the paper Robbie had given him. John and Rowan tittered as Robbie came up the steps with a smile.

"He bought it, hook line and sinker." Rowan gave a huge gasp of a laugh as Robbie and John chuckled, Skip shook his head.

"You are too cruel my friends, poor old Harry he has had the worst time of his life... although I must confess, I am curious as to what will happen at midnight." All of them sat watching Harry stood out near the trees, as he studied the paper Robbie had given him with a very strange look on his face. Chuckles and laughter seeped through lowered heads all along the long wooden porch.

CHAPTER FIFTEEN

STRANGE CURES

It had felt like a very long day of organising, Robbie had returned from having his bath and feeling clean, he had collapsed into bed in the cool long house deep in the Forest of Time. Furry Face who had been asleep all day at the side of the bed rumbled quietly in his dreams, all round the old house there was little movement as the exhaustion finally took its toll, and clean with full stomachs most of the group slept.

Jade was working out on the forge with Bear, as they did what they could to make minor repairs, to get it working again. Woody had found peace in the barn with the animals, and Una who had struck up quite a bond with the old Keeper, wandered around the lavish garden filled with vegetables, and picked the food for the next meal. Rune, who had already done a great deal of sleeping while she had waited for Robbie, walked into the forest looking for herbs and medicine plants. Everyone else slept quietly knowing that for a brief time they were safe, and protected by the power that shielded the forest from the powers of the Star of the Merle.

It was late afternoon when Robbie finally woke up and walked to the door, to look out on the wide cleared meadow surrounded by trees. The sun was still high in the sky and the day was hot, as the bees fanned out over the grass looking for buttercup and corn cockle to collect up their pollen. For Robbie it almost felt familiar, and the calmness held in the air reminded him very much of the Mere and home. Through the stillness of the air, he felt the tip of his open shirt move slightly, he watched as the trees ahead of him stirred in the soft breeze, and felt it run across the grass and gently stroke him, opening his unbuttoned shirt. Rune walked out of the trees with a small woven basket and gave him a smile as she waved.

He stood for a moment and watched her as she walked towards him, feeling that sense of contentment creeping back into his body. Rune wore her green woodsman attire, and she had plaited her hair into a long plait that hung round her shoulder like copper woven rope, her eyes danced with life as she came closer wearing that familiar smile. Robbie looked back to the trees and they were silent and still, and he gave a smile as she came up the wooden steps, and kissed him on the cheek. "Oh good your up, did you sleep well?" He pulled her into his arms and gave her a big hug.

"I slept like a log and feel a hundred times better, there is a lot to be said about being clean, fed and rested." She kissed him again and then stepped back.

"I need your help, I want to look at Rowan's leg, but you know how stubborn he can be. Can you get Mum and Jade for me while I organise the table, I gave it a good scrub earlier?" He gave her a nod.

"Yeah sure, but why do you need the table, why not just look at it while he is on the bed?" Rune smiled and kissed the tip of his nose.

"I am going to look deep inside it, so I will need his leg to be very still and flat. The table is a harder surface, it will make things easier."

Robbie sensed she was once again up to something, but he knew better than to question, he gave her a smile, and turned on the steps to go and get Jade from the furnace.

By the time Robbie arrived back with a very hot and sweaty Jade with her Mother, Rune was stood at the stove where a large copper pot was boiling. On the table was a mortar and pedestal, and a small cloth bag. Rune turned and crossed to the table where she opened the bag and took out some small dried green leaves. She crushed them into powder as Jade came round and had a look. From inside the bag came a very pungent smell, Jade took a deep breath, and coughed as she quickly stepped back. "God Rune what the hell is that?"

"It is a gift from our Lady of the Woodland; these are very special leaves with a powerful set of properties. This is the only place where they grow, and they will help you fix Rowan's leg." Jade looked confused.

"Help me? I thought you were going to do it." Rune gave a smile as Rowan hobbled in supported by Bear and Maddy, he shuffled up to the table and looked at Rune.

"You don't want me up on there do you? Can't I sit in a chair or something?" Rune gave a smile and patted the table.

"No, we need your leg flat, so come on Rowan stop being a baby and up you get." He was not keen, but Jade came round and helped, and soon he lay on the table as Rune cut away the bandages that held the splints tightly in place, and then started to carefully unwind the bandaged leg. Rune took a knife and slit the trousers further up, she smiled as she saw his face.

"Oh, stop frowning, you have some of the best seamstresses in Loxley here, your pants will sew back, really Rowan, you would think they were the last pair on earth." Steph gave a giggle with Jade as Rowan looked at Rune.

"I love these pants, they are comfy." Rune shook her head.

"You and Robbie are so alike; nothing is good enough unless it's comfy and smelly." Rowan frowned.

"They are not smelly... well not much. I have worn these in, and they are just right for being in the woods." Robbie gave a nod of agreement and Rune giggled.

"Have no fear they will be good as new when I have finished, but I do warn you Rowan, before I sew them back, they are being washed. Rowan gave a look that conceded defeat, as Rune took away the pads and looked at his knee. Just below was a large gash where the bone had come through; it looked very red and swollen, and most of the top of his leg was blackened and blue. Rune turned to the stove and brought the kettle over. From under the table, she pulled out a large stone bowl. She sprinkled a few pinches of the powdered leaves into a mug and poured in some hot water. The smell was instant, and everyone gave a puff as they smelt it and gasped out. Rowan looked a little worried.

"What the hell is this, it stinks, I hope I don't have to drink it?" Rune gave a big smile and nodded.

"Actually, you will find it tastes better than it smells, here just sip it whilst it's hot, and make sure you drink all of it, this will work miracles on your leg."

Robbie stepped back a bit; the whole room was filling up fast with a smell that was somewhere between turpentine and disinfectant mixed with rotten eggs. He shuddered as Rowan took a sip. Rune turned to Jade who had screwed up her face and was holding her nose.

"Ok Jade the herbs will help to remove the swelling, and they will help heal the bone, but before they can work, you must use your gifts from grandmother and fuse the bone together." Jade suddenly looked horrified.

"What? No way Rune, I cannot focus on Rowan's leg." Fear and panic swept across her face, as the colour seemed to drain from it. "What if I go wrong and it blows up?" Rowan shook his head vigorously as the colour faded even faster from his face, his eyes had widened as he looked in disbelief at Rune.

"Yeah... Yeah... What if... You should listen to her Rune, I mean... Shit Rune she blows whole trees up by mistake... God Robbie tell her she mustn't do it... Jade honey I love you, but you know how much trouble you have had controlling it. I mean...I want to walk again, what if you blow it off, I will be buggered."

Jade nodded her head as she looked at Rune. "Rune he is right, I keep going wrong and exploding things." Two tears ran down her dirty sweaty cheeks. "Please Rune you do it, I am too scared I will blow him up." Rowan nodded as he looked round at the others, he pointed to Jade with a long finger whilst holding the cup. A thick band of sweat formed on his brow and began to trickle slowly down his pale white face.

"She is right you know? I mean, we should listen to her, and let Rune do it." Robbie who had felt a deep jolt inside his stomach nodded vigorously at Rowan in agreement.

"Yeah Rune you do it, I need all of him not half." Rowan agreed panic in his eyes.

Rune turned and faced Jade, she lifted her hand and stroked the long blonde curls out of Jade's eyes, her voice was soft and caring as she spoke.

"Jade you are my sister and the start of a new line of power. The line of the Green Circle has some gifts from grandmother that did not come to me, I cannot fuse bones, I can help heal wounds and cuts, but this is beyond me. You have to do this or else Rowan will have to stay here when we leave, we cannot take an already injured man into a fight with us, it will risk his life and others." Jade looked at Rowan's white frightened face, as more beads of sweat formed on his brow, more tears ran down her face. Her lip quivered as she spoke quietly.

"Rune I am scared to." Rune pulled her close and hugged her, as Jade watched Rowan sat waiting looking terrified, even Robbie who was at a loss for words, felt very nervous and unsure Rune was right. Rune slid Jade back and looked her deeply in the eyes.

"Jade do you trust me?" Jade gave a sniffle.

"How stupid are you? You know I do." Rune smiled.

"Please trust me now. Jade I am here at your side, and I will be with you, trust me when I say, you can do this." Rune took her hands and gave them a squeeze; Jade gave a gentle nod and looked at Rowan who was immensely pale, and looking scared stiff.

"I love you Rowan." He looked round in disbelief unable to comprehend what was happening, Rune turned and looked at him, her eyes were already going pale violet, Rowan shook his head.

"Hey hang on a minute Rune, let's think about this, I mean..." Rune's fingers snapped loudly, and Rowan fell back and was caught by Steph who smiled at Rune.

"You know one day he is going to get really angry with you about doing that." Rune gave a smile.

"He will have to talk fast; it takes but a moment to click my fingers." Even Robbie gave a smile as he looked at the sleeping figure of Rowan on the table. Rune prepared the bowl, as Jade stood beside her looking very worried and frightened. Rune added the rest of the powdered leaves to the bowl and then filled it with hot water, the smell intensified in the room, and Robbie had to blink as his eyes began to water. Rune dropped the bandages in the bowl to soak and then looked round at each of them.

"Ok Robbie you hold his thigh firm, Mum if you could come round and hold his ankle, his leg must be perfectly still. Right Jade stand here, and just relax and feel the power build inside you."

Rune's eyes flared purple as she lifted her hand to Jade's back. Jade closed her eyes as she felt Rune blend with her, and as sisters together they prepared.

Although Rune's eyes were closed, she could see all that Jade could, and she spoke very quietly as she guided Jade.

"It's alright sis, I am here with you. Now focus carefully on Rowan's leg... try to look through the skin and find the broken bone." Rune's mind washed with the pictures from Jade, and she gave a small smile as she saw all of the particles that made up Rowan's leg swim around in Jade's mind. Rune let her calmness wash into Jade, as Jade slowly searched for the broken bone. Robbie watched as Rune's eyes flickered sending small flashes of violet across her white cheeks. Jade had her head down and her eyes open and he saw the faint green light grow in her eyes, as she looked down and deep into Rowan. Rune spoke in almost a whisper. "Alright sis, fade and focus your powers on that point."

Robbie watched as slowly the colour ran out of Jade and she disappeared. He smiled as he saw that there was the faintest out line left behind that shimmered in a very pale violet. His eyes met with Steph's as both of them watched and gave a smile. Rune was stood still her eyes closed tightly, but in front of her was a slightly shimmering Jade that radiated with a flowing purple outline, it was like someone had taken a picture of her and drawn it in the smallest droplets of violet water, and Robbie watched with wonder and awe, as one sister guided and protected the other.

Rune could see the structure of Rowan's bone and the gap where the break was. Using her mind, she guided and instructed Jade, and slowly she saw the structure of Rowan's leg bone begin to vibrate. Jade focused harder, and the bone began to extend to fill the gap and fuse together, even Rune was amazed to see how it actually happened. Fusing the bone seemed to take an age, although it took only ten or so minutes, the power that passed through Rune and Jade was draining, and as the bone sealed together Jade gave a slight gasp and Rune took hold of her.

"Relax Sis you have done it." Echoed into Jade's head, and she gasped as Rune opened her eyes, and Jade came back into view. Rune held her close as she smiled. "That was fantastic, come on sit down and rest a moment." She guided Jade to the chair near her mother, and Jade flopped down, her legs shaking violently. Steph let go of Rowan's leg and gave her daughter a huge hug.

"That was amazing darling, I joined with your sister and watched, oh that is so very clever Jade I am so proud of you." Jade gave an exhausted smile and looked up at the table at the sleeping figure of Rowan. Rune worked quickly, she took out a needle and thread, and soaked them in the hot liquid before sewing up the wound. Taking the soaked bandages, she bound the leg tight, tearing the end to create two thin tapers, she could tie to hold it in place.

"Ok everyone, the bone has started to fuse, but he will still need time to heal. Rowan must not put any weight on this leg for a few days, it's going to hurt like hell as it heals, but with constant soaking in the herbs it should strengthen very fast, and within the week he will be right as rain." Steph gave a happy sigh.

"Oh rain, how lovely that would be at the moment."

Robbie smiled, and then noticed the heavy perspiration on everyone, not only had it been a moment of anxiousness, it was also incredibly hot in the house, which was odd, as it had thick walls that usually kept it cool. Steph lifted a cloth and wiped her face. "Is there really nothing we can do about this heat Rune sweetheart, it is gonna cook us all?"

"As long as she uses that star, the heat will continue, there is nothing I can do until I get it off her." Steph gave a gasp and moved across to the sink where she lifted a wet cloth from a bowl and wiped her hot red face with it. Rune looked at Robbie. "We need to get him in bed before I wake him." Robbie gave a nod, and with Rune's help he lifted Rowan, and carried him past the chimney in the centre of the room, to the back of the house, where Rowan and Jade had their room. Jade curled up on the bed beside him and Rune gave a smile.

"Jade when he wakes, he could be a little... well let's say Harryish. Those herbs can have an odd effect on people." Jade looked a little concerned as Rune raised a hand as she stood by the door and clicked her fingers loudly. Rowan sleepily opened his eyes and gave a daft looking smile.

"Hey sweetheart, I just watched my bones leave my legs and walk on the clouds with little people, with bright coloured hair who blinked." Jade looked back at Rune who gave a little giggle.

"See, get some sleep the pair of you, rest heals faster." She turned in the doorway and watched as Jade snuggled into a very happy if not somewhat stupid looking Rowan, and Rune pulled the door closed with a sigh of relief, and turned to head back to the kitchen, time now would heal.

As the evening moved towards mealtime, members of the group began to arrive in the kitchen. Fagan had been nowhere to be seen all day, Maggs who had fallen into a deep sleep, now woke feeling very much revived, and joined Una in the kitchen as most of the others wandered outdoors into the blazing heat. Robbie and Jade had been down the forest road back towards Avalon to get a good lay of the land around them, and Rune had walked in the woodland with her large proud tiger, as she admired the trees and flowers that were strange to her. Harry had risen early and disappeared into the woodland alone carrying a large brown sack.

By the time everyone had returned and the meal was prepared and served, it was gone ten o'clock at night, although the sun still shone with great heat. Rowan was in pain but his leg felt better, and with the help of John, he had managed to sit out on the porch and rest with his leg up. Robbie and Jade sat with Rune and Steph, as they sat back after their long meal feeling well feasted and relaxed. Rowan was keen for news and Robbie filled them all in on what he and Jade had seen on the edge of the Forest of Time.

"It looks like we were right, the mist is thinning. Avalon has been dried out, the thick mists we saw, were the water vapour from the land, trees are turning yellow and the grass is starting to die, there looks like there are quite a few fires still burning on the grasslands."

"We have seen this before Robbie." Rune's voice was quiet as he turned to look at her; he instantly knew what she meant.

"In that dream everything was rotting and decaying, here it is simply being drained of liquid; she is turning Avalon into a desert." Rune gave a soft nod as their eyes met.

"It's a different symptom, but the effects are the same, either way she is taking the life out of everything. The green world is dying at her command, it is what she has always planned for us, and maybe this is her way of practicing before she moves on to Loxley." Rowan could see the sadness in Rune; he looked at all of them sat in thought.

"There must be something we can do to stop this happening?" Robbie shrugged.

"We keep fighting... We rest and re-arm, and then we go back, we have to find a way to get Amethyst back in power. I am not sure how, I just know that if we can find a way to unleash her power, maybe then we will have a fighting chance of defeating that star." Jade gave a solemn nod and flicked her fringe out of her eyes.

"We are sisters bound together with mixed powers, if we can team up and focus together, there must be a way of defeating her." Rune admired her spirit and didn't want to crush it.

"The only problem Jade is once we leave the protection of this forest that star will start to drain all of your powers again, and the harder you try, the quicker you will drain them. We cannot use the gifts we hold because they will increase her strength and we will never defeat her. As far as I can tell she has only one weakness, and I am the only one who can exploit it." Robbie turned to her with a surprised look on his face.

"No way Rune.... You can forget any idea of facing her alone." Rowan watched not quite understanding.

"What is this weakness?" Robbie looked at him with angry eyes.

"Don't even think about it." Rune placed a hand softly on to Robbie's as she looked at Rowan.

"She has what I am... Life, I can take what was given at the start of time."
Jade frowned. "But she has protected it by binding it to the Raven." Rune gave a small chuckle.

"She thinks she has, but her spell was flawed. Gwynfor knew the truth of the spell and told me, I tried to take her life force in the cave, but she threw the star at me and it broke the connection. I think she will have realised her error now and made preparations to protect herself." The atmosphere seemed to fall, as they all sat in silence, lost in their own thoughts and the time ticked slowly by. Robbie suddenly looked down at his watch.

"It's time, it's eleven thirty." Rune did not understand, as Jade and Rowan smiled.

"Why what's happening?" Robbie gave a big grin at her, as the others seemed to chuckle.

"We have to hurry and get up inside the top floor of the barn." Rune felt confused as the others stood up. Jade kissed Rowan, who for obvious reasons had no means of climbing the long ladder up, and had opted to stay. Skip, Fox, Hawk, and Smokes appeared in the doorway, followed by a grinning John, as Rune looked round at them all.

"What?" Robbie took her by the arm and giggled.

"Let's just say tonight is Harry's coming out party, come on we have to hurry." Rune was swept along with the others, who giggling, quietly made their way into the barn and headed for the tall ladder that took them up to the wide hay loft, where a long row of bales had been placed against the wooden rail.

Rune did not understand what was happening, and she looked at Robbie as he pushed her down out of sight behind one of the bales. "Shush, you will see soon." He gave her an excited smile, and then crouched down at her side as all the others got into place and settled down to wait. Rune watched them as they all stifled their giggles, and waited for whatever it was they had planned as the clock ticked towards midnight.

Far below the door creaked and Robbie stiffened, he lifted his finger to his lips as the others all gripped the top of the hay bales and slowly began to rise to peep over. Rune followed, curious as to what it was they were waiting for, John gave a gasp and covered his mouth quickly, Jade was already shaking with silent giggles. Rune carefully peered over the top of the bale and looked down, she almost screamed out with surprise, as she quickly brought her hand to her mouth to hold in the sound. Robbie was already shaking with giggles as he winked at her.

Far below in the doorway, Harry walked into the barn with his large brown sack. He was completely naked and painted blue from head to foot. She fought to stop herself from laughing out loud as her stomach muscles vibrated. Harry looked back outside checking all was clear, and pulled the door quietly closed. He lifted a crate from a stack and placed it carefully in the middle of the floor, and then he bent down and rummaged in the large sack.

Pulling out a large green piece of cloth he covered the crate, and then laid it out like a small altar. On it he placed a large sprig of coiled ivy and a branch of holly, two large candles, and a small stone bowl. Nervously he looked round making sure the coast was clear, as he muttered to himself, and then rummaged around inside the sack. Harry mumbled. "Oh yeah flowers in my hair."

Rune almost squealed as he sat on the floor and began sliding bright red poppies into his long sleek locks, creating a crown of vivid red, she grabbed Robbie's arm and squeezed it tight. All along the line, the group of huddled viewers shook as they fought to contain themselves.

With most of his preparations done, he laid the final piece of the puzzle down on the altar, as he checked each item off on the list Robbie had given him. "Blue, yeah, flowers, yeah, candles and cloth, yeah." He glanced nervously at the door. "Bowl and petals, yeah. Tonic, oh man I hope this works." Rune felt Robbie vibrate as Harry lifted the piece of paper and prepared for his ritual.

He lit the candles and took a breath. Lifting the holly off the altar he read the words on the sheet of paper out in a strong clear voice. "Hear me Green Lord, and see the spirits held in this stick." He gave himself a mighty whack on the head with it, and red petals shot off in every direction. He picked up the ivy and began to wind it round his waist like a belt.

"Fairy spirits, gnomes and sprites, make me cosmic with happenin vibes." He lifted the bowl into the air and began to hop and dance around the altar. Jade fell backwards onto the soft hay stuffing her shirt into her mouth, as Harry jumped and jigged around the altar. Rune felt the laughter rise inside her and pushed her face as hard as she could into Robbie's rapidly wobbling side. She wanted to scream in hysteria, and tried with all her power to fight back the impulse as Harry's voice echoed in her ears.

"Give me power of spirit and tree, take out the white flowers and set me free." He began to dance faster and faster singing his mantra over and over as he worked himself up into a frenzy. Jumping up and down, hitting himself with the large Holly branch.

Rune could no longer watch as the others fought with all their might to fight the laughter and hysterics inside them, and Harry danced around the naked flames, his bright blue body glinting in the light as the poppies on his head shed petals that fluttered softly to the floor.

"Give me freedom, give me power, and make me cosmic violet flower." He stopped gasping for breath, and knelt down in front of the altar panting. He lifted the small violet petals out of the stone bowl, and held them up in front of him.

"Restore unto me thy gifts." With a quick swipe of his hand, he put them in his mouth and began to chew. Rune fought hard to keep the tears from her eyes, as curiosity got the better of her, and she pulled away from Robbie and peeped back over the bale.

Harry swallowed hard, and then licked his lips rapidly; and then reached for the silver hip flask of tonic. Nervously he unscrewed the cap and held it out in front of him. "Oh man I hope this works." With a shaking hand, he put the flask to his lips, closed his eyes and took a long swig. His face exploded with delight and relief, as he swallowed the mixture brewed by Joe back in Loxley, and he gave a happy sigh of relief.

To Rune's surprise he jumped up on his feet and began dancing round the little altar. "It worked... yes it worked... I'm free." Happy chuckles of almost madness, squeaked from his lips, as he danced round the barn unaware of the loft filled with an audience in silent fits. Bright blue and as naked as the day he was born, he screamed into the air. "I AM CURED!" with a giant energetic leap; he jumped over the candles, and landed a little off balance. He staggered forwards and hit something on the floor and stumbled.

Woody opened his eyes, form his deep slumber in the hay, to see a bright blue face containing wild panicked eyes looking at him. Woody screamed in terror as he stretched for his sword, Robbie almost fell over the rail laughing, and Rune snatched at him quickly.

Harry screamed with abject terror, and leapt off Woody, who had grabbed his sword and had swung wildly at Harry. Covering his privates, Harry turned in panic and fled towards the barn door. Woody pounced into the air, and as quick as a flash he ran screaming after Harry waving his sword. Robbie exploded with the others in fits of laughter, as Harry fled from the barn followed by the enraged Woody. Screams echoed out in the woodland as Harry ran for his life, and Robbie fell on the floor with the others as tears streamed from their faces.

Jade howled with laughter, rolling on the floor. "That was so funny.... Did you see his face when Woody pulled that sword?" She screamed out with laughter holding her sides and kicked the floor as she gasped for breath in between laughing.

Rune wanted so much to stop laughing, but found it impossible. In between her gasps of laughter she tried to speak. "You... are.... all... evil...poor Harry ... how... could ...you?" She slid down the hay bale next to Robbie, and wailed with laughter, John was so red in the face he looked like he was going to have a heart attack. Jade thrashed wildly screaming with hysterics as the others hung onto the rail to stop themselves falling over. It was over fifteen minutes before Rune could find the strength to compose herself. Robbie sat in front of her, red in the face and sweating as he continued to giggle.

"That poor man, what have you done to him?" Fits of giggles broke out again and Rune looked at them all and tried to be serious, but she too began to giggle again as she wiped her eyes. "You have scarred him for life I am sure, and poor Woody he was terrified." Laughter rose up again inside the barn and the hayloft shook and creaked.

It was well past one in the morning, when they finally came down the ladder, and made their way towards the long house. Jade still giggled with John, and Rune found it impossible to look at Robbie without breaking out into renewed fits of laughter. Steph stood with Rowan and both of them kept emitting small giggles, the sight of him running for his life being chased by Woody had been so funny, Steph had almost peed herself, Rowan smiled a huge smile. "That was indeed very mean My Lord, but also immensely funny." Rune started to giggle again and put her head down, Robbie chuckled.

"It's unfortunate for Harry, but I think it's been a tonic for all of us." Everyone started to laugh again. Rune tried to hold it in.

"It was wicked, all of you should be ashamed, poor Harry he could have hurt himself dancing that close to the candles." She gave a gasp and covered her mouth, and the laughter began all over again.

Woody returned ten minutes later looking very hot. His sword was now sheathed as he walked back towards them. Robbie tried his best to be serious, but he could feel Jade and Rune stood either side of him shaking as they stifled their giggles. "Everything alright Woody, we heard a disturbance?"

Woody pointed back towards the band of thick trees trying to find the words. "I err... well you see... there was... err." He looked back and thought for a second. His hands made gestures, which conveyed his confusion. He looked at Robbie. "There is something very strange living out there."

Rune gave a blurt of air, and quickly turned away, and the rest of the group once again burst into laughter. Robbie giggling stepped forwards towards Woody.

"It's alright Woody, it was Harry." He looked very confused.

"Harry? But he was blue." Robbie smiled.

"We know, he had a very sacred ceremony to perform, it's an old Celtic thing." Woody looked back at the trees.

"He scared the hell out of me, I almost cut his... err... Oh! Poor bugger, I must have scared the hell out of him too." Robbie patted Woody on the shoulder with a huge smile.

"I am sure he will be fine, come on it's getting quite late, I think a cool drink and then we should all turn in for the night, I think Harry needs a little time to calm down." Woody gave a nod as he walked back towards the house, and the smiling figures of the group

It was over an hour later when Robbie lay back in bed and closed his eyes. Rune snuggled up at his side and put her head on his chest. Through the thick curtains enough light passed through to light her face dimly. He looked down at her as she smiled. "What?" She gave a big smile.

"Poor Harry, he is such an easy target." Robbie grinned at her.

"He is back on his tonic, and once again the fighter we need to get us through this. Everyone was lifted by tonight, and the others will hear about it in the morning and it will lift their spirits. To be honest Rune, after the last week, it might help them all recover a little, and that will work to everyone's advantage. You saw them all when they arrived here, they looked beaten, and tomorrow they will become a team again." She lifted herself up a little and gave a small giggle.

"I have to admit it was very funny, you surprise me at times. Whatever made you think of it?"

"I didn't."

"You didn't?" Robbie shook his head and smiled.

"It was all Rowan's idea, he was the one who suggested it to me, and I knew everyone would muck in, especially John and Jade." Rune frowned, and Robbie looked at her. "What?" She shook her head slowly.

"I always thought Rowan would kinda straighten Jade out. I am beginning to think she has corrupted him instead." Robbie gave a giggle and she giggled with him, and settled down beside him. "Poor Harry, he is so sweet."

"Don't you mean gullible?" Rune giggled as she curled up close to Robbie. There were a lot of quiet giggles that night round the old house deep in the Forest of Time.

Ursula slept in a small bed, in a room off the tunnel, just down from the main hall of the large labyrinth of caves underneath the Citadel Mount. Returning from the tomb of Arthur, her mistress had directed her here and told her to rest. The room was small but contained a small stove and table opposite the small wooden bed she now slept in. The flickering candle made the white walls of crystal sparkle, and she liked it, it felt like a very magical place, and she had enjoyed cooking a small meal and sitting on the wooden chair as she ate. She had eventually lost all track of time in her long wait and had undressed and slipped into the soft warm bed, while her mistress continued her work inside the vast main hall that had once been the court of Rhiannon and the people of Fae.

Ursula felt the bed shake violently; she snapped open her eyes to see the white drawn face of her mistress looking down at her with deep red eyes. "What?" She sat briskly up and rubbed her eyes of the sleep, as her wits recovered and she realised where she was. "I am sorry Mistress."

The Dark One gave a smile as she turned back to the table and lifted the cloth bag off the back of the chair, where she began to check the bottles and jars of powders. "I am glad you slept well, we have important work to do, and it will be a long day today." Ursula swung her legs out from under the covers and dropped them onto the cold floor; she reached for her blouse and skirt.

"What time is it?"

"It is a little after dawn, although there is no rising of the sun as it's been high in the sky for days now." The Dark One turned as she watched Ursula dress. "Today the cloud of my dissent will appear for all to see, I have been busy watching in the Raven's eye, and now I see all that is happening across many lands. My son has done well and as I speak his riders have spread his news of the fall of York. Our trap is working well, and my soldiers are busy gathering all the rotten eggs into one nice big basket for me to deal with later."

Ursula looked up and could see how pleased her mistress was, the Dark One gathered up the bag containing the bottles. "Today I wish you to sketch out the floor of the main hall, there is much to do and many charms to speak, for we will need to protect ourselves for the moment when I finally confront my accusers, and demand justice for my line."

Ursula hurried and slipped on her cloth shoes; her mistress led the way down the long tunnel towards the two large heavy doors that marked the entrance to the Hall of the Moon. The first sight of the massive hall caught Ursula's breath; it was bigger than anything she had ever known. Her eyes followed the large stone pillars up to the ceiling that was pure white and streaked with bright violet seams. Balls of light hung in the air vibrating slightly, they fascinated Ursula as they provided the main source of light in the great hall. The Dark One noticed her fascination with them and looked up.

"Those are courtesy of the Flower Girl, it was nice of her to leave them for us, it makes your job much easier. Come we shall work here in the centre of the room, ignore the statues, I shall entertain their living souls tonight."

Ursula scurried across the wide violet floor to where her mistress was emptying the contents of the bag out onto the floor. "I must leave here to prepare other things; you are quite sure you know what to do?" Ursula gave a nod as her mistress handed her a large roll of parchment.

"Follow this with great care, and say each charm as you draw the lines over and over, the forces of my line will guide you. I shall return before you are finished, and then we shall seal all the spells and enchantments into the land forever."

The Dark One walked back towards the doors as Ursula unravelled the large role of parchment. "You will be provided with sustenance and if you require anything at all, there are two of my personal Houlen through the first door to the right, alert them and I shall send you what you need. Work well Ursula, for this will be a great test of your own abilities." The large doors clunked shut, and echoed around the massive empty room.

Ursula stood for a few moments and gazed round the great Hall of the Moon that had been built in honour of Rhiannon with sheer wonder, it was hard to imagine such a huge room and fit all of it into her mind. Finally, she thought of her task and looked down at the large parchment containing the circle and stars and symbols that her mistress required her to draw out on the floor. She carefully examined the dimensions, and then she got on to her knees and hammered a small sharp spike into the floor. This would allow her to unravel the endless feet of cord she needed, to begin working on drawing out the circles. It was going to be a long and busy day.

CHAPTER SIXTEEN

FAITH IN THE HOODED REALM

The time at Lincoln had been one of wonder, as Father Warren wandered around the huge gothic cathedral with Father Simon. The atmosphere had felt very tense, and Father Warren had noticed how the bishop, and even his most trusted aid had been on edge around the many visiting clergy that now seemed to be everywhere within the grounds. He had not seen the bishop since his arrival, and he had guessed quite rightly that in order to protect him, Bishop Stevens had for the moment kept his distance. Father Simon the bishops most trusted aide had been instructed to give Father Warren a tour of the Cathedral. Warren liked Simon, he was still quite young, but seemed devoted to his mentor Bishop John Stevens.

Together they strolled out of the large doors, and down the steps, onto one of the only few remaining streets that had survived in Lincoln. The old buildings showed the signs of the raging hurricane that had devastated much of the old city shortly after the Red Death. Castle Hill still contained some of the buildings that had been admired during the age of modern man, and although they had fractures in the brickwork, and scars from the debris that had been tossed and hurled against them, they remained intact and served as a central focus for the church and the communities that surrounded the city.

Warren admired what had now become a local administration office run by the church for the area. The old black and white Tudor building had been repaired, repainted, and looked almost new compared to the worn and slightly crumbled buildings beside it. Side by side they walked down the street watching the view from the hill of the trees and fields, that rolled between what where large rough areas that Warren assumed contained the decayed remains of the rest of the old city.

The sun was hot, and Warren slowed noting the lack of others around, he turned to Simon who had been telling him of the efforts the church had made to help all of those in the countryside. "Tell me Simon, I understand the pressures of the bishop, but is the church really being split as much as I feel it is over the potential new king?"

Simon glanced round very nervously, to check they were alone, his face had paled and Warren noted his fear, Simon spoke in hushed tones. "There is much you do not know, Mason Knox is a very powerful man, and all of us must be very careful, he has many in the church who still support him as the only candidate for king. They have been bought by his promises of a completely Christian England." It was not what Warren had expected to hear.

"But that's outrageous, how can he promise such a thing? Half this country is Earth Faith, not to mention the few who have survived of other different faiths. Even as a Christian Church, we have no right to dictate the beliefs of others." Simon gave a solemn nod.

"You must not forget who he is Father. Mason has no care of faiths, he will wipe out any who oppose him, just look what he has done to York, which was only because they had a local government that he did not approve of. His brutality knows no bounds; do you really think that Mason will not slaughter all who oppose him? It's what he has been doing since he began building his wall in Devon."

Father Warren only had to look back to his time in the black city to understand, he shook his head in disbelief. "But Robert of Loxley is fighting him, he has half the country in arms against him, does Mason really think he can win so easily?" Simon gave a huge sigh.

"York fell, even after so many months of holding him back, at the end of the day, Loxley had to admit defeat and York went to Mason, it is a sign of the man's strength and ability, and the sad truth is that those in the church that have influence have seen that. They are now saying Mason will win, and those who do not support Mason, will not join a council of twelve behind the bishop out of fear of reprisals." Warren could not believe his ears.

"But that was a tactic to draw Mason in, it was planned all along by Loxley, they knew they would lose too many if the fight was taken to the walls, it's why Loxley emptied the city, don't they see that? Simon you must convince those who understand military tactics that was always the intended plan of Loxley. Mason is now sat surrounded by walls that are completely surrounded by the woodland forces; even Mason has not understood that Loxley has tricked him. He will never leave York there is nowhere for him to go. Simon as we speak the woodland forces have mustered, and are preparing for when he opens the gates. Do they not see that Mason has walked into a trap? The only safe road he has now is that from the Black City, and that is because Loxley wants him to move everything into the shelter of the walls of York so he can contain his whole force." Warren felt the urgency grow inside him.

"Simon you must talk to the bishop, I know he has had to avoid me a little because I am here with a member of the woodland forces, but you have to get me in to meet with him. He does not have all the facts, he is in a stronger position than he realises, and he must not involve any who support Mason in the council of the church, the man is about to get the surprise of his life." Simon was now the one who seemed to be surprised at what he heard.

"Please Father tell me you know this is the truth, My Lord Bishop is weighed down under the amount of pressure they are exerting on him, those who support Loxley are afraid to voice their opinions publicly in fear of retribution, if what you say is true, it would give the bishop a chance to resist until Loxley acts and brings new hope to the cause." Warren gripped Simon firmly by the shoulders.

"Believe what I have said here, I am fresh from Loxley and have spoken to their commanders at the stockade. You must believe me when I say that the woodland forces will rise up in an attack far more severe than Mason has ever known. He will not hold York for long, and when his forces fall it will deal a fatal blow to him, you must gather those who support a king of a true line, and tell them a new king will rule with a fair hand, Loxley will assure it, these plans have been on the table for over a year now."

It was clear that Simon desperately wanted to believe him, it was almost as if he did not dare to hope. His eyes sparkled, as he considered all that Warren had told him, but took a few moments to compose his thoughts before speaking. "I have no idea how we will get the word out, the men of Mason are watching every move we make, but I will find a way to get you in to see the bishop soon, but please I beg of you, tell no one of what we have discussed here for your arrival with a man of Loxley has created a great deal of attention." Warren gave a reassuring nod.

"You have my word, I will stay close to my quarters, and wait for you to get back to me, and I will speak to no one of this." The young vicar smiled.

"My lord has a very high opinion of you; I know your word to be true. I will let you know as soon as I can find a way to let you talk with my lord bishop alone.

The young Father made his way quickly back to the cathedral, and Father Warren walked on slowly, along the remains of the end of the street and looked upon the dense woodland at the foot of the hill. Several yards behind him Bowman Jersey in his long green hooded cloak kept a more alert watch. Without first realising, it was quite obvious that to Father Warren he had been caught in the middle of the two opposing sides of the Church, and he knew that failure to seat the new king would have a dire consequence, as Mason would seize control of the country and all the supporters of Lord Loxley would be sought out and slaughtered. With no news from Robbie, he suddenly felt the pressure rest on his shoulders, time was running out and the coming days would seal his fate forever.

As Ursula spent her time working on the floor of the large hall, her mistress had much to attend to. Samuel Knots, the commander of all the forces encamped within the realm of Avalon, had been ordered to move his force south towards the Forest of Time. The Dark One observed his soldiers stationed in small groups all along the long woodland road that marked the edge of the forest. She felt a strong sense of satisfaction as she turned to face the large brutal Cutter. "You know what to do?" He gave a nod of his head,

"Yes, Lady le Fey, nothing will get out of that woodland." She smiled a thin and crooked smile.

"Mason was right about you Knots, I must admit, I am more than pleased with your handling of the soldiers since I arrived. It is now your responsibility to keep that forest sealed and prevent anything from getting out, especially over the next forty eight hours. Believe me if you can do that, then you will see the true gratitude of my family."

He watched her closely, as she began to turn to return to her waiting carriage, she stopped and his eyes met with her cold red eyes. "Do not fail me Knots, even you a man who has seen the worst of people, has no idea of the horrors I can torment you with." He swallowed hard, and felt the cold shiver run down his spine.

The whip of the Houlen driving the carriage gave a loud snap as it lurched forward, drawing the dark figure of Morgan le Fey back towards the town, and the high peak of the Citadel Mount. Samuel Knots turned to a group of six scruffy and burley soldiers, dressed in the usual black bib bearing the familiar red dragon of the Knox Empire. "Right, you lot, you know what to do, get in there and find em. I want em watched every second they are there, and if it looks like they are making a move, you follow em and send word here OK?" The six soldiers jumped to attention and spoke as one.

"YES SIR!" Knots nodded at them.

"Right get on with it."

Under the canopy of the ancient forest, the light seemed to fade away, as the dense canopy of the old trees formed a heavy roof of matted twigs and branches covered in leaves. Far below the canopy, the ferns grew tall and thick on either side of the long winding path, and a strong heavy air circulated around the six Cutters as they moved with caution along it. The silence was eerie, as from the moment they had stepped onto the path; every bird had ceased singing, even the bees had moved as far away from the visitors as they could. The air felt hot and sticky as they walked watching every leaf along their route, the leader, Captain Banes, looked across the path at his two comrades, who seemed to be whispering quietly to each other.

"Hey, what's with the chatter?" The large red haired Cutter named Norris gave a shake of his head.

"It's Ovens here, he is bloody stupid, he thinks there are demons and ghouls in here." Banes gave a sigh, as Ovens moved forward to see his captain.

"I am telling you Cap, there have been all sorts of strange stories about this place up on the mount, loads of the guys back there were real happy not to get this detail, they were scared stiff of coming in here."

The soldiers behind him nodded their heads in agreement; they too had heard some very strange stories about a giant and talking trees. Banes looked back at them and then across to Ovens.

"What have I told you lot about listening to these old wives tales? The only thing you lot need to be scared of in here is me. Now shut your yap and keep them eyes peeled, we got to find this woodland hideout, and then get on with the job of watching them. I don't want to hear another bloody word about unnatural things creeping about in here, you all got that?" The soldiers nodded at the captain.

"Yes Cap."

"Right then, let's get a bloody move on." Ovens gave a cautious glance across the wide expanse of ferns and weeds, and lifted his crossbow up nervously.

Rune stood by the steps of the long house as Robbie came out with a steaming mug. "You haven't seen Fagan have you; I have not seen him since he brought the others back yesterday?" He noticed her eyes were closed. "Oh sorry, hadn't realised you were thinking."

"It's Ok, I am just seeing the surrounding area, I was looking for Furry Face, I think he has gone exploring. Fagan came back early this morning, he is in the barn feeding the animals with Woody, those two seem to be hitting it off very well." Robbie took a swig of his drink.

"Cool, I want to get the forge going and get straight into getting the weapons sorted; Fagan has some good long straight shafts for arrows somewhere." He began to walk towards the barn, and then turned back. "Has Harry surfaced yet?"

Rune gave a little titter. "Not yet, he is probably sleeping it off." Robbie chuckled as the memory of the night before came back; he walked off to the barn to see Fagan.

Harry snored loudly as the few remaining poppies vibrated in his hair. His sleep was now very deep in the heat of the early day, and his thoughts were filled with the dreams of all things funky and cosmic. So deep was his sleep he failed to notice the group of Cutters in the distance up the track.

Leaning against the tree, still bright blue and naked, with his hands holding the empty flask in his lap, he was relaxed and at peace. At his side lay two empty bottles, and his large bag containing his swords and weapons.

From the ferns in front came a loud sniffing noise, followed by a low pitched rumble. Furry Face had picked up a familiar scent, and worked his way slowly sniffing the floor towards the sleeping figure. Much to Harry's disbelief, Furry Face had taken a liking to the tall jumpy man in black; he wandered through the fern and found the search for the source of the scent was over.

Sniffing round his ears with a deep rumbling purr, Furry Face slipped out his tongue and gave Harry a long wet lick across his mouth and face and sat back. Harry disturbed and grunted lifting his hand to waft away the interruption to his mellow dreams. "Hey Chicken later, go back to sleep it's not time to get up yet." He murmured an inaudible few words, and slipped back into sleep. Furry Face gave a high pitched squeak, and lifted a huge fist like paw to Harry's shoulder and then leaned forward and licked him again.

The group of Cutters moved quietly down the track, Ovens was at high alert, as the stories of the others played in his mind, and his eyes darted from left to right. Suddenly his heart froze.

"ARRRRRRRRRRRRGH, UNCOSMIC MONSTERS!"

Up in front, the fern on his left, exploded open, and at high speed, the tall, naked blue skinned, blue faced Harry, came crashing head first towards him. Furry Face bounded down the path of crushed ferns behind him. Harry bounced to his feet like a coiled spring, and seeing the others he screamed in terror. "Oh man it's tasted me funky vibes and wants more." Furry Face gave a happy little yelp, and jumped up landing his two large paws across Harry's shoulders and gave him a long loving lick up the side of the face.

"ARRRRRRRRRRRRGH IT'S CHEWING ME VIBES! Help me, I am being karma chomped."

He staggered back under the weight of the large tiger, and then with a scream of a deafeningly high pitch, he wriggled free of the tiger's grasp, turned, and ran like the wind towards the Cutters. Furry Face bounded after him purring loudly and yapping happily. Harry looked back with large wide terrified eyes. "Save me it wants to eat me, I am like too funky and cosmic and the beast knows it."

The group of Cutters separated in panic, as the huge blue naked screaming man came towards them with wide terrified eyes. Ovens dropped his crossbow, turned and ran back down the track; the others dived into the ferns for cover. Harry came charging up with the large tiger bounding along happily behind him. Captain Barnes hit the floor next to a very shaken and white faced soldier. "WHAT THE BLOODY HELL IS THAT?" Ovens could be heard screaming in the distance above the chaos, as he ran for his life.

"DEMONS! GOD SAVE ME IT'S A BIG BLUE DEMON FROM THE DEPTHS OF HELL, HELP,HELP, IT'S DEMONS." Barnes jumped up as Harry drew level screaming as loud as he could.

"UNCOSMIC MONSTERS, RUN FOR YOUR LIVES AND SAVE YOUR KARMA FROM CHOMPING!" Barnes yelled to his soldiers who were popping up in amongst the tall ferns.

"STOP THAT BLUE MAN, YOU HEAR ME? I SAID GET HIM." Black shirts started to move through the ferns back towards the path, waving large shiny swords. Harry slid to a halt and turned, he began to run back towards the tiger.

"CUTTERS, RUN FOR YOUR LIVES, IT'S AN INVASION, WE ARE BEING ATTACKED."

The large happily yapping tiger halted on the path, as Harry ran past him, he turned as Harry looked at him. "RUN FOR IT BEASTY, THEY WILL HAVE YOU FOR A RUG." He flew down the path back towards the break in the ferns where he had entered the road. The Cutters came flying out of the ferns, waving their swords and screaming for all they were worth. They saw the huge tiger sat in the middle of the path looking at them. Furry Face opened his mouth and roared like a lion, exposing his long sharp white teeth.

The Cutters turned and fled back into the tall ferns screaming. "MAN EATING TIGER RUN FOR IT."

Furry Face watched not sure of what to do, as the Cutters scattered back into cover. He turned on the path and bounded down it to follow Harry.

Harry came panting back up to his pack; he knelt down gasping for air as he unrolled the canvass bag that contained his swords. He pulled them out and jumped back up to his feet, with a long deep breath; he turned and ran back towards the path. At the edge of the path, he vaulted as high as he could, and came over the top of the ferns like an enraged blue elephant waving his swords. He screamed at the top of his voice as he landed and looked back up the path.

There was no sign of any Cutters at all, Furry Face bounded towards him yapping happily, Harry panicked. "Oh no it's still here, oh man this is not cosmic, its gonna chomp on me vibes, I am buggered." He darted back into the ferns and headed for his pack. At the tree he didn't stop, he just snatched up his pack and carried on running like the wind. Somewhere behind him came the sounds of yelping, he swallowed hard and ran for all he was worth.

General Mark Richard Dale had taken his time to unpack and settle into the top floor of the Head Quarters in York, where he was enjoying having the very best of everything, and that included the housemaids. The sleeping pale slender figure with short brown hair moaned in her sleep, stretched out across the general's bed as he pulled the door closed, and made his way down to the operations room to begin his new duty. General Dale walked with confidence in his usual immaculately pressed uniform, as he turned the corner to the corridor containing the operations room.

Mason's voice echoed in the hall as the door opened and a young girl in uniform scurried out, dropping the towering pile of papers in her arms. Mason was in a temper and everyone was hearing it, as the general stooped and collected some of the dispatches that the young female soldier had dropped. She scurried about picking them up quickly not really looking at the man whose hand contained a wide pile to add to the already growing stack she had gathered herself. "Oh thanks, watch it the old man is in a foul temper." She looked up and saw the rank badges and the colour seemed to run from her face. "Oh sir, I am sorry, I meant no offence it's just...." Dale smiled.

"The old man sounds fierce." He smiled; she gave a look of relief and smiled back.

"Yes, sir he is, there has been bad news from London." General Dale gave a nod as the young female soldier stepped back holding tight to her load of paperwork.

"Thanks for the warning, I shall tip toe in." She gave a smile at him as he turned and opened the door.

"WELL WHAT THE BLOODY HELL WERE YOU DOING? THERE IS AN ENTIRE GARRISON AT WINDSOR, WHY THE HELL DON'T YOU BRING THEM IN?"

Mason's face was almost purple, as he turned from the officer who was literally shrinking away in fear, and faced General Mark Dale. "Can you bloody well believe this? They are being attacked all along the river, and instead of bringing in reinforcements, they just let the bloody woodsman right across the river to blow up and destroy everything they wanted to." Mason handed out a large white sheet of paper with a dispatch note on it from London, General Dale looked down and read the reports of the damage to all the factories, Mason turned and looked at the cowering officer.

"WELL DON'T JUST BLOODY STAND THERE, GET ON THE TELEGRAPH AND TELL THEM TO CALL IN THE TROOPS FROM WINDSOR."

Mason turned from the large table covered in plotting markers, and walked to a silver trolley where he poured out two large glasses of scotch, he turned to face Mark Richard Dale. "Sorry old pal I wanted to give you the tour, but it looks like I will have to head down there and sort this mess out. I hope you don't mind; I will have a word with Dana, I am sure she would be delighted to show you around, I will only be gone for a week or so."

General Dale gave a broad smile as he took the glass from Mason. "You have to do what you need to Mason. Leave York to me, I will be fine." Mason patted him heartily on the back.

"Good having you beside me again, we will show these peasants a thing or two now eh?" Mark smiled back at him.

"You leave it to me, and we will back on track before you get back here."

With clothes torn from the brambles, in their run of blind panic, the Cutters finally regrouped a quarter of a mile away from their meeting with Harry and the tiger. Ovens was very white in the face and shook with fear, as the captain walked down the path toward the huddled group looking very displeased. Ovens rambled on, the panic still coursing through his body. "I warned you, but oh no you wouldn't listen... Well you tell me what the friggin hell that was?" The others all nodded still feeling very shaky, Ovens was happy to finally be believed. "I was right wasn't I lads.... Big blue bloody giant of a demon that bugger was... Did you see his eyes? Oh shit lads we are buggered, anything that fights with a tiger for a mate is way beyond us."

A rough tattooed hand came through the fern and slapped Ovens hard on the head, and he flew violently sideways. "What the bloody hell were you doing dropping your weapon?" The crossbow came through the fern followed by the captain and landed at his side. Ovens looked up rubbing his cheek, the captain scowled at him.

"You should read a book or two on history, instead of listening to the tales of old women, the Celts of old painted themselves blue and fought naked to frighten their enemies. Bloody coward, I would slit your throat if I didn't need you."

Ovens sat on the floor and pointed a finger into the scrub. "He was eight feet tall, that was no ordinary bloody man Cap." The captain looked at all the group.

"Now you lot listen to me and listen real hard, I don't care if they are twenty feet tall, there was bloody six of us, instead of wetting your pants and pissing off, you group together and we face the bugger out. You all got that?" Still looking frightened, they all nodded at the captain. "Right then, grab your kit and let's go find the bugger." The Captain of the Cutter group walked out on to the track, and began to walk slowly back to where they had met with Harry. The others lifted their things and followed; Ovens stayed at the rear complaining quietly to the Cutter at the side of him.

"Bastard, he ran off just the same as us lot, big bloody pissed off blue demon running at us and he was off like a rabbit down a hole he was, I didn't see him waving a sword at it, friggin tiger as well, he expects too bloody much of us, we are as good as dead if we have to fight another of those blue buggers."

"Ovens shut your yap and get a move on."

"Yeah Cap." He picked up his pace with his colleague, and caught up with the rest of the group.

In the centre of the Great Hall, deep within the heart of the caves under the Citadel Mount, Ursula spent most of the day working with the piece of parchment, and countless bottles of sulphur dust. Working very carefully, she followed the complex design on the parchment, and drew it out across thirty feet of the floor. Her Mistress arrived back late in the afternoon, and paced the sides of the hall constantly returning to the small fractured doorway to the room that Rune and her party had rested in.

Ursula kept her head down as she heard her mistress muttering about Rune under her breath, she knew it was best to keep busy and avoid eye contact. Rune had a way of angering the Dark One in ways no other could. The fact that Rune had sheltered her group in a room that still carried a protection that prevented the Dark One from entering was more than just a little irksome to her. Quietly she walked along the top of the white steps, watching Ursula on her knees as she used a long piece of fine silk twine tied to a lead weight, to trace a perfect arc in sulphur dust on the floor.

The day had passed in a blur of dust and powder, when Ursula wiped her brow and sat back on her haunches with a long sigh of relief. With stiff legs, she slowly stood up and viewed her work with pride; the intricate design of stars and circles set round large silver candle sticks was impressive. The Dark One appeared pleased, as she walked up from the bottom of the hall. "Good work, that is perfect, you have learned much my assistant, and did you say the rituals with each marking of the lines?"

Ursula stretched her legs to stretch out the cramps. "I did Mistress, I was very careful to pronounce every word carefully." Her mistress seemed pleased.

"Good... Now leave me here, and go up to the Citadel and wait for me, I will be some time, as I wish to perform this one ritual alone."

Ursula felt the disappointment grow inside, as she saw her mistress place a small stone bowl on the floor into which she placed the finger bone of Uther. As Ursula walked through the doorway that led up the tunnel to the steps, she glanced back and saw the Dark One grinding the bone to powder with a pedestal of black shining stone.

It felt like a million steps up to the Citadel. Alone in the long tunnels her steps echoed, and a feeling of loneliness overcame her, somehow, she had expected to be a part of the ritual, and could not understand why she would be excluded. The old monks in the lower entrance hall were all busy, and seemed unpleased to see her walking about. One was kind enough to hold up a herbal tea to her whilst avoiding eye contact. It did not help her feelings of isolation, so holding the cup in both hands to warm them, Ursula walked up the newly constructed wooden steps, and out onto the wide platform at the top of Citadel Mount. Most of the broken and smashed lumps of white stone had been moved out of the way, and formed a long line of blocks not far from the edge of the steep cliff. It was early evening, although felt like midday, and she walked slowly towards the edge and sat on the stone, and looked out facing the east. Ursula watched as the sunlight shone down far away behind the hills covered with trees, she lifted the cup and blew the steam off the tea. It had been cool down in the hall, and it warmed her cold cheeks as she breathed out, and she sipped it slowly feeling the warmth run into her throat. Her eyes stared ahead at Avalon below, which now was just dressed in a very thin pale mist.

Far below her, on what had been the grasslands, smoke still rose from the black charred remains of the fires. The wide lake was almost empty, and the sunlight twinkled off the few small pools of water that remained.

In the east was a thick and lush green shimmering forest. It was a few moments before she understood what she was seeing, and she blinked just to check she was right. She looked down below her to the woodland at the side of the road and the stone circle, which was dull and brown. Across the bridge through the burial ground, and across the wide watery marshes the land seemed as it always had, yet further east where the trees grew in a dense blanket, that looked like it stretched for hundreds of miles, the canopy of the trees appeared like they were filled with sparkling diamonds.

"Is that the Forest of Time?" Her voice was quiet, and seemed lost in amongst the large white stones; it felt more like her thoughts were talking to herself.

"It is beautiful this time of day isn't it?" Ursula jumped with fright, spilling her tea, which ran quickly into the cracks in the stone and away from sight. The old monk in heavy shabby black robes that was stood beside her, had given her quite a fright, she had not heard him arrive and stand level with her. He stepped forward towards the edge, and stared out across the wide valley of the realm. Ursula could not see his face for the large frayed hood that hung low keeping his features shaded.

"I did not mean to startle you, but to see this sight once more is joy to any who view. When I saw you sat there, I could not help but walk up and watch with you, this is not a spectacle for one, it should be viewed and shared." Ursula was unsure of how to react; she looked back out across the land, and watched the light shimmer over the forest above the horizon.

"I have been told it is protected by magic, and was the first forest ever created." The old monk's hood moved.

"Your Mistress has informed you correctly, for there before you, is a place of great wonder and beauty. It was there that the first of everything was created, it is without doubt a magical place, for it was given life by the lady of this realm herself, and it encapsulates her beauty and spirit."

The mention of her mistress made her nervous, who was this black clad stranger, did he know anything of who she was, and why she was here? Her senses felt no threat, but unlike anyone she had ever met, this person gave no sense of who they were, which was very strange. Ursula had always been able to get the measure of a person just by being in close proximity with them. There had been few times when she had not been able to read the personality of those who stood before her. Her Mistress and Runestone were the only people she had ever met that gave her no signal at all. Her nervousness increased, yet she was stuck here beside him with nowhere else to go. She tried to think of something to say.

"You say the Lady of Life, I have not heard that title before, the Lady of the Woods is a title known to me." She watched the hood move slightly as the old monk replied.

"The Lady of the Woodland realm does reside here for a short time; the lady of this realm was once mistress here before she handed the guardianship over to Rhiannon of the line of Fae. The lady of this realm was Eve, and it is her vision of wonder that grows under that blanket of protection. Your Mistress is foolish to think she could rule there, for no amount of power could match the hidden power that created all the realms. Look more carefully Ursula of the boat people, and seer of human hearts, feel the force of the woodland lord and his lady. Their protection of their line is fierce, choose your own path with more care, it will take more than a star of black, and the blood of a failed king to overpower the force of violet."

Ursula gave a deep shudder, for the first time in her life someone had done to her what she had made an art of doing to others, and she did not like it, she turned away from the view of the forest and back to the shabby old monk.

"Who are you?" There was no one there. She looked from left to right, but the wide plain back to the Citadel was empty, just a few monks worked by the wooden scaffold stacking more timber for the day's work, but they were robed in brown. Her heart beat fast inside her, she had no idea at all of who it had been, was it a spirit or a sorcerer? The goose bumps ran from her neck down her arms and legs, she moved slightly and the floor crunched below her feet. Looking down at the hard stone floor, she saw a small piece of twig on which were two acorns, one of them had been crushed under her shoe. Ursula crouched down and lifted the twig to inspect it; the nearest trees were thousands of feet below her. She looked back out across to the Forest of Time, and then back at the small twig, two tiny green leaves had sprouted and were starting to grow out of it. She let go and dropped it, stepping away from it quickly in fear, and spilling more tea.

"What is this? It's not possible, the realm is sealed and none can enter." Her hands trembled vibrating her cup as she turned and looked out across the realm of Avalon. "Oh Mistress what is going on, why do the spirits seek me?"

Her dark eyes were wide as the sun filled her face, the wind rose up and her hair lifted spreading coldness inside her. As it blew past her ears the voice of the old monk whispered. "You have chosen ill my little boat girl, leave here now for it is not too late to change your path." Her arms stiffened, as the goose bumps increased and deep down inside her fear began to grow. Dropping the cup, she turned, and ran with all her might back towards the working monks, and the safety of the Citadel, and the protection of her mistress.

CHAPTER SEVENTEEN

DARK MISUNDERSTANDINGS

Rune's sleep had at first been restful, but as the night wore on, she began to have strange dreams, and she felt unease growing inside of her. In her dreams voices she did not recognise talked in an ancient language, mist rolled in and out of the trees and she saw shadowy figures walking in and around the edges of the mist. She woke with a start, and sat bolt upright, the sweat was thick round her neck and turned cold as it ran down her spine making her shudder. Robbie was fast asleep curled against her, and slowly she slipped his arm free of her, and turned to sit on the edge of the bed.

She could still feel a strong sense of unease and urgency; she slipped out of bed and dressed quickly. It was still and quiet in the dimness of the house, the morning was just beginning as she slipped out of the bedroom, and walked along the side of the stairs to the old brick chimney in the centre of the house. Fagan sat in front of the glowing embers of the fire smoking his pipe and rocking slowly; he gave her a kind smile, his eyes watching from under his thick white bushy eyebrows. "Ye have been called; follow the path east to the hot springs." He gave her a wink. "I thought I had felt something earlier, you will see, have no fear all here are safe."

"What awaits me, because the feelings inside me are of deep caution?" The old white haired keeper gave a nod of recognition, understanding some of what awaited her.

"This realm belongs to your line; ye have nothing to fear here."

His smile was kind and gentle, and yet the feelings in her stomach did not subside. Rune felt the nervousness rise, as she slipped on Robbie's thick green cloak and stepped outside. The woodland was calm and quiet, apart from a few of the first birds, who had risen and now sat high in the trees singing their own praise of the new day. Rune moved swiftly along the path, the grass swishing below her boots, her senses seemed to increase with every step, and yet she detected nothing at all in the woodland ahead. It felt cooler and she could not understand why, the sun seemed paler than it had been recently.

The water gave off thick clouds of steam in the cooler morning, as she passed the hot springs and took the thin dirt path that led round to the base of the high rock. The white mists began to swirl in front of her, and she felt her heart beat faster as pictures from her dream became a reality. Moving faster she walked into the mist and up the path that led to the summit, her breathing drew into her in small gasps, as she began to feel out of breath. With a pounding heart that seemed to pulsate inside her head, she reached the top of the large flat rock with the two twisted trees, and saw within the mist a distorted figure dressed all in black.

Rune stopped, and watched the figure as it appeared, and disappeared in the clouds of white. "Did you summon me?" The voice was kind and gentle and yet held a force of power and age.

"You have no fear here Runestone Sapphire, daughter of the line of this realm. Life is within you and protects you, as it has all your line in the past... Come closer child for there is need of council, for soon you will face what you fight." Rune did not quite understand and felt a little afraid, she sensed nothing ahead, and yet she could see the figure in the mists in front of her.

Her eyes flickered with violet light with each step, as she tried to keep the blurred figure in focus. "Are you the one who walked in my dreams? Will you not tell me who you are or why you wish to meet in secret like this?"

The mist rolled forward and the figure disappeared from sight, the blurred figure reappeared a little closer, and yet Rune could not make out a face for the long black hood.

"I am but a traveller who is passing with your interest in mind, be at peace here and take heed in my words, for soon you will meet with a spectre of the one you fight, and she will try to wield a mighty weapon, you have the means to defend yourself, but need my assistance for the jewel you hold is of my hand. With my touch you will find greater use."

Rune slipped her hand into her pocket, and felt the warmth of the small white stone, she clutched it tight in her hand, and for the first time she felt it give off a sense of pulsating.

"This stone was carved from this land, the land of my great grandmother and created by my grandfather, how was this jewel created by your hand, for it is said to hold the power of this realm?" Rune drew the stone out of her pocket and opened her hand to reveal it in her palm. The mist swirled all around her and she had no sense of where the mysterious figure was. Her hand grew hotter and she looked down, the voice of the stranger echoed in her ears.

"The power of this realm is life, and you hold within your palm the key to all of it, you and the jewel are one, for all is not as it first appears. This gift was given by my own hand in addition to the gifts of all of us, use it well Runestone Life, and be all that was written." Rune looked all around through the mists trying to follow the voice, but there was no sign of the shadowy figure. The voice seemed to trail away as if leaving, and she felt panic growing inside her.

"No! Please wait, do not leave... I do not know how to use this, please I beg you come back and guide me." She spun in the mist, looking for any glimpse of a returning figure. "Please I beg you, tell me your name, come back and help me for my friend's lives and the lives of the woodland lord depend on me. Please do not leave me alone, help me as you must have my great grandmother." She fell to her knees feeling frightened and overwhelmed. "Please stay just a little longer, I am alone here and need the knowledge of others."

Silence surrounded her, and the uncertainty flooded into her. "You have never been alone my child, hold it out in the sunlight and be who you were born to be." Rune looked up to no avail, and watched as the mist swirled up into the sky and the day below the mist cleared into the bright sunlight of the new day.

For the first time since her grandfather had left for another realm, she had felt a sense of hope, a hope that someone could give her advice like her grandfather had always seemed to give her. Now alone at the top of the rock she felt a million miles away from Loxley, and the woodland where she could speak to her woodland lord. Rhiannon had deserted the realm, and her grandmother was in the Hidden Realm out of her grasp. She could not travel back to her table, and the only source of power left was Amethyst, who herself was a prisoner, and had not received the gifts of her line as the Star of the Merle had blocked them. Rune felt alone and out of her depth as she knelt on the stone floor alone in the sunlight, and the tears of her helpless feelings welled into her eyes.

Her hand felt hot and crouching low she looked down at her closed palm, through the blur of her tears. She gave a sniffle. "What is the use of something I have no knowledge of how to use?" Wiping her eyes on her left sleeve, she opened her right hand, and stared at the white stone shaped like a star. Slowly she sat back feeling lost as she gazed at it. The stone did nothing, her feelings of loss increased, as she sat on the floor below the old Hawthorn, she stared at her hand to no effect. A few minutes passed, as she waited with no result, and then she gave a long depressed sigh, and slowly stood up. She brushed the dirt from her pants, and turned to look out over the tops of the trees towards the Citadel Mount.

"Hold it out in the sunlight, what sense does that make?" Rune looked down at her palm as the light flooded over her now stood upright, and out of the shade of the old tree. The star gave a loud crack. "What?" Rune watched as a faint hairline appeared in the topside of the white star shaped stone. The star glowed for a second, and although it seemed strange, she was sure it had increased in size, the hairline crack looked like it marked a fine lid to what now appeared to be a star shaped container. Using her nail, she pushed, and to her surprise the fine lid slipped off.

There in the centre was a flat round red stone bearing a single runic letter; her voice was quiet and resounded with her surprise. "My symbol." Rune tipped the container, and the stone fell out, with her other hand she slipped the lid back on the white container and slid it back into her pocket. "Crystal contains all powers; I should have known." She held up the red stone and looked at it; it was smooth and warm to the touch as she moved it round her fingers, although she had never seen it before, it felt odd, as if the stone seemed to be familiar to her. She gave a soft satisfied smile. "My runestone." She closed her hand around it.

The flash of red before her eyes felt blinding. Pain flooded into her mind, and she felt a sudden jerk in the small of her back. Rune fell to the floor, as her mind raced. She gave a scream of fear, as images and words flashed through her mind at horrific speed. Her stomach churned, and she felt like she wanted to be sick, and still the images of millions of old and ancient runic symbols passed through her thoughts, like millions of words were being shouted at her. It was like the dreams of the night before, where shadowy figures told her things, but it was so fast she barely had time to take in the information, as more and more ran through her head at a dizzying speed. Her legs felt weak and she stretched out her arms in hope of grabbing on to something, as her head reeled and she gagged for breath. The bright lights continued to flash, and Rune felt panic, and thought she would faint. With a final jerk, her eyes exploded in light, and she felt a thump on her back. Everything stopped and she was almost sick.

Rune lay on her back with her eyes closed, and felt like she was lay on a round table that spun at high speed. She took a long breath of air and felt her insides calming down; the spinning felt like it was slowing. Breathing hard she sat up and opened her eyes, and the world all around her was normal and still. She felt a small twinge in her temple and took another long breath. "Oh Hearne, what the hell was that?"

Her composure returned, and she opened her hand and looked down at it. The stone was gone, it was as if it had melted into her hand, she knew she had not let go of it, and just stared thinking at her hand.

"Is it inside me? Was it part of me?" She was not sure; it had felt familiar like she had always known it. It was hard to say, she had always been told about the reasons for being called Runestone, but now she had to understand that somewhere deep within her, the magic had taken everything that had ever happened and everything that could happen, and placed them deep inside her. "Be what I am... I am just Runestone." She was not sure if it made full sense just yet, all she could think about was her grandmother and the many insights and powers she held. Opals held water which was one of the keys to all life. If Opal was water, did she have a stone of water within her? And did that mean that her daughter who was Violet Stone, which was the meaning of Iona, did that mean the violet given her by Hearne would one day enter inside her too? "Oh God Robbie, you struggle with all my family, hell I am one of them, and I am still having trouble understanding all this. No wonder you look baffled when we all meet."

Rune shakily got to her feet, and brushed herself down for a second time. She had no idea who the stranger in the mist was, and in a way she felt a little bitter about it. "Strange men in the middle of the night with weird gifts, as if life isn't hard or complicated enough as it is. Hearne knows what will happen next."

She pulled her cloak straight, and lifted the hood and looked up to the Citadel Mount, her head was still fuzzy and her eyes felt strained. She was not aware of the violet light that surrounded her. Rune took a long deep breath and tried to relax, she felt a little strange, if strange was indeed the word to use. Somehow, she felt like a change had taken place deep down inside her and was not sure what exactly had happened, the only thing that she could think of was the time at Robbie's Mere when her grandmother had left, giving her the full powers of her line. It was a similar feeling, back then she had been surprised to suddenly feel the life within everything around her. It was something she had become use to over time, and now she could focus that sense on to individuals and read their life flow. Her awareness began to grow inside her as she stood on the edge of the flat rock of the Lookout high above the trees.

"I feel more than normal." Her words passed her lips as thoughts, but seemed to take on a new meaning as the understanding of what she had said began to work within her. Like a bolt of lightning, she made the connection, here in the land of her beginnings she had received her final gifts and become what she had always known she was. The words of the mysterious figure sounded in her mind again. "You are Runestone Sapphire daughter of Life, be all that was written."

Her eyes lifted to the sky, as she understood. "I have become the stone, for the stone is all that was written. Time and life are one within me, I truly am Violetline." It all made perfect sense and she looked up into the heavens, and lifted her arms and screamed. "Lord Albanlin you should have waited, your gifts to this world and my guardian grandfather created who I am, I want to thank you for all you have done for my life and future." She gazed high into the sky and saw just for a moment the twinkling of the stars as the sun flared and took them away. A small streak of light shot across the sky leaving a long white trail behind it, and Rune felt a huge joy rise up inside her and her face lit up with bright violet, as she gave a huge smile.

"Thank you, My Lord of the Whitelines and skies. Thank you for giving me the knowledge to know what to do, I love you brother to Eve and my line." Rune's full abilities had been restored and enhanced, and over the moments of thought she took stood alone, she began to realise that in her fight against the Merle, she had strengthened. Albanlin the high lord of the fellow creators of the world had visited the land seldom in its time, his life span had been spent travelling the universe and seeking out the knowledge of time, and the powers contained within it. It had been he who had taken the small life form created by Eve, and added his powers of time and lines of white to create Merlin.

Merlin had been taught and guided by the white lord long before he came down to the realm of the world. Albanlin had studied the Merle deeper than any, which was why he had created a Guardian of the Whitelines of Time. Rune suddenly realised that her grandfather's powers had flowed into her, and now mixed with her grandmother's. The Violetline was now complete, and she felt for the first time in her life that she was now equal to the abilities of her grandmother Opal. All of her doubts had been taken away, and as she turned to face the high wall of rock in the distance, across the wide lake of Avalon, she knew she was right.

Rune adjusted her hood, as her eyes glowed with vivid purple and she scanned the realm before her, her senses seemed to be more finely tuned, and she felt a greater sense of power. Her mind moved with greater ease, and she smiled as she felt the small figure that stood alone in fear by the side of the entrance to the Citadel. "I see you little witch, your time before me will come, but for now tremble in the knowledge that you are not as safe as you first thought."

Rune's powers flowed through her, as she began to search the wide expanse of the Mount. Her eyes focused in her thoughts, as she felt a sudden sense through the crystal rock that should have held her out. Her powers flowed, as she pinpointed her target deep down inside the Citadel Mount, and Rune felt a great joy in knowing that she was now invisible to everyone, yet she could see them clearly. Her words left her lips in triumph. "I see you Le Fey, hide if you want but now I have you, mix your potions and do what you will, for Life is coming, and yours is my quest. Say your spells witch, you will need them."

Deep in the heart of the large carved hall of Rhiannon, the Dark One worked quietly alone. The thick yellow design covered most of the floor as she had added a few small designs of her own. Even Ursula, who was stood high above her at the entrance to the Citadel, had no real idea of what her mistress was preparing. The Dark One's spirits were certainly higher than many would expect, this had been something she had planned for a long time. In many ways it had annoyed her that Rune had taken so much time in coming to the realm of Avalon. But now she knelt in the centre of her design of power and prepared the final ingredients with trembling excited hands.

"Long have I waited, oh the joy I will have when you all see the extent of my powers, such fools it's almost too easy?"

She stood in the centre of the huge seven-pointed star that Ursula had drawn on the floor in a thick band of sulphur. Around the star set in a circle, her runic symbols traced lines across the room to large circles set at regular intervals, and filled with old runic letters. She gave a deep laugh as she lifted her arms, and the sulphur ignited, burning deep into the stone floor, as it flared from tallow into a deep blood red on the amethyst crystal floor. The sulphurous fumes hung in the air all around her as she slowly revolved round viewing her work, and she chuckled as she lowered herself to the floor and began the final preparations for her ritual.

Morgan le Fey pulled the thick, woven, heavy black cloth bag towards her, and the round polished brown wooden handles rattled as they knocked together on the floor. Opening the bag she rummaged around, and carefully lifted out a wide piece of rolled white fabric tied round its centre with silk cord, there was an air of glee about her as she muttered to herself. "Long has my collecting been, finally I have all of you within my grasp."

She pulled at the cord, which unravelled, and then slid it from the roll of fabric. The Dark One placed it gently onto the floor and gave a wide smile, which resembled the smile of a child with chronic wind. Unrolling the fabric, it revealed the long row of pockets that contained the fine thin vials of glass, which were sealed with small cork lids. She gazed for a second at what she had always called her collection.

Her ritual alone felt very sacred, the vial's contained small fragments of a life's work, and as she drew each one out of its own sleeve she smiled, and named her precious pieces. "From the crown of a woodland lord an acorn. From his daughter while held captive, a fingernail." She lined the vials in order on the floor. The next vial gave her a little more joy. "A tear from a queen of the Fae, and oh how could I forget, the hair from the eyebrow of Eve, Life herself." She gave a small cackle as her excitement bubbled out of her. She placed the vial down and took a long deep breath.

"Now what have we here? The dried fragments of skin from the Queen of the moon, Rhiannon you were valiant in battle in your youth, you knew you would never defend Eleanor." The vial lay by the others as she lifted the next. "Gwynfor one of the hardest to collect, the hair from the shoulder of a queen in Scotland. Oh, the joy I felt knowing you had embraced her, and given me the part of my puzzle I most desired."

The thin silver hair in the glass vial seemed to glow as she placed it back on the floor. The next vial contained a red powder like substance; it was the dried blood of Merlin, which she had used to help revive Mason and Mordred. One vial remained in the long roll, and her face seemed to explode with delight as she looked upon it. Morgan le Fey lifted it up to the light, and admired her greatest piece of her collection.

"My greatest prize of all and if I may say so, the most unexpected find of my whole collection history. The eyelash off the star of the Merle." Her face was almost illuminated as she spoke the name. "Runestone Sapphire of Loxley, my flower girl and almost the complete collection."

Gently she placed the vial on the floor, and turned back to the large black bag. "Now to business, before this day is full, all of you will answer to me for the crimes you have committed. Now you will know what true power is for the darkness is upon you all."

Morgan le Fey lifted a large silver chalice out of her bag and placed it in the centre of the seven pointed star, which now glowed in bright red against the purple floor of the hall. She slid a small silver dagger out of her belt and placed it on the floor beside the chalice. The moment to begin was approaching and she felt the excitement tingling in her fingers. Morgan lifted the pedestal, and tipped half of the crushed powdered bone of Uther into the chalice. Taking the dagger she drew it quickly across the palm of her hand, and clenched it tight, the blood dripped off the bottom of her hand, and into the chalice. Her face seemed to cloud as she drew her focus and concentrated hard.

Her head slipped backwards as she faced the sky beyond the roof of the cave, and stretched out her arms. "Eternal powers on high come to me and take this offering to the darkness and draw in the light." The chalice gave a small puff, and smoke rose out of it in a thin slither. She squeezed her hand tighter and let more blood drip into the chalice. "With my body I call thee, using him who you supported I call thee. Council of eight I draw thee here to my summons, be you of this world or others."

The Dark One spoke the name of each of the council that had ruled, and as she did, she tipped the item belonging to them into the chalice. "Seven of the land, come to me." She tipped the vial and the acorn dropped into the chalice "HEARNE" His name echoed around the chamber as a flare jumped out of the chalice. "OPAL" The flame in the chalice rose in a burst of white and burned three feet high.

"Gwendolyn White Circle." The flame gave a huge burst, and rose to the ceiling high above her. "EVE LIFE." The flames burst like a torrent across the ceiling of the hall, giving off a roar as if fanned by a huge wind. The Dark One leaned right back and howled with joy as the flames blazed out of the chalice and across the roof. She screamed in delight as she lifted the next vial. "RHIANNON OF THE MOON!"

The floor trembled beneath her, and she screamed, more from feeling the huge joy within herself, knowing that she was now in control and drawing the council together. "GWYNFOR LYLE OSBOURNE." The fire streamed down the walls to the floor creating a room of flame that engulfed the floor around her. She lifted the vial of dried blood and tipped it into the burning chalice. "Merlin the betrayer, I summon you back. As the last of the seven, I call the council to order, and command you attend." The whole of the Citadel Mount shook violently, as Morgan le Fey stood up and looked to the heavens and the ceiling of fire.

"Albanlin, you arrogant lord of the Whitelines the council has been called, your presence is required, and I draw you to me as replacement to the heir of your family line." She lifted the vial containing the eyelash of Runestone. "I have no earthly possession of you Whitelines, but I hold the element of yours within the realm of this earth, come to me to be judged in her name." She spun on the spot, and her dress billowed out into the air, and from her back two large wings slipped out and flapped behind her, as the colour in her eyes intensified. Lightening bounced around the room, and the large fountain at the upper end burst into life, and flowed with the deep thick red of blood.

"I call to you in the darkness, and with the darkness, hear me and the will of the Merle. I summon all of you to my council, appear before me and be judged by the Raven of the Merle."

The flames roared turning a rich golden yellow, and then with a blinding flash of white lightening, the first figure appeared fighting and trying to resist the power of the Dark One. Gwendolyn appeared as a faint smoky figure, she stood as if bound in ropes and struggled, wriggling from side to side, her face was contorted as she fought to free herself, and the Dark One smiled with her pleasure.

"Hello again little fairy, did you miss me?" She howled with laughter, as she turned and saw the next figure slowly appearing in one of the circles drawn out by Ursula on the floor. Gwynfor did not struggle, but he looked in pain as the smoky image of him grew. Behind her the room flashed blue, and the Dark One turned to see the image of Rhiannon bold and straight. "Welcome home Moony, sorry your new queen is a little busy at the moment, and cannot be here to meet you." Rhiannon said nothing but stood resolute staring with hatred at the Dark One.

Hearne and Opal arrived together, and she was delighted to see the tall tree like figure trapped in the circle around his feet. "Watch the fire Old One, twigs catch quickly." She gave a chuckle as he scowled with hatred at her. Opal looked a little in distress, but she faced Morgan le Fey, and held herself taught trying to not show her pain. All was going well, and there were just two circles for the council of the land, and one for the realm of the skies. Merlin came next with a burst of white lightening, he arrived and turned in his circle as he looked round at the others, and then at the Dark One.

"WHAT IS THE MEANING OF THIS OUTRAGE?" His temples pulsated, as he looked right at her. "You have not the right to summon a council you were never worthy to serve." Morgan strolled round the group with a lightness to her stride.

"I knew you would arrive ranting as usual, my god Merlin, have you ever been happy about anything? Hold your tongue until we are all assembled, I am sure you will find the proceedings of huge interest, after all you never gave me any credit as a student, did you?"

"I am surprised it took you this long Morgan." The soft voice of Eve echoed as the flames fell to the floor and were extinguished. The Dark One turned around to see the red clad image of Rune, who was Eve, gave a curtsy to her, as her eyes sparkled violet. "I am impressed, although I believe much of the credit belongs to that rock you clutch so tightly in your hand." The Dark One gave a scowl at Eve who was still smiling.

"You are here are you not? It was not the rock that demanded you be present at this time."

A deep cough rumbled behind her. "But we are not present, all you have here is our conscious images, I believe I am still home resting in my cave Morgan... but you have my attention, so please proceed, although looking at your beautifully drawn floor, I believe we are one short." The deep booming voice of Hearne, echoed with coldness round the inside of the great hall, and the Dark One felt a small twinge of fear, feeling the lack of fear in Hearne. She spun on the spot.

"What do you know, you stack of old twigs?" Her eyes burned with red fire. "I have summoned the council to answer to me. All of you have played your parts in the downfall of my line, you must pay for what you have done, you all must be punished for the betrayal of my mother and father."

"Tell me of the betrayal you believe we all played our part in Little Morgan of Cornwall." Her head snapped to the side where the tattered black robed figure walked up the long hall past the fountain that sprayed blood into its base. Albanlin walked slowly to the circle, and looked down at the floor. "Your assistant is skilled; I believe you would like me in here?" He stepped forward as Rhiannon lifted her hand.

"Albanlin no!" He smiled at her, and turned to face the Dark One. "I am watched over, so will play my part if it pleases you, although I would appreciate an answer to my question. Tell me how you think we betrayed you?"

She screamed at Albanlin and lifted a long white finger with a black sharp fingernail towards Merlin. "HE HELPED THAT ANIMAL RAPE HER." There was no denying it was a subject that Merlin had agonised about over the years. Albanlin looked to Merlin and then back to the Dark One.

"You are quite correct Little Morgan of Cornwall, my guardian gave in to a king, and your mother bore that king a child, but isn't it true Little Morgan, in many ways your mother had a better life? She was of a high line of the Celts and was bargained by her own father to marry a Saxon. Was it not true she felt shame at the union?"

"My father was a great warrior, and great leader of men, how dare you stand there in your arrogance and foul his name. Any woman would have been proud to be joined in a union with his line." Her eyes burned brightly, and small flashes of red shot out of the ends of her fingers.

"He was a beast, I met him several times, and he was nothing more than an animal who took whatever woman that was there at the time, I am sure he had other bastards all over the region hidden in round houses. There was no honour for your mother being married to a beast like that. Cornwall was an animal who ruled using fear and brutality, his only good quality was he renounced the dark arts and sent his even viler mother back to Saxony. Uther had his faults, but he treated her with great honour, and I might add, he loved her truly and her alone."

Gwendolyn looked at the Dark One with abject disgust. "You know the truth of him, why do you play these games? Uther treated you well, he would have treated you better had you given him the chance. I spoke with him often, I know how he tried to show you love, which is more than can be said of your father Morgan. Is it not true he ignored you as he found your spoilt pampered tantrums tiresome?"

Morgan le Fey spun round in the centre of the circle, her face twisted with rage as she glared at Gwendolyn. "Uther never loved me, he spent his time searching everywhere for his son, he did not want a half Saxon daughter. I was nothing more than a shadow to him."

Eve stood beside Gwendolyn in the circle of sulphur. "You never gave him a chance to though, did you? You did everything you could to destroy the feelings he held for you. Morgan, you have called us all here for truth, but you are the one who is blinded by it. Your hate is such that you will not accept anything we may say, Uther was Celtic and gave great honour back to your mother in their union, and whether you admit it or not, she loved him deeply for it, so what is the point of this spell? You have wasted your time here tonight."

It resounded deep with the Dark One, who had felt a little side tracked by the council. "I have other things to bring to your attention, do not try to weave your way out of this, you are mine now. The charms that hold you will not release you until I decide." The smugness returned to her face, as she began to walk slowly round the circle, Gwynfor gave a cheeky smile, and she stopped at sneered at him.

"What do you find so amusing? All you could ever achieve was to follow your sister, and hope that her shadow did not leave you completely in the dark." He gave a nod of agreement.

"She was rather busy as I remember, but I must admit My Dark Queen, things have been a little boring recently, I am rather enjoying this, I find it's often quite good to get out and about."

"WHAT? This is not a holiday old man; YOU ARE MY PRISONER."
Gwynfor gave a solemn nod.

"Oh yes, I understand you have my spirit here, you just carry on I am quite looking forward to the climax." The Dark One looked dumbfounded for a moment; Opal gave a snigger, as did Rhiannon. Morgan scowled at Gwynfor. "I brought you here to punish you, smirk all you like it will be your last."

The Dark One turned to face Hearne. "I have taken control of this realm, it is sealed to all other realms, I have the new queen of this realm prisoner, and I will soon destroy her castle, and scatter her burned body to the birds of your precious forest. You have no power here to stop me, I will rule here and use my power to aid my son, it's time to give up the fight and deliver your so called new king to me. If you bring him here to me this day your lives will be spared."

Suddenly the room felt more sober. Albanlin watched from under his hood, Merlin looked outraged, his face turned purple as he looked at her in disbelief.

"Are you insane? What the hell are you thinking Morgan, did you learn nothing at all when you studied with me?" Hearne shook his head.

"You have gone too far Morgan; how could you think we could even agree to your request? The future of this land lies in the hands of the new king; we could never agree to this, it would be a death sentence to everyone."

Morgan's face whitened. "The King? He is a boy whose only similar quality is his arrogance, what can a boy do to this world to make it better than my son has? He is the one who has rebuilt this land; it's his factories that give people money to live, he is the one that saved the masses from the Red Death, while you sat in the woods and watched them die. Man had finally come of age and what did you do the so called creator of this world? You set the world back a thousand years."

Albanlin looked up from under his heavy black hood. "Mason has done nothing except pave the way to his own ambition. He has hurt many people on his road, even now he sits at York and plots the destruction of peaceful communities, his rule is not fair or even handed, and you know it. You use the truth in a strange way Little Morgan; the facts you give look very different in the cold light of day. There appears to be two truths in here tonight, the first is the facts we all know, the other is your version of events."

Morgan walked across the wide circle back to the chalice, which still gave off a small flame and strange odour. "Truth, what do you all know of truth? You are guilty of the persecution of my family; you have brought aid to that woodchopper and his flower girl, and misused the powers for your own benefit. Man was supposed to have free will, and yet you have interfered to get the picture of life that you all deem right." Her eyes glowed brightly, as she lifted the cup, and with the flick of her fingers she dropped more of the crushed bone of Uther into it.

The yellow circles on the floor glowed white, and then rose like crystals around the ruling council of old. Albanlin made to move away, but she had worked so fast, even he was instantly encased in the tube of white crystal. Morgan le Fey tilted back her head and screamed with hideous laughter, she knew that trapped as they were she could take their essence and destroy them forever. Spinning round, her laughter rose higher and higher, until she sounded hysterical, as her black feathered wings expanded, and stretched to touch each column of crystal as she spun, she had finally achieved her life's ambition.

"Fools, Fools, for all of your powers and you have not the wit to defeat me, look at you all caught like rabbits on a snare, sealed in jars like an old maid's pantry. I am the one with the power to rule, it is the daughter of a Saxon king that will take this land of Celts and use it as I deem fit. All of you will die screaming; as I laugh at the world you made for the rule of the Raven. I will be queen supreme forever."

Rune sat quietly on the edge of the flat rock, as she rested and came to terms with her powers. The influx of information had been hard to ingest, and had left her more than a little giddy. She leant against the old hawthorn tree, and closed her eyes; runic letters still seemed to be jumbling around in her head, as an old language seemed to reverberate inside her. As always, the sense of life was all around her and yet now it felt stronger, she scanned the woodland in front and felt the familiar presence of Robbie, he was awake and with Jade by the furnace. Some of the women were up and walking in the woodland towards her, she smiled as she sensed her mother and knew that the hot springs had attracted her, she knew how much her mother loved to lounge in the bath.

Rune turned her mind and swept across the north of the realm, her mind moved slowly through the marshes and further, could she really detect all that was happening in the world? She focused her thoughts on two things, far away her children opened their eyes in their cribs, Rune was able to connect with them and her heart soared. The presence of Iona and Hal spread deep down inside her, and she smiled as a strong warmth filled her. Her thoughts went to her children now safe miles away, protected behind the tall wooden walls of Loxley.

"Hello my precious angels, I am here in your hearts. I will be back with you soon, and I will never leave you again."

A black cloaked figure appeared in her mind as if standing in front of her, Rune gave a startled gasp and opened her eyes. There was no one there; it must have been her imagination, she thought as she blinked just to make sure it was not a trick of the light. She closed her eyes again and drew another breath, the hooded figure was there in front of her, and his voice was familiar.

"Time is short, open your mind and be the stone, now is the time to appear." As quick as a flash the image disappeared, and with a beating heart she sat forward and opened her eyes again.

"My Lord Albanlin." She was alone, yet the feeling of urgency grew inside her. Footsteps crunched on the path behind her, and she stood up quickly and turned to face them. The tall white haired figure of Fagan walked towards her with a very concerned look on his face. "Fagan can you feel it as well?" He gave a nod as he looked passed her shoulder to the high rock in the distance.

"There is great danger, but of what I cannot say, ye must go to them for I feel something strange but foul, and know that time is short." Rune spun round and looked at the Mount, she focused on the strong feeling of Albanlin, and instantly she saw the scene in her mind of the eight tall columns of white crystal, and the hysterical figure that danced wildly around them.

"The Dark One has them trapped, the Ruling Council have been caught, I must go to them." Fagan snatched at her arm.

"Wait." Rune's head snapped round.

"I cannot she will kill them." He held her firm.

"Use ye gifts My Lady of Violet, ye must not rush, ye will not make it on time by foot, so use the gifts ye hold and walk unseen as the lady of life did." Rune could see the concern in Fagan's eyes, and she understood he was giving her good advice. She turned back to face the scene and closed her eyes to scan the whole scene. The Dark One was about to perform another ritual; she could only kill them one at a time. Fagan whispered to her.

"Relax and be seated, I will sit with ye and ensure ye has protection. Come sit below the trees and gather all ye power."

Fagan gently took her hand, and pulled her back towards the ancient hawthorn. Rune sat down, and got comfortable, and then with her guardian beside her, she closed her eyes and moved through the realm unseen. Ursula was still at the Citadel entrance, and the Houlen were stood behind the doors to the Great Hall guarding the passageways. Inside the hall Rune moved around each crystal cylinder checking the inhabitants were still intact. Fagan sat still and watched her with great interest.

"Tell me My Lady, are they caught in spirit or body?" Rune's eyes flickered and violet streaked across her cheeks.

"They are all there in spirit, held captive in containers of crystal." Fagan gave a nod even though Rune could not see him as her eyes were shut.

"The Lady of Life warned me of this. The crystal belongs to the three of creation, they are safe within it and cannot be harmed, and Little Blue Eyes is of ye line, as is the white lord. For now they will be safe. Help those who are of other lines first." Rune understood and moved through the air towards the hall using the tunnels as her guide. Her spirit arrived as the Dark One began to move around the circle. Her red eyes burned in her pale face, which bore a hideous and contorted smirk of happiness.

"Darkness of secret and darkness of deed, flow to me and hear me, as I offer you these sacrifices as thanks for the powers you send to me. Hear me, and take from this world those who would enslave you forever, and banished you to the outer reaches of all time and space."

Red light glowed from her eyes colouring the whole room in a sinister red glow. The chalice now in the centre of the huge yellow circle and star began to smoke. The Dark One moved across in front of it, and went down on her knees, and bowed to the smoking cup.

"Eternal power of the Merle, through this vessel of the universe I will guide you to me, and your unrivalled power will live forever in this realm." Flames burst up from the chalice to the ceiling, and the white crystal containers glowed with a sinister flicker of reds and yellows. The violet clad hooded figure rose out of the floor in front of the fountain still running red with blood. The Dark One did not notice as she bowed, her back to Rune and facing the chalice, and prepared for the passage of power. The voice of Rune rose into the air and echoed loudly.

"Be wud an stun, skyn ant bon. From min nay trey, broat te lif thru min..." The Dark One's head snapped up as she recognised the charm of the undoing, and as she lifted her head to the silent violet hooded figure she screamed.

"NO, NOT THIS TIME BITCH!"

"Hark min ant gran min, I col te yon retie te min"

Violet light filled the room, and the chalice lifted into the air, and flew at speed towards the wall, where it collided and crumpled spilling its contents, which blew in a thousand directions. The violet cloak parted, and a thin delicate white hand bearing a silver ring with a large blue stone rose up at the end of a violet sleeve. Light exploded out of it, and the crystal containers exploded in violet light, showering large chunks onto the Dark One, and throwing her backwards across the room. The Sulphur jars exploded, and thick yellow dust blew up into the air like a thick cloud, and blasted at the Dark One as Rune's voice echoed louder.

"I warned you witch." The Dark One lifted into the air blinded, as she threw curses in every direction, trying to see through the thick yellow mist that burned at her eyes, and find out where Runestone stood. She landed with a bump, and slid on the smooth cold stone. Her hand shot into her pocket towards the black Star of the Merle, but as she entered the pocket, Rune's words echoed into her head. "Oh no you don't." Morgan le Fey felt something grip her arm tightly, and as hard as she tried, she could not force her hand down and around the black stone. She screamed in frustration as she fought with all her strength.

Sat by the tree as Rune's anger surged upwards inside her, she felt the hand of Fagan take hers and squeeze, then a softer and smoother hand took her other. The familiar voice of the black hooded lord spoke softly in her mind.

"Now is not the time, the others are free and returned safely. It is time for you to return and gather your strength for the real fight." Rune felt the calmness wash into her, and the anger subsided; she relaxed and felt her spirit leave the room, and return to herself sat below the old Hawthorn.

The dust fell slowly back to the floor as the Dark One coughed and writhed on the floor. She sat up like a viper ready for the attack, but was confronted by shattered crystal and swirling dust. The room was empty, except for the trickling sound of the water in the fountain, where it ran clear and cool. She spat the dust from her throat and screamed out in anger. "I will find you Flower Girl, and when I do you will know my fury." She leaned back her head and gave a loud wailing scream of temper and pounded on the floor with her arms and legs in temper. The large chunks of crystal from the containers rose up off the floor and spun in a large circle. As the Dark One gave another mighty scream of rage, the crystal hurtled down the long hall and collided with the fountain.

The statues exploded into a million pieces, and were thrown across the floor of the hall, as water sprayed wildly into the air. The doors all along the large hall burst open, and the Houlen came screaming inside and stopped instantly, as they saw the water spreading across the floor to the base of the steps at their feet. All of them looked round with angry eyes, and then noticed their Mistress sat on the floor dusted in yellow powder and screaming with rage.

They stood silently unsure of what to do, as Morgan looked round at them all, it seemed a little too much for her to bare and up came her arms, as lightening blasted out of her finger tips and bounced off the water hitting the Houlen guard, and throwing them back to the floor. "Don't just stand there like fools, get into that woodland and find me that purple bitch. Burn it and hack it down until you find her, and do not return until you do so."

The black elegantly dressed figures leapt from the floor, and screamed as they transformed into the tracking wild beasts of evil they had been made to be. With high pitch screams, and wails for blood lust, they all turned and ran into the tunnels. Several monks made the mistake of crossing their paths, and found themselves on the receiving end of their long claw like talons. The Houlen were free, and they wailed out of the Citadel and lower tunnels to hunt.

Rune opened her eyes, and Fagan gave a smile. "By heck ye can fight as good as Little Blue Eyes." She gave a small giggle and looked round, the fine figure of a woman dressed in red stood at the edge of the rock and looked out over the realm; Rune stood up and walked across to Eve.

"You have used your gifts well my Granddaughter of Life." Rune was unsure, and did not understand why she was stopped. Eve lifted a hand to her back and let it rest on her shoulder. "Now is not the time, it was important that the others were returned, and the Lord Whitelines returned to the outer realm. In time you will understand more, you have learned much this day, but it will take a little more time before all of it will make sense to you. We are all proud of you Runestone Life, for you have honoured all of us. You must harness your new powers and prepare to face all that have taken this place." She turned to face Rune, and her violet eyes shone in the light.

"A new queen must be seated before you face the line of the mortal le Fey. Once the black one leaves this realm you will have little time here. The power of the Fae will grow swiftly, and you will have to take those who have no link to that line out for their own protection. The power of the moon will rebuild the realm quickly, and then as in days past it will seal itself to remain hidden from the woodland realm. Only then will the passages of power be the gates in and out." Rune felt a little disappointed but she understood the reasons.

"I would like to be rid of her forever. I feel I have wasted my chances." Eve gave a smile as she turned.

"The Mount is sacred to the Fae and to take the life that is not fully mortal carries consequences, your time will come, you still have lessons to learn. Know this much Runestone Life. When the time comes to destroy her, you must have the sword bearers with you, read the words of those who saw this event and documented it, and you will know the moment and she will be destroyed forever."

Rune nodded at Eve. "I know the text you speak of; I have read it many times.

Although I am afraid that one is lost to us, and I cannot see them." Eve pulled her into a warm embrace.

"You are in the centre of your homeland, here the powers of all of you will grow in strength, use well those who can communicate to all forms, for there lies the path to discovery. I will see you again Runestone Life, but now I must return to rest, it takes great strength to maintain the shape I lost. Bring the star to me when the time is right. Now go with my trusted friend and prepare." Eve looked up and smiled at Fagan as he waited quietly. "Thank you, My Keeper and good friend, again you have been there to protect all I hold dear and precious." Fagan gave a very regal bow.

"I am ye servant My Lady of Life, rest now for a time and I will watch over all." Eve bowed to him and Rune.

"She will send her hunters; be ready for they will penetrate a little of the protections here." The figure of Eve faded slowly from view, and Rune felt sadness, she turned away from the edge of the rock, and walked with Fagan to the path that took them down to the hot springs, and back through the woodland to the house of logs.

Fagan talked none stop about Eve and her time in the realm, and though he often wandered off at tangents, Rune found it interesting, for it was the story of her family line and the start of time.

At the edge of the trees in front of the long house, Fagan stopped and turned to Rune. "Her guard will wait at the edges and prepare to attack ye, here in this forest my trees will protect ye. Ye must rest and prepare, the time here will be shorter than I believe ye expected, I will be sorry to see ye leave as there is much I would talk to ye about. Ye must promise me, ye will return to my home at times and talk with me."

Rune gave a smile, Fagan was a little eccentric in some of his behaviour, but in the brief time she had been around him, she had felt a fondness for him. "I will look forward to many visits with you in future days Fagan the Keeper, and with your permission I would like to one day bring my children to see the start of their line."

Fagan puffed up his chest with great pride; his voice was soft but filled with delight. "I would be tickled to pieces if I could see the little violet one and her brother of the thorn, for there has been many a thing said to my ears about them." He lowered his voice to a gentle whisper as he bent closer to Rune. "The beech are most excited about them, but I know my friends on the rock would feel great honour to meet them for a while, just don't tell the Ash, oh they can give quite a paddy at times if they feel other trees got more than them." Rune gave a giggle and took Fagan by the hand.

"I shall keep it very quiet, I promise." Fagan stood up and looked around to check they were not overheard; he smiled and gave a wink. Walking slowly and sharing their secret, they wandered over the wide grass towards the large house, where the sound of hammering steel rose up into the air. Jade stood up near the fire with a black sooty face and waved.

Robbie stood up and smiled next to Bear, who was pumping the large bellows, the sweat ran down his face as he gave a big smile, Rune left Fagan's side and walked across to him, as the other Specialists worked all around Robbie. Jay looked up from a row of the Specialists who all fitted brown spotted feathers to the long new shafts of the arrows, Jasper and Big John carried large stacks of old weapons on their backs, as they walked to a large pot on the fire, Rags gave a cheeky grin as she lifted the weapons and dropped them in to melt. Robbie put down his hammer and walked across to her, his skin shone in the sun with his sweat. "Hey beautiful." She slid her arms round him and pulled him close.

"Hi gorgeous. You look like John wielding that hammer."

He gave a smile and winked at the bright smiling face of Jade. "Not sure he would think me that good to be honest, but it's nice to hear the ring of the hammer, it reminds me of home." She held him tight feeling good to be close.

"This is our last hurdle and then we can return. It won't be much longer Rob." He kissed the top of her head.

"I can't wait to walk in the Mere; I think a few days off and picnics in all our favourite places." Rune gave a happy sigh.

"Oh that would be so nice, yeah home and the children, and a feast in the woodland. I love you Robbie."

CHAPTER EIGHTEEN

UNEXPECTED ANNOUNCEMENTS

The trees around the quiet wooden house rustled as the breeze lifted, the long grass around the edges of the Mere swayed from side to side shaking their nodding bright flowers of the wild poppy and columbine. Just short of the tree line, under the dense beech the dark mysterious figure dressed in a black hooded robe stood as still as a statue. From under the hood no visible feature could be seen, and all of the birds in the trees fell silent from their song, and the small animals stopped in their tracks and sat silent. The wind moved, whispering to everything and tapping the edges of the water, so that its ripples slowed to a soft lap. The presence of Albanlin received respect from all of nature.

A soft creaking sounded in the trees, and the hood of Albanlin twitched. "You were always aware of my movement's old friend." The tall treelike man of Hearne moved softly across the leaves towards the hooded figure.

"Not at all, I knew you would not be able to resist a look at what will be the centre of all things; I surmised you would visit before you left." Albanlin turned to greet his old friend and brother.

"You still doubt the choices we made; I felt it in the cave. I came to feel the presence of the Runestone, for I have never doubted the power of my sister, and I knew it the moment I met the red stone, as of all things that Eve was as always quite correct."

Hearne gave a long sigh, which sounded like the steam that flowed up from the hot ground. He shook his head slowly, and the hair from his chin swayed like the long grass in a summer storm.

"I loved her, and you know of the faith I placed in her, but I see the doubt that lives in my little Runestone at times and it concerns me deeply. The bowman has done much, but like the willow on the bank he has over stretched, and he is in danger of falling into the water." The black hood of Albanlin moved as he shook his head.

"You misunderstand him my old friend; can you not feel what they have built here? Below the bank is a mighty rock of support, and it is red in colour, little

Runestone has more power than even I saw. She will cling like a vine to her willow, and he will stand on that rock and lean out further, but he will never fall." Hearne gave a smile.

"I admire the faith you hold, and as promised I shall wait here and watch from my cave. The council ruled, and I will not undo what was planned in those times long ago. But as I have said in the past my friend, I will not allow a snake to rule in this land, and as before, I am ready to undo all I created to protect what was built here. This realm and all the others would prosper without man." Albanlin turned and walked out of the shade of the trees and into the brilliant sunshine.

"Man was flawed there is no doubt, but there have been times when those flaws were also strengths, I believe in my sister, and her faith that all would come full circle, I know times may look dire my old friend, but when you bend a tree like a willow backwards, it has no choice but to recoil and fire back with huge force. They will return with force, our old tree talker already has them on the road to recovery, and in his realm, things can grow stronger than we ever imagined."

"Yet they haven't, their power has entered the star, and soon if it is not stopped it will spew out its evil, and this world will become darkness and suffering forever." Albanlin looked back at the serious dark lined face of his old friend of the trees.

"It will never go that far. Hearlearn please I beg of you, give them the time, do not interfere until the final moment comes, think of what we discovered and built here. There is nothing like it anywhere, you cannot risk this for nothing more than a moment of doubt, if Rundalba was here she would prove you wrong and you know this." Hearne hesitated for a moment, and his voice dropped for a second, and it lost its deep rumble like thunder, and was as soft as a gentle foot on warm grass.

"But she isn't, she is gone, and now walks her realm as a lost image of a time long past. She lies encased in tears projecting herself to the eyes and minds of others, nothing more than a whispering spirit. Her faith was the reason the mother of the snake gained the advantage; she will never be allowed to use that magic again. Man now is her puppet and I will cut the strings if she tries." Albanlin saw the sudden pain cloud over the face of his friend, he walked slowly back into the trees and patted his soft moss like shoulder.

"Do not rush my friend; take your time before deciding the fate of so many. Have faith in my judgement, for the Runestone will harness what she needs and drive the darkness away; as we speak her awareness is growing as the seeds I planted in her mind germinate. Search your heart for the love of Opal and her children, and give them the time that they need." Hearne looked saddened and weary, and yet he gave a soft smile and nodded.

"You have always shown us all greater wisdom, I shall keep the bargain I made with the council, from my seat I will watch over my line, it will only be in the last moment of her breath that I shall act, have no fear Father of White Time."

Albanlin gave a nod of appreciation.

"I shall walk a little longer in your realm, and then I must return to my seat and like you, I shall watch what becomes of this and other realms. I have enjoyed this time my friend, may your beard grow ever greener, and the leaves beneath your feet ever softer."

Hearne gave a smile and turned back to the trees, his mind was now filled with a life lived long ago when all was first created, and the pictures of his beloved Eve flowed like water over the stones in his head. His pace was slow and silent as he made his way back to the large outcrop of rock; to wait and see what will become of all that Eve breathed life into.

Albanlin walked round the edges of the Mere and felt the life in the earth at his feet. The more he stood in Robbie's Mere, the more faith grew within him. As the day wore on in the unbearable heat of the sun, unaffected he turned and looked to the sky. "Be the stone all was written on my child of lines." His words a whisper, as in a flash he was gone.

Where he had stood a single white flower grew out of the damp soil, it was like nothing that had ever grown in this realm, and was only growing in one other. The time flower, or white star as some called it, grew in wild abundance in Avalon, and it marked the flow of power of the highest lord of the council, Albanlin.

"HARRY MAN! Oh my big brave baby, where have you been, I have been lost in a realm of uncosmic vibes that hassled my karma with worry." The tiny figure of Maggs ran for her life, as she saw the tall dark clad dripping figure of Harry walking out of the trees. Her feathers and beads bobbed into the air flapping, as her chains and bangles rattled like metal bones, Harry staggered towards her holding his sheathed swords, and looking like he had walked to the edges of hell and back.

Rune smiled as she slipped her arm round Robbie's waist. "It appears our wanderer has returned.... Ooh he looks rough Rob." Robbie gave a small smile as he watched the tiny blonde bushy haired figure of Maggs leap up into Harry's long arms, and hang from his neck as she plastered him with kisses.

"Hey Chicken, I've been to some radical and most uncosmic places, seeking my karma. Whoa, it's been intense." He gave a weak smile, and Maggs went into cosmic chick mode.

"Oh My Poor Big Baby Boy, Oh you poor Chicken, Come... Come let Mama take you to cosmic places, where I can make your karma happening and most funky." She cooed and kissed him, as he walked holding her up in his arms, as her bright pink boots covered with brightly coloured felt daisies dangled round his knees. Rune smiled.

"Funky boots, I wondered what she had on under that huge green skirt, think I might ask her to make me a pair." Robbie chuckled.

"Yeah, me too." She laughed as she squeezed his side.

"Good news is Rob, you got Harry back as he was... I am still not quite sure that's a good thing, but he will be Ok in a scrape." Robbie gave a nod.

"He is as mad as a hatter, but that's how I need him. He had me worried for a while, I am glad to see him back to normal. Although I wonder why he is so wet?" Rune shrugged.

"Not sure, maybe he fell in the river."

The truth of the matter was that as the tiger chased him and still very blue and naked, he had not paid that much attention to where he was going. His blind panic kept him moving much faster than he normally would in strange territory, and he trampled everything in front of him down. It was unfortunate that he ran into to a large clump of small Birch saplings that rose from the floor like ten-foot canes. Harry ploughed on through not realising they were on the edge of a rather steep rock wall. Screaming for his life, he ran right off the edge, and dropped like a stone into the deep cool pool below. Blue Harry, swords and bag, all descended to the bottom of the pool. For Harry it was a lucky escape, as Furry Face was not overly keen on taking a bath, and turned at the top of the high wall, deciding he would play with Harry later, and returned home.

Harry swam back to the surface and lay gasping on the soft grass for some time, before he dived back in to recover his things. Back to a normal pink colour, and dressed in his dripping clothes, he returned back to the long house of Fagan. He had been cured of the curse of the white flowers, but it had been a very long and difficult ordeal. With a new bottle of tonic, care of Maggs bag, he settled down in bed to be pampered by the love of his very strange life. A quick visit from Robbie who found it hard not to smile revealed that there were Cutters in the forest, and gave Robbie the chance to start to move forward, as he began to plan the rescue of Amethyst, and the freedom of the realm of Avalon.

It had been a long day, but Robbie was pleased to see the new stack of fresh arrows. Jade had worked all day with Bear keeping the furnace running, and apart from the stack of arrows, Big John had several buckets of arrow heads to sharpen, before fitting onto the new shafts. Robbie gave a sigh of relief, as most of the group gathered on the grass with a cool glass of nettle tea. In the forest, the powers of the group seemed to be recovering, and Crystal was delighted when she managed to chill all the drinks.

Robbie looked round the group, all of them looked pale and drawn; it worried him as he knew that the coming days were going to be tough on them. Earlier he had despatched Blades and Fox to find out more about the Cutters in the forest, he wanted more time, but he felt it was running out. Rune was the only member of the group that looked like she was at full health, but she had disagreed with Robbie and argued the group needed more time, Skip noticed him taking stock of the group.

"Something on your mind Robert?" Most of the group looked up at him, as he adjusted himself on the large log he was sat on. He gave a long sigh as he sat before the people he cared about more than anything.

"I feel like we have all been here before." Smokes gave a nod.

"Canterbury and Dunnottar were tough ones, but no tougher than what we face now Robbie, I cannot speak for everyone, but I know Harry and me are up for it." Every head in the group gave agreeable nods; John patted Smokes on the shoulder.

"Aye, we are here, and ready to finish the job." Robbie gave a smile, it never ceased to amaze him, how much loyalty he had around him.

"This will be tougher than before, we have all the soldiers and the Houlen to face, and for some of you, it may be without your powers. That little black trinket she wields will draw all your powers towards it and leave you defenceless." Maddy scoffed.

"We are hardly defenceless Robbie... I must admit my bow gives me a great advantage, but I am just as good with an ordinary bow. All of us have great skills from what we have learned from being together for so long, even without our powers; we are still superior to her soldiers." Rags looked round at the others.

"I know I am just a postie most of the time, but we aint got much choice have we? I mean, it's like I was saying to Blades earlier, we are trapped here unless we kick their ass good an proper aint we?" Robbie had to agree.

"Yes we are Rags... But the odds of getting out of here at the moment are greater than any of us have ever faced, I want you to understand that." Bear sat covered in sweat and grime from the forge, his large muscles rippled as he moved.

"We all know the score Robbie, we knew coming in would be dangerous, yet here we sit, I think I can speak for everyone when I say you have our swords, so find us a way out and use them."

"Ere, ere. You look at what we can be doing, an you will ave all of us up your back. Alley was my sister, and I ave not forgotten them Houliens, an what they did to her. We eez ready to show them our woody ways and even this score." Skip pulled Treen close and gave her a hug.

"I think my lovely fiancée has said all that needs to be said." Maddy turned with a look of surprise on her face, as did some of the others. Treen blushed.

"My Skippy has asked for my hand, and I ave said a big yes yes to im." Skip beamed a very large smile.

"Well, it was only fifteen minutes ago, I had meant to let you all know at dinner, but I feel her response has somewhat overwhelmed me and I slipped up a little." Robbie stood up and walked over to Treen. She stood up and he pulled her into a tight hug, as the others all gathered with smiles and embraced Skip. Robbie turned to them both; he took Skip by the hand.

"I am delighted for the pair of you, it's much needed cheer for all of us. All I have ever wanted for you is happiness." Skip smiled at Robbie.

"We have come far together Robert my friend." Robbie nodded as Rune came up at his side and gave him a kiss on the cheek.

"I am so happy for you both; I know you will make a very happy life together." Treen gave a giggle.

"You ave seen this...? Or are you just aving a guess?" Rune laughed as she embraced Treen.

"I know things; you know this my sweet sister."

The sudden announcement turned a normal meal into a full blown celebration, as Maddy insisted on putting up tables out on the grass, and organised a proper meal to mark the very special occasion. It was a loud and noisy evening under the hot sun, as some of Harry's tonic seemed to find its way into the fruit juice. For Robbie who sat up on the porch beside Rowan, it was nice to see them letting off some steam and enjoying themselves. Rowan smiled from his chair and saluted the happy couple. His voice was low as spoke to Robbie.

"Keep them together in whatever you plan, we almost lost her in the tunnels, make sure they both come through this side by side." Robbie smiled at the casual yet deep way Rowan expressed himself.

"I have it in mind, I want all the sword bearers together, and those closest to them. I think for this fight we will need to watch each other with far more care than normal." Rowan took a swig of drink.

"I would prefer it if we all stuck close... In the past we have split into groups, I think she will expect that, so let's disappoint her."

In front of the long wooden house, the group frolicked enjoying the moment and doing their best to keep their minds off what the coming days would bring. Steph watched as Rune slipped off and walked towards the trees. She quietly picked her drink off the table, as Smokes laughed with Big John, and ensuring everyone was occupied, she lifted an extra cup, and then headed towards the trees.

Rune walked off the path into the lush green grass, dotted with thousands of tiny flowers. Her mind was preoccupied as she tried to understand the thousands of voices that had given her endless amounts of information. From the moment the stone had sunken into her palm, she had felt different. She could not explain it, it was more than just feeling everything, and her awareness had grown a thousand fold. Robbie had done his best to understand what she had told him, but even she was finding it hard to fully comprehend the power of the rune stone. Her surroundings filled her with a sense of joy as she looked down at the flowers in all shades of colour, weaving in and out of the bright coloured grasses and ferns. Up ahead the trees thinned out, and she could see a large tree that had fallen, and was wedged in the crook of another large tree. It formed a barrier at chest height, over which the grass ran down to a large clear pool. In many ways it reminded her of the Mere and home, it was little comfort to her, knowing that before she would ever be able to walk there again, she must confront and defeat the Dark One.

She reached the fallen tree, and leaned on it as her mind wandered, ahead the water shone, reflecting the light in a thousand directions, at the far end of the lake reddish brown mountains rose high into the clear sky. It was so picturesque, and Rune thought it could have been anywhere in her world, but it wasn't, no matter how much she wanted to be as far as possible from this place, the reality was, she had no choice, her destiny was set out, and it meant confronting something more powerful than even the vast knowledge of the world could predict.

Alone in her thoughts, she did not notice as her mother came up behind her with two tin cups and walked up to her side. Steph looked out on the pool as she put the cups down onto the tree. "It's beautiful, isn't it?" Rune seemed to come out of her thoughts as Steph passed her the cup.

"What? Sorry Mum I was miles away." Steph took a sip of her drink.

"I felt the change when it happened, I cannot know what you are feeling, but I am your mother, and here I am sweetheart."

"I forget you too are from the line of Eve." She smiled. "I think sometimes I forget too much."

Steph lifted her hand across Rune's back, and holding her shoulder she pulled her daughter close. "You have a lot on your mind sweetheart; it has been a very long year." Rune lifted her cup with both hands and took a small sip, it was hot and she blew the coffee to cool it as her eyes wandered back across the lake.

"So much has happened." Her head turned slightly to her mother who watched her with care. "I feel it overwhelms me if I try to think about it all." Steph smiled.

"I know how hard it is for you sweetheart, you should have had more time and rest before coming here. It is barely a month since your children came, you look exhausted." Rune slouched on the tree, as she adjusted her stance, and looked down the bank to the water that gently lapped against the grass.

"I didn't want to leave them, but I could not let Robbie come alone." Two tears ran on to her cheeks. "Mum... I miss them so much; I don't think I can bare another moment away from them." Steph opened her arms, as Rune turned and burst into tears, she pulled her close and held her tight.

"It's alright Rune sweetheart, I know how much you miss them, come on let it out, you have been bottling it up since we left." Steph stroked her daughter's hair as she held her tightly, and Rune sobbed deep bitter sobs into her. "There we are, let it all out, I am here sweetheart." Rune's sobs mixed with her muffled words.

"I am so frightened, I did not get enough time with them and now I am not sure I will ever see them again, we are trapped here and I am not sure what to do, I am trying so hard to get everyone through, but I cannot think straight with all this stuff going through my mind. I want Iona and Hal; it is driving me insane thinking of them." Rune wailed into Steph's chest, and all her mother could really do was hold on tight and let Rune release some of her pent up emotions, after all on two previous occasions Rune had wiped out a large forest, and also a very wide circle of mountain range. Steph knew this would be a better if not a more old fashioned approach that could well save lives. She clung on to Rune and talked quietly to her.

"You are not alone Rune; you should not have shouldered so much of the burden. We are a family who all have gifts given for the tasks we face; you have to let others take some of this burden and help you." Rune gave a huge sniffle and looked up, her eyes were red, and her tears shone like small violet crystals on her cheeks.

"None of you can face her Mum; I am now the only one left who can do this." Steph gave a shrug.

"Rune sweetheart I am not exactly sure you are right." She smiled as she raised her hands and cupped her daughter's face. "Maybe alone we could not, be we are a circle... Rune together as sisters we have more power than she could ever draw down from the sky." Rune blinked as her tears left her eyes.

"But Mum, she has the power of the Merle. I have to face her and take back the stone, none of you could do that, she is too dangerous." Steph's green eyes shone with her love of her child.

"Rune, I have the power to make all around her sleep, Una can hold back her power, or at least some of it. Jade has an extraordinary gift; she can cause chaos all around her. Maddy has stored pains that can cloud anyone's judgement, not to mention Treen's ability to weaken minds. Hell, Crystal could freeze the bitch." Rune gave a slight giggle. Steph smiled.

"You see... You are not as alone as you think. The point is we have all these gifts; we could distract her and confuse her, which would give you the chance to disarm her. The thing is Rune; you have forgotten some of the things we have all done together, I remember a time when Runestone Sapphire called to her sisters in need, and as our centre we came to her aid. Maybe my sweet daughter you should remember those moments, because everyone of us is here waiting."

Steph kissed her softly on the head, as she saw the glint move in Rune's eyes, she knew her daughter well enough to know that Rune understood her. Rune nodded as Steph leaned back and lifted her cup off the trunk. "Thanks Mum." Steph gave a broad smile.

"Never forget Runestone Sapphire, you are my child. I too have the need to know I am needed by you, and I miss my daughter at times as well." Rune smiled and felt a little of the pressure inside her release.

"I am sorry mum, I never realised. I do love you." Rune gave her mum a big hug, and they stood together leaning on the tree and sipping their drinks.

"Rune never forget that it matters little whether you have power and abilities, nothing is more important than family, and who you are as a person. I know, I have watched my daughters grow, and they are the most precious things in my life. You have your own children now, and for them you must fight, because they need a mother." Steph stared out across the lake. "My father taught me that, he fought for me and my sisters all his life, all I have left is Gwinne, your father, and you girls." Rune watched the sadness wash over her mother's face.

"He has left us... I miss him, I really need to talk to him, when I saw him, last night sealed into a tube, my heart broke, because I realised how much he has taught me, and how much he has left to teach. What will we do without him?" Steph turned to Rune.

"I cannot see him Rune, but he will never leave me or you. Close your eyes and believe me he will be there, just talk to him as I do." Steph patted her daughter's arm. "Never forget he was the Guardian of the Whitelines, in all he did for you, there was deeper meaning." Rune gave a big sigh.

"He knows about the runestone Mum, he was the only one I could ask for understanding, and he has left me here alone." Steph turned and pulled Rune into her arms.

"Oh Sweetheart is that what you think? Oh no Rune you must not believe that." She slid Rune back and looked her right in the eyes. "The night you were born he knew, as you know Runestone was not the name we intended to give you, but my dad bless him, he saw how the magic had been woven and hidden within you. I was not sure at first why he had chosen that name, but do you honestly believe knowing how close I was to him, that he did not share certain information with me? He knew Rune, I have no idea how, but he made sure that if anything happened you would not go through this alone. I know Rune, its why today I felt you receive your gift, because your grandfather made certain one of us would be here for you." She gave her a smile and kissed her softly on the cheek. "I am here My Darling; together we will work out all the answers." Rune felt a great sense of relief wash over her and nodded her head.

"I am glad you are with me; I always end up in trouble, and you never fail to come along at the right moment." Steph smiled and picked up her cup.

"It's what we mums do." Rune gave a giggle.

"I suppose I have all this to come." Steph handed Rune her drink.

"It never goes away Rune, you will see."

Both of them stood and watched the lake, somehow the effects of the water instilled a great sense of calm in both of them; it was a special moment between mother and daughter. Rune's spirits lifted, and she began to smile more. They turned to walk back, although the sun was high in the sky, it was almost midnight, and Rune felt exhausted. Slowly they crossed back through the grass filled with flowers, and Rune thought about all that had happened, as they got back to the path she stopped and looked at her smiling mother.

"You have realised haven't you, that Jade inherited grandmother's gifts?" Steph gave a laugh and looked at Rune; she saw that Rune was being serious.

"Rune you are life, you are the one that has taken her place, not Jade."

"I have the gift of Life as Eve had, but the Green Circle is Jade's to use, she has gifts I can only dream of." Steph shook her head.

"That cannot be right Rune; mum passed her gifts over me, and chose you." Rune shook her head.

"No Mum, I have part of her gifts and some of Hearne's, they are blended with the one gift Eve never passed on, I got the stone on all that has been written. Can you not see what has happened, how can I have all these gifts, without a means of mixing the magic?" Rune stared at her mother. "Mum I needed a weaver, to take my powers and blend them into me." It took a few moments for Steph to completely comprehend; it hit her like a rock.

"I am the weaver... I never realised." She suddenly looked very surprised and lifted her hands to her mouth, Rune gave a solemn nod.

"Mum you are his heir, you are now the guardian of the Whitelines. I really am not sure if he told you, but I am positive he has prepared you... Think about it, there has only ever been two who could weave magic together from differing sources, the first was Albanlin, and the second..."

"My father." Her voice was almost a whisper, Rune started to chuckle, and Steph looked at her. "Why are you laughing?" Rune looked at her with astonishment.

"Why... think about it, finally it's happening to someone else, all this time has been me discovering all this information on who I am and who I have to be. Now it has finally happened to someone else."

Robbie lay in the dark in his bed and heard Steph and Rune as they came laughing across the clearing, full of giggles; Rune stumbled up the steps and into the kitchen. He gave a smile and turned over, he had a lot to think about, but he also knew that after tonight, so did everyone else.

The new morning brought the start of activity around the house of Fagan; he dressed and made his way into the main room of the house, where the old figure of Fagan sat quietly thinking and smoking his long white pipe. He pulled the tip of the pipe off his lip, and lifted it in silent salute. Robbie gave a nod, and wandered across the room toward the stove, where a large brass kettle smoked with the steam of the freshly made coffee. Fagan leaned forward in the chair.

"Ye will need to prepare, things will turn quickly and ye must take the opportunities whilst they are fresh." Robbie poured two cups out, and walked over to the fire; he handed the other cup to Fagan, and sat in the chair opposite, lifting his feet to warm them on the fire.

"I have arrows, I am grateful for the use of the furnace; I cannot thank you for the kindness you have bestowed on my team." He gave a long yawn. "We still need to sharpen our weapons, and repair any that will need it; I feel this fight will be a hard one." Fagan's bushy eyebrows moved up and down as he spoke and thought at the same time.

"Ye worry too much about numbers. In the past ye have defied the odds, why change fighting habits? Ye people have gifts that the enemy do not have, but I agree ye should prepare and be ready for a hard fight. A war can be won on what has been set up in advance. The enemy has prepared for a long time; I think ye have seen that much in recent days." It had occupied a lot of Robbie's time recently, the amount of Mason's soldiers was vast, after all he had expected the realm to be empty.

"We walked into a trap here, I underestimated Mason for the first time, and it has cost me." Fagan could see the concern, and also feel the heavy burden that Robbie shouldered. He tapped his pipe on the arm of his rocking chair, and fumbled for his pocket knife. He scraped at the inside to clean it as he watched Robbie in thought sat drinking his coffee.

"Ye have achieved what ye aimed, ye young prince has his jewel, and ye good lady is working out the means to use her gifts. It was a hard fight there is no doubt, but ye are not the kind of man to sit back and lick ye wounds." He gave a warm smile as Robbie looked across at him. "Ye have good people; ye are all quite young and came late to the fight." He leaned forward in his chair and his eyes as dark as the earth met Robbie's in a hard stare. "But the thing is my young lord, ye came anyway. Just remember to win this ye must be a bindweed."

"Excuse me." Robbie had waited for some great pearl of wisdom to break the suspense, and had been somewhat confused by Fagan's remark. "How exactly can being bindweed help me?" Fagan gave a hearty laugh as he rose out of his chair and patted Robbie on the shoulder.

"It's a bugger of a plant." He lifted his cup and drained it, as Robbie's brow furrowed in confusion. Fagan wandered across to the stove, opened the door and threw in two large logs. "It gets bloody everywhere, it's a fine delicate looking bugger, but mark my words it will sneak up and strangle the bloody life out of ye if ye are a tree."

Robbie looked back watching the old man; he was sort of getting the point. "I can tell ye this, my young lord, the trees bloody hate it, ye should see em when they feel it growing in the meadows, fair gets em in a tizzy it does, oh I can hear em for miles screaming and yelling like smacked babies, bugger of a plant it is, ye should be one and strangle the life out of that witch." Robbie noticed movement and turned to see Rune giggling quietly, she shrugged at him.

"Good advice Rob, you should take it." Fagan beamed across the room at her, she gave a bright smile, and walked across the kitchen towards him. "Good morning Master Fagan, I thought I would rustle something up for breakfast." Robbie sat back in the chair feeling even more confused.

CHAPTER NINETEEN

GOOD COUNCIL

Father Warren spent most of the morning working quietly in his room, the library at the Cathedral had provided some rare finds, and he had taken the books to his room to study and make notes. Halfway through the day he had been joined by Jersey, who after all was a woodsman, and Warren had a great opportunity to sit and match the two faiths for his work. It had been a long day, and the heat was now at its highest, even with the windows wide open there was little breeze, and Father Warren accompanied by his woodland guard, walked quietly down the long corridor to the dining room.

The accommodation for all the guests was a familiar feeling building for Warren, it was obvious that even here Mason had applied his gifts, the grey stone of the walls was something Warren would never forget, having spent many years within the large city at Scarborough. The dining hall had little decoration, except for the fact it had been painted white. Long tables marked out the eating area, and at the far end young women in long black skirts and white aprons with matching headscarves, scurried as they served the visiting members of the church, they were obviously novice nuns in service to the cathedral.

The room seemed to be fuller than usual, it did appear that every day more and more of the members of the church arrived as the time for the announcement of the new Church Council came closer. Warren sat down at the end of the one remaining empty table with Jersey beside him, two young women scuttled across the long hall with bowls of hot steaming broth, and large fat crusted cobs of bread. They gave a polite curtsy, and headed back into the throng of the busy hall at mealtime. Together the two of them began their meal.

It was not long before Jersey leaned over and quietly spoke. "I find it hard to believe all of these in here would be against Lord Loxley."

Warren gave a small smile as he tore the cob in his hands in half; many in the busy room sat eating their meal had noted the Father, and were watching him carefully.

"Not all of them are." Warren gave a nod to a monk who had caught his eye;

the monk had looked both ways and then given a reassuring nod. "Mason rules with the tool of fear my good friend, here we have a great deal of support, but until Robbie strikes hard at Mason, many here will stay in the shadows." Jersey gave a nod of agreement, understanding the power of Mason Knox. In his time with Father Warren, he had learned much of what it was like to live in a large stone city, he paid close attention throughout the meal, and he too began to see that there were some who made a discreet greeting towards the two men sat alone on the otherwise empty table.

Father Warren found he had little appetite, and he rose from his seat. As Jersey prepared to leave, he placed a hand on the woodsman's shoulder. "Finish your meal, I shall be fine, I am going to return to my room and work a while longer." Jersey seemed uncertain as he looked at the room, where many had noticed the Father had risen. Father Warren smiled, and Jersey gave a reassuring nod back.

"I won't be long, but go straight there, and keep the door locked until I arrive." Warren smiled.

"I am in my father's house, here I shall be safe have no fear."

The room had been hot, and now in the long corridors, it felt cooler as Father Warren unbuttoned his top buttons to let the air circulate. He breathed long and hard, as he felt the small amount of cool air move swiftly around his stifled neck. His pace was slow and thoughtful, as he made his way towards the end of the corridor, and the turn to the wings where his room was. As he turned the corner, he jumped back with surprise, to find himself confronted with the large frame of a grey clad monk. "I am sorry Brother; I was deep in thought and did not see you."

The monk scowled at him from under his heavy brown eyebrows. "You have no right bringing that heathen into this holy place." Warren was a little taken a back as the monk stepped forward and leered at him. "You don't belong here spreading your lies about a false king and his pagan witch protector."

Warren felt a burst of fear in his stomach, as the monk breathed his words, from the rotten breath of his decayed teeth. "We are all the children of our lord, and in his eyes all of us are worthy of his love." The monk jolted forward, and Warren leaned back, his face gave a grimace and then he gave a howl of pain, and he moved backwards quickly. Father Warren noticed the green shirt of a Loxley Woodsman, as the monk felt his hand dragged painfully up his back.

"This may be the shape of a cross, but this aint no crucifix is it brother?" Jersey gave a smile, as the monk gave a stifled gasp of pain, and Jersey slipped the long silver dagger out of his twisted hand. Warren's eyes widened with surprise as he looked at the monk's evil face, and then back to the smiling Jersey.

"WHAT IS GOING ON HERE? WHY ARE YOU ASSAULTING A MEMBER OF THE CHURCH?" Warren turned to see the black flapping robes of the Bishop's Secretary, as he hurried up the long corridor; Jersey roughly released the monk and lifted the silver dagger into the view of the oncoming secretary.

"I aint assaulting no one, I was just convincing the good brother that his dagger here belongs anywhere accept in the gut of my good Farther Warren." The steps of the Bishop's Secretary faltered as he came closer, the monk snatched his arm away from Jersey with a look of pure venom.

"Keep your filthy hands off me heathen." The Secretary looked astounded as he looked from Warren to Jersey, and then to the monk.

"Is this true Brother Maynard?"

The monk's voice rose as he addressed the Bishop's Secretary, he had no choice but to air his opinion, he had after all been caught red handed. "He does not belong here; he is unwelcome and pollutes all we hold dear in the church." The Secretary gave a long gasp of disbelief.

"Brother Maynard, the Father is a guest of the Bishop as are you, this is outrageous behaviour in the church of our lord." Brother Maynard scowled with his hatred.

"NO... NO... Inviting this filth into our sacred house is outrageous." He spat on the floor at Jersey's feet, turned, and stormed off as he lifted his hands and screamed. "Heathens and witches, and the foul smell of a pagan king, that's what they bring, you mark my words, things will change here. Argus will show you, he understands the purity of the church, not that leaf loving Bishop, you will see. It will not be long now and then you will regret it." His voice echoed loudly in the long corridors, as he stormed away and turned the corner, his voice still ringing in inaudible bellows, bouncing and echoing along the corridors. The Secretary was quite flustered as his pale white face looked apologetically at Farther Warren.

"Please Farther; you must forgive us for what I can only say is one man's opinion. You are very highly thought of here, but I hope you understand that with the country as it is, there are some who are very misguided." Warren gave a smile.

"Please, I am unharmed, Lord Loxley ensured that I would be safe, and my lord gave me an able guard to ensure it. Let us not dwell on this." The Secretary looked very relieved, as he lifted an arm to guide Farther Warren on to his room. Jersey gave a big smile, and slipped the dagger of some quality into his belt. The Secretary walked on slowly at the side of Farther Warren as Jersey followed a few paces behind.

"I am so sorry that my Lord Bishop has not been able to see you yet, I can assure you that he too feels very frustrated, but with endless lines of delegations arriving, he has been very busy. Simon has relayed your messages, and we do have considerable support from those who would wish to examine the documents of Professor Rimmer, but as you can possibly imagine, with the gossip and scare mongering of certain parties, it is a pressured time for the Bishop. I hope you will be patient a while longer, and accept the hospitality of our humble church." Farther Warren gave a nod as they reached his room.

"I will as always help the bishop in any way I can, and appreciate your words very much. Express my best to the Bishop, I will be here when he is ready." The Secretary gave a smile and a slight bow. He turned and shook hands with Jersey, and then hurried along the corridor back to where he came from, Jersey watched him as Farther Warren opened the door, he turned back to look at the Father.

"Don't say I didn't warn you; I have been in the trees a long time, you sense things others don't, now in you go and lock the door, I am only in the next room so shout out if you need me." Farther Warren gave a chuckle as he nodded understanding his guard was in fact right.

"Yes, indeed my good friend, I will follow your advice and lock myself in." Jersey gave a nod.

"Good... Good night then, and don't work too late."

"I won't, goodnight my friend." Farther Warren slipped inside, and Jersey stood waiting until the bolt slid into place, he gave a nod and then turned to his own door.

Father Warren sat down on the small bed, he looked at his desk next to the wide open tiny window, but his thoughts now were far from his work. The name of Argus had struck a deep chord with him, the pictures of his grim smile at the suffering of Sapphire as he gave his case against her drifted through Warren's mind. He had in his time heard many things about the old monk, and now he felt some fear, as he realised the power of the man behind the scenes placing pressure on the bishop.

Argus had gained much more power and influence since the night the council fell, even lost in the woods of Loxley, Farther Warren had heard of the movement behind Argus to reform the church back to the ways of old. A cold prickle slipped uneasily down his spine, as he realised how cut off from the church he had been. Sat deep in thought he knew now that the church truly had split into two, and he realised his only choice would soon be to choose a side and stand up to defend it.

It had been over a week since York had fallen into the hands of the black army. The woodland generals had expected Mason to advance fast, and come out of the south gate in force heading for Loxley. They sat in the trees with the walled city in the distance, waiting and wondering what Mason might be up to. The plans of Scarlet had been quite thorough, but there had been a few areas she had overlooked, and Rayne and Gwinne had added what they thought were important elements. The extra time had given the woodland forces a chance to prepare; the defence of Loxley was now everything. With no news of their hooded leader, they had no choice but to move forward and prepare, it now looked like the new General Mark Richard Dale had halted all of Mason's plans while he studied every aspect of what had taken place. The road from York back to the black city was still open, and carts had trundled daily along it bringing yet more supplies to the aid of Mason's men. Dale was suspicious, he knew that the Night Strikers were still attacking, and he had for the time being suspended some of the overnight supply runs, but what made him question the tactics of the woodland realm, was the lack of damage they had been inflicting. He now faced the difficult question, was the dynamite running out, or were the woodland forces just keeping up appearances as they prepared another surprise for the forces of Mason Knox?

Rune walked along the path as the evening lengthened, her mind had been active all day, as she put the pieces of her meeting with the mysterious Albanlin together. The forest seemed to feel somehow different from any other woodland that Rune had walked in before, the scents in the air seemed stronger, and although she recognised the smells of honeysuckle and sweet pea, there were many new scents in this mysterious old woodland. Looking up at the sunlit sky, she could see the thatch of fine twig work that made up the canopy, many of the leaves she knew, yet the trees here were far bigger than any she had seen before. Even the Sacred Oak, which was the oldest tree in Loxley, would look dwarfed and stunted by the size of the trees she was now underneath. The path was wide and lined with the dark vibrant purples of vetch and bright almost translucent yellow of the spearwort. Between them grew the now familiar white flowers that had dressed the grassed fields around Avalonia, but there were others that she had no names for. Rune slowed as she looked down at what at first appeared to be violets, but had more petals and were striped with yellows and oranges. "Thought ye might notice those little fellows." Rune smiled, as she heard the voice of Fagan behind her, she turned and looked back at the tall white haired old man.

"They are very beautiful, I thought for a moment they were violets, but now I see they are just similar, what are they?" Fagan gave a bright smile.

"Well now... Knowing ye would ask, I gave it some thought, but blow me if I can remember." He rubbed his chin and looked up at the trees above him. "Papa Oak here says they don't talk so much, but they sing like little angels if you stroke em." Rune gave a happy giggle as she pushed out a finger, and gently touched one of the petals; she was surprised to see a shudder run down the small green stem, and gave a chuckle as she looked back at Fagan. He stood still with his head to one side, his wide eyebrows twitching slightly as he listened. "Well if that aint the nicest I have heard em sing, ye have a touch of magic and wonder if ye don't mind me saying."

Rune gave another little giggle, as she looked down at what was now a thick row of quivering little plants. "But I cannot hear anything, how can you hear them?" Fagan gave a dreamy smile.

"Ye are Life; concentrate on the life that flows at your feet." Rune stared at the floor and thought of all that was around her, her mind seemed to slip and drift for a moment, and then she heard it. It sounded like a chorus of distant dreamy voices washing in waves up a misty bank. It was soft and delicate, and she felt waves of happiness flow inside and around her, for a moment her head swam with the wonder and her eyes flickered with violet.

"It is so beautiful; I have never heard anything like it." Fagan came up beside her and whispered quietly.

"That is the first sound My Lady Eve and the Green Lord ever created together; they sing the sound of pure innocence." Rune felt overwhelmed by the beauty and the pureness of it.

"It is a shame that it grows only here, how wonderful the world would be if it grew everywhere." Fagan gave a nod.

"It did once...they says it was everywhere in the beginning and all could hear it, then along come the badun's and before ye knew it, it had gone an died out with grief." He shook his head with a sense of sadness, as his huge eyebrows bobbed up and down. "Poor little loves, they only got here now." He gave the flowers a small wave as he looked down, and then turned to Rune. "Tis getting late, maybe ye should be walking back soon, the trees are chatting and watching, but they can only do so much if we need em." Rune felt a twinge run through her.

"We are safe here in the woods are we not? Le Fey would not dare to enter here." A shower of leaves fell from the trees and Fagan looked up.

"Ye can cut that out for a start, she is Life, and if she wants to name her she can, remember who stands below ye. Ye aint all too old to be shown a thing or two." Rune looked at Fagan.

"What did I do?" She looked nervous as he gave her a big grin.

"Oh ye want to ignore them old buggers, they get their roots in a twist too quickly these days, touchy bunch at times, I don't know why I waste me time on em. They don't like the sound of her name, but as I told em, ye have more right than any, ye being of the good ladies line. I won't have them show disrespect." He looked up and gave the trees a hard stare. "Behaving like that in front of the Lady of Life, ye should be ashamed of yeselves." Fagan looked down and gave a snort as he sniffed the air. "Moody buggers when they want rain." Rune smiled.

"You can't blame them, it has been so hot, it must be awful for them sitting in this heat all day." Fagan looked up as he pointed to Rune, his voice rose slightly as he shouted.

"Ye hear that did ye? Ye go chucking all ye leaves down, and just ye hear what she said, see how sweet and nice she is thinking of ye hot feet, and how do ye behave? It's shocking I tell ye." Rune couldn't help but smirk as she touched Fagan's arm.

"Honestly it's fine, please don't shout at them on my account." Fagan gave a rough nod.

"Don't like lack of respect, it needed to be said. Them buggers feel guilty now; it will do em good to think about things for a while. Come on let's walk back now."

Rune gazed up at the branches that were now very still, she gave a smile, and then turned with her arm pushed into Fagan's. He walked slowly along as he talked of the woodland and all the trees, Rune listened carefully enjoying his manner and fondness for all that surrounded him, as he told his stories of the moments in his life, alone in the woodland of the Forest of Time with just his trees for company.

"Aye, I dare say they can be grumpy old buzzards, but they are good friends." Rune loved the way he saw the trees, in so many ways she felt that Robbie had that same sense of them.

"You lived up in Avalonia, and yet you gave it all up to come here, why didn't you want to leave with all the rest of the line of Fae?" She had to admit to herself that it was something she had never quite understood. Fagan came to a stop, and just stared for a moment in to the distance; he thought for a second and then began to walk again.

"I had a good life as the Maker. But ye have to understand, that yes, I lived up there at the bottom of the rock, and I dare say for a man I had a lot." He stopped and thought again, Rune almost carried on walking still linked to his arm, and she gave a small giggle.

"Well, the thing is..." He began to walk again. "Thing is ye see, I made all manner of things, and in all honesty, I thought they were things of beauty." He stopped and scratched his chin Rune gave another giggle. "Then one afternoon Ned Butterbass came to me and asked if I would mend his cart, it appeared he had been down here chopping wood." Fagan began walking again, and Rune quickened her pace to keep up with him. "So, I come along with him and I saw this place filled with big trees, and I says to myself, blow me Fagan, this is a right nice place, so when I had done the job, I went for a walk to have a good look round like." He carried on walking and Rune listened waiting to hear more, but he just walked on as if lost in his thought, Rune looked up at him.

"Fagan?"

"What?" Rune gave a giggle.

"Well, what happened then?" His bushy eyebrows moved up and down, as he realised Rune wanted him to tell her.

"Oh... Right...Well ye see I walked about for a bit... actually it was two weeks later when I come out and that was it." Rune looked confused.

"What was?"

"Well ye know?" Rune blinked.

"Well actually Fagan, no I don't you haven't said." He gave a big smile.

"Oh course not, bless me I forgot... Well as ye see, I had walked round and I saw what real beauty is, well I says to myself, ye can't top that Master Maker so why try. So I went back to town and packed up me stuff and asked her ladyship if I could come an live here like." It seemed so matter of fact, and yet there was something in the way he spoke, his tone was somehow softer, and Rune could feel the huge sense of wonder radiate out of him.

"So you just gave up everything for the love of the woodland?" He gave a huge smile.

"I never thought of it that way, but yes, I guess I did. Ye have seen her, she was worth it don't ye think?" Rune felt the love of the woodlands surge through him, and she finally understood the old man, and in many ways, she felt the same sense inside him she had felt with Robbie in Caerleon Woods. Once again, she had been surprised, as she saw another who loved the life that had been created in the world, in the same way she had been surprised by Robbie. Rune gave his arm a big squeeze and without any words, Fagan knew.

"If I might be so bold My Lady of the Woods, ye have a very beautiful and I must say wonderful realm, it has been my honour to protect what ye line began here. The lady of this realm has given ye much of herself, and I think she was right to. I will live here and do everything in my old bones power to protect what she started; it has made me the man I am to live here." Fagan was indeed a very old man, and it was true he had lived alone for many ages, but as he turned to face Rune, and she saw the life and the love, and the utter sincerity in his bright eyes, she felt a tear well in hers.

"I am honoured Fagan, keeper of my woodland, your words do me great service." His eyes gave a twinkle.

"No tis I who have the honour My Lady." He gave a big smile and turned sharply. "Oh come with me and I will show ye the star poppies." He looked back with a look of pure excitement on his face. "They will be tickled pink to see ye, oh I do hope they explode with joy, it's a right nice sight to see them shoot seeds of every colour into the sky." He pulled sharp on Rune's hand, and with a deep chuckle, he led her off the path into the tall grass that seemed to part as he walked briskly through to a secret place, to show Rune the pride of the Forest of Time.

Farther Warren sat back in his chair, as the candle flickered with the soft breeze that blew through his open window, somewhere outside, the sound of foxes screeched in the darkness as they hunted. He lifted his aching hands and rubbed his eyes, and gave a long sigh as he felt the yawn build in his cheeks. He leaned right back, and stretched to get the aches out of his back, and then he heard the soft tap at the door. He turned uncertain at first. "Father are you awake?" It was Simon.

Quietly he opened the door, to see the bright eyes of the bishop's aid glowing in the dark, his voice was almost a whisper. "Father I am sorry to call you at such a late hour, but it is important the bishop sees you now." Warren gave a nod, as the tiredness seemed to leave him.

"Of course." He slipped out of the door, and pulled it quietly behind him. The corridors were very dark, and Simon carried no light with him, he walked quickly and Father Warren could feel his apprehension. He kept quiet following Simon through the labyrinth of corridors to a small brown door, behind which he could hear a quiet murmur. Simon stopped, and tapped four times on the door as the voices within died down. The lock gave a loud click and the door swung open, light spilled into the passage, and Warren blinked for a moment, before moving swiftly in, herded by Simon. The door closed quickly and the lock gave another click as Father Warren looked round the room at the gathered faces. John Stevens came forward with a smile as Father Warren's eyes adjusted.

"Peter, please come on inside you have nothing to fear here, you are surrounded by friends." Some of the faces that looked from the long table in the bishop's consultation room were very familiar, a few of them he recognised from the dining hall, as they had been the ones to give him the secret and silent nods of acknowledgement. Bishop Stevens led him around the table to an empty seat.

"Peter you must forgive all this cloak and dagger, but I am afraid it is of need at this time, please sit down and we shall have tea while I explain."

The hot tea was placed in front of him, as the bishop sat down beside him; he lifted the cup as the others all seemed to be happily sipping their own. John Stevens gestured to the group of ten sat round the table; all were men bar one, who was a middle aged woman, who gave him a wide smile.

"Peter sitting here before you are the new Church Council. All of them are loyal supporters of Lord Loxley; I hope you now understand why we have brought you here in secret?" Farther Warren suddenly felt wide awake, and for a moment he had found himself greatly surprised. Bishop John Stevens had indeed needed to be secretive, considering there was not one supporter of Mason Knox in the new council. Each of the group gave him a smile, and nodded towards him, the bishop continued.

"I am sure you are more than aware that here in this room are all of the people that Mason would strike out against if he knew we were here? As you can see my friend, we have decided to back Loxley against Mason, and as I think you are very aware this could create a huge split in the church."

Warren nodded feeling the surprise growing inside himself, an old grey haired man who sat just to the side of John Stevens smiled and leaned forward offering his hand, John leaned back to let Farther Warren take it. "This is Bishop Walker; he was until recently the Bishop at Exeter." The old man smiled.

"Mason is a bit touchy about telling the people trapped behind the wall what he is really up to in the rest of the country, John here gave me a safe place to hide out until he is removed." Farther Warren gave a smile and shook his hand.

"I am pleased to meet you, all of you, please forgive me this has come as a bit of a surprise." A large Monk further down the table gave a hearty laugh.

"Not as surprised as Argus will be when Mason finds out his spies have failed." The rest of the group all gave a chuckle. John Stevens turned back to Farther Warren, he looked tired and somewhat older; the strains of recent days had taken their toll on him.

"Peter, you see before you ten members of the church, including me that is eleven, we all oppose what Mason is doing in the country, and we are bitterly against the way he is trying to manipulate the church against those of the Earth and other faiths. Peter the council should be twelve; can you not see you are a vital link that we need to take the fight for our church to those who oppose all Loxley stands for? Peter, we need you, will you please reconsider and take the last empty seat on the council?"

In many ways it did not surprise him, he had sat in his room all night and thought hard of his meeting when he arrived at the Cathedral. Somehow, he knew that Bishop Stevens would put up a fight to convince him to join, and Farther Warren knew that he had a valuable role in a perfect situation to inform the church on the ways of the woodland peoples. The teachings of Column Cille had brought together many of different faiths in harmony before, and he had always thought that at some point there would be some contact as the Church tried to unite everyone behind one king.

It was after all, the only way that those from the old world could come together in the new world, and all night he had indeed pondered the point. Maybe in many ways this was to be his destiny, to help heal the rift and bring about a solution, where both faiths could join under one king. He looked round the large table at the faces that eagerly awaited his response. He turned to the new Arch Bishop John Stevens, and held out his hand.

"If you ask me as my friend and as my Bishop, then yes I will do all I can to serve the council to the best of my ability."

There were a few long gasps of relief around the table as John Stevens gave a big smile, and he took hold of his hand and shook it with vigour. "Thank you, Peter, I knew you would understand, this is indeed a wonderful moment for the future of the Christian Church, we are indeed very happy to have you aboard." Warren gave a smile as he looked at the others.

"This will not be easy; Mason Knox will not take this too kindly." A tall vicar with a heavy Scottish accent leaned over and took his hand.

"Farther Ivan McKay. Don't you worry about Mason, once we fix Argus and put the rightful king on the throne, what can he do?"

It was a very good question and one for the moment Farther Warren did not want to contemplate. Slowly the rest of the council came round and began to introduce themselves, many of the places they came from were very much in the woodland areas controlled by Robbie, and he understood then, that it was their people that were suffering the most under Mason. Farther Warren relaxed a little as he truly knew he was amongst friends as the names of places, such as Warwick and Cardiff and Carlisle were mentioned in connection to the people shaking his hand.

Over the following few hours, Farther Warren was introduced to those who would serve along with him, many he knew by reputation and he was delighted to find that the only female in the group was in fact a vicar and also John Stevens's youngest sister. It was agreed by all that the announcement of the council would be withheld for a little while longer, as it would allow the woodland forces a chance to make a move, by which time Mason would indeed have his hands full, and so they would have a small amount of leverage to move fast.

In the meantime, everyone would continue as normal, and Simon would circulate information to each of them. It was almost daylight when Farther Warren returned to his room and slipped into bed, although he had not had any sleep at all he lay back in bed and pondered his new situation; there was the nagging worry that when he had left Loxley there had been no word at all from Robbie. He now had to get word to Loxley that there would be support for the new king; he also needed to find out where Lord Loxley had disappeared to.

Deep in the Forest of Time, Robbie was curled up asleep with Rune. She had returned earlier from her walk filled with happiness, whilst he sat by the table in the kitchen with Rowan, Bear, Hawk, Skip and William discussing their situation, Rune had been out sitting on an old stump watching the brightly glowing star poppies explode their seeds into the sky. Fagan had sat beside her laughing with joy at a display better than any he had ever seen.

As the night grew late, Robbie with Rune had slid into bed, in his mind having some rest had done her the world of good, and he snuggled in beside her, and she softly brushed back the fringe from his face and kissed him. He slid back happy to see her so relaxed and smiling, as he gazed into her bright sapphire blue eyes filled with life, he too felt better for the rest, and he slid down under the sheets with her close and drifted into a happy sleep.

Outside in the sky darkness was falling, but it was not the night time, clouds rolled into the sky blotting out the sun completely, leaving the sky looking like a starless night. The trees stirred, and the grass moved rhythmically in what little breeze could find its way into the forest. It was still hot and humid, as those who were still awake watched in the sudden darkness.

Jade crawled up to the side of Blades, who was sat against a large tree; Fox was nowhere to be seen. Blades pointed through the gap she had cut in the fern and whispered. "Over there... Can you see them?" Jade leaned over, and peered through the gap, as Blades moved her finger. "We make it six, we think they are here to watch us and report back." Jade nodded as she saw them huddled together in two groups. Blades pointed behind her.

"There are two down there watching the house, Todd is watching them, we think that if we move, they will send two to let the rest of the soldiers know." Jade smiled.

"We should have some fun with them, I mean, it wouldn't be right to let them have an easy time of it." Blades gave a smile.

"I am not sure, although it would be fun to spook them. Robbie told me to keep well clear and just observe them; I mean we don't know if they have any more with them yet." Jade shrugged.

"I reckon if we spook em, they will run back to the others. I can fade and follow them in here and they won't see me. It will at least give us a clue of what they are doing here." Blades, wasn't too sure.

"Maybe we should ask Robbie, it's pretty late, and if they attack everyone is probably asleep by now." Jade sat back against the tree and looked up at the clouds rolling in across the sky.

"It's going really dark; I am telling you Blades; this is a perfect chance to catch them off guard. I say I have a little wander over and see if I cannot get some idea of what they are planning. Look at it this way, if I am invisible, they will have no idea, especially if it goes really dark." Blades gave a nod.

"Ok Pebbles, but be really careful, we are low on numbers as it is." Jade gave a devilish wink.

"You sit and watch, don't worry about me, it will take better than a Cutter to catch me out."

Ovens had been jumpy all day, the captain had managed to convince the others that they had been up against an ordinary man painted blue, but he did not believe it. As far as he was concerned, he knew of no man who could hunt with a tiger as a partner. He believed the stories of old about the strange spirit worshiping folk that had built the realm of Avalon.

As the darkness drew in, he glanced nervously up at the sky, and pulled his crossbow closer. He was on a rest break, but he had no intention of sleeping, there were way too many strange sounds in this forest for his comfort. The other three were sat huddled together talking about some of the strange things that had been said about the hooded man. One of them had been up in Scotland, and heard all the stories of the Cathedral at Canterbury, he whispered quietly about the little girl who cooked a man just by looking at him. It gave Ovens a deep shudder down his back.

He swallowed hard as he listened and leaned into the group. "They aint got a kid with em have they?" The fattish Cutter from Scotland was called Travis; he saw the frightened look on the face of Ovens and smirked.

"If they had, it's no possible for a lassie that small to do that, come on man get a spine."

"Oh I don't know, they say it's not possible to have a green eyed devil working for a man, but there is one working for the Hooded Man." Ovens nodded.

"I have heard that too, they say it just appears, and if you see the eyes, you are dead." Travis looked across at Ovens.

"What the hell are you going on about now?" Oven stared in the gloom at him.

"The green eyed devil, you know the one you were talking about." Travis looked at the other three.

"Is he all there or what?" He turned to Ovens. "Who said anything about green eyed devils?" Oven's voice rose slightly from a whisper to a squeak.

"You did just then, I bloody well heard you." Travis shook his head.

"No I bloody didn't, it's the first I have heard of it." He looked at the other two. "Did any of you say owt?" They both looked as confused as Travis. Ovens shook a shaky finger at Travis.

"Stop messing about, I know what I heard, you were talking about the little girl, and then you mentioned the green eyed devil, don't you go denying it, I heard you clear as day." Travis shook his head.

"Your bloody mad you are, I never said a sodding word, you want to watch it mate accusing folk like that, especially here in the dark, you could get hurt blaming folks and calling them liars." Ovens felt the fear growing inside him.

"I aint lying, I know what I heard, and if you say you didn't say it, then who friggin hell did?" Ovens went rigid as behind Travis, a pair of bright green eyes appeared in the darkness.

"It was me." Travis gave a jerk, and the long tip of a sword came out of his shirt. Ovens felt instant panic, and reeled backwards away from the blade, which had slid back into Travis. He rolled over and scrambled across the floor, clawing at the clumps of grass to pull him forward. Behind him there was a thud followed by a deep moan, and he knew another of his comrades was dead.

Filled with panic he scrambled to his feet, and without looking behind him, he ran in blind panic into the forest. A loud scream echoed behind him, and he screamed with all his might, and fought to push his legs even faster on the rough floor. With terror coursing through him, Ovens headed for the path and ran for all he was worth, and he didn't stop until he ran right out of the trees over an hour later and tumbled down the bank towards the road, wailing and screaming for his life, and ranting about big blue demons with green eyes.

Jade sniggered as she lent on a tree and watched the soldiers as they ran to his aid, all along the road she could see the soldiers preparing as they cleaned their weapons, huddled around small burning torches. In a small clearing just back from the road she saw the large group of finely dressed men and women in all black. They sat still staring at the trees and waiting to be unleashed, it was a cause for great concern as Jade counted to fifty.

Quietly and still invisible she withdrew and turned to head for the path, THUMP! She bounced back into the ferns in surprise, and grabbed for her knife.

"Ye want to be careful; ye almost trod on me toes." Jade sat up and smiled.

"Fagan, we better make a move, there are bloody hundreds of em. I got to get back and fast, Robbie needs to know." The dark figure passed over her and an old hand came down to offer help, Jade grabbed it and Fagan pulled her to her feet.

"Now don't ye go running off like strawberries in a heat wave, we are as safe as a thrush in its nest up here. This forest has ways of keeping out bog weed like them, we got all the time in the world, them foul black things is feared of coming in here, they have met with me before, and they know the taste of the old keepers wrath believe me."

Jade felt uncertain, she wanted to let Robbie know as soon as possible. "I think we should still hurry Fagan, if they attack, Robbie has no idea of what he faces." Fagan patted her shoulder as he walked casually down the path back into the forest.

"He knows, ye mark my words, he has the wisdom of my old owl he has, he don't go running off like dandelion clocks, he thinks stuff through."

CHAPTER TWENTY

BEHIND THE MASK

Sapphire opened her eyes with a start; her breath gave a sharp intake as she sat up in amongst the trees. "Who's there?" There was no response, and she slowly got to her feet and looked round at the giant beech like trees, which seemed to stretch for as far as her eyes could see. "Am I dreaming?" She turned slowly, trying to understand what was happening, she was in a huge forest, but she had no memory of how she got there.

Her head felt a little clouded, and she blinked as she tried to think. The last thing she had remembered was walking around the farm in New Avon, and then she was sure she had gone in and up to bed. Sapphire noticed the blue sleeve and looked down at her clothes, she was dressed as a woodsman, but everything was deep blue, except for her boots, which were her old familiar white leather. "What is happening to me, how could I change my clothes and travel here without remembering?"

The last week had been very strange, Sapphire's dreams had felt very real, but this one was far more realistic than she wanted it to be. The large woodland was totally silent and it made her nervous, she could hear no birds or insects, and it all felt very unnatural. The grass where she had been lay was flat, and on the floor in the grass was a long yellow coloured bow, with a quiver filled with long white arrows tipped with white feathers, that had the softest hue of pale blue. Feeling a little relieved that she could at least defend herself; she stooped down and picked up the bow and quiver.

Understanding what was happening to her was difficult, everything felt so real to her, the smells of the damp earth, and the breeze that lifted her hair on her shoulders, and yet she knew this had to be nothing more than a vivid dream. She stood and looked for a direction to go in, but everything just looked the same no matter which way she looked. Endless trees stretched everywhere and she gave a long sigh. "Great I get stuck in a dreamland with no map, well there is little I can do about it, until I wake up I am stuck here." She lifted the soft blue hood of the long blue velvet cloak she was wearing, and with the bow clasped firmly in her hand she began to walk.

Robbie woke in the darkness and rolled over; the other side of the bed was empty. "Rune?" He sat up and looked round the room that was very dark, which instantly made no sense, as it had been permanent daylight for days. He slipped off the bed and felt around for his clothes, the sudden darkness felt strange, and hampered his attempts to find his boots. Finally dressed he made his way towards the door feeling along the wall, and worked his way down the corridor and past the chimney into the kitchen.

The door was wide open, lit by the palest shimmer of violet. "Rune?" He whispered, as his hand clasped tighter to the sheath containing Destiny. A soft breeze blew into the room as he edged closer to the door, his senses now growing as he moved slowly. At the door, he carefully peered round to see if all was clear, and his breath caught in his throat.

Rune stood alone in the centre of the wide open grassy area in the total darkness. She wore her long violet cloak, and her hair hung down past her waist, shimmering as she held up her arms to the sky. From the sky, thousands of what looked like fireflies shimmered with the faintest lilac light, and flowed down towards her. They swarmed around her, casting a faint pale lilac light that illuminated her and the area all around her. Robbie leaned on the doorframe captivated by what looked like an enchanted vision before his eyes.

Rune smiled and softly laughed, as the strange creatures fluttered all around her and her face lit up in the radiant light, giving the appearance of a slightly violet aura, never in all the time he had known her, did she look more beautiful.

She giggled as she softly waved her arms, and the small glowing insects swirled around her arms and streamed back into the air. Her laughter rose into the air as she spun, and the streaks of light spun with her, and even Robbie gave a small laugh as he watched. Rune came to a halt facing him stood in the doorway. Her face was beaming with happiness and shone with life. Her bright blue eyes danced with delight, as the insects swept around her. Her voice was soft and yet excited.

"Robbie look how beautiful this place is, I am Life, and see how it responds to me, it knows me and has no fear of me." She gave a large giggle and lifted her arms and spun. The clouds of light swept past her, and flowed like a stream of light into the air, spiralling high into the sky. He came out of the doorway and crossed to the steps, and looked up at the sky as the shimmering insects flowed like water and then fanned out across the clouds, casting a violet like moonlight on the whole of the forest.

Rune scampered across the grass and up the steps, where she threw her arms around him; he smiled as he pulled her close, seeing the excitement of her face. She looked so happy, and he felt the warmth that flowed between them. Rune gave a gasp as she caught back her breath from spinning. "Robbie all this time they have told me I am the centre, but I never really understood what it meant." Her eyes danced with excitement, sparkling with blue fire. "Robbie tonight I think I really do understand, it is not just about being the centre of a table with people around it, I am at the heart of everything. This is where it all started here in the centre of every realm, and I had to come here to see that. I am Life." She flung out her arms, and let her head fall back as Robbie held her tight.

"I AM LIFE, AND HERE I AM THE CENTRE OF EVERYTHING!"

"Rune sweetheart, please it's still very early, and some of us have got a headache." Una trudged into the kitchen with a candle, looking very much the worst for wear. Her feet dragged on the stone floor from her unlaced boots, as she took a taper from the jar and lit it on the candle to light the stove. "Oh, I think that Fagan's brew is more deadly than Harry's tonic, so please don't shout, I fear my head could possibly explode any second." She set the large copper kettle to boil and shuffled to the chair, where she slowly sat down with her eyes closed, and rested her head in her hands. Robbie giggled and took Rune by the hand; they walked back out onto the porch and down the steps to the grass.

High above them in the clouds, the small flies still shimmered with soft light, and Robbie watched them swirl through the thick heavy cloud, Rune was filled with happiness and stared with joy into the sky. Robbie studied the sky above. "Rune?

"Yes Robbie."

"Where's the sun?"

"What?" She blinked, and then realised. She had got up and come out of the house to see the flies glowing as they hovered above the floor. It had captivated her so much, that she hadn't even realised that it had gone so dark. "I am not sure Robbie." He shrugged.

"It's been there for days, so where has it gone all of a sudden?" He turned and looked at her, and could see her surprise as she shook her head slowly.

"I am not sure, she is controlling the weather at the moment, so what is she up to now?" Robbie looked up at the dark sky.

"What is she planning that requires darkness?" His words passed out quietly with his thoughts and Rune felt a shudder run down him.

"I am not sure, but if she needs darkness, you can bet your last bit we won't like it."

Sapphire had been walking for some time, when the tall grass before her parted, and she stepped right out on to a wide open track, she stopped suddenly feeling very exposed. She looked to her right at the road that ran for miles. "Oh shit!"

In the far distance she could see the wide round clearing filled with red rock, and from its centre rose something that looked very familiar. Through the wide gap in the trees she saw the cold black stone walls rise into the air on a single tower, and on the very top of it stood a huge cold black stone Raven. The coldness ran down her back, as she felt her the hairs on her neck rise. "How can this be, Rune destroyed Dunnottar?"

"Dunnottar was merely a copy, to help her feel at home; as you can see the real lair of the Raven is considerably larger." Sapphire raised her bow and spun round as the old voice echoed in her ears. As she pulled back on the string, the arrow snapped and the bow flew out of her hand, she gasped with shock.

"You have no need to fear me Sapphire of the White Circle." In the centre of the path stood a small figure dressed in all white. She wore long robes, and her face was covered with a hood, from underneath it faint flashes of blue flickered as she spoke. Sapphire fell to her knees.

"My Lady of the Woods, forgive me, this is a strange land, and I am lost and in fear, I meant no offence." Opal gave a small chuckle; she put her hand behind her, and pulled out a small colourful looking child.

"Come on out and meet your mistress, I have been waiting for you child, come we have a great deal to prepare, your quest to find me is over, but we have only until the crow of dawn, before you must return to the realm that holds your life."

Sapphire slowly stood up not entirely sure of what was happening. "Was my quest to find you? I really am struggling to understand what is happening to me." She noticed the little childlike creature beside Opal and smiled at him. He gave a big blink of his eyes and then bowed to her. Sapphire looked at the white hood.

"Why am I this little boy's mistress?" Opal turned on the path.

"All in good time, first we must leave here... Come walk with me and I shall fill in the blanks for you." The little boy ran across to her, and took hold of her hand. The small figure had the brightest of blue hair, and very pale blue eyes, which were larger than normal; it was obvious he was not human. He was very small, being only two and a half feet tall. He wore a small heavy cotton jacket of green and pale blue trousers, and had bright blue soft leather shoes. Sapphire smiled, and he gave her a bright smile and blinked.

"Well you are a bright little fellow, what is your name?" His large pale eyes shone at her. Opal turned as she walked off.

"He is a Sandling, and he is linked to you as his mistress. He has no name yet as you have to be the one who names him, now hurry child time here is never on our side." The little Sandling pulled on her arm, and Sapphire began to walk slightly behind Opal, she felt warmth flowing through her from her hand where the little Sandling held it, and she gave another smile. Opal turned from the path and walked into the trees. "I have a safe place just a few moments from here, hurry Child, and we shall talk."

Sapphire hurried alongside Opal, suddenly she had a thousand questions, and she hardly knew where to begin. Opal walked without looking to the sides, the back of her long white hood bounced on her shoulders as Sapphire hurried to keep pace, and the little Sandling ran along at her side. "Where is this place, and why is the Dark One here?" Opal continued to move quickly forward.

"She is not, she is in Avalon... You have entered what many call the Hidden Realm, or to those of us in the know, The Hidden Realm of Sleep." Sapphire turned her head to Opal in disbelief.

"Where Rune and Robbie got trapped?" Opal paced towards a wall of thick trees.

"The very same, this place contains everything associated with the night and with sleep, it is where the Dark One feels at her safest to conduct her foul experiments, and where she imprisoned the Ruling Council during the Age of Sleep. This place overlaps all of the other realms, and is home to the Realm of Dreams." Sapphire felt a little panicked, she remembered her time on Iona and the great fear Rhiannon and Merlin had felt when Rune and Robbie had been trapped here.

"Am I a prisoner here like Rune was?" Opal gave a little titter, as the trees parted and they walked through them onto a large wide circular glade of lush short grass, which surprised her and she looked around.

In the very centre was a fallen long tree, which was white with age; in front a small fire heated a hanging pot that bubbled with an aromatic aroma. Next to it was a wide silver basin, the size of a wooden barrel, filled with clear cool water. It stood on a silver stand that formed the trunk of an old and twisted tree, at the end of which was a tall stand, on which a bright orb glowed white and illuminated the whole glade. Opal lifted back her hood and her long grey straight hair fell down her back, she lifted her arm, and a pale white hand slipped out of her fluted white sleeve. "Welcome to my home and in answer to your question, Sapphire you are to be the centre of the circle of sight, here you can walk freely whenever you need, and so will the sisters of your table, for this is where those who glimpse what could be will gather together."

It all felt like too much as Sapphire sat down with a bump on the old tree. Opal smiled as she knelt by the fire and lifted a bowl; she scooped out the food with a large ladle, and then handed the plate to Sapphire. "You are new to the power that grows within you, have patience child, all will flow in a natural way, and your understanding will grow."

Sapphire took the bowl, she did not feel very hungry, for several days she had waited with Rafe as he spent time with his mother, and she had done little apart from sit and eat. She stared into the stew that did smell very inviting, Opal poured out two large glasses of a clear liquid; Sapphire could smell the subtle scent of roses. Opal smiled and her bright blue eyes twinkled, Sapphire gave her a polite smile back as she took a sip of the drink. "Rune is very like you; I can see the resemblance." Opal stretched out a hand and stroked Sapphire's long auburn hair back from her face.

"I see much of Gwendolyn in you; it is very obvious to me that you are the right choice for her gifts."

"So why do I feel very wrong for them? I am so unsure of everything in my life, my feelings run so wild at times, and I get myself so worked up about everything, honestly I have difficulty handling the present, how will I ever be able to cope with the future?" Opal laughed.

"Oh my poor sweet child, you must look at what is around you and begin to learn from the facts, you have such a strong ability, have you not taught a future king and his sister for most of their lives? You have more than enough ability to cope with the gifts that you will learn to control, just show the same love and patience to your gifts as you did young William and Gaynor and you will be fine. It was no coincidence they were sent to you in Scotland." Seeing the old woman smile with such love and happiness helped to calm her and she nodded to Opal. The little Sandling sat on the grass eating from his almost empty bowl, Sapphire handed hers to him.

"I really am not that hungry." He gave her a blink and she smiled; Opal sat back with her drink.

"I think a good place to start would be here, and then we shall look further out for more answers... You will need a place to call your centre, and from there you will draw your power, is there a place that has deep meaning for you?"

Sapphire didn't need to even think about it, and without a moment's thought she spoke. "To me my home is Callanish, for my father is there, and every happy memory of my childhood with my mother." Opal was very pleased.

"See... Your instincts guide you well, Callanish is a very powerful place, and has been a site of seeing for a very long time." Opal looked at the little Sandling, who was busy devouring Sapphire's meal. "What about this little fellow? He will be your guide throughout the rest of your life; he will need a name that feels close to your hopes and dreams." He looked from his bowl, and his mouth was surrounded with a thick rim of gravy, Sapphire gave a laugh.

"I like the sound of Cal, it somehow seems to fit in with everything." Opal nodded and patted the little figure on the head; he gave a huge smile and blinked at her, Opal smiled.

"The seal is made; you and Cal will be linked forever, now on to things further away."

Opal stood up, and lifted the large silver basin towards her, and pulled it between her and Sapphire. "From here I watch many things from the past, the present, and the future." She bent forward and lifted a daisy from the grass, holding it in her hand carefully, she gave it a flick, and it spun from her hand, and landed in the clear water. Sapphire watched as the water turned white and began to swirl and pictures appeared in it. She leaned forward to get a better look and smiled as she saw herself standing on the edge of a harbour dressed in all white waving at a little blue boat. Opal touched her shoulder.

"My basin sees many things, the past and the present, and also it shows elements of the future, concentrate as I show where things stand today." The water rippled and a picture of Rune appeared dancing in the darkness surrounded by pale lilac light, she looked so happy and filled with joy, Opal leaned a little closer.

"My granddaughter has discovered much of who she is, and as we speak, she is surrounded by all that she loves."

Sapphire watched as Robbie appeared watching her in a doorway, she gave a smile knowing they were both safe. Opal watched her carefully. "You cannot enter that realm, so we shall move to other areas where you have work to do." The picture changed and she saw the dark outline of the black city walls. Flames seem to rise up turning parts of it orange, and Sapphire jumped as suddenly into the picture a dark figure cradling his hand ran out of the darkness. Opal watched carefully as Sapphire realised who she was watching.

"Billy..." She looked back at Opal. "What have I got to do with him? He betrayed Robbie; I could never help him." Opal pointed back to the basin.

"This moment is about watching and learning, the gift of sight walks hand in hand with the truth, no one can hide it from you, as you will see deep within everyone. Sapphire you must let go of everything you believe to be true, and learn the truth of everything from scratch." Sapphire looked back to the basin where she saw Billy run screaming in pain through the rough heather in the darkness. His eyes were wild with fear and pain, even though she hated him, she also felt a twinge of sadness for the look he bore in his eyes, Opal smiled.

"We all have choices, and the hardest ones to make are sometimes the best, yet some fear the path of the truth for it is not always free of pain. Young William took an easier path and it led to a greater pain than even he realised." Sapphire scoffed.

"He deserved it." She watched as he stumbled over the edge of a large bank, and fell into a large peat filled hole with large boulders. She shuddered as his head hit a rock and blood sprayed out and he fell still. Opal watched her reaction.

"It is never easy to deal out justice, yet I see your feelings. Would you really want to administer such justice, when even his brother and lord felt pity for him?" Sapphire shook her head.

"You cannot deny that he risked the lives of everyone, and placed even your granddaughter in danger. Robbie should have killed him for the betrayal he caused." Opal gave a slight shrug and Sapphire found it hard to believe. "How can you feel any different? My Lady, Rune's life was at risk every moment he was alive." Opal gave a nod of agreement.

"It appeared that way I must admit." Sapphire frowned at her, it made no sense at all, and she could not understand how Opal would not condemn him for his vile acts of treachery. "But he also saved not just my granddaughter's, but also Robbie's life." Sapphire was stunned.

"How? Where? When?" Opal pointed to the basin.

"See the truth and undo what you believe Sapphire of Callanish. Take your first steps into the realm of sight, and take off your mask of ignorance and lift up the face of knowledge."

The water rippled and the scene expanded and she watched as the sun rose and he woke up. Sapphire gasped as she saw the large hole he lay in, filled with his blood and tears, as he screamed in pain knowing he was still alive.

Billy looked broken and lost to the world, she almost felt sorry for him seeing his pain. She watched as he looked up to the sky, and her heart almost stopped as Opal walked up to the edge of the hole. "You helped him?" Opal gave a nod.

"I did... for all of his sins, he too suffered the equal of Robbie. On that night he lost a mother he loved without understanding how much, he lost all that had been his past, and he also lost the love of a brother he had protected." Sapphire looked back at Opal in disbelief, and Opal gave a solemn nod.

"In all of the things he did, he never once put Robbie at risk, if anything he guided him away from danger, I might also add that his love of Alice gave her great protection, even her kidnapping was to save her and her child from the clutches of his grandmother. Whatever you may think of him, he tried hard to save those he truly loved." Sapphire looked back into the basin and watched, as Opal washed him and healed his broken hand, she could not help but feel he was like a small child responding to a grandparent, even though she could see he was a man. Opal gave him a new set of green clothes and handed him a new bow.

Something stirred in Sapphire as she looked upon him dressed in all sage green, she watched as he knelt before Opal in shame and hid his face from her, and he pulled up his hood and bent low. It was a few moments before she began to understand the strange feeling growing inside her. "That hooded coat?" Opal gave a nod and smiled. Sapphire could not draw her eyes away as she watched Billy cut away his long hair and bind his head in a green bandana, she gasped. "No, he cannot be?" Billy lifted a long piece of cut tree from the floor, and cut away its white bark. She sat stunned as she watched him fashion the mask, using his knife blade as a mirror to ensure the fit was right, and finally she drew her eyes from the pictures and looked at Opal with shock.

"Billy is the Sage?" Opal touched her gently on the hand.

"The magic is all around us; it weaves its own path and influences everything. Now you see the truth for what it really is, Billy can no longer hide from your sight, sooner or later you would have discovered the truth, but you would not have understood it, which is why you must learn now while you have a chance to understand the magic that works in this world."

Sapphire liked the Sage; on the few times she had met him she had always thought of him as a kind and honourable man. To find out he was in fact Billy left her speechless. She looked at the basin where he travelled towards the coast of Wales. Opal voice sounded of compassion and gratitude. "He saved Merlin, it was he who went and rescued him. Without Merlin, Robbie and Rune would have been trapped here in this realm forever." She turned to Opal looking very shaken.

"They would have died here?" Opal smiled at her.

"See how the truth has a funny way of making everything clearer? Billy was ashamed of what he had done, but as hard as he tried, he could not find a way to put it right. He did try many times to undo what he had done, but he never understood the strength that he had, it was the touch of your grandmother that gave him his freedom." Sapphire looked blankly at Opal.

"How could my grandmother help Billy, she has passed out of this realm forever?"

"She was in the knife and the sword; her power flowed through the white bracelet, of an heir to her family line. Your grandmother saw the strength and the honour that lay hidden deep within a man who was raised to be a man of Loxley; it was she who brought together the elements that saved him in his hour of need. I understood what she had done and I went with my father's blessing to aid him."

The pictures continued as Sapphire watched him with his party head towards London and search for those who could help Robbie. "I would have shot him gladly, and I did not understand Robbie when he spared him, I saw it as a weakness, I could not understand why Rune did not go after him and finish the job."

"Runestone has deep understanding, she never wanted Billy to die, when she realised who the Sage was, she went to his aid knowing it was the man who betrayed her greatest love."

"Rune knows, what about Robbie?" Opal shook her head.

"Now is not the time, that day has been seen by a few of us, and it is best we allow the Sage his secrets, for not only did your grandmother save him, she also awakened his gifts." Sapphire looked at her.

"What gifts does the line of Knox have that could aid Robbie?"

"Sight."

"What?"

"Morgan le Fey has limited sight, but there have been many in her line that have had great abilities, Mason's daughter and her granddaughter will have abundant gifts, and even though she would never expect it, her grandson also has these gifts, which he has used with great skill. You will meet him here in this realm, as he also has a companion and often visits. I am sure he will be pleased to know his sister and daughter will be part of your circle." Sapphire almost fell off the tree stump.

"Judy and Jessie will be part of my circle?" Opal gave a nod.

"If my hunches are right yes, both of them have the mark of the sapphire deep within them, and in time you will be revealed to them, and help to instruct them in the ways of your circle." Sapphire smirked.

"My circle, ha! I am hardly able to cope with all of this, how will I ever teach anyone else?" She gave another small laugh. "Saff the seer with no table and no clue at all, if anything I am blinder than any other." Opal gave a hearty chuckle.

"Oh, my dear child, you must have more faith, you have a table, your centre has already given it to you, it's around your neck." Sapphire looked at her confused.

Opal smiled, and pointed to the golden butterfly set within the violet talisman from Rune. "At the right moment for your circle to form, that little trinket will separate, and inside you will find a five pointed star. It is set on a background of white and enclosed within a violet circle." Her eyes danced with excitement. "I must admit she stole the idea from Rhiannon, she carries hers on a ring, and Rune saw it in her own table, so when she made the talismans for all of you, she hid your table in the talisman. Can you not remember the words? Here let me remind you."

The water in the basin rippled, and then cleared as the pictures formed. Sapphire saw herself as Rune went round the circle at Dunnottar handing out her gifts; her voice suddenly rose out of the basin and echoed around the open glade. "I have carried my message through you many times my sister. You should have been placed, and I know of the sadness you felt. Take this butterfly, for it is the centre of my words, and the bearer of my news, carry my power with you always and know you are close to my heart."

Opal patted her leg. "A bit too cryptic for you? Runestone Sapphire Loxley, the centre of her name is that of yours, Sapphire is the mark of sight, carry her power always means the one gift she has had longer than any, her sight, and also her table. Rune's table centre has twenty points to it; yours is the same colour but has just five. Your table will come in time, have no fear."

Sapphire lifted the pendant and looked at it. "I had no idea."

"What you mean you didn't see it coming?" Opal burst into laughter and slapped her playfully on the leg; Sapphire shrugged and started to laugh.

"See what I mean? I am hopeless." Both of them sat and laughed at each other as the little Sandling Cal, watched and blinked at them with happiness. It took a few moments before Opal stopped laughing, and she felt Sapphire had begun to accept her destiny and calm down a little.

"Your time here is almost done, but now you know, you can come here whenever you have need. Just think of Cal and he will come to collect you and guide you here. One last thing, I have shown you the moments of Billy's life that took place after the attack of Lord Loxley, I must remind you Sapphire, what you have seen must be guarded. Runestone is the only other person in your woodland world who knows about the true identity of the Sage, you must at all costs keep him hidden. If Mason was to find out, or even Robbie, it could tip the scales for either side and create chaos." Sapphire gave a nod.

"I understand, you have my word, nothing will be learned from me." Opal smiled at her.

"This is a new road, and it is a long one, there is much to learn and even more to do. I want to you return and collect Commander Rafe, take him to London, and both of you protect the Sage at all costs. Events are turning rapidly now, and the coming time before seating the new king will not be easy. Mason has suffered heavy losses and his retaliation will be swift and very severe. Go with Cal, and I will see you again My Lady of Callanish."

Sapphire gave Opal a huge hug. "Keep safe." Opal held her tightly.

"I am always safe within my circle, go with speed and good luck."

Sapphire left the glade of Opal holding the hand of her new companion, they walked into the woodland of tall grasses and trees, and she felt a great relief build inside her. Cal trotted along beside her smiling, until they reached a wall of tall reed like grasses, where he stopped and pulled back on her arm. Sapphire looked down at the small figure that had let go of her arm; he stood quite still watching her. She crouched down until her bright sapphire blue eyes were level with his. "Is this where you leave me?"

Cal gave his usual blink and she smiled. "OK, I understand, what do I do now?" He lifted his small hand and pointed at the tall reed, she looked at it and she understood. "You will be here waiting when I come back yes?" Once again, he blinked; Sapphire gave a nod, and then stretched out and pulled him close to her embrace. "Watch yourself and keep safe, I will see you soon."

His tiny arms stretched up and held her until she let go; as she stood up he gave her a big smile. Sapphire gave him a small wave, and she turned into the tall reed.

She sat up in bed with a jolt, and took a long breath of air. For a moment she felt like she was still there and blinked as the dim room of the house in New Avon came into view. "Wow." She shook her head. "Was that for real, or just a dream?" Everything in the room seemed as she had left it, her clothes were folded neatly on the chair opposite in the dark, next to her bow and quiver.

She slipped out of bed and walked to the open window, the moon was high in the sky, as she pulled back the curtain and looked out on the clear night. "Another dream, this is becoming way too weird for..." Her voice trailed off as she saw the neatly stacked pile of clothes, which were no longer green, but a deep sapphire blue. "What?" She lifted up the cloak and looked at it in the moonlight; it was without doubt the one she had worn as she sat with Opal.

"It cannot be, that is not possible." The new bow and quiver shone in the moonlight and she swallowed hard. "What the hell is happening to me, I think I really am losing it?"

London had been relatively safe and rebuilt by Mason, but now his factories had become targets in his absence, and much of his work had been undone. The Sage had a great deal of knowledge of his father's efforts in London, and over the

past weeks he had pounded all the most productive factories. Mason now rushed
back to find out why it had all gone so wrong, his mood was not good, and there
was panic within the ranks of the commanders based in London. Mason's hot
temper was soon to explode, and several of his high command found themselves
on the receiving end of his pistol.

It was a subdued bunch that walked along the side of the river towards the blown
up bridge, and half sunken ships, that barred the way up the river. All over the
city smoke and the smell of many fires hung thick and heavy in the air, in every
direction the tall plumes of black smoke rose into the clouds as Mason turned at
the river with his party, and surveyed the bridge that no longer connected the north
and south side of the river.

Terence Jones had suddenly found himself promoted from general's aide to
general, and now talked fast as he briefed Mason. "I really cannot explain it sir, I
mean, it's like they knew every factory and place of industry we have, you could
say the attacks were almost surgical in their pattern." Mason stopped and looked at
him.

"Do we have a leak?" Terence took a deep breath and swallowed very hard.

"I have to confess My Lord Knox, it is something a lot of us have thought, but as
hard as we have investigated, we have not found one." Mason gave a nod, he made
great use of spies, and knew how effective they could be, it made sense that Loxley
would try to infiltrate his ranks, he crouched down, and stared at the water and
crushed metal of one of his transport ships as he thought.

"What of our man in their camp, did he give us no warning at all?" Terence
shook his head.

"The inner circle is very careful, there are few who can get close to this masked
Sage, by the time we got news the attacks had begun, we are finding it very hard
to get information out of their camp. Since we learned of the tunnels, we have not
been able to get near them, they are well equipped and have many guards, and in
such confined quarters it's impossible to drive them out."

Mason stood up with a smile. "Then we shall seal them in, we have enough
troops coming from Windsor, it's pointless rebuilding there. Use the new strength
of numbers, and seal up every hole on the northern side of the river, and then
when we have them caught in their burrow, send everything we have across the
river, and hound them out of their holes and kill them." He turned to Terence
and gave him a hard stare. "I mean every single one, find them and blow them up,
seal this side of the river first, we have not got enough forces to attack on the South
side yet, so we seal this side and then we line the river with troops and bring in the
new troops on the south. Let's see our masked friend find his way across without
being seen then." He gave a nod to Terence who shook his head vigorously.

"Yes, My Lord, what a wonderful idea, I shall see it is done immediately."
Mason gave a grim look.

"Yes, you better had, if I lose so much as a rifle bullet from now on, you will have no need to worry about fancy green masked men, I will level London with all of you in it myself." Mason turned, and walked back down the bridge to the riverside. "My son will be arriving later, we shall dine together tonight at the apartment, make all the arrangements and make sure we are left in peace, I have much to discuss with him."

Terence gave a resolute shake of his head. "Yes, My Lord Knox, will there be anything else?"

"Not for now, although I wish to see every dispatch as it arrives, we will need to do some rethinking on this place, but we have time now, Loxley is hiding in his trees and York and Lincoln are under control, without their wood chopper, they are all feeling at a loss, so for the time being we have the time and space to solve this so called Sage problem, if our man inside appears, send him to me."

"Yes My Lord." Terence gave a bow, as Mason walked on with three of his aides, he turned sharply, looking very worried, and began giving his orders to the gathered group of officials, within minutes they were despatched in every direction as Mason's new plans were implemented; London for now was back in safe hands.

Mason was not really that wrong. Robbie was to some extent hiding in the trees; his group were all tired and exhausted and needed some time to recover. Under the watchful eyes of Fagan, they were all slowly finding their way back to their own selves again. Outside the realm of Avalon, no word had reached Caerleon or Loxley, and for the woodland commanders it was a time of worry. Rumours flew around about why the hooded man had mysteriously disappeared. To all but a few it looked like the battle was lost, even Mason, although not without his problems could smell victory.

High up on the lookout above the Forest of Time a faint figure stood and watched through the darkened sky. Eve could see all that was happening below in her realm, her eyes were fixed on the Citadel where the torches of the carts filled with monks and supplies, burned in a long line as it snaked up the high pass to the summit, she smiled quietly to herself. "Build all you like my dark little queen, you will not last here long enough to finish it. A new power is coming of the like you have never known. Even you Little Morgan will one day bend to the power of the Runestone."

CHAPTER TWENTY ONE

MAKING RAINBOWS

Ursula sat with her knees up, and her head resting on them, as she watched from the safety of just outside the doorway of the Citadel. It had felt like a very long few days, and she now felt exhausted. Her mind played back all that had happened over and over, as she thought about the mysterious stranger in the black robes.

Ursula remembered the time from many years ago, when she had left the caravan people and taken up with the young boat Gypsy, named Ferdinand. He had been very kind to her and she had loved him deeply, but the lack of understanding of others, had led to his death at the hands of thugs for no other reason than he had not been one of them.

The night she met her mistress came to mind, she had been alone for two years on the boat reading fortunes to make ends meet, Morgan le Fey had walked into her in the small town, and recognised her talents instantly. The words of that night still resounded deeply within her. "You will have no peace in this life alone my girl, you are different from them, but there is a time coming where the likes of you and I will be free of the hate, and finally we will be treated with respect."

Ursula now understood what she had meant, for her mistress had grown in power and people trembled with fear before her, and as her assistant, she was always treated with the utmost respect by everyone who met her. It had been long and hard for her to understand the family that used its power and brutality to get what they felt they deserved, had she not once been so fearful she had tried to run away? For Ursula it had been a long journey, and now she could see more of the woman who was her mistress and mentor.

In many ways she felt she had a deeper understanding of the pain her mistress carried, and now she did understand why Morgan le Fey felt she should fight to defend what was her legacy. She was the first born of Igraine, the queen of a long Celtic line who had been robbed of her place in the world. It troubled her deeply now as she had to work out why the words of the robed stranger had bothered her so much, for many years she had felt she was on the right path towards her own destiny, but why now did she feel a huge conflict inside herself, did she really doubt the path she was on?

The sun was high in the sky, although even this high up on the Mount; the dark clouds that rolled in above her obscured the view. She sat and stared out across the rough stone plateau, and across the long dried up lake to where she knew the Forests of Time sat under the clouds in the far distance. Deep under the trees Runestone was preparing again, Ursula had no idea of what had happened that night and how after Rune had destroyed all her work, she had left her mistress to scream and holler at the walls and ceiling of the huge hall. The fountain lay in waste destroyed by the wrath of her mistress, and water now covered the floor she had marked in sulphur with such skill. Morgan le Fey sat at the top of the steps utterly exhausted from her tantrum, and moaned and complained to herself about the wrongs that had been done to her.

Ursula sat alone and watched lost in her own thoughts, filled with the doubts of not knowing where her own future lay. All around her the monks worked, as they began to create their own new building to commemorate the Church, and provide a sanctuary to all who followed the scripture of Old Brother Argus.

It had been a very long time since she had felt this alone and isolated, in all her years of service to her mistress, she had not felt such a deep pang inside her, and she could not understand why quite suddenly she would feel this way. She got up and walked out on to the wide stone plateau, and pulled her cloak tightly round her, with the coming of dark clouds, a strong breeze had risen and it buffeted her, grabbing the ends of her cloak and shaking it violently. The wind screamed into her ears, shouting her name and she shook her head and lifted her hood to prevent it, it was then she heard her name shouted out loud above the wind, and she turned and saw a young soldier dressed in black. He beckoned to her, and she moved back across the plateau towards him. The young soldier smiled. "Are you Miss Ursula?" She nodded.

"Yes, what do you want with me?" He smiled.

"Our Lady Morgan has asked me to escort you to the cave and pack Miss."

Ursula did not understand.

"Are we leaving?" The soldier gave a quick nod.

"Your mistress wants you to leave here, she has another job for you Miss, and she has given me details of where to take you and what to do." Ursula shook her head.

"No I cannot leave here, she needs me." The soldier shook his head.

"Look Miss, I am sorry, but she was very adamant that you and you alone were to do this. Please I have my orders, and I cannot disobey them, we have to hurry Miss the carriage is waiting."

"But I must go and see her, and say goodbye, I cannot leave without a parting word." The young soldier leaned closer to her and lowered his voice.

"She does not want any goodbyes Miss, that's like admitting she cares. Please we have to go." Ursula gave a nod of agreement; she understood her mistress, and she knew how expressing any sort of feeling would be seen as weakness. She followed the soldier back into the Citadel and down the wooden steps into the labyrinth of tunnels.

"Where are we going?" The soldier looked at her.

"To be honest Miss, I don't rightly know, she has arranged for one of them creepy folk to drive us, I have orders to open a package when we get there. I am sorry but that's all I can say, cause I don't know much more."

Ursula gave a small chuckle and it echoed off the walls, he smiled at her. "Sorry, but I have to say, I know they are on our side, but none of us lot like em, they are very creepy, especially when they turn."

"Yeah, I know what you mean; they are very scary at times. I tend to stay as far away as possible from them." He gave her a big smile and held out his hand.

"I am Thomas by the way, folks call me Tom." She took it and shook it.

"Ursula, I don't really have a short name." He gave a small laugh.

"Yeah I know, your mistress told me." She felt a little foolish.

"Right, sorry not thinking." They hurried down the long tunnel that would lead them out into the dried and scorched earth that Avalon had now become, to visit the cave before leaving the realm forever.

Fagan walked out of the trees towards the house, holding up two tied and gagged soldiers in each hand. Jade wandered along just behind him with Fox and Blades. Rowan limped to the steps as he saw them heading across the grass. "Robbie, you better get out here, we got guests."

Robbie appeared in the doorway, closely followed by Rune and a few of the others. He walked out onto the porch and stood beside Rowan, as Fagan gave a nod of a greeting. He thrust them down hard on the floor. "We found ourselves a few rats sneaking about in the honeysuckle, I thought ye would want to give em a talking to, and the trees were yelling like they had coral spot about em being on their roots." His bushy white eyebrows twitched as he viewed the two soldiers with distaste. Robbie noticed the captain's badge on the collar of the largest and gave John the signal to take his gag off.

John pulled it down hard a look of utter revulsion on his face, and dragged the soldier up onto his knees. The Captain stared defiantly at Rowan and Robbie. "Ask all you like woodcutter, you won't get a word out of me." He spat on the floor. "Even if you get your demon, I will die before you learn a thing." Rowan looked at Robbie with a confused look; Robbie understood having heard Harry's entire story.

"He means Harry." Rowan gave a nod. The captain looked up at both of them.

"You might as well kill me now, go on and get that blue bastard, and we will finish this." The mention of blue in the sentence brought understanding to the rest of the group, and a few of them smiled, the captain looked round at them all. "Laugh all you like, your days are numbered, the darkness is already here, and its queen will not be far behind, and then you will burn like the heathens you are." Robbie looked up at Fagan.

"Tie them to the forge, I would say put them in the barn but it will disturb the animals." He looked down at the Cutter Captain. "Thanks for the information, when I see your queen, I will be happy to let her know how helpful you were, although I won't be burning any time soon." The captain at the mention of the Dark One suddenly went very white.

"What do you mean, I told you nothing, she will never believe a word you say." Robbie smiled.

"Your men down there on the road will try to burn this forest, but I am afraid, thanks to you they will fail. As I said, thanks for the information." Fagan gripped him hard behind the collar, and hoisted him into the air as he wriggled and squirmed, he turned without a word and walked off towards the forge, the captain screamed back at Robbie.

"Hey wait; I said nothing about burning the forest, you're wrong. She will never believe you, and you will be dead before she finds out."

Robbie looked at the others. "We need to move and fast, most of this forest is tinder dry, we have to stop them. Everyone grab your kit, and get out in front in ten." The group scrambled as Fagan dumped the two prisoners down by the side of the forge, and bound them with a heavy chain. Captain Banes continued to rant and swear at Robbie, even though he had gone inside the house, Fagan pulled the gag back up and tightened it. "Oh my, ye can chatter, I know a good willow who would love ye, he rambles on spouting nonsense for hours an all."

Fagan straightened up and looked around the open grass area. "Right then guarding ye will take someone with a bit of power." He leaned back to try and get a glimpse of the open barn door. "Where is he?" The two prisoners sat and feared the worst, they both started to shout inaudible words into their gags, as they feared that Fagan was looking for the blue demon they called Harry. Fagan gave a smile as he looked over at the long grass. "Ah, there he is... Puss, puss, puss, puss... Come on lad and do a bit of babysitting for me."

The two guards breathed a sigh of great relief as they realised the giant demon that had terrified them was not around, the thought of the Puss doing it seemed a little comical, but it had to be better than a demon. They both relaxed as they waited, held tight in the chain thinking they had got off the hook nicely. Furry Face pounced out of the long grass and came running over to Fagan.

High pitched squeals came out from beneath the gags as the two white faced, wide eyed Cutters saw the large impressive tiger walk towards Fagan. It looked at the two Cutters and his lip curled, as he growled with dislike. They pushed on the floor with their feet to try and get closer to the forge wall, and away from Furry Face. Fagan patted the large tiger on the head with affection. "Ye keep a good eye on em, and don't eat em mind... well not all of em, we still need em talking, I am sure an arm or a leg will do."

The tiger walked up to the Cutters, he was taller than they were sat on the floor. He came very close and sniffed at them, both of them screamed under their gags as the tiger gave a loud ferocious roar. A stream of liquid ran out from under the young tied up soldier, as he shook at the side of his captain. Furry Face stepped back and roared again. Fagan gave a smile and walked off to prepare.

Rafe was sat at the table with his father eating his breakfast as Sapphire dressed in blue came down the stairs; he looked up at her and gave a double take as he saw the new clothes. "Where you get them from?" Sapphire gave him a blank stare.

"Get what?" He pointed at her.

"Them clothes." She smiled.

"Been shopping, you like them?"

"How?"

"You forget how we got here; I can leave whenever I want." He took a big swig of tea.

"So what's the occasion?" Sapphire rested her new bow on the wall.

"We have been called back to duty, we leave for London shortly, we have a task there before we move back to Loxley." Rafe looked at his dad who gave a smile.

"It had to happen sooner or later, stop worrying I will be fine." Rafe gave a solemn nod.

"I know Dad, it's just...." John Rafe patted his son on the shoulder.

"It's your job Johnny lad, go on you are needed, make me proud, we will be fine here, we have extra troops and more scouts, Mason won't walk this land easily."

Rafe gave a long sigh as he slid back his chair, he knew the moment would come, but he had hoped he would go straight back to the Specialists and Jett. The thought of a job in London felt boring and useless. Sapphire smiled as he passed her to go and get his kit, John Rafe came across the room and gave her a hug.

"I want to thank you for all you have done for us, I know it has not been easy for you, but I do appreciate everything, I am in your debt." Sapphire gave him a big squeeze.

"It was my pleasure, think nothing of it; I just wish I could have done more... Are you going to be OK here without him?" John Rafe let go of her and smiled.

"It's been wonderful seeing him, but I think I need some time alone... you know do those little things I promised her." Sapphire understood.

"Well as long as you are alright, don't forget, if you need us, send word to my mother at Loxley, I will have him here in a flash of blue." He smiled at the thought.

"Honest, I will be fine, and I think he will be when he gets back to duty, I can see the frustration in him, he has and always will be a soldier first." Sapphire gave a nod; it was probably the best way of describing Rafe.

"Take care then, I will wait outside for him, send him out when he is ready." She gave John Rafe another hug, and then lifted her bow and bag, then headed out towards the gate.

Rune stood by the bedroom door as Robbie grabbed his things. "Why won't you listen to me Robbie?"

"I have, but there is no way in hell I will allow you out there without us." Rune could feel his pride, but that just seemed to annoy her even more.

"That's not what I am saying, why won't you just wait and hear me out, you know I am right, they have had nowhere near enough time to recover." Robbie lifted his bow and stopped at the door.

"We fight as a team, and all of them have had enough time to rest... that's my last word, if you are coming, grab your bow." He walked past her and out through the door. She turned but knew he was not listening.

"But Robbie they will have way too many soldiers and no matter what you think, they are not ready for a fight that big."

Robbie walked rapidly out of the door to face his group of Specialists. "Jade, Blades, Fox and Hawk. Head off now, get as close as you can and watch them, if they strike before I get there fall back, and one of you high tail here to let us know, the rest of you get ready." The four Specialists turned, and ran off towards the trees as Rune came running out behind Robbie, she looked very upset with him, and his manner did show everyone that something was not right.

"Oh will you please listen to me, Robbie just hold up and don't go running off, they are not ready for this yet." He turned to Rune.

"We cannot wait, I have to stop them."

"But Robbie, just listen." He walked through the group to where Rowan leaned on his walking stick waiting, and armed with a new long bow made by Fagan. Rune ran after him as he waved to the group and they all fell in behind him. Rune ran up at his side panting as he stormed off at a quick walk. "Robbie we still need more time to recover, please hear me out?"

"Rune we don't have time, they are there ready to burn us out." He looked resolute, and Rune felt frustrated, she stopped on the path, as Robbie walked onwards leading the group; Steph came up at her side.

"Sweetheart he has no choice, this is the Forest of Time, he has to protect it."

"Not by killing everyone he doesn't." Her eyes burned a bright sapphire blue, and Steph could see the temper rising inside her. Steph lifted a hand to her shoulder.

"What other choice does he have? If there was any other way I am sure..."

"HE WOULDN'T LISTEN TO IT!"

Steph gave a jump as Rune screamed down the forest track at him. Rune's face looked like thunder, and Steph thought it better not to push it. Rune stamped down on the floor hard. "He will listen to me." She screamed down the track at him. "ROBERT JOHN LOXLEY, JUST YOU GOD DAM WAIT!" Lifting her fingers, she snapped them hard, and the group stopped dead in the middle of the track. Rune gave a satisfied nod at her mother, who could do very little but smile.

With a deep intake of breath, Rune marched up the track walking past the Specialists, who were frozen in place. All they could move was their eyes, and they watched as Rune walked passed them, and up to the front of the line. She stared at Robbie who she could see from the hard stare in his eyes was not at all pleased. Rune faced him and lowered her voice.

"Now I have your attention, just you listen to what I have to say. I realise you are Lord of Loxley, and when there we all obey you, but you are forgetting my dear husband that this is my realm, and for once I think you should listen to what I have to say, before marching off to your death." He blinked, and she smiled.

"Good, I am glad we sorted that out." Rune gave her fingers a loud snap, and all the others gave a gasp as they felt their limbs relax and free up, Robbie remained frozen before her, and he blinked rapidly, Rune smiled. "Not yet, I have more." Rowan gave a huge smile as he walked slowly up the line from the back leaning on his stick.

Rune softened her voice. "Robbie I love you, but you are frightening me. I know things have not gone well, and I know you need to prove yourself again, but please listen to reason." She looked at Rowan for help. "Tell him Rowan, they have the spirit, but they have not got the strength yet." Rowan gave a small nod; he could see her concern and did feel a little guilty that he too had ignored her pleas to slow down.

"What have you got in mind Rune?" Robbie's eyes shot to the left where Rowan gave a shrug. "Hear her out, we always take her input, why exclude her now?" Rune's fingers snapped, and Robbie lurched slightly forward.

"Because Rowan doing nothing is not an option, and letting her go alone is even more less of one." He turned to talk to Rune and she lifter her fingers and he stopped and waited. Rune shook her head. "Look, this is the Forest of Time, hard as it is to picture; this is a realm in its own right." Robbie and Rowan both looked confused. Rune gave a small smile and then continued. "This is the very first realm created, it is for want of a better word, the first home of Eve. It lies parallel to Avalon, and appears as if it is part of it, but it isn't. Avalon has an effect on it, like the weather, which is why it's been so hot here, but unlike Avalon, if you look around you will see the trees still have green leaves."

All the Specialist including Robbie looked up at the canopy high above them, it was true, they looked lush and green and very different from the shedding trees they had all see in the mist. Rune appeared to be very happy with her argument. "I am the true owner of this forest, and it has with it many protections."

"Like what?" Rowan was keen to know.

"Nothing can enter here if I so wish it, not a soldier, or Houlen, or dark sorceress, this is the one realm she will never be able to penetrate, it's something like the defences my grandfather placed on his house." Robbie gave a resounding nod as he understood; Rune gave a sigh of relief and lifted a hand to his face. "Robbie, I know it all went wrong in the caves and we lost Alley. I know how much that hurts you still, but please do not put your pride before your life, because I am frightened I will lose you. Stop for a minute and remember outside of this realm, think about the Mere and our children, and the promises we made to each other." He lifted his arms and pulled her close.

"I will never forget, you know that." She held him tight.

"Please this one time, I am the one who can control this. Let me lead and I promise, I will keep everyone safe." Robbie gave a long sigh.

"OK what do we do?" Rune gave a huge smile and kissed him.

"We use rain." His brow furrowed.

"Don't you mean hail?" She looked up at the dark brooding clouds.

"Oh no Robbie, she has finally made a mistake I can use. You can only make clouds that dark, by using a great deal of water." Rowan glanced at the dark sky above him and smiled.

"Nice one Rune, I've needed a shower."

Rafe said his goodbyes, and with a heavy heart he walked down the steps of the old farm, and through the large blue pulsating window that Sapphire had opened. He walked out on to the brick strewn basement of an old building, and looked round at the decay covered in grass and weeds. "My God what a dump, welcome to bloody London, and we are fighting for this shit hole, for what reason?"

Sapphire shook her head as she came through the window, and it closed behind her.

"There is no pleasing some people; come on it is this way." Together they climbed a set of stone steps, which brought them up to ground level; Rafe was less impressed as he looked at the endless smashed and crumbling buildings, covered in mosses and weed. He brought his hand up to his nose.

"What the hell is that bloody awful stink?" Sapphire gave a chuckle.

"It's the river, most of the waste is dumped into it, you will get used to it." She stood on what had once been the road on the south bank of the river. Along the edge of the river there were small groups of woodsmen behind barricades, and there seemed to be some commotion, as men ran about shouting at each other getting organised for what looked like an attack. Rafe gave a smile.

"Should have known it, I get called for duty, and guess what, it's a bloody war zone. I thought we were supposed to be babysitting some bloke?”

“We are, ignore that lot, and follow me. If all hell is about to break lose, I want to find the Sage before it does.”

Rafe stared across the river, as Sapphire began to walk towards four large trees; it took a few moments for him to work out exactly what he was looking at. In the trees it had always been so much easier spotting black and red against green, here in the rubble and stone of a fallen and still burning London it was not quite as easy. Sapphire turned. “Rafe come on will you.”

“Yeah, yeah, give me a minute will you?” He lifted his hand and shaded his eyes from the bright sun. It took a few seconds for his eyes to adjust, and then he saw them. At first it was a tiny glint of brass in amongst all the activity of black. Within a second he understood it was men rolling cannons up to the edge of the river. “Oh Shit!” He turned and ran for his life, he very quickly caught up with Sapphire, as she walked towards the entrance to a smashed up old building, he grabbed her arm and dragged her.

“Rafe what the hell are!” The boom was loud behind her; the whistle from the shell was louder. Rafe grabbed her and flung her down against the wall, and jumped on top of her, as the earth shook violently, and the explosion thundered into her ears. She screwed up her face and pushed it into Rafe. A cloud of dust swept down the street and covered everything.

Rafe lifted his grey coloured head, and looked down at her shocked face. “You OK?” She gave a nod, her ears ringing from the blast. He stood up slowly and offered her his hand, she took it and he pulled her up. All around was hidden in the dense cloud of dust; he spat as Sapphire coughed at his side. “Shit that was close; I see what you meant about this guy needing looking after. My God Mason wants this bloke deader than dead.”

He brushed the thick dust off his shoulders. “Where is this bloke? We need to move, that was the first, and I will bet my last bit there are more.”

Through the heavy cloud of dust, another deep boom rang out. Sapphire tugged at his sleeve and he followed at a run. Both of them swerved round a corner as the whistle screamed above them. Rafe slammed into the wall dragging Sapphire close. With their heads down they clung to each other as the floor shuddered, and the thunderous explosion went off.

The air was so thick with dust it was almost impossible to see, Rafe screwed up his eyes, as they stung with the fine bits of grit that were swirling through the air. Sapphire shook her head and the dirt rained out in every direction. She walked carefully back to the corner of the alley they had ducked into and looked round.

What had been the railway station was just a pile of burning rubble. Bodies littered the floor, and Woodsmen walked in a daze covered in blood. What had been the rough surface of an old road where Rafe had stood only minutes ago was now a huge open crater. Rafe wiped the dirt out of his eyes and spat on the floor.

"If your man was in there he didn't have a hope." Sapphire stared ahead slightly in shock, and unable to comprehend the nightmare in front of her. Rafe took her arm.

"It looks like everyone is heading out over there, let's take a look and see if this Sage bloke is with them." She gave a small nod, and he took her hand, and guided her into the clouds of swirling dust. Further up river more guns fired.

Jade watched the road as more and more soldiers moved into position in the darkness. For as far as the road stretched into the leafless trees of the lower vale of Avalon, burning torches flickered in a long wavy line. Carts filled with large barrels trundled along in amongst the soldiers; it was very obvious that the Dark One had every intention of burning everything in sight. Jade turned to a very nervous looking Blades. "Any sign of them yet?"

"Todd said they are a few minutes behind us." Jade turned and looked out at the thousand soldiers dressed in black. "You ready for this one?" Blades gave a nod, but she looked doubtful.

The Specialists walked four across the path, with Robbie and Rune in the middle. Rune told Robbie what she needed, and the rest of the group listened in. "Spread out along the edge of the trees, but please do not go any closer than two feet to the very edge of the bank. None of their arrows will enter the trees, and the Houlen will not be able to attack you. As long as everyone does exactly as I ask, you will all be safe. We can shoot, but no swords, you cannot cross the boundary, or my protection will fail. Does everyone understand that?"

Fox stood waiting in the centre of the path, and as the Specialists approached, they began to fan out and move into the thick undergrowth along the edge of the forest. Rowan with his walking stick and his bow across his back went left, and Robbie went right. Rune stayed on the path to lead through the centre; she grabbed Maddy by the arm. "Stay close to me, how are the new arrows?"

Maddy looked at the new bright silver arrows in her quiver tipped with brown flights. She still had a few bright white ones mixed in with them. "Not really tested one yet, my alchemy is not as good as my mums, but Una and Treen between them seem to have done rather well. I suppose we are about to find out." Rune gave a smile.

"Well we have plenty to test them on." She winked as they came up close to the edge of the tree line. Very carefully Rune looked left and then right. Robbie and Rowan held the line, and were safely within the boundaries. Rune gave a slight gasp as she saw the amount of soldiers on the road. Maddy raised her eyebrows.

"She certainly means business; I take it my targets are those big barrels?" Rune gave a nod.

"Even after all this heat, she will need a lot of fuel to get the green burning, I think we should wait until they start to unload the barrels."

Jade stood at the side of Robbie, behind a large fern and some small beech saplings, as they viewed the scene below on the road. Samuel Knots yelled and screamed at his Sergeants as they organised the men into large groups. He carried a long black whip, which he would crack as he shouted out his commands, it gave a very strong sense of who exactly was in charge, and the men would leap up to ensure they did not feel the tail sting of his lash.

It was very brightly lit, due to the thousands of burning torches, and from where they both stood, the roar of the flickering torches, as they burned sounded very loud. Fagan sat in a large bunch of small saplings watching, he would occasionally stroke the leaves of the small trees. "Now, now, don't ye go and fret, I know it looks bad, but we have the Lady of Life with us, and she is not going to let anything happen to ye, so hold it together and stand proud." He smiled as he listened to the small frightened little squeaks and gave a very reassured nod to them. "That's the ticket, see I told ye." He gave a big smile as he looked around at the rest of the trees with pride. "Did all ye big ones hear that? I am proud of this lot, right bunch of little troopers they are."

It had taken somewhere around an hour to organise, as the woodsmen finally sat in wait for the soldiers. Samuel Knots gave the signal, and groups of burly fighters took hold of the barrels and lifted them down to the groups of soldiers gathered around them. Rune gave the signal, and everyone prepared as Maddy lifted her bow and fitted one of the new arrows made by Treen and Una.

Ten soldiers dragged the large barrel onto its side and rolled it towards the edge of the road, where a huge Cutter lifted a heavy axe to chop into the side and begin the flow of oil. Rune nodded as he swung high, and Maddy took her aim and released the arrow.

WHOOOOOOOOOOOSH!! It exploded out of the bow like a missile, blowing Maddy right off her feet. Everyone watched as it flashed like lightening across the open area between the woodland and the road. It hit the barrel with massive force and before anyone could breathe in, the road was engulfed in fire. It swept in a mighty cloud of napalm burning everything in its path.

Soldiers dived to the floor in every direction, not quite understanding what had happened. Samuel Knots screamed with rage; not even aware it was enemy fire he was under. Maddy sat up with a huge laugh. "Wow, I think Master Fagan's ingredients are a bit purer than we are used to. What a weapon." Jade was already laughing in the trees, as she saw men scattering in every direction filled with panic. She held her sides as she pointed at them.

"Look at em run Robbie.... That scared the pants off em." A second arrow streaked out of the darkness into one of the loaded carts, and men screamed in fear as Jade wailed even louder with laughter. Bodies scattered in every direction as a thunderous cloud of fire erupted into the air. It flared up into the sky stroking the trees in front of Rowan. Jade screamed even louder with laughter, as Big John,

Harry, Bear, Hawk and Skip grabbed Rowan and ran like mad back into the woodland, and dived for cover under a thick Hawthorn.

Robbie gave the signal, as he saw the Cutter officer point to where the arrow had come from, the officers shouted to those not in danger of burning to aim for the forest and light their arrows. The Specialists rose out of the floor and took aim. Before a single Cutter arrow was fired, a volley a white arrows with brown feathers, found their mark in the soldiers, and they crumpled forward on to the floor.

In the chaos on the road, the soldiers tried to avoid the exploding barrels and Woodsmen's arrows. Samuel Knots screamed out from behind the cover of a turned over cart, and men gabbed the barrels that had not been hit and started chopping holes in them before pushing them off the road and towards the steep embankment.

Rune's moment arrived as the barrels rolled towards the trees emptying their volatile contents onto the floor. Two men tried to light the fuel with torches, but Robbie's arrows sent them flying backwards into the dead grass on the opposite side of the road. Behind his cart, Samuel Knots lifted a burning torch and flung it over the cart. Robbie saw it heading towards the grass in front of Rune, and he loaded and fired with huge speed. His arrow hit the torch, but it did not hit it far enough away to stop it igniting the floor.

A wall of flames thirty feet high, jumped up in front of the trees and the Specialists staggered backwards in the intense heat.

Rune's eyes went a deep vivid purple as she looked up to the sky, and with a snap of her fingers, a massive bolt of violet light streaked into the air. It hit the dark clouds above them and spread out wide across the sky. Robbie lay on his back in the fern and watched as the clouds above twinkled with violet flashes. He felt the first drop hit his face, and then it came down at speed and he blinked, the raindrop hit his cheek and bounced into the grass. Then came the second, and the third, and slowly the rain increased. The downpour hurtled out of the sky in huge raindrops; Rowan threw back his head and laughed with joy as he held out his arms, and stuck his tongue out. It felt like heaven, and in less than a minute the rain rattled down over the leaves and into the ferns drenching everything, including the Specialists who stood perfectly still and looked up, enjoying the first rain in seven of the hottest days ever known to man.

Jade and Blades danced together under the heavy drops, as Robbie turned to see Rune soaked to the skin, but wearing a big happy smile. Behind her the wall of fire raged, as the soldiers stood on the far side of the road and watched, thinking they had achieved their goal. The large frame of Samuel Knots walked with stature down the road, smiling with satisfaction at a job well done.

Robbie walked up to Rune who smiled at him; he nodded to the wall of fire ten feet behind her. "What you going to do about that?" She turned to face it.

"Oh, I almost forgot." She brought her hands up to her chest, and with palms facing out she stood fast and then closed her eyes. Robbie watched as she rapidly pushed forward with her arms, and a blast of wind erupted out of the floor in front of her. The wall of fire burned fierce as the soldiers watched feeling victorious.

From nowhere there came a loud roar, and the flames exploded out of the trees, crossed the burned out grass and engulfed the road. Soldiers ran burning and screaming into the trees, and threw themselves down rolling around in the dirt and dry grass to put out the flames. Panic swept through them as they patted each other and flailed around on the floor, but seven days of intense heat had left everything dryer than paper.

The grass and scorched fern ignited quickly, burning fast and creating a thick swirling cloud of dense choking smoke. Small trees and shrubs burst into flames spreading the fire faster. Tinder dry trees caught in the tall flames, and within minutes the woodland opposite the Forest of Time was like hell on earth, as it burned out of control. The air was filled with smoke and the screams of panicked soldiers, as they ran from the flames in every direction. The fire followed them engulfing everything, fanned by the winds of Rune. And as they headed away from the forest screaming and wailing, behind them the rain moved over slowly and quenched the fire and flooded the gullies.

Rune watched feeling a sense of great relief. "They will run for miles before it stops chasing them, we are all safe now."

Robbie pulled her close to his side as he watched the fire drop along the edge of the forest, and the water ran off his nose and dripped from his long lank hair. He was soaked right through his cloak, tunic and shirt, and yet it felt wonderful and refreshing.

"You did good Rune; it's nice to win one without a hard fight. I am sorry I doubted you, I should have realised by now, with each addition to your powers, you find new tricks to help us." She turned and kissed his cheek.

"It's alright I forgive you, after all, we all make mistakes when we are fatigued." She gave a giggle and her eyes sparkled with glee, Robbie nodded his head and laughed.

"Guess I had that coming?" Rune smiled and turned towards the path, and gave his hand a tug.

"Take me back and hold me in the darkness, with all this daylight recently, I've missed it." He gave the signal, and the Specialists withdrew, and holding Rune by the hand, he walked towards the old log cabin of Fagan's, feeling a deep sense of relief, and happiness.

Sapphire and Rafe staggered through the dust to a wide road leading off to their right, everyone seemed to be heading that way, as more cannons fired behind them. Rafe held onto her arm and kept close to a collapsed wall for some cover. In the blinding dust it was hard to see his footing, as he wove round piles of fallen brickwork. He constantly wiped his eyes to keep them clear enough to see where he was going as they made their way along the road and away from the choking dust.

Both of them looked like workers from one of the Knox factories they were so grey, as they were swept along in a long stream of retreating woodsmen. The air began to clear and it was easier to breathe, Sapphire coughed and choked and Rafe saw a few men sheltering against the wall, he moved over pulling Sapphire, and they both leaned back against the wall and coughed hard to clear the dirt and dust out of their lungs before drawing in fresher air.

Far behind them on the river edge, the cannons continued to pound everything the resistance could use; Rafe shook his head and heard the sand like particles patter on the floor. He looked up at the man at the side of him as Sapphire bent over and shook her hair, he was covered in grey dust and had a bad cut on his head, that trailed a mixture of blood and dirt over half of his face. "You ok?"

The man looked down at him with a blank stare. "Fine, it looks worse than it is." Rafe slipped his hand under his cloak and pulled out a crisp white handkerchief.

"Here use this, it's clean." The woodsman took it and lifted it to the side of his face. Grey dust ran like sand from his cloak onto the floor. Rafe stood up and noticed the flash of red, and the commander's bars, he held out his hand.

"The names Rafe, I have just come from New Avon." The woodsman took his hand.

"Silas... Commander Silas." Rafe smiled.

"Nice to meet you Silas... I don't suppose you would know if this Sage bloke is about? We were supposed to report to him as soon as we got here, but as you can see, we arrived as dear old Mason decided to vent his anger." Silas lifted a hand and pointed in the direction of the moving crowds.

"Follow the rabble, that Outlaw lot from Loxley set up a camp up there; it appears everyone is heading towards them. The Sage is always with them, so I would just follow the queue, and see if he is there, if not he is probably buried." He brushed the dust off his cloak and Rafe saw the distinct red lion crest of Caerleon, he smiled. "You're a ways from home?" Silas looked at the crest.

"Yes, mores the pity." Sapphire gave a tug on Rafe's cloak.

"Come on we have got to get moving, we need to find him fast, it looks like operations here just ceased." Her face was dirty and her eyes were inflamed and red looking. He turned to Silas. "See you at the camp." Silas gave a slight wave.

"It's a possibility." Sapphire moved off with Rafe at her side.

"He was fun." Rafe looked back at Silas stood against the wall holding Rafe's hankie to his face. Rafe shrugged.

"Looks like he is in shock, not bloody surprised, it scared the hell out of me for a minute." They headed back onto the road and walked with the long crowd of Woodsmen away from the river towards what they hoped was a camp that contained the Sage.

The clouds over the Forest of Time broke up as the water dispersed and moved with the gentle breeze towards the town of Avalonia. In the forest the rain was just a fine steady light stream, and as the clouds parted, the bright sun above shone through the canopy and lit the forest with a thousand rainbows.

Jade squealed with delight as Maggs stared in wonder. "Oh Rune, Sweetheart that is oh so beautiful, I feel positively recharged in a cosmic and karma building sort of way." She stood in the middle of the track in her pink boots and long green tie dyed skirt, adorned with a million feathers and beads and sets of silver jewellery and vibrated in tune with excitement. Rune gave a chuckle.

"I am pleased that you like them Maggs." Maggs rose with positive excitement.

"Oh Rune Darling, this will enhance the aura of all of us.... Oh where is my Harry Man? This is just what he needs to enhance his vibes and strengthen his karma. I shall snatch him quick, so we can mellow out and Rainbow bathe. Oh he has no idea of the wonders of it." She rattled off down the path shouting for Harry, as Rowan scoffed behind her next to Robbie.

"Rainbow bathe, she is madder than he is." Rune heard Robbie laugh and she tried to force her laugher down, as she watched Maggs grab hold of Harry and try ripping his shirt off him to catch the rays. Both of them fell backwards into the thick fern, and Rune thought it best, she didn't ask as they passed.

CHAPTER TWENTY TWO

SHRINKING THE NET

As the flames erupted, and the roar of the explosions burst into the sky on the south side of the river, from his high advantage point on the northern bank, Mason watched with keen interest and cold pale blue eyes. Most of the bank across the water was hidden deep below the thick blanket of dust and smoke, which swirled with the force of more explosives landing. Through the cloud, voices screamed and wailed with fear and pain, as the hundreds of resistance fighters fought their way to the surface, out of the deep tunnels of the underground, only to be pounded by cannon fire as they surfaced.

They ran in panic away from the underground exits, into the rubble and blinding, choking cloud, disorientated, as they stumbled and fell as more lumps of concrete and mortar whistled through the air all around them, propelled by the explosions. It was a scene of chaos and horror, as they scrambled together trying to find their comrades, and stumbled away from the terror towards some point of safe haven.

Mason rested his glass on the small wall in front of him with a clink, as he viewed the scene before him, beside him with an equally unemotional look in his eyes, his son Lance watched with less interest. "You should have waited until the wind blew the opposite way, we could have at least had a better view of them dying."

Mason gave a small nod; it was an interesting point, and one he had not considered in his preparation to wipe out those who had cost him so much of his stores. He lifted his glass, which twinkled, as it reflected the large explosion that shook the ground, as it went off across the dark and dirty river. "I think we have seen the best of it now, come on, we shall dine and discuss the girl." He turned from the rail, and with his son beside him, they walked slowly across the roof, to the small wall containing the steel door that led down to the apartments below.

Rafe grabbed Sapphire by the arm. "Hey, there he is over there." He lifted a grey dusty sleeve and pointed across the wide stone floor of a demolished building that was littered with the laid out figures of the wounded, of which there were over a hundred. Ox and his team were moving along the lines trying their best to help the injured and badly wounded, in what had become a temporary field hospital. All around from out of the gloom dazed and shocked figures walked silently like grey clad ghosts, as they homed in on the first place of safety they could find. Sapphire looked around in horror at the semi crushed figures with mangled limbs; their blood seemed to show more against the white and grey dust of their clothing. She looked back at Rafe as he viewed the scene with equal horror.

"This isn't fighting, it's slaughter." The whites of his soft brown eyes shone brighter in his dirt covered face as he looked round at the devastation, and long lines of the dead. Somehow, he could not find the right words, and looked back at her blankly, Sapphire's eyes showed her concern and feeling of helplessness.

"They cannot stay here Rafe; somehow we need to get them to a better place." He gave a nod still trying to find the right words. Sapphire turned and began weaving her way through the rows of the wounded towards Ox, Rafe stood for a few more moments as he watched the lines of wounded growing longer, as others appeared out of the dust clouds carrying yet more injured and dead. Finally, his silent words slipped out of his dust filled mouth.

"We need you here Rune." Ox looked up at the sound of his name, and saw the dust covered, blue clad, slender figure of Sapphire as she walked towards him, he tied a knot in the bandage he had applied to the arm of a soldier and stood up. "Miss Sapphire, what you doing here?"

Sapphire walked towards him along a strip of bare concrete soaked in blood, which splashed up onto her normally gleaming white boots. "Thank Hearne you are safe, I was sent here by Rune to help the Sage, but as yet I have not found him, do you know where he is?"

Ox gave a puzzled look, and then wiped his hands on his patched green pants. "Not seen him, but Miss Louisa will probably know, we been real busy here Miss, what with bombs and injuries, it's been hell for the last hour."

Sapphire could see the pandemonium all around, there were more wounded than there was men to attend them. Ox was doing his best, but all he could really manage was to bind the less serious wounds, and let Doc and some of the others tend to serious cases. All around them came the cries and moans of pain, set to a backdrop of explosions going off just a few minutes away. The ground below her feet vibrated constantly with the continuous impacts of Mason's cannon shells. Ox pointed a large thumb behind him. "You will find her back there sorting out them what we have left to fight." Sapphire patted his large shoulder.

"Thanks, you do what you have to do, we will see what can be done here, and hopefully find the Master Sage." He gave a grunt as he knelt down beside a man who had a huge hole torn in his shoulder, the wound was swollen and matted with dirt from the impact of a large piece of masonry, Sapphire felt her stomach churn as she saw the open, gaping wound surrounded by the glistening blood soaked torn sleeve.

Louisa was looking very stressed as Sapphire approached, two green cloaked men stood in front of her as she replied to their questions. "I am well aware of it, but look around, what the hell do you expect us to do with all these? You must try and delay them to give us more time here." She spotted Sapphire with Rafe following behind her, and her face changed to one of a little relief. "Sapphire, is Robbie with you?" Her face dropped as Saff shook her head.

"Sorry, it's just Rafe and me, Robbie is tied up with bigger problems." Louisa seemed to wilt as the two soldiers parted to allow Sapphire with Rafe through to her.

"For a moment then I thought I had a little hope, it's chaos, the tunnels have collapsed killing hundreds, the river bank has gone, I have soldiers and Cutters crossing the bridges in the east and west slowly circling in on me, and need about a hundred times the medical supplies we have, just to have a small chance of helping this lot." She gave a long depressed sigh as she looked into Sapphire's bright blue eyes. "We are trapped, if we do not get the hell out of here soon Mason will surround all of us, but with so many wounded we haven't a hope of getting away in time."

Rafe watched from Saff's shoulder as Louisa carried the agony of her decision on her face. "I don't want to leave them, as I am not sure Mason will care for them, but staying could kill everyone."

"We could send this lot to my dad... I mean, he has the space and the medical facilities, I am not sure he can save all of them, but hell, anything is better than dying here in this bloody awful place... I mean what was this place? It looks like a crumbled old factory." He looked round at the few parts of moss and plant covered walls, the only sign to show the size of the building that had once stood there, was the long wide empty concrete raft of the floor.

Sapphire gave a broad smile. "You know Rafe; you may be on to something... I can open a window and we evacuate as many as possible.... That's an unbelievably good idea, I can't believe you just came up with it, you are not quite as stupid as I thought you were." Rafe looked up with a surprised look, but Sapphire was already working and had turned back towards Ox.

"Hey hang on a minute.... What the hell do you mean stupid?" Sapphire shouted back as she walked away from him.

"Don't think Rafe, one good idea like that must have worn you out... now stop talking and get every able bodied man we have, if we are going to do this, we need to hurry." Rafe stared at her in disbelief as behind him Louisa gave a very relieved laugh.

"Come on Wolfie, help grab every free pair of arms we have." She patted his shoulder as she turned to the two waiting cloaked woodsmen. "Bring the watches in, and tell them to gather everyone they meet and get them here as fast as you can, we are going to take everyone out of here as quickly as possible, now hurry we have a lot to do and it's going to be a long evening." The two woodsmen gave a salute and moved off at the double, as Louisa turned and began to pull all those capable of helping others together. Rafe walked slowly back towards the Outlaws mumbling to himself.

"Stupid.... Who the hell does she think she is? I was top of my class in wood camp."

Down below in what had once been a first class hotel, Mason sat at the table opposite his son and waited until the maid dressed in black had served his plate. A hundred candles hung from the crystal chandeliers above them lighting the room, and they flickered as the mighty cannons outside shook the whole of the waterfront when they fired. The waitress leaned over Mason and slid his plate from a silver tray onto the table; he smiled as she walked away and noticed how his son watched her. "You like her? Take her if you want." Lance lifted his knife.

"I was ensuring she was out of ear shot, she has nothing of interest to me." Mason shrugged.

"As you wish... Now you were telling me about the girl... What was her name again?" He lifted his knife, and cut into the rare thick steak, Lance chewed on his beef for a moment before swallowing, and then continuing his conversation.

"Nadia... Her name is Nadia... It appears her father was killed on the moors, he was one of Franklin's men, apparently quite high up." Mason lifted his claret, contained within a cut crystal glass.

"Really... So she was not some whore for the town as I had thought? What did she do again?" Lance rested his knife on the edge of his plate and lifted his glass.

"She was the assistant to that oaf Walters, and then when Billy... Mordred or whoever the hell he was at the time came along, she was transferred across to him. I am sure you must remember her, she spoke to you daily when she brought the reports at the dock side." Mason sat up for a moment as if trying to recollect the girl; he took another sip of his claret and then seemed to suddenly remember her.

"Not that little skinny one with the dark hair? She was sort of prim and proper and dressed like an old accountant." Lance smirked.

"A bit before my time with the description, but yes that's the one, believe me looks can be quite deceiving, she may look quite meek and mild, but she has quite the fire in her belly." Mason gave a nod and his eyes twinkled.

"I take it she has quite a temper?" Lance gave a nod of agreement as he lifted a heavily laden fork of vegetables into his mouth.

"You have no idea, quiet as a mouse when I first met her, then she exploded like a bomb and screamed at me." Mason's eyed widened.

"And what did you do?" Lance shrugged as he cut another piece off his thick slab of beef.

"I let her get it all off her chest, and then told her she would be taken in my care." Mason stopped chewing.

"So it's definitely his child then?" Lance wiped the inside of his lip with his tongue and then lifted his napkin to wipe his mouth.

"I looked at all the statements, and yes I think there is no doubt, it's Billy's or Mordred's depending on how you look at it, although we have no idea of whether or not it's a boy or girl." Mason lifted his eyebrows as he watched his son talk; he rested his knife on the table as he considered the situation.

"Interesting... Looks like your uncle or brother however we look at it has given us another family member, there really is no doubt it was him?"

"None, looking at the scars, she looked like she had been attacked by an animal.... Although she still has a unique prettiness to her, I was quite surprised to see her at first." Mason gave a shrewd smile.

"So you find her attractive... mmm, that is interesting?" Lance gave a small smile, possibly his first of the day.

"She has qualities of strength and determination, with the right care and guidance; I think she will provide the child with qualities that will serve this family well."

"I have no doubt Lance; the question is which family member will she serve well?" Mason gave a chuckle. "Could it be you have an interest in her that is more than just a family interest?" Lance sat back in his seat.

"I have pondered my future, as I am sure you have. I will need someone of her character at my side eventually, it does not hurt to speculate Father, was it not you who advised me keep an open eye for such things?" Mason gave a hearty nod of understanding and lifted his hand almost as if to wave.

"I have complete faith in your judgement, you know that. If you think she is the one for you then of course take her for your own. I must admit it will make things simpler if you decide to raise the child as your own, I mean the family resemblance will be there, and the bloodline is the same, so the child will be part of the family regardless of whether you call it yours or not." Lance cleared his plate as he watched his father talk, and then wiped his mouth and reached for his glass.

"Of course at the moment she hates me, but I think I quite enjoy that, it will take time, which is why I will take her into my care, I think eventually she will understand that this is a family of power that will serve her needs."

"I think you show wisdom, under your wing she will witness the power you wield and understand that it is also her protection, no woman I have ever met would resist such a force. You are growing up so fast these days, I believe at times I can barely keep up, but I will say this for you Lance, you are very much your father's son and true to the name of Knox. I am very proud of what you have accomplished." Lance gave a smirk, which revealed the arrogance of him.

Outside as the evening progressed the explosions continued as the cannons increased their range, and their shells fell further into the south side of the river.

Sapphire opened a window and sent Rafe ahead to inform his father of their situation, as the explosions slowly crept nearer. Louisa stood with Ox getting reports from all around them as to the state of Mason's advancing Cutters. The bridge at Chelsea was still intact, and Mason's men were now in command as hundreds of heavily armed troops crossed and headed towards them. To the east three units were engaged in a brutal fight as they tried to hold the last remaining intact bridge under very heavy fire. Time was running out as the wounded were lifted and carried through the bright blue window and into the small town of New Avon. Rafe's father supervised with his son as they converted the large family barn into a field hospital, and long lines of Avon woodsmen hurriedly made make shift beds and stretchers to carry the injured to safety.

Sapphire took a breath as she stood next to Louisa, and was handed a drink by Tiny, all around was chaos filled with the screams of wounded men, and the panic of trying to ship them out as quickly as possible. Her ears rang from the constant bombardment of the cannons and her mouth was filled with the dust and grime from the swirling mists created by the explosions. It was hard to see anything past the edge of the green they were stood on, and she began to wonder if under the sea of smoke and cloud there was actually anything left at all. Louisa turned with a dirty tired looking face; it was so loud she had to almost shout so that Sapphire who was right beside her could actually hear her.

"The way it looks at the moment, I say we have about thirty minute's tops, after that we will be in range of the cannons and everything here will be pounded."

Sapphire shook her head to show she understood and leaned in close to reply.

"We have extra men from New Avon helping us now, all we can do is get as many out as possible, I will hold here until the very last minute to get everyone if I can." Louisa gave a nod.

"I am sorry Sapphire but we have no idea where the Sage went, he was seen earlier, so we know he made it out, but there has been no sight of him now for three hours, he could be anywhere."

Sapphire felt the disappointment grow inside her, Rune had seemed so insistent she find him and help him, but it looked now like he had used the event to slip out of the way to do something. She had no idea what he could possibly be up to in such a violent battle, nothing seemed to make sense to her, and she could not understand why at the most important time of all, he would desert those who had supported him.

As the evening drew into the night, Rafe and his father with the help of most of the town, ferried the wounded through Sapphire's window and into the large barn. Townsfolk appeared from everywhere with carts laden with food and blankets, as the floor was cleared by the farmhands, and long rows of soft beds were made from the straw bales. John Rafe organised the women who tended to the heavy cuts from the flying debris, as he and his staff attended to those with more serious injuries.

Rafe stood at the doors watching the scene of intense activity, he had never seen his father work so fast or so hard, and it brought a smile to his face, as he realised that this was probably the best thing for him. Keeping busy with so many to care for, would help him to focus and give him something to keep his days busy as he dealt with the death of his wife. It was quite late when he headed back through the window to see Sapphire covered in dust as the last groups of the injured were taken out of London and into New Avon. As he walked up he heard her talking to Louisa and Ox.

"I have to find him, Rune was very insistent and I think she might have had an idea that this would happen, go to New Avon and I will meet up with you there when I find him." Ox shook his head in disagreement.

"Not sure that's right Miss.. You know they have this place surrounded now and they are closing in, I would much prefer to be here if you need me, it aint safe for woods folk here now." Sapphire smiled.

"Thanks for your concern, but honestly Ox I will be fine, after all if it gets too dangerous, I will open up a window and slip back to all of you, now come on and get going, it will not be long before they arrive." Ox looked unsure but she pulled his hand and he gave her a nod and began to walk towards the open blue shimmering window. Rafe patted his shoulder as he passed him, and a cloud of dust puffed off it.

"Don't worry about her, she will not be alone my friend, I will watch over her." Ox gave a grunt of appreciation as he passed Rafe and Louisa gave Sapphire a hug.

"Ok Saff, watch yourself and hurry back." She gave her one final big hug and turned towards Rafe who was almost level with them. "Keep her safe and keep your own head down, Jett's waiting for her Wolfman, so just you get back to her in one piece."

The sound of Jett's name stirred deeply within him and he smiled. "I will, see you soon." He gave her a wink and with a bright smile on her dirty face she ran to Ox who was stood by the pulsating blue window, he turned with her arrival and they stepped through. With one final bright pulse of light the window closed, and in the fading light, they stood all alone in a cloud of swirling dust, Rafe suddenly felt very much isolated, he turned toward Sapphire. "So what's the plan?"

Sapphire wiped her face on her hankie.

"There is only one person I know who will be able to locate the Sage, so I think a quick leap and we will have an idea what he is up to."

Rafe looked round feeling tingles down his spine, neither of them had noticed, but for no reason the cannons had stopped firing. They stood together in the silence of the thick blinding swirling mist of dust, and somewhere out of sight they both heard the sound of moving feet. Mason's men were almost upon them, and nervously Sapphire took hold of Rafe's hand.

"Come on let's get the hell out of here." There was a flash of blue, and before he could speak, Rafe felt the pull on his arm, and he stepped through the window into a large forest of the tallest trees he had ever seen. The window closed behind him, as he leaned back and looked up at trees the size of skyscrapers, set below the darkest sky filled with millions of bright stars. His eyes opened wide as if to get the vastness of what he was looking at inside them, it felt like he had walked into a fairy tale giant kingdom, and he could barely speak he was in such awe. Sapphire smiled as she realised that finally she had found something that was bigger than his ego.

"Hey?" He blinked and looked blankly at her.

"What?" She pointed to the wide path edged with shrubs he had never seen before, and groups of ferns as tall as he was.

"We have to go, this place like any other has certain dangers." He looked round at the vast emptiness.

"Like what?"

"Like Darkmares Rafe, do you remember them?" He gave a shudder; there was not a single man who had been on Iona during the fight to protect the newly born infants Iona and Hal, who did not remember them with a cold shiver.

"Those creepy gits live here?" Sapphire gave a smile.

"Yes Rafe, this is their home, so stay alert, we do not have very far to go, but they patrol this woodland looking for the dream people, so come on and get a move on." Sapphire gripped her bow tightly in her hand and began to walk onto the path at the side of the tree they were stood under. Rafe looked up once more, and could see its giant limbs stretch out over the path about a hundred feet above him; he slung his bow onto his shoulder and at a steady pace followed Sapphire on to the path. She walked quickly, and it appeared to him she had been here before and knew just what she was looking for. He gave his head a shake, and spoke quietly to himself.

"Dream people? Man she has been spending way too much time alone recently; she will be looking for a giant and golden hen next." Sapphire walked onwards at a good pace.

"I can hear you Rafe, it just goes to show how stupid you are, only Rune knows where that hen lives, everyone knows that." He quickened his pace.

"What? No way, you are having me on aren't you?" She looked back and giggled.

"God Rafe, does Jett know you are this dumb?" His soft brown eyes twinkled as he realised he had been caught out, and with a giggle he hurried up to her side, as they made their way along the wide path watching out, and heading for Sapphire's only hope of finding the Sage, the white clad figure of Opal.

With the meal completed and cleared from the table, Mason and Lance moved to two chairs set by a small table by the open fire. Mason handed the large goblet shaped glass containing a brandy to his son and sat back in the soft leather chair. "Do you have to leave tonight?"

Lance stared at the flickering flame his mind lost in thought; Mason leaned forward in his chair. "It's going to be quite cool tonight, if you must leave, take the coach, it will be much warmer than the seat of a saddle." Lance came out of his thoughts and took a sip of his brandy; he felt it warm the back of his throat.

"I want to get back, I will be fine, the horses are swifter, and the road is well guarded, I can sleep when I am back." Mason watched him carefully, sensing his son's thoughts.

"You worry too much, leave the woodcutter to your grandmother, let her deal with him, and then when she has finished him off you can return to York with me." Lance looked up at his father and met the bright blue eyes of confidence that observed him; he paused for moment and then voiced his thoughts.

"Why don't you fear him?" Mason sat back about to speak, but Lance continued. "The last time you met he was too strong for you, what makes you think if you meet again, it will be any different?" Mason gave a smile.

"I have always feared him, and that my Son is why I show him respect." Lance felt the surprise inside himself hearing his father admit fear. Mason gave another smile. "Strange as it sounds, I have always enjoyed pitting my wit against him... I do respect him, for he is young and yet shows wisdom far beyond his years. Our last meeting was unfortunate, but I learned a great deal, our young lord will find me much different the next time we cross paths I can assure you."

Lance gave a gasp and sat back trying to work out his father. "I think you should avoid him; it makes no sense to put at risk everything we have built." Mason took a drink and appeared to be very relaxed, whereas the thought of meeting the lord of Loxley made Lance feel tense.

"Lance you cannot hide forever from what you fear... I admit there is much that can be done to ensure we never meet again, and I do try to ensure that will be the preferred scenario, but fate has a strange way of working against you, and I am sure there will be another meeting between us before all of this business is finished. If that is to be, then I will face him again and use what I have learned against him, destiny will then decide, as I am sure will be the case for you. What I will say is this, use the fear to drive you, do not show it, but harness its energy against him, and meet him with honour, for after all he has achieved, even you should show him the same respect as you would myself." Lance gave a scowl as his nose screwed up with distaste.

"I am not sure I could show him any respect, he is my enemy and will kill me given the chance, I will spare nothing to see him dead." Mason gave a gentle nod.

"Only you alone will know what to do when the time comes, how you deal with him will be your own affair should the matter arise, for now leave him to your grandmother." Lance's words almost spat out from his lips.

"She is only interested in the witch and that boy king; she cares nothing about the woodsman." Mason could see the anger in his son and smiled.

"Lance, never forget who she is... our dreams have been hers for much longer, she will not let the chance slip to help you by killing as many of them as possible, even if I may say it, she does seem to take a much more indirect route than we do." Lance flicked his long blonde hair back from his face and emptied his glass; he set it down on the table and stood up.

"She has them for now, I suppose all we can do is hope she finally gets things right, somehow I doubt it, her abilities of late have been very disappointing."

Mason stood up and gripped Lance firmly on the shoulder. "Have a little faith, and wait to see what becomes of her efforts, hurry back safely and I will see you when things have been finalised at Glastonbury, and remember when the area has been cleared of our woodland rabble, give it to that greedy monk and leave him to rot inside there, we shall progress much quicker without his constant meddling." Lance gave a nod and his father pulled him into an embrace.

"I will, although I have no idea why you pander to him, I find him repugnant."

"He has his uses for the moment, now go with speed." Lance walked up the room towards the double white doors with golden ornate handles.

"See you in York Father." Mason smiled.

"Good luck with the girl." Lance looked back and gave a small smirk.

"I will need it." Mason laughed as his son opened the door and disappeared. He turned and walked over to the cabinet containing the decanter of Brandy and poured a second measure, then headed back to the seat where he sat back sipping the brandy and stared into the flames, his voice was soft and thoughtful, and just an echo of his thoughts.

"I will see him again... He knows it and so do I, I fear mother has never really understood that pair, they will be mine at the end to kill."

"Where are we?"

"Shush!!" Ben was sat on the cold floor behind a large wall in the darkness.

Martin was sat beside him, huddled up close. For over three hours they had worked their way with Markus and the Sage across the river avoiding the soldiers, and had worked their way round through the crumbled remains of many old buildings back towards the riverside on the northern side of London.

Markus was forty feet up in front on lookout, and the Sage was nowhere to be seen, he had gone ahead on an errand he had told them was a task only for him and him alone. Ben knew that Martin was not very happy about it, but he had allowed the Sage to go under the understanding that they would stick together as they had in the past and work as his lookouts. Ben pulled his cloak tighter round him, it was very late and he felt sleepy, although hiding here so close to all of the soldiers was more frightening than anything he had ever done, and he was sure he would not doze off no matter how tired he was.

Martin was nervous and kept twitching as he watched all around him, making sure he had a good eye on Markus up ahead, who watched the Sage scuttle across the road into the shadows, and climb onto a drainpipe that rose high above him to the roof top in the darkness. Ben could barely see anything sat so low to the ground and pushed against the wall, yet he felt Martin stiffen and sensed there was some sort of danger. Martin lowered himself and slid back against the old brickwork as Ben strained to try and see what direction Martin was looking in.

The few tense moments that had the hairs prickling on the back of Ben's neck seem to drag, and then without notice Martin pounced on something a few feet away. Ben jumped with fear as his heart leapt up in his chest with fright; his wide eyes searched the darkness in front of him where there was a dim stir in the blackness that he knew was Martin.

The scuffle in front of him lasted just a minute as he heard the heavy gasps of two people, and he rose up onto his knees wanting to shout out and find out if his friend was safe. On all fours he stared forward trying to see what part of the darkened mass was Martin, and then he heard a whispered voice. "What the hell are you doing here?" It was Martin's voice and it looked like he knew his prey.

"I am bloody well doing the same as you, what the hell do think I am doing?" Ben recognised the dry tone to the voice, it was that of Commander Silas, a man who Ben generally tried to avoid. There was movement and Ben saw the dark mass move slowly towards him, Martin still had hold of the Commander as he pulled him close to the wall. Silas seemed unhappy at being jumped on and his voice showed it. "I did think you may need a handy sword or bow, but thanks to your little intervention it appears I am a bow short now. Why the hell did you jump me? I was coming to offer you help."

Martin's voice sounded a little irritable. "This was supposed to be a small secret investigation; you should have stayed with the others and helped." Ben moved about to speak, but he felt martin's hand push on to his shoulder and push him back towards the wall, and decided to stay quiet.

"Well you should have let all of us know, I mean all hell has been unleashed back there, they have pounded everything to dust, why the hell are you over here?"

"That is no concern of anyone but the Master Sage; let's just say the less people know then the better for everyone." Even Ben who had tagged along from the very first impact had no idea what they were up to, the Sage had spoken very quietly with Martin, before they had snuck off and taken a small canvass covered boat across the river. All Ben really knew was it was important to the Sage, and he had told him to stay close and keep very quiet. Silas rang out his cloak and seemed very annoyed.

"Think what you want, I know where you are going with this Jarrod, I aint your bleeding spy, I know I rub people up the wrong way, but believe it or not, I have done everything I can to help all of you out." Ben saw the light glint over the wall and catch Martin's face as he rose up a little to check on Markus, he did not look at all happy.

"Don't go weeping if your ego is hurt Silas, this has nothing to do with you or most of those men over there. The Master Sage has been with us from day one, and for that reason and that reason alone he trusts us, you are right though, someone has given away all of our positions and it has cost us dearly."

"So what now, three men and a boy are going to even the scales?" Ben saw the heavily scarred face of Silas as he lifted himself up to look over the wall, in the partial light he looked sinister and evil and Ben took a deep breath and slid back harder on to the wall. Martin pulled him back down.

"Look you are here now so you might as well be useful, to be honest we have no idea what the Sage has in mind, but we are here to make sure he does whatever he has come for and then gets out safely. If you really want to help, watch that area over by that street corner and let us know if you see soldiers. If it kicks off act fast and regroup here."

"Yeah fine, I will keep you in view, well actually I won't be able to see you, but I am sure you will have a clear view of me."

Without another word Ben heard him slip off across the rough ground, a few seconds later he saw the hooded figure as he crossed an opening and took cover behind a low wall next to the corner of the opposite street. Martin seemed to relax a bit and Ben felt him move to get comfortable again. He could hear Martin breathing slowly in the darkness, and tried to resist talking, but he could only hold his thoughts in for a short time.

"Martin... I don't like Silas, he scares me." From nowhere Martin's hand patted the top of his head.

"Not many do, but if you want my honest opinion Ben, I do actually think you would be very safe with him. He is arrogant, but he has very good skills as a woodsman." It surprised Ben, and he looked across the darkened ground to the small silhouetted wall, where he saw the Commander lay down keeping watch.

"Really? I just thought he was always angry at everyone."

"Well you are not wrong there, but he means well. Now shush we are supposed to be hiding here, and there has been too much chat already." Ben pulled his cloak back round him and brought up his knees and waited in the darkness, while he thought about Silas and how Martin thought he could be trusted. He was still not very sure, Silas was a frightening man at times, and he decided it would be better if he still kept his distance for now.

S apphire stopped on the edge of the path, and moved into the thick reed and shrubs. Rafe dropped to one knee as Sapphire moved her head from side to side. "Cal... Where are you?" Rafe looked round.

"Who the hell is Cal, and why are you talking to the plants?"

"For god sake Rafe shut up will you, I am trying to find someone." There was a faint rustle somewhere to the left and Rafe turned to face it. His hand slipped down towards his sword, as Sapphire moved forward into the dense undergrowth. Her eyes seemed to be glowing a faint pale blue as she moved forward sensing the air around her. Rafe had no other choice than to follow her off the path and into the low gaps below the thick heavy shrubs. Sapphire stopped and he crawled up to her side, she was smiling and looking ahead towards the large tangled roots of a monstrous tree.

It took a few moments for Rafe to actually realise what he was looking at. There in the long grass was a small child like figure with bright blue hair, and the largest eyes he had ever seen on a being. It was looking at Sapphire with a huge smile on its face; Rafe looked at her and could see she was equally as happy to see the creature. "You know it I take it?" Sapphire gave him an accusing look.

"It has a name, and yes he is my friend and companion, his name is Cal." She crawled forward passed the base of the shrub, and out into the grass, the tiny figure gave a huge blink and ran towards her.

Still on her knees, she embraced him with great fondness; Rafe crawled out to get a better look at the little figure, to which Sapphire was now speaking. "Why did you hide so deep? Could you not feel me looking for you?" The creature looked nervously at Rafe. "Oh him, yes I understand, don't worry about him, he is an idiot, but you are safe with him."

Rafe gave a smile at the small creature, which stepped back and moved round to Saff's other side. She ignored Rafe and continued to talk to Cal; Rafe sensed the urgency in her voice.

"You must find her and fast, tell her I am here with Rafe and must see her as soon as possible. I sense danger and need to find him quickly, now hurry; I shall follow the back path towards her circle." With a big blink of his pale blue eyes, he turned, and as quick as lightening he ran off into the tall grass.

"Wow, he is a fast little bugger." Sapphire stood up and looked at Rafe.

"Time is running out, we must hurry." Sapphire pushed into the tall grass, as Rafe moved quickly to catch up, and soon they found themselves on a thin path that wove round the tall trees heading uphill and north. Rafe was intrigued as he trudged along at a fast pace beside her.

"Well are you going to tell me or what?"

"Tell you what Rafe? Honestly there really is nothing to tell." He looked around at the strange landscape and back to her as she moved quickly.

"This is not exactly nothing Saff, I mean, I take it we have gone into some other realm because where I come from the trees aint this big and I am pretty sure our kids are not blue haired with huge eyes like that little bugger was." She gave a long sigh.

"Cal is a Sandling; he is a dream guide, a childlike creature that transports the dreams of everything living. This is his realm, or at least it was until the Dark One came here and set up her home. This place is known as the Chimerical Forest, by the Sandling's, you may have heard it mentioned as the Hidden Realm of Sleep." The penny dropped and suddenly Rafe felt a wave of concern pass through him.

"Hang on a minute, this is the place Jett's grandfather was kept a prisoner."

Sapphire gave a smile.

"Yep... Opal now resides here, and I need her to help me find the Sage, because he has hidden powers of sight like me, and he is connected to this place as all seers are." Rafe was starting to finally understand, and he was glad Sapphire was finally shedding some light on her thinking. He ducked under the low branch of a heavy shrub with large leathery leaves and soft red berries.

"But wasn't this place used as a trap, and that was how the whole age of sleep started? I mean, we just popped straight into this place, we can actually get back out when we need to, can't we?"

"Stop worrying Rafe, The Dark One used a lot of powerful magic to imprison the others here, Gwendolyn was the first to work out where she was, and it was then she realised that as a seer herself she could come and go. It was breaking the spells around her that held her here for a thousand years that was her problem, I can take you out any time you want me too." He gave a reassuring nod.

"Ok that's good." Sapphire gave a small giggle.

"We are fine, it's the Sage I am worried about.... Come on it's not far now."

It took about another thirty minutes of running along the rough path, before Sapphire slowed down gasping for breath. It was very hot and Rafe wiped his red face with his shirtsleeve as he stood breathing heavily at her side.

The woodland was thinner towards the wide path that ran down the centre of the realm, and Rafe could see that although the tall heavy trees were thinner, they were also of a much greater age, casting their canopies wide across the area into dappled shade. Below them there was little growth, and the bumpy surface of dry earth was littered with small clumps of grass. Seeing the wide path far across the open area brought a feeling of being exposed and caught in the open to him, and he turned towards the thick wide band of birch like trees that appeared to mark the edge of the tall trees and the start of something else.

"We should move in there where we have some cover, if this is her realm god knows what unnatural thing is lurking about." Sapphire gave a nod.

"That is the place I was looking for, don't fret once we are in there we will be safe. She pulled on her long hair and wove it round her hand to tie it back from her face, which was equally as red as Rafe's, he gave her a smile.

"You know this probably sounds daft, but why have we just run in this heat for over an hour, when you can open a window? Would it not have been simpler to just pop here?" Sapphire took a long breath and shook her head.

"In here it does not work like that, this part of the forest has protections that rebound the magic, it's how Opal remains invisible from the Dark One. Even if she invited me, I could not open a window under these trees, it's better to come in back there and follow the path. Rafe gave a nod, it didn't seem logical to him, but after all this was a magic thing, and in his mind most of it was not logical.

"So what now?"

"We walk into those young trees, and hopefully Opal will meet us there."

Sapphire walked forward at the side of Rafe, and parted the soft lush leaves to reveal a gap in the closely packed trunks. They walked forward along the narrow path, which wove from side to side through the dense band of growth, and after a few minutes they stepped out into the wide green round circle of short grass that housed a long fallen trunk of an Oak. Sapphire smiled as it was exactly as she had seen it on her previous visit, the black pot hung above the fire, set in a circle of grey stones, and bubbled as wisps of steam lifted into the air, scenting the whole of the open glade with an aroma of slightly garnished stew.

Opal stood dressed in her familiar long white hooded robe, her long grey hair rested gently on her shoulders, she smiled and Rafe could see how much Rune favoured her.

"Greetings my children, you have arrived just in time, come and sit a while and eat while I await the return of my messenger." She opened her hand and gestured towards the long fallen tree, which rested on its side in the centre of the circle. Sapphire gave a huge smile of relief and walked quickly towards her and embraced her.

"I am so glad I have found you, I have strong feelings of danger and yet I cannot decipher as to their origin, although my instincts tell me that the Sage is in trouble."

Rafe held back for a moment before walking slowly towards the white figure hugging Sapphire. This was the first time he had ever met with Opal, who after all was Jett's grandmother and a very powerful entity. Opal gave him a smile as he approached.

"Welcome Master Rafe, you have no need to fear me, I have shared the happiness of my granddaughter, and I am happy to see she has finally found a companion to warm the days of coldness that she felt. Please sit and eat for we have much to do."

She turned to the fire and the large pot of bubbling stew, and taking a carved wooden ladle she scooped it out into two delicately carved wooden bowls. Rafe hearing the grumbles from his stomach took it gratefully and sat on the log to eat; Sapphire held her bowl and stirred the stew as she looked to Opal for guidance. Opal sat at her side and prompted her to eat, Sapphire lifted the spoon to her lips, and Opal sat back with a smile. "Your instincts have served you well, I am pleased to see that you are listening to them, for I fear the Master Sage has made a move long since predicted, but I do feel it is too soon and it concerns me also."

Sapphire gave a deep sigh of relief. "I am not sure that this destiny for me is quite right, I think my instincts are all over the place at the moment, although I am glad at least one of them is half right."

Rafe lifted his spoon and began to eat with enthusiasm, as he realised with the taste of the hot stew how hungry he actually was. As he chewed on the large chunks of meat and vegetables, he half listened to the old woman clad in white.

"Your instincts are fine Sapphire, and I may say, so are that of Runestone, for I think she has long expected this move. You were right to seek me out, for I have sent for the Sandling that guides our Master Sage, and when she arrives, I think we shall both find that our green friend has indeed set in motion a plan to meet and kill the Snake." Sapphire's bowl gave a gentle thud as the spoon fell back into it.

"He is mad, how can he think for one moment he will get close enough to him? I must stop him."

"Listen to me child." Opal gently took her by the hand, and for a moment Sapphire felt a warmth flow into her, that quelled her anxiousness. "We always knew that there was a destiny set for the Master Sage, your grandmother herself spoke often of her visions of a strange white faced stranger that would bring aid unseen to the hooded man. When he played his part to free my husband, and in doing so saved the lives of Robbie and Runestone who were trapped here in this realm, all of us knew her visions had been right, but that task is long since done, so now we must ask, considering who he is, what else has been preordained for him?"

"You think this is also his destiny?" Opal shrugged.

"None of us have seen further than this moment, but we were destined to leave the future to those who came after us." Sapphire's head fell and her shoulders sagged.

"Please tell me you do not mean me by that?" Opal gave a hearty laugh.

"Oh my dear poor child, you really must look deeper within yourself and try to find a little confidence, this gift you hold is very precious, and to be given you by none other than one of the most powerful rulers of the Fae, she must have seen something within you that would be your strength, for she was after all, the White Circle." Opal patted her hand as Sapphire tried to find something in the turmoil inside her that would allow her to believe that Gwendolyn had been right to choose her. Rafe had no idea at all what they were talking about, and leaned across Sapphire to reach for the ladle and fill up his bowl again. Opal stood up and looked across at the trees sensing something approaching.

"Good... I think this may be the guest I am waiting for, and not a moment sooner, I fear our Commander cannot stay here for much longer, as he is mortal and his strength will begin to fail. It's bad enough that my granddaughter is lost to another realm, I fear if we tarry longer her intended may share a similar fate."

Sapphire looked up with a pale face as Opal began to walk towards the trees, her pale face turned to Rafe who had stopped eating, he looked concerned and she felt her heart skip several beats.

"What does she mean, lost in another realm, Jett is in Avalon with Robbie isn't she?" Sapphire felt the tingle run down her spine as the colour in her face paled. Rafe put the bowl down on the trunk at the side of him; she could see from his eyes that he knew that Sapphire was holding something back. "Jett is fine, isn't she? You know something, what aren't you telling me Saff?" She swallowed hard.

"It's Ok Jett is alive."

"What... is she hurt?" Sapphire's voice raised a little as she shook her head.

"No! She is fine and quite healthy from what I can gather."

"But?" Sapphire lifted a hand and took Rafe's in her hers. He shook it free as a strange look came over his face, and he moved backward standing up and knocking the bowl of hot stew on the grass.

"What the hell has happened? Rune told you something didn't she?" His face gave away the anger that was rising behind his accusing tone of voice. "What did she tell you? I know you know something; I can tell by your eyes... All this time and you have been hiding something, tell me now or so help me god Saff I mean it..." His hand dropped to his hilt on his sword, Sapphire jumped up and tried to calm him down.

"I told you Rafe she is fine, now calm the hell down will you." She reached out towards him, but he stepped back from her reach. "Rafe she if fine, it's just Rune asked me not to say anything."

"Like what? You better start talking Saff, and bloody fast."

"Rafe she is fine, it's just there was a fight and Jett had an accident... honestly she is OK and is well from what we know." Out came his sword in a flash to match his sudden temper.

"WHAT YOU KNOW, WHAT THE BLOODY HELL DOES THAT MEAN?"

Sapphire jumped backwards away from him, and went for her own sword, there was a loud ear splitting crack, and Rafe shot backwards as if something had grabbed him from behind and jerked him back. Sapphire trembled holding her sword as she watched him hit the grass and slide away from her. Across the glade, Opal had dropped her hood and looked very angry, as she stood beside a pale shabby looking small child like creature. Her eyes blazed with deep blue light.

"How dare you pull a weapon in my circle; you will control your emotions commander or I will see you expelled to somewhere you will require that and a lot more to survive." The moment was just too much and Sapphire felt her legs collapse as she tried to fight back the tears of fear. She dropped to her knees and the tears exploded out of her, as Rafe sat up feeling dazed and not entirely certain as to what had just happened, although he felt the bump that was growing on the back of his head. Sapphire sobbed a few feet in front of him.

"This is all too much, I really cannot cope with this, what with strange dreams about large fortresses and Gypsy girls, and my twisting stomach all the time, and then all the worry of Rune and Robbie trapped in that place and Jett missing I am not sure I can take much more of this." She lifted her hands to her eyes and sobbed harder, as her tears dropped onto the grass. Her words squeaked out as she blubbered. "I don't think I am strong enough.... It's been hell for the last year... I never wanted this. I miss my mum, and I want to go home."

Opal crouched down, and stroked the long auburn hair away from Sapphire's tear streaked face. "Come child, let all of this out, it has been building inside you for some time I see, let go of it and release the pressure."

Rafe sat watching and feeling the guilt rise within him as Sapphire was pulled into a gentle hug and Opal whispered quiet kind words to her. His anger fell as quickly as it had risen within him and slowly, he rose to his feet and slid his sword back into its sheath.

"I am sorry Saff, I didn't mean to... you know... my temper just got the better of..."

"You should save that anger for the Cutters Commander Rafe, Sapphire is bound to Rune as her centre, and if she was instructed to stay silent then that is an unbreakable vow. If you feel the need to spar your anger, then I strongly suggest that you do it with me, after all this is my home and you are my guest." Her tone was hard and he lowered his head in shame.

"I am deeply sorry My Lady, I hope you will accept my apology, for I meant no disrespect." Opal lifted Sapphire to her feet.

"Come child sit and I shall get you a drink that will refresh you and help you gain your strength again." She turned to Rafe with a flash of blue in her eyes, Rafe had seen it before in the eyes of Rune and he knew how much he had caused offence, her tone was a little less as stern as it had been. "If you would kindly fetch me that jug and two of the goblets."

Rafe looked at the end of the fallen trunk, where a small hummock of green stood, with a tall earth coloured jug and two wooden goblets. He was sure it had not been there a few moments ago, but understanding he had gone too far, he thought it better to do as he was asked and not question Opal. As she helped Sapphire sit down, he lifted the jug and poured out the clear liquid into the goblets, then walked back to Sapphire and handed her one, she took it avoiding his gaze, and he stepped back and sipped at the ice-cold liquid deciding it was better if he stayed out of the way. Opal spoke softly to Sapphire.

"It is quite normal to feel such fear at this time Child, we have all experienced the very same feelings of doubt and panic at the onset of our gifts, even as we speak Rune struggles with hers, and Robbie has faced overwhelming doubts in his own abilities." Sapphire looked up almost surprised.

"They have?" Opal gave a smile.

"We are in very uncertain times Child, no one truly knows what will become of the world we all know, for things are moving faster than any of us expected. The coming weeks and months will test all of us; even I have strong feelings of uncertainty, as many things have not been as we all thought they would be." Sapphire gave a hearty sniffle.

"Really?"

"Yes My Child. You must have faith in yourself and all of those of your circle, because it is in that faith of those you trust that all of you together will find a way through this." Sapphire pulled out a small lace edged handkerchief and wiped her eyes.

"I am trying, honestly, but my head and my heart feel opposed, my heart is torn and my head is constantly filling with pictures of reinforced buildings and people round a large table, and this small girl who is running away. None of it makes any sense, and then there is this voice banging on about a bridge all the time and I just carry on trying as hard as I can." Opal patted her knee.

"That is all any of us can hope for, now drink, it will give you strength and vitality for you must now do whatever you can to bring aid to our green friend, who I feel is making a mistake, but it is indeed a very brave one, so we must at least give him our support."

"He is trying to get Mason then?" Opal gave a small nod.

"I am afraid he is, we must do all we can to help him, and then I think you should return to me here, and we can discuss these voices."

Sapphire sipped her drink and relaxed feeling a little better; Rafe paced uncertainly around the edge of the trees, where he kept looking back at Sapphire sat with the small shabby looking little Sandling, Opal was talking to Cal and he was blinking at her.

Nothing made sense; all he could do was feel a huge pain inside him, he had missed Jett but had thought that he would be reunited with her soon, finding out she was lost tore at the pain he felt at the loss of his mother, and suddenly he was overwhelmed and feeling angry about everything. Standing around doing nothing was starting to get to him, he wanted to get a move on and then he would be free to find Jett, the frustration began to build inside him again.

Sapphire stared at the small dull and shabby little childlike creature, although she was unaware of the little figure in front of her. The liquid seem to fill her with warmth and she felt her strength growing, and with it began the twisting in her stomach and the pictures in her mind, she was lost in thought as Opal stopped talking and watched her, Sapphires eyes flickered with blue sparks as she softly spoke in a language that she had never heard of, Opal recognised it instantly, as

Sapphire repeated it again.

"Time breaks all circles, stretch it out across all time, lay it down in the void, a broken circle or a line. Return to the blind, cross the boundary you make shine, build a bridge of intention, take the circle to the line." Opal stared at her with shock as she watched Sapphire give a jolt and looked round at her.

"Sorry... what were you saying?"

Opal swallowed and was very shaken, she flustered for a moment as she tried to think. "You must leave here...Now!" Sapphire gave her a puzzled look as she saw Opal stand up looking very anxious.

"Is everything alright?" Opal shook herself to appear calmer; when inside her heart was racing.

"You must go and go now, time is no longer our friend, go quickly to those helping the Sage, take one extra who you trust above all others and give him aid, I have things here to prepare and there are things of great need I must attend to, we have tarried too long here. Leave now and when you have finished return here alone for we must speak on things of your future."

Opal looked down at the little shabby Sandling. "Go with Cal and lead them all to your master, be swift and guide them to his aid, all will not go well if you are late." The small female creature gave a blink and looked like she was about to cry, Opal pulled Sapphire close and hugged her. "Destiny awaits you and danger will walk in your footsteps, so hurry my child and complete your task, for this is the first step closer to a circle that must be built and built soon, now hurry."

There was something to the way Opal spoke and Sapphire sensed fear in her words, Opal grabbed her bow and handed it to her with a resounding nod and she pointed to the trees, the little Sandling grabbed at her hand and pulled, and before she could ask another question, she felt herself walking backwards away from a worried looking Opal as Rafe grabbed his gear and quickly followed. Before a word could pass her lips, she was in the trees being pulled along by the small Sandling onto a path that led her away from any parts of the forest she had seen before.

Alone in her circle, Opal hurriedly collected her things and almost ran out of her sacred glade towards the high rocks, and the cave under the mountain that contained the well of dreams, she muttered as she ran along the path. "Gwendolyn I always knew it, you met with her and kept it secret, oh why you fool, you should have told me I could have seen more if I had known where to look, what will befall all of them? Oh Sequana you were told over and over not to meddle, why did you not listen?"

CHAPTER TWENTY THREE

FATHER AND SON

Sapphire ran behind the small figure with Cal, Rafe ran along at her side and panted. "What's the rush, are you going to tell me, or is this your way of getting back at me." Sapphire breathed quickly her eyes watching the little creature in front.

"Grow up Rafe, not everything in this world is about you, there is great danger and we need to get to the Sage before he does something stupid."

"Bit late don't you think, after all this is a bloke who wears a white mask?"

Sapphire ignored him and watched as the small figure turned onto a different track. Her mind was racing as she thought of what Opal had said, take the one you trust echoed in her mind as the little Sandling in front of her ran into a wall of tall bamboo stems, Rafe panting followed her, as she jumped into the tall canes, and on to the small path that the Sandling had taken. It was suddenly very confined as she wove through the wide stems keeping her eyes fixed on Cal and his little companion.

The Sandling broke out of the bamboo and entered into a wide circle of cut grass, Sapphire stumbled through and almost fell as she came into a sudden bright clear space, Cal stood with a smile watching her as she staggered to regain her footing, and then stopped gasping for breath, somewhere behind her she heard Rafe cursing to himself as he fought his way through the bamboo toward them.

Crouched down and breathing heavily she thought for a moment, and then made her plan to help the Sage, Rafe parted the tall canes and staggered out into the open, he stood breathing heavily and watched as Sapphire stood up and turned to him. "Sorry Rafe."

"What?" Before he realised, a circle of blue light opened up at his feet and he began to sink into the ground. "Hey what the hell is this?" Sapphire shook her head.

"You pointed a sword at me, sorry Rafe but I no longer feel I can trust you, you're suffering from grief and your temper is out of control, go back to New Avon and sort yourself out."

"Like bloody hell I will, you need me." He lunged forward to grasp at the ground to pull himself out of the hole of light below him, but Sapphire clicked her fingers and the circle widened out of his reach, and before he could call out, he dropped like a stone through the hole. In New Avon everyone had stopped as they saw the blue light hover about three feet off the floor, it hung pulsating, and then suddenly it shot ten feet in the air and a body came falling through. Rafe landed with a heavy thud, and the light went out. He jumped from the floor and screamed upwards, but he knew it was too late. "Saff you need me, stop being bloody stupid."

Sapphire smiled at Cal. "Does our friend have a name?" He gave a shrug and blinked, Sapphire understood him in her mind and nodded back to him. "Ok if she is nameless that is OK, as long as I know she is the guide of the Sage that will do fine, what I need her to do for me is locate her master exactly, so I can go straight to him, can she do that?"

Cal gave a blink and then turned to look at her, she was very drab and looked very miserable, she gave a thin smile, as she understood what was expected of her, and Sapphire turned her attention to someone she could trust, she closed her eyes for a moment and tried to focus, it was a few seconds before she located the person in question, and with a little extra thought a bright circle opened on the floor in front of her. The circle of blue light rose slowly into the air revealing the feet, then waist and then the rest of a very surprised looking Louisa, Sapphire opened her eyes and smiled.

"Sorry I hope you don't mind, but the Sage is in trouble and I need someone I can rely on." Louisa gave a shrug and looked up at the bright circle above her as it closed.

"Yeah, no prob's, although that was really weird Sapphire, you gave me quite a stir for a moment."

"Yeah sorry, I am in a bit of a rush and have not got much time to find him and get to him, it's a little unconventional but it gets the job done." Louisa gave a smile and walked toward her.

"I am assuming Rafe is not up to it, although he is a little preoccupied at the moment with the lump growing on his head." Sapphire gave a chuckle.

"I owed him that for being a jerk, call me Saff by the way, everyone else does."

"Ok Saff, so where are we off to, I assume he is still somewhere in London." Sapphire pointed to the two small Sandling's, and Louisa gave a little jump as she saw them, they were not something she had expected at all.

"This is his dream guide, she is looking for him as we speak, as soon as I know we will go to him, I just hope he has not done anything stupid."

The air above London was filled with the smell of burning. From the south side of the river smoke wafted across in thick clouds, and in the darkness faint plumes of orange could be seen through the smoke where the decayed remains of large buildings still burned. Martin Jarrod crouched behind the crumbled wall with Ben, as he watched across the roadway, to where Markus hid inside a deep doorway and signalled back to them. For over an hour they had sat in wait, and he was now becoming anxious as there was still no sign of the Sage. Silas who had appeared to help, had disappeared from his post and was nowhere to be found, the Sage was in an alleyway hidden in the shadows as he crept slowly forward watching the back of the tall hotel which was his intended target.

The tall frame of Pat appeared at the end of the wall and the Sage gave a sigh as he saw Brian's advisor look cautiously about. He pulled his cloak tightly around him and lifted his hood, the Sage moved closer to the wall to stay out of sight, he knew what he had in mind was a job for one and did not want Pat tagging along. Pat crossed the alley into the shadows on the other side, a voice echoed through the darkness. "Oi you twit, you forgot your bow." Another figure came out from behind the hotel carrying his bow, and for a moment the Sage felt his heart skip a beat. From nowhere a long dagger shot through the darkness hitting the man with the bow, and then a scuffle broke out where Pat had just walked, the Sage could hear muffled voices and moved quickly along the alley to help out Pat.

As he approached the narrow passage that led down behind the row of riverside buildings the Sage heard the heavy grunt and the fight stopped, he grabbed at his dagger and crossed quickly to come round the wall and investigate the scene. As he swung round he saw the large mass on the floor in the darkness and another man bent over it, it took a few seconds to register before he understood what he was seeing, and looked back into the alleyway to look at the fallen body hit by the dagger. Slowly the pieces fell into place as he understood that it had been a Cutter who had carried his bow out to Pat, the other figure above Pat was Silas as he attempted to drag the body out of view of the guards, he noticed the Sage.

"Come on hurry up and help me, if they find these we are all done for." The Sage quickly ran into the alley and grabbed the feet of Pat, it still felt a little surreal as he helped Silas drag the body through the gate.

"You were right, I am sorry I doubted you, you said it was someone close to Brian." Silas gave a smile in the darkness.

"Don't look so disappointed, I know I can be a bit of a shit with the ladies, I never was top of the list when it came to being popular with the officers, but even I wouldn't turn on those I fight with. I have few morals, but I do hold true to those I believe in. Right, you keep watch and I will nip back and get the other one, he is only a little un, I should be able to carry him."

The Sage gave a nod as Silas nipped out of the gate, and he looked down at the dead body of Brian's most trusted man, and the man who had convinced him to come on board in London. He felt the bitter pain of anger rise inside him as he realised from the very first day, Mason had been aware of everything Brian had planned. It was a sick feeling and he felt a sudden chill run through him, as he realised that the sickness he felt must have been a hundred times worse for Robbie, it was a cold sobering moment.

Silas came back quickly and dumped the dead Cutter on top of Pat. "Right, they should be safe here for a bit, I am assuming you have something planned, which is why you are here, so what do you need?" There was a long tear in his cloak and the Sage could see the blood shining in the little light from the alleyway.

"You are cut and bleeding. Look, get back to Martin and the others and tell them what has happened here, tell Martin to head for Mason's lock up and I will meet him there as soon as I can." Silas pulled out a piece of cloth and stuffed it on to his cut with a gasp.

"We cannot leave you here now, what with Brian dead and most of the organisers dead, who the hell is going to take command?"

The Sage gave him a pat on his good shoulder. "We have done all we can here for now, I have other things in mind, get back to the others and I will meet up with you all soon, trust me Silas, I have a few things that only I can do, for now get to his lock up and get Markus to look at that arm, you will need it cleaning before it gets infected. Remember Mason's lock up, Martin knows all about it, he was stationed there before he went to Dunnottar for a year." Silas felt uncertain.

"No offence but I would feel better knowing you had a lookout with you, I am not sure you should be sneaking about this side of the river without back up." The Sage gave a smile.

"Believe me I am not alone, I have other forces at work to watch over me, she is shorter but very effective, now go on go, neither of us should be hanging about with two dead Cutters." Silas gave him a strange look.

"Well Ok if you are sure, I mean I don't mind."

"It's Ok Nathan believe me, go on you have done all of us a big service rousting him out, we should all be a little safer now, you go and protect the others, get them away from here as quick as you can." Silas gave a nod.

"OK just watch yourself and we will all see you in a little while." The Sage watched as Silas ducked out from the gate and disappeared into the shadows, he gave one last look at the two dead bodies and then slipped round the gate and headed back towards the rear of the hotel.

Against the wall with his bow over his shoulder and across his back, the Sage slipped on his fingerless gloves and lifted the hood of his long green coat over his head. With one last look to check all was clear, he vaulted up and over the wall, dropping silently to the ground on the other side. As quick as a flash he crossed the yard, grabbed the drainpipe and pulled himself up, he climbed quickly reaching the fire escape in seconds, and slipped over the rail onto the metal platform without a sound.

For a moment he gained his bearings and then with his route in mind, he began to ascend the stairs slowly and quietly, he knew that just above him somewhere if he was correct, his father would have opened a window to his room to let the air in.

Mason Knox sat in his chair by the fire and dozed, the meal with Lance and the several glasses of Brandy has sated him, and after a day of victory finally wiping out the resistance to him in London, he relaxed and slept feeling all was well in the world. He gave a grunt and jerked in his sleep and opened his eyes, the hooded stranger sat opposite gave him quite a stir as he reached for a sword that was no longer there. The hooded figure watched him as he shook the sleep from his head and sat up with a start.

"You have more than a nerve to come, what the hell are you doing sneaking in here? You are aware I take it, there are guards outside and one call from me and you will be dead?"

The Sage did not move, his father looked older to him and he had put on a little weight. "Call out if you must, you will die long before I do."

Mason gave a smirk at the coolness of the character, he eyed him carefully, noting through his open coat there was no sword, just a dagger, but his bow was carefully placed at the side of his chair. Mason noticed his own sword standing beside it, he moved in his seat to get more comfortable, but it was not enough to fully see under his hood, and view the mask he had heard so much about.

"Well, you are not the hooded man, as a lot of my people thought, so just exactly who are you my masked guest, and what is your purpose for coming here this night?"

The Sage lifted his hands and let his hood fall down behind him, exposing his head wrapped in a green bandana and the silvery white mask of Birch. "I am seen as your enemy and therefore a threat, although as to the outcome of this night I am still not certain." His piercing blue eyes sparkled behind the thin slither of wood that covered his identity, and the rest of him was hidden under a thick layer of white stubble giving him a much older appearance. Mason gave a nod.

"So my death was not your complete intention... that is interesting, so if it is not my life you wish, what else brings you here?" He lifted his glass from the small table and swallowed the mega contents, the Sage folded his hands across his lap, Mason had not recognised him and it had surprised him. Mason lifted his empty glass.

"You don't mind if I get a refill, would you be obliged to join me? I do feel a gesture of some respect should be shown, after all you have proven your worth against my forces." He poked his thumb as he held his glass behind him, and the Sage cast a glance across the room to the small table and the crystal decanter, he gave an agreeable nod.

"You may fill your glass, but at present I must decline your offer."

Mason gave a broad smile and rose slowly from his seat, the Sage watched his every move with care, although Mason had no intention of raising the alert, he found his guest quite intriguing and wished to know his true reason for coming, and he decided for the moment he would play along. He crossed to the table and took the shiny top out of the decanter and poured a good measure of the French Brandy.

"I am sorry you won't join me; this is a rather fine brandy I get from France, most of them over there are peasants, but there are the odd few who have a talent for fine things. It's a sad reflection of the times I fear, there was a time when rivals would meet over a meal with fine wine and cigars and thrash out their difference's before going on to battle, everything today is bitching and whining over grass and stone."

He turned back to the Sage and stopped with a feeling of complete shock; the Sage had removed his mask and stood before him in the dim light, his voice was soft and calm.

"But you were the one to start that now weren't you Father." The surprise subsided and Mason took a large swig of his drink and raised his glass in salute.

"William...?" He thought for a second and then gave a mighty laugh. "My God boy." He shook his head as he laughed and lifted his glass again, before giving a reassured nod. "I should have known... the targeting across the city was far too accurate, you of all people knew where everything was stored and manufactured.... I have to admit it boy, I admire your cheek, even if you have gone woodland on me. Still, I am actually very pleased to see you are still alive."

He walked slowly back to his seat and sat down with a chuckle. "Well, this will be news your grandmother never expected, like all of us she thought the hooded man had killed you when he ripped out that vile uncle of yours." His eyes met with Billy's. "Just for the record Son, I knew nothing of her plans with the sword, had I known anything I would have killed the sword maker long before he got to her, I am glad you made it out, I've got to hand it to you William, if nothing else you have my complete respect, even if you have blown up most of my stockpile." He gave Billy a fond smile and winked, Billy felt a little anger rise inside him, whether he knew about Mordred or not was irrelevant.

"I wasn't looking for your respect; I was trying to stop you... The damage has set you back years, hopefully now you will stop and think about what it is you are doing, as for grandmother I hope I am there when the hooded man sticks her, I could care less what the old harpy thinks." Mason turned a faint shade of red; he jumped up from his chair and pointed a long finger at Billy who stood just a few feet away, his voice rose to match his anger.

"What I am doing boy is trying to ensure the future of my family, my god have you not learned anything sat up there in the trees? All this was meant for you and your brother and sister, hell even old Loxley built a small empire for his children, even if it was just a stack of logs, mind you, the old goat never did have much vision." Billy stood his ground; he was bigger and stronger than in the old days where he had been afraid of his father's anger, he gave a slight chuckle.

"For me... Yeah that's a plan, how would you even know if I would want it? I was stuck in a town with strangers living a lie, you had no idea at all of what I wanted, so don't bullshit me and pretend like you cared, you sold me off for your own vanity Father. All you cared about was making sure your little scheme was safe and hidden from the one man you knew would come after you and kill you." Mason watched his son and calmed a little as he took another drink.

"That is not fair.... It was not like that William and you know it, I made sure you were safe and well protected, you were never in danger and as I have told you before all you had to do was spend just a short time longer, and I would have pulled you out safely." He looked at his father in disbelief.

"You haven't got a clue... Protected.... You call that feeble old man and that animal protection? Oscar was incapable of helping anyone, and that animal Moores had no intentions of letting me live, he was looking for the first clear chance he could get to slit my throat. If the Specialists had not killed him at Caerleon, he still would have come after me, and probably you, I cannot believe you never saw it in him, the man's wet dream was slicing up the son of a Knox." Mason gave a snort.

"Don't be so bloody dramatic, he was protecting you, but you made life very bloody difficult and you know it, you never did a thing he asked. Moores just wanted you to follow the plan to the letter and you had to be awkward and make waves, he had to keep you focused that's all." Billy's eyes flared at his father.

"Well he managed that when he chose to threaten the life of the girl I loved." Mason gave a long bored sigh and headed back to the table for another drink.

"God are we back to this again? When will you ever learn? I was building you an empire, you will be able to have any woman you want by simply taking one, have you any idea at all of the power this family now wields? My God if you would just open your eyes you would see the huge strides we have made towards ruling everything. If you would just come down off that pile of morals you found up there in leaf land, you would see that you have more power as my eldest son than any other man in this land." He poured his drink and looked back at Billy; there was almost a pleading look to his face. "You more than any know that, William you are my eldest child, believe it or not it actually means something." Billy stood resolute and shook his head at his father.

"You are so wrong Father, none of it means anything to me, can you see how blind you are? It's always about power and money with you... I never wanted any of it, I wanted a family, you know what that is don't you? A father who cared about me and a mother to love me, it's pretty much what most of us want, would you even recognise that?" Mason's voice rose again, Billy felt he had hit a raw nerve, Mason lifted his long finger and pointed at him.

"Don't you dare preach family to me boy, my whole life has been dedicated to this family. We were robbed of everything that was rightfully ours, and I have moved heaven and earth to redress the balance, no one alive has done more for their family than I have, how dare you stand there and preach to me. Those bastards stole everything from your grandmother and it's been me alone who has clawed it all back." Billy's voice rose higher with his disbelief.

"It was over a thousand years ago." Mason snapped back feeling even more anger growing inside him.

"That is irrelevant; it was a deed that had to be undone. That crown was ours and they took it, and I intend to bring it back to this family if it's the last thing I do."

"It will be.... Can you not see how insane this all is, it's past history? You have more gold than anyone stashed away in that pile of bricks you call home; you have a private army and fertile lands right at the foot of your door. Are you honestly telling me that taking every square inch of this land is really going to make a difference?" Mason's eyes burned with a hint of red to them.

"It's mine.... All of it, I am the true heir of this land and I mean to get back everything." Billy quietly shook his head as his eyes locked with his father's, but his voice was quiet and gave away a little of his emotion.

"But you are not, hell even Leenard proved it, Uther was the rightful king and his line were set to rule, just because he stole a woman off our line does not make you a king, hell she was not even Saxon, you have to stop this Father, it's insane, none of it matters anymore that world has gone forever, it died back in 2012. This is a new world and you should be helping everyone carve out something better than before... Listen to me Father, you have to stop this and let the old ways go and embrace the new, you will have a place in it just like the rest of us." There was almost a sadness to his tone as he begged his father to change his course, Mason was resolute and snapped back defiantly.

"What would you know, look at you, you let those leaf lovers and that crazy old fool Rimmer into your head, and they have brainwashed you in their ways of thinking, you will never understand the struggle this family has had to regain the power it lost, you have gone woodland forever and picked the wrong side. I was right to focus on your brother you have no true understanding of anything."

"I understand everything better than you realise, I am not a cold robot like Lance, I see all that has happened and I am neither yours or theirs. You forget that they too see me as their enemy, and thanks to you I am forced to live in the central ground of this conflict."

"Then what the hell is all this for?" Mason pointed out of the window, where smoke rose through the night from the pounding of the southern side of the city, and mixed with many of the fires still burning from the fuel dumps and weapons factories destroyed under Billy's orders. "If you are his enemy why the hell are you helping him?”

“I am not helping him; I am stopping you... What you are doing is wrong, no one has the right to claim control and dictate to everyone. Father you have no right to slaughter thousands because they disagree with you, Loxley just wants to be left alone to live their own way, they were peaceful before you came along.” Mason began to pace round his chair, it was obvious to him that his son had completely missed the point and he felt the frustration mixing in with his anger.

“They were building an army in secret, my god you were there; don’t tell me you didn’t see it.” There was desperation in his eyes as he tried to reason with Billy, but Billy just shook his head and would not accept his father’s view of things, after all he did know the truth. He stared at his father and shook his head.

“As always Father you have it all wrong, they had hunters and gatherers and farmers and they used the stockade as a focal point for the area. All they did was send envoys and parties to help others in the area, it wasn’t an army, it was the fulfilment of the woodsman code, just rules on a parchment that said they had to help anyone who was in need, and help unite all the towns and villages in a bid to prosper everyone and help them survive.”

“Oh William you are blinded by their sentimental claptrap, but who the hell cares now? What’s done is done and there can be no going back, Loxley will fall and that rabble will be rousted out and I will rule, they have no hope against the might of my army, and I have no intention of stopping now I am so close.” Billy gave a long sigh and lifted his mask off the chair.

“Then I have failed and have no choice but to stop you Father.” He lifted it up to his face and pulled on the string to tie it back behind his head. Mason gave a mighty roar of a laugh, and lifted his arms in the air.

“Ha.... Finally.... You see? Now you are starting to sound like a man with some power... You challenge your old man, and for the first time in your life you sound like a Knox.” Billy’s voice rang with a note of sadness as he shook his head at his father.

“I am nothing like you, I would have had the sense to stay in Cornwall supported by a people who saw me as their saviour, you could have been a respected ruler of the whole region and you would have earned it for the lives you had saved.” He shook his head slowly. “Yet you chose to throw the whole country into war using up the resources that were needed to survive, I do not want the blood of thousands on my hands like you have, and if that is what I have to do to prove I am your son, then there is no hope for me and I will return to the woodland and destroy everything you have built.”

Mason gave a nod of understanding, as much as he respected his son for his bold move to confront him, he was now the enemy and Mason fully understood the implications of that.

“Then so be it William.... You always had your mother’s sentiment, I knew you were weak even then, I just chose to ignore it." He dropped his hand inside his jacket and pulled out his silver pistol. "Maybe I should have let Moores kill you back in Loxley and saved myself the trouble. Go on and join your mother and leave this for those of us who have the stomach for it. GUARDS!!"

The gun gave a deafening explosion as it fired, there was a blinding blue flash of light, and from nowhere four arms gripped Billy's hood and yanked hard, Mason surrounded by the smoke of his pistol fire stared at the floor to see where his son had fallen, but there was nothing there except for a few drops of blood.

He moved quickly to the open window and pushed it wide as he popped out his head to view the fire escape, but there was no sign of his son at all. The door behind him burst open as four guards in black came storming in with their swords raised, Mason stood by the window and smiled still holding the smoking pistol. He turned back into the room feeling cheated again by the woodland world and looked angrily at the first guard.

"Where the bloody hell were you? I have half the hooded man's realm dropping in through my windows, and what the hell are you doing while I am forced to defend myself?" He lifted the pistol and fired a second deafening round; the guard lifted off his feet and crumpled into the wall as the other three watched in fear. Mason pointed to the floor over by the window. "Clean that blood up. It's going to stain the carpet."

The guard gave a frightened nod and quickly moved across the room to view the stain, as Mason returned to the small table and poured a new glass of Brandy, he stood staring out of the window at the smoke and the flickering of light from the fires. Behind him a man with a bucket ran into the room and began to scrub the carpet, Mason glanced back at the man, but all he noticed was his sword stood next to a long thin bow made of Yew, somehow it seemed to symbolise everything his life had become.

Eight miles to the south of the city, in amongst the rubble of a broken old house covered in moss and trees, there was a blinding blue flash in the darkness. Sapphire and Louisa stumbled backwards out of the light dragging the masked figure of the Sage. They crashed to the floor with a squeal and rolled over each other in the turmoil. Sapphire sat up in a blink and shook her head in the darkness, a flint ignited and the small candle lit the scene as Louisa looked down at the moaning figure on the floor.

Down the sleeve and across the front of his coat the red patch of the bloodstain was expanding. The Sage gritted his teeth in pain as Louisa leaned over. "That's not good, we need to get you out of here and back to Avon." She lifted the jacket carefully to peer inside as the Sage grabbed her wrist, he was in pain but he was quite adamant as he held her tightly.

"No... Get me to the lock up and Martin." Sapphire leaned over and looked inside the jacket.

"No offence my green friend, but we are going nowhere, that bullet has to come out and we need to stop the bleeding; going anywhere now is out of the question." She looked at Louisa. "Don't suppose you have taken a bullet out of someone have you? It's just arrows tend to have a shaft so you can follow them in, bullets is not my strong point."

Louisa looked scared as she looked at the blood seeping out onto the floor. "I have not done one, but I have seen it done, not sure I am in a rush to learn, but we have to do something before he bleeds to death." His face was ashen and he was beginning to shiver, Louisa gave a big sigh and rolled up her sleeves. "We are going to need more light and lots of hot water." She lifted the coat and took a closer look in the dim light and Sapphire gave her a nod.

"Ok hang on for a second, I will be right back." There was a blinding blue flash, which illuminated the wound better and Saff was gone, Louisa gently did her best to lift the jacket, and taking out her knife, she cut it away down the seam.

"I hope Saff is good with a needle, because I am terrible." She folded back the cut coat and grabbed the shirt and tore it away to reveal the skin and the large gaping hole in his shoulder. "Erg! It looks like chopped liver."

The Sage was out cold, with a cold sweat running down his face under his mask of Birch.

CHAPTER TWENTY FOUR

THE DARKNESS RETURNS

Amethyst had been the Queen of the Fae of the Moon for a week, and in all of her time in the glorious and lavish Crystal Castle in the centre of the Mirrored Lake, she had been a prisoner. The excitement had soon drained away, when she noticed the stone in her ring had not shone with the light of the moon. As the days progressed, she became despondent, and had taken to sitting in the large library trying to find something that might help her, on the many hundreds of shelves of books. Fish felt her concern but was helpless to do anything; he began a vigil in the tower next to the seat of the queen as he watched the lake and the long dark shapes that constantly encircled the castle.

Altman, one of the servants who had served for many years under the previous queen kept him company, and helped to educate him in the role of the queen and her consort, and although this did help distract him, at times he had felt it was pointless as he began to feel a need to walk out in the trees and swim in the water, and understood that he was a prisoner, and it looked like he would remain so for a great deal longer.

As dawn approached and Amethyst awoke with a start, having fallen asleep for the third night in a row on her books, a bright blue light exploded on the edge of the circle of Opal deep within the hidden realm. Sapphire dashed through the trees expecting to see the familiar old woman dressed in white, but the circle was empty except for the old fallen log at its centre. Cal pulled hard on her arm and she looked down at his bright wide eyes, he gave her another tug and she followed his lead toward the log. Sapphire gave a giggle as she understood and saw the cauldron filled with steaming hot water, and a neat pile of bandages and ointments at the side of the fire; she looked round the circle with a smile. "Thank you, my lady of the woods, we have great need and as always you are with us."

She picked up the bandages and ointment and placed them in her bag, and there behind them was a bottle of pink liquid. Sapphire gave a grin as she lifted it knowing it held a potent brew that would help heal the Sage and give him greater strength to recover. Lifting the steaming cauldron, she carefully walked to the edge of the trees and out towards the wide path, and then with a bright flash of blue she was gone.

Louisa padded out the wound applying as much pressure to stop the bleeding as possible, on her hands and knees working by the low light of the candle she did her best to clean the wound and pad it. The Sage lay motionless lost in a daze of pain and delirium, and she counted the seconds whishing Sapphire would hurry, with a flash of bright blue she was back. "How is he? Oh he looks quite pale round the mouth." Louisa went to work quickly washing the wound and cleaning her knife ready to probe for the bullet, she felt the sweat forming on her brow, as she prepared to insert the knife into his shoulder. She stopped and looked at Sapphire.

"We could use some strong alcohol about now." Sapphire nodded.

"Yes... I must admit I am not a lover of it, but I think a drop now would steady my nerves." Louisa gave a giggle.

"I meant for him, you know, numb the pain and knock him out while I do it." She gave a smile.

"Sorry, I guess I am just nervous for you, I mean, you are about to go in there and in a way I am sort of glad it's not me, but I see what you mean... I can sit on his other arm if you want... you know stop him lashing out at you." Louisa gave it a thought.

"Yeah, good idea, he is well built, I would imagine a blow from him would hurt." Sapphire slid over and sat on his arm pinning it to the floor, as Louisa straddled over the arm of the wounded shoulder and took a long deep breath. "Here goes then."

It was the start of a new day in the Forest of Time, and deep inside the protection of the trees, the Specialists slept secure in their bunks having had a day of relaxation after the fight in the forest. The fine drizzle from the rain created by Rune and Jade had remained, and after over a week of intense heat, it had lifted the spirits of everyone and given the forest some much needed water. Fagan was especially happy hearing his trees and plants give out bursts of delight, and he had wandered around the group giving good advice and cheering everyone on in their duties. Rune was already up and sat on the grass outside the house delighting in the new rain, and starting to come to terms with her new powers. Since the coming of the red stone she had fought the heavy headaches and managed to cope with the constant stream of pictures flashing through her mind, but her body was again learning to adjust and she could manage to block it all out, and free the peace of her own private thoughts.

It had been such a hectic week, in which for the first time she could sit and really revue what had happened and her mind turned back to Jett and Amethyst.

Amethyst was safe, but with the uncertainty of the Dark One, Rune was worried that all alone in the castle and with no powers Amethyst would become despondent. Robbie had spent all day planning, but he had a difficult fight, and she was not convinced the Specialist were recovered enough for it, Rune felt the moment looming as a strange feeling began to grow inside her.

Her biggest fear was for Jett, she had spent as much of her free time searching as possible, but trapped in a sealed realm it was harder than ever to find out where she had been sent to, and with Jasper unable to connect with any who could advise him as to her whereabouts, Rune was starting to think she would not be able to get her home safely. It all swirled around in her head as she sat alone in the fine rain waiting for the others to rise.

Inside the cabin sat at his table and watching through the window, the white haired old figure of Fagan thought deeply about all he witnessed and the plight of the group. He had been alone for so long, and yet over the past week he had gathered together more people under his roof than he had ever known as friends in his time as the Maker in Avalonia, and all of them were so nice and respectful, that he had found himself becoming very fond of them.

Their loyalty to Robbie and Rune had won them great favour and, in his mind, knowing of what difficulties they faced, he knew it was time to offer them a little wisdom and aid as he had promised his greatest and dearest friend Eve. He stared at his plate and his half eaten sesame bread as he gave the matter some thought, and then having decided his course of action, he looked up and through the old window, Rune had stood up and he saw her walking towards the trees, he gave a smile. "Ye will find answers if ye let the trees talk away your worries my little Redstone, aye walk under their green wonder and hear em chattering like bashful maidens, the answer is always under their roof." He lifted a finger to his large ear and stuck it inside to give it a good wiggle, and when he pulled it clear he could hear the trees whispering to each other and chuckled to himself.

By the time the others had woken, Rune had walked deep into the forest, she walked slowly taking her time and enjoying looking around a world that was similar in many ways to Loxley, but also had some stark differences. The air was hot and humid with the rain, and her nose was filled with the scent of heavy blooms and damp earth, there was a feeling in the air of joy, brought on by the light rain after a long and intense heat wave. Somehow, she felt the grass was greener and the leaves more resilient from the addition of the water, and all around her the air buzzed with busy insects, and the branches sang with the chorus from the birds. Every square inch felt filled with life, and it lifted her spirits as she thought of the coming days. Lost in thought, time passed slowly as she wandered round in a wide arch that brought her back to the large pools near the foot of the Lookout, where Una sat on the edge of the water washing her green trousers.

She smiled as Rune walked up, her face was red as she rubbed the pants with vigour before slapping them across the rocks to pound the soap into the fabric and remove the dirt. "I thought you would wander off, this is a very beautiful place, and it's a shame you had to visit it during such a time of upheaval."

Rune often forgot that Una had visited here as a small girl with her mother and father, Rune gave a smile as she sat down and watched as Una plunged her pants into the water to rinse out the soap.

"You never lived here did you?" Una squeezed her trousers hard and the water bounced off the rocks and ran quickly back to the pool.

"I did actually, but just for a few years when I was very little, the cottage Robbie visited was home for a couple of years, but shortly after I was five, mum decided to head to France, and for a short while I lived between the two. It's nice being back, a lot of things have not changed, it's a shame the town is empty, it was a pretty exciting place when I was little."

"So you do remember Fagan then?" Una gave a nod.

"I was surprised he remembered me, but yes I remember him in the town as Maker, although he was a lot younger then, he had thick black bushy hair, and the same kind smile. His mum was nice, although I only met her the once." Rune thought for a moment.

"Sequana, she was a seer wasn't she?" Una laid the pants onto the rock and sat down.

"She was, she gave the queen at the time very accurate counsel, and mum said she lived for most of her time on the Citadel as she visited the queen daily." Rune stared at the water lost for a moment in thought; her voice was quiet and reflective.

"I remember a man coming to visit my grandfather and asking lots of questions about her, he got quite angry with the man and told him to stop wasting his time." Una gave a smile that showed her understanding.

"He always did avoid talking about her, there are some who said she guarded a big secret, my dad always said it was myth, although there was one occasion when he told me about her, and at that time he felt quite certain that she did indeed hold the key to something very mysterious, he told me that Fagan had become the new guardian which was why he stayed behind."

"I think my grandfather discovered it and used it Una, I think it is why I cannot find him." Una looked puzzled.

"How do you mean?" Rune turned to look at her and her eyes shone in the brightest of blue.

"My grandmother left this realm, and yet through my table I can contact her in the hidden realm, I feel her at times, yet with my grandfather there is nothing, tell me you have not tried to search other realms and look to him for help?" Una gave a small chuckle and gave a nod.

"Yes Rune I have, and I must admit I have thought the same. If this is the centre of all the realms, then from here we should have a sense of him, or Jett come to think of it, I have tried to contact her, but there is nothing." Una rested her hand on Rune's. "Don't forget the Star of the Merle, this realm is set in the heart of Avalon and overlaps it, none of us are sure if the power of the Merle has not had an effect on this one, I mean if you think about it, it was affecting the weather patterns in Loxley before we came here, there is nothing to say that if we dispose of it we will not be able to contact either of them." Rune gave a nod but she was not convinced.

"Maybe, I just thought with my powers now complete, I would be able to see into all the realms like I did when I connected with Iona, I have been trying all day to see if I could find them, but there is not a trace of them at all." Una gave her wrist a soft squeeze.

"Give it time Rune, you will see things have a habit of working themselves out, have some faith and wait a while longer."

Rune gave a weak smile. "Yeah, I suppose so."

They sat for a while as Una finished her washing, and then together they walked in the shade of the large rock along the path. The fine drizzle finally stopped and the floor began to pale as the heat from the sun took over and dried the paths, Una could sense the many thoughts going through Rune's mind, and decided to voice a few of her own.

"This will not be an easy fight for you, I hope you have realised that the Citadel is sacred to the Fae?" Rune had thought of nothing else for a week, she gave a slight nod as she tried to find something she could say that would put Una at ease.

"I really am not sure what I can do if she remains up there." Una stopped and Rune looked at her. Una looked very serious.

"Don't go, stay here and fight her from this place, let the others in and you watch over them, this will be a fight like no other you have faced, and as long as she has that rock in her hand, she will drain your powers. I mean it Rune, stay here and use your powers where you are protected, I have already told Robbie and Rowan and they agree."

"What! Una how could you?" Rune felt the sudden panic rise inside her at the thought of Robbie knowing; she had not said a word to him and had hoped he would not figure it out. Una stood her ground even though she saw that Rune was angry with her.

"Shout if you must Rune, but you are my centre and I am sworn to protect you at all costs, in you lies the future and whether you agree with me or not, I will not disobey the oath I gave to protect this circle."

Rune was defeated and she knew it, she respected Una a great deal, and felt a deep bond with her, but her deepest fear had been revealed and she knew now there was no hiding it from Una.

"I cannot let him walk into her traps, and she will be prepared, she knows that we will have to approach the castle at some point to help Amethyst, how can I leave him alone down there, when the last time she almost had all of us?" Una gave a nod.

"You are right she did, but last time we did not have you using your new powers of the stone, I am sorry Rune but you are life, and you have the gift of Eve, you can see and walk where no others can, and you do not have to leave here to do it. I think with you to guide us in there we should be well enough protected, and if needs be you can move to the sacred sites round the realm to help us, the stone circle is a protection even the Merle cannot overcome it, its power has resisted the star since it arrived, as does the tree of souls and the Isle of Tears. I think you would be wise to use them and guide us, she will not expect that, and your power will be at full strength, where as ours will weaken the longer we are in there." Una's eyes shone with bright violet in her tanned face, it was clear that she too had been giving the matter a great deal of thought. It was easy to see the look of disappointment on Rune's face.

"I don't want him to be alone in there; I want to be at his side as I always am."

"But you will be." Una lifted her arm round Rune's shoulder. "It will be just like when you were pregnant, you will be there in essence to guide him as you always have, and let's be honest he will hardly be alone. Look, we already know that for some reason Steph was not affected by the star, she was able to maintain contact with all of us, with her at Robbie's side all of us will know where he is and what is happening. Jade resisted for longer than most of us, so she too will be a big help, and Rowan will not leave his side, it hardly seems possible to prize them apart these days. We also have Fagan, and he knows the tunnels as well as she does, and I am sure he still has a few tricks we have not seen yet, use the strengths we have at their greatest advantage, and stay here where you can be protected and protect us, you know it makes sense." Rune gave a long sigh.

"I hate it, but what can I do now? Oh Una I wish you had said nothing, you know what he is like."

"That is why I told him, I knew you would keep quiet, I am sorry Rune, but while she carry's that star we have to plan a smarter game, and I think it's the one thing she will not expect. I think she is banking on you being there in person to stop her, play a thought out game this time and do what she least expects, that way the element of surprise will be ours and not hers." Rune had to agree that it did make sense, although the pangs in her stomach made her feel like she wished it didn't.

They walked together along the path, until the long wooden house came into view, Blades was out on the grass in front teaching Will a few tricks with his sword, and Rags was showing Gaynor a few things she had picked up with a bow. Rune knew that Robbie would be inside with Rowan and Steph planning ways to help Amethyst, and so as Una carried her clothes to the rail to hang them to dry, she skirted the house and took the small path up the side of the barn that led round to the large vegetable garden at the rear. Maddy was working in the tall maze plants with Crystal, and Bear was knelt on the path next to Big John, as they tended the tall beans under the wary eye of Fagan. Both of them with fat large hands fumbled with the fine cord as they tied the plants to the tall canes, and Fagan's eyebrows would twitch and jump as he watched like a nervous parent.

"Oh ye take care now, she is only a slim one and you might choke the poor dear... Oh treat her like a woman and be gentle there John, ye would not hold a maiden by the waist in that manner." John gave a gulp and twitched trying not to pull too tight on the string, he gave another look back as he slacked the knot and Fagan gave a broad smile. "There now that's the parchment, she will be wriggling like a worm in a dung hole soon she is so happy. It's like I always says, ye give em some room and they will dance with delight." He gave a broad wink and John sat back and gave a deep sigh of relief, and wiped his face. Bear looked deeply focused as he held his tongue in his teeth and gently tied a knot to hold the plant in place; Fagan gave him a broad smile. "I see ye have held a woman or two, oh she likes that she does, look ye have given her the wiggles." Rune gave a chuckle as she watch the bright wide smile on Bears face; John nudged him in the ribs.

"Bet ye give Alice them wiggles an all?" Bear looked a little pink as he gave a small smile back to the large smiling face of John. Rune walked along the path and thought of home and Alice, she had never realised how much she missed her, and gave a smile as she remembered those first few days on the road from Kirklees to Good Hope, it had all gone so very fast and now she stood on the edge of her most trying time, she wished that Alice could be at her side again.

Rune stood by the fence and looked out on the trees that had halted with the lack of breeze, the sun beat down hard and it was starting to feel even hotter now that the rain had stopped, everything felt oppressive and her mind wandered back to her conversation with Una, how could she let Robbie walk alone into a trap? Her stomach gave a twist and the uneasiness grew inside her again, her mind churned over and over as she became lost in her thoughts, and had not even noticed she was walking again.

Inside her mind the intricate puzzle of the Star of Merle played in her thoughts, she was not even aware that she was talking quietly to herself. "My mother could communicate easily, but she is my grandfather's successor so she has great power in the Whitelines, I know Una was always meant to protect and warn of evil, so that must be why her powers lasted much longer than everyone else's, although Jade was strong for a very long time, and she is the new force of the Green Circle. Amethyst can withstand the Mirrored Waters, as she is the heir of Rayne's line, but that does not make sense."

She stopped for a moment to think and found herself up on top of the high rock that formed the Lookout, next to the old Hawthorn as the sun burned even brighter. Rune lifted her hood to shield her eyes and then slipped down under the cool shady canopy of the tree; she got comfortable and then began to mutter again.

"Maddy is the heir of Gwendolyn, not Una, so why does Una resist better than Maddy? All the others are heirs and therefore stronger than the rest, Una is the twin of Melanie, she should not hold such powers, and why did granddad pass his staff to her? By rights the staff should go to my mother, this is not making sense at all, what does Una have that makes her stronger?" Rune pulled up her knees and leaned her head on them, as her dark hood kept the sun off her face, she didn't even notice as a cloud passed across the sun, blotting out the bright light for a moment, she was so involved with her puzzles, that for the first time in a long while she missed the importance of the moment.

Morgan le Fey walked with the large black bag of Ursula's on her shoulder out of the long tunnel and onto the start of the long ornate bridge of white stone. In the distance across the Mirrored Lake, she could see the white castle glowing in the ring of light that swirled around it. She hummed as she made her way to the edge of the bridge and peered into the water where her Bronteal swam on guard, she gave a smile and closed her eyes, and lifted her arm with the Star of the Merle firmly clenched in it, she muttered quietly under her breath.

From all around the cave there came a deep rumbling sound, the mirrored surface of the water rippled and began to bubble as air rose from the depth below, and raced to the surface. Fish who was in the tall tower watching nothing in particular for the fourth day running, suddenly jerked into alertness.

Looking over the high tower wall, he watched as the bubbles rose to the surface of the water and spread outwards, looking back quickly at Altman, the servant and soldier of the Fae he spoke quickly. "You better get Amethyst, something strange is happening."

The servant gave a short bow and turned quickly to the stairs, Fish looked back at the water, and to his surprise he saw a long road of white stone break the surface and rise up to meet the castle steps. Slowly he looked down the length of the road and realised it had joined at the other end, where only five days ago he had waited with Rune and the others, for Amethyst to return and take him to the castle.

In a way it explained the short bridge to nowhere that they had found when they came out of the labyrinth of tunnels, and he began to understand that in the past, this would have been how Rhiannon received her guests in the castle. For several long minutes he watched the water drip as it ran off the bridge, before Amethyst appeared at his side. She looked tired as she leant out of the window and looked down to where the bridge came right through the wall of swirling light that surrounded the castle, Fish watched her carefully. "What do you think this means?"

Amethyst held up her hand to where the ring remained the same. "This is nothing to do with the phase of the moon, if it was the ring would glow with moonlight. No this must be some trick of hers, because we have heard nothing from Rune or Eve." She shook her head as she spoke. "No this is the Dark One, and if she has been able to lift this out of the water, I think the time has come to bar the doors." Fish gave an eager nod.

"If she is planning a visit, I think we better get all the staff together and get down to the main hall." Amethyst looked very worried and she agreed with him.

With Altman, both of them rushed down the stairs, and found all of the staff had gathered, Amethyst ran across the long hall towards them and shouted. We need to close those doors and secure them tight." Altman was not far behind.

"Please My Lady, you must not alarm yourself, even if this is not the doing of our line, she cannot enter without the express invitation of yourself. Nothing may walk in these hallowed halls without consent of the Queen of this realm." Amethyst halted and allowed him to catch up.

"The problem is Altman; I am not the queen.... Well not yet, the power of the Fae has not yet taken over, and so for now she rules here, and I am not very confident we will be able to keep her out." Altman shook his head.

"No, My Lady, the powers in this place are older than any, and are forged with secrets that have never been disclosed outside of the people of Fae, she will not walk these halls I am certain of it." Fish stood between the both of them.

"I say we bar the doors just in case." He shrugged. "Call it instinct... To me it makes better sense to play on the side of caution, we all thought the water was safe, but look at those beasts she has released into it... Let's get them shut, and if this place has extra hidden powers, then that's fine by me." Amethyst gave an assured nod.

"Yeah, me too." She turned and walked toward the doors as several of the servants took hold, and began to swing the large old wooden doors shut. They met with a thump that boomed all around the inside of the castle, and Fish and Altman slid the heavy wooden beam across the two doors and slowly lowered it into its locking bracket with a dull clunk. Amethyst looked at them both. "What now?" Fish looked at Altman and then back to her.

"Find somewhere close to watch from and wait and see what happens."

"My Lady and Lord, if you follow me, I will take you to the balcony above the doors, from there you will be able to observe easily, but still be inside the protection of the walls." Both of them gave a nod as he turned and followed him.

Morgan le Fey walked with arrogance along the white bridge, a look of sadistic confidence on her face, her eyes were the deepest blood red, and were illuminated in her pale white face. In her hand, which had blackened skin, she clutched the Star of the Merle, and all that Amethyst and Fish could do as they reached the balcony above the large doors, was watch the figure of malice grow as she came closer toward them.

Morgan noticed the movement above the doors through the bright light that swirled round the castle; she gave a smile that made her thin black lips look crooked, she slowed as she approached the wall of illumination and gave a snort of impatience. Her red eyes met with the violet of Amethyst above the doors on the balcony. "Do you really think such things can protect you from the Star of the Merle? Honestly girl, you call yourself a Queen and yet your powers are as outdated as the décor in your halls."

Fish gave a frown and looked at Altman. "What protection? I thought she did that to keep us in." Altman gave a shrug and looked to Amethyst.

"This is nothing to do with the Fae of Moon, if it was it would shimmer blue." Amethyst looked back to where she saw the Dark One lift her palm to the wall of light, her face looked focused and also a little confused, as her open palm moved very close to the wall of the light it rippled.

Rune's eyes flared with bright violet light and her head snapped up under her hood, her legs slipped down to the floor from under her chin, as her head moved and twitched and she sensed the realm in front of her, her few words followed her gasp. "No... Not yet... we are not ready."

As she rose quickly to her feet, and stood on the edge of the high platform of rock, Rune saw for the first time the swirling mass above the Citadel Mount and gasped with surprise. She had been so preoccupied with trying to work out her riddles, sat below the tree and hidden by her large hood, she had not seen the swirling mass of darkness that had swarmed out of the sky and engulfed the top of the Mount. Rune felt a cold tingle run down her spine, as she saw the blackness swirl round in the air and then begin to spread like storm clouds slowly across the rest of Avalon. A rumble sounded at her side and she looked down and saw the yellow eyes of Furry Face as he stared at the mass of black in the sky. She slipped her hand into his deep fur on his head and scratched. "It's OK Baby Boy, she has not won yet, but we will have to hurry if we are going to save this place."

Far away from the darkness, and under the bright sunlight on the outer southern edge of London, the Sage moaned as he began to awaken, and the pain in his shoulder reminded him of his previous night's encounter with his father. He opened his eyes and looked to the bright sky, and lifted his arm to shield his eyes, the pain seized him and he jolted it back to the floor and lifted his left arm instead. Louisa leaned over and peered down at him. "Good afternoon, one too many late nights I think, you have slept away most of the day." He felt weak but tried to sit up; Louisa helped him as he blinked in the bright light.

"Where are we?"

"Safe out of his way, Sapphire is looking for your friends, I am hoping she will be back soon, this is not the safest of places to be." He looked round at the mounds of broken stonework covered with trees and grassy weeds, he appeared to be sat in a corner of the remains of what once was a tall wall, and in front of them a small fire crackled with a pan and a black kettle on it, his stomach gave a long whine and Louisa smiled. "Hungry?" He gave a nod as his senses returned.

"What happened to me?" Louisa spooned a large amount of thick soup like substance out of the pan onto a wooden plate.

"Mason shot you, to be honest had we been a split second later, he probably would have hit your heart, the snatch into the light moved you just in time." His mind filled as the memory of his meeting with his father flooded back into his mind, he noticed Louisa watching him.

"What?" She handed him the plate.

"What the hell did you think you were doing? I mean I understand you have your secret ways and all that, but honestly how the hell could you think that you could just climb in his window and try and kill him? Here eat this, it's not much, but we were in a bit of a rush when we left."

"Thanks... I have my reasons, as you know there are places I can go where no other can, I thought it would help if I could stop him." Louisa stared at him, but he could see she was uncertain as to whether or not he was telling her the truth, she spoke before he could say anything more.

"Why is that I feel you never tell everything, and that what you say is just the tip of the iceberg?" She stared at him and he felt a little nervous, his charade had lasted longer than he had thought it would, and yet now he felt the tension as Louisa's sharp mind worked on him. "You talk of things with too much authority and I don't really know why, but if I am honest with you, I will admit it bothers me. None of us with the best intelligence we can gather knew which places were the best ones to hit; you must have been an insider once, is that why you hide behind a mask?" He gave a smile.

"You are brighter than most people realise, let's just say that I walked away from a past of disgrace, and chose to hide who I really am in order to protect a great deal of secrets." Louisa gave a nod.

"Yes, I thought as much, so you are an enemy of high value that has turned from him, which is why you thought you could get close to him to kill him?" The Sage gave a chuckle and lifted the spoon to his mouth; it felt awkward holding it in the wrong hand.

"I was once in a very high position with Mason, yes Louisa you are right, although I would ask that what you have learned does not pass further than us two, many people could be hurt if my true identity was revealed."

"I take it Martin does not know, or he has not figured it all out yet, you do know at some point he will work it out as I have? I give you my word nothing will leave us two, although if you are working for us why hide who you are, that mask cannot be a comfortable thing to wear?"

"It's not the best thing I have ever worn, but believe me Louisa, it's better I hide my face." He gave a chuckle and ate his soup, Louisa sat back and spooned out a bowl for herself, she glanced back as he ate.

"Your face must be very well known to both sides if you hide it, I mean if you were just a general as Martin was, then it would not matter that much, from what I can tell, the only face that would stir up a great deal of problems would be that of Mason's missing son, now that would get you in anywhere and also cause a great deal of havoc." Her lip dropped and she stared at the Sage, as the sudden burst of her inspiration left her with a cold chill running down her spine, her head shook very slowly as she stared into his bright blue eyes. "No... I am wrong... Please tell me you are not William Knox?"

The Sage placed his bowl down on the moss covered floor, and reached with a painful arm for the ties behind his head. "I wish I could, but it appears I cannot hide from you Louisa."

The mask fell to the floor and her bowl clattered as she looked on the face that had created so much talk within the ranks of her home barracks at Caerleon, her breath seemed to run from her lungs with complete shock. "Shit! I really wish I had kept my big bloody mouth shut."

CHAPTER TWENTY FIVE

STRANGE TRUTHS

Louisa ate her food quietly, as the Sage fitted his mask back in place, her world had been temporarily turned upside down, and now her thoughts raced as she tried to make sense of the fact that the man she had admired and respected, had turned out to be a man she had despised over the past year, since she had talked with Jett at Caerleon shortly after she had discovered the truth about the identity of Billy. He felt her apprehension as she sat opposite him and ate. "You are upset Louisa, I can feel it, now maybe you understand why the mask was so necessary?" She rested her spoon on the side of her bowl and looked at him.

"You sold them all out, and you hurt Robbie and Rune deeply." Louisa stood up and pulled out her sword, she pointed it at the Sage. "How do I know you were not selling us all out again last night as you had your cosy little chat with daddy?" The Sage did not move, he gave her a shrug.

"You don't.... Although as you witnessed, he did try to shoot me, even you said if you had not pulled me at that moment, it would have entered my heart and I would be dead now, would that be proof enough to show you I have no interest in supporting him?" She felt an overwhelming confusion, as she stared down her blade at him and shook her head.

"That could very easily be staged; it would give you the perfect alibi."

"Maybe...But there again, I had no idea that Sapphire and yourself were about to make an entrance. I will not sit and tell you I am blameless Louisa, I am not, but what I will say is this, no matter what you think or feel, I did what I did, for believe it or not, honourable reasons. I will not bore you with the details, but I had my own reasons for my actions, right or wrong I was trying to do the right thing." She hated the fact he would not deny any of it, and his refusal to justify it made her even angrier.

"What about Eric? Was killing him an act of honour? He was just a kid who wanted nothing more than to prove to his lord he was worthy; he did not deserve to die so early." The Sage gave a sigh, and for a moment he dropped his head.

"Eric was never meant, and I regret that more than most things, he was not my intended target." She gritted her teeth as she spoke.

"No Robbie was... My God after all you had been through together, I only know a small amount from what Jett has told me, and even knowing so little, I cannot believe you would try to kill your own brother, because it matters not that you were not blood, in everything but that you were true to each other as kin would be." He could see the anger in her eyes as she spoke, and he understood the loyalty she felt for him, his voice was low and calm as he replied.

"We both had our chances to kill each other, I was angry and confused, when he faced me out, he was beyond angry, and yet the bond we share was stronger than both of us. Eric was an accident, believe me we would all take those accidents back if we could, I know Rob regrets killing my mother as much as I do Eric."

"What?" Louisa looked stunned. "Robbie killed your mother... When?"

"At the Cathedral, he shot and my mother leapt to protect my father, it was not unsimilar to the act that Eric did for him. I believe with all my heart it still haunts him today, as he like me, has to live with the actions of the moment. Louisa I am sure if we all had our time again, we would do things very differently, I think both of us have learned that lesson well. I cannot speak for him, but I will say that when I finally got out of the turmoil that surrounded me, I used the act of a friend and took full advantage of it, and now I work very hard at trying to undo some of the wrongs I have done. I feel on days like today, it will take me a lifetime to do it, but that is the path I have chosen to walk, and I will not stray from it." Louisa lowered her sword, and crouched down in front of him, as he sat against the wall with no weapons and heavily bandaged.

"But why go back? What the hell were you thinking when you climbed in through your father's window?" He gave a small laugh.

"Hard as it maybe to believe, I was hoping to get him to stop and simply go home to Cornwall and be content ruling over that region. I told him that if he did, I would not attempt to stop him, but if he continued, I would be the one to smash all his plans and stop him once and for all, and I meant it. You know we may not have had that much time together as father and son, but he knew I was serious, and in a way I think he knew I would do it, that is why he chose to try and kill me... He did it before I killed him."

Louisa sat back on the grass. "That was insane. I cannot believe you could think for one moment he would stop, if that is an example of your decision making, I think you should talk to others before you make certain choices in life, what the hell made you think you could do it?" He gave a slight shrug.

"I never thought I could do it, let's say it was important to me that I gave it a try, to be honest I may have a hole in my shoulder, but for once and for all time, I truly know where I stand now, in a way it's feels quite liberating just knowing."

"So where do you stand in this new liberation you feel, because I am buggered if I can work it out?" The Sage gave a broad smile.

"I am still in the middle, both sides will kill me if they discover who I am, and so I must walk my own path and in doing so I choose to walk one that will aid my brother of the woodland. Even though he will never know of my identity, I feel I owe him that, which is why I have been doing what I have for the last year, and I do know for certain, I have made a difference in his favour, it's up to him now to take the lead and help stabilise this land."

Louisa was not sure what to think now she had listened to his side of the story. She had thought he was a very honest and genuine person, but that had been shaken by the discovery of who he really was. Now she felt caught in a trap, she really did like him and held him in very high regard, but the stories of his actions with the hooded man said he was the opposite of the man she knew. She slumped back on the grass and felt at a complete loss, he closed his eyes and waited for her to talk, by the time Louisa could think of something she wanted to say. She noticed the steady pace to his breathing and realised he had drifted off into sleep, all she could do now was wait for Sapphire and the others, and for now say nothing at all about their conversation.

Morgan le Fey stood with her hand in front of the bright wall of light as she tried to decide what it was that she was going to do, after all she had thought the protections would have been put up by Rhiannon, something she could easily defeat with the Star of the Merle. The wall of protection before her was very different from anything she had ever encountered, and although she had tried to focus her mind using the star, she found it impossible to get through to the other side and the steps that led up to the castle doors.

Amethyst was anxious as she watched, and also trying to work out where the light had come from, after all it was not violet, so she thought it was nothing to do with Rune. Altman was positive it had nothing to do with the protections left by Rhiannon, and she knew she had not done it; she looked back at Fish and Altman as they studied it from the edge of the glass doors to the balcony. "Well, someone put it there guys, she is looking as stumped as us, but we better work it out and soon, because it's not just keeping her out, it's keeping us in."

It was a possibility that Fish had not actually thought about, he looked to Altman who he was finding to be a very useful and reliable aide in a castle filled with women, but it was clear he had no idea at all. "Who else is in this realm?" Amethyst turned to him.

"How do you mean?"

"Well, if not her, Rune, or your grandmother, there must be someone else wandering about doing stuff like that to help us." Altman shook his head.

"No other power would enter during the moon phase rebuilding, the power of the moon would kill all who were not born of Fae, it is a ruling of our line to expel all when we use ways of the old that are secret and guarded. No other life form can walk here and use their powers like this."

Amethyst watched the long white bridge, where she could see the frustration rising in the Dark One, the Bronteal were coming closer to the bridge and she felt the suspense rise in her heart as she waited for something to happen.

"Well I hate to say this boys, but obviously there has been a mistake, because something somewhere is watching our back, and maybe it's not a human form, because it's got some power to hold her back as it is."

The Dark One lifted the star in the air and began to chant, Amethyst braced herself, as she saw four large dark shapes in the water swim away from the bridge, and then turn back towards it coming at great speed. She stepped back away from the edge of the balcony putting her arm out to push Fish back, and the large beasts leapt up out of the water, their long necks waving as their oval heads revealed the long rows of sharp pointed teeth. Their bodies rose above the surface of the water to show their long fins and short stubby legs, as they towered into the air, and then fell flat against the bright wall of light.

There were deafening, horrendous, squeals of pain and a mighty flash. Amethyst felt the wave ripple through the air, and she was lifted off her feet and thrown like a match in the wind, back into the wall eight feet behind the balcony. She landed on top of Altman and Fish, who hit the wall with a thud, Fish yelled out in shock from somewhere behind and under her.

"What the bloody hell is...?" He gave a cough as the air was knocked out of him, and Amethyst grasping wildly at nothing rolled off the men and slid across the floor.

The women servants screamed, as they came running down the corridor towards them, Amethyst was shaken, but also saw the funny side and began to chuckle. Fish sat up looking very shaken, as Altman crawled out from behind him, he looked out across the balcony and then back to Amethyst. "Well My Lady whoever made it, we should thank them because for now it appears to have held them out." The maids came fluttering around Amethyst as they lifted her back to her feet and tried to straighten her clothes, she brushed them away impatiently.

"I am fine... I said fine, oh please do not fuss, I have had far worse knocks than that." She slipped out from the circle of fussing women and looked out through the doors, down towards the bridge and the water.

Morgan le Fey was twenty feet away from the wall of light; it looked like she too had been blown off her feet, she was soaking wet and dripped as she scowled up at Amethyst. On the surface of the Mirrored Waters, four large bodies floated motionless, and the water around them bubbled and frothed, and she gave a long sigh of relief.

"Well, whatever it is, it's monster proof. Those four things have been well and truly grilled." The other Bronteal surfaced as she watched, and they began tearing large slices off their dead companions, she gave a shudder as she witnessed the ferocity of them as they ripped what had been part of their own group apart to feed, in a cold brutal frenzy of hunger.

The old witch scrambled to her feet and snatched her black bag off the wet floor, she turned and pointed a long white finger at Amethyst and screamed out along the bridge of dripping water. "This will be finished soon, I can assure you this is not over yet, I will be back and you will have more to fear than my monsters. When I return, not even the White Lord himself will have the power to protect you."

Fish looked over Amethyst's shoulders and saw the Bronteal feeding; he screwed up his face in disgust. "Urgh...! What has the White Lord got to do with this?"

Altman appeared at his side looking a little ruffled. "What indeed? He has not walked this realm since the loss of his sister, he came here with the Green Lord to help create the Isle of Tears as her resting place, but even then he had to ask the last queen of the realm to enter. I think it's very unlikely she would give him entry without her own presence, although he is pure Whitelines, so his power would be revealed as such, I must admit I find this all very strange." Fish gave a smile.

"No kidding, before I got here the strangest thing, I had ever seen is a girls eyes flashing with purple light, this place is a whole bag of new tricks and no mistake." He looked at Amethyst who was watching the Dark One walk away down the long white bridge, she seemed lost in thought, and he nudged her, she seemed to snap out of her thoughts as she looked at him, he gave her a smile. "You OK?" She nodded.

"Yes, I was just thinking about what you both said." She looked at them and her eyes seem to sparkle with her thoughts. "You know when I went to save Jett; there was something else, something more than just Rune and myself. It felt strange almost distant, but it was there working between us... I guess with all this being so new to me, I did not understand what I was feeling. Does that make sense?" Altman gave her a reassuring smile.

"I think My Lady at this moment in time, I would believe that just about anything may be possible, if the last queen cannot gain access, she may very well assist the White Lord, for he too has many gifts not possessed by the Fae." He took her gently by the hand and guided her off the balcony back into the corridor. "I think My Lady you would be more at ease if you were to change into something dryer. Please both of you go and attend to your clothes, and I shall remain and watch for you, if there is need, I will send for you." Amethyst looked down to her dripping robes.

"Yes I think I will, a hot drink and a dry dress might not be such a bad idea... Come on James, we will see you shortly Altman." He gave a polite nod as they turned, and then he stepped out onto the balcony, where he could see the small black speck that was the Dark One, far across the waters, hurrying along the bridge.

Rune took a deep breath and gave a sigh of relief; she opened her eyes and looked at the large fat cat in front of her. "She is safe for now." The voice of Fagan gave a wheeze behind her and she turned, it felt strange that he could appear without her knowing, and yet he seemed able to just walk up to her undetected, it was obvious he had been there for some time. Fagan gave her a smile.

"Ye has noticed I walk unseen, it was a gift to aid me in me work, and one I prize above the others, for it helps when the willows is moaning and groaning, I can sneaks off without them knowing ye see." Rune gave a giggle.

"You certainly have become my guardian since I arrived; it is nice to know someone looks over me as I do the rest." He gave a courteous bow.

"I promised that ye would be safe in my forest, and it's my privilege to watch over ye. For as long as ye remain here, like the trees ye have my eyes and ears working beside ye." Rune walked slowly along the top of the lookout to the Hawthorn where he stood, he had his strange ways and mannerisms, but she had become very fond of him.

"I have been watching your new queen and she is safe for now, but we must act fast if we are to aid her, I fear we do not have as much time as I would wish, and regardless of what Robbie may say, he knows as well as I do Master Keeper that the Specialists still need more time. I would ask you to aid them all you can in their next task, for I fear I may not be able to walk as freely as you can."

He gave a nod of understanding; the law of sacred ground was very old and seated in strong magic from the start of time. Although he knew that Rune was unaware, it had proven as great a hindrance to Rhiannon in her time, when it came to the removal of Morgan le Fey. Fagan looked at her, she was so small and delicate compared to him, and yet he could feel the power radiate from her, he knew she was worried and he gave her a kindly smile.

"Ye must not worry so, I will walk at his side in place of ye, and no harm will afford him while I watch the path, although I would ask a favour if ye would permit me?" Rune watched as he became a little discomforted and nervous.

"If there is anything I can do for you, then please you must ask me." Fagan put his head down.

"I does feel cheeky about it, but I am sworn to an oath and caught in a bind tighter than the weed." He looked almost embarrassed as Rune gave him a sweet smile; just for a moment he had almost reminded her of OX and his boys.

"You have done so much for us Fagan, if there is anything I can do in return for your kindness I would gladly do it." He nodded his head as she spoke.

"Ye are as gracious as I always dreamed of, if it's not too much of a bother, I would be as happy as ragwort in the hedges if ye would let me borrow miss Una, and ye good Shepard Woods for a while." Rune felt the surprise rise inside her, and was not entirely certain as to what he would want Una for; she gave a reply without thinking.

"Of course... Are you romantically inclined towards Una?" Fagan almost jumped back with surprise.

"Eh! What?" He lifted his arms and shook them in front of him. "Oh no... I mean no My Lady it's nothing like that, I mean.... Oh dear my what a to do, no what I wants is for her to take a walk with me." He suddenly stopped and looked panicked. "Oh... No that's not it." Rune started to giggle. "Ye see I gave my word, so ye see it's my task to take her where she must go, if ye understands? I mean it's not like she is not pretty and that, she is, I find her pretty as a buttercup and as sweet as sesame bun... It's just I promised in confidence that I would show her the way to a task set long back by her father." Rune stopped laughing.

"My grandfather?" Fagan gave an exasperated gasp and wiped his face with a large green rag.

"Aye that be so, he swore me to tell no other of the task set long ago by him, and he told me that when the red stone faces the dark clouds, then shall be the time to awaken her memory, and take her to a set place to wait for his command. It's a place that will make the horses jumpy as a buttercup with black fly, and I have seen the special bond ye Shepard has with all beasts." Rune saw how uncomfortable this made him, she could see him struggle as he tried to keep his promise to her grandfather, but felt the tug of his loyalty to her, she felt sorry for him and her voice softened.

"Fagan my grandfather has gone forever; he is no longer here to command any of us." Fagan gave a sharp nod.

"I know My Lady, he said he would, but he still made me promise, and I feel duty bound to him as my friend." Rune understood, and as much as she wanted to enquire more, she knew she had already asked too much of the old keeper.

"I trust my grandfather, and if these are his express wishes, then I have no doubt there is good reason, ease your heart my good friend, for his wish shall be so. Take the Lady Una and follow your instructions, then return to us when you are done." He suddenly looked very grateful and relieved.

"I thanks ye My Lady, I promise I will not be long, and shall be back to stand by the wooded lord's side quicker than a poppy can bursts its pods I will." Rune smiled at him.

"Go and do your best then." Fagan gave a regal bow and turned on the path, she watched as he scurried off, and his bright tufted white hair bobbed away down the path, then she turned and looked back at Furry Face as he watched her. She gave him a smile and scratched the top of his head, and then looked back across the wide open land toward the dark clouds building up over the mountain.

Rune sensed the tension in the air, and deep down inside, she felt the worry building as she knew that her moment of truth was coming, the following days would test everything she had learned from those who had spent a lifetime preparing her, and even though she was surrounded by those she loved, suddenly she felt very much alone. The Citadel was sacred ground, so she had to find a way to temp the Dark One out, but with the Star of Merle in her enemy's possession, she knew that her powers would drain and she would lose, and everything would be lost. Standing alone stroking the large head of the tiger at her side she felt a sharp pang of real fear rise swiftly inside her chest. "There must be something I am missing, Oh Furry Face how will I ever get that rock out of her hand?" The large animal gave a mellow squeak and rubbed his wide head against her leg, it wasn't much, but Rune smiled and for a moment felt a little bit less alone.

Back at the old wooden house deep inside the Forest of Time, it was cool, as the thick heavy walls kept at bay the intense heat of the day. Robbie and Rowan had spent their morning with Bear and Skip looking at the old maps given to them by Merlin, and Fagan had provided one of his own, which had a lot more detail on it. Knowing the time was drawing near, Rowan had sent an advanced party off to scout around the area of the fire from two nights ago, and try to get a little closer to the edge of the lake to see what they could find out. Hawk had chosen Blades and Todd, backed up by Big John and Harry, who had finally come out of his room now that Furry Face had grown bored and gone off looking for Rune. They skirted the burned out woodland, and slowly made their way east to where they were in deep tree cover at the very far end of the Lake of Passing, and would have a perfect view of the large mountain that contained the Citadel.

They had been met with a big surprise as they stood in what remained of the ancient woodland. Hawk walked slowly up in front, it was hard to believe his eyes as the sun burned down on what should have been a thick forested area of dappled shade. The heat of the sun had dried up everything, the grass that poked up around the base of each tree was withered and brown, the trees were stripped of leaves, which they now waded through, as the pile was higher than their boots. Like a sea of brown and yellow, all that remained was a woodland of skeletal trees, as the sun beat down on the leafless landscape. In some places the remaining branches of the trees had become so dry, they had cracked and splintered, and fallen to the floor. To a woodsman, it was the worst thing on earth that could happen, and the small group began to see and understand the evil that the Dark One had wrought. John shook his head. "Oh this aint right guys, if Hearne saw this it would destroy him, we definitely should not bring Rune this way it will break her heart." Hawk stopped next to the fat trunk of a bare old Hawthorn.

"I think that's her plan to be honest John. She wants to show us her power, and destroying so many trees in just a matter of a week is her way of telling Rune and our lord that she is now in control." He turned to look back at the others as they moved closer to him. "I tell you what? Robbie and Rowan aint going to be too happy, with no cover it will be easy to spot us from up there." He gestured behind him with his thumb, and the small party came up to his side and looked out on the deep bowl of dust that had once been the lake, and across to the bridge and high wall of rock that rose high into the sky and the Citadel above. Blades gave a shudder.

"It makes me feel sick to the stomach looking at it, I can understand her wanting to show she is ruling, but honestly no matter how dark you are, do you really want to live looking out on this?" Harry took off his hat and wiped his head with his bright red handkerchief.

"Whoa man this aint cosmic, I saw stuff like this when I was a kid in picture books, these like big companies filled with bread heads, cut and burned everything for building and grazing land, it was totally unradical and vibe jangling, but man, money back then talked and we all had to like live with it going on, it looks like the Mason Dude has learned a lot from the past." He gave a deep sad sigh and put his hat back on. "I say we split before the uncosmic monsters see us, it aint too funky here, we have like seen more than we need, this aint good for your karma dudes, I like feel it sapping my vibes as we speak."

It felt strange agreeing with Harry, but Hawk's sharp eyes looked out from the tree at the top of the hill that ran down through the long grass and reed to what should have been the water's edge. All that remained of the huge lake was a wide flat expanse of thick dark mud, the water had evaporated leaving the mud to dry and crack into dust. In the distance the high white wall of the rock face of the Citadel looked less beautiful without the deep clear blue of the water to reflect off it, and the skeletal frames of the thousands of trees that covered the land looked grief stricken. The air was hot and silent, and it made him shudder, there was no sound at all, every bird had left for the green lush forest that edged the border of Avalon, and it added to the building feelings that oppressed the joy of life deep within him. The only sound he could hear, was the distant rumble from the mass of thick black cloud building above the Citadel Mount, as he stared at it swirling in the sky above it, Harry patted his shoulder.

"That aint cosmic either, I am telling you man, there is one big uncosmic storm coming and we need to like split." Hawk gave a nod and shouldered his bow.

"Yeah Harry, I think we have seen all we can, let's get back to where the trees watch over us, I hate this place it's not natural." Feeling the sadness of the moment, they all turned, and with Harry more vigilant than normal, they trudged back through the deep piles of dead leaves, heading in the direction of the living Forest of Time.

Woody had never really found a place that he truly fitted in, the Cutters had attacked his home in Cumbria and in one day of brutality, they had taken every security he had ever known away. With his mother slaughtered and his herd carted off to the boats, he lost the only family he had ever had and his only chance of survival, as his sheep provided his income and primary source of living. From that day on he had wandered trying to find a place he could belong with his only companion his faithful sheepdog, Bess. For a time, he had found a way to survive as one of the Outlaw group, and then with Robbie and the Specialists, but deep down inside he knew he could never be truly at ease, and the death of his greatest companion Bess, had brought it all to the surface.

Since his arrival at the long wooden house of Fagan, he had isolated himself by living in the barn with the animals; there in secret he had grieved alone, and finally found a place of peace where he could simply be himself. Caring for the animals he found his nerves subsided and he spent most of his day feeding and cleaning their pens and shelters, as he talked softly to them. Being around sheep again re-ignited his skills as a Shepard, and for the first time in a very long time, he felt like he had a place where he truly felt at one with the world around him. He had thought that hidden inside the barn it had gone unnoticed, but it had not escaped the attention of Robbie or Rowan, and Fagan had duly noted it too.

It was late afternoon and Woody was feeding the horses when Robbie came inside the barn, unlike the others Robbie still looked very tired as he leaned on the wooden rails and watched Woody fill the rack with fresh greens and hay for the horse to eat. Robbie gave a smile as Woody looked up from the rack. "I have been looking for you Woody; I would like to talk if that's OK?"

Woody gave a nervous nod, as he straightened up and looked at Robbie who appeared quite serious. Robbie thought for a moment picking his words with care. "Woody you have been a huge help to all of us, in fact Hawk tells me that it was your skills that guided everyone safely across the marshland." His dark eyes stared at Woody's as he thought for a moment; Woody gave a nervous nod in recognition for his task. Robbie gave a sigh. "Yet you hide away in here and keep yourself separate from the group, and I have to confess my friend that it worries me a great deal." Woody fidgeted not very certain of himself.

"I... I like to be useful... You know...? Busy hands and there is a lot here I can help with... I mean... You know, this is what I am good at My Lord." Robbie gave a solemn nod.

"Yes, I know of your background, and I must admit when you first joined the ranks with Todd, I thought out on the moors with Harry you were starting to feel a part of us, but if I am honest with you, and I don't mean this in a bad way at all, I am beginning to think more and more that your place is around the care of animals." Woody took a step forward looking a little more than nervous.

"I don't mean to displease you, it's just this is what I have been trained to do, I would never let any of you down... I would fight to the death with everyone to stop Knox." His voice contained a little desperation and Robbie lifted a calming hand.

"You misunderstand me Woody; honestly I have no problems with your abilities in the group... No, what concerns me is that I see how hard you try, and yet if I am brutally honest, it looks very much to me like you find it impossible to fully fit in, and that has concerned me a great deal of late, and I came here to talk to you because I want everyone to have a place in this world, and maybe I thought if we talk, I could find out where your place lies." Woody put his head down and Robbie felt bad about upsetting him, Woody mumbled.

"I have never fitted anywhere, and losing Bess has made it worse, I really am sorry for the trouble I have caused you, I don't mean to be a cause of trouble for anyone." Robbie could see and hear the hurt inside him.

"Woody listen to me, I am not looking to hurt you or upset you, if anything I want to help you." He gave a long sigh as he watched the sadness rise in Woody's face. "Woody Fagan has asked me if I will let you do a special task for him." Woody gave a sniffle and wiped his nose on his sleeve.

"I will help anyone who needs it, I hope you know that My Lord." Robbie smiled.

"I know, Rune especially has seen the kindness you show to everything, which is why I have told Fagan I will speak to you and then let you decide what you wish to do."

"What can I do for Master Fagan?"

"Fagan has asked if I will let you be a companion and guide to Lady Una on a special task set for her, the problem is Woody, if I let you go you may be some time, and when you return we could have left here to go and try to free Amethyst, which as it stands could mean we may never return here again depending on what happens." Robbie watched as he saw that Woody was starting to understand what Robbie was saying.

"I would get left here and not be able to get home again?" Robbie gave a nod.

"It is a risk all of us have to take, but yes, you may have to stay here with Fagan for the rest of your days, at the moment nothing is certain and none of us can know the outcome of a fight with the Dark One. The thing is if we defeat her, we may have to leave here very fast, as some of us are not of the lines of Fae, and so may be harmed by the old powers of the realm. We may have to leave at that moment of victory, and if you have not returned in time, even though you will be protected in the forest, I cannot give you an assurance I will be able to come back here to collect you." Woody understood what Robbie was saying. "Will I be stuck here forever?" Robbie gave a shrug. "I just cannot say with any degree of certainty, we hope that after the new queen is in power and the balance is restored, we will be able to return and collect you if you get left behind, but at the moment I cannot be completely sure. I suppose what I am asking you is this, do you want to guide Una and risk being trapped, or do you want to come along with us not knowing if we will win or lose this fight?" Woody gave a nod.

"I understand... if I come who will guide the Lady Una?"

"Fagan can only take her part of the way, after that she will have to go alone, Una may not return to us in time, if you do go it will be because someone will need to return the horses here, as Una must face her task alone and where she is going may spook the horses, which is why Fagan asked for you, as he can clearly see you have a deep bond with all his animals.”

“And if I return and you have left, where will I live and what will I do?”

“You will reside here with Fagan and care for his animals and become his assistant as Keeper of the Forest, unless we can get back, in which case you will help him until that time. I would like to give you longer to consider this proposal, but I am afraid that time is not on our side and so can only give you about an hour, I am sorry for such short notice.” Woody gave a small smile.

“Lady Una has been kind to me, it would be wrong to leave her alone My Lord, I think I should go with her and be her companion and watch the horses. I am better with animals than people, and if I get stuck here to be honest there is not much left for me out there. I have never really known what I would do if we won, there is nothing left for me to go back to. If I am honest with you My Lord, this place is better suited to me, being trapped here is better than being alone out there.” Robbie gave a nod as he looked at the sad figure that had proven himself in his service.

“It can only be your decision, but I promise if I can get back for you, I will not abandon you. Una is lucky to have a man of such honour to guide her, your loyalty to her and us is a credit to you as a man.”

“Thank you, My Lord, it is nice for you to say that.” Robbie gave a smile at him.

“I say it because I mean it Woody, you know you should know that whether you feel it or not, everyman here holds you in their respect, and you alone earned that, I would say there are few men in the world who could claim that honour, you should think about that.” Woody gave a smile and his face seemed to brighten.

“Thank you, My Lord, I too respect them as much, for they call me friend, and that does mean a great deal to me.”

“You are one of us my friend...I also think it’s important you understand, that whatever the outcome of everything, you will always have a place to call home at Loxley, a man of your skills will be very useful where there are herds to tend, and Loxley has a great many animals. I will let Una know to prepare, you will need four horses and supplies, I need to find Fagan and get everything arranged, we will speak again before you leave. Thanks Woody, you will ease my mind knowing she is not alone.” Robbie left the barn and Woody lifted a saddle off the rail and talked softly to the horses as he prepared them, in a way he knew that this would be for the best, after all if the new queen came and balance was restored, he would be able to walk in Avalon, which meant he would forever be close to the grave of his beloved Bess.

CHAPTER TWENTY SIX

SECRETS

Rune stood alone on the top of the flat outcrop of the Lookout, and looked across the trees and onto the plain of Avalon. Her blue eyes shone in her pale white face as she took in the scene of what was once a lush and green fertile land.

What had been the large lake in front of the high stone rock face, was now a vast deep empty mud filled crater, and the green banks of lush grasses and reed were brown withered and tangled with the death brought by the searing heat. In her heart she felt the sadness build, for she had looked on Avalon when she first arrived, and felt a deep love of the life that had been contained in everything. Smoke rose from large areas that now were empty bands of black soot from the fires that the soldiers had lit, in hope of finding the Hooded Man to hunt down and capture for their mistress. A tear ran down her cheek as she slowly took in the devastation of the Dark One.

High above the high wall of rock on the Citadel Mount, the air was filled with the swirling dark clouds, which were starting to radiate out across the whole of the realm, shutting out the light from the dazzling sun, and casting a sinister shadow across the land. Behind her hidden by her long violet cloak, a deep murmur came out from under the low growing Hawthorn, and Rune blinked and gave a small smile. "I know... I sense him too." The large yellow eyes of the tiger closed, and he lay his big round head down on his paws, as on the track behind came the familiar crunch of the clay and loose stone under a leather boot.

Robbie walked up the path and came round the side of the large boulder; he walked slowly as if not to disturb Rune's thoughts, as he crossed the small stone top of the rocky outcrop and walked up at her side. His hair lifted on his shoulder as the faintest of breezes washed across his neck, and he stood motionless beside her and looked out at the swirling darkness heading towards them. Rune lifted her hand and slipped it into his, it felt warm and pumping with life as he gently closed his around hers. His head turned slightly towards her, and he noticed her eyes shining in the brightest sapphire blue staring ahead. "What is she up to?"

She gave a gentle sigh. "I'm really not sure... I can feel her evil in the air, she is planning something, and whatever it is it will not be pleasant." Robbie understood and gave a slight nod, his eyes never leaving her soft pale face.

"Una has told me, I know you are worried, aren't you?" Rune stared out into the dim light.

"I am safe here in this realm, she has no power here, not even with her little black stone." He felt her pause and waited for her to continue as he watched her, Rune blinked and turned, she looked up and he could see the full beauty of her blue eyes surrounded by the lilac of her whites, they were stern but serious, as she moved closer and lifted her arms to him and pulled him close. He sensed her concern and brought his arms up behind her to hold her as she rested her head on his chest. "I don't want you to go there Robbie, stay here in safety and wait for those who can face her to deal with her, there is great danger lying in wait for all of us." She gave a shudder and he pulled her tighter as he looked back towards the darkness rolling in over Avalon. Robbie took a long breath enjoying holding her close, as his mind searched for the right words. His voice was soft and gentle.

"I never wanted any of this Rune.... Not for you or any of them." She moved slowly almost knowing what he was going to say, and she turned and looked up into his dark brown resolute eyes. He smiled and lifted a hand to stroke back the copper red strands of hair from her soft pale face. "They chose me, and I accepted knowing that it would be dangerous. I love you more than life you know that, but you also know that I gave my word. I cannot break it Rune, too many depend on me now." Tears welled into her eyes, and she pushed back braking away from him.

"I cannot help you." She shook as the tears rolled down her cheeks and she slowly shook her head. "If I enter the realm while she has the star, it will drain everything from me and I will be powerless to defend you." Rune gave a huge sob and looked back at him through the streaming tears. "You cannot go and leave me here alone; I will not watch you walk to your death." Rune fell to her knees and wept. "I can endure anything except that; if you go into Avalon without me you will have no protection and be at her mercy."

Robbie lowered to his knees slowly and pulled her close; she sprang into him and held him tighter than he had ever known as she trembled with fear. "I finally have the power to face her and kill her, but with that stone in her hand, I will be rendered powerless. Oh Robbie... What is the point of all these trials if the gifts I received are drawn into the star the moment I appear? How can I fight her here, miles away on top of this rock? I want this over, I want to go home and be with the children, why oh why can we not have a normal life like everyone else?"

He held her close, and stroked the back of her long golden and copper hair as he let her wail out her worries and fears, feeling her pain inside himself at having to witness such deep distress. There was so much about the magic that had surrounded him and Rune since the moment he had first seen her as a young boy, and he was the first to admit that a great deal of it left him lost and confused. He had never really understood how the magic had twisted and weaved its way through time to create everything that had led to this point, but somehow deep down inside, he had always known it would find a way to help them both.

In many ways he understood that he had at times forgotten the power that had bound them together, maybe it was here in this moment of Rune's doubt that he had truly began to understand it, or he had simply lost hope for a while in it. Kneeling on the rock with her trembling in his arms, he felt a strong sense flow over him, almost as if he was free in the woodland and using his senses to hunt. He lifted her face and smiled as he wiped the tears from her eyes, she gave a sniffle as her eyes cleared.

"I will never believe that we have come this far simply for everything to fold in on itself like this." She blinked. "Rune for over a thousand years this destiny has been preordained for us... I cannot say what the following days will have in store for us, but I will never believe that you alone were chosen to wield these powers simply to have them fail in the moment of truth. I have Destiny and the other swords at my side, and you have your sisters, and it is no coincidence that the power of the red stone came to you at this moment." Rune gave another sniffle and swallowed hard.

"But Robbie, you are one sword short... I mean Jett is still lost to us, and she has the sword of truth, every prophecy ever written states all five swords must be as one to fight her." Robbie stood up and lifted Rune to her feet, he looked out across Avalon and his voice was defiant.

"That maybe, but somewhere out there Jett Amber is alive, and as long as she is, then there is hope that we will defeat Mason and his vile mother. I trust in Jett's instincts, she might be as flaky as hell at times, but when push comes to shove, she has never let me down, and I am sure as hell certain that one way or the other, Jett and me have business to finish as a duo.... Trust in her Rune, she will find her way back I am sure of it, and until she does, then that just means I have to find a way of parting that bitch over there from her precious little jewel, and when I do, I know you will have a way of finishing this and getting us home again. For now, we are safe enough to gain our strength and restock our weapons, you have these new gifts and you must use them to get back my wild sword touting banshee, believe in her Rune and find her for me."

Rune suddenly felt the fires grow inside her as Robbie rose in stature before her, she felt the power rising inside him like it had on so many other occasions, and she began to understand the words of Eve. Rune knew he had fought against his own fears and doubts since they had arrived in the realm, and now she watched as she saw him find his own way back to who he was.

"Yes my Hooded Man." He turned, a slight look of confusion on his face.

"What?" She gave a giggle, and he felt a surge of joy seeing her face lit up as she smiled at him.

"You were chosen because the magic is very strong in you, you are the Hooded Man returned to us, I think both of us forgot for a moment, but I see it clearly now. I trust your instincts; I always have for they have never been wrong, and so I will trust them now and I will look for Jett using all that I have." She slid closer to him and stretched up and kissed him softly. Both of them stood together on top of the Lookout facing Avalon for some time watching, still holding each other as the warmth passed between them, until Robbie stirred.

"These rain clouds will help, come to think of it a bit more rain will help us a lot, this heat saps everyone's strength, a little downpour will cool things, off and give everyone good heart."

"It's not rain Robbie; those aren't even clouds." He frowned at her.

"They aren't?" She shook her head.

"No Robbie... That is the Merle.... She is drawing it into Avalon to soak up every ounce of the power of the Fae to use against us. To you it looks like clouds, but when I look at it, I see long strands of smoke like fingers filled with grotesque figures who suck the power out of everything growing in the realm, that is why everything looks dead to you... the Merle is killing everything." He gave a shudder.

"What like the Smoggets at Dunnottar?" Rune gave a slight nod.

"Similar... it's just these are far more evil and dangerous."

"How much more evil Rune?" Her tone seemed to change as the seriousness of the situation was absorbed into Robbie.

"Let's just say that when Harry says they suck out your karma and leave you unfunky, well in this case he is not that wrong, only these suck out your soul and don't leave you unfunky, they leave you dead." Robbie gave a deep swallow.

"How do we fight them Rune?"

"That's what worried me; you can only fight something if you can see it, and for now that's just me." Robbie pulled her close as he scanned the land in front, his mind filled with all the possibilities, and he found it hard to believe that after all that happened and with the weaving of the magic there was not some way to defeat her. His eyes caught the glint of metal as it flashed with a ray of the sunlight, and he slid his arm down from Rune and into his long waistcoat pocket, Rune moved sensing his thoughts.

"What is it?" Robbie slipped out his old brass telescope and pulled it apart, and lifted it to his eye, as he focused over the great distance.

"I was just wondering what she was doing with all her soldiers, we don't just face her, we have all them to deal with as well." He scanned along the edge of the dead trees up towards the large castle near the town, and then panned across the empty lake to the fork shaped island in its centre. "It looks like she is preparing her troops, Avalonia is full and by the look of it she is moving more across the other side of the lake on some sort of bridge towards the Misty Bank. I think she is planning to fill the woodland all-round the lake to force us out."

Rune closed her eyes and sensed the realm in front of her, her cheeks flashed with small flickers of light, as her eyes moved underneath her closed eyes watching the lake and woodland, Robbie smiled as he watched knowing she was trying her hardest to yet again find a safe way in, she gave a small smile.

"I can feel you watching you know?" He chuckled

"So what are they up to?"

"They are preparing, it's not easy under all that cloud, but I think they are preparing a defence, they expect you to strike within the week." Robbie gave a nod.

"Rowan thinks we should strike sooner than later, and try to catch them off guard."

"When does he think you should go?" Rune opened her eyes and stared out in front avoiding Robbie's gaze.

"Late tomorrow, or the morning after, although I think the timing is irrelevant, it's neither day or night here anymore, the sun just shines all the time." Rune gave a slight nod of her head.

"Go the morning after, let them have one more day with Fagan, in his home they are growing stronger, but they are not yet ready, if you let that cloud grow a little wider, it will bring with it darkness, and that you can use it as you would the leaves in a woodland to hide in. Stealth is more important now than it has ever been, and with a little more time I can prepare, I have a few things in mind for the soldiers that will help you, and once you are in the tunnels, I can guide you even if I cannot be with you. She is not the only one who can see through the rock now; the main difference is, I do not need a rock in my hand to do it." He could see the concern in her eyes, and also hear the determination in her voice; it worried him that she would do something stupid, his voice held a note of caution as he asked her the question most in his thoughts.

"You do mean from here though don't you? You know no matter how much you hate her and want to get her; you will stay here and do nothing that might risk your powers? That mount is sacred ground Rune; you cannot kill her there, no matter how unfair this all seems, you must not set foot on it and face her."

Rune didn't look at him, she knew what he thought and did not need to be told, but she also knew that she would never desert him and find a way to protect him at all costs. "This is not the only safe place, on the Isle of Tears, or in the stone circle I am also protected, I can watch you from a closer point if needed. I know I cannot kill her up there, but if she steps off that rock for one moment, I will attack her to protect everyone, in that one thing Robbie, you will not stop me."

He understood that her hatred of the Dark One was deep, but he could see she would abide by the rules set at the start of time, and he felt a little relief knowing that no matter what happened she would be safe and protected. Robbie took her small soft hand in his. "Come on, we have seen all we can see here, let's not brood on what has not happened yet, I think you need to get away from this rock and relax a little."

Rune turned to him and he smiled. "I think a walk in the forest and a picnic would do both of us good."

He felt a deep pleasure as he watched the radiance light her face as she smiled and her eyes danced, slipping her arm round his waist, they both walked off the top of the Lookout and onto the path of loose stones that led them down and back into the woodland, Rune's melancholy lifted as she realised, they would be spending some precious time alone, and she gave a happy giggle as he pulled her close and stopped to lift his bag from the path where he had left it.

The place he had in mind was some distance away, but coming down from the high rock and moving into the trees under the dappled shade made a huge difference to Rune. He walked with his arm round her waist under the trees, he saw how some of her concerns slipped away as she relaxed and enjoyed being close with him. For Robbie it felt a little like old times, and although this was not Loxley, walking slowly along talking reminded him of home.

They followed the brook as it babbled along at their side, and made their way slowly down past the meadows of poppies, and on to a rough grassy trail that wove through the trees until it met back up, where the brook chatted happily under a small carven bridge of pine. Here Robbie turned and followed the brook as the sound of crashing water echoed through the trees, Rune was happy and giggled at his jokes as she rested her head onto his shoulder. "You need a shave." Rune reached up and kissed his cheek.

"I need a bath as well; this heat is driving me nuts, just breathing makes me sweat." Together they walked through the trees in the dappled shade, it felt like it had been years since they had been alone under the trees, and Rune was happy just to have the time away from everything with him. Robbie guided her along the path and soon they came out of the trees onto a wide flat shelf of stone, on the edge of a vast pool surrounded by huge walls and thick trees. On the far side of the pool was a giant waterfall, which dropped from the top of the high cliff into the deep cool pool, Rune gasped at the beauty of the place and stood for a moment to take in the idyllic view of the walls of rock, decorated with heavy clinging vines and masses of brightly coloured flowers.

"Oh Rob, this place is beautiful."

He gave a smile, pleased with his discovery that she obviously adored. "Yeah, Harry told me about it, apparently that is the cliff he fell off when he was being chased by the Cutters, I think if you look hard enough you will find small splatters of blue on the grass where he washed himself clean." Rune gave a giggle as she thought about poor Harry and Robbie's trick to cure him of the white flowers; her excitement bubbled up with her joy.

"Come on let's swim and get clean ourselves." Robbie put down the bag as Rune slid off her top.

"What about the picnic?" She gave a giggle as she dropped her skirt on the rock and turned to the edge of the water.

"We can eat as we dry in the sun, come on." With a happy chuckle, she turned and dived naked into the deep wide pool of cool water, Robbie gave a deep laugh as she rose above the surface ten feet in front of him with a squeal. "It's freezing, but it's wonderful, come on hurry up."

Within minutes both of them were happily swimming in the cold pool, washing away the sweat and grime of the intense heat that had lasted for over a week. Rune came up from under the water in front of him and slid into his arms, her hair was smooth across her head and away from her face, and her eyes shone with her happiness and twinkled with a dazzling sapphire blue. She kissed him slowly and pulled back with a smile, and he saw the girl he loved shine with radiance and her happiness.

Rune looked back over her shoulder and then back at him, she moved closer and kissed him again. "I love you Robbie, come on let's go under the waterfall, I want you to make love to me." She slid back away from him and took his hand, and together they made their way to where the water came crashing down into the pool, and slipped giggling out of sight behind it.

Far away across the vast land of dense green trees, Fagan walked between the two horses carrying Una and Woody, the heat of the day beat down between the gap in the trees above the ancient woodland road, and Woody found the gentle pace in the heat almost hypnotic as he rocked gently backward and forward. Una who had been very surprised to find a task had been set for her talked quietly to Fagan, as Woody half listened opposite her. "But Fagan you must have some idea of what my father had in store for me?" The old man gave a gentle nod.

"I am sorry but I can only tell ye what I already have. He came up to the door one late July evening many, many years ago, he was as wild as a bee who had been robbed of his honey, he took me firmly by the shoulders, and says almost in a gasp, ye must promise never to break this secret he does. Then after drinking most of me Crocus beer, he gives a huge gasp and says, take her to the old house on the lake and tell her to wait for me, but only do it when the clouds are dark and swirling, and the stone has come to the little red one."

"But there must be more, how will I know what he expects of me?" Fagan scratched behind his large ear, and rubbed back a thick tuft of his snow white hair.

"Well, I was as lost as a Willow with his feet in dry sand, and I says to him, well Father Whitelines, what would be the point in that? It's right on the edge of the lake and where no man would ever wander, you see there's the Briar Wood to think of, I mean that place is a jungle, and them trees in there are wild and proper thugs they is. The place is so filled with bog holes and deep pools; no one would ever get out alive if they had not been in before, so I says to him, how can I take her in there alone? It would be like planting a sweet slender Birch in a patch of Bindweed; the poor thing would be swallowed and torn apart in no time." Una looked a little worried as Fagan rambled a bit, she was now more uncertain of her task as Fagan described the place he was taking her too.

"What did my father tell you?" Fagan slowed a little.

"Well, I must say, that's the bit what really foxed me, ye see he just looked up with them bright green eyes filled with more love than a Chestnut when it sees the first leaves come through a Conker, and he says all serious and wizardish, fear not my old friend, for my staff will be her guide and my voice will flow from lands unknown. I got to tell you Lady Violet Eyes, it was as eerie as the moment before the thunder hits the rocks, and proper gave me the wobblers it did. I am not a man that is easily frightened but that just about did it for me it did."

Woody was suddenly very alert, and gave a shudder as he swallowed hard and looked across at Una, she was no comfort, and looked as frightened as he felt.

"This place is err... you know... safe... isn't it?" He watched the trees to his side with a nervous attention, even now below a bright sky filled with sunlight, the woodland looked dark and mysterious under the canopy. Una gave him a small smile.

"We should be safe, after all I trust my father, and I know the love he holds for his children, he would never put any of us in harm's way, would he Master Fagan?" Fagan gave a bright happy smile, and his thick bushy white eyebrows twitched with delight.

"Ye should never fear the trees Master of the Woods, I will lead you through the ancient sleeping fellows onto the Whispering Dunes, and then all ye need to do is cross them to the side of the lake and the old cottage, and ye will see that ye have been blessed to be placed in such a spot. Just ye stay clear of the wood there and ye will be fine. As long as ye keeps clear of them briar ye will find there is plenty of fruit and other foods, just keep ye eyes on the briar, they have teeth like needles, and a grip that is tighter than a soldiers lover, but not so caring if ye gets my meaning?"

Woody gave a vigorous nod, not at all feeling in any way calmer, as Fagan strode with a satisfied smile between them leading them on towards Una's task set her by the old wizard of the Whitelines.

Robbie slid the blade of his knife slowly down his cheek, shaving off the last remnants of the thick stubble, as he watched Rune sat slightly higher up the rock, as she plaited her long fiery red hair in the sunlight. She smiled to herself with contentment and happiness as she wove the strands of hair together and hummed quietly to herself. Her skin was whiter than milk against the lush greens and bright colours of the high wall of plant life across the wide pool, and in the bright sun he could see the faint dusky freckles than ran across her shoulders and down her back onto her slender thighs. He slowly cleaned the knife as he watched her; she was without doubt the most beautiful woman he had ever seen, and in that moment he thought of all she had become in his life since that very first archery lesson.

To him she was the girl he thought the most attractive, the woman he married and the mother of his children, she was small and slender and almost frail looking, and yet he knew that deep down inside her there was a force so strong it could destroy the Earth. It was hard at times to understand that part of her life, but watching her sat naked on the rocks happily drying herself in the sunlight, for the first time he saw the wild natural being that was at one with everything around her.

Here in the land that began her line, he knew he had found the perfect setting for the true vision that was Nature in a human form. In so many ways his life at times felt like madness, and yet just for a brief moment sat on the rocks at the side of the Flow Falls, life away from this place seemed to have stopped, and just for a little while his life was simply that of his and Rune's. He gave a long contented sigh and lay his head back on his pile of clothes, closed his eyes and drifted in his own contentment and happiness, as Rune's soft humming voice echoed around the inside of his head.

It had taken most of the day to reach the woodland Fagan was looking for, and they had turned from the road into a wide valley of very ancient trees. The canopy towered above them, the sunlight dimmed by the vast ceiling of leaves, and in the dappled shade, they walked with their horses across the leaf strewn floor.

For Woody, this was without doubt the most impressive woodland he had ever encountered, and he appeared lost in his thoughts of wonder, as they made their way slowly towards the edge of the tall grassed lands known as the Whispering Dunes. After what felt like the whole day walking, on the outer edge of the woodland, Fagan took the horses and tied them to an old broken branch, this was to be their first camp, and it was here that he would leave them. Woody came out of his dream and began to gather dead wood for a fire, as the old man of the forests gave a reassuring smile to Una.

"Here I must leave ye, for there is much to do as the time draws near." He pointed behind him with a thick fat thumb. "Ye will find a stream and small pond back there, so fill up your bottle and skins before ye leave in the morning, the dunes can be hot at the best of times, but under this sun it will not be easy going."

Una gave a nod as the old man smiled; he lifted his arm to her shoulder as he saw the concern in her eyes. "Fear not, whatever it may be he has in line for ye, I know with all my heart that out of all his children, he thought ye best suited the task." She smiled feeling the warmth and kindness in the old man's heart.

"Thank you, I know you are right." She gave a big sigh of relief. "At least I know the house, although I came from another direction, I only realised when I saw the grasses swaying on the hilltop that I have been here before, it is a little comforting."

It was Fagan who now looked surprised, and his thick bushy eyebrows twitched below his mass of wild white hair.

"Ye have been here before; it is strange that I have no knowledge of this?" Una understood the secret on which she had been included, and yet she knew that in Fagan she could place her trust.

"No one at the time knew, but when I came here it was shortly after the death of Eleanor. I came here with Rhiannon and my mother, we bore her body to its final resting place across the water, I had just given birth to my son." Una gave an embarrassed smile. "His father was a married man and I was a young girl filled with the illusion he painted, my mother thought it best I stay out of public life, and so brought me here to help take care of Eleanor as I had Arthur. I ended up loving the lake so much I stayed on for a short while and it was a good thing in many ways, because while I was safe here Maddy and Mel were both caught by the Dark One." Without realising Fagan suddenly finished Una's sentence.

"When Eve was killed ye mother told ye to remain here longer hidden from her." Una was a little surprised, as at the time no one had known she was here alone with Mac, she could see that there was something going through Fagan's thoughts but was not sure if he was going to share them, she thought that maybe he was offended that he had not been informed and felt she should somehow apologise.

"You do know that at the time you were still in Avalonia working as the Maker? It was Rhiannon who suggested it to my mother, at the time my father had gone missing and we were all worried. When Eleanor was killed and my sister's taken, everyone knew then that it was Morgan who had struck at the heart of the council, and was planning her revenge against those she saw as traitors to her father." Fagan shook his head as if understanding, he had not really got the right to question, Una looked into his old eyes. "Fagan you were not the Keeper at the time." He gave a smile.

"Ye is right and it's not something ye should worry about, just the old mind of an even older man thinking, don't ye fret now, I am at least happy to know that you will pass across to the house with an easy heart. I will leave now and go to the aid of ye friends, good luck, and I will listen to the trees and look to the road for ye returning."

Una watched as the tall old man turned, and with long strides, he soon disappeared into the woodland and out of sight. Woody prepared the camp as she stood still watching the path Fagan had taken, deep down inside she had sensed that there had been something important he had wanted to ask her, and yet he had chosen not to, and for a very strange reason it troubled her.

Robbie lay on his back on the warm rock with his eyes closed. He felt her soft warm skin stroke on his leg as she gave a soft giggle and slid over him, the bright light that burned into his closed eyelids darkened, and he opened them up as Rune slid on to his waist and leaned over looking down at him. Her eyes sparkled with joy and happiness as they danced in the brightest of blue within her pale white face. "Hi gorgeous." He gave her a large smile.

"Hey beautiful." She leaned down and softly kissed him, his arm lifted around her and pulled her closer, as he enjoyed every second holding her soft warm body close to his. It had felt like such a long time since they had been this close and intimate, and he relished the moment. She broke apart and lay on his chest snuggling her head into his shoulder with a happy contented sigh.

"Oh Robbie I have missed this, I wish we did not have to leave and go back to face her, I just want to go home and lie in bed with you, take care of the kids and get some of the life back we have lost." He turned his head and kissed the side of her face.

"We will Runestone, but before that we must finish what we have started, and then we will have eternity together and live out our life deep in the woodland."

"Oh, if only it was that easy. Oh Robbie, I have loved this time with you, but I know that we will have to leave soon and I don't want to go. Just for this one moment in time I have forgotten all the pain and worry of what you have to do. Now I think my heart is going to break as we leave here, it's so beautiful and peaceful, I had almost forgotten where we were." Robbie slid his arm underneath her, he sat up and lifted her on to his lap and held her close, he too had been lost for a moment and now he felt the pressure starting to build again.

"We have maps and plans, and Fagan has something in mind for us, so please wait and see what we have, I do not want you getting yourself all upset Rune. This is the land of Fae, believe me it knows we are trying to help and I know deep inside there is something waiting for the right moment to reveal itself, please Rune trust me, I know I am not wrong." Her eyelashes burned with fiery light as she gazed into his deep brown eyes.

"I do trust you, and I have always believed in your instincts, but you are my love, my husband and my life, there will never be a moment when I am not afraid for you. Robbie you are the Hooded Man, and because of that there will always be something in the shadows, and I will always be looking out for you." He understood, he too felt the same, and he gave a soft squeeze and smiled.

"Come on then, let's get dressed and pack up, we will need to get back before Fagan to prepare for him." Rune slipped off his lap with a sigh, and he watched as she gathered her clothes and began to dress, slowly he packed up the bag with the remains of their picnic, and then slid on his clothes and waited, as Rune walked slowly round having one last look at what had felt like a small slice of paradise for her. When she was ready, he took her hand in his, and together they walked into the trees and headed back to the path, which would take them weaving through the forest, back to the long wooden house where the Specialists waited and prepared for their new orders.

Below the mountain of the Hidden Realm, Opal looked into a deep pan and tried to see if her hunch was right, she stared at the water in hope it would reveal the answer to her thoughts.

"We were not supposed to see further than this time, show me what Gwendolyn did, she cannot have found it, none of us could know what is beyond these days, it was agreed that everyone could only see so far, so what did she know that she would pass on to Sapphire?" She flicked the water and her nail flashed with green light, which bounced up out of the pan and lit her face.

"If you passed it to Sapphire, you were not breaking the rules, but she is not ready and your meddling could have dire consequences, show me what you saw."

The water rippled but nothing appeared, and she gave a gasp of frustration, and took her face away from the pan with a sigh of disappointment. "You and your secrets, we are on the same side and yet all of you have hidden your ways from us. You learned nothing that's why the Fae almost died out, will you and Rhiannon never realise? Bloody stubborn fairies, you will be the death of us all one day."

CHAPTER TWENTY SEVEN

COMPLETING THE CIRCLE

The arrival at the Lockup caused quite a stir, Martin had served there briefly, so he was quite accustomed to the place, and although he was unaware of it, the Sage as Lord William had been there with him. For the rest of the group, it came as a huge surprise, as they stood on the edge of what looked like miles and miles of metal boxes stacked ten high. For as far as the eye could see, row upon row of steel containers had been stacked and filled with the valuables and the ill-gotten gains of the Cutters.

Sapphire felt the cold tingle run down her spine, as her bright blue eyes scanned the scene. "Is this place safe? And just where the hell are we?" Silas wore a huge smile as he looked up at the towering heights of steel with wide excited eyes.

"Who cares, this place is paradise, sealed and contained just waiting to be picked over." Martin gave a small laugh as he walked up to the side of Sapphire; Ben was stood in awe as he looked on the scene next to the Sage.

"This is the safest place in this country, although I wouldn't get your hopes up just yet Commander, this is the deserted sector, most of these are empty awaiting the arrival of more stock. This place is a massive storage depot for Mason, this is where every bit of scrap and salvage has been brought and sorted for over twenty years, it's known as Area Eight, although over the years it has been referred to by those who know of it as Mason's Lockup." Sapphire glanced sideways at him.

"Yeah, but just where about are we exactly?"

"Oh yeah, sorry." Martin turned and pointed just off to his left. "About two miles that way use to be Eastbourne." His arm swung to the right. "Over there was Brighton and then Worthing, all of this was once pretty much seaside and fishing places, London is behind us, we are not that far from the coast, as you can see by the Seagulls." Sapphire watched the sky as the birds flew up and swirled around each other.

"So why are we here?"

The Sage with his arm in a sling walked up behind them. "We need to hole up and re-evaluate just exactly what we are going to do next; Mason has got the upper hand for the moment, although he has very little left in the way of supplies. This place is safer than anywhere else; I thought it would be a good place to make camp and rest up until we have another plan of action." Silas turned.

"Like what? Look at us, we have hardly any weapons and there is just eight of us." The Sage nodded, yet behind his mask of white birch, his eyes gave a very reassuring twinkle.

"I know, but believe me more will join us, there is support for the Hooded Man everywhere, and when those people see what is happening, they will seek us out Commander, have a little faith for even though we have suffered a great defeat, what has been lost shall return by other routes."

His voice was soft and yet carried a tone of authority, and just for a moment it was as if something had struck a deep chord with Sapphire, she felt a strange tingle inside and turned to him with a questioning look on her face, her voice was low as if asking something she wanted only him to hear.

"You have seen something haven't you?" He gave her a soft smile.

"Your circle is forming Saff, and there is other work intended for you, go to Avon and return here with the Outlaws, and when you have finished return to Opal, Rune was right to send you here, but now is your time and you must prepare, go... Time for the moment is not on our side, you must be ready when the moment comes." The tingles inside her increased and she gave a shudder.

"Will you not tell me, or at least give me an idea of what it is you have seen?" He shook his head slowly.

"That is not my task or my place, trust me and you will be fine, all I will say is it's time for you to stop doubting yourself and become what you have always known inside, put aside your past and your fears, and walk into your destiny with happiness and confidence that is all I can tell you, except that from now on you will become a centre of your own."

She gave a sigh and flicked her long auburn ponytail over her shoulder. "You have been spending way too much time alone with Opal; you are starting to sound like her."

He gave a happy laugh as Sapphire opened up her round blue window; she turned and looked back at him. "What is it with mystics and seers, why doesn't anyone talk straight? You know it would save a hell of a lot of buggering about, and would make things so much simpler." Her ears rung with his hearty laugh, as she stepped through the window, and back into New Avon in search of the large scruffy Outlaws.

The day had been quiet in London, the shelling had stopped, and the dust settled as the soldiers of Mason Knox combed over the area, which was just piles of burning rubble after the intensive bombardment. Mason felt a little uneasy, his encounter the previous night with his son had caused him to lose a lot of sleep, and instead of going to his room to sleep, he had sat in his chair as the flames across the river flickered on his closed windows.

For most of the day reports had been arriving from all his military units, and although he had tried to concentrate, his mind kept going back to his son.

The reports confirmed the full extent of the damage done to his factories and stores, he carefully checked what he had lost, and he knew that Billy had been serious about attempting to stop him. He gave a sigh and sat back in his seat, his blue eyes set in his lined face appeared older than they had when he had left York, and he could not help but feel the disappointment within him. His son was now an enemy, although as far as he could tell, his identity was still a secret, he looked down at the papers on his desk, and the order that was to condemn the Sage for his treason, without sitting forward he lifted the brass stamp off the pad of red ink and with more force than normal, he plunged it down with a heavy thump on the paper.

He lifted it up to reveal the stamped seal of a red dragon that officially confirmed the papers, and warranted the death of his son. It had not been an easy decision, but after all Billy had given him no other choice, he placed the stamp back on the pad and lifted the paper and dropped it into the out goings tray. The paper below it carried the emblem of the messenger at Lincoln and he lifted it up to read.

Holding the paper in his hand, Mason got up from his seat and walked across the room to where a wide silver bowl sat on a carved ornate stand, and gave off a strange fine stream of coloured smoke. Mason pinched some red powder from a small stone bowl and sprinkled it into the wide basin; dark smoke swirled up in front of his eyes and formed into a rough image of a face. Slowly the smoke thickened and two dark red eyes glared back at him from a cold cruel face, the voice was high and contained no aspect of caring.

"What? I am busy, can this not wait?" Mason looked equally as unemotional at his mother.

"No, it cannot, and I would like to add that I too have much to do." Her expression changed although it looked equally as cool.

"What do you want Mason is there more trouble?"

"No Mother, I have everything under control, actually we have eliminated our problem in London, although it appears we have a problem building in Lincoln, which is why I am contacting you." Her eyes narrowed as she studied her son.

"What has the bishop done now? Don't tell me, that fool of a monk has failed?" She gave a laugh that was very high and almost a shriek, Mason knew how much she hated the monks crawling all over the place as they organised the building of their new monastery. "I told you didn't I? That fat greedy fool should have gone personally to deal with the bishop." Mason hated her being right, but he knew it was pointless to argue.

"The new council of the church has not been announced yet, but it will soon, and if my source inside is right, it will support the new king if they crown him, just you make sure he does not leave that place." Morgan gave a sly smile, which gave her a slightly pained expression.

"He will go nowhere, I have everything in hand and I am preparing as I speak to you, fear not my son, when he slips out from under the trees, I will have him like a rabbit in a trap. By one means or another, the only way he will return to Loxley is in a box."

"Make sure he does, the last thing I need now is to have a church rally the masses with hope to the leaf lover and this boy king."

"It's taken care of fear not. What do you want to do about the monks?" Mason gave a flick of his head, as he flicked his long white hair backwards over his shoulder away from the smoke.

"Do what you will with them, just make sure that not a stone is laid, our fat little friend will have to look elsewhere if he wants to survive the woodland witches, I have withdrawn my support." The eyes of Morgan le Fey seem to grow with excitement at the thought of removing the source of her irritation as she planned.

"Good I will deal with them and fear not, for not one will leave here, I shall enjoy some sport before my games with the leaf lover begin." Mason gave her a nod.

"Alright Mother, I am going to finish up here and then head back to York, I think it is time we began the last phase of the removal of that pile of logs, I will talk to you tomorrow."

"Until then my Son." Mason lifted some yellow powder from another bowl and dropped in into the basin, with a small puff, the smoke broke apart and his mother vanished.

Mason turned from the basin and looked at the half open door, behind which the sounds of men moving around and talking quietly slipped in. "JONES!" There were hurried steps and the newly appointed general appeared at the door.

"You called My Lord?"

"Yes... Gather together all your commanders, and get the despatch riders for the garrisons at Area Thirteen and Fourteen at Birmingham, we will be activating the next phase of the plans, so I want everyone here with me in one day, I leave for York after I have briefed them."

"Yes My Lord." The door slid closed as the general disappeared, and Mason moved to the stand and lifted the whiskey decanter to pour a glass before consulting his maps and notes.

It was early evening, the sun was still bright and burning in the sky above the Forest of Time, although over Avalon the thick mass of swirling black cloud had sunken lower and most of the realm was in shade, as the high wall of the Citadel Mount slowly disappeared into it. Rune laughed and giggled with her happiness as she skipped along the path holding Robbie by the hand into the wide clearing around the long wooden hut of Fagan.

On the grass most of the group were busy, in Robbie's absence Rowan who was walking much better, had gathered everyone together and told them to check their weapons and supplies, to prepare for moving out. Blades sat smiling sharpening her swords, and winked as Rune walked up with her radiant smile, Robbie wandered over to Rowan who stood by the door and smiled as he approached, Rune walked across the grass to speak with some of the others.

"Rune looks very happy; I take it sometime alone has done both of you some good?" Robbie came up the steps.

"I think both of us needed it, thanks Rowan." Rowan slapped his shoulder.

"Glad to help, it's about time you took a little time out for her, you spend too much time trying to organise everything, after all the both of you have been through it's important you don't lose sight of what you are to each other."

Rowan entered through the door with him, as Robbie dropped his bag. Maggs was busy with Crystal preparing a meal, Jade and Steph sat at the table looking over a very detailed map Fagan had provided of the Citadel tunnels. The map was much larger and far more detailed than the one Merlin had sketched, and it was very clear from the way he had colour coded each different level that he knew the mount better than anyone else. Jade glanced through her long fringe at Robbie.

"What exactly are we going to do in these tunnels Robbie? Because from what I can see, Amethyst is protected by the Mirrored Waters, and the Dark One could be anywhere inside there?" It was a good question and one that had occupied most of his thoughts for days.

"Fagan has a plan that might just help; I take it he is not back yet?" Steph shook her head.

"Not yet... where has he taken Una, have you any idea what he is up to, because her keen sense for danger could be a life saver in those tunnels?" Rowan sat down at one of the chairs and rubbed his leg.

"Hornet is our key there, she will sense her quicker than any of us, and with Rune on watch I think we can say we will be very well covered."

"I am not worried about Le Fey, eventually she will come out into the open to confront us, she thinks she has the upper hand, it's her soldiers that bother me. From what I can tell they are everywhere, no my worry is that they have massively superior numbers, to be honest in the tunnels we will be safer, because it will restrict what they can throw at us." Robbie seemed more confident than any of them; Steph felt more than a little unsure.

"I hope you are right Robbie, it was no picnic last time, if anything I would say it was the hardest fight we have ever had, there just wasn't enough room to move." Robbie nodded his head as he looked at the map made of many colours.

"That is just what I am hoping for, if we exploit it right, we could create our own advantage." Steph and Jade both looked up at him, and he turned and smiled. "Hey, trust me I'm a woodsman."

Deep within her cleared circle in the Hidden Realm, Opal worked fast muttering to herself. "It's not possible, they always said it could not be done, Oh Gwendolyn you should have been more careful and given these things more thought." Opal suddenly stopped and straightened up; it was as if she felt something in the air. For a moment she stood frozen and then in an instant she sprang back into action. "It's too soon, she is not ready." Her words whispered to herself as she stretched out her arm and clicked her fingers, and the pot on its stand above the fire disappeared, and the small moss covered humps slowly sank back into the floor.

For a moment she fussed and fidgeted, and then she felt the presence of Sapphire as she came up the path, towards the thick band of trees that grew around her glade. Opal took a deep breath and tried to compose herself, she was worried but did not want it to show when the nervous girl arrived.

Sapphire had eventually found all of the Outlaws, who had been doing whatever they could to help out with Rafe; she had then taken them with supplies and new weapons to meet up with the Sage at the Lockup. The Sage and his group had quickly checked the area was indeed as safe as it had been previously, and then set up a small camp using three of the empty large steel containers.

Sapphire did not wait, once she was certain everything was alright, she handed Rafe a small blue dragonfly pendant which he could use to call her back if they got into trouble, and then she opened her new window and walked through to Cal, who stood patiently waiting in the deep thicket down the path from Opal's Glade.

When Sapphire entered the open area, Opal stood robed in white looking calm and relaxed with a bright smile to greet her, Saff felt a sudden sense of calmness as Opal waved to the old stump. "Come Child, for it is time to sit and talk, for there is much that we must now organise as the forming of your circle approaches."

Sapphire still felt unsure about herself being the centre of a circle of power, but somehow having Opal as a guide helped her relax a little, after all hadn't Opal aided Rune through her transformation? She crossed the wide circle of grass and sat down on the log; Opal sat beside her and took both of Saff's hands in hers. "There is much we must discuss as it appears the time is closer than any of us thought, and on this day your circle will become complete."

Sapphire gave a little frown. "I know it will probably sound silly, but all this talk of my circle is confusing and no one seems to be able to tell me clearly what is going to happen." Opal gave a broad smile and her voice lowered to a gentle and soothing tone.

"You will be centre to a circle of five, as most of us only command five others, Runestone is the exception, as she was able to create a new line of power, and the Violet Circle contained within the Violetlines is the centre of many circles, of which one will be yours, and so she will remain your centre. Actually, if you think about it, it is a very good thing, because that means she will always be with you to guide you." Sapphire nodded understanding.

"I get that, but what I want to know is why does it have to be now? I mean if I am going to be the centre, then why can I not form it when I feel more prepared?" Opal gave a smile as she remembered asking her own mother the very same question when it came to forming the Table of Life; she gave Sapphire's hands a squeeze.

"Before we begin you need to understand the fuller picture, and I will tell you in as simple a way as I know how. Firstly, we have now entered into the Age of Dreams, and it is very important that you understand that, because there have been three other ages prior to it. The Age of Power was the time when all was created, and then came the Age of Knowledge, and the Ruling Council took what it had created and learned from it, and passed their knowledge into all of their creations, and so men and the Fae learned all of the ways to live together within all of the realms that were made." Sapphire nodded as Opal spoke; this was something she had learned alone with her mother on Callanish, Opal gave a smile seeing that Saff was following.

"During the Age of sleep most of the council were imprisoned as you know, and the evil Morgan took control of man and corrupted all he had learned, to a certain degree some of this was seen coming and we did what we could to prepare, for we all knew a time would come when a lost kings line would return to undo her evil and balance the world again. More importantly though, what we did not know, was when exactly it would happen, and what would come after." Sapphire was surprised.

"But you had some of the best seers; surely someone must have an idea?" Opal shook her head.

"I have doubted many things, but I am certain that in this I am right, Sapphire of Callanish, you are the one chosen to see the future and lead the way forward from this point on. I believe it because of a very precious and special gift given to Gwendolyn, and she was told that you were to follow her, and in doing so she found a way to help everyone. The fact you can recite the rhyme written before her birth confirms it, as none of us could see past this time. The White Lord Albanlin who invented the notion of time, made it very clear that when the time came our powers would diminish, and we would pass our gifts on to others. I am sorry to say Child that all we can do now is speculate using the wisdom we have gained. Our time is over and the time of Runestone, Jade, Amethyst and yourself is upon us, it is within all of you that the eyes of the future are now contained. All that I know is that Gwendolyn marked you with a very powerful gift, and if I am right, it was a gift she was given, but even in that I cannot be completely sure. I have tried hard to see what will come, but all I can see is what is happening now and what has been, you are now the future, and it is in the forming of your circle that others will be bonded to you, and with you, they will see what is to come."

"But I do not know who they are, and I have no way of knowing, so how can I form a circle?" Opal smiled as Sapphire gave a long desperate sigh.

"I do not think it is that hard to work out, and as it forms, the circle will bond you in a way that you will know the moment it is created, you already know that Iona the coming queen of Fae will be part of it, and if I am not wrong Jessica Sapphire will certainly play her part, as to the others I can only speculate."

"But they are just babies, how can they help me?"

"Sapphire you must understand, that once the circle is formed, it is their existence that matters not their age, look at how Iona has helped both Treen and Robbie, you were there at Gwendolyn's circle, did you not see a woman of great power rise from the table, even though you knew she was a child at home in her crib in Loxley?" Sapphire gave a small laugh.

"I still have no idea how Iona could do that, I saw it with my own eyes, and yet it made no sense at all."

"You are from the line of the White Circle with a special gift given by its queen, I am Green Circle and although I have gifts you will never hold, your line of Fae have gifts also. We both have the power to wield the magic, and to many it will make no sense to them, but either way we have that ability and you like all of us, will learn its secrets and learn to use it with authority. The thing that makes me smile is that Iona could only ever learn to do that by being taught by her greatest teacher." Sapphire gave her a surprised look.

"Who could teach her that, do you think they could teach me?" Opal gave a hearty chuckle.

"Oh my Sweet Child she was taught how to do it by her centre, how else could she learn such a deeply kept secret of the Fae?"

"What?" Opal could only chuckle more at the look of stunned disbelief on Sapphire's face. "But I have no idea how she did it, how can I teach her something I don't even know?"

"Your circle has not formed yet, but when it does you will find with it will come secrets hidden inside you at birth, it has been the same for Runestone who has had many things inside her awoken by her table." Sapphire slumped slightly and gave a deep sigh.

"She is lucky enough to have one, I have no idea at all how to get mine out or even build it."

"You have your table already Child, I have told you, it's around your neck on the talisman given you by your centre." She lifted her pendant and looked at it; Opal gave a soft smile and leaned forward taking the pendant carefully in her fingertips.

"This is a table of extreme quality and power, it has been made by Runestone

Sapphire the direct descendant of life herself, and I might add the most powerful of our line. I think the time has come for you to face your destiny and begin the start of your circle, for it must start today." Sapphire suddenly looked scared.

"Will you show me what to do?" Opal stood up and offered her hand.

"It would have been nice to have taken my time in teaching you more, but that is no longer possible, events are turning in unexpected ways and we must act for now is the time, only you can do this, but I will guide you to the best of my knowledge. I would however warn you now, my powers have diminished greatly since Runestone replaced me, and so we may need her help, which will mean we may have to walk unseen into another realm. Fear not for I will help you to do that."

Sapphire stood up nervously and took Opal's hand, and together they stood beside the old fallen log. Sapphire removed her chain and slid the pendant given her by Rune off the chain; she took a deep breath and looked to Opal.

"Ok... How are we going to do this?" Opal lifted her own hood and then slipped the dark blue hood of Sapphire's up over her head.

"The light will be bright, but you must ignore it and focus on your pendant. The table cannot be made until Runestone commands it, but after, you will only have to think and let it fall at your feet and it will appear. Focus only on your pendant and allow the forces within you to come forth, I will take the lead and tell you when to release what is contained within you." Sapphire nervously nodded her head, and tried very hard to keep her hands from shaking, Opal moved close to her side and raised her left hand and swept it across in front of them. "I am Opal of the Green Circle, and guide to the white, hear me and obey me."

Sapphire felt the ground vibrate beneath her feet, and swallowed hard as she wobbled slightly, for a brief moment she felt her eyes blur, and then right in front of her on the outer edge of the circle, the ground erupted and where the grass split and the soil parted, a tall pillar of stone rose out of the ground creating a huge column. To her right another began to rise and she turned slightly feeling afraid, the warm hand of Opal took hers and held it firmly. "Have no fear we have to replicate our destination, it's quite exciting really, it will feel like having a holiday."

If she had not been so nervous and frightened, she may have laughed, but her legs shook more violently, and she was not entirely sure if it was the other stone columns appearing out of the floor, or her legs quaking in fear. The huge stones rumbled to a halt, and everything went totally silent, Sapphire could hear her heart pounding deep inside her head, and she knew it was fear as her legs continued to shake. Opal smiled at the sight of the large stones all situated around the outer edge of her glade.

"I must admit I really like this; I wonder if I could keep them here permanently? It adds a little character to the place." Sapphire was unsure if she was kidding, the stones must have weighed tons, and yet Opal who had told her that her power was diminished had raised them with a wave of her hand.

"You know I hate saying this, but you can be really scary when you use your powers." Opal gave a chuckle.

"Command of the earth is a gift of the Green Circle, believe me in a year or two, you will achieve greater feats with a flick of your wrist."

"Ok... so what now?" Opal squeezed her hand gently.

"Now we use some real power."

"What... Like that wasn't enough?" Opal shrugged.

"Runestone cannot come to us, so we go to her, this is where we walk unseen, have no fear for in a way we will remain here, but to everyone else that meets us, we will be very solid to them, it's not unsimilar to when you walk here in your dreams."

Sapphire clutched tighter to the pendant and tried her hardest not to worry about what was happening around her, the stones all around her began to glow with a silvery white aura, Opal lifted her arm again and clicked her fingers hard, the loud snap echoed, and feeling the fear rise inside herself, Sapphire dropped her head and looked at the floor.

The grass had gone and she was stood on a smooth surface of the brightest gleaming white. The light flooded up out of the ground and she screwed up her eyes and squinted. The cool surface of the floor turned blue and she let her eyes open a little as she lifted her head and looked across to the stones. The blue was instantly recognisable as it was the bright sapphire blue twenty pointed star of Rune's table. Her eyes opened wider as she saw the star set in a white disk begin to rise slipping slowly up her legs, her boots were gone from sight as it rose slowly into the air and her heart began to beat faster.

Clutching tighter to Opal's hand, she could only watch as the table rose slowly up her chest absorbing everything, she stretched her neck as it approached her face and felt the tension stiffen her whole body. Holding her breath, it came slowly on to her face and her head tilted slightly, but she knew there was no way to avoid it or stop it. She could not understand why she was afraid, after all this was her centre's table and she had always been protected by it. It came slowly over her cheeks and she wanted to scream, her eyes exploded with bright blue light and the table passed her eyes and she disappeared below it into a blinding world of the purest white light, she snapped her eyes shut as the light burned into them, and she felt her knees buckle.

The cool surface of the floor chilled her knees, as her legs gave way, and she collapsed still holding tightly onto Opal, she gasped in fresh air as she began to breathe again, and felt the tears roll down her cheeks from her stifled eyes. The front of her hood tugged forward and she opened her eyes as the blurred hazy image of Opal appeared at her side. "Give it a moment and let your eyes clear Child we have arrived."

Sapphire took another giant gasp of air, and lifted her head, which was pounding in rhythm with her heart. "Where are we?" Her throat was dry and it was hard to talk, she opened her eyes and could see nothing but white light all around her. Opal came into focus and smiled.

"You are sitting in the circle of my mother in Avalon, only those who enter the circle can see you, to everyone outside nothing has changed. Do not fear Child we are protected more here than anywhere else." She pointed to the sky. "Have a look and see for yourself."

Sapphire's senses returned slowly, and she felt the soft warm grass on her hand, as she lifted her head, she could see the giant circle that was much bigger than the one in Opal's glade surrounded her. Between the stones it was like fine net curtains had been hung, through which she could see the vague shapes and colours of the trees. She lifted her head and slid back her hood, and followed Opal's finger as she looked up. High above her was the star of Rune's table, which had sealed the roof of the open circle giving it almost an opaque window like appearance. Opal released Saff's hand and stood up. "Right, that for now is my bit over with, all you have to do now is summon Rune, I think considering it's been over a thousand years since I was last home, I shall take a little peak and see how the place is doing."

"WHAT? You're not going to leave me, are you?" Opal gave her a soft gentle smile.

"My part is played; remember I am the past and you and your equals are the future, you are safe here and Runestone is aware of you for she prepared this. Take the pendant and give it a squeeze and she will come to you." Opal turned and walked through the curtain out of the circle.

Back in the Forest of time Rune took Judith by the hand. "Walk with me for there are things we must do."

Judith got up off the floor from where she had been cleaning her bow, and Rune took her gently by the hand, and walked slowly with her into the trees, there was a flash of bright purple light.

Fagan stood on the road in the hot sun and wiped his brow on his old black neck wrap, the air was changing and he sensed it. He looked up at the edges of the trees all around him and sniffed the air as his white bushy eyebrows twitched, his eyes moved to the upper branches of the towering Beech. "Aye, I feel it, there is change in the air and no mistake, and ye keep your roots firm, it's not going to disadvantage ye. Aye if anything I would say things is moving faster than even we thought, still it's going to be a change for the better in my book, ye watch the skies and let me know."

He rolled his neck wrap up and slid it back round his collar and tucked it in below the shirt. "I best make tracks, things is going to get a bit ruffled from now on." And with a slight jump to his stride, he moved off along the track at a much faster pace.

Sapphire waited nervously rubbing the pendant between her fingers, even though Opal had promised she would be safe, she could not help but feel exposed. She stood on the grass and stared at the wall of trees blurred and obscured behind the stones where Opal had disappeared, but there was no longer any sign of her. The walls began to shimmer in the softest of violet light, and she gave a happy sigh of relief, Rune walked out of the bright burst of violet accompanied by Judith, and gave her a smile. "Greetings Cousin."

"Oh Rune." Saff swept across the circle and pulled her into a tight hug. "It's so good to see you safe." Rune squeezed her hard.

"We are all fine; it's nice to see you too, now come we must prepare for your circle is forming and you will have need of those who surround you."

Rune released Sapphire who gave Judith a hug, and then she walked into the centre of the circle, Sapphire gave a brief sigh of relief seeing that Judy looked just as nervous as she did. Rune stood in the centre of the circle and looked at them both stood waiting for her to talk them through whatever was about to happen.

"Sapphire, Judith has been placed at my table and protected by it, she was tied to me as her centre, but her line has gifts that are more attributed to your table, and so I will release her to the table of sight, and she will be the first of the five you will place." Sapphire went to speak but Rune continued. "She will remain by my side and under my protection, and as with yourself she will remain seated at my table, for the Violet Circle binds all in my care including the tables that will form all around it." Sapphire looked at Judy who gave her a nod and a smile, she turned to Rune.

"So my table will not be the only table in your circle?" Rune smiled and pointed to the large stone pillar in front of her, both Judith and Sapphire turned to look. "I am the Violetlines and all will respond to my call to connect and build a power of the good, there are those who will join as those who already exist have joined within me."

The large pillar in front of them gave a slight shimmer, and out of the stone as if carved in light, a symbol appeared of a bright white star. "The Lord Albanlin has granted us his allegiance, and so has my grandfather of the woodland realm." On the next pillar the symbol of a white stag appeared, the next one revealed the circle of life of Opal, and then the table of swords appeared on the column at its side. Rune turned as more symbols appeared. "The table of Amethyst has already gained allegiance, although she has yet to claim it, as has the table at Carnac which has recognised Treen as its new mistress." On the next pillar a circle set with a golden tree on a violet background appeared. "The Queen of Fae shall come in time as will that of my sister." A green table with a white star on it appeared, and in the centre of the star a green hazy circle drew itself. Rune turned back to Sapphire. "As you can see we are one short, and that is the place for you to make your allegiance, will you form your table and join us Sapphire of the White Circle?"

Sapphire stared at the empty pillar. "I am not sure I am ready and I have no idea who will join with me, but as my centre you will always have my support and full allegiance." Rune gave a nod.

"Then it is done, come bring me your pendant." Rune lifted her hood and gave Judy the signal to do likewise, and Sapphire walked over to her and held up the pendant in her sweaty hand. Rune took it and then took Sapphire's hand and held it out flat; she kissed the pendant and then placed it into the centre of Saff's hand. "Welcome my sweet sister, join with me and open the gifts of your line in aid of White Circle and those you defend."

The circle flooded with violet light and Judy fell to her knees as Sapphire screamed with fear, Judy looked up in the air where Sapphire rose spread eagled against the background of the twenty pointed star. Light flowed out from her eyes and filled the circle as she wailed in pain, and Judy slumped to the ground and buried her face in the grass as the wails grew louder. Violet light swirled around the inside edge of the circle and then erupted up into the air and entered into Sapphire who shook violently. Rune had disappeared into the mass of swirling light as Sapphire's wails echoed in Judy's ears. She pushed her face into the grass and shook with terror, trying to block out the fear and pain she now felt as Sapphire connected with her, and she became a part of the table of sight. Her tears dripped onto the grass as she sniffled afraid to lift her head, when she felt a soft hand move her hood and touch her face.

"Judy... Hey it's OK it's over now." Judy lifted her head slightly, and saw the soft white leather of Sapphire's boot; she slowly sat up and looked into the bright blue slightly flickering eyes of Sapphire. "I am sorry you were frightened; please do not cry I am fine honestly." Judy lunged forward, and pulled Saff into a tight hug.

"I felt the terror and pain." Sapphire stroked her hair softly.

"It is fine, it was a little scary but I understand now, come on it's all over and you have nothing to fear." Sapphire stood up and lifted her back onto her feet, Judy looked round to see Rune smiling back at her, and on the pillar of stone behind her was the symbol of a white round disk surrounded by a violet ring, and on the disk was a bright blue five pointed star, Rune smiled and looked back at it.

"The Violet Circle is complete, we are all one, bound together in our quest to strengthen the Violetlines." Rune walked over to them and embraced Judy, Sapphire looked at Rune.

"So, what happens now?" Rune reached down and lifted Sapphire's hand and opened it, the pendant was as it always had been depicting the symbol of the dragonfly. She turned it over and the back had changed, it no longer carried the golden flower on a violet background, it now had the blue star set in white contained within a fine violet ring. She lifted it up and on the palm of Sapphire's hand was a blue star.

"As your table forms the points of the star will disappear." Rune touched the top point and it began to fade. "Judith is now at one with you, and my daughter joined with you in the cave, although you were not aware of it at the time." The second point of the star began to fade, followed by the third, Saff looked up at Rune.

"Three have gone, but that is only two I know of." Rune gave a smile.

"Jessica Sapphire is aware as we speak and the process to connect her was started by me, you must sit here and wait for the return of my grandmother, and as you do, concentrate on the star, then the other two will be revealed to you, by the end of this day your circle will be complete. I have to return now and so must you, for this time has come sooner than any of us saw, and the reason has not been revealed to any of us yet. Complete your circle and prepare, for soon your destiny will call to you, go with a happy heart my sweet sister for the world will open before your eyes, and you will see all that are beautiful, which will heal your heart and calm your feelings."

Rune took Judith by the hand and walked to the edge of the circle, Sapphire stood staring at the pendant and her palm lost in thought. Rune stepped into the misty curtain and Opal smiled.

"It is done, what have you learned?" Opal placed a small white daisy into Rune's hand.

"We will talk soon, I will wait here a moment longer for her to connect, go for it is not safe for you outside of the circle, come and see me when it is done." Rune leaned forward and kissed her grandmother on the cheek.

"Return safely and we will speak, thanks for helping her." Opal hugged Rune tightly.

"I will always help where I can, keep safe and stay as far from that star as you can, never forget she knows many tricks as well as her magic."

"I won't, I love you." With a burst of bright light Rune and Judy disappeared, and Opal waited as she watched Sapphire sit down on the grass and concentrate on her hand.

In the long wooden house in the Forest of Time, Rowan and Robbie had all of their maps spread across the table as Jade and Steph looked on. Rowan followed the lines in different colours across the map and he looked up at Robbie. "This could well be what we are looking for; this mine is about fifteen minutes outside the forest and tree lined. All we have to do is get into this mine and the tunnel runs under the lake all the way to the back of the Citadel Mount and the start of the Mirrored Lake."

Robbie followed the line with his eyes; Jade stood on her tiptoes and leaned over the table to see. Jade gave a gasp and slipped back holding her stomach.

"Owwww!" She took a deep breath as Rowan turned looking concerned; she slid back to the edge of the table, and leaned on it as she gasped again in pain. Steph gripped her and looked at her.

"Jade what is the matter?" Rowan slid down the table and took hold of her.

"What is it tell me?" She screwed up her face and clutched her stomach.

"Owwww... Oh Rowan it hurts make it stop." Fear crossed his face as he looked to Steph for answers.

"What is wrong with her?" Jade lifted her knee to her stomach as she bent forward in pain.

"Oh.... Owwww.... Oh, it hurts.... Rowan, please make it stop."

She nuzzled in pain clenching her teeth, as he pulled her closer and held her as tight as he could. Robbie could do little but watch feeling her pain with Steph unable to do anything. Rowan was quickly filling with panic, as he tried to hold her close as muffled gasps of pain came from his chest, where Jade now buried her head. His heartbeat increased as the panic flooded up inside him, his eyes met Robbie's and almost pleaded with him.

"What's happening Robbie? What the hell do I do, what is doing this to her?" It was Rune's voice that answered from the doorway.

"Do nothing and it will pass?" His head jerked towards her.

"What do you mean do nothing; can you not see she is in agony?" Rune stepped into the room where Maggs and Maddy both had stopped and were watching, Crystal stood smiling in the corner gently nodding as if she understood something. Rune lifted Jade out of Rowan's arms, and turned her round, she pushed her hand on to Jade's stomach and smiled as Jade relaxed, and a soft violet light glowed around Rune's hand.

"Is that better?" Jade gave a gasp and breathed in.

"Oh much.... What the hell was that?" She slid to the floor and breathed a deep sigh of relief. Rune gave a broad smile as she looked up to Rowan and then back at Jade.

"That was your daughter telling you she has become connected to the table of sight, quite an achievement for a two week old." Rowan stared at Rune as Jade gave her a double take.

"What.... Oh no no no.... not yet.... I am not ready yet Rune, how can I...?" Rune smiled, as she nodded and Jade's words faded, as she fully understood the moment. "But how?" Robbie gave a mighty laugh as he slapped Rowan on the back.

"How... my god I am amazed the way you two have been at it you don't have ten already." Rowan slipped to his knees at the side of Jade, he looked stunned as she turned to face him.

"It is alright isn't it...? I mean you will be a daddy like Robbie is." Rowan snatched her into his arms, pulled her close, and hugged her tighter than he ever had before. Rune smiled and looked up at Robbie with tears in her eyes, and he nodded with a smile, she understood. Maddy sniffled and wiped her eyes on her apron and Maggs beamed with delight and her hair sparkled with beads and feathers as she shook with joy, her jewellery rattling in tune.

"Oh how groovy and wonderful. Oh the road of womanhood is so cosmic and karma filled, I feel the world filled with an aura of wonderment and happiness around us, we are all truly blessed... Oh I must find my Harry Pops and give him the tidings of this blessed event." With that she gave a skip and rattled off through the door her jewellery playing a soft melody.

At the very same moment deep inside the cave below the Citadel Mount, Amethyst swooned and gripped the back of the chair, she too felt the pains of a daughter who was to connect with the table of sight, and James held her in his arms a look of concern on his face. It soon turned to a smile, as a maid rushed across the room, and looked Amethyst deep in the eyes, and then with a proud smile, gave her the good news that there would be an heir to the throne of the crystal kingdom. James danced with delight as the old servant knelt at the foot of the chair and helped her ease the momentary cramps.

Opal smiled as she turned to Sapphire, who watched the last point of the star on her hand fade. "It is done, now we return." Sapphire gave a deep sigh of relief and looked up at the sky above her.

"Hey look, Rune's table has changed, it's no longer blue, it's purple." The sapphire coloured twenty pointed star set with a decorative runic R of platinum in its centre glowed in a bright violet. Opal gave a nod and took Sapphire by the hand.

"The circle is complete and the Violetlines now command everything, she no longer has need of blue now Child, that task has now passed onto you." Opal lifted her arm and waved it, and the table of Runestone dropped to the earth and disappeared, leaving only the ancient stone circle set in the trees on the banks of the dried up lake in Avalon. The air was still and hot and there was no sound from any living creature, the old stones stood proudly facing each other across the large circle of grass, as if waiting for some moment of great importance.

CHAPTER TWENTY EIGHT

FINAL TASKS

The visit to the stone circle by Rune, Saff and Judy, had not gone unnoticed, but the protections within the sacred stones had hidden them safely. At the moment when Sapphire had risen into the air, a massive burst of bright violet light had streamed down from the sky into the circle. On the nearby Queens Road, monks had jumped from their carts in fear and scattered onto the fields, they fled screaming in the opposite direction of the woodland containing the sacred circle. The soldiers in Avalonia had watched the thick black clouds in the sky sweep aside as if they feared the bright violet light, and it had worried them a great deal, the rumours of the Violet Witch were not easily brushed aside. Morgan le Fey had been below the ground when the ritual to complete the Violet Circle began. She had felt the power flare up inside her as a feeling of creeping coldness, and had rushed to the summit of the mount, where she had instructed her vile Houlen to attack. The creatures rushed into the sky, but it was more out of fear for their mistress, as even they feared to fly into the violet light that hurt their eyes, and filled them with a cold icy fear. Morgan screamed at the top of the mount, but it was to no avail as the bright light pulsed down from the sky into the circle, a place she knew that even she could not enter. When the light went out and the clouds of black swirled back in above the circle, she scanned the whole of Avalon looking for the source of the power, but there was nothing to detect, which was a cause of great concern. She was not sure how Rune had arrived and left undetected and it did bother her, as she slowly made her way back to the great hall where she was preparing for the battle that would inevitably arrive.

Back in the Glade of Opal, Sapphire felt a little dizzy, suddenly her mind had opened and connected with the five members of her circle, and although she still had many questions, as her thoughts mixed with the many pictures that had flashed into it, she swooned slightly and Opal steadied her.

"It has taken a lot of your strength, come Child and sit for a moment, I will prepare food and I think for the coming night this should be where you rest." Sapphire slipped down onto the old log as Opal went about her duties; she placed a pot on the fire and prepared a soft bed that rose up out of the grass. Sapphire's mind swam as Opal chatted happily; she did not notice at first the slowly fluttering eyes of Sapphire.

"I am so tired and my head is pounding, I will just take a small..."

Opal smiled as she watched her slip off into sleep, she waved her hand over the sleeping figure and sat with the bowl of rabbit stew on the log as she watched.

"Now is the moment of change for everything, I can only wonder if I am right, and if I am then please understand and forgive me for what I do."

Opal's eyes flickered for a moment with bright blue light, she lifted her hood and rested the bowl of steaming stew on the log, and held her palms to her face and a stream of light flooded out of her eyes into her hands. When she took her hands away from her face, a ball of bright blue spun inside them as she gently cupped it. Opal turned to Sapphire's sleeping figure and gave a gentle bow, and wisps of fine smoke rose out of Sapphire and drifted towards the ball of light in her hand. The smoke swirled around the light and then the ball of light gave a pulse, and the soft wisps of smoke were drawn into it. Cal came out of the trees and walked across the glade towards her, he gave a bow, and with his large blue eyes he blinked and then raised a finger to the ball of spinning light. The moment he touched it, the light divided into two, and both of them spun faster in Opal's hands. Cal lifted one of the balls of light and gently carried it to Sapphire as she slept; the light expanded in his hand and rose into the air as his eyes began to flicker with the same blue light. It floated above her momentarily, and then like a cloud bursting, it gave a loud pop, and small particles of light fell like snow on to Sapphire, and as they rested onto her sleeping figure, they soaked into her like dew drops and vanished.

Cal turned and walked back to Opal, and with another blink of understanding he took the second ball of light, and he lifted it from Opal. It turned into a bright opaque bubble and stiffened; he opened his pocket and dropped the ball inside, Opal smiled.

"It is not what I wished, but it will save her if that moment comes, go now and wait for her in the dream forest." Cal gave a bow and turned away, Opal watched as the small figure walked back into the trees, and she gave a deep sigh. "If I am right, you will walk the stair of no return, but Cal will have the compass to bring you back. It is all I can do, and I hope it is enough precious child of the White Circle."

It had been a very long hot day of rest and preparation, and once they had all eaten, everyone helped to clear the pots and clean the long wooden house of Fagan, before sitting down to join in the debate with Robbie and Rowan. The coming hours and days were going to be the toughest they had ever faced, and for the first time ever, Robbie had decided he would voice his thoughts and let everyone offer their opinions, as to how they could confront Morgan le Fey, and free the land of Avalon to restore Amethyst as its queen.

The kitchen and living space were full, as everyone found a place to sit or perch where they had a clear view of the kitchen table where Robbie sat with Rune, flanked by a much recovered and happy Jade, Steph, and Rowan. Skip sat opposite with Bear, William, and Treen, as they looked at all the maps and plans, they could find to help guide them in their choice of way into the high mountain of the Citadel Mount. Robbie sat back, having told everyone he wanted to ensure Amethyst and Fish were safe, and then he intended to seek out the Dark One, it felt like a no hope mission, but he could not see any other way, Skip gave a nod as the others watched.

"I must say Robert, it is not my first thought to attack her head on, but I agree, I feel we have little choice in the matter, and we must take the bull by the horns." Bear and Rowan agreed, yet Rune's voice carried a note of caution.

"You all know that your powers will diminish the closer you get? You must understand that when you confront her you will all be just mortals attacking her, none of your powers will be there to help you as they have in the past. If any of you try to use them in the presence of that star, it will strip your gifts away forever and I will not be able to prevent it." There was a long moment of quiet as they thought which was abruptly shattered by Treen who banged on the table and everyone jumped.

"I am no afraid of that witch! I care not for the powers, she took my sister and she eez going to pay for it, I ave a sword and that is all I am needing." Treen looked fierce and unafraid; it was a quality that had gained her a great deal of respect on the front lines of York, Hawk nodded as he watched her.

"I am with you." Everyone turned their eyes to him and he shrugged at them. "Let's face it guys, this bitch has been getting in our way since we began, I say we face her out and finish this, I mean hell there is twenty one of us, it's got to be enough to get one of us close enough." Rune smiled.

"No one from my line or that of the White Circle can spill her blood, it is forbidden, and she knows it." Rowan gave a long gasp of air.

"Well, that suits me fine, I will happily do it for all of you, I must admit her line has caused me great pains, I will happily stick it to her if everyone else can keep her busy." Agreeable nods and mumbles came from the whole room. Robbie shook his head.

"Ok, let's not get carried away, as much as I appreciate all of your commitment, we need to think this through, she has proven herself to be very tricky, none of you should underestimate her. Remember she has ways of getting inside your head, this will not be an easy fight, we cannot just run in and slit her throat, which I think is what most of us would like to do. We need to be very careful, never forget she has some very vile guards, and we know she has the ability to produce more evil beasts if she wants to."

"It matters not, we ave no choice but to play it by the ears and get all around her, then we will know ow we can take her, she may be a snake but she as only the one pair of eyes, and snakes can be captured like all beasts." Her bright orangey brown eyes smouldered at Robbie and Rowan, it was very obvious she had no fear and would confront the Dark One no matter what. Steph gave a shrug and looked at Rune.

"You will be able to see us wherever we are now, it will be up to you to distract her if you can, just keep your feet firm on sacred ground and do what you can." Rune gave a nod, although deep down inside she was feeling very worried, the fact she could not be with them was making it very difficult for her to deal with. Her eyes looked down at the table for a moment.

"I will use everything I have to protect you all; I will not fail any of you." Robbie felt her turmoil and gently slipped his arm round her waist and gave it a gentle squeeze. He knew the pressure was on, but none of them would feel it more than her. Big John was sat on the sink observing everything.

"I am ready, my sword is extra sharp and my bow is taught, I have arrows and the will to fight anything that crosses my path. I never doubted the leadership I have had, and trust you to lead us all now, General Loxley, and My Lord of Loxley my sword as always is yours." Bear slapped his heavy hand down on the table.

"And mine! Bugger the bitch; she will get a fight like she has never seen from me." Skip gave Bear a heavy pat on the back.

"Here, here." And each in turn followed suit, Rags wiped her nose on her sleeve.

"I aint big and aint that good with a bow, but it's yours, I aint never welched on a mate and I aint gonna start now." She gave a big cheeky smile across the room and Robbie and Rowan both appreciated her sentiment. Bear eyed the two leaders in front of him.

"Well that about settles it, so how are we going to play this?" Rowan unrolled the map on the table.

"Fagan has drawn us this map of the caves and tunnels, I think we are better off going in via the old mine here outside the forest, this way we can slip into the tunnels below the mount unseen." There was a loud thud and everyone sent their hands to their sword hilts.

"Ye cannot be going in down there, they was sealed just before the queen left, she wanted to keep her precious things intact for the new queen. My aint ye all more jumpy than a leaf hopper with a spider on its back?" The entire group had turned to the very large frame of Fagan stood in the doorway, who had just dropped a large grey sack on the floor. He pointed down at it and gave a smile as his bushy white eyebrows twitched.

"Ye will find another six of these on the cart out there, this is all I got left from the old shop in the town, I brought it here and hid it, I figured that it will serve ye as ye fight for the realm of my queen." Robbie had slid round in his chair as he looked at the large sack in front of him.

"What is it Fagan?" The old man bent down and gave the sack a tug, and from the open end, weapons and thick leather armour rolled out across the heavily polished wooden floor.

"I knows ye all likes ye hoods and vests and stuff, but I got to thinking she will have a lot of soldiers, and if ye comes across em, well I thought to me self, a little bit of extra protection never hurt, so I figured ye could all take it and use it."

Rowan leaned down and lifted a chest piece off the floor. It was well made with great skill and care, and polished to perfection, it reminded him in many ways of some of the books he had read as boy about the warfare of old. "These are mighty gifts Master Fagan; I take it this is all your work?"

"It is indeed, as I have said, I once served my queen as the maker of all things, but I vowed I would never make any of this again when I came to the forest. This being all I have left from those times and ye all needing every protection, I feel I have not broken my vow by giving it to ye, as its not been made here. Use it and live, the armour of the queen was once very famous for its ability to hold off many swords." Rowan smiled as he looked at the wide array of other leather garments.

"We are very grateful, I am sure this will be of great assistance to all of us, thank you Master Fagan we are...have been since arriving here, very much in your debt."

Out in the open glade in front of the cabin was a small handcart loaded with sacks. They contained chain mail and wrist protectors and even a few very heavy leather hard hats. The group delighted in sorting through them picking out what fitted them and then swapping with each other until all of them had found something that fitted them comfortably.

Robbie only chose two leather wrist guards, to him the leather chest plates felt heavy and cumbersome and he did not want his movement restricting, it worried Rune that he would be more exposed than the others, but she could not convince him otherwise, Jade and Blades both also refused to wear anything heavier than their ordinary clothes, although Jade made good use of some nice leather belts on to which she knew she could strap on extra knives.

When everyone had made their choice, Robbie suggested that they all make it an early night, it was already gone nine, and he wanted to be up early to prepare and get underway. Slowly the house cleared leaving just Rowan and Jade sat with Rune and Steph, as Robbie poured himself another cup of Fagan's herbal tea. Rune's eyes never left him, and as he turned, he saw the bright shining blue glisten at him from her pale face.

"What?" He knew her well enough to know she was thinking of something, she blinked and then stared at him.

"I want you to leave Jade with me." Both Rowan and Jade turned to her at the same time, as Jade let out her surprise.

"Why Rune?" Rune turned to them watching her.

"Do you trust me?" Jade knew she did not even have to answer; Rowan gave a slight nod of his head.

"I find it strange you would ask me, but yes Rune, you know I trust you more than most, although I am curious as to why you want Jade to stay behind?" Jade nodded her head.

"Yeah Rune, why do I have to stay? You know that I am more use to them at their side, I hope you don't think I will pee myself or something silly, because no matter what happens I will be there as part of the team as always." Rune smiled, and took her sister's hand in hers and she glanced back to Robbie.

"I have never doubted your bravery, but that is not why I ask. Jade you have gifts of the Green Circle that will diminish when you walk within range of that star, but if you used your gifts from my side here in the centre of the Forest of Time, then you will be a mighty force that is invisible to the enemy, and can help create a massive diversion to aid the rest of the group." Robbie was beginning to understand as he moved away from the stove back to his seat.

"You are talking about using windows?" Rune gave a nod.

"Think about it, if both Jade and myself open windows on opposite sides of the soldiers, we will not leave the forest, but we can push our arms through and drop a stick or two of explosives to aid you. Potentially we could create so much confusion that it might divert the enemy from their real goal of seeking you out." Rowan gave an approving smile.

"I like the way you think, I must admit Robbie, if we can get them running in every direction it will draw a lot of heat off us, after all, the one thing we know is that they are setting up and waiting for us in very large numbers."

"It's alright with me, what say you Jade?" Jade looked up from under her long blonde fringe.

"I suppose so, I mean yeah I can do it you all know that? If you want mischief and mayhem well I guess that is my special talent, although I will worry about you Rowan, I always watch your back and if I am not there, then who is going to watch out for you?"

"I will be watching everyone Jade, believe me if he gets into trouble, you can open your window and go to his aid, but I will have the Violet Circle around all of you." She gave a big smile.

"Cool, let's do it then." Rune gave a smile as she saw the bright green twinkle in her sister's eyes.

"Ok it's you and me Sis, let's even up the score for the Green Circle and granddad."

The heat of the day had risen steadily, and as the group of Specialists settled down to sleep under the safe watch of Fagan, high up on the Citadel Mount the thick swirling mass of cloud was spreading fast. Unbeknown to the sleeping Specialists, the mass of dark cloud had completely engulfed Avalon and was now creeping its way around the outer edges of the Forest of Time. For those who had toiled hard under the blinding sun, to be suddenly engulfed in almost darkness was bliss. The water to the soldiers of Mason and the Raven had been rationed as the lake dried up, and so as the darkness descended, even though it was still hot and dry, somehow to them it felt cooler just to be shaded.

The day had been spent positioning soldiers in every part of the realm. As the sky darkened, the word on the lips of everyone was vigilance. Darkness would aid the hooded men of the Specialists, and so long lines of men stretched out linking all the command stations to Avalonia, where the giant fearsome figure of Samuel Knots waited patiently for any sign of attack. For Morgan le Fey it had been a frustrating day, she was still unsure what the bright violet light had been inside the stone circle, and she had been less than pleased to see her Houlen fly away from it in fear. For almost a week they had appeared skittish, and even though she had screamed at them, none of them had admitted that they were afraid of the bright sword wielded by the Hooded Man.

In a final fit of frustration, she visited the deep cells under the mount, and felt great cheer to see the array of beasts and extra soldiers that she had been silently preparing for some time. The rooms below echoed with the wails and snarls of her many beasts, and she felt a tinge of excitement as she viewed them and tried hard to suppress the joy it brought her, knowing that for over two years she had been preparing the trap that she knew the woodland group would eventually have to walk into. The tall sturdy guards from Dunnottar sat silent, devoid of all emotion, dressed in all black leather with black metal hats. It was an eerie sight that unnerved the guards as they stared with black emotionless eyes into space waiting to be commanded. The Marsh Hounds prowled along the metal bars eagerly awaiting a meal, they had been kept fed to the minimum, and they anxiously felt that the time was coming when they would be free, the sight of their mistress raised their hopes, and they howled as she walked along the side of the large run of steel bars.

Morgan had no idea when the group would come out of hiding and make their move towards her, all she knew was that the time was coming and with each passing moment, she felt the grasp of her dreams of ruling everything. The whole realm was sealed and she alone held the keys, sooner or later the Hooded Man and the pretender of a new king would walk into her arms, and she would rip them to pieces and be free of them once and for all.

It was almost dawn when she came up the long passage that led to the small town of Avalonia lit by a thousand torches, Samuel Knots was waiting as she came out of through the ornate metal gates. Across the small square set at the back of the town, the Houlen prowled waiting for their orders, as she walked slowly with her general. "Everything is in place?"

"It is My Lady, the woodland is full and the road is watched by many eyes."

They came to the crossroads in front of the tall fortress of stone, where a long line of wooden carts waited and stretched back down the long white Queen's Road. The monks had pulled in for the night to sleep, Knots pointed at them. "The gates will open up top soon and then they will clear the road, the road at the curtain is now closed and sealed, there will be no more until this is all over." The Dark One gave a smirk. "There will be no more period... The church has failed my son General, when they are risen and on the move, let your soldiers use them as target practice, keep the supplies and add them to the stores." Samuel Knots stalled for a moment. "My Lady? Is that prudent? The church carries a great deal of influence, is it wise to alienate them at such an important time?" She gave a cold laugh as she saw the worried expression on his face.

"Believe me Knots no one will even know they have gone, after all when they entered this realm no one really expected them to return, as for alienating the church, I think that the church needs to readjust its priorities and honour its agreements. You are wasted here as a soldier Knots; I think maybe you are better suited to politics, although not too many of them of late appear to have lived, so maybe you are best placed here. Fear not about the church, they too will find in time backing the wrong horse will be their downfall, I intend to deal with them personally at some point, and we shall see if that god of theirs is any match for me."

Morgan le Fey strode onto the road and looked round in the dim light, as she appraised her defences; she turned and looked up at the tall wall of white rock that disappeared into the thick swirling blackness of the Merle. "Tell your soldiers not to throw the monks off the cliff, it will create too much damage and mess down here, it's bad enough they have been under our feet for weeks, they can drop them off the other side, no one really visits that part, and I am sure it will give the animals somewhere quiet to feed." She turned on the path that led back into the town, in the direction of the large Inn. "I shall rest up in my rooms, join me later for breakfast, and we shall look at further tactics." Samuel Knots gave a snap of his feet and saluted. "Yes My Lady, I will be honoured to join you." The Dark One walked ahead with a shrill titter.

"Of course you will." Samuel Knots had worked all his life for the Knox family, he knew them and understood them better than any, but even he felt a small pang inside him as he thought of the orders he would have to give. He had tortured women and slain children without so much as a care, and yet standing watching the black robes of his mistress blow behind her, as she walked up the white cobbled street, he felt a great deal of uncertainty about murdering men of the Christian Church.

CHAPTER TWENTY NINE

UNEXPECTED ALLIES

For Una it had felt like a very long night, she had sat by the fire on the edge of the grassy covered sands of the Whispering Dunes, and watched Woody rolled up in his blankets as he slept. For a while she had been distracted, as Woody had been surprisingly good company, and his quiet wit had made her smile. As he slept and she sat in the quiet, her mind filled with a thousand questions, and for the first time in a very long time she had felt that she really missed her mother and father. Coming back to the area had triggered all the memories of a time long since gone, when she had returned shortly after the birth of Mac with her injured mother, it had been the last time that all of them had been together and she let the tears of remembrance silently roll down her cheeks.

It was a place she had never wanted to return to, and yet under the instruction of her father, she was now about to do so, and Una suddenly felt frightened and alone and scared of the power of the emotions that would rise up inside her, as they had during that bitter struggle to save her mother's life. It was a life that had cost her the life of a child in the life for a life rule, and even though she had always been certain that she had done the right thing, it was still hard to live her life knowing Mac had betrayed her, and the life given in trade could have been a child who would be her support now. Feeling lost to the world, all she could do was try and wonder about what good could come from returning here, and why had her father knowing the pain this place held, had asked her to return?

Over a day's ride away across the Forest of Time, Rune stood alone in the sunlight watching from the lookout. Her mind was alert, even though she had slept little as she scanned the trees and the roads all around her to work out what was happening. Her mind drifted as she felt the mixed emotions flowing through Una. Rune closed her eyes for a second and focused.

"Hear Me Sister of my circle, for I am Runestone and your centre."

Una's eyes flickered with flecks of violet and she gave a sniffle and sat back against the tree.

"I hear you Runestone."

"Una what is the matter, are you both safe?"

"I am sorry Rune I was not thinking, we are fine, I just had a moment of melancholy, I think it is being back here, there are so many sad memories here for me."

"I am not sure of where you are, although I feel you strongly. Have you been in this forest before, I was not aware you had?"

"I came here to nurse my mother just after Mac was born, it was here I had to choose to save her, I guess just being here brought it all back for me."

Rune felt the wave of sadness and recognised it, for she too still had moments when she felt the loss from the bitter choice, she had made to save Jade.

"I am here Una, you are not alone, and I will stay with you always." Una gave a big sniffle as she talked with her mind and her eyes closed.

"I know, I am just being silly, I have no idea why my father would want me to return, I have tried all night to think about what returning could possibly achieve, and to be honest I cannot think of a single thing."

"I must admit Una, it has been on my mind also, but at times the logic of my grandfather was not always very transparent. All I can say is that if this was a task he thought you must do, then it must be very important, as he trusted you above all others. This must be something to do with your mother and the White Circle, so trust him for he would not let you suffer if it was not vital to all of us."

"I guess so, don't worry about me Rune, you have enough on your plate, I will follow his instructions and trust in his wisdom. Keep everyone safe until I return."

"I will, but remember I am here, if you need me just call."

"I will... Thanks Rune, I love you."

"I love you too, take care." Rune opened her eyes and gave a sigh, there was so much at the moment that made little sense to her, for the whole of the night she had tried to work out what everything meant in hope of finding a way to help Robbie and defeat Morgan le Fey. With the stirrings of life in Avalon she knew the day would turn bloody, and the true fight for Avalon would begin, all she could do now was watch and hope that she could take the lion's share of the burden away from Robbie.

The time passed slowly as she sat on the edge of the rock with her eyes closed, sensing the realm in front of her. Far below in the long wooden house all of the Specialists had awoken and prepared for their day, Maggs had cooked a hearty breakfast for every one of thick smoked slices of bacon and fried eggs with tomatoes. Fed and feeling wide awake, thanks mainly to the last of their coffee beans, they trudged out of the house, and made their way to the hot springs at the bottom of the Lookout.

Robbie walked up the hill with Rowan and Jade; Bear followed carrying a very large and heavy looking wooden box. Rune opened her eyes and turned her head, she smiled as she saw Robbie with his long green cloak flowing behind him, he gave her a big smile and lifted his hand to show he had something wrapped up in a brown cloth. "You missed breakfast, Maggs made you two good bacon sandwiches, she thought you should keep your strength up."

The smell wafted down to her as he passed it to her, and she happily took it and unwrapped it, suddenly realising how hungry she actually was. Rowan was stood watching Avalon as Robbie handed the sandwich to Rune. "It looks dark over there, I am not sure if that is a good or bad thing."

Rune chewed for a few moments and then swallowed. "It's a bit of both I think, the darkness will replace the lost leaves and give you cover, although it is that darkness that will absorb the powers of my line if not protected." Robbie patted Rowan on the shoulder.

"If it makes it hard for us, remember we are better trained, so it will make it one hell of a lot harder for them." Rowan gave a nod, but his slate grey eyes stared forward as he tried to find his bearings in the dark haze below the cloud.

"Yeah, I suppose so, we must be on our top game this day Robbie, for today all of us must show the measure of the woodland realm. Today we strike first and hard, there will be no room for error, everything we fight for and hold dear hangs on a thread one hundred times thinner than cotton, if it snaps, we lose everything for everyone."

His tone was sombre, and yet mixed inside it all there was the slightest glimmer of hope, it was not much, but it was enough for Rowan to take his fight right on to the Dark One's doorstep, and he had a determination in him that showed it was exactly what he intended to do. Rune understood him as she sat and chewed the last of her sandwich, she was not sure if it was the good food, or just the feeling in the air, but as she swallowed, she felt the hope and knew no matter how hard the fight would be, it would be the best they ever gave.

Robbie gave a sigh as he felt the moment, he did not want to happen looming; as Rune stood up he turned and slipped his arms round her. Being separated at such an important moment felt wrong, but he knew it was right to keep her safe, and felt a little comfort knowing Jade would be with her. "I am going to miss you at my side."

She pulled him tight and squeezed him hard, her hand slid along his to the wrist where she felt the white bangle.

"I will be with you, I could never desert you in your hardest hour, my spirit will be all around all of you protecting you at all times. Be careful and do not take any careless risks, and if you get into big trouble, I am bringing you all straight back here." He looked down and smiled as he saw her fiery red hair pressed into his chest, he stroked it down onto her back and she looked up at him with her bright blue eyes. He leaned down and gently kissed her, and felt the warmth of her pass into him.

"I love you too, and yes we will be very careful, keep your eyes peeled for me and give me as much warning as you can." She nodded and smiled.

"I will." Slowly he let his arms slide free, and with one last look at her, he turned to head down the track and prepare for Rune to open a window back into Avalon. Jade still hung from Rowan's neck as she kissed him passionately, and Robbie pattered her shoulder.

"Sorry Pebbles but I need my general back for a while." She released him with a giggle.

"Ok, watch out for each other guys, and if it gets too hairy, call me and I will be there in a flash. Don't worry about Rune and me, we have got a few tricks planned to keep em real busy." She patted the large box Bear had carried up for her.

"Fagan has made us a few useful tools; you will know when I start to use them." She winked and gave a giggle.

Bear, Robbie and Rowan stepped onto the track that led back down the high rock, and Rune called him back. "Robbie wait a minute." Her eyes were vivid purple as she turned back to face Avalon and her eyes closed. Her body was taught and Robbie knew the signs well, he walked back across the top of the rock to her side.

"What do you see?" She did not move.

"The soldiers are attacking the monks... Robbie they are slaughtering them."

"What? That makes no sense at all." Rowan was at his shoulder.

"Maybe they have not kept their bargain with the Dark One?" Rune stayed motionless.

"They are fleeing off the road into the trees, and the ones at the top of the mount are running down the track away from them... Robbie, you must help them."

"What? After what they have done?" Rune's eyes snapped open and the whole area flooded with violet light.

"They are defenceless, they cannot fight for themselves." Robbie gave a shrug.

"I am not sure about defenceless Rune, I mean they had no weapons but that book of theirs certainly almost brought about the end of Sapphire's life." Rowan agreed.

"That maybe so Robbie, but we want to throne a king, and let's be honest here, if we save their lives, then they owe us, and it won't hurt having some of the church on our side." It was a good point.

"But what about Amethyst and our dark mistress?" Bear gave a deep cough.

"She is up there Robbie and we are sort of heading in her direction, I figure we can start with the monks and work our way up to her, or at least take a few of us to help, and give you a very good diversion." Robbie shook his head.

"No that sounds like suicide." Bear gave a hearty laugh.

"There are twenty odds of us against hundreds, whether we help the monks or not, the whole bloody day pretty much looks like suicide... Let me take half and try to help, you and Rowan get inside while we do what we can, it might take their eyes off you long enough to pull this off." Rune agreed with Bear.

"It makes sense Robbie, I can watch both groups and use Jade to give extra help, if you can get those monks out in safety you will win a great deal of support, especially if they make it back into the Woodland Realm. Their stories alone will prove Mason has lied to them; it could swing the balance for us in getting William on the throne." He understood what she was saying and it did make sense, but there was so few of them as just one group, splitting them into two made him very uneasy. He turned to Bear.

"Ok you take half, but I want them to volunteer for it, the church has not been good to us and I will stand by any who do not feel they want the extra fight, our priority is still to Amethyst and Fish." Bear nodded.

"Understood." He turned and headed down the path, Robbie turned to Rune.

"Can you help them?" She gave a nod and closed her eyes.

"Get ready to move out. There are few things I can do to give Bear some time, you get everyone ready, we will be going fast your group first followed by Bears." Robbie looked at Rowan who was smiling.

"I feel another adventure starting." He gave a laugh.

"This may be even too adventurous for both of us." With a laugh both of them shouldered their bows and headed down the path toward the waiting group, Rune focused on the long white road, where the monks were screaming and dropping from their carts in droves, and the soldiers of the Dark One fired hails of arrows into the wooden carts, the road was littered with the dead.

The screams and wails of the injured and dying echoed in the dim light, as under the trees monks scrambled blindly in panic trying to get away from the jeering laughing soldiers. With wild eyes filled with terror they ran and stumbled, crashing onto the floor as they tripped, screaming frantically as they clawed their way back to their feet and escaped the madness that had over taken the soldiers of Morgan le Fey.

Along the wide stretch of burned grass that had been the meadow that bordered the white Queens Road, the Cutters and the soldiers laughed as they fired yet another volley of arrows. They walked almost in a leisurely way, taking their time and enjoying their sport, making jokes to each other as they reloaded their crossbows.

Out on the road just in front of them, a long green line drew itself in the air, and the soldiers slowed not sure of what it was they were seeing. Two bright green eyes appeared in the air above the carts and the soldiers stopped in fear. From nowhere four fizzing objects flew out of the sky and rattled across the stony surface at their feet, there was a brief moment's pause before the soldiers understood what had happened.

The flashes were blinding and the explosions rocked the floor deafening those out of range. Soldiers were tossed into the air and as the explosives blew massive holes in the ground, over in the woodland the monks fell sprawling as the ground vibrated below their feet.

The Group had divided, and Robbie flanked by Rowan and Smokes waited as the window opened in front of him. Without pausing they flew through the bright violet arch and into the dry leaves of the woodland on the North Western side of the dried up lake. Steph bounced through behind with Maggs and Rags, then came Harry, Blades, Todd and Maddy. They hit the leaf littered floor and looked for cover as Fagan stepped smiling through the arched window and looked around. Robbie took a moment to see where he was, and then up went his hand, and the group moved into formation, staying close and headed for the rocks up in front.

In the woodland on the southern side of the dried up lake, the monks ploughed on driven by their panic trying to get as far away as possible. Behind them in the dark trees came the laughter and jeers of the hunting Cutters, which filled the monks with terror as they moved as fast as their old limbs could carry them. Slowly bunching together, they headed in the opposite direction to the sounds of the Cutters, wailing and moaning in fear.

As they hurtled down the central path that wove towards the dry lake bed, there was a blinding flash of violet light, from nowhere a loud voice bellowed in the darkness. "DOWN...NOW." Whether it was just the instinct to survive taking over, no one was really sure, but without thinking all the monks dived in unison and hit the floor hard, gasping and panting as they rolled badly and smashed into each other.

Above them came the faint whistle of passing arrows followed by grunts and squeals in the woodland behind them, there was the sound of steel sliding on steel, and figures bounded over them, as the monks buried their faces in the ground expecting to die. The sound of clashing steel and the grunts and screams of battle, echoed back through the trees, and the exhausted monks began to realise that someone was trying to help them. Slowly they got up from the ground, and looked in the direction of the violet light.

Behind the battle continued mixed with loud explosions somewhere off to the far side of the road, sense began to work its way back into their minds, and they all turned to the light and began to walk calmly towards it. Framed in the bright light stood two figures, one was that of a young man and with him was a small female, both of them beckoned the monks to hurry, and they picked up their pace and headed towards the light.

William and Judith guided the monks quickly through the window and out onto the large flat rock shelf above the hot springs, where the monks collapsed and gasped heavy sighs of relief. They grabbed at friends they knew and hugged them in relief, happy to see they were still alive; some were total strangers who just hugged simply for the need of feeling another living soul close to them. Many sat on the rocks and wept, and others knelt and prayed for being saved, and rejoiced that they had life.

William came through carrying a badly bleeding old monk on his shoulder, three others help lower the old man to the floor as he knelt down to ensure the old man was alright. His face was cut very badly, and one of the monks tore away some of his robes to bind his head. The old monk shook with fear as he looked into the bright green kind eyes of Will; his voice was soft and quiet. "Thank you, I owe you my life, but I am sorry, I do not know who you are. Please tell me the name of my saviour." Will smiled at him.

"You are safe here, for this is a realm protected by the Hooded Man and his wife, no harm will come to you here." The Old man gave a gasp of breath.

"Are you he?" Will shook his head and smiled.

"No he is leading a party to free the true queen of this realm, it was half of his men that came to your aid, and it is to him you owe your life." Will stood up and turned to see Judith smiling at him, she lifted a small green bag.

"There are first aid supplies in here; Milly thought you might need them." A young looking monk gave her a bow as he took it from her, William passed her to head back into the woodland to help others, Judith turned to follow and then stopped, she looked down at the monk who was watching her as others bound his wounds. "The man who saved you is William Pendragon; you owe your life to your future king, for he is the true heir to your realm not a pretender like Mason Knox." She disappeared through the light as the monks sat stunned staring at the old monk on the floor.

Out on the long white road the darkness echoed with squeals of pain. Bear was in no mood to be messed with and came out of the trees in a rage, swinging his sword in one hand and his axe in the other. Behind him from the trees came a hail of arrows as the others picked their targets with skill. Bear roared into the Cutters and soldiers, followed by the might and power of Big John, as Skip, Treen and Jaz came out of the trees further up and cleaved into the mass of startled soldiers. Crystal glowed like a ghost dressed back in her white, her eyes glowing looking like she had no pupils at her enemy, several of the soldiers took one look and screamed thinking she was a ghost, dropped their weapons and fled into the darkness as she screamed at them with the rage of a demon.

In the large fortress of the Keep at the far end of the long white road, the alarm bells sounded marking the arrival of the Hooded Man, and the road echoed with the crunch of running feet as the commanders yelled their orders to muster the troops. Deep in the thick of the gathering soldiers, a tiny line of green drew itself in the darkness between the gathering ranks, there was a gentle thud and the light went out.

Seconds later with no warning at all, the sky lit up and the floor shook with the explosions as the soldiers were blasted to the floor and thrown against the wall of the fortress. Men blackened by the blast that blew out many of the windows in the nearby houses, walked dazed and slashed unaware they had even been injured. There was chaos, as those who were not injured screamed out they were under attack, and yet in the chaos they could not find an enemy to fight. Several more massive explosions rocked the crossroads, throwing everyone to the floor as fear rose against an invisible enemy.

Back in the woodland Jay and Milly helped guide stray wounded monks towards Rune's window, and Hawk kept watch tracing his bow in the direction of any sound that might be an enemy, with lightning speed he would release his arrows, and from deep inside the darkness of the trees would come a squeal of pain.

A familiar wail rose into the sky and screeched like a banshee, and everyone knew it was time to leave. The Houlen were coming and quickly they moved backwards into the trees. Grabbing the last of the wounded, and under the cover of Jay, Hawk, William and Judith, the Specialists led by Bear made their retreat and headed back towards the violet window. The few Soldiers that tried to follow fell to the keen eyes of Hawk, as the Specialists moved rapidly backwards. The Houlen wailed down with great speed into the trees, and came driven on by their wild lust for death, but to no avail, by the time they reached the spot where the scent of their prey was heaviest, it was clear and the violet window had closed.

The woodland was filled with the screams of the wailing Houlen as they searched the ground for a sign of the Specialists, but they had vanished without a trace, and they were left to tear and slash at the dead soldiers already scattered on the floor in their madness.

Bear looked round at the Specialists, who were wiping their faces and drinking from their canteens. "Is everyone OK, no cuts or wounds?" They were sweating heavily but all were fine, he gave a smile as he shook his sword arm. "I needed a good warm up." Jaz gave a giggle as he rested his arm on Milly's shoulder, Jade came down the hill towards them wearing a big bright smile.

"Rune says if you are ready, she will put you on top, Robbie is almost at the cave and will be heading inside soon." Bear gave a nod and looked at the group.

"Are we ready for round two?" The Specialists prepared their bows and fitted the first of more arrows to fire and gave the signal. A few moments later the violet window reappeared and with a nod to the others, Bear followed by the group ran back into action on the top of the mount to rescue yet more of the trapped monks.

Rune stood on top of the Lookout watching the group in her mind, and at the same time she was connected to the white bracelet on Robbie's arm tracking his movements. She felt the stranger as he walked up the path behind her; he saw her stood looking small and slender dressed in all violet with her eyes closed, and small flashes of light flickering across her pale white cheekbones. For a moment he stood and simply watched, Rune smiled.

"Welcome... I believe you are to be addressed as Brother, is that correct?"

He gave a slight nod, unsure of whether or not she could see him. Jade had her back to him as she poked her head through her green window and dropped bombs on the soldiers running towards the Specialists, her hand would reach out, and grab the long cylinder made from Bamboo with a fuse, which she lit before dropping through the window. The explosions could be heard through the gap, and each time one went off the monk would twitch and jump.

"I am Thomas... Brother Thomas." Rune's eyes flickered as she moved from Bear back to Robbie and then back again.

"Welcome Thomas, I see you are curious as to why the Violet Witch would save you, when you are seen as my enemy and have played your part in plotting my destruction." Thomas gave a gulp, and Rune smiled.

"I would not have phrased it such, but many lives have been saved this day by the Hooded Man and yourself, and I suppose yes, I am very curious as to my saviours and their actions." Rune gave a slight nod understanding his curiosity.

"You have a strong faith in your God and yet not in your fellow men, for we are all human are we not?"

"We are, and yet times are hard and many are divided."

"The answer you seek is simple, although I am not sure that you will understand. The Hooded Man fights for all of those who cannot defend themselves, and so he gave the order to send his men to your aid. The fact that you have conspired against him, and helped those allied to Knox to try and plan his destruction is irrelevant. To us a man without a weapon who has no ability to fight should be protected, it is why we oppose those like Knox who use pain and death to control those who are unable to stand up against him. It is as I believe a value known to your Christian brethren?" Thomas did understand her, and yet it still made little sense to him.

"We came here seeking harm to no one; our aim here was a life of solitude and prayer."

"We understand that, but your church was to be built to the glory of Brother Argus I believe? He is a known enemy of the Hooded Man and the future king, and so you have been tarnished by your association with him."

"Brother Argus has used his influence to gain this land for the church; we have no quarrel with your Hooded Man."

"I am sorry Thomas, but Argus is a corrupt man who tried to gain influence and power to his own ends, this land does not belong to Mason Knox, and so therefore he cannot give it to your church. The heritage of this land has ownership that predates your Christ by thousands of years, it was given as a gift to the people of Fae and it is rightfully theirs, we will ensure it is returned to them."

"But what will become of us, we seek only peace and solitude."

"As do we Thomas, and yet we have had to fight to save what little land we have to live peacefully on. Your people will leave here unharmed, and can return to your original homes and lands, you must remain here for a little while so we can assure you all safe passage, fear not, none of you are captives, but you owe your life to the Hooded Man and the future king, never forget that." For a moment Rune opened her eyes and looked at him, Thomas jumped back in fright.

"But you... you are... I mean how can we trust?"

"A witch?" Rune gave a deep laugh.

"I mean no offence but you are." Rune closed her eyes and continued to chuckle.

"You trusted her and I can tell you this for sure Thomas, she is darker than I could ever be, if you can place your faith in her dark words, then none of you should have any problems in believing I mean you no harm. Go to your brothers and tell them that when the queen of Avalon rules again and the gates of this land are once again opened, all of you may walk freely back to your old lives. Then and only then will you have to decide whether or not I am right to trust. Once you are all safely home you can choose freely which side you want to support, but remember this Thomas, a new king will rule the land of your forefathers, and his name will be Pendragon, not Knox."

Rune turned back to face Avalon and Thomas knew it was time to leave, for a moment he watched the curious sight of Rune and Jade, and then he turned and headed back down the path towards the growing numbers of rescued monks.

Robbie wove with skill through the trees; to his left he saw the flashes of Jade's explosions over the tops of the trees far across the other side of Avalon. The diversion seemed to be working as all eyes were now facing in that direction; he took a long breath as his eyes stared into the dim gloom below the thick mass of clouds above. It was hard to believe that far above the cloud; the sun was burning as brightly as it had for over a week now. He came out into an open space and recognised it instantly, high above him came the faint sound of tinkling chimes in notes that lifted his heart in the gloom. He stopped close to the thick wide trunk that had been his protection not that long ago, and waited as the others caught up to him. Smokes smiled as he saw the tree and walked into the clearing, he thrust his long silver spear into the ground and wiped his face on his sleeve. "Well at least we know we are safe here."

Robbie smiled noting the black leather breastplate he wore, that bore the indented crest of a moon surrounded by stars, it felt slightly comical to see all his men in armour, and he leaned back against the tree to catch his breath. Rowan crouched down in front of him and wiped his face, it was very hot under the cloud and all of them were sweating heavily. Robbie looked down at Rowan and the others around him.

"Take a few moments, this place is safe to us, this is the tree of lost souls, and is protected by the Fae, you have nothing to fear as long as you are below its branches. The entrance to the cave is not much further now, and with luck we will be underground in cooler conditions soon." Rowan took a long breath and stood up to stretch his leg, which although felt a great deal stronger, still ached a little.

"I knew we were safe the moment I saw your sword handle, it's moonstone, and it glows in defence of the Fae." Robbie looked down at the hilt of his sword, and he noticed that the large stone set in the top of the handle glowed in a faint almost unearthly glow.

"How strange, I never noticed, although as I told you before, the Houlen feared it when they confronted us here."

Fagan walked into the circle with a hearty smile. "Oh my this place makes you feel as happy as a daffodil, well ye have come to the right place, strange ye did not ask me though." His bushy white hair and eyebrows seemed to glow in the dark, it reminded Robbie of Crystal and he smiled wondering if there really was some distant family connection. Steph looked up at him from where she sat on the floor.

"Ask you what Fagan?" He looked confused.

"Well how to wake em up... that is why ye came here... isn't it?" Robbie stared at the old man.

"Wake who up?" Fagan leaned back and gave a roar of laughter.

"Well, I will be as pickled as a walnut on Michaelmass." He looked so surprised as he pointed to Robbie. "Ye has the sword and he has the spear of Moon, does ye not know that they are keys to the trees?" Robbie looked round at the others who all looked as confused as him, his eyes landed on Maddy.

"You are White Circle, have you any idea what he is talking about?" Maddy looked as lost as he did.

"I have heard of the spear, it was once said to belong to Eleanor, but apart from that I have no idea at all." Fagan roared with laughter as he began to almost dance around the circle, he pointed up at the trees and gave a large wheeze and choked he was laughing so much, all Robbie could do was watch wondering if all the years alone had finally snapped, and Fagan's sanity had left forever. Fagan came to a halt in front of him chuckling as he wiped his eyes, he landed a large hand on Robbie's shoulder as his stomach continued to shake.

"Oh thank ye, I have not laughed this much since old Barley Winesdrum fell off the bridge and almost drowned." He chuckled and his eyes sparkled with tears, the others couldn't help but smile his laughter was so infectious. Fagan took a large breath to compose himself.

"My blessed Queen Rhiannon would never leave her realm unguarded, as I keep telling ye, there is magic in here deeper than Little Dark Eyes knows. My people have powers that no one has ever seen or learned, and there are ways of unlocking it for those who wish to defend this realm, I thought ye knew? Ye are of

Fae and I saw the sword and spear and just thought well he is as crafty as a squirrel in a Chestnut tree."

Robbie lifted his hands and gripped Fagan by the shoulders. "We have aid here? Please Fagan I have no knowledge of what you say, tell me and quickly because I have people over there that will need others to help them." Fagan gave a good cough as he cleared the last of his chuckles, and he suddenly looked very serious.

"That sword and the spear are the keys to unlocking the Marshals of Avalon. Push them into the soil side by side below the tree and you will unlock them and bring aid to the plight of my people and new queen. As Fae you can command them in the defence of this realm, I thought ye knew?" Robbie wasted no time, he drew the gleaming sword of Destiny out of its sheath as Fagan stood back and gave another little titter, he walked over to Smokes and plunged Destiny into the soil at the side of the spear.

"Now what?" Fagan gave a happy smile as all eyes fell on him.

"Ye wait."

CHAPTER THIRTY

THE KEYS TO THE TREES

Robbie watched the sword and spear as the sweat ran down his face, there was almost silence except for the quiet little titters of Fagan, as he wiped his face and smiled at the thought of them not knowing of the keys to the trees. For a few moments everywhere felt as still as the grave, and then from the soles of his boots Robbie felt something.

The ground began to shake slightly, as he looked down to the parched dry grass he heard the tinkling of the tree above, festooned with small tokens of the Fae that shook and vibrated together. The shaking increased and the sounds above him grew louder, like that of a cupboard filled with fine glasses being shaken. The rattling increased as the earth moved, and the entire group lifted their arms to steady their balance stood on the shaking earth.

White light erupted out of the floor all around the outer edge of the huge tree, and Robbie looked as the clouds above him parted and the wide white circle of light flooded into the sky. Rune turned up on the lookout. "What the hell is that?" Jade fumbled as the bright white light filled the sky and streamed up into the heavens, she looked down as the small bomb rolled off the edge of the Lookout.

"Oh crap!" Far down below in the trees there was a massive explosion, she peered over the edge. "So sorry Squirrels."

Rune watched, and began to smile as she felt the power of Rhiannon flow into the air. "Oh Thank you my queen you have no idea how much we need you now." Jade looked back at her.

"What is it Rune?"

"I am not sure exactly what, I just know that Rhiannon left a few things behind to help Robbie and Rowan, and I can feel her all over Avalon going to his aid." A small tear ran down the side of her face, and she gave a gasp as she lifted her hand to her mouth. "No one will ever know how frightened I was for him, we have so few against so many and I was terrified I would lose him."

Jade walked over and pulled her into a hug, as Rune's eyes sparkled with her tears. "Rune he is with Rowan, believe me he was always going to come back to you, Rowan promised me that." Rune gave a smile as she sniffled and hugged her sister.

"Rowan is a good man, I am so proud of the life you have made with him, and I am also very excited about being an auntie, we are both very lucky Jade. Come on we still have much to do."

Robbie watched in disbelief as all around him the trees seemed to glow in the darkness. High above him in the sky he could see the faint outline of a large moon surrounded by stars, and he smiled as he understood that even the Merle could be weakened enough to allow the oldest powers known to gain a little advantage. Fagan walked out of the circle where to the surprise of everyone small specks of light were forming and coming out of the trunks of all the trees, Fagan gave a royal bow as the specks of light gave a bright pulse, and where they had hovered previously stood a golden haired soldier dressed in the same black leather armour, and wearing a long cloak of pale blue.

They stood proud in front of Fagan, who looked suddenly like a great leader of authority; his voice was loud and powerful. "Ye have a new queen to serve and a realm to protect, go to the mount and into the tunnels, protect the monks and give them safe passage to the Forest. Help and guide those who are allied to the spear and sword, and do your duty to this realm and the queen."

There was a loud roar as from nowhere thousands of blue clad soldiers raised their weapons and roared into the air, all Robbie and the group could do was watch and stare as Fagan instructed the soldiers of his line. Steph stood at the side of Robbie quite taken aback by all of it. "So what do we do now?" Robbie gave a big smile and patted her shoulder.

"We lead them, come on, we have a job to finish."

As the Marshal of the Fae ran into the trees, Robbie lifted Destiny high in the air, and ran into the trees followed by his Specialists, as he made his way towards the cave and back into the labyrinth of tunnels below the Citadel Mount.

High on the mount, the monks fled down the long path that led to the top of the only path down the high cliff to the town of Avalonia, and their only chance of escape down the white road. High above them the Houlen squealed with delight as they dropped with speed, snatching the screaming, terrified, monks in their talons and ripping them to shreds. Bear and his team loaded stinger arrows on their bows and fired, trying their hardest to take out as many as possible.

The Houlen swirled like gathering swallows at autumn, and turned as a single group in the air, like flies in a swarm they headed straight at the Specialists. Jay and Hawk were side by side crouched as they aimed; Crystal and Treen moved in unison as they followed the vile twisting beasts in the air with their bows. Bear and

John took the front line with their swords and waited for the moment of impact, and Gaynor and Will with Hornet at their side faced the rear where the soldiers of the Dark One gathered for their assault. Skip and Treen took the centre ground as the monks threw themselves to the floor, and Jaz and Milly flanked them waiting as the Houlen swept low over the high cliff and came screaming and wailing for blood towards them.

John planted his feet firmly onto the rock and raised his sword up to his shoulder as he prepared for impact. The wild eyes of the lead Houlen glowed red with blood lust as she wailed with terror at them, John gripped his blade firmly and felt Bear doing the same, he gave a chuckle as the he looked at the wild grotesque women coming towards him.

"I never did attract the pretty ones, even as a kid I always got the ugly one." Bear gave a laugh as the Houlen wailed across the last ten feet, and John swiped his blade across in front, and took the head of the screaming Houlen clean off. The body shot sideways and crashed to the floor in front of five monks and splattered hard spraying blood everywhere. They screamed in terror and pushed their blood streaked faces into the floor, as the rest of the Houlen swooped above them and crashed to the floor with arrows embedded in their skulls.

Those who survived rose back into the air and twisted to make their second sweep. Bear gave a laugh as he brought his sword back up. "See your luck is changing my friend that one there is a little better looking." The wild banshee like women screamed round as the Houlen made their return, the group braced for another attack and clenched tightly to their weapons, as the Houlen again swept lower this time almost at shoulder level, John spat on the floor.

"Keep it low people this time is going to get rough and nasty." The Houlen were now wilder than ever, they had lost members of their ranks, and their blood lust was more intense. John and Bear held the front line and stiffened as they brought their swords up ready for the attack. The Houlen closed ranks as they came across the long stone plain towards them. The leader buckled and smashed into the floor, and then others followed, from inside the group Skip shouted.

"Who the hell are that lot?" John turned taking his eyes away from the Houlen to momentarily see whom Skip was talking about; across the top of the cliff from nowhere a mass of pale blue clad men had appeared. They all stood in rank with those at the front down on one knee and fired a hail of arrows into the Houlen. John turned back to the Houlen who veered to the left as a large number of them crashed to the floor writhing and wailing with pain. The Houlen swept up and over their heads out of range, and John at that moment did not care who the strangers were, they had saved his skin and that was fine by him. Blue cloaked soldiers flooded the top of the cliff, and began gathering the monks together and herding them back to the pass at the edge of the wall. A large section moved forward to meet them and Bear gave a smile as Crystal came up to his side.

"I have no idea how they got here, but those are Rhiannon's Marshals, they are the elite guard to the Queen of the Fae." Bear wiped the blood off his face with a rag.

"Well whoever they are, they are very welcome to join in, handy lads with a bow if you ask me, we can use em." He turned and looked back at the group of Specialists who were all bloodied but intact and free of injury. "Will we have Cutters to kill; it's about time you took a command, lead on we have help to back us up."

Judith beamed with delight at his side, as she saw him rise a little in stature, he was still very young and not unlike Robbie had been when he first left Loxley, he was covered in blood and his hair fell lank with the sweat, but somehow he appeared a little older and had an air of some authority. He shouldered his bow and pulled out his sword, and as loud as he could as the Marshals of the Fae fell in behind, he pointed to the black clad Cutters that were heading down the path towards them. "The Queen of Fae is in need, CHARGE!"

Rune watched as Robbie with his group reached the mouth of the tunnel, and drove into the large group of soldiers stationed in front. Surrounded by the Marshals, he cut and sliced into the soldiers, dealing out heavy forceful blows. The soldiers were overwhelmed and did not have the time to send up a signal, as Rowan and Robbie side by side cleaved a path for the following members of their group right through into the tunnel entrance.

Robbie and Rowan ran down the wide white tunnels followed by hundreds of the Marshals. As other tunnel entrance's appeared at their side, the Marshals would veer off into them, Rowan figured they knew the place better than any and was happy to leave them to it.

They ran out of the tunnel into a wide circular hall and Robbie skidded to a halt as the group all came to a sudden stop breathing heavily. Robbie lifted the folded map and he gasped in new air and looked at the large round room lined with about forty other tunnels.

"I don't remember this place, one of these leads down to the lake at the side of the castle." He scanned the map trying to get his bearings Fagan tapped his shoulder.

"Tis that one, although I think ye will find it occupied." He pointed to a wide tunnel just off to the right, where the sound of deep rumbling growls came up from the darkened depths. "She has let her hounds out I fear." The growls were getting louder, it was obvious it had got their scent and was heading their way. Robbie dropped his bow off his shoulder and pulled an arrow from his quiver.

"Ok let's give em a traditional Loxley salute." He fitted the arrow to his bow and readied his stance as the others followed suit.

The growl intensified, and then with an almost lion like roar, a huge mass of dirty matted snarling hair belted up out of the tunnel and launched itself into the air. The arrows whistled and then there was an ear piercing squeal, and the huge dog crashed to the floor with a heavy thud and skidded on the smooth crystal surface. As they reloaded, a second and third came bounding out of the tunnel with fierce roars and snarls, Robbie and Rowan reacted in an instant, as side by side they lifted their bows and fired.

Harry screamed with fear, Steph ducked as Smokes bumped into her side, sending her sprawling onto the floor, he rammed the spear into the polished floor and pointed it upward as the huge dog came snarling down at him. Smokes disappeared under the massive creature as it slammed into the floor, Steph screamed and jumped to her feet, Blades bounced across the room towards her, as another dog came leaping out of the tunnel. Panic flooded across Steph's face as she screamed for Pete, and clambered over the dead foul smelling animal.

"Hey baby I'm fine, but I could use a lift." The enormous head of the dog was lolled to one side with its massive mouth open baring its sharp fangs and needle like teeth, Pete was just below where the dogs tongue hung limp onto the side of his face, as a thick jelly like gue oozed out mixed with blood. Pete took a deep breath and tried to hold it in. "My god it stinks." He tried to hold in his retch as the foul slime oozed down his face past his nostrils and mouth. Steph scrambled up to his face and gave a heavy gasp of relief; she recoiled slightly from the smell and lifted her hand to her mouth.

"Oh sweetheart... That is disgusting, Oh God please help me get it off him, I think I am going to be sick." Behind her Blades and Fox dealt with the last of the creatures, as it howled at the end of Blades swords.

Now that the dog was dead, Harry found the courage to approach it with Fagan, and with Robbie and Rowan both smiling, they grabbed its large flea infested ears and pulled back with all their strength. The large dead brute slowly slid off Smokes who gasped for air as he pulled out his scarf and wiped the slime quickly off his face with utter repulsion. Fagan gave a hearty smile as he offered a hand to the pale looking Steph on her knees.

"As I said, they are the most vile beasts ye could ever wish to meet, it makes no sense that their meat is so sweet." Steph shook her head, trying to breathe and calm her reeling insides.

"What is?" She looked at Fagan who was staring at the dead beast with an almost affectionate look on his face, he pointed to the dead dog.

"That... Ye know, the Marsh Hound?"

It took a few moments for it sink in as everyone came up to speed, Steph's eyes opened wider than Robbie had ever seen them, as she lifted a very shaky hand and pointed to the dead dog, her voice rose higher and higher.

"That is a Marsh Hound!?" Fagan gave an agreeable nod, the colour drained from her face.

"Aye tis Lady Whiteline, why?" It was like watching a volcano preparing to erupt as Steph's hand shook more violently still pointing the dog and her eyes fixed on her husband in terror and disgust.

"YOU FED ME THAT!?" Steph staggered back as Smokes looked at the dead foul dog; he turned to her with an almost apologetic look on his face.

"Well I didn't know it looked like that Honey, Jade just gave it me as meat, so I cooked it."

Steph turned, staggered a few more paces, and then was violently sick. Everyone cringed as the splatter hit the floor, and screwed up their eyes, and turned away. Steph stood frozen unable to stop as her body gave a large spasm and shook with disgust. Fagan walked over and gave her a gentle pat on the back.

"That's the ticket, it's no good festering inside ye, just get it all up and out." Steph panted in between bouts of retching.

"Not Helping Fagan... Sorry. Urgh!" Fagan stepped back quickly.

"Oh my, I see ye ate quite a bit." He took a few paces back and then turned to the others. Blades looked a little paler than normal, as did Rags; he gave them a hearty smile. "Tis not to everyone's liking, right time is pressing and I think ye should be back on ye way." Rowan gave a nod as Maggs hurried over to Steph; Smokes stood up and scraped the slime off his shoulder with his knife. Rowan turned to Robbie.

"Get Mother composed, I will take Blades, Todd and Harry and do a bit of scouting ahead, catch us up at the end of the tunnel." Robbie gave a nod as Rowan grabbed Harry and the others, and ran off into the tunnel; Maggs offered her lavender scented hankie and uncorked a small bottle.

"Take this my dear, it has just a hint of Sloe, but it will cleanse you as it goes down and sterilise any beast left in there. I find at difficult moments it cleanses the karma." Steph took the bottle, which she knew must contain something made by Joe and took a huge swig. She swallowed and her face turned red as she breathed out and then coughed violently, her voice was just a hoarse whisper.

"Wow.... Thanks Maggs." Her coughing subsided as she wiped her face and took long breaths, and several minutes later she felt ready to move on. Robbie gave the signal and they moved into the tunnel on Rowan's trail.

Rune opened the window at the top of the Citadel Mount, and the Marshals of the Fae helped the wounded and terrified monks through to safety. The arrival of the Marshal's had given her great relief and Rune wanted to personally thank them, Jade had gone down to the bottom to collect one of their officers, as Rune watched Robbie in her mind and continued to ensure his safety, she wore a relaxed smile even though seeing her mother's revulsion was not something she should laugh at, it had made her giggle.

The tall officer of the Marshal's came up the path with Jade, and as she turned, he recognised her and instantly fell to one knee. "My Lady of Life, I had no knowledge that you had returned." Rune smiled as she walked toward him.

"I am not her, she was my great grandmother, although I believe I carry her likeness, I am Runestone Violet Circle, and this is my sister the Lady Green Circle, I am pleased and very relieved to see you, as it has eased great pressure from my Lord of Loxley who fights the cause of your new queen, and is the daughter of my aunt, and the son of Rhiannon, Rayne."

The officer lifted his head and looked up at Rune. "My Lady, it was your lord who called us back, without the sword and the lance of Eleanor they would not have been able to unlock the trees and summon us. The safety of the new queen is our duty; we are honoured that he would respect us so highly and request us to service."

Rune was uncertain how exactly Robbie had achieved such a feat, but at that moment as the battle raged on it felt irrelevant. "Tell me how the battle goes, for I feel a slight change in the air and would say that your queen is growing in strength." He rose to his feet and marvelled at her beauty, for she was not of Fae who were known for their grace and elegance, and yet to him Rune would rival all of them.

"My Lady, we are slowly gaining the advantage, these crude soldiers are no match for the fighting skills of my men and women. As we speak the town and keep have fallen to our forces, and we are deep within the Mount fighting those who have fled. The new queen has an escort as we bring extra powers and protections to her, once she is safe and protected in our keep, then the hunt for the dark witch will begin, her beasts and vile demons will fall to our arrows and swords have no fear."

Rune understood his loyalty to his men, but cautioned him. "Be aware My Lord that the witch will not fall easily, she has planned this assault of your realm for a long time. She has in her possession a thing of great evil dark power, and if not approached with great care your men will find they are no match for it." He gave a nod of understanding.

"We have been warned by the keeper of trees, we shall take every precaution as this thing she wields is known from the legends of our past. The Citadel is sacred to us and all who walk it, blood will not be spilt to defile our land you have my word."

Rune was satisfied that he understood the importance of the situation, she offered her hand and he knelt and kissed it, as was tradition amongst the Fae. "I will move to the mount at the final moment, for I wish to be on hand when she is taken, removing that star from her grasp will not be easy, it is a task that I alone can do, so do not sacrifice the lives of your men." The Marshal gave another bow and turned.

"With your ladies' approval I shall return." Rune gave a nod and he walked off down the path, Jade looked at Rune with a shrewd stare.

"You said nothing about it being your task alone to remove the star; I thought none of us can touch it?"

"None of us can, but it is still my task and I am the only one with the means to do it."

"You are getting very like grandmother; you do know that don't you Rune?" She gave a slight giggle.

"I thought she was your hero?" Jade smiled.

"She is, so is Fagan I think he is pretty cool for an old bloke, he is like a really weird version of Joe." It was a strange thought, and Rune gave a chuckle as she walked back to her lookout to ensure the safety of the others.

Rowan peered round the corner and took stock of the situation. The castle glowed as it had the last time he saw it across the wide smooth water, the bridge that ran from the point where they had confronted the Dark One to the castle was new, and looking at the sides of the stone pillars holding it up, it was obvious the water level was dropping. The smooth path that ran round the edge of the massive cave was a lot wider than before as the water receded back, but apart from that everything appeared quiet. He gave the hand signal and Blades and Fox came forward. "You check out the tunnels along that side, Harry and me will check these out. I want everything clear for about a hundred yards, Ok?"

Blades gave a nod and slipped off quietly with Fox, and Rowan stepped out of the tunnel followed by Harry. Carefully they crept along the path to the first tunnel and Harry peeped inside. His voice echoed as he spoke. "Hey man these aint tunnels, they only like go back for about twenty feet, although they are kinda cool." Rowan shook his head.

"It's a passing point, they use them all round the cave so that they can get past each other without blocking the main path." Harry shook his head approvingly.

"Cool man, these fairies are pretty funky you know." Rowan tried to ignore him and walked along the line of passing points to the first real tunnel and looked round the corner, everything was quiet. "You know man you shouldn't sneak off like that, it aint cosmic." Rowan gave a jump as Harry whispered in his ear, something he had not expected.

"Sorry Harry but I want to make sure all of us are safe."

"I don't no man, this place is like radical and cool, and all with its white walls and really funky stripes of violet, but there is like some weird psychic funky thing going on here that jangles my vibes." Rowan gave a shrug, somehow it did not surprise him, after all Harry found spooks in just about everything he encountered, he could not imagine why he thought this place would be any different.

"You think too much, chill out Harry." Rowan stepped back onto the path and looked the whole length of the Mirrored Waters; along the far end of the bridge in the distance he could see pale blue clad soldiers walking along the bridge to the castle. "That's good news the soldiers have arrived, down here must be pretty secure, come on let's get back to meet Robbie."

Harry watched as the long line of soldiers drew level with them across the pool and marched towards the steps of the castle where a white wall of light pulsated around it, he gave a chuckle as he screwed up his eyes and watched the light streak across the water like blurred lines. "Harry hurry up Robbie should be here soon."

Harry watched as the ripples ran across the surface of the water and lapped up against the path, he screwed his eyes again and watched the light bounce off them and jump into the walls. "Whoa that is so cosmic man."

The soldiers arrived at the steps of the castle and stood at attention with their backs to Harry in a defensive line of protection the whole length of the bridge. Rowan headed back to the tunnel as he saw Blades and Fox turn and begin to make their way back, he gave a sigh of relief as he walked to greet them.

Harry stopped and looked at the water; he felt the vibration run up his legs, as his inner strength seemed to stall momentarily. The sounds in his larynx failed, as he lifted a shaky finger, and pointed to the large oval head that rose out of the water silently on a long thin slender neck, between him and the long white bridge. Rowan slowed his pace as he saw Blades and Fox suddenly stop and stare in fear, a cold prickle ran up his neck. Somewhere behind him, Harry found his voice and screamed.

"UNCOSMIC MONSTERS, RUN FOR YOUR LIFE!"

Rowan turned quickly and was not at all prepared for what he saw. Harry was running like a wild man, the huge monstrous beast had noticed Harry shouting, and it turned its oval shaped head and saw him. Rowan watched as its large mouth opened revealing a thick row of what looked like sharp long pointed teeth, it moved without a sound in the water and lunged its massive head towards Harry who was almost on top of Rowan.

It was an instant reactive moment, as Rowan stepped back into the passing point and snatched at Harry's hood as he thundered past the opening. He heaved with all his might and yanked Harry as hard as he could into the tunnel, as the big grey coloured head came whipping past with a loud snap.

Both of them fell backwards with Harry screaming for his life, they rolled on the floor in panic, and Rowan scrambled to his feet. He gripped the wailing Harry by the collar and pulled him up using every ounce of his strength. Harry's eyes looked wild and terrified, but there was no time for words as Rowan saw the huge neck twist, and he knew it was coming back. "Harry for Hearne's sake run."

Both of them fled back up the twenty feet of tunnel as the giant head came directly towards them, they reached the end of the tunnel and Harry screamed for his life as the giant head came straight through the entrance, and slithered up the tunnel like a hideous snake. Rowan pushed Harry back into the wall with his right arm and felt his own back press hard against the cool wall; he closed his eyes and waited for the final moment.

Rowan could hear his heart pumping in his head, and had become aware of everything around him, at his side he felt the shaking of Harry's body and could hear Harry drawing deeper and deeper breaths, the scent of something rotten and decaying filled his nostrils and he felt his stomach twist, but the inevitable had not happened so he opened one eye, and gasped with shock.

The large Bronteal had got trapped just a foot away from them. The mouth was so large it was impossible to open it in the restricted space, and so its long white pointed teeth were exposed and bared like an old growling dog. The hot breath smelt foul, and Rowan tried hard not to breathe it in as the monster breathed out. "Oh that is disgusting, what the hell does this thing eat apart from woodsman?"

He turned his head to Harry who was flat against the wall with his eyes tightly closed, shaking violently and silently mumbling. It felt very odd being trapped by such a terrifying beast, and for no reason at all, Rowan began to see the funny side. He gave a slight chuckle not sure whether it was relief, humour or fear.

"Well Harry, you finally got it right, there is such things as uncosmic monsters after all." Rowan started to chuckle and felt for some very mad reason light hearted. "Hey Harry, I dare you, open your eyes." His chuckle grew deeper as he started to laugh. Harry shook his head violently.

"No man I just know." Rowan gave a deep belly laugh.

"Oh Harry you have no idea, go on open your eyes and meet your guest."

Harry's whole body shook from top to tail, and he forced his eyes closed tighter.

"Oh man I just can't I know it, if I look it will be real, and my vibes won't hack it man honestly."

"Well, we aint going nowhere for a while Harry, it's about time you faced your fear and acted like a man about it, look at it Harry, I do believe it likes you, go on give it a kiss." Rowan could see the small dark eyes up near the roof of the passage watching them as he started to laugh, he nudged Harry who flinched and gave a whimper. "Harry we have to deal with this, you are safe for the moment but with a head this big I am assuming the body is just as huge and powerful, so we either deal with it and live, or stay like this and die together, it's up to you."

Rowan felt the sweat rolling down his face as the breath of the beast filled the tunnel heating it up, he wanted to lift his left hand, but was not sure putting it any closer to the monster was safe, Harry took a series of very long deep breaths and Rowan gave a titter as he waited for Harry to see their visitor.

Harry opened his eyes and stared at the monster. The scream was long, loud and almost deafened Rowan who could not help but burst into laughter again. Harry looked more terrified than Rowan had ever seen him, the monster reacted by trying to roar at him through gritted teeth, and for a moment it felt like a competition between who could scream louder, Harry or the monster. Rowan's mind was working fast as Harry ran out of energy and quietened down.

"Can you get your swords out Harry?" Harry shook his head vigorously.

"No man the roof is too low, I won't get them over. Oh shit man I am going to be chomped by this voodoo beastie, this is so not cosmic." Rowan gave a smile.

"Hate to tell you this dude; non cosmic monsters are like that... what about your flask?"

"Whoa dude, one last one for the road, that's funky. You know I think you are a cool and cosmic guy don't you man?" Rowan smiled.

"Hang in there and don't get more weird than you are now, pass me the flask and your lighter if you can reach it." Rowan carefully slid his arm across Harry as he fumbled in his pocket. He felt the warm metal of the flask touch his fingers, and he gently moved his hand back across Harry where he took hold of it with his left hand. Carefully he moved his hand back to Harry who remained as flat against the wall as possible, to get the lighter.

"Thank god for Joe and your addiction, this might be the only time where this poison actually enhances your life Harry."

"How do you mean man?"

"Watch and learn my friend." Rowan gently slipped the flask up to his lips and he pushed himself as flat as he could against the wall, the monster watched with his dark small eyes, but was not aware of what Rowan was up to. Gripping the cap with his teeth he unscrewed it and let it fall to the floor, Rowan filled his mouth with the hot burning alcohol made by Joe.

Bringing his left hand holding the lighter up to his mouth Rowan took a long breath through his nose and held it. His finger slipped on the wheel and the lighter sparked and ignited, and pushing all of the air inside his lungs into his mouth Rowan forced out the alcohol, and sprayed it through the flame onto the face of the Bronteal. The flames erupted as the liquor ignited. The Bronteal gave an horrendous squeal of pain, Rowan opened his eyes to see the huge head sliding away from him back down the tunnel covered in flames, and gave a resounded gasp of relief.

Harry was pressed tight against the wall with his eyes closed tight, although his eyebrows had gone, and most of his goatee. Rowan seized the moment and grabbed him. "Harry run for Hearne's sake we are free."

The two of them ran for all they were worth back down the tunnel and out onto the path, where Robbie and the others were shooting at over twenty identical creatures. Across the water on the bridge, the Marshals of the Fae were slashing at the beasts as they fought them off with swords.

Rowan gave a happy sigh and filled his lungs with fresh air as he pulled the dazed Harry along the path back to the group, Robbie looked back in relief to see them safe, and Maggs gave a squeal of delight as she ran at Harry and threw her arms round him. Rowan pushed both of them into the long tunnel and slid out his sword.

In the castle of crystal, Fish had his sword and bow and was waiting for the light to stop so he could join in with the Marshals and help. Amethyst dressed in pale blue pants and a long top waited impatiently, with a bow, quiver and sword, she felt the moment was approaching as her ring had gained a small glimmer of light, and she was ready for battle to claim her realm.

The violet figure of Rune rose out of the floor and Amethyst gave a squeal of delight as she hurriedly threw her arms around her. "Oh Rune, I have missed you." Rune smiled as she embraced her cousin.

"I have missed you too, I am sorry it has taken so long to get here, but there has been much happening which I needed to do to ensure the safety of everyone." Amethyst's eyes sparkled with tears.

"I knew you would come, when I saw Robbie and the guys on the path, I knew it would not be much longer, is she dead yet, can I leave this castle and walk outside again?" Rune gave her a bigger squeeze.

"That time is not here yet, but it is coming, you have your guard so I think you will be safe enough to leave in their care, just wait a moment longer while I take care of her watchers at your door."

Rune walked out of the castle and through the curtain of white light, on to the long white bridge, where the fighting was frantic as the Bronteal swooped down biting and snatching at the slashing Marshals of the Fae. She lifted her arms and violet light flickered in her eyes. Rune's voice boomed and echoed around the vast white cave containing the Mirrored Lake. "Circlee ant ston, eskith nay bon, bern en Terraphantisum."

The water within the lake exploded up engulfing everything and rejecting the Bronteal who flew up into the air above all of them, their massive slimy ugly bodies writhing in pain, and then with a click of Rune's fingers they ignited. Maddy stopped looking stunned as the water covered her; Robbie looked at her with a very worried look on his face. "What is it?" Maddy gave him a very stunned and shocked looked.

"She named it; she named the realm we never name." He shrugged.

"So what?" Maddy took a long breath.

"It is a realm none of us name out of fear, wow Robbie, I don't think you have any understanding at all about how powerful your wife is becoming. Eve created and named that realm, and as far as I can tell, that was the last time it was ever spoken, she truly is the heir of Eve and no doubt."

Robbie turned back to look up at the Bronteal writhing in agony above him, as he watched a long line of flame draw itself across the ceiling and then separate. As the gap widened he could see the black tortured figures engulfed by fire deep within it, the Bronteal gave one last terrifying scream and were sucked into the gap, which snapped shut extinguishing their sounds, and all around the inside of the cave suddenly went very quiet.

Robbie watched as the violet shimmering figure of Rune walked back along the bridge to the castle, and the bright white curtain of light fell to the water and was gone. Amethyst walked onto the bridge as the Marshals of the Fae held up their weapons and cheered, for the New Queen of Avalon was free. Rowan came up at his side.

"Ok that was intense, now we face the hard bit, we head upward and find her, it has to end here and now, Loxley will have need of us."

CHAPTER THIRTY ONE

LAST ARROWS

It had been over a week, and the ring wore by Amethyst still did not shine completely, showing the authority of the position she held. No one appeared to notice, but for Amethyst it was very important, and her eyes often wandered down to her hand. Fish was feeling much happier, being trapped in the castle had its merits, but he had lived a life where he could roam free, and so as the wall of light fell, he was quickly onto the bridge, where he delighted in the company of the Marshals.

Robbie and his group were hot, tired and hungry, as they walked the long length of the Mirrored Waters to the end of the white bridge, there they sat against the wall and rested as the long line of blue clad guards celebrated the coming of their queen. Maggs passed around oat biscuits and dried fruits, as they rested and waited for Amethyst and Fish to be reunited as Specialists, and gave sympathetic looks towards Harry, who was looking much paler than usual.

High up on the flat shelf of hard stone, Bear and his group finally rested as the Marshal's cleared up the last remaining fighters of the black clad army. In every direction there were bodies littered from what had felt like a day of fighting, even though it had only been half of the morning. Sweating and tired they made their way to the littered rocks and rows of burning torches, on the edge of the high wall, under the dark clouds there was little relief from the trapped heat, but the edge of the cliff provided a small amount of breeze, which after a long fight felt like heaven.

William broke a thick slab of a fruit filled cake made by Steph into pieces, and passed it round the group, as they drank from their canteens and slouched against the cool stones, watching the Marshals of the Fae surround and secure the perimeter. All of them bore the signs of a fight in the form of blood splatters and small nicks and wounds.

Bear eyed the countless bodies of headless Houlen scattered all around them, the few that lived had fled in fear, and he was not sorry to see them leave. He looked round at the tired faces of the Specialists and smiled. "We took the measure of them second time around, what you say people?"

Closed eyes on smiling faces just about said it all, in a way it felt like evening things up, their first encounter had served the bitter blow of yet another loss to their ranks, so it felt better to have survived intact, and dealt a lethal blow to Morgan le Fey and her hideous creatures.

Will slumped back with his eyes closed next to Judith. "Thank god that is over." Judith did not feel as confident as he did.

"She is still around Will, I feel her somewhere beneath us." He opened one eye and looked at her.

"Do you know what she is doing?" She shook her head.

"That is not how it works, I am of her blood, and she had the gift of limited sight, I can sense her presence, but I am not privy to her thoughts.... I am glad about that, I do not want to feel what she thinks, her mind is filled with hatred and I do not want the burden of seeing it." He understood, so did many of the others as they listened quietly to her. "I will know if she comes near to us, you will not have to fear being surprised by her."

"This eez good Hornet, your gift will be a good aid to us, I am glad we ave you with us this day, she eez hiding but I think she knows we are waiting; I think it will be not long before she comes to greet with us."

The fact she had not been seen was a point of concern for Rune. It seemed strange to her that after such a long time of making the plans for her very elaborate scheme, she had not appeared anywhere to stop the slaughter and taking prisoner of any of her men. In the town of Avalonia hundreds of black vested soldiers sat on the burned grass tied together and watched by the Marshals of the Fae. It made little sense to her, in Rune's mind it would make more sense to appear and protect those who fought her cause.

Rune paced up and down on the Lookout, as Jade sat in the shade of the Hawthorn and chewed on fresh fruit and cheese. Rune stopped and turned to her. "Why all the plans, why the traps and closed doorways if you are not prepared to fight to keep them? She has the Star of the Merle, what the hell is she playing at Jade?" Jade chewed on a grape.

"It does seem odd, but to be honest Rune who cares? To be honest if she never comes back, I will be happy and Rowan will be safe."

"But Jade if she has gone into hiding, we can never go home again. Avalon will never be restored and the balance will be tipped away from all of us, everything as we know it will end." Jade shrugged.

"Then she wins and gets what she wants, I mean that is the point isn't it? Maybe this is just part of her plan, she is devious enough to have more up her sleeve, she probably thinks if she hides, we will think we have won and let our guard down, after all Robbie is always saying we should stay focused and be prepared for anything."

Rune walked back to the edge of the rock, her frustration was building inside and she wanted to get Robbie back at her side and safe. "Maybe we should go over there and have a look around for ourselves?"

"Well, that is one way of tempting her out; she cannot kill you if she can't find you." Rune looked back at her sister.

"That's not very nice." Jade shrugged.

"It's true though, oh come on Rune, she would love to get rid of you, let's face it, we are all in the way of her plans. Robbie wants you here safe for a very good reason, I know you are bored, I am too, but we must stay here until we know what she is up to, just be patient and let her show her hand, you're smart enough to figure it out when she does." Jade lifted a large chunk of pink looking cheese with blue streaks in it. "This is really weird cheese but I think I am becoming quite fond of it." She took a large bite and smiled as Rune sat down on the edge of the rock and let her legs dangle over the edge, she gave a big sigh.

"I hate having to wait around." Jade gave a small giggle.

Fagan led the way, and soon the group containing Amethyst and Robbie and his party arrived in the large Hall of Rhiannon. The Specialists moved round the room quickly checking all the doors were secure as Robbie and Rowan viewed the devastation. The floor was covered in water and thick clumps of what looked like yellow and red sand, the fountain was smashed to the floor, and water trickled out across the floor and down to the lower doors. Most of the ornate wooden doors were filled with long scratches that showed the anger of the Houlen, and the white walls had large splashes of blood across them. Robbie looked at the destruction of what had been a very beautiful place, as the group splashed round looking for any signs that the Dark One was still around. "This was her hiding place, maybe she is heading up top, and somehow I think being out in the open will not be a bad thing, I like to see what is coming at me."

High above Robbie around the scaffolding left up by the monks, Bear and his group decided to wait for Robbie. For most of the day it had been dark, but as the day moved on it felt like it was becoming much darker. Skip and William ventured below ground and found some extra torches, which they lit and brought back to the surface. Big John and Treen organised several large bonfires from the piles of scattered timber that had been destined for use as scaffold. With bonfires spread every forty feet the light helped illuminate their surroundings, and the Marshals of the Fae spread out to watch every possible route onto the Citadel platform.

Bear had been sat for well over an hour when the first signs of more trouble began. The watches to the rear of the Citadel sounded the alarm, and everyone was up on their feet. Bear and his group walked round the ruined building and passed the long rows of make shift tents, to look out across the wide plain that sloped away towards the back end of Avalon and the mountains behind it.

At the base of the slope there were twenty very large men dressed in all leather, clad with long steel spikes. They wore full face helmets in which there was a letter box type slit, behind which burned dark evil eyes. All of them held on to a thick steel chain, on the end of which was a thickly matted snarling savage Marsh Hound. The row of men stood waiting as if expecting the Specialists to do something, Bear watched with a keen interest with Skip at his side. Skip was curious.

"You don't think they want us to run down and challenge them, do you?" The others were all thinking the same; Bear loosened his axe in his belt.

"They can wait there all day for me, I aint leaving this place, if it comes to it, this is the best place to make our stand, so if they want me, they can see me."

"Well, I suppose so, one would think she would have sent more, after all we do have a few hundred of these Fae chaps with us." Treen nodded.

"This eez just the start, she eez as slimy as her son, there will be more giving it the sneaky to catch our guard off it, Bear eez right, this eez the best place to stand."

Bear took stock of the situation checking out where the Marshals were positioned, he knew Treen had spent more time with Scarlet than any understanding the fighting skills of the enemy and he agreed with her.

"We stay and we hold until Robbie gets here, this place for now is the prize, it's the highest part of this rock and it's ours, and nothing changes till I say so, agreed?"

The rest of the group all nodded and voiced their agreement, and Bear planted his feet firm to show they were not moving; the black clad soldiers remained where they were.

Rune sat very still and watched the scene unfold. "Jade get ready, it's starting again." Jade looked up from under the tree, but Rune was as still as a pillar, she hurriedly got to her feet and walked across the rock to her sister's side, the sky above the whole of Avalon was now a thick jet black blanket of cloud.

"What do we do Rune? It's so dark over there it must be like midnight."

"I think it's time to get closer, we may have very little time to act, and over here we are just too far out of it."

"But Rune we are supposed to stay here on safe ground."

"I have been thinking about it, the site of the Mount is sacred, and so is Arthur's grave, she knows I cannot kill her on the mount, so she will not leave it, but if we are closer and on hallowed soil, we can use our skills to get that star from her." Jade shook her head slowly.

"I am not sure Rune, Robbie and Rowan were pretty insistent we remain here." Rune suddenly jumped up and Jade gave a startled squeak.

"Robbie and Rowan do not understand her like I do, they think they can do this, but they can't, I am the only one who has the skills to deal with that star, it is my destiny alone, they have done what was meant for them, now it's time that I fulfilled what was destined for me, you can stay if you want to Jade, but I am going across there to protect the people I love."

"Chill out Rune, I didn't say I wasn't going, wow you get moody when your left alone, honestly you can be as crabby as granddad at times, I love em too you know." Rune gave her sister a smile.

"Sorry Sis, I am worried about them, and I just want this over so I can go home, I really miss it don't you?" Jade nodded.

"Yeah, I do, I can't have noisy sex next to your room here, Rowan says I have to be quiet, at least at home I can have a good scream and swing from the lights if I want." Rune gave a giggle as she waved her arm and a violet window opened.

"Alright Jade, remember we have to stay out of sight, and do not try to go invisible, the moment you do the Merle will start to drain your powers, only use them as an absolute last resort."

"Ok got ya." Rune took Jade by the hand and both of them stepped through onto the top of the Rest, the large carved rock into which Arthur's tomb had been placed. In the distance across the top of the rock the large fires flickered through the darkness. Jade crouched down and stared across the wide plain. "Wow it's dark here; I can hardly see a thing."

"I can and for now that is all that matters."

In the darkness behind the line of silent soldiers holding back the Marsh Hounds, the blackness of the air appeared to move. Hawk had the keenest eyes but even he was unsure of what was happening. "I can see something, but I am buggered if I know what, I think we should prepare because whatever it is, I am sure it's coming this way."

Arrows slid out of quivers and were fitted to strings as the long row of Specialists began their preparation for their second clash of the day. Somewhere ahead there was a faint rumbling sound, and the group all tensed unable to clearly see anything. Suddenly from nowhere a massive glowing ball of fire came hurtling out of the darkness towards them, the group ducked quickly as the ball hurtled overhead and landed behind them with a massive explosion blasting fire everywhere. John looked behind him with a startled look on his face. "Where the friggin hell did that come from?" Hawk pointed.

"There.... SHIT!" Four more large fireballs came out of nowhere, and hurtled across the Citadel and landed spraying fire over the monks' tents and supplies, the Marshals scattered as the flames brushed across the floor like liquid and poured off the edge of the cliff and down onto the town below.

The Marsh Hounds snarled and began to roar and bark like the savage beasts that the Dark One had made them, the black clad guards pulled back on the chains to hold them, but they looked like they were finding it difficult. Bear lifted his bow.

"Looks like dog is back on the menu, just don't tell Mother." He sighted his bow and waited as the others followed suit, Bear knew it would not be much longer now. "Aim at their heads and reload fast; these bastards want us on their menu."

From deep inside the darkness came a loud roar, and the black clad guards let go of the chains. The Marsh Hounds snarled and ran up the slope towards the line of Specialists and Marshals, behind them out of the darkness came a mass of black leather clad soldiers who screamed and yelled as they thundered up the slope to meet the waiting protectors of the Citadel.

Bear took aim and fired, his arrow hit the dog square in the forehead, and it crumpled over rolling into the stone floor, his hand dropped to his axe as the mass of soldiers pounded up the slope towards them. Behind the Specialists long rows of archers lifted their bows, and as Bear planted his feet firmly into the floor and raised his axe, the hail of Fae arrows whistled over his head. The arrows came down like rain and the front lines of the black army fell into the floor and were swallowed by the mass that followed.

Somewhere behind them Robbie shouted his orders as he arrived at the surface with the rest of the Specialists, and as the front line prepared for the clash, the gaps in the Specialists ranks filled as Robbie and the rest of the group joined them with their swords out. From the left Marshals of the Fae flooded onto the rocks, to meet with those coming in from the right, over a thousand blue clad members of the Fae lifted their bows and fired into the mass as it reached within ten feet of them, hundreds of soldiers fell riddled with arrows, and yet more still came.

They met like a crashing wave, as the Specialists brought up their swords and cleaved into the onslaught of the black army. It was bedlam, as screams and wails of the dying and wounded rang into the air.

Deep in the thick of it, the Specialists carved their way forward, blindly hacking and slashing with all of their might. The Marshals fought with power and agility and soon a wide circle began to form as the Specialist took their ground and protected it. In the centre of the open circle Maggs Gaynor, and Milly fired at anything looking like it could threaten a Specialist, Rags worked with Jay lighting her explosive arrows, which she fired with skill into the dark mass of enemy arms and legs. Fagan stormed into the centre with the strength of twenty men, he swung round with a huge gleaming scythe, to which no one had the faintest idea of where he had got it from, large sections of the soldiers folded into the floor as he brought the lethal blade whizzing back round.

Explosions erupted as limbs flew into the air, and bits of soldier fell out of the sky like rain. Maddy panted as she stepped back into the open circle dragging a blood splattered Crystal back with her. "Screw the bloody Merle Crystal, if we can get just a few extra special arrows into that lot it will help." Crystal nodded understanding as Maddy dropped her long white bow from her shoulder. "Oh mother, give me all my gifts of the White Circle now when I need them most."

She lifted her bow with a long white arrow and a barbed tip, and pulled back on the string aiming high.

The arrow exploded off her bow like a rocket, and disappeared into the blackness above her; a few seconds later it fell from the sky like a blazing missile, and landed in the thick of the black soldiers. There was a huge burst of fire that blew up into the sky and an area the size of a small football pitch exploded into flames, snuffing out the soldiers in a roaring inferno. "Thanks mother." She winked at Crystal who lifted her bow and aimed to the other side of the heaving mass of enemy ranks.

Crystal aimed through the gaps in the fighting mass and picked out one extra large individual. She closed one eye and took a deep breath. "May the power of the Fae be with me this day and protect this land of my sister." The arrow released.

The massive man in black pounded towards them up the slope swinging a large steel club, behind the others charged with raised swords, through the gaps in the fighting men Crystal's arrow streaked like lightening, and found its mark. Ice sprayed out from the arrow instantly stopping everyone within fifty feet, those behind bumped into the frozen figures and they watched in horror as their fellow soldiers exploded into a million tiny deep frozen fragments.

Maddy had her second silver arrow on the string and took aim at another large group, her arrow flew through the mass and struck deep, the flames exploded out taking out half as many as her previous arrow, she knew the Merle was absorbing her powers and it was pointless to use a third, Crystal released her second, freezing yet another large group, but as with Maddy's arrow, it was only half as effective.

Rune lifted her bow with Jade. "I know we are well out of it here, but focus on me and release when I do, your arrow will count Jade and every arrow at the moment will help, she has not appeared yet, but I think she will soon, until then we will help out all we can." Jade lifted her bow and closed her eyes.

"OK Rune I am ready."

"Fire!"

Robbie and Rowan were side by side slashing and blocking as five soldiers fought them, two arrows came out of nowhere and hit two of them in the forehead, and

Robbie and Rowan stepped back as the bodies fell at their feet. Rowan swung a heavy blow into one of the soldiers with a grunt. "Urgh! I never saw an arrow turn in mid air before....Urgh!" He pulled his sword out of the soldier and twisted ramming it into another.

"Yes you have... oomph!"

"Where?" Robbie twisted Destiny and swiped taking off two heads.

"Windsor... Remember the birds and the castle?"

"Rune and Jade, right I am with you now, where the hell are they?" He brought his elbow into the face of a soldier and twisted his blade backwards thrusting into the stunned man.

"If I am right, they have disobeyed us again, and are probably not that far away." Robbie cut upwards hard, and the man in front screamed with agony drowning out Rowan's reply, two more arrows came out of nowhere taking out yet another two soldiers.

As the battle raged, slowly the Marshals of the Fae formed a huge circle around the Citadel and began to slowly push the enemy backwards clearing more space. Inside the circle was littered with the dead and dying of both sides. Amethyst was not allowed into the fray, and surrounded by ten guards; she used her bow to help out the Specialists.

Big John was covered in blood and sweat as he sliced up anything in front with his wide sword. Fish fought his way across to the side of him and gave John a huge smile as he stood once again at the side of his old fighting comrade; John gave a grunt as he drove his sword deep into a soldier. "Who are you? Hey lads, look we got a part timer helping out." He cut down in a massive slice, and the soldier in front fell to the floor. Bear and Jaz both laughed as they saw Fish fighting amongst them.

"Nice cloak, not bad for a grain thief." Fish laughed out loud as he worked his way forward.

"Go on laugh all you like, I am telling you guys be nice, or you won't get an invite to the house warming."

"Have you got any ale?" Fish laughed in the thick of the fight.

"We got a cellar full John, why are you thirsty?" John gave his usual big smile.

"I am working one up real special for you Fish." They all moved forward into the thick of the fighting with sweat running down their faces in the stifling heat, the Marshals of the Fae worked their way closer together and soon were mixed in between the Specialists as the fight raged on.

Milly and Judy worked fast as they tended the wounded, those who were lost were covered with their cloaks by Maggs and Rags as they moved round the widening circle doing the best they could for the dead. Judith stopped and slowly stood up; over on the top of the rest Rune lowered her bow and stood still for a moment. Judith closed her eyes and Rune could feel her connect to her, Rune understood and lifted her hand to Jade's shoulder. "Wait Sis, I think she is coming."

The Marshals of the Fae gripped at the cloaks of the Specialists, and pulled them back as others filled in their places on the front line. Covered in blood and grime the Specialists stepped back away from the fight as the Fae closed ranks creating a ten wide wall of men that encircled the Citadel Mount. Right in the centre of the cleared circle the small cloaked figure of Hornet stood alone as she sensed the world around her, her eyes flickered with pale blue light, and then she turned to where Robbie had suddenly noticed her and lifted his arm to Rowan, Judith screamed across the space. "SHE IS HERE!"

For Robbie there was no time to react, the floor gave a lurch, and from the opening of the tunnel at the entrance of the Citadel, blinding white light blasted out and up into the sky, engulfing everything and burning at their darkness adjusted eyes.

The floor lifted and exploded upwards throwing everyone off their feet and knocking them heavily to the floor. Boulders and chunks of stone rained out of the sky as a hole twenty feet wide appeared in the top of the mount. The Specialists were strewn across the open space covered in dust, rubble and blood. Judith lay stunned, half buried next to Maggs, and several of the Specialists groaned under the weight of the falling fragments.

The whole of the mount had shaken with such a massive blast that Rune and Jade had been knocked off their feet, and thrown across the top of the Rest. Jade moaned as she found herself lying on the rough hard floor in the doorway of the tomb of Arthur. Rune lay on her back high above her, slightly stunned from a bad knock to the back of her head.

Robbie coughed and spat as he crawled out from between two large boulders covered in grime, as around him the others moaned and slowly sat up coughing and choking. Robbie shook his head to get all the dirt out of his hair and blinked to clear his eyes.

His ears were ringing and his head pounded, as he slowly tried to stand, for a moment he felt dazed and confused. The noise around him seemed dull, as he tried to take in what was happening. Behind him the clash of steel and the roar of fighting soldiers of the Raven intensified, as they saw the arrival of their mistress. They thundered forward with renewed vigour, crashing in waves on the thick ranks of the Marshals.

Morgan le Fey hovered in the air taking in the scene with relish, the thin smile on her withered lips showing the pleasure she felt in her moment of victory. Her red eyes shone with satisfaction, as she took in the view of the group of Specialists as they clambered from between the boulders, and struggled to get to their feet, and gave a small laugh.

"Look at you, how pathetic, how could any of you honestly think you could match my army? You honestly think those old inadequate fighters of a long past era can match the might of my modern soldiers?"

Rowan spat the dirt and blood from his mouth as he looked back at the wide line of blue holding back her forces, he had dirt all over his face and a long line of blood ran down from his temple and glistened, his eyes were fixed like cold steel as he rose slowly to his feet and turned back to look at her.

"I don't know, it looks to me like our boys are kicking your soldiers' arse, I don't see any of them getting through to protect your skinny bones." He lifted his sword and stared at her with hatred, as the others took hope and began to stand all around her. The Dark One glared at Rowan.

"OUT OF MY WAY YOU IRKSOME FOOL, I DO NOT HAVE THE TIME TO BANDY WITH IGNORANT PEASANTS, GIVE ME THE BOY WHO CALLS HIMSELF KING!"

There was a flash of blue as Rowan lifted his sword, and he was thrown backwards into the air revealing the dust covered figure of Robbie behind him.

Rowan smashed to the floor as Big John jumped forward sweeping with his blade. It collided with yet another bolt of light, and he was lifted into the air and sent crashing to the floor several feet away. Jay let a stinger fly, and it shot at speed towards the Dark One, she gave a swipe of her arm and it bent in the air and exploded behind her. Maddy lifted her bow containing a white arrow, but it snapped from her hand and clattered across the stone as the Dark One squealed with laughter. "Fools all of you, you cannot match the power of the Merle, you are nothing compared to the force I wield."

Her cloud floated lower, and they all saw the dark red eyes flash with her evil malice. Robbie was still stunned as he lifted his head, and looked up and his eyes looked deeply into the dark red eyes of Morgan le Fey, he felt the hand on his throat, then the jerk through his body, as he swung upwards into the air. His ears instantly cleared as he heard the cold cruel familiar droning voice. "Got you... Give me the boy king, and where is your witch log chopper?"

He could feel the pressure behind his eyes, as the grip on his throat tightened, and the air restricted from his lungs. He tried to move and thrash out at her, but his arms and legs felt paralysed with the coldness running through him, as he swung from her hand unable to fully understand the strength of the pale white woman who was holding him aloft.

Her deep red eyes stared at him with curious pleasure from her white cold face, her smile was cruel and her laughter cold as she threw back her head and laughed at him. "Fools, all of you, did you honestly think you could outsmart me? You foul woodland dwelling parasites, you are nothing compared to the life I have built, all of you look at your leader hanging like a mouse I caught in the trap of my making."

Rune sat up as Jade clambered back over the edge of the rock on to the top. "Rune what happened?"

Rune was on her feet in seconds, as her eyes blazed with violet, Jade saw the urgency in her face and quickly scrambled to her feet. Her head was bleeding and she wiped the blood from her face as she crossed to the side of her sister. Jade connected to Rune and gave a gasp of horror as she saw the Dark One slightly raised in the air, on a black cloud holding Robbie by the throat with one hand.

Morgan le Fey gave a sinister smile as she watched Robbie's face starting to turn blue. "Give me your witch and the boy, then I will drop you and let you live."

He fought as his lungs felt like they were ready to explode, he wanted to scream 'Never' as loud as he could into her cold white face, but there was no way any sound could pass his air tight throat. She lifted her black hand, and through his straining tear filled bulging eyes, he saw the Star of the Merle, and he knew that it would soon be over; he closed his eyes and concentrated with all his might.

"I love you Runestone."

"No fight her, I am here."

Rune turned looking at the floor, she saw the bow and bent down and snatched it up. Rune went for her quiver, but it was empty. "Jade quickly I need an arrow find one." There was panic in her voice as one of Rune's tears hit the floor and a small violet sprung out of the stone. Jade twisted searching the floor as she panicked.

"There all gone Rune, we used them." Jade's eyes covered the whole surface of the Rest in the darkness, but the quivers were empty. "Rune I can't find any." She started to cry as her heart pounded, and she ran to the edge of the wall and looked down to see if any had rolled off the top and fallen below. "Rune please, you must do something." Her tears were streaming from her eyes as she looked to her sister in desperation. "Save him don't let him die." Rune was blurred in Jade's vision as the terror took hold of her.

The panic was surging through Rune as she turned back, her eyes exploding with violet light, and deep down inside her a voice and pictures from some past moment entered into her mind.

Eve pulled an arrow that was woven between the laces of Rune's empty quiver out and looked at its split shaft, and tattered white feather. "This place has a forge, it does appear you need more arrows, and some repairs to your equipment." Rune gave a smile and gently took the arrow from Eve's hand.

"This arrow will never be fired; I carry it with me always as a memory of my first time hunting with Robbie. It was damaged and unusable, but I kept it as a keep sake." Eve smiled.

"The last arrow of your woodland realm, and one it appears that carries much of the love that binds you both together. Keep it safe, for if the love it holds is as deep as the love I see in your heart, then it carries the hopes and dreams of all the realms."

The moment hit in a burst of clarity, and she twisted grabbing the quiver tied to her waist. Her hands shook violently as she pulled at the laces on the only arrow she had left, an arrow made of love in Loxley. She tugged at the laces as she felt the force on her heart of Robbie's last attempts to live, and her heart screamed out with her voice. "JADE HELP ME, I AM LOSING HIM!"

Jade flew across the top of the Rest, and with the glint of steel, her hand grabbed the arrow and her dagger sliced through all the laces pulling the arrow free. Rune snatched it from her and twisted back to face the mount, the arrow came up on the string and Rune closed one eye as she sighted the bow. Jade gave a gasp. "This is sacred ground, you cannot kill her."

The arrow was straight and clean, without a mark down its long smooth clean shaft, the touch of Eve and mother of life had given life back to the love that Rune held for Robbie. Rune took a deep breath as she saw the Star of the Merle in Morgan le Fey's hand give off a slight glint. "For the love we hold together, and the love of all this realm is to us, may you be straight and sure and give life to those who fight for it."

The string of the bow gave a twang, and on the opposite side of Morgan le Fey, a loud snarling roar echoed off the stones, as Furry Face jumped on to a rock level with her.

Just for a second the Dark One turned to look at the large ferocious looking tiger, and out of the darkness to her opposite side, violet glinted. The arrow hit the star and exploded with a huge burst of violet light. The Dark One screamed in pain as her body was torn from the star, she let go of Robbie and he crashed gasping and choking to the floor.

Furry Face pounced at the Dark One with a massive roar of hatred, and she slipped backwards and fell from her cloud and smashed into the hard floor.

Violet light exploded everywhere and Rune came out of the light in a raging temper. "YOU EVER TOUCH HIM AGAIN, AND SACRED GROUND OR NOT, I WILL RIP OUT YOUR HEART BITCH!"

Morgan recoiled back on the floor with the shock of Rune's sudden appearance right in front of her. She flinched as Rune grabbed her by the scruff of the neck and dragged the startled witch up on her feet, and with a reaction quicker than a striking cobra, her fist swung with all its might into her face with a resounding crunch.

The Dark One screamed in pain as she hurtled backwards flapping and flailing on the rubble, there was a blast of bright green light and Morgan le Fey was lifted into the air and tossed over the edge of the cliff.

Everyone was scattered in the rubble covered in dust having been blown backwards again, and stunned as they saw Rune and Jade side by side raging in anger. It was an awesome spectacle and very scary, Robbie gasped as Rune turned and dropped to him, she pulled him into her arms and held him tight; Jade gave a smile at the group. "Hey guys, how's it going? We figured we would pop up and lend a hand." Big John gave a deep belly laugh and winked at her.

Amethyst gave a giggle and got to her feet, as her guard jumped up and checked all around her was safe. The battle still raged, but black clad soldiers having seen their mistress fall, were starting to move backward down the slope in retreat.

Amethyst looked down, and just short of her foot lay the black star of onyx, she bent down to pick it up. "DON'T TOUCH IT!"

Rune's slender white hand gripped her wrist and lifted it away from the star.

"Innocent as it may look; this is still very dangerous to those who hold powers." Rune put her hand in her pocket, and took out the white star shaped crystal container, from her other pocket she took out a pair of tweezers as Robbie sat watching breathing in more air. She gently lifted the star and dropped it into the white container, it vibrated inside for a moment and Amethyst gave a shudder, Rune placed on the lid and ran her finger round its edge, the white star shaped container that had been the container of the rune stone glowed with violet light and Amethyst watched as the gap sealed tight.

"That will keep it safe and free from more harm, and we still have a queen of goodness, had you lifted it Amethyst you would have found the darkness still here."

Rune stood up and looked at the sky where the thick black clouds were fading away and melting into a bright blue sky with a burning sun. "It's still daytime, but as the moon passes through its full phase tonight, with the rising of tomorrow's sun, your kingdom will have its new queen and Avalon will rebuild itself anew." Jade gave a cheeky grin at Rowan.

"It will go dark tonight, and there will be stars and stuff." Rowan gave a cheeky smile back at her and walked over to hug her. Amethyst pulled Rune close and held her tight.

"I owe you so much, you and everyone else have done so much for me, I just have no idea how to thank you." Rune pulled away and gave a soft smile.

"I am your centre and always shall be My Queen of Avalon, I will always be here for you, and all of us will be frequent visitors you have my word. We will have to leave soon because the rule of the Fae is as it always has been, when the new queen takes the seat and the realm builds itself anew, no one who is not Fae can be present. Those who are not of your line will die, so we shall prepare and then take our leave." Amethyst gave a sad nod of understanding and Rune turned back to Robbie who was on his feet with the rest of the Specialists. "Judith how are you?"

She stood at the side of William looking very shaky and pale, but she gave a smile.

"I am OK, and yes before you ask, she has gone, she is not in this realm." Rune gave a nod.

"Thought so, come on we have much to do."

Covered in dirt and dust John stood at the edge of the high cliff wall and looked down on the small town and dried up lake, his sword was still gripped tightly in his blood soaked hand as he looked all around the base of the high wall to make sure the Dark One was really gone. He spat as he realised that for now they were safe, Bear and Hawk both walked up to his side, understanding he was just making sure, Bear patted him heavily on the shoulder and a cloud of dust wafted up off it.

"We are safe my friend, without her little black rock she is like a wolf with no teeth."

John gave a snort and spat again. "Aye maybe so, but a wolf still has its claws, and can do enough damage to a man I reckon, I won't be relaxing any time soon."

Hawk understood the deep protection he felt for Rune and Robbie, as he too felt nervous and scanned the entire valley for any signs of movement. "We will not be here much longer; it looks like the Marshals have everything pretty much in hand. Robbie wants to leave straight away and get back to Loxley, Bear keep up front and watch the path, John stay close to Robbie, I will watch the rear, get your bags and prepare to move onward."

CHAPTER THIRTY TWO

MERLIN'S DOORSTEP.

With the taking of the star, the large army of the Dark One slowly withdrew and then fell to their knees and surrendered, the Marshals of the Fae took control and disarmed them before taking them prisoner and leading them off. After quite some time of checking each other to ensure all were unharmed, the Specialists gathered together their things, and waited for Robbie to give the order. Rune led the group off on the hour long walk along the path cut into the rock, which took them past the tomb of Arthur and into a small canyon. As they reached the top of a deep pass she stopped and turned to the Specialists. "This place is known as Merlin's Door. Inside that cave at the base of the hill, is a secret passage back up to the Tor at Glastonbury, she never knew of it and so we hope it was never sealed, we shall go through it and then I will open a window into Loxley. Say your goodbyes and make your way down the pass, I have one more thing to do and then I will join you."

For many of them it was hard to say goodbye to Fish and Amethyst, both of them had been very popular in the group and there were several tears as they hugged and said their final farewells. For Crystal it was the hardest of all, and she hugged her sister and wept, as she knew that after all of the years they had spent growing up together, the moment had finally arrived, where she would have to leave her sister behind to rule Avalon.

Amethyst held her tight for a long time as she whispered words of love and hope for her sister quietly. Rune took off her sword belt and rested it with her quiver on the top of her bag; she stood up and opened a window, and walked alone out on to the top of the Isle of Tears where the transparent figure of Eve waited for her.

"You have done well Runestone Life, and the power that grows within you as was written long ago is twice the power I once held." Rune felt the lump in her throat as she looked at the almost invisible shape of her great grandmother, who stood within the white stone star on the top of the Isle, and at her feet was the small star shaped hole.

Rune opened her hand and revealed the white star shaped container. "When I place this in that hole, you will be destroyed forever won't you?" The tears welled in her eyes as the faint figure came forward.

"This has always been my destiny Runestone Life, for I have handed the torch of life to you to carry, do not be sad, my life has been fulfilled and I have known love so deep and so powerful, it will take me into the cosmos and beyond."

Rune shook as she felt the grief building inside her. "But why do you have to die, why can you not stay as a spirit to others as you have me? It makes no sense for you to end here and now, I will always need you close, if I am twice the power, then take some back and stay with us." She gave a long bitter sob as her heart broke, and Eve surrounded her with her love, for she no longer had the form to take her into her arms and hold her.

"Our time is coming to an end, it is the time for you and your Hooded Man to go forth and rebuild everything to your view of the world, just as I did many thousands of years ago. Dry your tears My Lady of Life, for inside you I will always live in the gifts I bestowed on you, now place the stone in the seal and leave. I shall take it where it will never be found again; happy in the knowledge you will always be safe because of this. Go with love to your children and hold them for me, for there is the key to your future."

Rune wiped her eyes and gave a big sniffle. "Goodbye Great Grandmother, thank you for all you have done to help me, I love you and always will."

She knelt down and took one last look up where she could just make out the outline of Eve; she smiled down at her and gave a nod. Rune placed the white star shaped container over the hole, and let it slip into place. Quickly she stood up and turned back into her window, and with a flash of violet she reappeared in front of the departing Specialists.

Fagan patted Robbie on the back with great affection. "Ye made a good Bindweed, go with speed, that liquid will bring ye words back soon, remember a squeeze on the neck like that will take a few days before ye can speak again."

Robbie silently nodded and turned onto the path as Rune walked up to Fagan. The old man smiled, and for the first time since she had met him, she saw a little sadness in his face, Rune wiped her eyes and smiled. "You will miss her more than most; I know how fond you were of her." He gave a sad smile.

"She was a good friend to an old man of the trees, knowing she is not wandering around will be hard for the trees, they did love to feel her ye know."

"I will keep my promise and I will return with the children; this is their centre and they should know it." Fagan gave a big smile.

"Ye would make me happier than any daffodil if ye did, I must say that the thought of little violet eyes coming here, brings spring to me heart." Rune pulled him into a big hug and fought back her tears again.

"Goodbye my good friend, and Keeper of my forest."

"Fare ye well my Lady of Life, until we meet under the high branches again."

Rune wiped her eyes and turned to the path, as Steph and Smokes both hugged Amethyst and Jade stood with Rowan in front of Fagan. Her green eyes sparkled as the sadness of the moment resounded on her; the white scruffy haired old man beamed a broad and happy smile as he lifted a hand and touched Jade's cheek. "I think I am going to miss ye most Little Green Eyes, the forest needs a nymph like ye to scamper through it."

"ROBBIE!"

Everyone turned as Rune screamed, she ran quickly to the start of the path yelling and screaming, and then down the roughhewn stone steps to the foot of the hill and into the cave, where she hammered on a wall that wasn't really there. Rowan turned in panic and ran as fast as he could down the steps, slipping and sliding on the dust and crumbled stone as he skidded into the opening of the cave. He moved swiftly to her, as Rune's eyes exploded into violet light and she wailed into the wall and he screamed with all his might.

"RUNE WHAT THE HELL IS IT?" Her voice was filled with panic.

"It's a trap and he is walking into it, all of them have gone through, and the doorway has sealed, Rowan help me I need to get in, she is there waiting to kill them, they have no idea they have been tricked."

He ran over to where she stood, and crashed into nothing, he bounced backwards onto the floor, as Rune screamed at the top of her voice, and violet light flooded out in a blinding burst "ROBBBBBBBIE!"

He scrambled to his feet as his heart began to pound in his chest restricting his breath, and pulled out his long sword to slice through whatever it was that was stopping Rune, who had disappeared behind the blinding glare of violet light. Rowan lifted the Sword of Honour, and swung it with every ounce of strength and desperation he had.

There was a tremendous explosion and everyone else who was arriving outside looking white faced and wide eyed, were thrown to the floor with a violent blast, the violet intensified as Fagan staggered to his feet and yelled at the top of his voice.

"STOP HER SHE WILL DESTROY THE WHOLE REALM!" He lunged forward into the blinding light that obscured both Rune and Rowan.

Rocks exploded and crashed from the walls, and bounced onto the path rolling dangerously close to the group, who staggered as they tried to scramble back to their feet, the violet light radiating out of Rune with her screams was blinding, and they had to shield their eyes to avoid getting them burned, as they dodged the tumbling stone and bouncing rocks.

A white hooded figure hurried down the path, and quickly walked passed them towards the mass of violet light that was Rune, Jade knelt on the ground bleeding, filled with terror and panic as she felt Rune's pain surging into her, and she shouted out with all her might. "GRANDMA HELP HER!"

The white hooded figure reached into the mass of light, and there was a loud resounding 'SNAP' as she clicked her fingers.

The violet light died leaving a white robe on the floor, and the limp figure of Rune unconscious in the arms of the dark sinister figure of Morgan le Fey. She gave a loud cackle, as her dark cold eyes viewed the stunned looks on the faces of the group, and with a spiral of black smoke, she lifted into the air. Steph was up on her feet first, but it was too late, as the Dark One screamed with delight from the sky.

"Fools, you never had a hope, you are so pathetic and predictable, and now she is mine and all of you will suffer for your meddling in my affairs, prepare leaf lovers your death is coming, years of planning and now all my traps have been sprung."

Jade screamed out into the air as Rowan fell to his knees in shock, Amethyst was defenceless as her powers would not come for another twelve hours, and somewhere out of their reach Robbie was walking into a trap. All they could do was watch as the dark laughing figure shot into the air holding Rune in her arms, Jade screamed and wailed but there was nothing she could do, with a flash of bright light, the Dark One with Rune in her arms streaked into the sky and was gone.

Deep in the forest of Loxley, a young girl cloaked in a heavy black robe fell to her knees and wailed out into the air with pain. "Lord of the woodland save me.... Hear me lord, for I have run away and she will kill me, save me lord, and let me repent and undo the pain I have caused." She buried her head in the grass and cried with deep bitter pain and terror, wailing with her fear. "Please I beg of you save me, future days will stain the world if you do not, please I am begging you to help me stop the destruction that is coming."

From a few feet away a kindly old voice spoke. "Ursula of Fae, you have wronged many in my house, why should I now take you into my care?"

Ursula looked up as her tears flowed down her face. "Save me Lord of the Green Realm, I have deserted her and wish to undo the pain I have caused, please I beg you show me mercy or we all shall die." She lowered her head and shook with fear, and the old lord felt the turmoil within her.

"Come lost child of Fae, I will protect you from the darkness, and she will not find you where I shall take you. Do not fear and take my hand." Hearne stepped forward and his robes rustled like the leaves blowing in the autumn wood, he leaned down to the small huddled shaking figure, as she slowly lifted her tear filled face. Hearne smiled and stretched out his hand, Ursula reached up and with a sudden lunge; she stabbed Hearne in the leg. He stood up quickly and felt the pain shoot through his insides as his temper rose, and his deep voiced boomed filling the woodland.

"What is this trickery?" He gave a gasp of pain and staggered back as smoke began to curl up out of the floor. Looking down he saw his leg turning black where a small fine slither of black stone stood out from his skin, his eyes flickered with green light as he tried to stagger backward, but he was stuck to the floor where the smoke now funnelled up and around him.

The voice of the Dark One screamed out of the smoke as Ursula got off the floor looking terrified, she turned and ran back down the path, to where a young soldier stood waiting for her, he grabbed her hand and both of them ran quickly into the trees. Hearne fought with all his might and tried to reach out to one of the trees, but it was no use, the smoke billowed out of the floor and with one final attempt to hold himself in the realm, he was dragged surrounded by black smoke, down through the floor to her lair.

In less than a moment he was gone, and the woodland was suddenly quiet and empty, the leaves floated softly to the floor, but little had changed apart from the wide ring of burned earth where Hearne the high lord of the woodland had stood last.

The years of complicated elaborate planning by the Dark One had finally taken shape and proven effective. No one had seen it coming, as she had studied her enemy deeper than anyone had realised and seen their weakness. Robbie had always warned of complacency, and it had been something that Morgan le Fey had learned from him.

In a cruel twist used against him, her plan had never been to take over and occupy Avalon, which had been the brilliance of the whole charade. Morgan had studied Merlin more than even he realised, as she lived in Avalon and studied the Fae. She had always known the old law of legitimacy to claim a throne supported by the powers of the spirit worlds, and at some point, a new king would have to return to the realm of old to take up the sceptre for a coronation to be fully accepted.

In that single fact, she had invested all of her patience and planning. Merlin had warned of her devious ways, and as Rowan and Jade were forced with Steph and Smokes to return to the house of Fagan, knowing they were trapped and unable to do anything to aid Robbie and Runestone, down in the depths of her castle within the centre of the Hidden Realm, Morgan le Fey screamed with joy knowing she had Hearne and Runestone trapped forever.

Her attention now turned to her Darkmares, as they silently surrounded the glade where stones of power had risen, and she felt a stronger sense of victory knowing that although she could not enter the secret hiding place of Opal, she could contain her within it forever, and the rest of the world was now free for her son Mason to conquer and rule. The age of sleep had been long and exhausting, but in the last dying moments of the long age, she had taken the initiative and wiped out all her enemies at once, and the new age of dreams would come to pass as the age when all of the Specialists and their hooded man would die, and through her son, she would rule supreme, her one final task would be to clear the land of everything built by the ruling council, and destroy everything the Woodland Realm stood for.

In her wild ecstasy of finally achieving her life's ambition, she felt almost light headed and gripped the edge of her long table where a long glass box awaited her new prize. The sands of an old hour glass were running quickly into the base, as the old doors at the top of her long room creaked open and a breathless and red faced Ursula slipped into the room. The Dark One lifted her hand to wave her assistant down the room towards her.

"Come... Quickly girl, come and see as the sand runs clear, the time is almost here." Ursula picked up her pace as she hurried down the long length of the work room towards her mistress's table. She came up to the side of the Dark One and looked at the large ornate hour glass, it appeared as if there was just a few minutes left before the top bottle was completely drained into the rising point of the sands below.

"What is this for, what does it mean Mistress?" Morgan le Fey did not take her greedy excited eyes from the jar as her voice almost whispered through her dry withered lips.

"This my dear girl marks the final moments of their leaf lover, everything is finally finished, and as the last grain falls, their prized Hooded Man will be lost forever as his life ends. There is nothing they can do, it is over, time has run out and all of them will die, my task is finally ended. They have fired their last arrows, and now I alone will rule everything and decide the fate of every kingdom."

More Author's
From
Violet Circle Publishing

Mike Beale. (Children's Book)

Crumble's Adventures.
ISBN: 978-1-910299-06-7
Digital ISBN: 978-1-910299-08-1

Colin Smith (Play)

Heaven knows I'm Miserable Now
ISBN: 978-1-910299-16-6
Digital ISBN: 978-1-910299-23-4

Ted Morgan. (Poetry and verse)

Wordsmith's Wanderings.
ISBN: 978-1-910299-04-3
Digital ISBN: 978-1-910299-09-8
Peregrinations of the Wordsmith
ISBN: 978-1-910299-18-0
Digital ISBN: 978-1-910299-21-0
Silhouette Soldiers
ISBN: 978-1-910299-19-7
Digital ISBN: 978-1-910299-22-7
A Menu of Memories
Digital ISBN: 978-1-910299-32-6
Digital ISBN: 978-1-910299-33-3

Robin John Morgan. (Fiction/Fantasy/Slice of Life)

Heirs to the Kingdom.

Book One, The Bowman of Loxley.
ISBN: 978-1-910299-00-5
Digital ISBN: 978-1-910299-10-4
Book Two, The Lost Sword of Carnac.
ISBN: 978-1-910299-01-2
Digital ISBN: 978-1-910299-11-1
Book Three, The Darkness of Dunnottar.
ISBN: 978-1-910299-02-9
Digital ISBN: 978-1-910299-12-8
Book Four, Queen of the Violet Isle.
ISBN: 978-1-910299-03-6
Digital ISBN: 978-1-910299-13-5
Book Five, Crystals of the Mirrored Waters.
ISBN: 978-1-910299-05-0
Digital ISBN: 978-1-910299-14-2
Book Six, Last Arrow of the Woodland Realm.
ISBN: 978-1-910299-07-4
Digital ISBN: 978-1-910299-15-9
Book Seven, Bridge Of Sequana.
ISBN: 978-1-910299-17-3
Digital ISBN: 978-1-910299-20-3
Book Eight, The Circle of Darkness.
ISBN: 978-1-910299-26-5
Digital ISBN: 978-1-910299-29-6

The Curio Chronicles.

Part One, Abigail's Summer.
ISBN: 978-1-910299-27-2
Part Two, Curio's Summer.
ISBN: 978-1-910299-34-0
Digital ISBN: 978-1-910299-35-7
Part Three, Curio's Christmas.
ISBN: 978-1-910299-38-8
Digital ISBN: 978-1-910299-39-5

Other Works.

Rise Of The Raven
ISBN: 978-1-910299-30-2
Digital ISBN: 978-1-910299-31-9
The Countess Of Darkness
ISBN: 978-1-910299-40-1
Digital ISBN: 978-1-910299-41-8

Han's Cottage.
ISBN: 978-1-910299-36-4
Digital ISBN: 978-1-910299-37-1

Find out more about our authors and their books at
www.violetcirclepublishing.co.uk

9 781910 299074